The Mythag

Volume

The Mythago Cycle

Volume 2

THE HOLLOWING
&
GATE OF IVORY, GATE OF HORN

ROBERT HOLDSTOCK

GOLLANCZ
LONDON

The Hollowing Copyright © Robert Holdstock 1994
Gate of Ivory, Gate of Horn Copyright © Robert Holdstock 1998
Illustrations © Alan Lee 1988

The Hollowing first published in Great Britain in 1994 by
HarperCollins *Gate of Ivory, Gate of Horn* first published in Great
Britain in 1998 by HarperCollins

This edition first published in Great Britain in 2007 by
Gollancz
An imprint of the Orion Publishing Group
Orion House, 5 Upper St Martin's Lane,
London WC2H 9EA
An Hachette Livre UK Company

A CIP catalogue record for this book
is available from the British Library

ISBN 978 0 57507 9 724

1 3 5 7 9 10 8 6 4 2

Typeset at the Spartan Press Ltd,
Lymington, Hants

Printed and bound at Mackays of Chatham plc,
Chatham, Kent

The Orion Publishing Group's policy is to use papers that
are natural, renewable and recyclable products and made
from wood grown in sustainable forests. The logging and
manufacturing processes are expected to conform to the
environmental regulations of the country of origin.

www.orionbooks.co.uk

THE HOLLOWING

For Wendy, Brian, Alan, Marjya and Robert, fellow travellers in the realm . . .

and for Hilary Rubinstein, with much appreciation.

My thanks, for a variety of reasons, to Chris Evans, Jane Johnson, Sarah Biggs, Malcolm Edwards, Andrew Stephenson (chats scientific), Dave Arthur (chats mythic) and Garry and Annette Kilworth. And of course, to the unknown author of *Sir Gawain and the Green Knight*, and the long-forgotten dreamer who inspired the tale.

'Now certainly the place is deserted,' said Gawain.
'It is a hideous oratory, all overgrown,
And well graced for the gallant garbed in green
To deal out his devotions in the Devil's fashion.
Now I feel in my five wits, it is the Fiend himself
That has tricked me into this tryst, to destroy me here.'

From *Sir Gawain and the Green Knight*

One of the deep silences fell on them, that seemed so much more natural than speech, a timeless silence in which there were at first many minds in the overhang; and then perhaps no mind at all.

William Golding: The Inheritors

PART ONE

From the Unknown Region

The Green Chapel: 1

Each dawn, since the hollyjack had come to the cathedral bringing her strange dreams, the boy had started to think of waking as the opening of petals, or a form of budding. At this time the light was not green, it became green later, but he could never wait to wake, and in the same way that flowers opened to the sun, and leaves turned and unfurled, so he unfurled, so he opened. At first curled up on the inscribed marble floor, arms and legs gathered in for warmth during the night, now he began to straighten, then stretch, face to the open sky where the roof had been, mouth agape and damp with dew.

His eyes remained closed but he knew the cathedral was not yet green, it was still in *stark* light, and the world was not yet *quick*. And like the pores of the leaves, still closed, the water stayed inside him. He liked the feeling of the water. It pressed painfully against his belly, but he kept the water with him, waiting for green light. He rolled on the hard, cold marble, touching the grooves in the slab, the hidden names of the dead carved in the floor that guarded their bones. He listened to the cathedral stir, to the forest beyond begin to wake, to the hollyjack as she woke and moved restlessly, like a bird, in her nest of vegetation at the end of the aisle, against the great outer doors of the church.

The hollyjack had been here for days, now, weeks perhaps. She had changed his dreams. He could dream more widely, and feel his way over great distances of the forest, peering up from the roots, or glimpsing the ground as he flowed through the branches. She still frightened him, but until she had come he had been unable to see anything at all. With her arrival he had seen how like a leaf he was, unfurling with the new day. But last night, the dream last night had been startling. He didn't want to let it go.

The sun moved over the line of the trees. The ragged edges of the cathedral's fallen roof caught its warmth, its light. On the cold marble the brilliant edge of the green light spread, moving like a growing thing, an unfurling plant, towards the unfurled boy.

He felt it touch his legs. He woke fully and cried out as the light spread across him and birds fled from the nest where the hollyjack chattered. The bones of the dead below him shifted as roots prowled among them. The cathedral shuddered into life, from nave to chancel. The rotting wood of the pews began to steam, and he could smell this, and the carved dancing men drew deeper into the knots and rings of the old trees, their night of freedom and exuberance finished for a while.

He let the water go, now, adding his own moisture to the heavy dawn as his belly deflated. The water stank of nettles as it passed, and this mingled with wood sorrel and anemone in the rising steam of the chapel. He was relieved, out of pain, and felt at last that it was time to open fully. To open his eyes. To let green light shape him for the day.

The hollyjack had left her nest. He saw her moving up the ivy-covered wall towards the high arch of a window, where tree branches reached into the ruins of the cathedral and stone faces grinned down at him. She hesitated for a moment, glancing back at her nest, and at the boy, then had gone, outside into the forest.

He wanted to call to her, to tell her about his dream, but it was too late. He stood and stared through the leaning trunks of oaks at the rows of rotting wooden pews, some of them crushed, others raised above the floor as the forest grew from below them. The altar space was a distant grove among white-flowered thorns, the gold cross sparkling through the leaves. Saplings were sprouting everywhere, coming up from the crypt below. Only the marble slabs, with the names and dates of the dead, defied the forest as it struggled to emerge into the cathedral, keeping a clear channel to the high altar. Since the hollyjack had come to him, he had begun to imagine how the roots and branches in the crypt, and the bones themselves, were all entangled, all pushing at the floor, a great pressure ready to erupt upwards.

It had been *such* a dream. It had been his first *real* dream since he had come to the forest. He said the words aloud into the decaying church. *Real dream.* For so long his dreams had been of endless snow, and endless forest, and endless running, and endless water, an endless flight across unchanging lands. All that had *broken* with the first dream of the unfurling leaf. And now this one. He had begun to remember so much again.

'They danced!' he shouted, staring into the brightening sky, through the crossing branches of the trees, through the green light. As if to answer his cry, one of the carved wooden faces on a pew moved slightly, then stretched forward from the end of the stall, poking out into the aisle. It turned and peered at the shouting boy, who watched back through the sunlit mist that hung heavily in the great space. It looked like the hollyjack, branches extending from its mouth, leaves around its face. As quickly as it had stretched to look at him, it withdrew and was silent again. The boy blinked, then laughed. He was still dreaming. Last night that same figure and twenty others had come all the way out of the wooden benches, small, gnarled shapes with willow-thin arms and legs. They had led a wild dance up the stone walls and into the branches, among the stone faces in the high eaves, which had laughed and twisted too, stretching out from the pillars and cornices of the cathedral, peering at the wild activity below them and around their vaulted positions.

In the stillness of the new day, the boy went to the hollyjack's nest and peered through the small hole into the stinking mass of rotten wood and foliage, grass, bracken and dead birds that the creature had compacted against the tall cathedral doors. Above those doors, half of a stained glass window began to glow purple and red as it was struck by first light. He liked the shape of the knight with his lance and silver armour, but now – another question! He was so full of questions these days – now he wondered what the knight was fighting – he could just see the creature's legs – what was missing from the shattered area of the window.

Away from the nest, he went into the gloom of the sacristy and looked at his disjointed reflection in the cracked mirror. His hair was long and filthy now, falling in a lank, black mass around his pale, smooth face. A new thought occurred to him (he smiled at the pleasure of it) that he looked like the picture of an Apache Indian boy he had seen in a book at school. The boy in the picture had worn animal skins. The boy in the mirror was naked. The picture of the Apache now blurred and shifted in his mind, then faded. The chapel boy's teeth were still white when he grinned, shifting his head across a distorting fracture in the glass.

The deep scratches on his chest and right arm were healed, now no more than bright red lines. They no longer hurt. The skin around them was still yellowed with bruising. He could hardly remember the attack, now, it had been so fast, and at dusk. He hadn't even seen the creature, just heard its awful laugh. He thought of it as the giggler.

He was grimy with dirt and remembered that he should wash, so he thought of the well, but the well was at the edge of the clearing outside, and the wood was dangerous there. When the giggler had snatched at him and ripped him, it had hurt him badly, and when the hollyjack had tried to help him it had torn her leaves before retreating into the deep bosk of the wood. She mightn't help him again.

The moment of apprehension faded as fast as the memory of the Indian boy from the book. He was suddenly on the ivy 'ladder', hauling himself up the stonework to the open roof, over an empty gallery, then across a broad sill that was carved with intricate rose and leaf patterns. He held the long neck of an ugly stone animal, and peered back down into the body of the church, swinging gently in the vast space and watching the wooden seats below, but they were quite lifeless now. Then he had clambered over the gargoyle and out onto a branch, crawling into the daylight and slipping down the twisted beech tree and onto the slate roof of the porch. The clearing stretched around him, ending at the wood. A few granite headstones poked from mounds in the tall grass and nettles. The stone well was half in shadow. The crowding wood was dark, crushing, and he felt a tingle of apprehension again. The giggler came and went, usually at dusk, but he couldn't be sure it wasn't there now, watching him from the shadows. He needed to drink, though.

Without really thinking, he reached the well and drew up the bucket, splashing water into his mouth and over his body, liking the cold touch on his bruises. Some impulse, faintly remembered, made him rub water between his toes.

Something moved suddenly in the dark wood, startling him, and he scampered back to the open door of the porch, yelping at the stings he received from the dense nettlebed. It was only the hollyjack, in fact. She hovered in the gloom, then stepped quickly past the well, crouching against a headstone. He knew that her eyes would tell him of fear, but her eyes said nothing. They gleamed from deep in the holly leaves that wreathed her face. The thin twigs that stretched from each side of her round mouth were wet. She had been feeding, then. She was fat, these days, and her body often moved as if she was being kicked from inside.

In her hands she held a selection of colourful fungi. She offered these, and he came forward and picked carefully, knowing that some would make him dizzy and sick. The rest he ate gratefully as the hollyjack quickly examined those he had rejected. She was trying to learn.

The hollyjack was disturbed. Her mouth flexed and she made bird noises. Her long fingers stroked her body leaves restlessly, almost nervously. He wanted to go back into the chapel, to safety and security, away from the strange men and creatures who so often prowled among the trees. But he sensed that the hollyjack needed him, so he stayed in the shadow, listening to furtive movement in the woodland and the fluttering of wings in his friend's body.

He realised quite suddenly that she was inviting him to dream again, and his heart surged.

He had had a dream last night, in the cathedral . . . as he ate the last of the mushrooms he struggled to recall the details. There had been wild dancing. The green men in the church stalls had slipped out of the wood and ran amok. He was like a leaf, unfurling at dawn. The giggler had stepped from the wood and walked into his dreams, hiding there . . .

But as he tried to remember these things, so they faded, leaving him blank again, empty and restless, lonely and isolated. The details had gone.

A bigger dream was on offer, now. The way the hollyjack crouched and trembled, watching him and chitter-chattering in her funny way, all of this told him that she had heard something. Big Dream, he wondered as he chewed, or Little Dream?

When he was full he left the porch and went over to the hollyjack, curling up in her twiggy arms. The prick of holly leaves made him shudder, but after a while the mixing of blood and sap soothed him, and although the inside of her body shifted and fluttered restlessly, he felt himself slip out into the wood, flowing softly, spreading widely, connected to the forest around him through her roots, now embedded in the earth of the graveyard, and touching the tendrils of wilder trees.

She was sending him on the Little Dream, and he heard his father's voice again, for only the second time since the hollyjack had come. His father was in the wood. His father was coming closer. He was looking desperately for his son. There was someone with him, a man like a bear, dark-featured and fierce. There was excitement, running, they were afraid. The wood shifted around them, tripped them, snagged them, sucked them deeper. The giggler was watching them, but they weren't aware of it.

Then he touched his father's dreams again, his memories, and he shouted with pain at the anguish he felt, the sadness. The hollyjack wrapped her arms more tightly around him, soothed him, rustled and twittered at him with her voice. Blood and sap mingled more deeply. He lay back in the hollybush and started to cry. But he dreamed his father's dream for a while, feeding on it, bringing himself close again to a man he remembered only as a picture. He moved out of the cathedral and into the wood, a wraith, anxious to touch the man who was searching for him.

Out of the Dark

It was to be an evening of rain and strange encounters. There would be a return from the dead, and the beginning of the ending of a life.

Richard Bradley hastened along the road to his house, at the edge of Shadoxhurst, hatless and drenched by the torrential and freezing late September downpour. The whole town had become dark. The few shops had their lights on, and at four in the afternoon this made a depressingly wintry scene. Richard was wearing only his suit, the collar of his jacket drawn tightly around his neck in a vain attempt to stop the rain coursing down his back. Bedraggled and fed up, he broke into a run as he neared his cottage, then slowed abruptly as he saw the woman dart away from the back gate towards the fields.

She was wearing strange clothes. She too was saturated, he could see, her dark hair plastered to her scalp. He didn't see her face, only the army trousers, tucked into muddy, black boots, and a full and heavy-looking green anorak drawn tightly around her neck. She had something slung across her shoulder, and although it was hard to be sure, Richard thought it was a short bow and full quiver.

He quickened his step, puzzled by the fact that she had been at his back door, but by the time he reached the gate she was a bulky and distant shape, running through the downpour towards the stream that led to Ryhope Wood, on the estate. The rain made the wood seem grim, as always.

He opened the back door and peered inside the house, noticing the wet footprints that led across the kitchen and into the small parlour. The footprints were small. He assumed at once that they were those of the woman, but what on earth was she doing here? Nothing looked disturbed. The cash box, clearly labelled as such (it contained only coppers), was still on its shelf.

Richard followed the footprints. They ascended the stairs and showed clearly, though slightly faded, how the intruder had looked into each room. The carpet had dried the wetness from her boots by mid-landing of the return, but downstairs, on the bureau, he found a note, which he read with astonishment.

Why aren't you here? Everything's OK with Old Stone Hollow. I really hoped you'd be here. I miss you. It's been too long.

IMPORTANT: Lytton reckons he knows how to locate the boy's protogenomorph, but we need YOU there. Come to the Station. I'm going back into the wood by the old brook, taking path through Huxley's Lodge. Follow me the moment you get back. This may be our only chance to find the true Cathedral! Just do it! I miss you.

The note was unsigned. The paper was wet where she had held it, the pen, a cheap biro, flung on the table. She had rested a hand on the polished wood and he placed his own hand upon the vague outline, noting its smallness, the details of her fingerprints, three of which were crossed with scars.

A thought had occurred to him, that he should fetch the police, but he stood there unwilling to do so. He just looked at the handprint, and the note, savouring its strangeness and its incomprehensibility. And remembering the image of the woman, wet, dark-haired, bulky with clothes, but fast, running along the bridleway towards the wood that had so fascinated Alexander's young friend Tallis Keeton, before she and her father had so tragically and mysteriously disappeared, over a year ago, now.

Alex came bounding up to the front door and rang the bell. Richard folded the note and tucked it into his trousers pocket, then opened the door to the wet, excitable thirteen-year-old. The boy ran straight to the kitchen and poured himself a glass of orange juice, then crashed upstairs to get ready for the school play.

On impulse, Richard followed his son to the 'treasure house', as he and Alice called Alexander's room.

'Do you want tea?' he asked from the door, watching the boy poring over some typewritten sheets.

'No thanks. Had crisps and two Lion bars.'

'Well, that sounds healthy enough.' Alex didn't respond. 'We'll be leaving at six, if they want you there at six-thirty, so don't lounge around reading for long.'

'I'm not reading – I'm memorising. Mr Evans and me wrote a new scene today.'

'Mr Evans and *I* . . .'

Alex groaned tiredly.

Richard looked around the room, reaching out to flick one of the many model planes that were suspended from the ceiling. Alexander's costume – he was to play the red-bearded Lord Bertolac in the third year's production of *Sir Gawain and the Green Knight* – was draped around a tailor's dummy. The red beard and hair had been fashioned from two very old wigs and looked hilarious upon the boy. Another pupil would be playing the Green Knight himself (who was, in fact, Lord Bertolac in otherworldly form) as the change of costuming was too difficult.

There was something about Alex's den that both embraced and unnerved Richard. It was a difficult feeling – there was so much obsession here, so much passion, from the paintings of knights, with odd insignia and helmet crests, to the drawings of dinosaurs and the carefully ordered trays of fossils and crystals, gathered from all over Britain, all labelled and all imbued with mystery. Chunks of iron marcasite from chalk pits were questioningly labelled 'Spacecraft remains?' The intricate patterns of fossils were related to Star Creatures, lost in the chalk seas in primordial times. Models, in plastic and wood, were everywhere, and the boy could tell a story about each one.

It was an imagination inherited from his grandfather (along with a love of toy soldiers), but a trait completely missing from Richard himself, although he tried hard to remember what had been his own childhood dream: he had walked, lazed in the sun and swum in the freezing seas off the Welsh coast. He had very little to show for growing up.

He realised that Alex was watching him anxiously. He asked, 'What is it?'

Alex said simply, 'You can come in, if you want. You can test me.'

Feeling awkward, for no reason he could identify, Richard turned to go downstairs. 'I'll test you in the car, shall I? I'd better get some tea going.'

Leaving Alexander to memorise the final few lines of his part in the heavily adapted play, he went down to the kitchen, taking out the note and re-reading it. It had an odd, foreign quality to the language – *Lytton reckons he knows how to locate the boy's protogenomorph.* It had an American twang to it. And what on earth was a *protogenomorph*?

The rain drummed monotonously. He heard the sound of the family car, an old Rover that roared and spluttered as the engine was turned off. Alice struggled out onto the kerb and cursed the rain.

He had hidden the note before she entered the house to begin her relentless domestic routine and preparing for the evening out. She had little time for idle chat. Richard prepared tea and wrote two letters, but he was distracted and disturbed – indeed, he was enjoying a welcome if vicarious experience.

The note had surely been intended for someone else, not for Richard Bradley. But he couldn't get over the odd and thrilling sensation that nine words in the woman's hand gave him.

I really hoped you'd be here, I miss you.

Alice was half asleep in the passenger seat, her head rocking as the car bumped slowly over the uneven road, leading back to Shadoxhurst. The headlights cut a bright path through the rain. Houses appeared grey, windows reflecting dully; trees were dark, looming shapes that appeared and disappeared from vision in seconds. The road curved across the country; two foxes scampered across the path of the car, casting gleam-eyed glances, hesitating as the vehicle approached.

Behind Richard, Alexander stared at the night land, awake, alert, excited. He was still dressed in his Lord Bertolac costume, all but the bushy beard. His performance had been warmly applauded.

In fact, it had been a spectacular performance all round, from the mad chase around the stage for the Green Knight's severed head, which took on an unintentional role of its own, to the sub-Gilbert and Sullivan words of the songs, all written by the children.

Even now, Richard found himself singing the 'Wild Man's' Song:

> 'I am a Mountain Wodwo,
> 'I live on leaves and fish roe . . .'

There had been no subtleties, of course, simply an adventure, with monsters and supernatural entities. The Green Knight's beheading, his magical return to life and subsequent challenge to Gawain, to meet a year later at the Green Chapel (an ancient burial mound) for a return stroke, were powerfully played; the three attempts at seducing Sir Gawain by the enchantress Morgan le Fay, disguised as Lady Bertolac, were excruciating, as the boy playing Morgan couldn't keep the pitch of his voice constantly high. Alex's innovation to the story had been to make the pagan Green Knight the guardian of a fabulous talisman. At the end, Gawain, disguised as a hunting falcon, tricked the monstrous knight out of his chapel, entered the mound to the fairy Otherworld and stole the treasure.

Alexander had been singled out for special applause. Richard and Alice had felt very proud of the lad and joined heartily in the encore, a refrain from the final song ('One bloody nick at the side of my neck – All for the sake of My Lady's Green Girdle').

Headlights cut through the dark, swinging across trees, hedges, walls, briefly illuminating a land that was silent, saturated and sleeping.

The man who suddenly staggered in front of the car was wearing only a dressing gown. He waved both hands helplessly as Richard swerved to avoid him. He was holding what looked like a round, white mask.

For a second, in the headlamps, the man had been startled like a wild animal, frozen in the road. Then he flung himself aside to escape hurt. Richard saw only his white body, naked beneath the gaping gown. He had been thinly bearded, and everything about him had glistened like oil, the effect of light on rain-drenched skin.

The car stopped heavily and Alice woke up abruptly.

'What the hell is it?'

'A man just ran into the road. I nearly knocked him down.'

'You should drive more slowly,' Alice said predictably.

Richard was already outside the car, peering into the darkness behind. He listened through the rain but could hear nothing.

Alice said, 'I'll drive, shall I? That way we might get home safely.'

'I didn't *hit* him, Alice. And he *did* run into the road . . .' But Richard was disturbed by the man's appearance. 'I just thought for a minute . . .'

He got back into the car and sat quietly. As Alice woke more fully from her drowsy state so her shock and her irritation passed away. 'Let's get home.'

'I thought I recognised him. I only glimpsed him . . .'

'Probably a farmer's lad, drunk. As you said, you didn't hit him, so let it alone. I'm cold.'

'He was wearing a dressing gown. Gaping open. Did you see him, Alex?'

Behind him the boy nodded palely. His eyes were wide and he looked upset.

'Alex?'

'It was Mr Keeton,' the boy said quietly. He was shaking. Richard went cold as the man's face became clearer to him. 'It was Tallis's father,' Alex repeated. 'It was Mr Keeton.'

'Nonsense,' Alice said, but she frowned when she saw the look on her husband's face. 'Jim Keeton and Tallis disappeared over a year ago. You know that, Alex. He hasn't come back, now. If it was Jim, then it's his ghost.'

Richard was trying to remember something from those distressing days, when the countryside had been searched and no sign of the two Keetons found. 'When Jim vanished . . . wasn't it in the morning? He'd run out of the house in his dressing gown. Don't you remember what Margaret told the inquest?'

Alice shrugged. 'I remember. But they've been gone for over a year. You're not telling me that a year later he's still wearing his dressing gown . . .'

Richard looked round in the darkness. On the small back seat of the car his Red Knight son was hunched, knees drawn up, eyes wide as he stared at his father. He was crying silently.

Five hours later, James Keeton came to their cottage. The rain had eased, but he made a miserable and bedraggled figure, standing at the bottom of the garden, staring at the dark window where Alexander watched, the mask held against his chest. He opened the gate and ran quickly to the back door, tapping on the glass. Alex struggled to see the man from his bedroom, but Keeton had moved through the rain to stand outside the dining room. Like a bird, tapping with its beak, Keeton kept tapping with his fingers, pressing his face against the glass, hand raised, tap-tap-tapping as he peered into the darkness of the cottage.

Alex stood on the landing, shivering. His pyjama trousers came undone and he struggled to tie them more securely. He listened to the noise of the beak on the glass downstairs, and remembered his friend Tallis's tales of birds, and bird creatures, and nights filled with wings. He slowly descended the stairs, and in the dining room approached the half-moon face of the man outside, coming closer until he could see the beard and the curve of pale flesh above, stepping right up to the window where the half-naked man tap-tap-tapped in slow desperation. Alex gently tap-tap-tapped back. Keeton's nose was squashed against the glass. A trickle of rain ran down between eyes and windowpane. He held the odd piece of rotting wood in one hand, and Alex saw the crude face, the moon-like curves, the cuts for eyes. He recognised it as one of

Tallis's masks. It was Moondream. He pressed his hand against the glass where the mask watched, remembering his lost friend.

The water on the pane, outside, mingled with the tears that Mr Keeton shed.

'Don't run away,' Alex called, and the man closed his eyes. He seemed to slump against the glass and continued to tap with the mask, as if he were a weary Punch and Judy man, using the cold-eyed wood to entice the children's fancy. Moondream tapped the window and Keeton sank down into a huddle; mask-face and man-face disappeared from view.

Alex went outside with the Persian rug from the hallway and wrapped the heavy fabric around the freezing man. Mr Keeton was silent, now, hugging the mask and watching the dark, damp night through eyes that were unpleasantly blank and watery. Alex tried to help him stand, but he wouldn't move.

'Don't run away again. Promise? Stay here.'

The man made a strange sound, then curled more tightly into his saturated dressing gown and the thick, dry rug, pulling the knotted ends around his neck.

Alex went upstairs and woke his father.

'Mr Keeton's come home. But he's very sad. I think Tallis must be dead.'

Moondreaming

There was something very curious about James Keeton's condition. When he had been bathed, shaved and his hair brushed, only a desperate, haunted look in his eyes suggested any difference to the robust and over-nourished man who had disappeared, presumably to live rough and wild, one year and fifteen days ago. His wife Margaret was very distressed, hardly touching her husband, but staring at him as he was examined by a local doctor, and talked to and tested, but without responding in any way.

Keeton's skin was scratched in places, and his two big toes very bruised. The growth of beard, now removed, had been that of four or five days. His dressing gown, though the pockets were torn, once dry was as good as new – not the raggy robe that might have been expected from a year in the wild.

Oddest of all, the elastoplast on his index finger covered an almost healed cut. The day before he had disappeared, Keeton had cut himself carving a shoulder of lamb for the family lunch.

Had he been looked after somewhere during his absence, only to be returned to his original appearance (minus pyjamas!) a few days before, to run blindly along the country lanes around Shadoxhurst? Only James Keeton could answer that question, and Keeton was saying nothing. He rocked slightly in the armchair, and seemed, at times, to be looking into the far distance. He cried silently, and his lips moved, but no sound emerged.

The doctor made a tentative diagnosis of shock, inducing a temporary catatonic state. He might emerge from it at any moment, or he might become dangerous, to himself if not to others. He should be taken to hospital for further and more expert examination, he advised.

Throughout all of this, from two in the morning to the new day, Keeton held firmly onto the crude mask, his grip tightening like a child's when Richard tentatively tried to take it.

'Tallis was always making those things,' Margaret murmured from across the room. She was pale, exhausted with confusion. 'Which one is it?'

Alexander said, 'It's Moondream. She told me more about it, but I've forgotten.'

At the sound of the boy's voice, or perhaps at the mention of the mask's name, Keeton's unfocused gaze hardened and he sat up straighter, his lips smacking together for a moment. When Alex put his arm around the man's shoulder, Keeton curled into the embrace, apparently relaxed.

At his own request, Alex drove with the Keetons to the infirmary, fifteen miles away, near a secluded village on the county border. Richard and others from Shadoxhurst spent the next three days searching the countryside for any sign of Tallis, but for a second time they found nothing. The owners of the Ryhope Estate scoured the edges of Ryhope Wood and the area adjacent to the mill-pond, but reported that they, too, had found no traces. Twice, Richard went across the fields to the wired-off road, and stood where the old road entered the gloom, to the ruins of Oak Lodge where his son, and other children, had once played. High, barbed-wire fencing and notices of the prosecution of trespassers, were unfriendly reminders of the detached and hostile attitude to the local community that now resided in the Manor House: the two children (now in their thirties) had inherited the property after the death of their father.

Alex was a regular visitor to James Keeton over the next four weeks, and Richard and Alice both became concerned at what appeared to be the boy's insatiable curiosity about the silent man. Keeton sat immobile and silent, staring into space, the Moondream mask either clutched to his chest or propped up on the mantelpiece of his small, private room, overlooking the woods. But although Richard talked to his son, tried to discourage him from the obsessive visiting, Alex would not be persuaded. He could cycle the fifteen miles to the hospital in just over two hours. His homework suffered. He was always glad if Richard drove him to the secluded place, and seemed unbothered by his father being in the room.

What Alex did was to whisper stories to the frozen man. As he spoke, he stroked Keeton's hands. Sometimes he held the mask up for him, and invariably Keeton leaned forward to peer through its eyes. It was the only voluntary movement he made. Everything that Alex did sounded reassuring. He told jokes, wild adventures, he talked of Tallis.

'Come back, Mr Keeton. Come back home,' Richard heard him saying once. 'I know you're still wandering. You can come back now. Everything is safe.'

In the car, driving back to Shadoxhurst, Richard asked his son what he had meant by those words.

'It's just a feeling,' the boy said. 'His body's here, but I think his spirit is still wandering, still searching for Tallis.'

'This sounds like a fairy story.'

Alex shrugged. 'Sometimes he whispers things that make me think he can see other lands.'

'Like the land of the Green Knight, eh?' Richard said, and then the implication of what Alex had said struck him. 'He *whispers* things? He talks to you?'

'Not to me,' the boy said, shifting in the car seat and staring out at the darkening landscape. 'But he talks . . . Not very much, and always in whispers. It doesn't make much sense, but I think he's wandering somewhere, searching hard.'

A month to the day after his committal to the infirmary, Keeton recovered consciousness dramatically. By the time Richard and Alex arrived at the hospital he was in a state of high excitement. He didn't appear to recognise Richard, but began to talk almost incoherently to the boy, even as he peered through the face of the mask on the mantel-ledge.

'I can see her, Alex. I've caught up at last! She's on the other side of the mask. I'm not sure if she knows it's me, and she can't hear me, but she's there, among big trees, with several riders. She seems well. But she's so grown up.'

Richard watched and listened as the older man poured out his vision to the thirteen-year-old.

'Her face is scarred. She's become so tall. I think she must be a hunter of some sort. They're in a deep wood, near a river, among stone ruins. An old man is with her, and he keeps crying. There's something very strange in the trees – like a creature . . .'

'May I look?' Alex asked.

Keeton passed the boy the mask and Alex held it to his face, peering *in* through the eyes, turning slightly as if adjusting his view. From his expression it was clear that he had seen nothing but the room. Keeton took the mask back and placed it on the mantelpiece, touching the smeared moon-shapes, the crudely gouged eyes. His white shirt was saturated with sweat, his grey flannels creased and drooping. His hair had turned completely white in the last month, a startling change that occurred overnight, as if a ghost had touched him and he had been unable to respond.

He sat down now and sighed deeply. 'Alex?'

'Yes?'

'It was her. It was my little girl all grown up. Wasn't it?'

'Yes,' Alex whispered.

'Oh dear,' the man said, then slumped a little. 'Oh dear . . .'

And then he was silent. Within moments he had slipped away again.

He came back two weeks later, raving and angry, screaming as he stared inwards through the eyes of the mask. He had to be sedated. Thereafter, every three or four days he would emerge from his catatonic state and address an aspect of the reality he could experience through his daughter's childish creation.

As often as possible, Richard took Alex to see him, aware that the two of them shared a rapport that was quite exclusive. Keeton described wild visions, of journeys across marshlands, of great snows, of thudding and frightening skirmishes, fought out in bloodstained mud, of fires on hills and mad dancing at fire-lit dusk. And as he described these visions he seemed at peace, as if he knew that his daughter would return to him.

The periods of lucidity were short-lived, however, the longest being only five hours. And the longer the lucid phase, the longer the time in silence, empty of dreams, empty of life. Quite often, at weekends, Alex would beg to visit the hospital, only to be frustrated and saddened by a day of sitting with a dead man. Not even the touching of the precious mask could draw a flicker of response from James Keeton.

Alex must have heard the rows between his parents, but said nothing, just became more withdrawn himself. Alice had become increasingly angry and concerned at the time Alex was spending at the hospital. She wanted to end the relationship. Richard argued that there was a special trust between the two, and that Alex might be the channel through which the man would return to full sanity.

'What the hell is the attraction? They hardly know each other—'

'I know. I don't know what the attraction is. Perhaps it's Tallis, a link with her. All I know is, Alex seems to comfort the man, and he's happiest when they're talking, sharing visions.'

'Visions!' Alice's frustration made her face contort, anguish and anger ageing her. 'We've got to put a stop to it, Richard. He's not himself any more. I don't recognise him.'

'Give him time, Alice. If he *can* help Jim . . .'

Alice, exasperated, closed her mind to the argument. 'You're a fool.'

Alex, certainly, heard it all, and sometimes he would try to reassure both parents, but only by touch, never with words.

One night, in the early spring, he crawled on all fours into his parents' bedroom, reached up and tugged his father awake. Richard peered over the side of the bed and groaned. Alex silenced him with a finger to lips and beckoned him to come downstairs. Blearily, Richard followed, as Alice slept restlessly and full of her own unexpressed – perhaps inexpressible – pain.

At the back door Alex pointed into the March night. 'There's a fire by the wood, people dancing. They've got drums. It's very weird.'

Now that he looked carefully, Richard could see the faint, flickering glow of light from near Hunter's Brook, at the edge of Ryhope Wood. When he investigated his tall son with his fingers he could tell that Alex was wet with rain, and cold with night air. He was also dressed in jeans and windcheater.

'Have you been *out?*'

'Come and see! Bring a stick. They're all dancing with sticks around the fire.'

'Have you been *out?*' he whispered again. 'At three in the morning?'

From the far distance the sound of drums swelled on the night breeze. It was an odd rhythm, faintly audible, a fluctuating murmur in the cold night.

'Come and dance! *Please*, Daddy. Get a stick. Do it for Tallis.'

Richard stared at the pale features of his son. 'For Tallis? What do you mean by that?'

'I was dreaming of her. And the fire. Then I woke up. It might help Mr Keeton to find her again.'

Confused, very cold, aware that he was operating in a game that he didn't understand, Richard nodded. 'What sort of stick?'

'Anything. Anything wooden. Tallis's call was always wood.'

Richard went upstairs and dressed quietly, then explored the playroom, searching behind cartons, trunks and camping equipment until he found his old school cricket bat. 'Willow,' he said as he closed the door, walking down the path with Alex. 'Will that do? It's signed by Fred Trueman.'

Alex had no idea what his father was talking about. Impatiently he said, 'Let's go!'

Six months before, Richard had watched a rain-saturated woman in army fatigues run along this bridleway. Now he used a heavy torch to illuminate the way to the small fire that burned by Hunter's Brook.

The air pulsed dramatically with the fierce drum sound. As he drew closer he could see dark shapes twisting wildly in front of the flames. He was reminded of Indian dancing from Western films, but there was no chanting or singing, just the rapid, turning dance of eight or nine cloaked human figures, whose death-white faces caught the firelight as they spun.

The land dropped slightly to a muddy brook, then rose again. Alex scrambled up the slope in the darkness, an eager shape picked out in the beam from Richard's torch. As Richard struggled through the freezing brook, gasping as cold water soaked his feet, he became aware of the sudden ceasing of the drum beat. At the top of the rise he stared at the fire close by, but the figures had gone now, and the March night was still and silent, save for the murmur of wind.

Alex ran to the fire, crying out and running around the flames waving his stick. As Richard flashed the torch around, he picked out the tall, feathered pole that had been pushed into the ground. An odd twig-doll dangled from the top, clattering against the wood as the wind whipped up. A light but steady rain began to fall, driving in gusts at Richard as he stood and watched the fire. The glowing embers sizzled as they were quenched.

'They've gone!' Alex cried again, staring towards the woods.

'Let's go home,' Richard said.

Alex turned back to him. 'We should dance. Dance round the fire.'

Richard raised his cricket bat and looked, by flamelight, at the faded scrawl that was the signature of his cricketing hero. The face of the bat was dented and discoloured from years of use at school. Where the handle joined the willow blade there was a deep split, making use of the bat dangerous.

'Alex—'

'Daddy! Dance with me! It'll bring them back . . .'

'I'm afraid I'd feel rather foolish.'

'That's what you always say! That's why you never do anything!'

Alex ran to the feathered pole and knocked the twig-doll down, turning it in his hands, examining it minutely. He was shuddering, and Richard realised the boy was crying.

The rain suddenly started to fall more heavily, and the fire hissed and spluttered, burning more brightly before dimming. Disappointed and distressed, but unwilling to take his father's hand, Alex followed back through the pitch-dark of the night, back along the mudtrack, to the dark house where Alice slept.

Richard crawled gratefully back to bed, but slept badly, his dreams centring around dancing and fire. He was not a man given to intuition or premonition, but he felt nevertheless an eerie sense that something was about to happen.

The phone woke him at six in the morning. He stumbled out onto the landing and snatched the receiver from its cradle, groggily acknowledging the caller. It was Margaret Keeton. Her husband was awake and raving. He kept asking for Alex. The specialist in charge of his case felt that this might be a last moment of lucidity before a total collapse; so could the family and friends come at once?

James Keeton was standing at the mantelpiece. He was fully dressed and stooping slightly to peer in through the moondream eyes of the ragged mask. He was calling softly for his daughter. He was hardly raving, but Alice took one look at him and turned, walking stiffly away down the corridor. 'I'll go and keep Margaret company at reception. She's had a night of this. She must be exhausted.'

Alex went up to the man and touched his arm. Keeton looked round, glanced over at Richard and smiled.

'Where's Margaret?'

'Downstairs. Shall I get her?'

Keeton shook his head. 'Poor Margaret. She's aged . . . This must have been a hard few days.' He stroked the mask gently, then seemed to change his mood, a glow entering his eyes. 'I think she's coming home,' he said to Richard, then repeated the words to Alex and squeezed the boy's shoulders.

'Tallis?'

'Yes. Tallis. Coming home – but I'm afraid – I'm afraid she's coming the hardest way of all.' A moment's shadow, then a vigorous voice again. 'There has been such a battle, Richard. Crows on the field, feeding on the dead, and ragged folk dismembering and carrying off the corpses. Through these eyes I can see her, but she's so old now. Such a full life led. I wish I could have been with her. I don't know if she even hears me.'

He turned to the mask and called again. 'Tallis?' And after a moment, the name again, and again, before a sad yet smiling resolution. 'She can't hear me.'

Aware of Alex, Keeton rested a hand on the boy's shoulder, then took down the mask and placed it against Alex's eyes. 'What do you see? Do you see anything? Perhaps she'll speak to you.'

'I can't see anything,' Alex confessed.

Again, Keeton placed the mask on the mantelpiece, then went to the armchair and sat down heavily, letting his breath out slowly, his eyes half-closed as if with effort.

He watched Richard for a moment, then asked, 'How long was I away?'

'Away?'

'Before I was brought to this place.'

'A year, Jim. We thought you were dead. We thought – suicide.'

Keeton laughed dully, shaking his head. 'Why not? There's no life left, now. I've lost her, Richard, just as I lost my son before her. There's nothing, now. I didn't believe her when she told me stories of the wood, what a strange place it is – but she's gone there, and she's gone for good. Four days ago she went away. She won't come back. And I'm a dead man, as good as. I've seen what's happened to her—'

'She's been gone for a year and a half, Jim. She was gone a year when you turned up again.' Richard felt awkward. 'You were gone for a year yourself . . .'

'Four days,' James Keeton repeated. 'And a lifetime.' But now he frowned, watching Richard curiously. 'A year?'

'A year. Not that you'd have known it from looking at you. You've been in hospital for six months.'

'A year,' Keeton said, savouring the words, his eyes closed. 'Dear God, it was a strange place. The stream into the wood. Ryhope Wood. I saw her riding. There were four men with her. I tried to follow, but they were too fast, and I was so cold – and then the strange place, and the gentle ghosts, and they took me by boat across the sea to a lovely island, but I was so unhappy and they brought me back. A moon-faced girl showed me the way from the wood. And when she left me, a demon started to laugh and tear at me, and then the rain . . .'

'What strange place? Can you tell me, Jim? Can you remember?'

Keeton's eyes opened, looking wild for an instant, then with a long sigh he said, 'It comes over me and traps me. It's as if everything is sucked from me, all energy, all thought, all hope, all intensity. I become empty, clinging by a thread. I am aware of you, but can't respond. I don't even have the energy to scream inside.'

Richard realised that the subject had changed. Keeton was talking about his existence *now*, how it felt to be home.

'Time means nothing,' he went on. 'Alex's voice is soothing, but even that is just like water, lapping over me. There is no pain, Richard, no anguish. And then suddenly there is a flow of energy and Tallis is back. She's on the other side of the mask, do you know that? The mask is her, and the eyes can see her. When she's close I can hear her, see her, almost touch her. I've watched her in glimpses, growing old, fighting, loving. She bore three children. Three. But they all died. She's nearly gone now. When she goes, I go too. I have nothing left.'

'You've got us,' Alex said. 'Especially me.'

Keeton laughed and hugged the boy.

'We don't want you to go, Jim,' Richard said. 'We want you to come home. Come with us. Keep yourself well.'

'If I could I would,' Keeton said. 'But I have no control over the ebb and flow of my life. Margaret means nothing to me any more, and she knows it, and I feel it is the same with her. When Tallis went away, part of me went with her. First Harry, now her . . . Whatever is beyond that mask controls me.'

Nonsense, Richard thought, looking at the scrap of wood. But he couldn't bring himself to articulate the dismissive word aloud.

A male nurse came into the room and spoke briefly with Keeton, then Richard, and left. Richard, weary of the other man's sentimental ramblings, aware that he was really addressing everything to Alex, excused himself for a while and went down to sit with Alice and Margaret. But he had been downstairs for only a few minutes when he began to feel uncomfortable, even alarmed. The two women talked quietly together.

'I'm going back up,' Richard said, and hastened away from reception, taking the stairs three steps at a time, breaking into a run along the stark, grey-carpeted corridor.

Breathless, he arrived at Keeton's room, and saw the man again standing at the mask, stooping to peer through the eyes. Behind him, Alex was a hunched, crying shape. Tearful eyes turned on Richard, and the boy shook his head, mouth quivering.

What was happening?

Richard stepped into the room.

Keeton said, 'Tallis?'

Then more loudly, 'Tallis!'

A look of relief touched his face. 'We were worried about you,' he said through the eyes of the mask. 'We thought we'd lost you.'

And a moment later, smiling, Keeton added, to no one in particular, 'Well, thank God for that.'

He turned from the mask and went to the window, looking out across the grounds of the hospital. Then, with a small laugh and a sigh, he came to his chair, sat down, closed his eyes . . .

Richard went over to him . . .' Jim?'

'He's dead,' Alex said.

Richard felt quickly for Keeton's pulse. 'He can't be.'

'She came home,' the boy said, trembling as he spoke, looking very frightened. 'That's the end of it. Mr Keeton found what he wanted. Tallis came home.'

Alex had crossed the room and was peering through the eyes of the mask. Richard felt for the pulse in Keeton's warm wrist, found none. He listened at the man's mouth, stretched open an eyelid, then dragged the body down onto the floor, stretching it out.

'Get a nurse!' he said, but Alex kept staring through the mask. 'Alex! Go and fetch help. I don't know how to do this. Alex!'

Thump.

A fist to the dead man's chest, then a more controlled, careful placing of one hand over the sternum, and a thump with the other. Dear God, how should it be done? Press, then hit. Press, that was right . . .

'Alex!'

He pushed down on Keeton's chest, four times hard, then opened the man's jaws and pressed his own mouth against the cooling lips. He inflated Keeton's lungs, then watched the air drain away.

'I don't know what to do. I never trained . . . Alex, for Christ's sake get some help!'

As he shouted his son's name, as he turned in desperation, aware that footsteps were pounding along the corridor outside and that a cacophony of screaming and shouting had erupted from the other rooms, as he looked desperately to Alex for help, so the boy screamed 'Mr Keeton!' A second later he was *blown* across the room. The air stank suddenly of wet earth and wood and for a moment the space between mask and boy writhed and rippled, like the distorted reflection in disturbed water. There was a distant sound, like harsh laughter, then all air was drawn from the room and the windows rattled, the door slammed back on its hinges.

Frozen with shock, Richard watched Alex hit the wall and slump. In the instant before he collapsed his eyes were wide, his face a mask of terror. Then he fell forward, folding into himself, curling up like a leaf, and Richard was on him in moments, unrolling him, cradling him.

Laughter – echoing, then dying – mocking laughter . . .

'Alex! Alex!'

The boy was still conscious, but his whole body was shuddering uncontrollably. Wet, empty eyes stared up at his father. His mouth worked, his tongue licked his lips.

'Alex . . . what happened? What happened?'

Alex stared at his father blankly, his gaze unfocused. Then, like a small child, he reached up and put his arms round Richard's neck, drawing himself closer, curling into the heavy frame of the man, nestling there.

A male nurse was at work on James Keeton.

'What happened? What's that smell? Oh Christ! Adrenalin! I need adrenalin—'

'He suddenly collapsed,' Richard said, as he crouched, cradling Alex in his arms.

'He's gone,' the man said anxiously, shaking his head. 'He was so fit. This isn't right. I'll keep trying. *Where the hell's the adrenalin?*'

Two female nurses ran into the room, one to look after Alex. Richard stood up and bit back his own tears, watching the black eyes of the boy, the wet lips moving silently. The nurse whispered to the lad, then looked up.

'You'd better go to your wife. She and Mrs Keeton are walking out in the grounds.'

Richard nodded dumbly. But instead of going downstairs, he felt impelled to go over to the mask, to pick it up—

('He's dead. I can't get him back. Damn! Get Doctor Warren up here.')

It was an odd and eerie sensation, but where before when he had handled the mask it had tickled his senses, making the hair on his neck prickle, now he saw just a childishly-daubed piece of bark. It was quite lifeless, rotting; dead-eyed and meaningless.

Later, when he went over the events of that morning in his mind, Richard could no longer be sure that Alex had been *blown* across the room. He had run back and struck the wall in his excitement or panic; he had stunned himself. Everything had been happening so fast, with such urgency, that the boy's movements had taken on a surreal quality.

Nevertheless, something had shocked him, something so startling that it had caused him almost to fly backwards with surprise.

Alex slept, then woke and was silent for the next few hours, not responding to his parents' attentions. Then he slept again, deeply, restlessly.

By the end of the second day Richard's apprehension had begun to develop into terror. Alice, grim-faced and cold, talked and talked to the boy, but Alex just responded with incoherent murmurs. His eyes were wide, almost depthless. He stared at things without thought, without real sight. He seemed immune to suggestion. He was in his own world, a new world. The only words he used, at this time, were 'chapel' and 'giggler'. When he murmured 'chapel' he seemed agitated, perhaps puzzled. But 'giggler' was a sound he used in his nightmares, waking screaming this word, or name, shrieked from lips that were flecked, wet, the expression of a boy terrified by his vision.

He no longer read books. He no longer took interest in the radio, or music, or the events in Shadoxhurst. His models meant nothing. He sat in his room, surrounded by the treasures of his imagination, and stared at the insubstantial air in front of him. The Bradleys kept him away from school, and when the school's inspector came to interview them it took no more than five minutes to convince him that Alex was seriously ill.

Perhaps it was this humiliating and embarrassing visit that broke the wall of resistance in both Richard and Alice. A day after the inspector's visit they arranged for Alex to be taken to the same hospital where James Keeton had spent his last days.

The boy came home every weekend. The three of them walked, and tried to talk, and Alex was calm, pleasant, responsive to the simplest of things, but without any engagement of intellect or imagination. He might have been two years old again. He showed no wonder, no surprise, no interest. Only at night did he scream. When they walked in the woods when the light was gentle, Alex would sound wistful and point into the distance.

'Chapel . . .'

Perhaps he was remembering the school play, Gawain, the Green Knight, the woodland chapel below the fairy hill. Richard could never find out, because Alex had no words for him, and quite soon Richard gave up trying.

Late that summer, Alex disappeared. The windows of his room were locked, but his door had been left open – there had seemed no reason not to leave it so – and he had probably walked out of the hospital at some time during the night. His day clothes were missing. There was no note, of course. One of the nurses told Richard that for two or three days before, Alex had been more vocal than usual. He had seemed frightened, jumping at shadows or unexpected movements around him. Twice he had locked himself in the small toilet at the end of the corridor, only emerging when his favourite nurse encouraged him out. It was to her that he had spoken his last word, before disappearing from the hospital, a wistfully breathed 'chapel'. He had been looking into the distance, from his window, over the trees towards Shadoxhurst. Perhaps he had been thinking of home.

His badly decomposed body was found a year later, half-buried in the leaf litter and wild growth of a boggy elm wood at the edge of a local farm. Rooted up by an animal, probably a fox, the traces had been sniffed out by the farmer's dog. The skull had been so badly crushed, by two or three blows, that precise dental association was impossible, but from the size of the bones, the male features of the pelvis, scraps of clothing in the same grave, and the fact that it was found so close to Shadoxhurst, the conclusion at the inquest was that the remains were those of Alex Bradley, unlawfully done to death by person or persons unknown. The police investigation lasted two months, and the file was kept open when local activity ceased.

Alex was buried in Shadoxhurst church in May 1961. His parents' wreath was shaped like Alex's favourite model plane.

Tallis Keeton's moondream mask was buried with the bones.

PART TWO

In the Wildwood

The Green Chapel: 2

It had been raining for hours and he sheltered high on the east wall, curled up below the wide stone arch of an empty window. From here he could see down into the cathedral, where the hollyjack moved restlessly among the saturated trees.

She was upset again. He could tell this easily from the chattering sounds she made, and the way she passed from nest to altar, kicking at the wet benches, gabbling at the wooden faces and watching the boy from behind rain-glistening leaves. The wood in the cathedral rustled continually, occasionally juddered violently as new growth stretched the trunks, the marble floor buckling suddenly as each tree, its roots in the crypt among the bones, thrust a boy's length upwards, feeding on the rain and the new life that flowed through the earth.

In the big wood, the giggler came and went, its face thrusting from the edge for an instant only, time enough for the boy in the high window to see a gleaming eye in the black face, a second gouged socket, a grinning mouth, white tusks thin and deadly.

Other creatures hovered at the edgewood too. During this long time of rain he had seen wolves on their hindlegs, men with the heads of snarling dogs, a pig of vast size, and bird-men of all descriptions. Most disturbing was a woman in torn green robes. Her hair was a rich and full tumble of red around a noseless face that was as white and dead as a fish, the eyes cold and unblinking, her mouth open and wet. She had watched him for an hour, unmoving, then had stepped carefully back into cover. A minute later the giggler had taken her, noisily and terribly, and fed for a long time while the crows had circled in the rain above the trees, disturbed by the stink of flesh.

Other humans came, peering at the high stone wall of the cathedral. Some had weapons, others were mere shades, cloaked and hooded. One was half-armoured, his face covered with metal, the features of a fox, his heavy cloak red around the green bronze. He watched the boy for a long time, then waved and withdrew. The giggler tried for him, but failed to secure the life and retired howling for a while, before it recovered, parted the undergrowth and leered at the watching boy.

Why was the hollyjack so disturbed? She had embraced him and let him travel on the Little Dream, and when he had cried she had soothed him with bird song and thorny caresses. Although she often accidentally poisoned him with her forest offerings, she was always careful with her touch, and never drew blood except when dreaming with him. When the sadness at dreams of his father had passed, she had taken him into her nest, and they had slept for a day or more. When the sky darkened and the rain began to fall, they had both moved back into the sanctuary wood, and while she had explored the area near the altar, he had ascended to the window on the east wall.

She called for him now. She was a bristling, beckoning bush in a thicket of red-berried thorn by the Lady Chapel, gleaming as the rain ran from her leaves. But she was calling for him and he swung carefully down the ivy, touching dog-stone face as he passed it, to pacify it, and entered her embrace again, letting her thorns prick his skin, flowing through her roots into the crypt below the marble, out through the rootweb, past the giggler and the other creatures at the edge.

Where are we going?

Big Dream!

Deeper and deeper through the earth, through glades and hollows, by river cuts and high banks, through beech and elm and lime, willows by lakes, and aspen on chalk downs, flowing through the wildwood like blood through water, spreading, thinning, yet always touching the stone-place and the holly bush.

He came up in a misty place, near a river among silent trees; and the greenjacks were here, the *daurog* as he heard them named. He was in a place older than stone, at a time before words and language, but he felt the presence in the wood of men, though men with eyes and ears only, no mouths or tongues that could articulate, no way of calling save like the birds or wild creatures of the forest they hunted. He peered out into this ancient grove from the face carved in a tree.

The greenjacks were waking from their winter forms, the new growth on their bodies vibrant and sensitive. They moved through the wells of light, scratching at bark, scooping fingers into the earth, or brushing water from the stream along the curving branches that erupted from their mouths. He could see the different forms of the creatures, the oakjack, large and densely leaved, the birch female, quivering and restless, a thin silver shape by the water. Willow and a smaller oak were still rooted, although their heads turned to the light, willow's fringed arms rising as if he was stretching on waking from a deep sleep – and of course, in one way, that was precisely what this family was doing, although it was only the conscious parts of their sylvan minds that had slumbered within the stalking bodies of their winter forms.

There was a hollyjack among them. This evergreen had emerged from hiding, now that the new growth was on her family, and she ran among them, tending to them. She was aware of being watched by one of her own kind, and the hollyjack that cradled the boy quivered uncontrollably as she observed the much younger form.

The greenjacks were moving towards the cathedral. They were advancing steadily through the seasons and the wild-wood, closing on the stone-place, but as yet the hollyjack was puzzled by the reason. All the boy could understand from the faint flow of thought, whilst sharing the rootweb, was that the *daurog* were coming for him – and there was great danger if they came in winter.

But the boy was in a waking dream, still, his mind half on his father, half on the terrible creatures who waited for him beyond the sanctuary. Each day he felt a little more alive, although he thought of it as 'seeing further'. Memories shaped, like images in rippling water that was suddenly still. He felt frightened of the greenjacks, but took comfort in the pricking arms of his nesting friend. He was aware of her own fear, the great fear of the still and silent time of winter, the black time for trees among the heavy white of snow on the earth. A terrible death stalked the wildwood at that time.

Later in the day the skeletal form of the shaman approached the face in the tree, emerging from the darkness of the denser wood. Ghost-of-the-Tree, as the shaman was called, was badly broken. Fragments of bark hung from him like stiffened flaps of brown flesh. One side of his face was ragged, the branch tusks shattered (they would grow back with his own first bud). When he lifted his forelimbs to the watching boy, the fingers were bent, some missing, the nails cracked. He was caked around the mouth and chest with a rust-like paint, the last vestiges of blood from his winter hunting.

But before he fed now, on the reviving nutrients and water of the natural forest, he came to the tree, watching the carved face through those sinister eyes, the glitter of steel encased in wrinkled oak.

After a while, bolder, he approached and scraped the bark face with a nail. The thornwood entered the hard skin of the tree, creating a new cut among the old scars.

There are not sufficient seasons to prevent us from finding you. We'll find you soon—

The thought flowed through the root web, frightening and threatening at first, yet perhaps it was more of an exhortation, a fervent wish. The greenjacks were gentle. They were lost on this journey and exuding desperation. Whatever they wanted from the boy in the cathedral, they could not communicate it clearly. They were just coming to find him. The seasons would not stop them.

Boy and hollyjack flowed away from the face in the tree. The rain fell steadily, pouring from ledges and stone faces, pelting the trees inside the cathedral where bush and boy curled together.

Don't let me go. Hold me. Don't let me go – I want to see him again.

The hollyjack closed over him; rain filtered through the leaves of her crown and dripped onto the boy's closed eyes. He flowed with the Little Dream again, drawn by the feelings of confusion and anguish from his father.

The man was alone and frightened. He was hiding in a clearing, striking at shadows; the bear-man was gone, and his father was lost. The power of his fear and his loneliness writhed like a twisted vine through the rootweb, and the boy followed this scent and surfaced at the edge of the glade, his head full, now, of the lost man's inner voice, memories that were fresh in the man's mind, recent events that had much to do with his son . . .

Out of the Pit

The drive from his London flat had been long and tedious. Beyond Oxford the traffic had been slow and Richard had been unable to pick up the Home Service on his new car radio. He had been forced, instead, to fill the car with the sounds of rock and roll coming from either the Light Programme or Radio Luxembourg. He had enjoyed Procol Harum (though the lyrics to 'A Whiter Shade of Pale' left him bemused), Pink Floyd and the jaunty sounds of The Kinks with 'Waterloo Sunset', but he couldn't get away, it seemed, from a syncopated piece of trivia called 'Puppet on a String' and an appalling piece of crass commercialism called 'I'm a Believer', and their performance, as he drove the last few minutes to Shadoxhurst, had been punctuated with his cries of Dear God, oh dear God, this can't be called Music!

You old man, he lectured himself as he finally stepped out into the cool country air and stared over the thorn hedge at the small spire of Shadoxhurst church. He ached from the drive. He was thirsty, hungry and haunted.

He was home for a short break from work, back to the house, back to bad dreams. But for Richard this trip was an annual pilgrimage – his fifth – that he felt he had to make.

The footpath to Shadoxhurst was overgrown with early nettle. He kicked through the weeds, crossed an open field, and clambered over the locked gate of the small churchyard. It had rained earlier in the day and everything was fresh and moist. His desert boots soon became saturated as he approached his son's grave and knelt down, his heart torn between grief and peace.

Someone had put fresh flowers in the small porcelain pot on the green gravel. Bird droppings were smeared across the name on the granite headstone and Richard spent a minute or so cleaning off the lime. His fingers, touching the sharply inscribed letters of the name, felt only stone.

He's not down there, not all of him, only part of him. What happened? What in God's name happened?

The loss was too much, and the return to the village too strong an event to resist: emotion surged; and for a while he sat, letting the sodden turf saturate his skin through his jeans, and cried, and missed Alex, and thought of Alice, long gone Alice.

He was startled by the sounding of the church bell. It was three-fifteen. The bell rang a second time, then was silent. A moment later the side door of the church opened, closed, and was noisily locked.

Richard returned to his car and drove to his house, parking on the street and spending a few minutes greeting neighbours. It was clear that his absence from the village, and from the house, was a source of criticism. But he had found it impossible to stay here after Alex's body had been found, and had moved to London, where he now worked in a bank.

Entering the house through the back door he was at first overwhelmed by the smell of damp. During the winter there had been a leak in the bathroom ceiling, and the carpets were encrusted with fungus. Giant spiders scuttled across the enamel of the bath itself. He trod the floor warily, but the soaking wood was firm. Below, the ceiling of the utility room sagged badly, and he sighed as he thought of a peaceful holiday now inclining towards repair work.

Everything otherwise was as he had left it. He had fresh bedding and a bottle of wine. The bookshelves were full of old favourites. There was no television. He would not miss it.

Inside the front door was a scatter of letters. He picked them up and leafed through them, the accumulation of nine months' absence. Among them were two scrawled notes on paper that had been folded and not enclosed in an envelope, and as he opened the sheets he was disturbed by the handwriting on one of them. It seemed familiar.

The first note, written in a robust, upright style, read: '*Mr Bradley – I have some information for you of urgent interest. No one in the town knows your forwarding address, but I'm told you return here regularly. I've left an instruction with the manager of the Red Lion. I'll drop by just before Christmas and hope to catch you then.*'

It was signed *Alexander Lytton.*

The second note, in a slanting but precise hand, read simply, '*You're a hard man to pin down. But we'll keep trying. Believe me, Mr B, you'll want to talk to us. I don't want to be more specific right now. We need*

44

to talk. If you come back to the house in the next few months, can you go out to the brook, where the bridlepath crosses it, and tie a green ribbon to the signpost there? And check to make sure it stays? One of us will notice it and stop by. We move in and out all the time. Sorry to be so mysterious.'

It was signed *Helen Silverlock.*

When the Red Lion opened, at six-thirty, Richard went into the lounge bar and ordered a pint. He was served by someone he didn't know, but Ben Morris came down later and greeted him.

'Showing your face again, eh?'

'Time to come home, Ben. Time for a holiday.'

'There were some folk looking for you, a few months back.'

'Yes, I know. They spoke to you. Left a message or something . . . ?'

'Last summer. Strange pair of tourists, strange dress. The bloke was small, sturdy, a Scot, very irritable. The woman was very pretty, like, long black hair. A right head-turner. She was American, no doubt about it. Not a hippy, though. Not a student. But both of them queer, like. Odd clothes. They were looking for you but wouldn't say why.'

'What did they ask you to tell me?'

Ben nodded and frowned. 'If you came home, you were to tie a ribbon out by the old track, by the brook. Nobody knew where you were, Richard. You didn't leave an address . . .'

'I know. I wanted to be away. Did they say anything else? Did you get an idea where they worked?'

Ben shook his head. 'He was some sort of scientist, working out on the Manor grounds, there. I heard them talking about "The Station". That's all. As I said, queer, like.'

It was a fine May evening, very tranquil, very warm, the light almost lucid. Richard walked along the bridleway to the brook, found the signpost, and tied a strip of green rag, torn from an old shirt, around the top. Two riders galloped over the hill, from Ryhope Manor, he imagined. Ryhope Wood, on the Manor estates, was shimmering, a solid wall of green and orange, just across the fields, beyond the rights of way. Alex had been fascinated by Ryhope, as had his friend Tallis, but probably only because it was reputed to be haunted.

Having left his marker, he returned to his house and began the process of unwinding, with fish and chips, red wine and *Cold Comfort Farm*, a school favourite of his.

*

Two days later, she was waiting for him when he returned from a shopping trip to Gloucester. She had found the green ribbon and arrived in Shadoxhurst as fast as she'd been able. Finding the house open she had entered and called for Richard, but then gone outside and sat down against the base of the elm at the bottom of the garden.

As he stepped through the gate she rose from the ground, startling him. She was dressed in a dull brown anorak and baggy trousers, tied rightly around hard working-boots the colour of mud. Her long hair was jet black, save for a silver streak at each temple. Her skin was tanned and her eyes an intense green. For a second she had seemed a part of the tree and its root system, but now she stood, breathing hard and extending a friendly hand.

'I'm Helen Silverlock.' She tugged the streak of white and grinned. 'My grandfather named me "Frightened of Foxes" but I buried that one years ago. I left you the note. I *guess* you're Richard Bradley?'

'Yes, I am.' As he stepped closer to shake hands he became aware of her smell, stale breath and the damp, rather rank scent of wet under-growth. Her gaze was startling, flickering over Richard's face in a penetrating and inquisitive way that unnerved him slightly. As his grip curled around her fingers, he felt the scaly, bark-hard skin on the back of her hand, and was so taken aback that he broke the greeting prematurely and obviously.

She smiled at him, rubbing the skin – which was almost black. Had she been burned? – and said, 'It's OK. It doesn't cause me pain.'

'Looks nasty.'

'Necessary,' she said cryptically, and then, as if slightly embarrassed, put her hands into the deep pockets of her strange anorak. She was not tall, and her American accent gave him no hint as to where she was from in the States. As they walked to the house he asked the question.

'Nebraska. A small town called Watanka Lake. I'm Lakota Sioux. Not pure blood, but not far off, I've lived in Brazil for four years, and here in the UK for over a year now, so home seems a long time ago . . .'

'Well, you're more than welcome in my own damp and humble home,' Richard said as he let her into the house.

She confessed that she'd already entered once. 'I forgot where I was. Back home it would have seemed normal . . .'

Richard was easy about the intrusion, but then he began to remember the running woman of eight years ago, the intruder who had scrawled a note to him, an incomprehensible message. And connections, nagging connections, began to be made.

Helen sat at the kitchen table, biting her lip and clearly not totally at ease. Richard offered tea, coffee or red wine.

'Not wine,' she said. 'Coffee, if it's made from beans.'

'I'm afraid I only have Camp Coffee. It's a liquid. Quite thick. Quite strong.'

She grimaced, showing her teeth and just a hint of tongue, but smiling too. 'Tea would be just fine,' she said.

'I agree.'

As he poured water into the kettle she asked, 'Do you have a TV? A paper?'

'No TV, I'm afraid. And I've chucked my paper away. Why?'

She shrugged, loosened the zip of her overcoat. 'This is going to sound odd,' she said. 'But what's today's date?'

He had to think for a moment. 'It's . . . I think it's the eleventh. Yes, the eleventh of May. Does that help at all?'

With a laugh, walking over to the window and peering out at the evening, she said, 'Just helps me orient.'

Richard leaned against the sink, watching his odd guest. He noticed a film of moisture on her forehead and, unsure as to whether she was hot or just nervous – she was behaving nervously – he suggested she shed her coat. Without response she unzipped the anorak and tossed it on the floor by the back door, returning to her chair at the table. The heavily lined, baggy trousers were tied about her waist with a belt of gadgets. Her undershirt was a startling affair of green webbing, a body stocking that hugged her slim frame like a skin. Watching the man watching her, looking at her body, she smiled sympathetically. 'It keeps me warm, it keeps me cool. It's based on what the astronauts wear on Apollo.'

'I was staring,' he said, reddening. 'I apologise.'

'I don't mind if you stare. It's OK.'

With a laugh he said, 'You look and sound as if you've just beamed down from the Starship Enterprise.'

'Isn't that a neat show? I miss it. I miss a lot of TV. Did you ever see *The Twilight Zone?*'

'My son did. I watched it with him sometimes. The programme I always liked was *Quatermass*. Did you see that in America? *Quatermass and the Pit?*'

She shook her head. 'I certainly heard about it. Some of the British guys at the Station grew up on it. Ancient Martians, right?'

'Ancient Martians,' Richard agreed. 'The Station?'

'That's where I'm based. Old Stone Hollow Station, Hollowstone for short.'

The kettle boiled and Richard made the tea. His heart had started to race. Helen watched him, more relaxed now. The evening sun, through the window, made her hair shine. The musty, dank smell of her clothes was heavy in the air, but the scent of the tea became stronger for a moment. He was too aware of the gnarled skin on her right hand. He thought of the hand as ruined, but she flexed it easily, the black scales stretching like a lizard's. He was more aware of her eyes. She seemed so familiar with him. Indeed, she seemed familiar *to* him. He thought of her note. He thought of the running woman. The thought nagged its way to expression.

'How long did you say you'd been in England?'

'About a year. In *England*.'

'You wouldn't have been in Shadoxhurst in 1959, then?'

She seemed startled, frowning, then quickly said, 'Damn it. No. No I wouldn't. Why? I was still at college. Why?'

Disturbed that he had alarmed her he turned and stared, then brought the teapot to the table. His head was in a spin – he consciously thought this as he tried to clear his thoughts – and he tried to visualise the writing on the note that the running woman had left all those years ago. Although he had long since lost the scrap of paper, he was sure that the writing was similar to Helen's. And the running woman had been small, short-haired and bulkily dressed.

What had that note said? He struggled to remember. Some of it came back. 'Do you have any idea about . . . pre-morphs?'

'Pre-morphs?' She looked puzzled.

It wasn't the right word. 'Proto-gamma-morphs?' he suggested hesitantly.

'Proto *gamma* morphs? You *have* been watching too much *Star Trek*. No. It means nothing . . .'

But for a second her face clouded, a moment's concerned thought before she again shook her head and confirmed, 'No. Nothing at all. Why?'

'I feel I've known you before,' Richard said bluntly, and Helen laughed.

'Great line. I've only heard it a hundred times.'

'I feel I've known you before,' he insisted solemnly, watching her face carefully. She was upset.

She stared at the table, good hand covering the black scales of the other. 'Please don't,' she said quietly.

'Please don't what? I'm not making a pass. I feel I've known you before. You're very familiar.'

'Don't,' she insisted. 'Just pour the tea. Don't talk about it. Not yet. I didn't come here for this. I'm not ready—'

'But I'm sure it was you—'

She erupted with anger. 'Stop it, Mr Bradley! Stop it now! You don't know what you're doing. Shut up about it!'

Her fury was heavy in the room. Her eyes had widened and her whole facial demeanour had knocked the breath from Richard's body. She had not just been angry: she had been terrified, and had covered the fear with a look of such draining aggression that he was incapable of speech for a moment.

It was she who spoke finally and her words were an apology. Then: 'I came to tell you something.'

'Tell me then,' he said stiffly. 'You've obviously been after me for some time. Tell me what you have to say.'

'Don't be angry with me. Please! I didn't mean to upset you, Mr Bradley. I can't explain yet, but you were touching difficult ground for me.'

Her candour softened him and he regretted the bitter tone that had touched his words. 'Please feel free to call me Richard.'

'Richard,' she echoed, 'I bring you tidings of great joy, yet great difficulty. Greater than I'd realised, since you're obviously in deeper than you know. And I've been in the deep end for a year, now . . .'

'You're not making any sense, Helen. What ridings of great joy?'

'We've found your son,' she said in an urgent whisper, leaning toward him, trying to instil confidence.

Richard's heart stopped. He banged the cup into its saucer, his face reddening, her words touching anger in him again. 'Alex? Alex died a long time ago. What is this? What are you doing?'

'Please!' she said urgently. 'Just listen to me. Alex *isn't* dead. We've located him. He's not dead. He's alive. We've made contact with him. He's been communicating with us since late last summer. He's still alive, Richard.'

Confused, wanting to feel anger yet aware that the certainty of the woman's words, her assurance, were pointing up his own uncertainties about the fragile, sad remains that had once been discovered in the woods, he drew breath and closed his eyes.

Dear God, he thought, I'm beginning to have hope again. Then he grew black. Alex was dead. Whatever this woman was talking about, whoever they had found, it was not his son.

'Who's we? "We've" found him?'

'We're explorers. I'll come to that later.'

'What does he look like? Alex? How does he look?'

Helen looked confused, now, shaking her head, angry at herself. 'I'm not making a very good job of this. Lytton should have been the one to talk to you. Richard, it's not as easy as perhaps I'm making it sound. I'm sorry. It's hard to know how to approach it—'

'Approach what?'

'We've made *contact* with your son. But we haven't exactly *found* him. Not yet, at least.'

'He's telephoned you?'

'No. Nothing like that. We *have* found him. We're going to need your help to bring him home . . .'

Tears stung Richard Bradley's eyes and he stood, facing the garden through the misting window, hands in pockets.

Six years since Alex's body had been found. Six long years, six empty ones. He could still remember the stink of the wood as he'd trudged with the police through the saturated bracken. The skies had been overcast, a dull, depressing rain falling. Beneath the trees it was stiflingly humid. Their footsteps, crushing through the undergrowth, had been the only sound in the world. A solemn group of men had stood around the cordoned area where the litter had been swept away and the distorted torso exposed, its empty skull upwards, the face no more recognisable than a crushed pile of autumn leaves.

'I'd given up hope,' he said from the window. 'I can't believe you. My son went away. He's never coming back. It's too painful to give me this hope again. You shouldn't have come.'

There was no sound from the woman save for the gentle clink of her cup returned to her saucer.

He went on, 'The bones were very corrupted. Very rotten. They were an inch or two too short. Or were they? Who could tell what changes had occurred with a skeleton so decayed? The forensic tests were done hastily. They all knew it was Alex. It was easy to bury him and give up anguish. If I've had doubts about his being dead, they've ceased to gnaw at me. So I suppose I've accepted it.'

'You've accepted that he's not coming back, not that he's dead. I spoke to the barman at the Red Lion. I know about your doubts.

Forgive me, that's why I was so blunt. I thought you'd be glad of the news.'

'What news? You've brought me no news. You can't give me evidence of Alex. You confuse me.'

He had turned from the window, angrily watching the calm woman at the table. She leaned forward.

'You said the bones were rotten – what exactly was said about them at the inquest?'

'They were woody.'

'They weren't bones,' Helen said dogmatically, her eyes alive with certainty. 'It wasn't Alex. We have a word for what it was. A *mythago*. A false thing. And the boy we've located *is* Alex. Believe me.' Her face darkened. 'The only problem is . . . we don't know where he is *exactly*.'

Suddenly suspicious, Richard came back to the table and leaned down on it. 'The *boy*? How old is the boy who's been speaking to you?'

'About thirteen,' Helen said.

Richard laughed sourly, walking away from her. 'What is this? What sort of sick game is this?' But he couldn't look at her as he chided. 'If Alex is alive he's nineteen, twenty years old, now. He's a man.'

Why was he crying? With disappointment? Anger? He didn't want to be angry with Helen Silverlock. He didn't want her to go. Perhaps hope had surfaced for a moment, but her words had dashed those hopes again.

She said, 'He's still a boy, Richard.'

Perhaps he was retarded . . . perhaps he sounded like the boy he'd been, even though he would be bearded, deep voiced . . . NO!

Helen went on, 'We've learned a lot from him, including where he lived, this house, and we feel him strongly. He's a boy, and he's not complete. His mind is not complete. But he has strength, and he is drawing his world back to himself. It may take a long time, and it's dangerous. He's in great danger. Dr Lytton doesn't know if we *will* be able to help him, but we can't do anything until we get our hands on him. That's why we need you. We want to help you, and Alex too. But you have to be involved, which means one weird trip.'

After a moment Richard sat down, tried to pick up his cup but the china rattled so badly in the saucer that he abandoned the simple act. 'You've hit me where it hurts,' he said with a thin smile. 'And I think you have something else to tell me. I can sense it. There's something very wrong. Where is it you *think* Alex is?'

'He's built himself a defended site in a ruined cathedral. The cathedral is in the heart of Ryhope Wood—'

'Ryhope? I doubt that. It's on the Estate. An unpleasant and dangerous stretch of wood. But it's far too small to have had a cathedral built within it.'

Helen Silverlock laughed delightedly, shaking her head as she watched the man. 'You'll be surprised by what can be found there. But I'm not the person to show you. There's more than a ruined church, Richard. And Alex is there too. We can get him back, with your help. But he's a long way in. Maybe three months . . .' she said awkwardly, watching him.

'Three months?'

'Maybe three months to get to him. It's hard to tell. There *may* be a short cut.'

'Three months? In Ryhope?' Richard was laughing at the absurdity of what he was hearing.

Helen ignored him, finishing, 'And we don't know what's between the edge and the guarded zone he's constructed. There's an anomaly, an abnormality, something we can pass through, but can't *access*.'

'Lost,' Richard said kindly. 'Totally lost.'

'Who?'

'Me.'

Helen stood and fetched her coat from by the back door, shrugging it on and zipping it half-way up. 'It's late. I have to get back, and you need rest.' She seemed undecided and disappointed.

Richard toyed with the cup, half-watching the woman, very much wanting her to stay, despite the pain he was feeling.

She couldn't be right. He shook his head. Alex would be twenty! They had the wrong boy. She couldn't be right.

'I've got to go,' she said. 'If you change your mind, leave another marker. And have good walking boots, weather-proofing, a good book, any medication you need, some food, a good brandy, two changes of clothing, and a rucksack, a good-sized one. Have them ready.'

'I have a job in London. I have to be back in two weeks.'

'You won't need that much time.'

'You said three months. Three months to find him. I don't understand.'

'I know. I know you don't. I'm sorry, but it's as hard for me at the moment. Will you come to the Station? It's not far. Six or seven hours' walk. Come tomorrow?'

He shook his head. 'I don't know. You have a boy at the end of some sort of communication network and the boy is thirteen. And my boy is twenty. And unless his voice has failed to break, they can't be one and the same. Is it possible he's older than you realise?'

'Maybe,' she said with a shrug. 'I doubt it. We think he's in a timeslow.'

'Something else I don't understand.'

'Sorry.'

She turned to go, opening the door to the gathering dusk.

'Helen?'

Glancing back, she hesitated and smiled. Richard stood and went over to her. 'Thank you,' he said. 'I'm sure your intentions are quite genuine.'

'I'll come back,' she said defiantly, smiling. 'Don't you worry about that!'

As she walked down the path he called out, 'Next time he calls you, ask him what stick I danced with round the fire. It was our secret.'

'That's a good idea,' she said dully, mocking him.

He called again, 'I'm being honest with you. I'm not sure I believe you've found what you tell me you've found. But I'll know him when I hear his voice. I'll know him. If you can arrange it.'

Helen had zipped up her coat and was running along the bridleway, towards Hunter's Brook. Richard recognised the gait, and his confusion was compounded.

Helen Silverlock *had* been here before, despite what she'd said.

Oak Lodge

At dawn, a grim grey mist hung over the land, a subdued and flowing sea in which the dark features were the taller trees of the fields and woods.

Richard stood in his bedroom, fully-dressed, hands in his pockets, and stared at the wreathed land, thinking moodily of the woman, her message, her enthusiasm, her strangeness. Crows circled close to the house, flapping and vanishing through the wraithed branches. One detached itself and swooped towards the garden, gliding low over the gate and rising towards the bedroom window with the merest flap of its wings. Richard could hear the scrabbling of nestlings in the disused chimney and waited for the great bird to continue its curve, up to the roof, but the creature came straight on and smashed startlingly against the window. The whole pane shook. The crack of beak on glass seemed deafening. When Richard opened the window and stared down, he could see no sign of the bird, but its dreamlike and dramatic action had disturbed him and he went downstairs.

At nine o'clock he rang Alice in London. She had just arrived at work and was tetchy and tired. She became almost hysterical when he told her, as simply as he could, what Helen Silverlock had implied to him, but when she heard that the boy was thirteen years old she laughed scornfully, then began to get angry. She wanted to know why he had *really* called her.

'For just that reason,' he said. 'I thought I should keep you informed.'

'You have something on your mind. What is it, Richard? Why don't you be honest about it?'

'I rang to tell you what I've told you,' he said wearily. 'Goodbye, Alice.'

He put the phone down, wondered if she would call back and when the phone stayed silent went back upstairs and sorted out his weather-proof clothing.

By midday the grey gloom had been replaced by a bright and overcast sky, a fresh wind bringing the land alive. Richard trudged in heavy boots along the bridleway towards Hunter's Brook. He had not brought a rucksack. He intended only to look a little more closely at the wood where Helen had said she and her team were stationed.

The stream was in wild flood, and along its edge he could see the spoor of deer, probably from the Manor park. A high wall bounded the Estate on most sides, but a right of way passed over several fields, and here the boundary was marked by fences and a stile. Ryhope Wood was a dense and solid wall of trees to his right as he crossed the field towards the old road. He followed this to the wood itself, and was mildly surprised to find that it ended abruptly, overgrown by dense bushes and scrub elder. A 'Keep Out' notice had been recently fixed on barbed wire.

He walked on round the wood, conscious that he was now on private grounds. The Manor House was hidden by trees, half a mile away; the only sign of life was a gallop, five riders exercising the horses from the Manor's stables. They crossed open land, then turned and came back, thudding past Richard without taking any notice and passing away toward the ridge where an earthworks had been built, long in the past.

Was this where Alex had come to play with his friends, Tallis and the rest? Tallis had always been so quiet, a mysterious girl existing in a rich fantasy world of story and invention. Alex had always wanted to play rougher games, when outside, exploring woodland being one of them. But he had never talked in detail about Ryhope, only referred to it darkly as a place where 'Tallis talks to statues'.

What had he meant?

Years after the boy's death, Richard began to miss him again, and to miss the lost opportunity of knowing his son, of sharing his mind-games. Alex had always liked comics, and they had read together in peace, or watched TV, but had so rarely spoken or explored ideas. Alice had always been too busy doing things, arranging for trips, for picnics, for journeys to London, for schoolbooks and clothes. She had known Alex's strengths and weaknesses and had been nurturing him towards areas of intellect and interest where he might do well at school, such as playwriting and biology. Even so, she could not have known the inner boy, the adventurer.

He felt sorry for himself, sat for a while head bowed and thought back over the years. He allowed himself tears, and the wind, freshening and gusting, made the enclosed scene all the more mournful.

Alex had been in his grave too long. The pain had passed away too many years ago. The tears, the melancholy, were short-lived, and Helen Silverlock was standing before him again, mysterious and inviting.

An intense curiosity now began to push away the sorrow. The edge of the wood was thorny and grassy, too solid, too dark. It was as if it had never been broken by the passage of people or animals. Sunlight caught the sign across the road, and Richard's interest peaked.

He eased himself through the barbed wire and entered the gloom of the undergrowth, brushing at branches and ivy as he felt his way carefully along the hard surface underfoot that told of the crumbling road. When the wall of a house suddenly loomed before him he was startled. He touched the brick and pushed through the stifling tangle of creeper and briar, following the wall until he reached the back of the house. Sunlight dappled above him now, and by its flickering light he could see the blackened, rotting shape of a tall wooden idol. It was leaning heavily against the house. If there had ever been carved features they were long since obliterated by rain and time, but he thought he could faintly discern a gaping mouth and the outline of a wide, blind eye.

Crouching, he crawled below the statue, still feeling along the brick wall, and after a moment stepped into a cleared space, now grassy and filled with flowers and nettles, extending from what had once been French windows. He saw, too, that people had been here recently.

He stepped into the house. The vegetation in the room had been scythed down and the smell of fresh sap was still strong. Through the covering of nettles and ivy he could see the fragmentary remains of furniture. A tree, a substantial oak, grew in the middle of the room, and Richard was puzzled: this was old; had the owners built their house *around* the oak?

He was startled as birds moved noisily above him, where the ceiling had collapsed and branches entwined, and stepped outside again. A small beaten path led from this glade to what had once been a back yard, and here a wider space had been cleared, bounded by thick saplings, but quite light. A ramshackle shed still stood here, and he could see the remains of a fence and gate forty yards away, where the trees grew thick and dark again. The garden area spread away from the creeper-covered hole of the back door, through which he now passed.

Inside he found the kitchen, a heavy marble work-surface, and the remains of fires and food on the floor. He saw, too, the gleam of light on a tracery of wires, and investigated more closely.

There were five wires in all, each the thickness of fuse wire. They had been run to and from various points, out around the perimeter of the garden clearing. There was no electric charge in them. They were just higher than Richard's head and did not seem designed to trap anything. Where they joined the house they were attached to tiny terminals, and around each terminal a gold spiral had been impressed upon the brick.

A sudden wind gusted and the wood swayed restlessly, then was still again. In the sudden silence Richard heard the sound of electricity deeper in the house, and he followed the murmur to its source. In a box in the middle of what might have been a parlour – he could still see the wallpaper and a sodden, fungus-covered armchair below the ivy – he found a small machine, like a miniature radio. It had two needle dials, one of which was flickering. Gold and copper wires led from four sockets into the ground around it, and from a fifth vertically to the exposed laths of the ceiling where the plaster had fallen. The machine emitted the faintest smell of ozone.

As he stepped away from it, the needle on the active dial registered something strongly, then faded. As he approached again the needle quivered but remained essentially inert, only to react suddenly with great swings to the extreme, even though Richard had neither moved nor breathed. It was not responding to him, then.

At this same moment the birds outside fled through the foliage and something crashed away from the house, making a sound that might have been a cry, or perhaps laughter.

Unnerved, suddenly claustrophobic, Richard kicked his way through the tangled undergrowth and out of the overwhelming gloom of Ryhope Wood, back to the field. His head ached and his vision was askew. He rubbed his eyes but they kept watering, the edges of his vision blurred. He was getting a migraine, he imagined, something from which he suffered when he was very stressed.

Oddly, he felt quite relaxed at the moment, merely a little spooked.

He lay back on the damp ground and watched the swirl of grim, grey clouds above. Slowly his vision returned to normal. The breeze made the moisture in his eyes sting with cold.

The gallop was returning. He could hear the drum of hooves, the shouts of delight and encouragement as the five riders stretched their charges to the limit, galloping up the slope, a hundred yards or so from where he lay.

As they passed, Richard still stared up into the sky, but he was aware that one horse had reined-in and was now trotting towards him. He sat up and stared at the young, grey-faced man who rode around him, watching him with the pallor and arrogance of the Manor's new owners. This was the eldest son, a man of thirty or so. In his green parka and flat cap he might have ridden straight from Windsor.

'These are private estates. What the hell do you think you're doing here?'

'I'm walking,' Richard said. 'Or rather was. At the moment I'm resting. Good morning.'

He had meant it to sound dismissive, but the rider kicked his horse forward and came threateningly close. The horse watched Richard through big, tired eyes. Steam was coming off its coat. It was a magnificent animal, seventeen hands at least, gleaming black, its mane tight and trimmed. It watched the man on the ground as if sorry for him.

'The right-of-way is half a mile to your left. Return to it at once.'

'The road into the wood . . . that was once a right-of-way too, I imagine. Where did it go exactly? There's a ruined house in the wood . . .'

The horseman came closer and leaned down, waving his crop menacingly in Richard's face. As Richard started to stand up in alarm, the young man thrust the short whip towards the bridleway. 'Over there! The right-of-way is over there! If I catch you trespassing again I shall have you arrested.'

And he turned and galloped towards the Manor.

Exasperated and angry, Richard walked slowly back to his house, kicked the kitchen table and poured himself a large glass of red wine.

It was an hour later that he finally noticed the message pinned to his kitchen noticeboard:

A cricket bat? You danced around the fire with a cricket bat?

That evening he wrote a brief letter to his parents, and an almost identical note to his place of work.

If you don't hear from me for a while, please don't be anxious. I'm teaming up with some people for an expedition into what I'm told is a pretty remote place, and it's hard to know if I'll get back in time for autumn. I can't talk about the trip in detail, except to say that I've just realised it's something I need to do: full story when I get back. Just one thing: if anybody from a place called Old Stone Hollow should call you, take what they say very seriously, even if you think it sounds a bit bizarre.

He took the letter to the Red Lion to be posted, had a glass of light ale, then returned home and slept well for a few hours, the result of the nocturnal distraction and alertness that had kept him awake the previous night. Nevertheless, he was up at three in the morning. He dressed quickly, then packed his rucksack with brandy, apples, sandwiches, a compass, an adventure novel and changes of clothing; an hour later he was walking through the same heavy mist that had encompassed the land the morning before. Now, though, he walked with purpose and at first light, when he arrived at Hunter's Brook and found the signpost, he spread a tarpaulin on the ground, sat down, then curled up to keep himself warm.

He felt strangely relaxed. The chill on his cheeks reminded him of his school days, and camping on the moors, or along the Wye Valley.

He knew without knowing that someone would come for him.

The Wildwood

He was being shaken gently. He opened damp eyes, glimpsed the huge, dark shape above him, and for a second thought that he was being attacked by a wild animal. He yelled with fright and twisted away, looking for a rock or piece of wood with which to defend himself. When no pursuit immediately occurred, he turned back to observe the new arrival.

The man was wearing a heavy bearskin robe, dark brown and black fur splattered with mud. His hair was long and jet black, as was his beard. A red and green feather hung, tied with twine, from a single ringlet on his right temple. Intense brown eyes sparkled with humour from below heavy brows. His boots were dun leather and filthy, their tops fringed with circlets of yellowed animal teeth, which rattled as he moved, crouched on his haunches. From his mouth came a powerful odour of cheese and wild onion.

He was watching Richard, grinning.

'You sent for me, sir?' this behemoth roared with a throaty chuckle, like a smoker's laugh, Richard thought as he wiped dew from his face. The man's accent was French. He extended his hand, quite slim-fingered and cool, not the brawny paw that might have been expected, and Richard shook it. 'You *are* Richard Bradley?'

'What's left of him. You've just scared the living daylights out of me.'

'I'm Arnauld Lacan, and I'm quite harmless. Good morning! I'm watching the edgewoods for a while and I noticed your summons on the way-marker. Good man! Helen will be glad you've come.'

Glancing at his watch, Richard realised that he had fallen asleep for three hours. It was seven in the morning.

'Where is Helen?'

'Beyond Hergest Ridge, looking for a *trickster*. It's a long way from the Station. She went off yesterday, so she might be away for some time. But we think everything should be all right.'

Richard reached for his pack, conscious both of the powerful smell of animal sweat coming from the friendly man before him, and of his words. 'Why shouldn't everything be all right?'

'It's too deep to be sure,' Lacan said with a concerned frown. 'It always makes us nervous to go there. But she's been beyond Hergest Ridge before and come back OK. She knows what to watch for. Are you stiff?'

Richard reached out a hand and the other man hauled him upright. As he stood he realised how tall the Frenchman was, probably six feet four. Without being asked, Lacan twisted Richard round and ferociously massaged his shoulders, powerful fingers stretching and bending the joints of his shoulders and back. 'Better?'

'Ça va mieux,' Richard muttered as the pressure-shock faded.

Lacan laughed loudly. 'A man who speaks my language!' he said. 'I think I'm going to like you!'

He probed around in his own pack, a bulky affair of stitched hides, and finally proffered a long, dark piece of bone and meat, which reminded Richard of a charred turkey drumstick. 'How about some breakfast before we journey?'

'What is it?' Richard asked queasily.

'Bear. Very rich, quite dry, very good.'

Richard stared at the tatters of flesh and sinew being waved below his nose. 'May I ask from what part of the bear?'

With a grunt, Lacan sniffed the offered gift. 'That's a good question. Hard to tell, after all this time. Does it matter?'

'I think I'll stick to apples and cheese,' Richard said quickly.

Lacan shrugged. His smile was ambiguous. He returned the dry joint of bear to his pack, then indicated Richard's own rucksack. 'Customs inspection. Do you mind? It's what you English would call "a formality".'

Hesitating for only a moment, Richard passed the pack across to Lacan, who undid the buckles and reached inside. 'Aha!' he said, withdrawing the brandy bottle. But his smile vanished as he stared in disbelief at the label. Without looking at Richard he muttered, 'And this, I suppose, is what you English would call "medicinal".'

'Best I could find. Sorry.'

Lacan sighed sadly. 'So am I.'

The bottle was replaced, the pack returned. Then more seriously, 'Come on. We have to get you into the wood. It's a slow process, learning to go deep. Lytton is very keen to talk to you as soon as you are acclimatised. That will take a few days, perhaps, and you must be ready. First, I have to check some instruments at the old Lodge. But I'll have you comfortable by nightfall. Don't worry.'

'I'm not worried – just intrigued. Who found out about the cricket bat?'

'The *cricket bat*? Is that some sort of ridiculous English animal? Sounds preposterous.'

'Helen thinks my son – Alex – is still alive.'

'We all think Alex is alive. One of us has talked to him. But not me. Come on, now. Save your questions.'

Richard hefted his rucksack onto his back and followed the enormous man along the bridleway. Lacan walked fast, hair and pack bouncing with each stride. He constantly paused to smell the air, and used his hands like an insect's antennae, waving his slender fingers as if sensing for a change in the breeze.

They crossed into the private estates of Ryhope Manor and left the path, ascending the fallow field to Ryhope Wood. As Richard had begun to suspect, Lacan led the way through the tangle of wire to the ruins of the house in the wood, following a narrow path that Richard had previously missed and which led directly to the small garden. In the parlour, Lacan broke open the back of the small radio-like machine, pulling out a roll of white paper covered with ink marks. The Frenchman unfurled a few feet to scan the recording.

'Looks like one of those hospital traces,' Richard said. 'An ECG?'

'Very like,' said Lacan distractedly. He seemed puzzled. 'Something has been generated. Someone has been here. There has been activity.'

After a moment Richard said, 'I was here yesterday morning. I came exploring. I noticed the needle on one of the dials started to dance around. It didn't seem to be in response to my own movements . . .'

Lacan scratched curiously at his long beard, staring at Richard and thinking hard, then shook his head and furled up the roll of white paper. 'You came here? Then maybe it *was* you. You've had an effect already. Quite remarkable!'

'What *is* this place?'

Tucking the record into his pocket, Lacan looked around at the ruined room. 'This place? It's where it began. Where it began in *this* century, at least. A man called Huxley lived here, with his family, a wife and two boys. They didn't own the house, they rented it. Huxley's father had been a good friend of the then Lord Ryhope. But something which had been quiet for four hundred years woke up again when

George Huxley began to study here, not in this room, but in another part of the building. We're trying to find what that thing was. The house is called Oak Lodge. The wood around us is very old, very old indeed. This crude piece of equipment,' as he spoke he loaded a second roll into the back of the machine, 'this little item is my own adaptation of Huxley's "flux drain". It's a monitor. Very simple, really. It monitors life, new life, spontaneous life, the life of heroes, ghostly heroes which we call *mythagos*.'

The odd word was vaguely familiar to Richard. Of course: Helen had used it, just a day or so before. He repeated the word aloud, questioning it.

'There are some things you should know,' Lacan said, leading the way outside again. 'You have to start understanding soon, if you are to help get Alex out of the wood, and it will take some time. Sit down. Perhaps a little of that brandy would help . . .'

George Huxley and his family had occupied Oak Lodge for twenty-five years, until his death in 1946. He had died leaving two sons, Steven and Christian, but they had both disappeared from the area in 1948, and had not been heard of since. Huxley's wife, Jennifer, had died tragically some years before.

Huxley's training had been as a scientist, initially in the field of psychology (he had studied with Carl Jung for some years) but later broadened his horizons to include research into the dating of archaeological remains and the variability of time. He was a man fascinated, even obsessed by myth, and by the spiritual presences in the wood. He had been a jack-of-all-trades. For many years his collaborator and colleague had been another academic, Edward Wynne-Jones. The two men, during the thirties in particular, had explored the odd nature of the forest and its startling occupants. They had documented its inner realm to the extent that was possible in their day, leaving a crude map, a fragmentary journal and many unanswered questions.

From one small, semi-cryptic passage in Huxley's research journal, which was now in the possession of Old Stone Hollow, it was clear that he had kept a second record, a private journal in which he had recorded aspects of his research, observations and discoveries that he had not wished, or had been too ashamed, to share with the world.

No trace of that second diary had yet been found.

Ryhope Wood was primary woodland. It had been untouched,

essentially unmanaged, for eight thousand or so years, a tiny stand of primordial wildwood that Huxley believed had survived by *defending* itself against the destructive behaviour – slashing and burning in Neolithic times – of the human population that was settling around it. Over the millennia, the concentration of time and spirit in the wood had made it into something more than just trees and bracken, dog-fern and bramble. It had become an entity, not conscious, not watching, but somehow sentient and to an astonishing degree timeless. It communicated not through the normal channels of plant and animal life – the transpiration, the pheromones, the ecological balance of its predators, prey species and decomposers – but through the eyes and ears and mouths of *mythagos*, and it was these spirit forms, solid and substantial, though destined for short lives, that gave time, perspective and fascination to the wildwood.

The word mythago – Lacan pronounced it with the stress on the 'a' – was Huxley's coinage, and derived from 'myth imago' or image of a myth. From the moment of first human consciousness, Huxley had believed, the need for heroes, heroic acts and a belief in the mythological attributes of nature had been the empowering force behind human psychological development. Archetypes common to all human life across the globe had arisen spontaneously in the collective unconscious and each culture had fleshed them out with human or animal attributes appropriate to their own environment and social situations. These characters, often based on historical figures, more often on imaginary but *needed* figures, had become an integral part of the human mind, existing just across the mysterious boundary between full awareness and that state of acknowledgement of an underconscious process at work – dreams, rituals, visions – that might be called intuition and insight.

Listening to Lacan talk, Richard experienced no real difficulty in accepting either the existence of ancient wild-wood, or the persistence of archaic memory. But he baulked for a while at Lacan's further explanation, that the combination of the two primitive states, powered by the dual tensions between the right and left hemispheres of the human brain, and the aura that existed within unspoiled organic structures, as represented by Ryhope Wood, could produce the solid *forms* of those mythagos. They condensed out of nowhere, to become real, to become aware, to carry language and purpose, to live a brief life in unnatural conditions before dying and soaking back into the vortices of the forest.

All mythagos were shaped by the moods and needs of the creator. A gentle Hercules would die quickly. A compulsively brutal version would forget the code of honour of the Mycenaean Greeks and become a killing machine. It was a complex creative process that begged caution, but told much about the existence of a realm of 'sylvan' time, as well as being able to answer many questions about the nature of the human mind in the past.

At the edge of his vision, the woodland seemed restless. Richard became aware of occasional movement and it broke his silent contemplation. Lacan had gone back into the house. Richard found him in the room behind the old French windows, checking the tracery of fine wires, polishing the unobtrusive lenses of the cameras positioned around the walls.

'This was Huxley's study,' Lacan said. He slapped the dark tree that grew from the floor, then reached through the ground ivy to take up a decayed book, its spine too faded to read the title. Tossing it aside, Lacan went on, 'It's a room that is visited often, but by a ghost we can never photograph. As you can imagine, this house is a powerful focus for activity. The echoes of the family that lived here are still in the wood, and they come back to touch the place before dying. We can glimpse them occasionally.' Lacan's eyes shone as he looked around, balanced precariously on a sagging floor beam. 'Such an amazing amount of magic starts with this room, Richard. It has been Lytton's obsession for many years, now. For myself . . .' He caught his words and glanced at Richard defensively. 'Well, never mind for myself. We all have our dreams.'

He escorted Richard outside again. 'We've excavated the place. You see? We've opened it up like an archaeological site.'

Now that it was explained to him, Richard could see how the cleared spaces around the house formed a pattern. Lacan and his team had cleared 'trenches' through the woods. The Frenchman pointed down one narrow pathway. 'Through there is a stream. Huxley refers to it in his journal. It was his own route in to Ryhope. In his own time the stream was at the woodland's edge, with a field between here and the house. From his study, he could watch the big trees at that edge, and he saw many creatures and other mythic entities. Then, at some time in the last twenty years the whole wood *grew out*. At an astonishing rate! It consumed everything in its immediate vicinity, including the Lodge. It is as if it needed to take Huxley into its heart, to *eat* him.'

'Didn't the owners of the Manor think that strange?'

Lacan grunted as he swung his leather pack onto his shoulders. 'Now there's a question. And a good one. The Ryhopes know more than they pretend, but they say nothing, give nothing away. It's very peculiar.'

He walked down the wide path away from the Lodge, and then entered the wood itself. Richard followed at a distance. As Lacan was consumed by shadows he called, 'Come on. Let's get to my camp. It isn't far, by an old stone shrine. You need to rest, to acclimatise.'

'I'm fine,' Richard said. 'I'm not tired at all.'

'You need to rest. You'll need to adjust. Your eyes especially . . .'

'My eyes?' Richard queried. He strode quickly and nervously after the other man, into the gloom. 'Adjust to what?'

There was silence for a moment and Richard stopped, staring into a well of light that marked a clearing in the trees. Lacan was a tall silhouette in the clearing, watching him. He stepped back to Richard, brushing aside the foliage. Brown eyes gleamed intensely as he breathed softly and smiled. 'To sights they have never seen before. To a light that illuminates from within.'

And adding only, 'Be patient. Write things down. It's cathartic!' he set off across the glade again.

Lacan's camp was a tiny clearing in a stand of beech, from the centre of which grew a grey monolith, deeply carved with the crude shape of a horse. Tatters of leather still draped over the stone, tied in places around the yellowed, weathered fragments of bones. This then, was the horse-shrine.

The light was quite intensely green. Lacan's shelter was an A-frame, made of poles stacked against the low bough of a large tree, a perfect roof-beam. The poles were tied with creeper, filled in with turves and covered finally by strips of black tarpaulin. Inside this cramped hut were two sleeping bags, skins, bones, brittle wooden weapons, tins of food, empty wine bottles, a clutter of machine bits and a small camping gaz.

'Not much, eh? But very comfortable when all there is to do is sleep. And this is your sleeping place, my friend. I will be leaving you for a while. But don't worry. We know you're here, now. We'll keep an eye on you.'

Lacan vanished for a while, returning with a plump, quiescent wood pigeon. He seemed triumphant. 'There are traps all around,' he said. 'Before I leave I'll show you. This beauty was almost waiting for me. What do you say Richard?' He held the bird by its breast, allowing the flapping of wings. 'Shall we honour that beauty and let her go? Or shall we eat her?' He looked anxiously at Richard. 'You must choose. You are the guest in my house, such as it is.'

Richard stared at the bird, so calm in the big man's hands. 'Let her go. I have plenty of dried food. I can last without a killing.'

The Frenchman shook his head, sighed with mock displeasure, then laughed and turned away. 'You are the sort of house-guest I usually cannot stand – the one that gives the wrong answer!' His right hand twisted suddenly. 'But on this occasion I forgive you.'

Grinning broadly, he tossed the bloody head into the undergrowth and began to pluck the pigeon. 'Now you must make a fire. Wood smoke is better for flavour than butane. You *do* know how to make a fire, do you, my friend? You just put two sticks together and rub—'

'I know how to make a fire,' Richard agreed, not knowing whether to smile or frown at the man's performance.

After they had eaten, Lacan took Richard through the tight woodland, showing where he had set his traps, three in all, designed to snare rabbits and small birds. 'We all become a little prehistoric in Ryhope Wood,' he said.

'Surely not . . .'

'But fresh meat is so much better than our supplies. If you see equipment, you mustn't touch. It's very delicate.'

'I shan't.'

'You will need two days here, two full days. To acclimatise. So I shall leave at dawn and be back for you at dusk, day after tomorrow.'

Back at the clearing, Lacan used Richard's tarpaulin to make a second crude shelter, long enough to cover his tall body, all but the booted feet. Richard was to have the comfort of the A-frame. He huddled below the turves, feeling the moisture rise through the earth, feeling chilled, feeling as if he was alone and exposed at night. The fire burned vigorously, and Lacan idly kicked wood from a small pile with his left foot as he relaxed himself below the weatherproofing.

'You may have disturbing dreams. It's how it begins.'

'Thanks.'

He stayed awake for an hour, then began to doze, still crouching. Movements in the woods alarmed him at some time after that, and he eased out of the shelter and stood, by the glowing embers, watching the pitch darkness around, and the glimmer of stars visible through foliage and cloud above. Whatever was in the woods was moving very deliberately. He hissed Lacan's name and the Frenchman stirred, muttered irritably in his own language. 'Go to sleep.'

'There's something in the trees.'

'Of course there is. Go to sleep.'

'We've got company.'

'Then get down or it might shoot an arrow at you.'

Richard dropped to a crouch, alarmed by the words and startled by the sudden swift movement of a figure around the edge of the clearing. His eyes, adjusting slightly to the darkness, were able to discern the full form of the watcher. A moment's gleam of eyes, the quiet withdrawal into cover, the surreptitious movement away from the glade. Richard reached for more wood and piled it on the dying fire. Crackling, smoking, the flames took again and Lacan groaned, kicking feebly as if to smother the noise and light with earth that his boot could not find.

'Go to *sleep*.'

In the event, Richard didn't dream at all. He woke at dawn to find Lacan brewing coffee and cutting thick slices from a hard loaf. 'But don't worry,' Lacan said, half apologetically. 'I have something very special to go with, it . . .'

This turned out to be an over-ripe brie. 'Some home comforts are always necessary. But my supplies are low. Thankfully, English cheeses can sometimes be quite good.'

So they breakfasted, and Lacan produced water for washing and paper for comfort. Again he said, almost wistfully, 'I've been too long here. I'm going *bosky*. I shall have to get out for a while, go and experience some of your exciting English night-life.'

'Not in Shadoxhurst you won't.'

Again, the instruction to remain within the glade. 'It will be very boring. Think of it as a test of character.'

'I brought a book. Helen suggested I did.'

'Good. I repeat, if you wander away from the glade you are in trouble. You'll get lost.'

'In Ryhope Wood? Hardly . . .'

'In Ryhope Wood! Definitely! Do this our way, Richard, or I'll take you back home now. This is no joke.'

'I don't intend to joke. And I'll stay here. And see you – tomorrow evening?'

'I'll bring some wine,' Lacan said with a friendly pat on Richard's shoulder. 'I'd brought some before you came, to greet you in case you made the right decision, but someone must have drunk it while I was sleeping.'

And with that he shrugged on his pack, picked up his staff, and walked deeper into Ryhope Wood, his last words a grunted 'goodbye', the sound of his movement through the forest loud for a few minutes, then suddenly gone.

Ghosts

Alone in the horse-shrine, sitting in a light-well close to the huge, carved monolith with its equine image, Richard began to realise how *wrong* it felt to be here. He could hear nothing but the breeze and the birds. Surrounding him was a claustrophobic darkness, through which the thin shafts of sunlight illuminated only colour and shape, without perspective, without definition. He felt trapped. By late afternoon he was panicking, stumbling his way back along the path which he felt sure was the track he and Lacan had followed the day before.

He walked for over an hour. This was not possible! The trees crowded in on him, the atmosphere heavy and resinous. He veered off the path and tangled with sharp thorns. He felt stifled and sick, increasingly enclosed, increasingly afraid. He called out, then screamed out, and the woodland shook to the startled flight of birds, then was abruptly silent.

Again he shouted for Lacan, then ran on, ducking and weaving, trying to keep as straight as he could, desperate to find the ruins of Oak Lodge and the way out of this forest prison.

He came back to the horse-shrine, emerging at a run into the clearing, thinking it to be the garden of the Lodge, then stopped in shock as he saw the carved monolith, the A-frame and the drifting ash from the dead fire.

From the corner of his eye he saw someone, or something, move fleetly through the undergrowth. Startled and frightened, he swung round, but the wood was still. He could hear nothing. It happened again, then: a ripple of activity to his right, vanishing as soon as he glanced that way.

'Who's there?' he called nervously. There was nothing but silence and dappled light.

This was the beginning of his waking dreams.

He built the fire again and made himself a pan of stew from Lacan's supplies. He regretted for the first time that Lacan had guzzled the entire stock of wine. He made himself tea instead. He started to feel feverish, his vision blurring, his head beginning to buzz. When he closed his eyes he felt better, but whenever he stared into space the swirl of activity and colourful movement dominated his peripheral vision. It was not nightmarish, nor frightening, but alarming in the extreme. Although he had never taken LSD, he knew of the effect of hallucinogens, and imagined that this was how it must be experienced. Had he unwittingly eaten magic mushrooms? The thought of last night's meal of wood pigeon came to mind. Had Lacan, in his culinarily unpredictable French way, stuffed the bird with the fungal contents of its own crop? Feeling sick at the thought, Richard reminded himself that hallucinogenic drugs took effect quickly, not twenty-four hours later.

He could not resolve the images. It was as if he saw the activity of people and creatures in a thin strip of highly distorting glass at the corner of his eye. The more he concentrated the more he realised that these were indeed human figures, shifting and blurring as if in a heat haze. Sometimes they came close and seemed to be peering through the glass at him. Sometimes they moved too fast. Faces passed his awareness in an instant: here a bearded man leading two enormous horses, there a youth in long, blue breeches, singing in a wild way; then a cloaked woman, her briefly-sensed glance, as she hesitated before hurrying on, one of sensuousness and curiosity.

There was a new vibrancy in the glade, now, a tension in every leaf, a murmur in every branch. He knew he was being watched, and he sensed the hair on his neck prickling as his adrenalin surged. He was anxious, reacting instinctively to an unseen threat. He crept into the A-frame and curled up, staring out into the clearing, mouth dry in anticipation. When he closed his eyes there was peace of vision, the clutter of figures and the sensation of movement fading. But birdsong became intrusive, and as he listened so he realised that the cries and calls from the canopy were wrong, that they mocked him, or taunted him. Sudden crashings and cries from the deep of the wood were startling and frightening. Towards dusk he removed one of the strong poles that formed the side of his shelter arid used a knife to sharpen the point. He stoked up the fire. Glowing embers streamed skyward, seeming to illuminate elemental creatures that hovered, staring down at him, just out of true sight.

He began to hear incomprehensible sounds, recognising them as voices, the murmuring of languages, the laughter and shouting of strangers, but the words were incoherent, a blur of sound, surging and ebbing, like the babble of noise on a foreign beach.

What was happening? Lacan had talked of furthering his sight. What exactly had he said? To learn to see the light . . .

What *were* these living dreams, these edge visions? What had Lacan fed him, or set him up for?

At dusk a wolf glowered at him from the far side of the glade. Richard watched it silently, despite the panic he felt. He held the sharpened stake forwards and prayed that the fire would keep the beast at bay. After twenty minutes of silent contemplation, the wolf rose onto its hindlegs, a massive, grey shape. It used its forelegs to break off a small branch and examined the implement carefully, hefting it and testing the broken edge. To Richard's astonishment it then stalked around the edge of the glade, upright and slightly hunched, murmuring and growling before abruptly disappearing from sight. It had seemed to be saying his name.

Richard had no difficulty staying awake and alert for the rest of the night, although in the morning he was frozen, his shoulders aching. He realised he was drifting in and out of a restless half-sleep in which an odd, disturbing dream of Alex running along a woodland path pursued by a hollybush haunted him. The boy, in his dream, had hovered at the edge of the clearing, watching him excitedly, before the hollybush had absorbed him and dragged him into the undergrowth.

He had wept whilst in this semi-conscious state and the moisture was now cold on his cheeks. With first light he felt more depressed and despairing than he had for years. An incapacitating loneliness smothered him. He thought of Alice, of their first years together, and succumbed to bitter regret that he had let their relationship drift into such remoteness. He thought of his small flat in North London, and the piles of newspapers and magazines that were never tidied, the TV that was always on, the phone that rarely rang. He became conscious, again, of the silence of the place, two large rooms which were never used to entertain his acquaintances. What had happened to him? He had slipped away, he realised, not for the first time. He had become isolated in his life. He had ceased to have direction, to make initiatives. Like a bear in the longest of winters, he had hibernated for the last six years, living off the decreasing supplies of mind-fat, of old memory.

With a sudden, angry shout he snapped himself out of the mood of incriminatory self-pity, crawled from the shelter and beat the fire with a length of wood, making grey ash swirl up in the new light.

A sudden movement in his peripheral vision startled him. He swung round, but of course there was nothing. And yet, there had been something eerily familiar about the human shape that had suddenly walked towards him then darted away. Something in the way it moved . . . He couldn't summon the image back, and the distortion had been too great to resolve the features clearly, and yet, again he felt that Alex had been watching him.

'I've had enough of this,' he muttered.

The wood was restless, Richard was unnerved. Determinedly he began to retrace his steps to the edge, pack slung over one shoulder, crude spear held tightly in his hand. There would be no turning back this time, no disorientation. He'd had enough. If Lacan, if Helen, had anything more to say to him they would have to come to Shadoxhurst.

'Enough is enough!' he declared, ducking below low branches, keeping his attention firmly on the narrow but beaten track.

Oak Lodge was just ahead. He could see the clearing in front of it, a place where the light was intense.

He stepped into the horse-shrine, faced the grey stone and screamed his frustration. 'How? Why? Where did I turn?'

A figure darted in panic from the A-frame, the sudden movement shocking Richard. It was a young man, his skin stippled and whorled with blue tattoos, his face quite black to the mouth line and lined with red below. His clothing consisted of a short, hide kilt, leather shoes and crossed bands of green fabric over his patterned chest. A long braid of black hair, gleaming with bits of bronze, hung from his right temple. He grabbed at a pack and a long knife before whirling round twice, shouting loudly, defiantly at Richard, then streaking away into the undergrowth.

Someone blew in Richard's ear. He turned in panic, bringing up the sharpened spear.

Lacan stood there grinning, a brace of red-furred hares slung over one shoulder, a tied bunch of wild garlic on the other.

'Been for a little walk?'

'Take me home,' Richard said, shaking.

Lacan ignored him and held up the hares. 'Look at these. Aren't they magnificent? Look at the nervous elegance of their sweet faces, the perfect and refined shape of the forepaws, the exquisite colour of the fur. Mountain hares, my friend, of the *finest* breeding. Which makes them French, of course. I shall make a meal fit for Vercingetorix himself!'

'Lacan, get me out of here! For God's sake take me home.'

'Why? Because a tattooed Prince from your Wessex of five thousand years ago has called you by the ghost name *pukk katha 'nja*—' he laughed. 'Condemning you, incidentally, to spew up demons in the shape of rocks every time you wish to speak! Great for hangovers! Shout back at him, my friend. Don't be afraid. It's good for the soul.'

'I don't know what you're talking about. I just know I'm scared. I'm claustrophobic. Lacan – I want to get out of this place! I'm hallucinating. I can't sleep. I need a drink.'

'A drink! *Now* he talks some sense. I need a drink too. Don't worry, I know where we can find one.'

Furious, Richard hauled the Frenchman back. 'Lacan. Take me home! I don't know what's happening to me!'

Frowning, but reassuring, the big man placed a hand on Richard's shoulder. 'It has happened to you fast. Faster than usual. Perhaps it is because Alex is in the wood. Lytton said you should stay here for two days, to acclimatise, but I think I must take you deeper right now. If we walk fast, if we encounter nothing more sinister than that wild, ghost-singing youth, we can be at Old Stone Hollow in four or five hours.'

'I want to go home,' Richard said, hardly finding the breath to speak, feeling his despair rise as tears.

Lacan shook him gently, then squeezed the lobe of his left ear. 'I know you do, my friend. But by this evening, fed, well-wined and surrounded by good company, you will feel very differently. If you don't, then I will take you home personally. That is a promise. But trust me for the moment, Richard. There is nothing to be afraid of. Truly. You'll soon get used to what is happening. Will you trust me?'

Helpless, Richard nodded. 'I'll trust you,' he said dully.

Lacan laughed in his falsely enlarged fashion and walked to the A-frame, Richard following. 'What a foolish man you are, then! But I *still* can't help liking you. I must be going bosky. Come on, we must hurry, or those other drunkards will consume all the Burgundy.'

The Green Chapel: 3

The hollyjack was fat with birds, crows by the sound they made as they shifted inside her. She had extended her nest until now it was a massive structure of dead wood, yellow grasses and thick briar, covering the whole of the double doors below the broken window where the knight challenged the half-glimpsed monster. She shrieked now, rather than chattered. Her activities were directed solely to expanding the fat sphere of the nest. Alex watched her curiously, usually from the high window where a rain gutter, stretching out over the graveyard, gave him a position to swing from. Whenever she looked up at him and bristled her smile, he called down his name.

'Alex! It's come home to me. Alex! My name. It's come home. I'm *Alex*!'

Chatter-shriek-chirrup. (That's a good name. Has it brought good dreams with it?)

'Yes. I dreamed I was playing in fields. I ran through long grass, full of thistles. I flew *kites*. I caught fish in the pond near the fallen stones. I lived in a small house, which was very dark, but it had a big fire. My mother was always writing letters. My father walked up and down a lot, and watched cricket. He seemed very sad. I made things with wood. I'm *Alex*. I'm going home.'

Flutter-shriek-chatterchatter-rustle. (Your father is looking for you. He's in danger. The *daurog* are calm now, but the seasons are changing quickly again. Call to him to be careful.)

'He can't hear me. I'm going home, though. He's coming to me. My name is Alex. Alex has come home. The giggler won't get me now.'

He swung down the ivy ladder and ran past the fat hollyjack, tugging at her leaves mischievously, to stand and stare at the figure in the window.

A name was close here, too, a certain recognition. He was waking from a long sleep. He felt his eyes open and his head expand. At first it was strange, but soon he began to grasp that a form of memory was returning. His name had come home, a bright bird that had flown through the wildwood and entered him, like an old friend. And now he knew the knight in the window, and the creature that he was killing, but the name still eluded him, even now he had become conscious of searching for it. And the faces at the edgewood were familiar too, all save the giggler, which changed so much that he could never be sure if the creature was there or not.

But the other inhabitants tickled his imagination now, suggested stories to him. They brought thoughts of sea voyages and great monsters, sword-fights and silver armour, wild rides in the night, with baying hounds, and great castles encased in rose briar and blackthorn.

He began to name things, feeling the words and the identity flow into him from the air as if they were a fine rain, drizzling through his hair and eyes and ears, into his mind. He screeched with pleasure as each name returned, 'Gargoyle! Crucifix! Gravestone!' And as he remembered the faces at the edgewood, 'Robin Hood . . . Lancelot . . . Jason.'

Some of these names frightened him because when they had appeared to him they had horrified him – they had been death's heads, or wolf's heads, on the bodies of men, and although the names should have been comforting, the men were not.

Nevertheless, as dawn crept through his head he alarmed the hollyjack as he scampered past her through the sanctuary trees, sending one of the uplifted pews crashing to the ground from the thin branches that supported it, shattering the small face at its end.

The dancer.

The whole bench was rotten. Alex picked up the pieces of the face. They were soft, like fungus, crumbling at his touch. He joined them together and placed them safely at the side of the wooded nave. He thought of taking the shattered dancer down to the bones and stone vaults below the floor, but he had heard something moving about down there, occasionally thumping at the marble slabs as if trying to get through to him, like the trees, and he kept the heavy door closed and barred with a branch.

The hollyjack shrieked suddenly. He turned quickly, staring at her from the altar, close to the golden cross that gleamed from its protective thicket of thorn. She seemed rooted. Her arms were over her leafy body and her branch tusks clattered. She was watching him in earnest, but a moment later she turned away and scurried awkwardly to her nest from which, for a long time, came the sound of her chattering, a sound of pain.

Helpless, Alex left her in the nest, leaving her sanctuary through the window, by the stone falcon, and dropping to the wet grass of the graveyard. Everything was still. He went to the well and drew water, drinking and staring at the wood a few feet away. Someone was standing in the cover, hardly breathing. He could feel the gaze on him, detect the shallow intake of breath, the betraying thump of the heart. When he moved slightly, as he lapped water from his cupped hands, he glimpsed dull grey fabric, a shawl and long dress, and red hair in a wild tumble. The glitter of watching eyes eventually resolved from the sparkling points of light that were wet leaves. These eyes were fierce, yet the hesitancy suggested fear. And a name came to him, drawn from the figure, finding a roost in his head.

Guinevere . . .

At once, as if the name on leaving her had released her from a spell, she screamed and ran. And at once the wood a few paces away erupted into a second flurry of movement. Alex backed towards the cathedral as the giggler broke through the tangled wood, a giant, stooping form whose stench emanated suddenly from the undergrowth, and whose voice rose from a growl to the braying laugh that haunted Alex's waking dreams. The woman stepped out into the open for a second and Alex grimaced at the face below the flowing hair, the twisted features, the vile mouth. This was not the beauty of his story-dreams. Her clothes were the rags of shrouds. She seemed to stare at him with pity, or perhaps uncertainty, but a moment later she had vanished into the wood and for a long time the sounds of the hunt told of her speed, and the giggler's determination.

Alex withdrew to the porch roof, below the ascent to his sanctuary. Rain came and went, and there was further furtive movement: a boy, then a figure in red uniform, then a hooded man. All of them glanced out from the wood, then retired: but not before he had named each of them, a whisper of recognition, a second's delight.

Suddenly the giggler grinned at him, fresh blood on its white face and teeth, the briefest of apparitions in the undergrowth, so quick that Alex could hardly grasp it. It chuckled as it withdrew, moving heavily away to the right.

A touch on his hair made Alex jump with fright. The hollyjack had eased herself down the ivy rope so carefully, because of her size, that he had not heard her approach. She crouched on the porch now, shaking like an aspen in the wind. There was something very final about her. In as much as Alex could tell her expression from the oddly shaped eyes, deep in the twisted wood of her skull, he perceived anxiety. She wanted to show him something.

She led the way to the ground arid reached around in the grass until she found a place in the earth where she could root. Alex curled into her, and flowed with her on the Big Dream . . .

It was the height and the depth of summer and the *daurog* moved through the stifling wood like shadows in the green. It was thick with heat. Where the forest thinned they passed through the deep wells of light, raising faces to the sky so that the sun shone on their polished tusks, emerging now from full, thick leaf on their fat bodies. Oak and Ash led the slow journey to the cathedral. Hazel and Holly kept to the fringes of any clearing. Beech, Birch and Willow walked slowly, using tall staffs to keep touch with the ground. Behind them, moving carefully, always watching, always listening, always feeling for the eyes and ears that came to him through the rootweb, the shaman was a sinister presence, never quite visible, taking deep root quite often so that he trailed behind the family, catching up with them by moonlight, as the others of the group formed into a spinney to rest.

The shaman had carved a face on his thick staff. Sometimes when he pushed the gnarly wood into the earth, Alex was drawn up to the face, and the shaman watched him, silently and closely, scratching the face with thorny nails, then clattering his tusks before walking on.

They were in summer, then, and safe. They were closer than before, and searching for the stone-place, for Alex. But there was something wrong with them, an emptiness that could not be conveyed, only touched. They sought something more than Alex, and they were in great pain.

Now he reached again, journeying on the Little Dream, feeling for his father, and touching the man, expecting to find sadness but finding a new joy. He was close and he was with a woman, not his mother. They were dancing by a fire. There was contentment and excitement in the air. The boy edged closer, came closer, and slipped back into the earth, draining towards the dancing man, expanding through the giant roots, curling around the deep stones, the hollow tombs, the bones of the dying-down and the being-born that littered the vast wood. When he could hear the sound of song and pipes, feel the drum of the dancers in the earth, he rose from the rootweb, and called for the man he loved . . .

Old Stone Hollow

(i) The Bone Yard

Five hours later, Lacan led the way out of the tangle of dark wildwood into clearer, lighter forest. Tall columns of stone rose among the trees, ivy-covered, weathered, some carved with the shapes of armoured men, others inscribed with glyphs and symbols reminiscent of those to be found in the Minoan remains of the Aegean. Further on, they passed below four corroding bronze pillars, each decorated with the faces of lions, one fallen at an angle and resting against an oak.

Lacan led the way carefully, taking a winding path through these majestic ruins. A huge wooden building, steeply thatched, had slipped to one side, folding into itself. Elm saplings had begun to penetrate the roof. Fallen idols, crudely hacked from stumps and sarsens, littered the ground before it, and Lacan ducked below the cracked, oakwood lintel to snatch a photograph of the interior.

The place was known as the Sanctuary. It was a collection of shrines and temples, and according to Lacan was dangerous.

'At least two *hollowings* lead away from here. We're not sure where exactly. We know a safe path and we keep to it. But this is where Dan Jacobi went missing, over a year ago. There's his marker . . .' Richard saw the grey and rotting doll, hanging loosely in an ivy trail from a tall column. 'I think he must be dead by now,' Lacan went on. 'I have a feeling for such things. But it's still all we can do to stop his wife going after him. She won't believe he's dead. Good for her! All love is blind to reason, and maybe that's why some people are so strong.'

'A *hollowing?*' Richard asked. 'What *is* that, exactly?'

Lacan was impatient to continue. He brushed aside foliage, and walked in the lee of an immense, marble wall, from which spectacularly grotesque faces peered out through the forest.

'A hollowing is a way *deeper,*' he said unhelpfully. 'We are going further into the wood, but there is a way under us. Not in physical space, you understand. Just *under,* going to other planes, other lands,

79

other *otherworlds*. It's dangerous to enter a hollowing. The wood is crisscrossed with them, woven with them. Another system of space and time. The only ones that we know are safe are close to the Station. We know where they come out. But there are many others. Helen will show you, later.'

His voice had faded as he strode ahead, out of sight, striking at branches with his staff. Richard struggled to keep up, noticing the furious activity in his peripheral vision, alarmed by this and distracted by the sense of being watched from within.

Suddenly Lacan was in front of him, a huge, broad back, blocking out the light. The Frenchman urged silence. Ahead, Richard could hear the sound of rapids. This was beechwood, the land sloping gently down, the light intense in places, shifting. Two figures moved slowly through that light, approaching the river. When Richard came closer he saw that they were children, crudely cloaked, flaxen-haired, each carrying a painted staff. Their movements were so deliberate that it took a moment for him to realise that it was sluggishness, not caution, that governed their actions.

'It is not pretty, up ahead,' Lacan whispered. 'Not pleasant at all. Harden your heart against these two. And just remember – they exist in other places. They are alive, they are not alive. These are dying—'

'Dying? Why?'

'Because this is a dying place,' Lacan said coldly. 'We made it so when we built the Station. We made it so when we set up the protective field to keep ourselves apart from the wood. These mythagos, these helpless creatures, are drawn here, drawn to us, and the closer they come the more their lives are drained. You must remember something: they are just dreams. Like dreams, they seem so real for a while, and then they disperse and are soon forgotten. Harden your feelings until you can understand better.'

He walked on, skirting the frail, shuddering figures. As Richard passed them, forty yards distant, one turned slowly. A sweet face, full of pain and puzzlement, watched him. The boy's head shook slowly, then his eyes closed and he subsided slowly, kneeling, then hunching, to remain quite still.

His companion was standing in a thin stream of brilliant light, looking up at the sky. Gradually her arms dropped and she remained immobile, stiff, not breathing.

'Who are they?' Richard asked.

Lacan shrugged irritably.

'Who knows? If you're that interested we can set up a study programme. That's what we're good at here. Hold your breath. We're
coming to the bone-yard.'

They were in sight of the river. The sound of it, fresh, powerful,
clean, was a welcome sensation as Richard looked around him. To
right and left, the wood was filled with the rotting figures of what Lacan
had called 'mythagos'. He stared in numbed horror at the wooden
bones. He was reminded of sculpture. Faces, skulls, shapes, their limbs
were cracked, their postures awkward, as if they had died crawling,
reaching for the river, heads thrown back with the effort of gasping for
air. It was as if a graveyard had been unearthed and scattered. Leaves
sprouted on drooping jaws. What appeared to be piles of firewood were
hunched, agonised figures, their ribs returning to the earth. Coloured
rags of clothing, and the dull reflection of metal ornaments, suggested
the rotting vestments of these sad dead.

They were all facing towards Old Stone Hollow, Richard noticed.

'They are drawn to us,' Lacan murmured again. 'It is a function of
these creatures. They are compelled to find and touch their maker, their
creator, whichever one of us it might be. We have had to defend
ourselves powerfully. But each time one of these things dies, someone
in the Station dies a little too. There is a connection which we don't yet
understand.'

Behind them, the cloaked girl began to sing to the sunlight, her voice
faint, very weak, very final. Lacan watched her for a moment, then
turned away quickly, looking very grim. 'Come on. There's nothing we
can do for her. And besides, I'm hungry.'

(ii) Sciamachy

'There is something wrong,' Lacan murmured as they came in sight of
the rough palisade that marked Old Stone Hollow. 'It doesn't feel
right.'

'In what way?'

'It's too quiet. There should be someone to hail us.'

They were on the slope of wooded land that led down to the
turbulent stream. A flimsy-looking rope bridge spanned the river. The
gate through the palisade was open, revealing a wide compound, several tents, and the end of a turf-roofed longhouse, from which smoke
rose. But for the moment, Richard's attention was taken by the two odd

figures that stood outside the wall, one on each side of the gate: they were made from poles, simple structures that suggested crucified men, leaning forward. The heads were grotesque bulges on the skeletal frames, draped with skins, rags and the black, rotting carcasses of carrion birds. Unquestionably, Richard realised, these hideous scarecrows were designed to discourage entry. Indeed, as he looked from his vantage-point at the trees around the compound, he could see masks, shields and weapons slung in the branches, and the shapes of totems rising behind the tents. The door of the longhouse was framed by the extended, elongated and lurid blue effigy of a tusked boar.

The defences of Old Stone Hollow were not, then, restricted to the thin barrier of electronics and infra-red that could be glimpsed as gleaming traceries extending between trees and bushes.

At the far side of the cluttered compound was dense scrubwood, white with elderflower, and otherwise coloured by pennants tied to branches. This wood separated the clearing from the awesome rise of a rock face, a cave-riddled cliff that towered against the bright skyline and cast deep shadow over the Station below, making Old Stone Hollow seem uninvitingly gloomy.

There was a slow, cautious approach behind them, as they watched, and something – someone – stumbled and was still, although a piece of rock rolled for a while down the slope.

'Lytton?' Lacan called, and his face registered his concern. 'McCarthy?'

There was no response. When the breeze shifted, though, the scent of beef stew came on the air. Someone, somewhere, was cooking.

They crossed the bridge, Lacan warning Richard of the dangerous nature of the river, which was often a 'through-way' for 'Wild Riders', and entered the compound. 'Wait here. Watch the bridge approach,' he said before moving swiftly to the canteen tent, a small, green marquee from which the smell of the stew was emanating. He emerged a moment later, chewing, shook his head, then checked the other tents and the longhouse. 'Deserted!'

Finally he hacked his way through the tanglewood below the looming wall of rock and called into the deep overhang, his voice echoing clearly.

While Lacan was otherwise occupied, Richard strolled warily around the Station. By the back wall of the rough longhouse were piled weapons, armour, helmets, bits of wagon, the broken hull of a narrow boat. It was a junkyard of the past, fascinating and repelling at the same time. An Etruscan helmet still contained the mummified skull of its owner; the patterning on a browning long bone proved, on closer examination, to be an intricate series of pictures of canoes on a river, each action dominated by beasts, animals, or unidentifiable half-human shapes.

The longhouse itself had a fire in its centre. Richard stooped and entered the smoky interior, light flooded the room from gaps in the turf roof, and from the slatted windows that had been shaped in the wattle and daub of the walls. There were tables here, and charts on crude frames. Chairs were scattered about, and there was a sectioned-off dark-room and a clutter of photographic equipment. This, then, was the research centre.

Richard was hailed and he stepped out of the lodge. Lacan appeared again from the undergrowth, tugging at his beard and shaking his head. He looked worried.

'McCarthy is here. I'm sure of it. I can see signs of him. I think he must be slipping away. He'll need help.'

'Slipping away?' Richard asked, then realised he meant 'going bosky'.

A thought occurred to Lacan. 'The lake. Of course! He'll be there. It's the natural place to be.'

Richard dropped his pack and followed along the bank of the river, which eventually narrowed and deepened, flowing between sheer, mossy rocks and stunted trees. Holding on to each other, and grabbing at roots and rocky prominences, they waded into the freezing water and edged through the ravine.

The confinement suddenly ended and the river opened out into a wide, ice-blue lake. It was cool here, and across the shimmering water the woodland was in the bite of winter. Richard could see snow on the dark trees, a stone tower rising above the branches and the wrecks of ships piled in disorder against the length of the rocky shore. The middle of the lake was hazy, the forest beyond visible as if through frosted glass. Richard didn't know it then but Helen told him later that this was 'Wide-water Hollowing', and was believed to connect ancient seas, meres, streams and lakes, from Tuonela to the Aegean of Odysseus, from the magic waters of Manannan and the lake of Excalibur to the river gorges of the Lorelei. None of the teams at the Station, however, had yet risked a journey to the watery worlds of legend beyond, and most of their understanding was guesswork, based on the mythagos that had come through to their own world of Old Stone Hollow.

Just off the shore, where Richard and Lacan crouched, a small boat bobbed as the breeze sent waves against it. Two fishing lines stretched out from the lakeside, one of them flexing under tension, suggesting that its bait had been taken. Lacan strode to the glass-fibre rod and reeled in the catch, holding it up on the hook. He looked at the five inches of thrashing juvenile perch with silent disappointment before returning it to the water.

'I have no time for *morsels*!'

A few minutes later they found McCarthy. He was hunched up in the rocks, totally naked, his hair draped with green vegetation, his body streaked with blue and black dyes, which at first glance looked like bruises. He was staring blankly out across the water. He appeared to be shivering.

'Is that what you mean by "bosky"?' Richard whispered.

'First signs,' Lacan confirmed quietly as they watched, adding in a whisper, as he fiddled with the bear-tooth necklace around his broad chest, 'It's very sad, Richard. Very disturbing. He will become more and more primitive, wearing animal furs, and charms, becoming very *strong* in smell, very wild in his look. It is a most unpleasant change. We must resist it at all costs.'

Richard glanced at the big man, almost unable to believe what he was hearing, thinking Lacan must be making a joke. But the Frenchman was impassive, impossible to read. He said, 'You see? He's sitting there dreaming, listening to the wood. There's nothing to hear. Not in *here*, at least,' he tapped his right ear. 'But there is so much to hear more deeply. McCarthy is a talented *sciamach*. They often go first.'

'Sciamach?'

'Shadow dreamer. They use the wood, they probe the wood, it's a sort of journey . . .'

Stepping into the open, Lacan shrugged off one of his heavy furs and flung it at the dreaming man.

'Get dressed.'

His words, abrupt and angry, seemed to shake McCarthy from his daze. He looked up through watery blue eyes and smiled.

'Arnauld! What's happening?'

'Put the fur on. Quickly. You'll die of cold.'

McCarthy stood awkwardly. Richard noticed the huge scar across the left side of his torso – he had been gored by a boar, Lacan whispered – and he looked like a wasted man, all ribs, pelvis and prominent knees. When he tugged the dark fur round his shoulders he looked pathetic. He was still trembling. He reached a hand through the cloak to shake

Richard's. His face was deeply etched, very drawn, and in the way of dying men his teeth seemed too large for his mouth, his eyes loose in their sockets. But he seemed at ease, was content to be led and followed Lacan obediently back to the Station, not complaining as he waded through the cold river.

McCarthy's speciality was dreams, although from the brief summary of his area of study Richard gathered that he was no psychologist. As he drank tea, and almost literally came back to earth, he talked of 'lucid dreaming', 'dream travel' and 'dream correspondence'.

'Ghosts,' he said, as his enthusiasm returned, 'dreams and creation – Ryhope Wood resonates with all of these things, and condenses them. If I can find the key to mythago-genesis, I can unlock the Big Dream, the First Dream.'

'I wish you luck,' Richard said encouragingly, again not understanding a word.

Lacan laughed. 'I can't understand him either,' he said loudly, bringing the hint of a smile to McCarthy's morose features. 'He speaks in tongues. But I like him! He may not be able to unlock the Big Dream, but he unlocks a very good *cassoulet*!'

When the Station at Old Stone Hollow had been established, three years ago by the time-standard of the world outside of Ryhope Wood, there had been twenty assorted scientists and anthropologists, all gathered in by Alexander Lytton, all with a specialist field, all made privy to the secrets and oddities of the realm of the wildwood. They had been divided into ten teams of two, but only five of these duets remained extant. Three had disappeared more than two years ago and were presumed dead. Helen had lost her husband Dan, although under circumstances that were unclear. McCarthy had been unable to save his partner from a lance wound, inflicted when they had been exploring one of the medieval castles that could be found in the deeper wood. Alexander Lytton and Arnauld Lacan had proved to be so temperamentally unsuited to each other that they had willingly and gladly separated and were the only two members of the research establishment who went on solo missions.

Helen was currently beyond a zone named Hergest Ridge, but was with Elizabeth Haylock, a specialist in first millennium Europe, and Alan Wakeman, a palaeolinguist and expert in 'glyphs'. Two Finlanders were due back within a matter of days.

Helen's team were several hours overdue at the Hollow, but

McCarthy, before his temporary lapse into the *bosk* (it was his first, it would not be his last) had sensed the three of them returning, quite close, quite safe. They were vibrant shadows in the wood, and McCarthy could communicate with those shadows, although in a way which was unclear to Richard at the moment.

Exhausted by walking, made tired by wine and McCarthy's gamey and substantial stew, Richard slept in the mid-afternoon. He awoke to the sound of voices, hailing the camp from a distance, and went out into the Station in time to see Helen carefully crossing the rope bridge. Haylock and Wakeman were already entering the compound.

Helen looked wretched, her clothes matted with mud, her face a tracery of thorn scratches, nothing serious enough to worry about. She greeted Richard very wearily, but managed the echo of an amused smile as she said, 'How's the man who dances with cricket bats?'

He noticed that moss was growing on the blackened bark of her right hand. Aware of his helpless glance, she covered the blemish, rubbing at it self-consciously.

'I really have to wash and rest,' she murmured. 'I've been two weeks in the wild—'

Richard was astonished. *Two weeks?* He'd only seen her the day before yesterday!

'—I'll talk to you later. I'm really glad you've decided to come.'

'I'm glad to see you too,' Richard said. 'I've got a lot to learn. A lot to talk about.'

'And a lot to see,' she added as she walked tiredly to one of the sleeping tents. 'And a lot of travelling.'

Wakeman and Haylock had unpacked onto a trestle table, displaying their finds, some of them quite gruesome. Stripped of their over-clothing, stretching their limbs after shedding the weight of their equipment, they made a strange pair, naked but for the tight, green body-webs both were wearing. Elizabeth Haylock was a tall, robustly-built woman with an angular face and restless eyes. Her hair was in a long, black pigtail which draped over her right shoulder as she talked to Lacan. She seemed shy of Richard, or perhaps uncomfortable with simple social graces. When he was introduced, and asked about her speciality, she was sharp; when he admitted his lack of understanding she seemed impatient. Perhaps she was just tired. He understood that she was also an expert on the Late Pleistocene, a part of the Upper Palaeolithic characterised by wide-scale treks of the hunter-gatherer clans, and the laying down of two separate streams of mythology, of which later echoes could be seen in the richly painted Magdalenian caves of the Pyrenees.

Her rambling words, her apparent hostility, blunted Richard's relationship both with the woman and with her conversation. She walked off after a while, and emerged from one of the tents wearing a towel and carrying soap and a scrubbing brush. She joined Helen in the river, which earlier Lacan had called dangerous, and floated lazily in the turbulent flow, seemingly quite unbothered by the prospect of Wild Riders passing.

Wakeman too was distracted and exhausted. He was in his fifties, tanned, wore his grey hair in a ponytail, and was intricately tattooed with Celtic symbols on each of his muscular arms. A powerfully-built man, he reminded Richard of the sort of wrestler who appeared on television on Saturday afternoons. Wakeman was triumphant over a find relating to his own speciality: the Urnfield and Wessex cultures of the Bronze Age (a term he hated). The bronze mask was very tarnished, and quite battered, but the face it depicted was imbued with a terrible evil, and was unquestionably, he thought, related to a particular magician of the third millennium BC, a terrifying spectre who used the river-ways of Europe to trade in the then current form of spells. His name, Wakeman believed, had been *Mabathagus*.

Possession of this mask then, was dangerous, and Lacan was not happy that it had been brought into the Station. He pumped up the generator power and made a circuit of Old Stone Hollow, checking the wires, ribbons and talismans of the defences.

(iii) Spirit Ghyll

An hour later, Lacan led Richard between the highly-coloured warning poles at the back of the Station. The path wound tightly through a scrub of knotty hazel and elder in full, white flower, into the deep shadow cast by the high, overhanging rock wall. It felt suddenly cold below this great cliff, and the smells of earth, damp and vegetation were concentrated powerfully. Richard could hear the distant sound of rushing water, but the scrub was heavily silent, eerily deserted. Their movements became loud.

Lacan indicated markings on the rock and as Richard's eyes became accustomed to the shade, so he saw the painted patterns for the first time. The activity of his edge-vision intensified, a swirl of colour, the sensation of two figures running towards him, a ghostly movement that set his hair prickling and caused him to glance round.

Lacan watched him curiously. 'Have you seen such designs before?'

Lines painted in parallel, complex spirals, rows of brilliant blue circles, cross-figures and stylised human forms and faces. The under-hang was a tapestry of primal patterns and surrealism. Everything seemed to flow towards the earth, gathering towards the place, behind dense bushes, where the sound of water was a constant, distant murmur.

'Some of them are like rock carvings,' Richard said. 'Those old tombs, the megalithic ones . . .'

Lacan nodded, satisfied. 'Some of them are very like that indeed. Where I come from, in Brittany, the tradition is even older than in this country. But there are patterns here that are like those of the Bushmen. In the Kalahari there are caves and rock faces with the same sort of configurations. It's like two cultures fused together. Have you ever been to the Kalahari?'

Richard hadn't, although he was familiar with the rock paintings from school studies. Lacan beckoned him on, pushing through the brush until the low cave itself opened before them. 'This is only the beginning,' he said. 'There's much more inside. Be careful.'

The open cave lowered and narrowed as they edged through. It became a cramped passage, curving and dropping in alarming fashion into the earth. They crouched, then crawled below the oppressive weight of rock. Richard could hear the sound of rushing water, far away, deep down. The damp, depressing smell of wet stone and stale air, familiar to him from potholing days in the Yorkshire Dales, was at once comforting and threatening.

'This leads the way to a most dangerous hollowing,' Lacan said. 'We've lost three good people through it, right at the beginning of the expedition. And more mythagos emerge from it to our world than from anywhere else. Look there . . .'

Lacan had suddenly pointed the torch at three hollow-sticks wedged into a crevice in the rock. The passage had widened slightly, and two narrow tunnels led away into the darkness, one above the other. One of the wooden figures was clearly female: the carver had shaped crude breasts on the thick twig that formed the body. All three had winding-sheets of green cloth tied around their middles, pouches to contain the relic that gave power to these spirit guides.

'We're coming to the main chamber. It's very slippery.'

A moment later the crushing rock lifted and Richard was able to straighten into the echoing, cathedral space of Old Stone Hollow. Lacan switched on the lamp that was placed here, and a pale yellow light set sudden illumination and deep shadow to the cascade of shape on the rock walls and the formations of thin stalactites on the ceiling. Water gushed from a narrow crevice to the right, tumbling through a fine mist of spray into a wide ghyll. The floor was strewn with fallen chunks of the roof. The mouths of smaller tunnels opened everywhere.

All of this, impressive though it was, Richard took in at a glance. Because above him and around him was a swathe of movement and colour that was breathtaking in its expression and overwhelming in its power.

He had seen the prehistoric cave paintings in Les Eysies and Niaux, and of course knew of the paintings at Lascaux and the Spanish Altamara, but these startling images of animals, elongated, deformed, yet brilliantly executed and astonishingly coloured, were like nothing from those ancient shrines. As he stared at them, so they seemed to move, to shift and extend further, their bodies draining down towards the deepest part of the cave, as if, again, being sucked by the mouth of the earth itself – or perhaps running towards it. Odd, disturbing patterns, dizzying to focus upon, seemed to interweave with the spirit creatures. They appeared to dart between the pounding legs, to pass straight through the ethereal and stretched bodies of bison, stag, horse and wolf. And other forms between these stampeding creatures re-minded Richard of men, hunters dressed in strange garb, not at all the sticklike figures of the Bushmen caves with their stylised weapons, but rather shapes that drew as much from the world of trees as from the world of human beings. And yet it was clear that they too, as they hunted, as they ran, were moving into the shrine, apparently racing inwards towards the swirling 'pot' at the cavern's deepest point.

Richard slipped and slid across the wet floor, bracing himself on fallen boulders, and cautiously peered into the deep well. Someone had fixed a rope to the rock, the cable dropping into the darkness. It was then that he noticed the vague shapes of humans in the rock itself. He used his torch to pick out the details more clearly and realised they were hollowsticks, but petrified now, hardened by the calcium-rich water that had been dripping steadily upon them.

'Who were they?'

'From another age,' Lacan said. His own torch ranged restlessly about the well, picking out other stone dolls, perhaps as many as twenty. 'They're very old, more than a hundred years from the amount of petrification. It's where we learned about the spirit guides. People went down this swirl-hole, reaching for unknown lands, knowing that they needed to mark the place of their departure to ensure their safe return.' He reached out and ran fingers down the smooth stone that now covered the dark figure below. 'These have obviously failed. Their makers are trapped somewhere.'

A thought occurred to Richard, something puzzling about several of the figures. They were *inside* the well, and they seemed to be facing into the claustrophobic darkness. Could they have been the guides of people *emerging*? he suggested. Maybe coming *from* the hollowing to Lacan's own world, and marking the way back?

'It's true,' Lacan agreed, turning his dark gaze upon Richard approvingly. 'That's what Lytton believes, when he isn't attributing everything to George Huxley. Our own world is the spirit world as far as some- mythagos are concerned. They emerge to touch their maker, the mind from which they were drawn.'

It was bitterly cold in the cavern, and even Lacan was shivering through his bearskins. He led the way back through the crawl-space to the welcome airiness of the overhanging cliff, below he confusion of painted symbols. 'As you have seen, Richard, this is a dangerous place. Avoid it, and avoid following anyone or anything *into* it. But whatever you witness here must be reported at once. We are three good travellers short.'

Lytton

A beautiful twilight spread across the Station at Old Stone Hollow, the sky on fire, the canopy bright with dusk colour. The painted symbols and shapes on the wall of the overhang, where Richard walked with Helen, deepened in tone as the light caught them, so that the ochres began to round out, to burn redly on the bodies of the animals, those that caught this last of the light.

They returned to the compound and sat at a trestle table, quiet and relaxed, save for the conspicuous shift of movement at Richard's edge-vision, the glimpses of a world forming from his mind in the vampire wood around him.

A few minutes later an odd breeze started to blow through the camp, a pulsing wind tingled with ice and movement. Birds flew in panic, and the screen of trees rippled with movement. The hanging masks and artefacts clacked and knocked against the poles.

From somewhere in the camp, one of the team called, 'Elementals . . .'

At once Helen rose to her feet. 'It's Lytton,' she said. 'He attracts elementals like some people attract flies. We'll have to be on our guard.'

Lacan was already scanning the twilight skies, turning in a slow circle, one of his hand-sized machines held against his chest.

'He's coming from the north,' he called suddenly, and there was a general movement toward the trees at the edge of the great overhang. The breeze grew in strength, and from the branches, eyes watched the camp, tantalising faces that flickered in and out of vision.

Lytton, Richard discovered, was returning through a hollowing which opened between the fallen boulder and the curved trunk of a lightning-struck elm. It was a narrow gap, leading to a bright glade, now tinged with evening's orange. It was easy enough to see how the wind, arid an oddly formless flow of shape, was coming from that area.

Something pinched his cheek and Richard slapped at it, turning quickly and in time to see a pointed face and quizzical eyes. Then his hair was tugged and blown as if by a sudden breath. He tried to follow the shape, but it had vanished.

He saw Helen struggle irritably with thin air, then look to the river where the waters became turbulent for a few seconds, a fish thrashing, perhaps, or something invisible exalting in the cool flow.

'Here he comes . . .' Haylock said, her voice calm.

Lacan called out, 'There's something behind him. It's coming up fast!'

The generator whined and Richard got the sense that extra power had again been pumped into the circular network of wires, beams and cables around Old Stone Hollow.

Between boulder and elm, the air pulsed, the view shrank, then expanded, whitening, as if looking into snow, then becoming intensely red. A man's shape was silhouetted there, frozen, one arm reaching out from its body, but as if hurrying. It hovered in the frame, a shadow against the red glow, immobile. Behind it a fainter shadow began to grow, looming up into the trees, then bending towards the frozen image of the running man.

A second later the tableau broke, and a tall, thin figure stumbled into the Station, yelling violently, the space around him contracting dizzy-ingly, almost swallowed, colourless, before becoming once again the twilit glade, the stone, the dark tree.

The ground trembled. Lytton turned and stared anxiously back to the hollowing, then grinned and shouted, 'Close, but not close enough, damn your eye!' After a moment he relaxed, ran a hand through his grey-streaked hair and tossed his slim backpack to the ground. His shirt was made of skins held together by bronze pins down the front. He was wearing the army-issue trousers and boots that Helen sported. As he walked into Old Stone Hollow he waved a hand at the air behind him, then slapped at his cheek. Richard sensed laughter and curiosity from the bushes near to him, and subtle, flowing movement, not unlike the movement of the cave paintings, half there, half not there.

Lacan, staring at his machine, pronounced, 'It's gone.' Then with a slap on the new arrival's shoulder, he asked, 'What have you been dragging up this time, eh, Alexander?'

'God only knows,' said Lytton with a grim smile. His way of speak-ing was very deliberate, and his accent distinctly Scottish. 'One of Huxley's nightmares, I imagine. But I've some good photographs.' He passed a small camera to Lacan, who took it and peered at it as if he had never seen such an object before. 'I need to change,' he went on, pulling the restraining pins from the ragged skin shirt as he walked over to Richard. 'Mr Bradley, I presume. Of course.' He shook hands.

His eyes were like ice, a pale grey. Richard couldn't engage with them. He sank through them. Lytton looked old, his lean features heavily lined. His teeth behind the engaging smile were yellow and bad. But those eyes, the depthless feel to them, that gaze was disorientating. He was shorter than Richard and smelled rank. His ribbed torso was heavily scratched, but very tanned. He exuded strength and certainty. He was very curious about the other man, and slightly apprehensive. 'I shan't be long,' he continued. 'I lost my shirt and had to rifle a corpse for this uncomfortable piece of rabbit skin. No sense of style, the Jutes. Not in 800 AD, at any rate. I'll just freshen up. Then there's something I'd like to show you. You're not in any sort of hurry, are you, Mr Bradley?'

'Not at all.'

'Of course you're not!'

He smiled again, slapping Richard's arm in a curiously stiff show of welcome, then stripped off the shirt and his heavy army gear before walking naked (and unconcerned) to the river, there to stretch out in the cold flow, his voice a murmur of pleasure, punctuated only by his irritated shouts as one of the elementals prodded or probed too close to him.

'As I'm sure you've been told,' Lytton said later, his words slow, the tone dropping as if always making statements, never questions, 'I'm plagued by Huxley's damned elementals. They must like my blood!'

He was leading the way through the undergrowth along the side of the cliff. The path began to rise steeply, away from the deep cut of the cave, and they dragged themselves up through wiry trees, stumbling on the mossy boulders that stuck from the ground like broken teeth. The sounds of the camp dropped away, behind and below. The wood was restless, bird life – or perhaps Lytton's attachments – frantic about them. The twilight played tricks with perception. The sun was brilliant as it sank low, although there was something almost diffuse about the orb, about the clouds reflecting the intense orange light. Stretching away, to the side of him, as Richard climbed, the canopy was a misty sea of shape and silence, a few tall trees probing the heavens, bony, storm-racked limbs spread out above their smaller charges.

Dressed in faded Levi's and a rugby shirt, Lytton grunted with effort as he picked his way up the steep and tangled incline. When he stopped for breath, he smiled and patted at the large, leatherbound book below his arm. The covers were new, the pages inside were old and crisped with time. 'Have you read much of George Huxley's journal? Did Lacan instruct you?'

'A little.'

'You have a treat in store, Richard. Truly, Huxley was a man of genius—' He broke off sharply, pointing through the trees. 'Look! Look there!'

A sudden flight had signalled the dusk departure of an immense heron from its nest in an elm standard high above the wood. Its throat feathers were blood-red, its back striped with black and grey. It sailed out over Old Stone Hollow and disappeared into the glow of the sun.

'Magnificent!' Lytton said with admiration. 'Do you know what nature of bird you've just witnessed, Richard?'

'A heron. A bloody big one.'

'A bloody extinct one! It was hunted out of existence by tribes living in what is now the Atlantic basin, west of France and Spain. But that was in the last interglacial, fifteen thousand years ago. Can you *imagine*, Richard? Fifteen *thousand* years. And now someone, some *thing* in this place, has brought the bird with it. A lost legend, a forgotten hero, a creature associated with that hero, and there it is, exquisite in its flight, beautiful, timeless, a brief glimpse of something our world has lost.'

His voice was still breathless, but his pleasure at this giant heron radiated through the wide smile on his face as he watched its last shadow in the distance.

Richard said, 'Lacan would smack his lips and wonder how it tasted.'

Lytton laughed and turned away, climbing again. 'You're not wrong there. The man's a true barbarian.' Then he slapped at the air in front of him. Richard smelled something rotten and felt a brush of icy breeze. '*Damned* elementals!' the Scot shouted furiously, reaching for a sapling as he hauled onwards. 'Do you understand the notion of them, Richard? Do you know what we *mean* by an elemental?'

'Something fairy-like?' Richard suggested. His legs were getting tired, but he could see the leading edge of the overhang through the foliage. The climb was almost at an end. Lytton brushed irritably at his left shoulder where, if the light was a certain way, Richard could just discern the small, hunched shape of an elfin-faced creature, lank hair waving. It was riding backwards, staring at him and grinning.

Lytton had been highly amused by that answer. 'Fairy-like! Indeed! But what exactly *is* a fairy? Have you ever cast your mind around that question, Richard? Something with wings out of a Victorian fancy, perhaps? Not in the least! Then maybe a wee, green guardian of pots of gold? That's the Irish for you, boundlessly optimistic! But a leprechaun's no fairy. A fairy is something corrupt, Richard. Something shrivelled and shrunken. Something so old that the flesh of myth has withered from its bones, and the bones of its story dissolved to a thin marrow.' He spoke slowly, his voice almost a growl. 'Like the terrible creature which rules them, elementals come from the first of times, the worst of times, the time of the first forests, the first fires, the first *language* that consisted of more than simple signals. Do you get my drift? The time of first insight, first irrational fear. First nightmares, if you will. Lacan calls them "shape-memories", from the earliest time of human consciousness. They are all we have left of the savannah, of the great lake cultures around Olduvai, of the long walks out of Africa. But because they *are* so old, they are *tenacious*, by God. They have lingered in our minds, as unshakable as our shadows on a bright day. And in this place, this wildwood, they condense and exist as easily as an English rain.'

Lytton led the way from the tree-line onto a grassy slope leading to the cliff edge. Dusk was deepening and they would be staring into its reddening mask on the horizon. Both men were exhausted with the walking and talking, but Lytton drew a deep breath, his eyes closed, smiling face to the heavens. Richard had been about to respond to the mini-lecture on 'elementals' with a question concerning the role of toadstools, but thought better of it.

'Come on,' Lytton said suddenly, taking the book into his hands. He brushed irritably at his left shoulder. 'Is there something there?'

'There is.'

'Damn! Anyway, let's sit, talk, and look at the world George Huxley has made.'

And as he strode to the edge, he lit a cigarette, choking as he drew the first smoke.

'Are you beginning to understand us, Richard?' Lytton asked in his slow, Scots drawl. 'Has Lacan been a good instructor to you?'

Sitting close to the edge of the overhang, Richard felt overwhelmed again by the spread of forest before him. As he stared into the great distance, regular shapes began to expose themselves among the billowing waves of the trees. He could see the crenellations of a medieval castle, the broken point of a spire, the solid columns of totem trunks, nearly as tall as the great elm standards. In the farthest distance, the wood seemed to burn, and beyond that flickering illusion of fire, the suggestion of mountains.

In answer to Lytton's question he could only say, 'I understand his words, but not how they add up. I just can't grasp the whole of *this* – all in one tiny patch of woodland . . .'

Richard had accepted the vastness of Ryhope Wood as if in a dream, but every hour or so the incomprehensibility of it struck him with surging, stifling power. It was a dizzying feeling, sickening. He was a *real* presence in an unreal world, listening to talk of spirit-guides and space-time warps, of elementals and a dead boy, now alive, and who had not aged at all over seven years. He lived a lucid dream, a dream of need, because that boy was his son, and he missed him and longed for him, but he was caught in this dream, fully aware, between sleeping and waking.

He realised suddenly that Lytton was watching him with a curious intensity. The Scot raised his eyebrows, asking, 'A dark twilight of the soul, is it, Richard? What are you thinking? Tell me about it.'

'*Is* my son alive? Is Alex alive? Is it possible? I saw his dead body.'

Lytton nodded and ground his cigarette into the sparse turf, then stared out across the wilderness. 'Alex is most certainly alive, and if I could show you where he's hiding, I'd do so, and gladly. I can show you a *bit* of him, that castle, the fortress. We're pretty sure it's from Alex's mind, and not Huxley's. Did he have an interest in knights and jousting?'

Richard thought of the models, the castles built of tiny bricks, the stacks of books on Arthur, and the paintings of Green Knights and Red Knights, even a knight dressed in gold, and one called the Ghost Knight that Alex had made into a Christmas presentation when he was eight, a silly little play, but wonderful fun for proud parents to watch. 'Yes,' Richard said with a smile.

'I'm not surprised. The castle is like the White Castle on the Welsh Marches, near Ludlow. Do you know it? The site of a fortress for thousands of years, mentioned in the *Mabinogion*, the old Welsh tales of Celtic adventure. In the manner of Hamlet's father's ghost, Alex haunts that castle. McCarthy has glimpsed him in the passages. Lacan too, I think. It's a place from which he watches us at times, and it was there that we first contacted him, first heard him talk, so to speak.'

'Sciamachy . . .'

'Indeed. The contact of shadows. It's a two-week walk to the castle, although it doesn't look it, and you'll go there with Helen. But as to where he *is* . . . all I can tell you, Richard, is that he is out *there* somewhere, hiding from us and defending against us, and against the creatures that would gladly render him to corrupted flesh and bone. He is in great danger. But you already know that, because Helen would not have kept it from you.'

'No. No, she didn't . . .'

'You can't see him, but we have an idea how to approach him. What you saw, all those years ago, the remains of the boy, they were probably, yes, probably a *form* of Alex. But they weren't Alex. He's here, around us, and he's destroying what Huxley has created.'

The words took Richard by surprise. Lytton indicated the wilderness. 'Do you not *get* it yet? Everything you *see* is Huxley. The wood was here from the first seed after the ice, yes, of course. And people came and went and seeded the wood with the products of their myths. Yes. *Yes*. But not until Huxley was it *shaped*. Whatever the man did, he touched its very heart. Huxley is dead, but lives on around us. We are living *in* the man, in the mind of Huxley himself. And somewhere out there, somewhere at the heart, is the key and the clue to what he did, thirty years ago. But Alex . . .

'When Alex came he began to disrupt everything. He is like a tumour at the heart of the world, eroding, destroying the subtlety and the beauty of Huxley's creation. His mind, roaming free, is like a fire, burning and charring. It's an evil thing. That's why I want him *out* of here, Richard. And *bloody fast*! That's why we need you. He'll come to you . . . I'm sure of it. And when he does . . .'

Lytton was suddenly angry; his words had taken on a tone of menace and Richard was disturbed. Very pointedly he said, 'And when he does . . . *what*? What will you do? What are you implying?'

For a second the fire continued to burn in Lytton's narrowed eyes. Then he frowned and shrugged. 'I apologise. Huxley's hurting and it grieves me. You may grieve too.' He glanced up, spoke softly. 'You see, there's something I have to tell you, something else about Alex. It may be bad news for you . . .'

'Go on.'

'There is something wrong with the boy. His mind . . .' Lytton tapped his temple, squinting at the other man as he growled the words. 'Something lacking, or something . . . twisted. We can't be sure, Richard. What the boy is creating, what is generating in the wood around the cathedral, is warped. It's not right. He has defended himself against these creatures, but it can only be a matter of time before those defences fail. This is a dangerous enough place as it is, without seeding it with, the twisted and cruel products of a child's grimmest imagination.'

Imagination. The key word. Richard thought about his son, that sad, blank face that had stared at Alice and him during the long, final year of the boy's life. He relived the pain, the attempts to draw something, some imaginative response from a child who seemed to have shed all emotion, all feeling, all fun, as a snake sheds its skin.

Lytton reached out and gripped Richard's arm, a reassuring squeeze. 'I'm sorry if that hurts. It's best you know.'

'I knew,' Richard said. 'Something happened to Alex, a year or so before he died . . . vanished. He was staring through a mask, trying to see into Ryhope Wood. I thought it was a game. A madman's game. But he was struck by something. I only caught a glimpse of it . . .'

Lytton was excited, his eyes intense again as he listened. 'I need to know everything,' he said. 'Every detail. A mask, you say? I need to know about it. Everything, Richard. The more we understand about the boy, the quicker we can winkle him out of hiding and send him home. Come on. Come on.'

He was standing, brushing at his jeans, impatient to be on the trail again.

Richard stared at the castle walls, now just shadows among shadows. He thought of Alex coming home. He tried to feel what it would be like to have him home again, as if he had never been away, the same age, the same bright-smiled child, the same enthusiast, the same little boy, longing for someone to help him with his models.

It was too much for him, too powerful, and Lytton came back and crouched down, staring impatiently out across the forest, but waiting until the sadness had passed.

Echoes

In the warm longhouse, Richard relaxed with the smell of fresh turf and the sweet woodsmoke that came from the central fire. Lytton unfurled a map of Ryhope.

'This is the perimeter, the easy part of Ryhope Wood to draw, though you still won't find it marked on any Ordnance Survey map.'

Ryhope was more-or-less circular, though a deep path cut into it from the south-east, leading to a mill-pond. Two streams flowed into the wood, only one flowed out. Inside the perimeter were bands and enclosures, with names like Oak-Ash Zone; Elm Track; Primary Genesis Zone; Quick-Season Gorge and Wolf Caves.

Lytton tapped the map. 'There are four ways into Ryhope that we know. One is across the pond, a difficult entrance through a thick stand of oak. It's the place where Huxley's boys saw various apparitions back in the thirties. Huxley's own entranceway was here.' He tapped a stream marked 'sticklebrook'. 'He found he could penetrate quite deeply by following the stream for a while. Ultimately, of course, the wood turned him around, disorientated him, but he managed to map the zones near Oak Lodge, and found the Horse Shrine, which is a very powerful site. The other two entrances into Ryhope are "hollowings", which run into different planes and different times, if we're not careful. One here is where we think the girl got lost, your son's friend, Tallis. From what you tell me, she probably went in through Hunter's Brook. The fourth way in is through an abandoned Roman tin mine, just here.' He indicated the solid edge of the wood, on the side facing the village of Grimley. 'The workings were abandoned in about 200 AD, probably because of what was happening to the miners . . . The shafts are deep, but were sealed in antiquity.'

Now Lytton unrolled a second chart, smiling as he saw the expression of complete bemusement on Richard's face.

'The underlayers,' he said. 'Otherworlds we think are accessed through hollowings.'

The map showed five Ryhope 'perimeters', one above the other in a staggered display, connected by thin tubes that curved down between them, some connecting adjacent planes, others running deeper and usually ending in a question mark. Old Stone Hollow Station was clearly marked on the top plane and, like some ancient and mystical site radiating ley-lines, seemed to be the source of several hollowings.

'We're in the top plane – topwood. It's the Ryhope that Huxley knew. Here we are, at the cave. Two hollowings leading from here are short, and have been successfully explored. One drops to a dark lake-filled land, in three-wood, probably from Slavonian legend. And this one . . . where does this one go?' He twisted the map slightly. 'Oh yes. To a valley filled with stone tombs in two-wood, late Neolithic Europe. But the hollowing that leads from the cave must go very deep indeed, the same with Wide Water Hollowing. So far we've detected five levels of underworlds. There's more than a lifetime's exploration here, Richard, and all we can hope to do is establish safe routes down and back, so that later explorers can at least have more than a hollowstick to guide them.'

Richard stared at the confusion of tracks, tunnels and shafts for a while, then gently rolled the chart up again to expose the simple plane of Ryhope Wood. He had seen, previously, the small spire marked in the outline, and pointed to it. 'You think Alex is in topwood?'

Lytton cocked his head and raised his eyebrows. 'That's not easy to say. He *seems* to be. But the cathedral itself might exist in more than one level. The question is: in which wood is Alex hiding? If he's deep, then we'll need to find a hollowing. If he's in topwood, then we should be able to get to him directly. The problem is, we can't. There's something blocking us, Richard, a barrier, about five days in from the Station. If it *is* Alex putting that barrier up, then perhaps – just perhaps – he will let you through. Are you willing to try?'

Richard was surprised at the question. 'Of course. I'll try anything, now that I'm here. Never mind that I hardly understand a word, that my vision is full of dancing, my dreams are like some prehistoric commedia dell arte, chaotic, colourful, confusing – frightening. If Alex is alive, then I want him back. Just tell me what to do.'

'You'll get used to the dreams,' Lytton said kindly. 'And the chaos at the edge of vision fades in time as well. That's just part of the process of *generation.*' He smiled broadly. 'Mr Bradley, you're creating life, although you don't know it. Out there, the wood is listening to you, feeding off you, enriching both itself and its underworlds from you. It's drawing out your dreams, your memories, your fears.' He slapped the back of his hand against Richard's chest. 'It's giving them *flesh*, but ennobled and empowered by the form of the Hero!' He laughed quickly. 'I like your metaphor of the *commedia*. It's more apt than you might think. Wait until you are an audience at your own show! It can be quite enthralling!'

As night closed over the Station, and a second generator powered-up to bring light to the compound, an odd and musical wind began to blow from the cave, carrying with it the distant sound of voices. At once, Lacan started recording. Helen went through the scrub to the overhang, to observe and to listen. Richard, finished for the moment with Alexander Lytton, sat with Elizabeth Haylock, the sketchy map of the wood spread out between them on a trestle table, and shivered as the voices rose and fell in eerie pitch.

'They sound in pain,' he said.

'It could be no more than distortion . . .'

'Can you recognise them?'

She shook her head. One voice, deeper, began to chatter. The words ebbed and flowed, but were meaningless. Then there was an anguished cry, high-pitched, falling away in volume, lowering in tone.

Soon the wailing from the cave passed away, and Helen returned. She came to the table where Richard sat and glanced grimly at Haylock.

'One of them sounded like Ben Darby.'

'Oh God.'

'You said you always wanted to know . . . I might have been wrong.'

'I *do* want to know. Thanks.'

'Need to talk?'

'Not necessary. Thanks anyway.'

Helen went into the longhouse. Elizabeth Haylock stared at the overhang for a while, then rose and walked stiffly to the river. She lay face-down on the bank, trailing a hand in the cold water. After a few minutes she stood again, walked along the river bank, searching for something, in fact a long stick, and crossed the bridge with this simple weapon, striking angrily at the vegetation as she was consumed by darkness and the forest.

*

Richard followed Helen to the lodge. She was eating a sandwich and writing notes in a thick pad. A mug of tea was cooling beside her. 'Elizabeth's just crossed the bridge. She seems very upset.'

Glancing up, Helen nodded, swallowed her food and motioned Richard to sit. 'She'll be OK. Ben was her lover. He's long dead and she knows it. We found his body a year ago. But his ghost pursues her in more ways than one. He and his partner must have passed through a timeslow, so he's still alive in the wood, just for a while. Sometimes the echoes come through.'

'Did the same thing happen to Dan?'

Helen watched Richard, her eyes narrowing slightly. 'Lacan told you about Dan, did he?'

Richard nodded.

She took a huge bite from the sandwich, staring into the middle distance, then scrawled a few more words on the pad. 'He knew the risks,' she muttered eventually. 'We take risks just by living here. But Dan'll be alive, still. I'll get him back. Lacan is wrong. McCarthy is wrong. They say there's no shadow of him in the forest, but I don't think that can be right. Dan knew the risks – he'll have been on his guard. Don't talk about him any more. Please?'

'I'm sorry. I didn't mean to distress you.'

Helen laughed. 'How English. There's no need to be sorry, I'll tell you about Dan later. I just don't want to think about him now, OK?'

'OK.'

'Now. Have you made your hollowsticks? You'll need to make four or five. You'll find wood behind the long-house. You need hair, blood and . . .' she smiled awkwardly, 'semen? If you've got any to spare. It's a good spirit link.'

'Witchcraft,' Richard murmured and she raised her eyebrows, nodding enthusiastically.

'It also works!'

Richard hesitated to point out that three hollowsticks by the cave entrance did not seem to have been effective, indeed, that Dan's token up in the Sanctuary ruins was growing fungal with age, but Helen saw his reservation and intuited his doubts. 'They work more than they don't. And sometimes it takes time to call the traveller back. We use the hollowsticks to mark our passage through the hollowings, to know who has gone. In this world, Richard, time is strange, so patience takes on a new meaning.'

Richard fetched twigs and twine from the small pile behind the research lodge and shaped five little effigies, ready for the incorporation of his 'body relics' later.

'Do you need any help?' she asked, mischievously.

'I can manage, thanks.'

'I'm sure you can.'

When Helen had finished her notes she cracked a beer – Richard took a second – and relaxed more, recounting her trip out to Hergest Ridge. She soon grew tired and went to the river's edge, splashing her face with water and singing softly to the night-dark across the flow. Richard was entranced with her voice and went over to crouch behind her. The song had an eerie tune, and the words were in the language of the Lakota. When she had finished singing she told Richard to look away and quickly used the river.

As they walked back to the tents, Richard said, 'Was that a folksong?'

'A charm,' she said, and smiled. 'A trick. It's the only way to catch a trickster. And catch him I will! Mark my words.'

And with that she ducked into the tent where she kept her pack, to sleep.

Genesis

The hares had hung for two nights and a day. At *reveille* Lacan, dressed only in torn-down denim shorts and his magic tooth-necklace, began to prepare the feast for the evening, skinning the creatures, talking to them, loudly celebrating their elegance, and issuing instructions to everyone, as they woke and emerged from the tents to wash, as to what they should each do for him.

'This meal is *Lièvre à la Royale* and only a Frenchman with an intense Celtic ancestry can do it justice. Ah, Helen – good morning – when you've finished your womanly ablutions, your job is to make a rich sauce of the congealed blood – brandy will thin it out—'

'I'll make a rich sauce of *your* blood if you give me *that* job . . .'

Irritably, Lacan hacked the head off one of the hares. 'Then sacrifice some carrots and cloves of garlic, finely, very very finely.'

'Much better.'

'I wish them to be *practically molecular!*'

'No problem.'

Richard was told to build a fire in the pit where meat was barbecued. McCarthy accepted the task of thinning the jugged blood. Lytton and Haylock gathered wild herbs and edible mushrooms before settling to a study of artefacts and a further hour's conversation with Richard about his son's last years in Shadoxhurst. Lacan fussed and sang, bellowed and criticised, but the morning passed and the 'first operation' was declared a success: the hares were slowly braising.

Richard made only one mistake. Watching Lacan from outside the blue ribbon cordoning off the cooker area from the 'uncivilised' part of the Station (Lacan's little joke) he said, 'Of course, the *true* Celts would never have eaten hare. It would have been sacrilege. Did you know that?'

Lacan looked up sharply, his eyes wide with surprise, then scowling.

He leapt the 'cordon bleu' and grabbed Richard by his shirt lapels, glowering down at him.

'Which *madman* told you that?'

'It's a known fact,' Richard said evenly, trying not to smile. 'The hare was a sacred animal . . . to the *true* Celts. They worshipped it.'

Lacan breathed slowly, gaze meeting gaze, then he released Richard and smoothed his shirt. 'Well, of *course*!' he said loudly. 'Of course we worshipped it. We worshipped it alive. We worshipped it dead. Best of all, we worshipped it when *cooked*!' He shook his head despairingly as he returned to the cooking area, muttering, 'Foolish man . . . he knows *nothing* about worship . . . he must be going bosky . . . it happens . . . perhaps I'll ignore him . . . maybe he'll go away . . .'

Richard had slept late, his dreams disturbed by thoughts of Alex. After talking to Lytton again, he looked for Helen, and found her at the lake, swimming. 'It's freezing!' she called. 'But wonderful. Come on in.'

He stripped naked and shuddered and shivered into the cold water, finally diving head-first to get the shock over and done with. The lake was crystal clear. Helen trod water, her limbs an unnatural pale hue, but slender and shapely as she slowly cycled. When he surfaced in front of her she was smiling. 'You need to lose some weight.'

'In water this cold I'm glad of the blubber.'

'Swim with me . . .'

She somersaulted in the lake, legs kicking as she dived deep, then surfaced, yards away, striking powerfully toward Wide Water Hollowing and its warning markers. Richard's best stroke was the crawl and he followed in her wake, soon warm enough to enjoy the cold. When they stopped, bobbing vertically in the deep water, Helen peered downwards. 'There's a castle below us. Can you see?'

Richard dived, descending as far as he could before the pressure-pain in his ears was intolerable. He saw the walls and weed-covered structure of a stone building a long way down. A mass of sinuous movement in one place resolved itself as eels. Two vaguely human figures seemed to be crouching by one of the ramparts. He was astonished at the clarity of the ruins, at how much light reached them. But they were too far down to explore without proper equipment.

Breathless, he surfaced again, to see Helen on her back, stroking lazily to the shore.

When they were dry they sat by the water and pitched stones across the shimmering surface at the haze that marked the hollowing. Richard asked, 'What's come through in your time?'

Helen shrugged. 'Boats, mostly. A selkie, a serpent, but mostly boats. They usually end up on the far shore – I guess they don't like the look of this one. The most dramatic was a Viking long-ship, wonderful sail, bizarre creature carved on its prow. It had only two men crewing it, one dressed in white skins and helmeted in gold, the other holding the ends of the sail in his hands, guiding the vessel. We didn't recognise the legend, and the mythago vanished into the deep-wood as soon as they'd beached.' She pointed further round the lake shore. 'The vessel is over there, somewhere. Lytton uses it when he sails round the lake calling for Huxley, which is something he does frequently.' She glanced at Richard, jade-green eyes curious. 'What do you make of Lytton?'

'Scots – obsessive – bad breath – romantic – probably brilliant . . .' He thought of the uneasiness in the conversation above Old Stone Hollow, the evening before. 'He's angry with Alex. He seems to think the boy is a *malignancy*, destroying some unseen and subtle structure in the wood. I'm sure he doesn't mean it.'

Helen's laugh was sour. She took her jacket from around her shoulders and shrugged into it, looking hard at Richard. 'He *does* mean it. He's frightened of what Alex is doing. He *does* mean it, and you should never let that thought leave you. Don't trust him. Listen to him, yes. He understands Ryhope Wood better than any of us. He's the one who called us together in the first place. He knows Huxley, and mythagos, inside out. Yes. But Richard – be careful of him. Watch him.'

'He wants to get Alex out of the wood. He wants to help him.'

'He wants Alex out of *Huxley* – he'll do anything to achieve that.'

Richard stared across the blue water. Everything was so quiet, so peaceful, so remote. He had just thought this when, distantly, Arnauld Lacan's voice roared faintly, another demand, another irritation during the preparing of his brace of hares.

Helen frowned as she listened. 'Something about "the first removal of the fat being completed"?' She shared Richard's grimace. 'Thank God all I had to do was cut vegetables.'

'He's a good man, is Lacan.'

'Yes he is. And a good friend.' She was suddenly wistful. 'He'll never find what he's looking for. There are times when I feel very sad for him.'

'What *is* he looking for?'

Helen looked down, shook her head. 'If he didn't tell you, I shouldn't talk about it. Sorry. It's a sort of rule, here. A part of the ritual.'

'That's OK. How about you? What are you seeking?'

'Me? Trickster. As I told you last night. That Ol' Trickster Coyote. Old Man Fox himself! The haunter of conscience. The first deceiver. The laughing friend, the gloating foe. Trickster. He's here, I'll find him. And when I do, I'll . . .'

She smiled, breaking off her flow and tugging at the silver lock of hair that grew from her temple. 'I'll find him,' she repeated. 'He and I have something to say to each other.'

'Everybody's looking. Everybody's seeking. Everybody's dreaming.'

'That's why we're here. You too. Except that, unlike us, your goal is not a mythago.'

'Yes, I know. I was astonished when you found out about the cricket bat so fast—'

Again, Helen laughed. 'It took a week! McCarthy encountered the shadow of Alex on one of the castles.' Richard remembered Lytton talking about this and said, 'Sciamachy?'

'Something like that. Alex is in difficulties, but he *can* move through the rootweb. He's got help. Someone's helping him. When he appears, it's literally as a shadow, but someone like McCarthy – and sometimes me – can communicate with him. We ask a question, we get a dreamlike reply. Like talking to someone who's in a lucid dream? When McCarthy asked the shadow about the fire-dance, it unleashed a storm of emotion. A lot of memories, almost overload. That night was important to your son. More important than perhaps you realise.'

Richard whispered, 'I let him down. I wouldn't dance. I was embarrassed. And he was so desperate for me to dance.'

'You wouldn't dance? Why you old *square*.' She smiled. 'It was more than that. It was the moment when he linked with the heartwood. We all do it, we all get trapped. If there's a significance in that evening, it's to do with the dancing figures, the fire, not your cricket bat! We'll find out eventually. For the moment, only one thing is important.'

He glanced at Helen, then looked more deeply, drawn to her looks, her eyes, and the warmth and strength she offered him. Beads of lake water had formed on the braided locks of dark and silver hair. She breathed softly, watching him, then said, 'Do you believe Alex is here? In your heart? Do you believe us? We won't find him unless you do.'

'I so much want to. The cricket bat – how else could you have known? Unless you can read my mind.'

'We can't read minds. Talk to ghosts, yes, but not read minds.'

'I do so much want to believe he's alive. I gave him up so easily after the accident. I gave so *much* up so easily . . . But I saw him dead and I buried him. Something came for him, struck him through a mask, took him away from us. When he finally died – oh God, I'll say it. I'll say it. When he died I was *glad*. It was such a relief. Like a depression lifting. I felt free again. I felt there was something to live for again. But that didn't happen.'

'Alice drifted away . . .'

'And I drifted on. I stopped living. I just started to get old.'

Helen's hand was a gentle touch on his shoulder, then she shuffled closer and put her arm around him, surprising him. 'Is this OK? Does it bother you?'

'No. Not at all.'

She squeezed him harder, grinning at his discomfiture, his reserve, looking hard at his profile, teasing. 'Then why are you so stiff?'

'You can tell *that*? Without looking? Amazing.'

'Why are you so *tense*?' she corrected with a laugh. 'Don't you do this in England? Get close to a friend when you know they're sad?'

'Maybe I've been thinking of more than friendship—' His face burned as he said the words, wondering where in the name of heaven he'd found the nerve to blurt out such an obvious truth.

Helen hesitated, then glanced away, thoughtful for a moment, but her arm held him tightly. 'That's OK,' she said suddenly. 'Why not? I'm attracted to you too. I was attracted to you the first moment we met, all those weeks ago.'

'Three days ago, if you don't mind.'

'Three days, five weeks – I've been in *deep*. I've had longer to think about you than you have about me. You're a hard man to shake off, Richard Bradley. You feature in my dreams. I like that. And I think Dan will like you too. And it's OK, before you start getting edgy. He's not the macho, possessive type.'

'Not a Jack Daniels and Marlboro man, then?'

She laughed. 'No way. The occasional Southern Comfort and lemonade, maybe. Marijuana, of course, but then who doesn't? But how about you? I know Alice left you. You still on your own?'

'A regular bachelor boy. Cliff sang about me and no *body* but me.'

'Cliff Richard? He's too pretty. Mick Jagger, now . . .'

'The Stones? With you all the way. The only music I'll dance to, these days. But I still have a fondness for The Shadows . . .'

Helen laughed loudly. 'Then, Mr Bradley, have *you* come to the right place!'

A horn blast brought everyone running to the river's edge, through the gates of the compound, and a great cheer went up as two bulky figures appeared among the trees at the top of the slope. They came down through the bone-yard, and again the man raised the bone horn to his lips and emitted the deep, sonorous call, laughing as Lacan shouted to him to be silent.

They came over the bridge and flung their packs to other members of the team, then stripped down to sweat-stained skin suits. They were Finnish mythologists and had been coming home for some weeks, vaguely tracked by McCarthy. Their arrival was sudden and unexpected and a special delight for Lacan, whose *Lièvre à la Royale* was sumptuously ready to eat. The woman of the new team, Pirkko Sinisalo, had an arrow nick in her right wrist and Elizabeth Haylock led her to the medical tent.

A few minutes later they came over to meet Richard, Pirkko reeking of antiseptic, her partner, Ilmari Heikonen, holding a half-finished bottle of *snapsi*, ice-cold and fragrant, which Richard happily tasted. They had been searching for Tuonela and the hero Vainamoinen, but had ended up on the tundra of an early Siberian myth-cycle, fighting for their lives against mammoth hunters.

As dusk drew close, music started up on an old gramophone, a loud country song, up-tempo and jaunty, made unusual with the voices of Lacan and Helen adding their own accompaniment.

The hare was served, so tender that it melted from the bones, so tasty that everyone forgave Lacan for his temper and his tantrums, and the jobs he had given them.

After the hare, and the compliments, and Lacan's voluminous and voluble acceptance of his culinary genius, there was dancing to Breton jigs and waltzes, supplied by Lacan on a set of ancient bone bagpipes, which he played with immense vigour and much foot-stomping, and Ilmari on a violin. Richard was quietly pleased that Helen danced with him early on, taking him through the steps of the country dances that, familiar in tune, he had only ever seen, never tried. The coals from the fire, plus dry wood, had been used to create a bonfire in the middle of the clearing, and the occupants of Old Stone Hollow wheeled and skipped around the flames, voices adding hysterically to the singing and guitars from the scratchy records.

'What, no cricket bat?' Helen called, as she waltzed with Lytton, who kept roaring out words of song in such a broad Scots accent that it sounded like a battle-cry. Haylock's black hair flowed around her like a veil as she and Wakeman pirouetted, the man holding himself rigidly upright, like a robot, his movements sudden and jerky. Richard and Pirkko, dressed only in the body-webs against the heat of the fire, performed a sort of sedate Regency to the slower Breton rhythms. Pirkko sweated, kept saying things to Richard which he couldn't hear, pressed close to him and laughed familiarly. He concentrated on Lacan and McCarthy, tussling with each other as they danced awkwardly, the small Irishman trying to control the monstrous Frenchman as they twirled together, at arm's length, scowling and insulting, stumbling and laughing.

The dancing stopped abruptly, almost shockingly. Ilmari Heikonen was screaming at them to be quiet. He was by the gates through the palisade, pale and frightened, illuminated by the fire.

'Turn the music off!' he shouted, and the strains of the Celtic dance ended suddenly, leaving an eerie silence broken only by the crackle of burning wood and Heikonen's words. 'There's something coming towards us. Out by the Sanctuary. It's coming fast, through the roots . . .'

Richard had never seen such activity. Within moments everyone was jacketed up, swinging cameras and monitors onto their backs and running to the river. Helen flung Richard's heavy jacket to him, and he struggled into it, following, confused, behind the others, over the bridge and up the dark incline towards the Sanctuary, stumbling as he went, aware of the torchlight ahead.

Suddenly the wood was very silent. Lights flashed in the dark, spread in a wide arc. Helen was breathing hard, leaning against a tree. Suddenly she shouted, 'He's here!'

At once two figures slammed themselves against trees, hands outstretched, scraping against the bark. Richard noticed Helen rubbing the blackened, coarse skin on the back of her own hand. He smelted blood.

'It's rising. Concentrating,' came McCarthy's voice.

Then Helen's, 'It's the boy. He's hesitating. He knows we're here . . .'

'It's your son,' she whispered a moment later. 'He's aware of you. He's probing for you. Quickly . . . we might get a chance to see him.' She dragged Richard forward.

Lacan bellowed: 'He's shifted through the web . . . to the right, forty degrees . . . He's in the Sanctuary!'

Helen changed direction, running between grey stones and carved columns, following the flash and flicker of torches ahead. Bulky shapes crossed in the light, or loomed up and scrambled away, each trying to find a position, to feel the flow of whatever energy Alex was projecting. Their voices merged and mingled.

'Here!'

And then a flight of birds and a wild crashing through crisp undergrowth.

'He's rising again!'

'But where? Where?'

'He's close! Who's got his shadow? McCarthy?'

'I'm with him. He's stretched thin – he's searching very hard. I can see his trail – he's frightened.'

All around him Richard could hear movement among the trees and the ruins, but suddenly he felt cold, isolated, standing with his back to an oak, facing the sombre shadows of a wood whose outline was broken, high above, by a fragmentary moonlight.

And then someone called him 'daddy'.

The voice had seemed to come from the edge of the world, but had shocked him. It was a boy's voice, a whisper only, not recognisable, yet powerful. A single word, a dream word, and he felt weak and leaned heavily back, staring at darkness.

It started to rain, warm and sticky. The tree against which he was leaning began to ooze and he pulled away, shocked by the unpleasant sensation. The whole glade rustled and trembled as the sap squeezed from the leaves. The atmosphere became heady, heavy, quite stifling, and the air pressure built until his eardrums began to hurt.

From the corner of his eye he saw a camera flashbulb triggered, a brief glare. The air was sucked slowly from his lungs so that he gasped.

An immense and ghostly face rose suddenly from the dark ground, a grey luminosity in the night, a half-glimpsed image of eyes and nose, a flop of hair, a mouth that worked silently, the gigantic visage of a boy thrusting up into the glade. As it rose, so it dispersed, fragmenting at the edge, but re-forming and leaning towards Richard, who backed again into the weeping tree. The spectre's eyes were wide, and in the glowing grey shape he could see what looked like tears. The face rose further and shoulders and arms appeared. A hand swept through him, tenuous fingers seeking to touch him. The figure began to enlarge then, spreading thinly through the trees, expanding unnaturally, then silently bursting, like a flock of white birds scattering in sudden alarm.

The pressure in the glade changed and the sap-scented air freshened. Helen came up to Richard and took his arm. 'What did you see?'

'I saw Alex. His ghost. His face.'

'Are you *sure* it was Alex?'

'He called to me,' Richard said. 'I think he recognised me. And he *did* sound frightened.'

Before he could say more, before he could allow the sudden sadness to arise and express itself, Lytton called out in a low voice, 'Let's get out of here. He'll have seeded the glade, and this is a primary genesis zone. Did anyone see where he came through?'

Lacan said, 'The arch. It must be a hollowing.'

'Good! Then we've got him!'

Helen tugged at Richard, an urgent gesture. 'Don't wait around.'

'A seed?' he asked as he followed.

'Genesis,' she murmured stiffly. 'Alex has come to have a look at you, but he's generating mythagos and we don't like what he generates. It's how we'll follow him, though . . . McCarthy will have seen shadows of the land between us and the Cathedral. We should be able to follow Alex home . . .'

The team moved back through the darkness. Richard listened to the glade behind them, but heard nothing.

In the night, though, the silence was broken by an almost human cry of pain and frustration, coming from a distance, lasting moments only.

The Green Chapel: 4

The hollyjack was in pain. She was certainly close to death. She had returned to her nest and lay there, emitting sounds that made Alex sad. He kept whispering, 'Don't die. Not yet. Don't die . . .'

It was dark, the sky laden with storm clouds, a cold wind blowing through the roofless sanctuary, this huge cathedral. Alex moved restlessly below the trees, waiting for the rain. He watched the dark maw of the nest, calling to his friend, but she was beyond his help now. He didn't fully understand.

She had told him that what was happening to her was merely part of her life and death, even though she had escaped from her own troop, and had not been with a male for several seasons. He knew only that there would soon be carrion birds. They would not harm him, they would simply fly to occupy the high nests of the wildwood. But the hollyjack was so weak she feared for her sapwood. She was already dry to the point of cracking.

Alex was so confused. He had left the Little Dream abruptly, dramatically affected by the sight of his father, who had looked so old, so different to the man of his recent dreams. He had surfaced in a place where there were traps – he had felt a pulse of hostility, like a raw wound, a savage threat to him from among the men around him. The anger had not come from his father. From his father there had just been desperation and longing, and the man had called to him, and Alex had answered, calling that he wanted to go home, that he longed to go back to the house with its shadows and its warm smells of food and the pictures and models on the walls and shelves.

He could see the house as if at the edge of his vision, not quite clearly yet, but it was welcoming, an old friend struggling to be remembered. He belonged there. Something terrible had happened to him, though. His father had seen it, and on one of his journeys to the Little Dream,

Alex had glimpsed the terror through his father's eyes, a boy blown across a room, a dead boy, a vacant boy, a boy buried in the rain. Something bad had happened, and that something was out in the wood, waiting for him. The giggler had struck once and it could strike again, if it could just break through the defences of the sanctuary.

The giggler had followed him through the wood just now. It had flowed behind him as he'd surfaced to see his father, and had run amok, dispersing the men and women who had set the traps. It had laughed and screamed, then skulked back through the rootweb to the cathedral again, to hover in the leaf shadow, waiting its chance. Or perhaps just waiting . . .

The hollyjack was silent. Alex walked up to the nest, conscious of the powerful smell of rot and decomposition that flowed from the round entrance. The hollyjack stirred in the darkness. Alex could hear the distant sound of cawing crows, muffled, painful. The hollyjack gasped, and her tusks clattered. Above the nest, stray light from the storm sky struck the shattered knight . . .

'Gawain . . .'

The name came to him just as thunder rolled and a sudden, freezing wind gusted through the cathedral. The light shifted on the coloured glass. The green legs of the monster shone briefly. Behind the headless figures, the green chapel beckoned, its dark doorway in the fresh green mound like a gate to peace. Alex smiled. 'Green Knight,' he said. 'I remember . . .'

The glass shook as a second peal of thunder rolled across the sky, followed by a strike of lightning and a farther crash of sound.

The hollyjack screeched. Birds erupted from the nest, a hundred of them, flowing like a black cloud from the bower. White-billed and black-winged, they struggled to the entrance and filled the air, brushing Alex back as they streamed into the thunder, swirling, crying, circling above him as they found birth and freedom.

When the nest was silent, Alex crawled into the soft interior, reaching to feel for his friend. She was still alive. Thorn-ripped fingers brushed his skin and she rustled. Alex wanted to fetch her something, anything that would help her recover. 'Water? Shall I get water?'

She emitted a feeble chatter, and he left the sanctuary, racing through the storm to the well. Lightning broke the dark cover and he watched the wood anxiously as he raised the bucket, then carried a scoop of cold liquid in a leaf pouch back to the nest. When he got there, the hollyjack had crawled out onto the marble floor, and was partially entwined with an oak root. She looked like a small bush, but raised her head and opened her arms to embrace the boy, who curled into her empty belly-space, aware of the gnarled backbone and the black feathers that were scattered between her browning leaves.

She sipped the water messily. She was very weak. When he dreamed the Big Dream with her, it was faint, a hazy view of the greenjacks as they made their way through the wide woodland, and the shifting seasons.

The shaman led them, his summer growth now browning with an encroaching winter, the flowers and grasses that decorated his body withering and losing colour. He stood in a rain-swept dell, watching the watcher, while around him Oak and Ash, Hazel and Willow, moved through the thickets, making slow progress towards the cathedral. They were agitated. Soon they would start to shed their leaves, grow monstrous and transform. Winter Wolves.

How far from the cathedral were they? Alex had no way of telling. But he felt his soul touched as the shaman scratched the face on his staff, and sensed a new direction, a new path through the forest.

What do they want with me?

To touch you. To enter the sanctuary. To pass through the chapel.

Why?

They are incomplete. They are searching for full creation. They are drawn to the source of creation. This place is at its heart.

Her chattering, whistling words were so soft in his mind that Alex could hardly experience them. He knew, though, that his friend needed to rest, and to grow in strength. She was an evergreen, and he was aware that she did not go through the shedding and renewal of strength of others of her species. But there was no nourishment in the marble slabs above the crypt. Alex rose and helped the *daurog* into his arms, but she was too leafy, and the leaves pricked and drew blood whichever way he tried to carry her. So he used ivy to make a sling, and hauled her to the window, lowering her to the porch, and then the ground. She found a soft-earth place, behind a slanting stone, and put down deep roots, folding into herself, quivering violently for a while, before becoming still.

Alex watched the thundery skies and felt the cold wind, but he sat beside her, watching the wood, protecting her as she struggled for life.

At some time during the night her arm reached out, and fingers touched him gently, and he heard his father's voice, and the sound of running and horses.

'We'll soon be safe,' he said. 'My father is close, and coming closer. We'll soon be safe . . .'

Jack

Very early the following morning, Richard was woken by Lacan shaking him roughly. It was dark, damp and cold in the tent and Richard's sparse beard was wet with dew.

'I've come to say *au revoir*,' the Frenchman said. 'I'm getting an early start.'

Surprised, Richard could only repeat, '*Au revoir?*'

The big man was a heavy, featureless shape crouched over him. 'You'll go inwards in an hour or so, with Helen and Lytton, maybe McCarthy. For myself, I like to take the Otherworld by surprise.'

Dazed with tiredness, distressed by what Lacan had just said, Richard propped himself up on the bunk. 'I don't understand. I thought you were coming with *us* . . .'

'Alas, no. There is something else that calls me.'

Richard shook his head firmly. 'I'm sorry, but that's just not possible. Quite out of the question! Consider yourself under tent arrest, Lacan.'

'Alas . . .'

'You're upset because I didn't eat bear for breakfast . . .'

'You want some bear? I have plenty . . .'

As Richard's eyes adjusted to waking, he saw that Lacan was suited-up, his backpack in place, lucky charms dangling from neck and jacket flaps below his heavy bearskin cloak. He had tied his hair into a ponytail and his high forehead was streaked with green and brown camouflage. 'You're still tired, eh?' Lacan said. 'Still the visions?' He indicated the side of his eye.

'I feel exhausted. I wake wearier than going to bed.'

'Bad dreams?'

'Indescribable.' He swung his legs from the crude frame, rubbed his eyes vigorously, then stared at the big man. 'Where are you heading? I'm sorry to see you go—'

'A big journey,' Lacan whispered. 'I've been planning it for some time. I'll be gone maybe six months, maybe less. I'm going in through the cave. I'll be OK. I have a nose for returning to where there's good, French wine!'

Perhaps Lacan saw the sudden concern that shocked Richard as he realised that his friend was about to enter the most dangerous of Ryhope Wood's hollowings. Lacan's hand was a firm and friendly grip upon the tired man's shoulder.

'It will be a great adventure! There are so many underworlds where Old Stone Hollow can emerge. I feel very *lucky*. Please *don't* worry about me. This sort of exploration, my friend, is what life in Ryhope is all about.'

He hugged Richard, kissed his cheeks three times, grinning all the while. 'The dreams *will* get easier. Write about it. It's good catharsis! And when you find your son, everything will be easier still. For all of us! Trust Helen. She's a fine heartwooder. She has an eye for you, too. Trust me! And McCarthy has seen much of the trail that Alex left when he came last night to visit—'

He stood and turned to go, but Richard reached out and grabbed his sleeve. 'Arnauld?'

As if sensing what was coming, the Frenchman stood quite still, quite silent, staring out into the new day.

'What is it?' he asked eventually.

Richard's voice was a mere whisper. 'What are you looking for? Can you tell me?'

Lacan glanced back, his features dark behind bushy hair, flowing beard and heavy fur hood. His eyes sparkled, though, and not with excitement. His breathing was slow as he said, quite simply, very softly, 'The moment of my death.'

Embarrassed, uncomfortable with himself both for this potentially offensive show of curiosity and for the curiousness of the answer it had elicited, Richard said, 'I don't understand – but I hope you find it. . .'

'Thank you. Me too. It would be good to live again.' He paced out of the tent into the pale dawn. A moment later Richard called after him, 'If you ever need help, just whistle! Do you hear me? You *do* know how to whistle, don't you, Lacan?'

The Frenchman's raucous laugh sent birds panicking through the trees.

They left within the hour, Lytton leading Helen and Richard the way over the bridge and up the wooded slope to the Sanctuary. McCarthy paced along behind, dreamy and distracted.

Once at the Sanctuary they quickly assessed the damage that Alex's 'seeded' mythago had caused: four deep slashes in the trunk of an ash, oak branches broken savagely, one showing the unmistakable pattern of a bite, long, pointed teeth, wide-jawed.

'We are beginning to reconstruct your son's childhood pleasures,' Lytton said with a smile. 'His imagination is loose. It affects everything he creates. This was a reptile of some sort.' He cast a thoughtful look at Richard. 'Did Alex, maybe, have a passion for dinosaurs?'

'Show me the child that doesn't.'

'Indeed,' Lytton agreed with a vigorous nod. 'This one was small, though. It has left traces of itself. Can you see?'

Richard looked to the upper branches of the battered oak and saw strands of greenish hair. There was a torn fragment of clothing, thick linen, also green. 'Two creatures?'

'I think not. Alex is creating oddities, combinations of passion and myth. What did you say was his favourite Arthur story?'

'Arthur? You mean King Arthur? All of them. He went through a phase of wanting to be Sir Lancelot. There was a series on the TV. That and Robin Hood were great inspirations.'

'But those serials were very shallow. He must have read more in the genre.'

'As I've told you, *Gawain and the Green Knight* always intrigued him. He performed one of the parts the same evening we found Jim Keeton running along the road.'

He looked up at the trailing green hair in the tree. Suddenly the idea of the monstrous form that had ravished this glade changed into something almost comical. And yet, its power was manifest. 'Half-reptile, half green-bearded giant?'

'Why not?' Lytton said pointedly. 'There are odder things in Ryhope Wood than that.'

A few minutes later, and with an awkward formality, Richard placed the first of his hollowsticks at the base of the Greek arch where the hollowing opened, adding his own crude figure to the three others. Lytton said, 'Don't hang about, now. We've got a long trek ahead of us. Come on . . .' and stepped between the stone pillars, somehow *melding* with the background, then fading.

The moment he had begun to blur, McCarthy followed through, then

Helen. Richard hesitated, watching as space seemed to swallow her bulky shape. For a few seconds, his heart racing, he stood nervously in a fragment of Ancient Mycenae, below dancing figures in marble and lush creeper, and then he, too, summoned his courage and took a few steps forward—

The light changed. It was still deep forest, but this was high summer, and the light was brilliant, blinding, the heat suffocating. A high earth bank rose to the left, and somewhere ahead a river broke over rocks. There was no sign of the others and Richard called for them, suddenly concerned. A moment after his second cry, Helen stepped naked into the light, from the direction of the flooding water. She was gleaming wet, her hair saturated, her face a solemn signal of her irritation. Silently she reached for her shirt, which was piled with her other clothes against the roots of an oak.

'I'm glad you finally decided to come!' she said angrily, wringing out her long hair as she watched the man across this dazzling glade.

Astonished, Richard could only protest: 'But I only waited a few seconds.'

'Don't!' she said sharply, tugging on her trousers. 'Didn't you hear what Lytton said? Don't ever do that again! Do you understand? I've been waiting a day and a half for you. The others have gone on ahead. McCarthy saw three colossi which might mark the edge of Alex's defence zone. Lytton thinks they can get that far without your help.'

'A day and a half . . .' Richard repeated.

Helen sighed, running fingers through her drying hair. 'I didn't know it would happen. Some hollowings are more time-friendly than others. Richard, don't make assumptions about this place. Please? I want to get on. I want to get moving. We had no idea whether you'd chickened out or were just getting up courage. Do you see?'

Richard did see, and apologised. But he added, 'If you were getting worried, why didn't you just step back?'

She looked grim as she hefted on her backpack. 'I tried.'

'And failed?'

'And failed. This is a way in only. And that's bad news.'

'But Lacan—'

Richard was confused. Lacan had told him that hollowings were two-way gates. Why should the rules have changed?

As Helen led the way to the river, all she would say was, 'This is a fragile, tentative land. It's in a state of flux. It's changing all the time with the minds around it. The rules are flexible and that's that. I don't know what the *hell* happened here. But this hollowing is different and there's no way back through the Sanctuary. And that's bad news. And I'm worried! And so is Lytton. Apart from that, and your abysmal time-keeping . . .' She glanced over her shoulder and smiled. 'Everything so far is going well.'

Richard had lost her again, and floundered in the cold and the darkness, uncomfortable with the constant sheen of wet on his beard, his legs aching with the effort enforced upon muscles from constantly keeping balance on the rough and slippery terrain of a wildwood. He was sitting on the moss-slick and softening trunk of a dead and fallen tree, enjoying dappled sunlight in an otherwise stifling gloom, when Helen's distant cry eased faintly through the heavy silence—

'Where are you? Richard! Come over here! Come this way!'

He found her crouching below a grey, overhanging rock. Whorled patterns were faintly visible through the lichen, which grew in rosettes across the towering face of the monolith. The remains of a tall man were crushed below the stone. Helen was turning the shrivelled head in her hands, peering at it matter-of-factly.

'It's a Hood,' she said, then added, 'Robin of the Greenwood? We call them Hoods. This one has very obvious attributions, almost certainly a child's. Probably Alex's. Interesting bow, though.' She nudged the longbow with her toe. Richard noted only the dark stained shaft, the red fabric tied around its ends, the small white feathers that radiated from its centre. 'Did Alex know a lot about archery?' Helen asked.

'No. Not that I remember.'

The dead man had been more than six feet tall and of substantial build. What remained of his clothing consisted of brown leather and dyed cotton, the predominant colour red. Around his neck he wore a thin chain of crude silver on which was threaded an amber stag's head, penny-sized and exquisite. The cause of death was all too clear – he had been disembowelled. His corpse was already corrupting, the limbs breaking away (as had the head), fungal growth intruding through the shrivelled flesh, ground ivy struggling to drag the remains down again into the soft ground.

'Murdered?' Richard asked.

Helen shrugged, then stooped to part the clothing and examine the open wound. 'A tusker, I think.'

Richard was astonished. 'An elephant?'

'A boar!' she said with a laugh, but sobered quickly. 'Which might still be around. Not a good idea to argue with the big pigs. When they condense – become real,' she added with a glance at Richard, 'they tend to have one particular mythical attribute: they're bloody gigantic!'

She tossed the skull to Richard and shrugged on her pack again. The head was light, like balsa wood. But the shock of touching it made him drop it, and the shrivelled bone cracked as it struck his foot, spilling grey, dusty remnants of a mythago brain.

'It isn't very interesting,' Helen said again. 'A very obvious phenomenon in Ryhope. There are hundreds of them in the wood, the stereotyped Robin Hood. It's a combination of race memory and enriched imagination. Everyone has a similar idea about Hood. Errol Flynn has a lot to answer for! I'm still intrigued by the bow, though. Everything else suggests a child's mind has generated the figure. Children have great power in this place. But that bow . . . It's not right . . .'

An hour later the wood changed character. It became very noisy with the chattering and shrieking of birds high in the brooding trees. The temperature of the dank and misty underwood dropped, becoming icy. Helen was agitated. She circuited the light wells, keeping to the gloom, persistently glancing up at the heaving foliage, then holding her hand out to Richard in a gesture that clearly said *stay still*.

'What is it?' Richard asked. His frozen breath spread before him into a half-lit grove of hornbeam and juniper. An animal track led away from the moody place, towards more open wood, and Helen beckoned Richard to follow her into the misty brightness.

But as Richard began to follow he heard movements in the grove, and a fleeting sound, high-pitched and human, the sound of pain. He dropped his pack, watched where Helen was going so as not to lose her again, then stepped between two trees into the flower and grass of this dell. The bird cries increased in agitation, the sound of their wings became louder as they took to flight.

A hump at the side of the dell resolved into the figure of a man, back arched up from the enclosing earth, arms spread to his sides. He was dead, Richard thought, and as he drew closer, peering down, he could see how the earth itself was open around his torso, and strands and tendrils of vine and sucker, were swathed around him, dragging the corpse back into the body of the wood. His face was scarred with flat fungal growth, his hair, which was fair and long, seemed to be rooting into the bracken. There was a dull gleam of metal around the body's neck and chequered red and yellow showed through the weeds on the torso, the remains of its shirt. The man's mouth was open and Richard glimpsed furtive movements in the hole. The eyes were closed, tightly, an expression of great pain. He could see no wound.

There was a sudden step behind him and he started with fright. Helen grabbed him by the shoulder. 'Get the hell out of here. *Fast.*'

'He's dead. Another Hood, I think.'

'Another Hood nothing. Quickly, Richard. Get away from here.'

Behind him the dead man, perhaps still dying, uttered a high, slow moan and shifted slightly in the sucking earth.

Helen was back on the track. 'Did he see you?'

'No. His eyes are closed. He's dying.'

'He's being born! Come on, let's put distance between us. If he sees you he'll fix on you. It's a Jack, and I don't like his colours. He's bad news.'

Being born?

Richard stumbled away from the dell, recasting the image of the corpse in his mind. Not being sucked into the earth then, but pushed out of it, the grey and green fungal growth being absorbed into the skin, not absorbing the decaying flesh.

'A Jack? As in Beanstalk?'

'As in Giant Killer,' Helen called back stiffly. 'Didn't Lytton show you Huxley's diaries?'

But before Richard could recapture a sudden memory of the dead man's writings, a more concerning thought struck him: *his pack!*

He turned back and ran to where he had dropped the bulky back-pack. Snatching it up he turned to follow Helen again, into the thinner forest, away from this icy womb. He caught a glimpse as he rose of a shape, mansized and stooped, standing deeply in the shadows of the grove watching him. It leaned an arm against a tree-bole, breathing hard. Light caught its eyes, which were narrowed, sinister, and staring.

Richard was in no doubt that it had seen him.

Huxley had written:

13th May '28. A Jack has come to the edgewood and watched the house. The boys are at school, and Jennifer in town. It seemed unsure at first, then, like all mythagos, it came towards me as far as the gate. I might have hoped to see a goose below its arm, the glint of a golden egg, but this particular echo of folk myth was hungry, bloody and heavily armed with whatever it had been able to find in the wood: this meant crude spears, a heavy club, two knives in its belt. Its clothing was reminiscent of Northern British Roman, the leather kirtle and short trousers especially, although it was warmed by a heavy sheep skin round its shoulders. There was something of Hercules about the jack in this form. Its long hair and wild eyes made it seem less intelligent than the tricky customer I have come to expect.

And later, in summer 1930:

Jack be nimble, Jack be quick . . . Jack change shape! In the Oak Ash zone I encountered a Celtic bard, a gentle creature who carried a complex set of bone pipes, elbow pipes of a very early design, and indeed his own story was linked with their first invention and use in magic. He told me four tales:

And one of them:

Finally, a Jack tale – I have called it 'Jack His Father' – close to the 'core legend', I think. Jack is a shape-changer. His name in the story is Cungetorix, son of the clan chief Mananborus, who was an historical figure. This early legend contains only an ingredient or two of the later folk-tale about the Beanstalk that it will become in the telling.

All of this Helen whispered to Richard as they rested in good, thick cover, catching their breath after an hour of running and weaving through the forest, away from the source of the Jack.

She went on, 'Jack His Father is one of the very few tales that George Huxley was able to interpret from his encounters in Ryhope. Mostly he saw mythagos as glimpses, or brief and incomprehensible meetings. But Jack His Father is a tale of the British trickster, so it interests me – and it means our pursuer is not to be messed with . . .'

'Can you summarise the tale? I suppose it would be useful to know what we're up against.'

Helen took a long drink from her water bottle, listened to the wood for a moment, then leaned forward, arms around her knees.

'Very briefly: it's a tale of mutual trickery and Jack's revenge. While Jack is out in the fields, sowing wheat, a raiding party attacks and slaughters his father and three brothers, taking their heads. Jack doesn't know this, but when the raiders come for him, he knows he's in trouble. He bargains for his life with three seeds which he claims are magic: one will grow into a house in which there will always be a feast cooking; the second will grow into a boat fit to sail over any magic lake. The third is the seed of a tree which will grow so high that from its top a brave man can see the fabled Isle of Women. The warlord believes Jack and offers in exchange the prize of all the pigs captured in his raid; the best singing voice that Jack could wish to hear; and offers also to make Jack a better man than his father. Jack accepts; the seeds are revealed as wheat, to the warlord's fury; but then Jack is given his father's head: his father was the best pig captured in the raid; his voice sang sweetly as he begged for life; and since his father is dead, jack is now the better man.

'But Jack invokes the Crow Goddess to exact revenge and she shapechanges him into his father's gory head. Strong-winged geese carry the head to the warlord's camp, where it first shapechanges into the feasting house, then the valiant ship, and finally grows into the giant tree. The warlord, being greedy for the Isle of Women, climbs to the top, but the Jack-in-the-tree keeps growing, snaps off at its base, and the warlord falls to his death on the rocks of the very isle he has coveted.'

Richard digested the tale. 'So we're on our guard against – what? A house, a ship and a huge tree?'

'Against a shapechanger,' Helen said. 'It's how Ben Darby probably died. From now on, Richard, assume that nothing, however simple, is as it seems.'

Inside the Skin

Unnerved by the incident in the juniper grove, Helen ran through the beech forest like a deer, apparently unconcerned at the noise she made as she crashed through the choking underwood. She was an occasional figure in the distance, half-lit, tenuous, no more substantial than the flicker of a shadow, but it was enough for Richard to follow.

After an hour they stopped to rest by a fall of water in the cool protection of rocks, huddling into the moist shade. The sound of the fall made it difficult to hear whether or not the Jack was following and Richard went up onto the overhang, where the air was warmer. The wood was quite still and he listened hard, but the only movement was a furtive rustling close by that resolved into the figure of a tiny man, who watched, hesitated, then fled, uttering a bird-like cry.

When he reported this to Helen she dismissed the small man, but was concerned at the silence behind them. 'Is it possible? He can't have . . .'

'Can't have what?'

'Overtaken us. Not already . . .'

'The Jack?'

She tugged apprehensively at her long hair as she stood above the waterfall and stared into the distance.

'He's fast. I should have remembered that about him. He's nimble Jack. He'll wait for us, somewhere ahead, so be vigilant.'

They camped that night in a crumbling wooden building that had once been used as a shrine. It was in a clearing in the wood, and had begun to dissolve into itself, the dark thatch rotting. Carved beams supported a thin, stone lintel on which the traces of painted runes could still be discerned. Inside, there were stone heads and limbs, and the shattered remains of patterned urns. It was an easy enough place to barricade against roaming wildlife, and a low door in the back made a convenient escape route, should anyone try and enter. It had seemed unwise to sleep in so open and obvious a location, but Helen shrugged off Richard's concern as soon as she was satisfied that this structure was not a manifestation of the Jack.

'It's going to rain.'

And rain it did, for most of the night, and although the air became damp, the thatch was intact enough to keep them dry.

Richard woke early, startled by the dead, grey face, blank-eyed and gaping of mouth, that was staring at him. He shouted out in alarm and crawled across the floor as he emerged into full consciousness.

Helen, in her body-web, was sifting through the pottery urns. She grinned as Richard finally calmed down and stared at her. She had placed the votive offering by him out of a sense of mischief, she confessed.

'You nearly gave me a heart attack!' he complained.

'Revenge, that's all. That's a powerful snore you have there, Mr Bradley.'

'I was snoring? That's not like me.'

'More impressive than a tusker. Boar, not elephant, that is.' She cast an amused glance at him. 'These are Urnfield. Lovely designs, excellent craftwork. The urns are full of stones painted as eyes' – she held out a handful of the oddities – 'and shards of reflecting crystal, including some lovely amethyst and opal. I think this must be the shrine that the Hunter-Child Vishenengra sought, to win back sight for his family, blinded in a Kurgan raid. It's a sort of *argonaut* adventure from all over Europe and West Asia, but going back five thousand years.'

Her certainty, her knowledge, was quite startling. How could she tell this from such a corrupted and shattered place? Helen reminded Richard that all things in Ryhope Wood were connected with legend, not just the heroes, be they Palaeolithic hunters or chivalrous knights, but also the structures and landscapes associated with the lost tales. At some time in the past, this crude shrine had been not *real* but mythic, a place of aspiration in the dreams of people, a place unreachable, unattainable except in story.

She had recognised the eyestones from a legend mentioned briefly in Huxley, circa 1940.

'This is a magic place, but I don't remember how. The Guardian hides from visitors, watching through the eyes of the Dead . . .'

They looked as one at the stone heads, and Richard felt a sudden shiver of apprehension. Helen's earlier tease suddenly seemed far less amusing.

'I suggest we get out of here,' Richard said, and she agreed.

They scrambled for their packs and Richard ducked out through the sloping doorway, stepping info the damp but bright glade and almost screaming with shock as a huge horse snorted in his face, then shook its head with a ranting of chains. It towered above him, black as coal, decorated with crescents of bronze, polished bone and coloured ribbons, stamping restlessly on the ground as its rider held it back. The tip of the man's lance was a broad and saw-toothed stone, tied firmly to the heavy haft with cord and now pressed painfully against Richard's throat. Against the restless light through the canopy Richard could see that the warrior was partly armoured. His hair was cut short, spiked with chalk along the right side and worn in three long, feathered braids from the left.

Further movement at the edge of the glade announced the cautious arrival in the clearing of two more tall horsemen, leading their mounts from the scrub. The lance tip was prodded at Richard again, indicating that he should move to the side, and he complied quickly. Helen was silent, still in the shrine, but Richard was helpless against this huge man. He hoped she was ready for the attack, or already making good her escape through the small door at the rear of the structure.

The horse-lord's two companions dropped to crouching positions, lances across their knees. They were both bare-armed, bodies protected with dull-coloured leather corselets. They wore heavy trousers and boots. Feathers and grasses, tied in bundles, decked them from braids to belts.

The horse-lord slipped down from his saddle blanket – there was no saddle as such, and no stirrups on the trappings – and stooped to enter the shrine. Suddenly afraid, Richard stepped forward, intending to call out, to draw the man's attention away from Helen. A spear sliced the air across his eyes, and struck the door beam with tremendous force; quivering there. Both the other men were standing, and a second spear was drawn back and ready for flight. The two horses grazed the long, wet grass unconcerned.

Richard put up his hands in a gesture (he hoped) of supplication, but called anxiously, 'Helen?'

From the shrine came the murmur of the man's voice. Richard heard him say one word several times: *Kyrdu*. He talked on. The eyestones were shifted, sifted, the pottery shards of the broken urns clattered about. *Where was Helen?*

Richard looked around, scanning the edge of the wood for movement that might indicate her lurking, hiding presence, but there was nothing, just these wild men, now relaxed again, crouching down and staring across the clearing as their horses fed.

The horse-lord suddenly appeared from the shrine, bent low, then straightening and examining a handful of the stones and crystals. He was looking for treasures, no doubt. Under his arm he carried the stone head. Behind him, stepping out into the glade, came Helen. She glanced at Richard and motioned him to be quiet.

The warrior placed the eyestones in a pouch which he tied at his belt. He tossed the head across the clearing to one of his men, who reacted with total surprise, the momentum of the catch sending him sprawling backwards, to his friend's great amusement. The head was then wrapped in cloth and slung over the grazing horse, which reared up and whinnied at the sudden weight.

'Are we in trouble?' Richard asked Helen.

As if reacting to his voice, the tall man suddenly came over to him, glowering at him, pushing him back. But then he worked the spear from the door-post, checking the stone point with his fingers, and appearing satisfied. His breath was fruity, although his body exuded a stale, sweaty smell.

Helen said, 'No. We're not in trouble. But they are. Our friend here has just taken the head of the god Mabathagus. Remember the mask Wakeman brought back? Same necromancer. I should have recognised it last night. These three will pay dearly for what they're doing. But with luck, not before they've helped us to the ravine and the colossi.'

They were three of the Sons of Kyrdu, part of a cycle of adventure that had been widely told across the forests and tundras of northern Europe, as far as the Altai Mountains in the east and the rocky coasts of Ireland in the west. These men were *Kurgans*, not the earliest form of the legend they embodied, but the first that had begun to draw influences from other cultures. The Kurgan people had been farmers and raiders, and like the Norsemen who were a much later reflection of their ethic, they were an odd mixture of rustic, warrior, land-grabber and superstitious monster.

An early form of their story had entered North America, probably with the Clovis Point hunters, and was best preserved in Iroquoian mythology, although it had been rapidly subsumed into a simple tale of a raiding party on another clan's totem land, elements of which Longfellow had recorded in his account of Hiawatha.

It was a rich cycle, with elements of quest, of revenge and of hubris.

The five sons – these three were all that remained at this fairly late stage of the story, the raid on the shrine – were determinedly seeking the way into the Underworld, to plunder the treasures they believed to be hidden there. On the way they accumulated talismans of various forms, but the stealing of Mabathagus and the Skinning of the Drum, whatever that would turn out to be, was one of the actions that would contribute to their terrible fate. The head was reputed to carry far sight and silent thought, an aspect of the 'long gone long to come', and Kyrdu's sons wanted that facility for the moment when they would cross Black Pike Lake.

Mabathagus, rising from the earth, would have something to say about the act of vandalism.

That fate remained in the future. From the brief, cautious exchange in the shrine itself, Helen had determined that these raiders were aware of the ravine, and the wooden colossi that probably marked the entrance to the zone where Alex had erected his best defences. The Kurgan would accompany her there, and Helen had agreed to trade for the privilege: their presence would be protection against the Jack, which she was convinced was now dogging Richard's trail.

For the moment however, they stayed in this silent, wet clearing. The Sons of Kyrdu had spread blankets and were seated now, busy with industry, one working an awl through a long strip of leather, the other re-securing the stone head of the spear he had launched in front of Richard by way of discouragement. These were Herkos and Kyrki. The horse-lord himself, Etherion, picked through the contents of Helen's pack, but dismissed everything as useless. Richard heard her say 'damn', and she glanced his way, looking apprehensive. 'Can he have a look at what you're carrying? I don't want him getting ideas about *me* . . .'

'Of course. He can have what he likes.'

But as he saw Richard preparing to offer his own backpack for consideration, the man shook his head. He drew a slim, stone knife and cut one of the long, silver locks from Helen's hair, braiding it with facility in his big hands, and using a thin twine to tie it to his own front lock. It dangled there, silver at the end of black, and he smiled broadly and nodded at the woman.

'It's a little bit of my spirit to protect him against the "shadow that comes from shadow". He's just paid me an enormous compliment. And do you know what, Richard? I actually feel complimented.'

'Good. Now let's get on.'

'Unfortunately . . .'

Their time at the shrine was not finished. There was a sense of expectation in the air. The birds around the glade began to fall silent. The awling stopped, the spear was laid aside. The three dark men watched the light through the canopy, ears pricked and expectant. Helen sat quietly, just inside the temple itself, waiting out the hours, waiting for the murder.

The drum started. It was distant at first, but came closer. It was high in frequency, like the Irish bohdrain, a single skin round a wooden frame, beaten with a bone. The drumming circled the clearing. The horses twisted against their tethers, and Kyrki stroked their muzzles, calming them as he watched the woods, alert for movement. The other two stood and drew their short, bronze stabbing swords.

The man who ran suddenly into the clearing was wizened, bent double, clothed in swathes of brown rags, with a fur hood drawn tightly around his weatherbeaten face. He beat the wide drum frantically and screamed at the three men, twisting where he stood, using the drum as a weapon, thrusting it at each of them in turn, as if its sound would stop them in their tracks.

The Sons of Kyrdu circled the wild man, wary, unsmiling. They seemed genuinely afraid of him, but purposeful in their movements.

'Time to go,' Helen said, and left the shrine.

Richard stepped out after her and edged away from the confrontation. She stood at the edge of the clearing, watching the dance. 'I don't want to be a part of this.' Her face was full of pain. 'It won't be pleasant . . .'

Richard looked back at the warriors. Kyrki had snatched the drum from its owner and sliced it into tatters, stripping the leather away from the frame. The other two were unfurling the old man, as if in some bizarre party game. He twisted and screamed as the rags came away, until his grey, scrawny body was exposed, naked and richly tattooed with distorted figures and strange faces. Suddenly he stood still, his hands resting against his skeletal thighs, his head drooping over a hollow chest. Kyrki stepped towards him, bronze skinning knife drawn.

Richard followed Helen into the dense undergrowth, into the welcome darkness. The old man's shrieks followed them for a while, and then there was a sudden silence. Helen turned and without a word put her arms around Richard, holding him very tightly. She was shaking. Richard felt sick, and as the old man's ululating death tones seemed to echo everywhere, he asked, 'Will they kill us too?'

'No. Of course not. Be quiet, Richard. Just hold me.'

Richard realised she was crying. She felt very small against him. In silence they stood against a leaning oak, the breeze shifting, the smells of the wood fragrant, calming. It was very still, very peaceful. Slowly Helen's anguish dissipated.

'It's one of the things I find hard, very hard,' she said softly, still with her face against Richard's chest. 'The violence. So much of myth, so much of legend, so much of it is turned around deeds of heroism, and bravery, and revenge, and war . . . and it all comes down to one thing: death. Violent death. The duels between heroes. The burning of saints. The skinning of old men. Dan hated it too. Even a good and chivalrous knight can become a killer in this place. We don't get innocent Jack, the Beanstalk boy with his pleasant trickery . . . we get Jack who kills, Jack who tricks, Jack who murders for gain.' She trembled suddenly and Richard put a hand against her neck, welcoming the closeness and the sudden deeper contact she initiated. 'God I miss him,' she whispered. 'So much. So much. I miss him so much . . .'

If Richard had thought she was talking about 'Jack', he soon grasped her meaning.

'He'll come back,' he said, pointlessly. 'As Lacan told me, time plays silly tricks. He's probably on his way home even now.'

But she shook her head. 'I've been deluding myself. He's dead. Trickster's got him. It's happened again and I've been a fool to insist otherwise. There are some things that you know in your heart, Richard. And in my heart I've always known that Dan's dead.'

She drew away and sat down against the swollen root of the oak, folding down into herself, head below her arms, the sounds coming from her faintly and sadly. Distantly a drum was being beaten and a deep voice shouted words which suddenly resolved into Helen's name.

The Sons of Kyrdu were calling her back.

Kyrki welcomed Richard into the glade by beating gently with the handle of his skinning knife on the new drum, the thin, stretched skin colourful and patterned with symbols of the moon, reindeer and swans. The sound it made was faint, as if the skin was tired, or distant, singing out its pain from another realm. The others had stretched sections of tattooed skin across their round shields. A red carcass lay sprawled in the door of Mabathagus's shrine. The horses, distressed by the strong stench of raw meat, were almost out of control, twisting, rearing and whinnying as Herkos held their tethers.

'Come on! Time to go!' Etherion shouted, smiling. Not in those words, of course, but his gestures and intentions were clear enough.

Helen stepped into the open, silently gathered up her pack, and grimly followed the riders into the woodland opposite.

Richard was glad to leave the place. He was gladder still of Helen. Her calm behaviour in the presence of these Bronze Age Kurgan mercenaries was very reassuring to a man who would have preferred to be running in the opposite direction.

And when it came to running, these men were more demanding than Helen herself, moving as they did at a fast jog through tracks that hardly existed, their horses snorting and trotting behind at the end of a short tether. There was no open country. All packs were slung over the animals, which made running easier, but too often the Kurgans ran so far ahead that Helen and Richard lost sight and sound of them. Etherion, perhaps honouring his promise to help the woman, was impatient with the two outsiders, but always waited for them to catch up. Richard noticed how he feasted his eyes upon Helen, but he seemed afraid of her, sharing smiles and looks, but not touching. What Helen thought of him wasn't clear. Richard assumed she was keeping him happy. He knew – it was not hard to realise – that Dan's was the only face she saw with love.

Etherion used sling-shot to bring down a plump pair of red squirrels, which he spit-cooked in the evening, when a very welcome rest from the relentless wildwood run was called. The fur was stretched over improvised drying frames, the entrails cleaned and twisted into a thong, also to dry, the flesh warmed over the wood fire. Kyrki produced dried plums from his pack and some thin cakes of mashed grain, perhaps emmer wheat, unleavened, in any case, and very dry, very bitter.

The squirrel was strong, in flavour, and demandingly tough. The raw skulls were carefully detached from the carcasses and put in a pouch with some earth. Richard assumed the idea was to make a necklace, but Helen said they would more likely be bartered in communities where animal totems were held in reverence.

Etherion wanted to reach a place, which he called the Silent Marshes, before evening of the next day, and so they left the small encampment literally at first light, and ran on. The Sons of Kyrdu smelled the air, and listened to the woodland breezes, watched the flights of birds and discussed shadows in clearings, using their daggers to make points to each other. They had sought long and hard for the shrine of

Mabathagus, and having found it they now seemed to be well aware of where they were going. Some guiding voice, some insight, some reading of the forest entrails had told them there location in the legend-heavy wood. The band moved cautiously towards the ravine, but Etherion was alert to the changing conditions, the land around him, the elements of myth that were in constant flux and shaping his quest, and that of his brutal brothers.

They reached the ravine in mid-afternoon, after stopping to rest in a grove in the middle of some young hazels. It was a welcome break as far as Richard was concerned, but Kyrki had scouted on ahead and his voice suddenly hailed the band from a distance. At once the other Kurgans packed the horses and led them away from the hazel grove at a fast trot. Helen and Richard followed, increasingly excited as the wood opened out ahead of them.

Kyrki was standing on a prominent spur of rock, a tall, dark shape, peering down the steep, forested slope to the gleaming thread of a river below. The far side of the ravine was close, a vertical wood of oak, elm and hazel standards. His voice echoed in the narrow space as he called to his brothers.

For the next few hours the horsemen picked their way carefully along the lip of this gorge, Etherion looking for the way back into the forest, Helen scouring the descent for a suitable passage to the river below, and the colossal wooden statues that McCarthy had clearly seen in his dream.

'There!' Helen said at last, pointing ahead and down into the forested gloom.

Against the contrasting light and gloom, for a moment it was hard to make out the shapes. But slowly the three figures below resolved into more than shadows, although only the tops of their heads could be seen at this distance. They were braced across the river, and for the moment seemed small.

When the horsemen were almost above the statues, the Sons of Kyrdu abruptly turned away from the edge and with no smiles, but loud exhortations which Richard took to be expressions of good luck, led there steaming horses back into the deep wood, seeking the open land that led to the Silent Marshes. Kyrki rattled his horse chains, Herkos howled and Edierion grinned at Helen, who raised a hand in a gesture of parting. Richard, however, just felt relief. He was not at all sorry to see them go.

They descended the steep side of the ravine, dropping from tree to tree, clinging on to each other, passing there packs between them, often slipping and coming perilously close to a head-first tumble to the river. As they descended, so the size of these wooden constructs became clear. Colossal was right. When Richard came level with their blind heads it was an eerie experience, particularly since the third figure was turned slightly, and seemed to be listening for him. The wood of their bodies was dark, cracked and was already beginning to sprout seedlings. The figures were naked, that at the front stooping forward slightly, as if peering up the ravine. The middle figure watched the sky through hollow eyes, its mouth a leering gash. They might have been three naked giants walking in single file up the river, legs braced across the water. When Richard reached the bank, he could see how the feet of the monsters seemed to grow from the land, joining at the belly. They were trees, then, that had been trimmed and carved to create these gargantuan shapes. They stood a hundred feet high, and looking up at them, against the skyline, they seemed to move and creak, as if straining to draw their legs from the deep rocks. Almost immediately Richard felt a familiarity with them, something about them that suggested a painting he had seen, perhaps, but the thought refused to resolve.

Behind the figures the gorge narrowed suddenly to form a roofless cavern, dark and deep, the source of the icy water that flowed below their towering forms.

This, then, was the way into Alex's domain. Not a hollowing, but the gateway to a place that seethed with the boy's lost passion, and which was convoluted and impassable, a block to the normal passage of human travellers.

And at once, as Richard thought of this, it occurred to him why the colossi were so familiar! 'They're his soldiers!'

'His soldiers?' Helen followed his gaze upwards.

'His model soldiers. Of course! I bought him a set of Second World War "Desert Rats" to play with. He had an obsession with them. My father gave him cannons and tanks. They fired matchsticks. He was obsessed with soldiers for a couple of years, encouraged by his grandparents! And being Alex, he used heat to soften the plastic of the models. They were only three or four inches tall, of course, but he twisted them into all sorts of attitudes . . . marching, searching, dying, hiding. He made a real army, set it up in a model wood, around a brick castle. I recognise these figures, the attitudes . . . they're his *men*. No guns, no clothes, but the postures are right. Why *are* they naked? That seems odd . . .'

'Not odd at all,' Helen said. 'When Alex created these monstrosities, he drew on several parts of his unconscious: personal imagination was just the model; forgotten folklore was the shape. These giants are part of an older myth.'

'Which one?'

'I wish I knew,' she said with a quick glance at him. 'But one thing I do know. I hope they stay rooted!'

Above and behind them there was a furtive movement in the trees. Rocks slipped and tumbled down towards the river. Richard watched as the boulders came to rest, leaving a sudden silence. A hundred yards away, a flight of birds took noisily to the air. A tree bent out into the ravine under the weight of something leaning on it, then was still, as if the creature was aware that it had been seen.

'It's the Jack,' Helen said, ending their moment of rest. She clutched her pack and stepped into the water, wading awkwardly towards the wooden giant, to the gap below its oaken legs. Richard followed apprehensively, stumbling through the cold stream, aware that the earth was shaking slightly and alarmed at the lumps of moss and rotten wood that fell from the cracks and crevices of the huge figures above him. He was glad to enter the narrow gully, with its wet ferns and slippery floor, and ducked with relief into the tunnel through the rock, scrambling towards the bright, yellow light at the far end where Helen was already emerging into the new land.

The Hunted

Lacan was right. There is a catharsis in writing about the events that have not just surrounded me but overwhelmed me.

I tried to keep a record in Old Stone Hollow, but was too fascinated and confused by the supernatural (no other word fits) that my record at that time consists only of fractured thoughts and fragmentary descriptions. When I followed Helen through the gully, away from the Colossi, I found even less opportunity for reflection, since we spent long hours running the forest tracks as we strove to catch up with Lytton, and the castle where Alex's ghost had once been seen. But I am aware now, as I was then, that a new vigour had crept into my soul.

From the moment I emerged from the narrow gully and the cold river, I knew that Alex was close. I could almost touch him – and yet there was nothing to touch. I could speak to him, but there was no child to speak to. I could embrace him – he seemed to be embracing me – but there was only the land, and the strange figures that littered that land, and the shadow of my lost son, reaching for me.

Helen was sitting on the bank, among the drooping and scintillantly yellow branches of a willow which formed a sort of bower in which she rested, half-naked, squeezing water from her clothing. Striking though this vision was, it was impossible to ignore the two huge effigies that rose on each side of the river, facing the gully, as if guarding this entrance to Alex's world.

The figures were made of straw, each the height of a tree, but both beginning to rot with the weather, to fragment with the rain. One of them was the martyred Christ, the once-extended arms now lost, so that just the stumps remained. Crows had nested in the socket of the left arm, below the drooping, ruined head. Across the stream was the figure of a second martyr, arms behind its back, body flexed. Black rods of thorn, emerging from the straw, suggested spears or arrows. The head was gone, but the identity was clear, for here was St Sebastian, shot to death by arrows.

As soon as we could we left these effigies of agony behind and followed the river into the deeper wood. The land was rising toward hills which we had glimpsed distantly and Helen had pointed out the fires that burned on the skyline. We found few traces of Lytton, the vaguest of tracks, until we came upon a fire, set back from the river, below a rock overhang, where traces of a bark and branch shelter could be seen. The fire had been constructed between stones, on one of which was a small pile of half-burned tobacco, the leavings of Lytton's pipe.

There had been a skirmish. Helen traced the slash-marks in the trunk of one of the trees, and pointed out the furrows in the damp earth near the river, where someone had slipped or been dragged. And when we searched the area around the rock, I found a shallow grave, its head marked with a crude cross.

Without a word, Helen scooped the dry earth away, and exposed the contorted face of a man, his skin greening fast, his teeth now brown and fragile. He had been pistol-shot through the left brow. By uncovering part of his torso, a rustling metal breastplate was revealed, and a coloured linen shirt. The creature looked just like one of Cromwell's Ironsides, a trooper from the Civil War in England.

I covered the corpse, remembering the boxed set of model Royalists and Roundheads that I'd bought for Alex one Christmas, forty soldiers on either side. We had reenacted the battle of Edgehill on the dining table. Somehow, as is the way with such things, a small patrol of plastic American GIs entered on the side of the Parliamentarians, and Alex had won the skirmish.

Many legends, many heroes, came out of those bitter years of Civil War in the sixteen hundreds. There were as many heroes from Cromwell's army as there were from the more romantic Royalists, but Alex had always been fascinated by the rigour of the commoners' army, and less romanced by the swashbuckling reputation of the King's Own Men.

Whatever this unfortunate soldier had done, Lytton had dispatched him dispassionately.

Alex was everywhere, in the high hills, with its earthworks, over which we toiled during that first day's journey, in the crumbling fortresses that peered greyly through the matted greenwood, in the falls of water with their huge stone guardians, in the rattling chariots and steaming horses, colourful riders full-cloaked and armed, that broke noisily across our path, clattering or galloping along their own roads, too busy in the pursuit of adventure to stop and hail travellers from another time. In all of these things I recognised a reflection of the land around Shadoxhurst, of Alex's dream-castles, created from fairy tale and our family explorations, on holiday, of the wonderful Norman fortresses along the border between Wales and England. Alex had always seen faces in rocks, or bodies in the hills – it was a game he had played, fitting features to the vision, a sleeping giant here, a witch petrified in limestone there.

The land beyond the gully pulsed with that life. Each hill hid a giant, whose movement was reflected in cloud shadow. Each woodland stirred as creatures rode through the hollow trunks, inhabiting a world out of sight behind the bark. All rocks watched us with eyes behind the cracks and holes formed from frost and rain and water. For Helen, the experience was frightening. She was continually apprehensive, edgy, sometimes deeply fearful. For me, there was a strange comfort. At least, there was little fear from the land itself – it was Alex.

It's so hard to describe, but I felt, for a while at least, that Alex was guiding me. He filled my dreams, but I would have expected that. He was a strong presence in my life again, perhaps I could say in my heart. I seemed to smell *him – socks and stale sports gear, the odour that had pervaded his room – and to hear him too, a clatter of activity, running through empty rooms with new model planes, or plastic knights, singing at the top of his voice. All this in a claustrophobic wood, where the only real sound of any permanence was water, the languages of birds, and the murmuring, barking, chittering signals of deer, fox and weasel.*

For the few days in Old Stone Hollow, Alex had been a sadly remembered loss, talked about by madmen in a mad world info which I had gone willingly, and which I kept at bay, as one always strives to keep the incomprehensible at bay. Not even the encounter near the Sanctuary had fully impinged upon me, although the feeling of Alex calling to me had been a terrible and saddening moment in the dream. At that time I was fascinated by Helen, and I will write here that I miss her, now, more than I can express. Like Alex, she continues to haunt my dreams, but I suppose it's too late. In Old Stone Hollow something happened to me, something fast, something of which I had had no previous experience. I can't use a word like love. I came to love Alice, after we had married because we had feared breaking the relationship that had existed for so long. I came to not love her. I probably never felt more than affection for her. I simply don't know. But when Helen came to me, that night in Shadoxhurst, and when she emerged again from the wildwood, wild and naked, wild and swimming, my God, I had such feelings for her, sexual, yes, but more than that: I felt strong in her presence, I felt vibrant with her.

And she, too, was not backward in coming forward about her attraction to me. Dear God, I must have seemed so fumblingly shy. After Alice walked out on me I had only two, tentative, terrible relationships with women. I must have been such a bitter man, such a detached man, not a lover to linger with. Those years in London are like a bad dream. A form of limbo. Suddenly there was Helen, an American Indian (not pure blood, I think she said) who reminded me of Cher from the pop duo Sonny and Cher, who was attractive to look at, whose presence excited me – such a good feeling! – who at first seemed abrasive towards me, but who was fond of me and let me feel that fondness. I thought Alex dead. I didn't believe in life after death. Helen was a stronger need than Alex, even in this unnatural realm where I should have known that the impossible might be happening, that the lad might truly be alive.

And then we passed beyond the gully, and it was like living inside Alex's skin. Like being in my private room, aware that my son was behind me, watching my every move, hearing my every sigh, my every word, and gripping my shoulder, urging me forward. The presence of Alex was so powerful that he came back *to me. I began to flounder, to cry, to need the boy so much. And Helen, in those first hours of our journey, comforted me greatly. She seemed to understand what was happening. 'My God, we're going to find him,' she said, and for the first time I was not chasing a dream, for the first time it was not a photograph of Alex that was being talked about, but the real boy, the living boy. He was here. He was alive. And he* was close.

Helen said that previous explorations of this part of young Alex Bradley's mental landscape had led to confusion, to circularity, to unwitting, unwilling return to base. But now Helen and I, following Lytton and McCarthy, entered more deeply than anyone before, save the sciamach*, McCarthy, whose shadow had flowed with the clouds and wild beasts, to reach as far as the castle, although not to the cathedral itself, where Alex was hiding.*

I began to have such hope . . . and yet though I felt comfortable in this place of family memory, the darker products of Alex's imagination also populated the confused and entwining landscape, and on the second night of our journey we encountered two of the more threatening of the boy's mythagos.

Lytton and McCarthy had marked their route well, and with more than tobacco ash; they left chalk arrows, and on this occasion a short note, which Richard discovered, rolled inside a tube of bark and marked, where it was hidden, by a cross. It was hard to read, because it had been written in such haste, but Helen managed to decipher it by firelight.

'*You are entering a part of Alex that has been influenced by Conan Doyle. This is the Lost World, even though it is not located at the top of a plateau. Last night our camp here was attacked by a small, ferocious reptile, the size of a child, with murderously sharp teeth, a velociraptor, we believe they're called, like a small version of a tyrannosaur. There were four of them and they reacted satisfyingly to fire. Since memory of such creatures cannot exist within the human unconscious, these are creations from his own learning.*

'*An ursine of immense proportion, a form of cave bear, has its den close by. It will attack if provoked. Don't underestimate its speed. McCarthy did, and only just escaped. It runs faster than a hound, but fortunately is reluctant to climb trees. I am fascinated by this mythago-genesis. It defies Huxley's understanding and account of the process, which is that a mythago is a remembered hero, a hope figure, or a place of aspiration, such as a castle, or a cathedral . . . unless, of course, such beasts are part of Alex's private hope, but I cannot work out the mechanism. Be on guard, and hasten to find us. Alex's castle is close. Once there I can give you two days to catch up with us before the final strike for the cathedral. There is something moving between our parties, however: a shapechanger. McCarthy senses it through the shadows. We are being hunted. Take special care.*'

'Hunted? Could He mean the Jack?' Richard asked as Helen finished the note.

'Of course he means the Jack,' she said, scanning the scrawled words again. 'It's got ahead of us. Damn!'

She was agitated and irritable and Richard kept both his curiosity and apprehension concerning the giant ursine to himself. They were in a place of massive trees, with wide spaces below the heavy canopy, a hard encampment to defend. Lytton had made a windbreak of dead wood in the overhang formed by a low bough. The river flowed on the other side of a raised bank.

During the early evening, the creature moved cumbersomely from its den, among the rocks on the high ground behind the encampment, and padded down to the river. Breathless, Richard watched it from cover, hoping that Helen, who was at the water's edge, washing, would hear it coming. The beast was familiar, its body bearlike if huge, its long muzzle thrown up into fleshy ridges. Overlapping canines pressed outside its mouth. Its shoulders were covered with a thick shawl of spiked, black hair, on a body that was otherwise grey and brown.

Close to where Richard crouched in total silence, waiting his moment to warn Helen, it rose onto its hindlegs and browsed at the foliage twenty feet above the ground, its stomach rumbling loudly, its breath a series of muffled snorts. When it dropped to all fours again, it hesitated half-way down, front paws with spreading claws held expectantly, the whole beast hunched as if listening.

When it moved on to the river, Richard followed it, spear held firmly. He wished sincerely, at that moment, for Lytton's pistol. There was no sign of Helen by the flowing water. The cave bear approached the tree-fringed river and drank.

There was a furtive movement opposite and it reared up to its full height, arms extended. The wood was suddenly full of chattering and three sleek, lizard shapes dropped from the overhanging branches onto the huge beast. The bear screamed in an oddly human way and turned, slashing at the reptiles. One of the wide-eyed lizards had its teeth in the bear's neck. One hung onto the black shawl with tiny hands, slashing with a blade-like hind claw at the ursine's eye. The third was kicking at its bulging and exposed paunch, trying to rip through the hide with its glinting knife. The whole attack held a fascination for Richard, probably because of the thought that these were *living dinosaurs*, engaged in the hunt: he eased down the bank, crouching in cover to watch the kill. Absorbed by the bloody mayhem by the river, he failed to notice the narrow, grinning face that was staring at him, until the reptile chattered suddenly and dropped toward him, killing jaws open.

He cried out as the sleek body swung down, ducking away from the claws that flashed before his eyes, narrowly missing him; the creature's whip-like tail struck him across the face. A second later, a bloody iron point erupted from the wide jaws of the creature and the dinosaur wriggled, gurgled and finally went limp. Behind it stood Helen, lowering her spear before working the point out of the skull.

'You should pay more attention!' she said angrily to Richard. 'This vicious little bastard had been watching you for over a minute.'

Richard watched as the hind claws flexed in the death throes, six inches of razor-sharp curved horn. 'Thanks. That's one down; only three to go—'

By the river, the ursine had broken the back of one of the rapacious reptiles. It used the limp body to thrash at the others.

Then, unexpectedly, a fifth reptile appeared, running like a sleek bird along the river bank, nervous, jerky, its long tail horizontal until it stopped, at which point the tail undulated stiffly. It glanced at the humans and uttered a croaking taunt, then ran to join its kin. Oddly, the two dinosaurs had detached themselves from the bloody fur of the giant mammal, leaving it to lumber away, still roaring with pain. They were spitting and tail-flexing at the newcomer. Richard sensed their panic, as they circled on the spot, watching an animal that was identical to them, but which they clearly did not recognise. The bear appeared suddenly close to Richard, but it ran heavily through the trees toward its den, shaking its massive head to alleviate pain, spraying blood to right and left.

By the river, the fifth reptile rapidly grew and changed its shape, and as the two killers turned to flee it hunted them down, so fast that its actions were a blur. It bit through each neck, severing the head, then stood on its hindlegs, the corpses in its hands as it tore and nibbled at the muscle and tissue of the bloody necks.

It was ten feet tall. There was a human quality to its face and limbs, though the tail, held almost vertically, quivered and flexed at the tip. It was a lurid red on its belly, bright yellow and green on face and back, the colours of the Jack that had been born in the hornbeam glade.

As it ate, it croaked a challenge to the woods, certainly intended for the human observers.

Richard withdrew discreetly, following Helen who had fled the location long seconds before. A last glance at the river afforded him the glimpse of a man, shaggy-haired and clothed in coloured rags, standing by the water watching the wood, the dead dinosaurs held easily in his hands.

'Why didn't he take us? The Jack – why is he taunting us?'

Helen had rolled up her sleeping things and filled her pack, then squatted down behind it, an arrow nocked to her bow, her iron-bladed spear to hand. 'I don't know. Part of its nature would be my uneducated guess. We can't move until dawn, in the meantime let's defend ourselves as best we can.'

In the event, the night passed swiftly, with only the grumbling roar of the wounded bear, high in the rocks, disturbing the snatched sleep of whichever one of them was not on watch. With first light they followed Lytton, cautious and apprehensive, but nothing was waiting for them, although Richard could not shake off the feeling of their tracks being dogged quietly. It was an understandable anxiety, he imagined.

Helen's apprehension did not lighten. On the third evening they heard the sound of fife and drum coming from a clearing in the wood, and she skirted widely, anticipating danger. Richard crept close to the small fire and saw the three tunicked soldiers, seated in the fire's glow, one of them practising the thin flute, a second drumming happily on his side drum, the third smoking a long, clay pipe. They were British soldiers of the eighteenth century, redcoats, and in Alex's mind would probably have been associated, from the Grimm brothers' tales, with giant dogs whose eyes were as wide as saucers. Indeed, the baying of a hound sounded later, but by that time they were ensconced inside the walls of an old tavern, huddled in the canvas tent as the night's dew formed. Empty oak barrels, stacked against one wall, were a tease to Richard's appetite for a pint or two of strong beer.

For warmth they slept in the same roll of blanket. They had come to this arrangement without really addressing it. Although intimate, in its way, it was also too practical for either embarrassment or exploitation. In the morning, Helen's arms were round Richard, her breath soft in his ear, the flop of silver hair tickling his nose. When he stirred, stiff and damp with dew, she murmured softly and tugged him back. 'This is too comfortable,' she said. 'Let's have a few more minutes.'

This welcome lie-in was rudely interrupted moments later when the bushes outside the ruined tavern were crushed violently and a tall shape peered over the wall, startling them. Against the brightening sky it was hard to see detail save that the figure was a man, a tall, lean man of huge height, carrying two staffs. He peered at the tent quizzically for a few seconds, then spoke in a deep voice, guttural words whose intonation suggested a question. He repeated the query, frowning at Richard's silence. Again he spoke, a single word, 'Helpen!'

Richard called up to this fairytale figure, 'We don't need help. Thank you for offering.'

He laughed huskily, then reached over the wall and with a hand the size of an armchair picked up one of the tuns, shaking it then discarding it with a sigh. A moment later he withdrew.

From the doorway Richard watched his unsteady passage through the trees, his short cloak ragged, his breeches tied with leather in the Saxon way, his face grey with a bristling beard.

'What the hell is *he*?' Helen whispered.

'A Long Man,' Richard said, and there was little else to add. That the visitor was a Long Man was obvious: he was the living reflection of the chalk figures that could be found on the English downlands, and whose origins and identities and functions remained a mystery.

Just before he was out of sight, the Long Man turned and called again, pushing aside the foliage with one of the staffs, bending the high branch easily. When Richard shook his head he shrugged, then turned and reached out his arms, a tall pole in each hand, an absolute image now of the Long Man of Wilmington, in Sussex. He stepped forward and faded, both poles following him into obscurity.

Behind Richard, Helen gasped and laughed at the same time. 'He carries his own hollowing!' she said. 'We should have made friends with him . . . he could have saved us hours!'

A distant rumble, a freshening breeze, told of the storm approaching. They had set off from the ruins, anxious to make the rendezvous with Lytton, but had gone no more than half a mile when the thunder came closer, and the sky darkened to such an extent that they lost the track below the canopy in the gloom and the constant, wind-whipped motion of the undergrowth. When the first rain began to trickle through the foliage, Helen led the way swiftly back to the tavern. They re-erected the tent and crouched in misery as the heavens opened and the downpour began.

For a while there was nothing but the drum of the rain, but the hound that had bayed in the distance grew closer, its cry a mournful sound at first, then more of an angry challenge to some hunted beast. Helen had folded into a tight ball, her arms around her head, as if blocking the sound, but after a while she looked up, drawn and misty eyed, a grim set to her features. Richard grew concerned and asked her why she was frightened, and she replied quite simply, 'Trickster.'

She wouldn't talk further, not for the moment. Richard established only that, although she was hunting Trickster, she could not be sure whether or not he had risen from the earth in the wood at her own instigation. The Jack that dogged their steps, the shapechanging relic of pre-Celtic myth that shadowed them like a lie, was probably Alex's creation, imbued with the darker side of the frightened boy, who was protecting himself so intensely against the products of his own imagination.

She could not be sure. She had expected to encounter Trickster in its AmerIndian form, yet this Jack was quintessentially European. This, however, might be the trick that Trickster was playing on her, hiding himself from her in confusing guise while he waited for the moment to destroy her, as he had destroyed . . .

At this point she slumped again, then looked up sharply at Richard, reaching for her bow and quiver. She said, 'It's an odd story, and I can only explain it in the simplest of terms.'

'Good. Then I'll understand it.'

'Five hundred years ago, Trickster destroyed my family; it didn't end at that time. The destruction has continued down the family line to the present day. And I'm going to stop it. Or die trying. And that's my story.'

She brushed aside Richard's question, his concern, his offer to come with her. Heavily dressed in weatherproof jacket and leggings, her head protected beneath a hood, she tested the bow, selected six arrows, and went out into the rain, walking fast towards the awful baying of the giant dog.

If it *was* Coyote, she would have a fight on her hands.

When two hours had passed, and the sound of the dog had been swallowed either by distance or death, Richard followed Helen through the wood, calling for her. Emerging onto open land, where tall, wild grass was being crushed by the heavy rain, he saw her distantly, coming back towards the stone shelter. Stray light, penetrating the thunder-clouds, caught on her rain-drenched waterproof. Her head was down, she was walking normally. As she came close Richard could see that she was unwounded.

Back in the shelter she ate food and tried to dry her saturated hair.

'Coyote?' Richard asked.

She shook her head. 'I let it go. It was what Lytton calls a wildhound, an early form of dog. You see them regularly. They're solitary animals, more inclined to help than hinder. All for food, of course.' She smiled distractedly. 'The story of the dogs' downfall.'

After a while she relaxed. In her absence Richard had built a ditch around the squalid shelter, the floor was dry, and it felt warm with the small fire that smouldered at its centre. Richard asked her what had happened five hundred years ago, and why she felt she could end the curse today, in 1967.

'Because I carry the curse in my head,' she said. 'As do all my family. Trickster is in here.' She tapped her skull. 'And he shares his spirit between all the minds of my family. There's only one of him, and if I can just entice him out . . . if I can just make him come out of the shadows . . .'

She was in a dreamy state, her eyes closed, her body swaying. For a moment she sang, but so softly that Richard strained to hear the words, then realised they were in an older tongue than his. When the song had finished she began to speak, eyes open but watching the long-gone, her voice rhythmical. The story was entrancing, *chanted* by the speaker as the rain lashed down.

Richard established afterwards that it was more than a family story, passed down from generation to generation: it was literally a family *dream*, and the dream of a family that had been regularly attacked, abused and destroyed by Coyote. When he came to record the story he could not recapture the sense of time and land that she had elicited in his mind, the rhythm of a lost land, reflected in the rhythm of her words.

The first dream is still with me, though I haven't dreamt it for years, now.

When we are children, the past is closer. It passes through the lands in our heads more easily.

Young Grandfather, who was named Three Crows Flying, was a fine hunter, and later a flier with eagles, which we would call *shaman*. He was born in the time before horses, when the great plains were covered with grass, and the best hunters were the fastest runners, or the most skilled at setting hidden nets and blind-alleys of wood for a single buffalo.

At the best time of summer, the grasses were very high. When the buffalo came down to the tribal lands, they entered the grass like a man entering water, slowing down, wading carefully. At this time the herds would spread thinly. The calf and the cow would follow the bull, but the families would move widely, leaving great passages in the grass, the trails which the hunters followed.

No hunter would follow any trail that led to the setting sun, or the rising sun. Those buffalo had a special spirit.

The hunters would dance in the great flat place, where the herd had gathered and the grass was trampled, and by song, by dance and sometimes by courting coup, they would select the high-grass trail to follow. They would run through the tunnel toward their prey on all fours, never allowed to stand high, because this would bring them above the grass, and make them vulnerable to the dark spirit that watched the herds from, the distant rocks.

Young Grandfather became a fine hunter. If a buffalo turned back along its track, it was considered right for the hunter to lie down and let the beast walk over him. It was a painful and humiliating thing. But when this happened to Young Grandfather, to his surprise Coyote appeared at the edge of the grass track, disguised as a musk rat. 'Next-Buffalo-Meal is walking away from you again. You can hunt him, now. He will not trample you. I have done this, and this is my gift. But don't forget you owe me a name.'

'What name?' cried Young Grandfather.

Coyote revealed himself for what he was. 'The name that was stolen from me at your birth. If you don't yet know this, you soon will.'

Sometimes the hunters would take up their coup sticks and arrows, their feathered lances and stone skull-crackers, and run across the hills to dance war. On one occasion Young Grandfather had stumbled in a snake-hole, and his enemy was screaming above him and about to crack skull. Coyote bit the enemy and the black stone club whistled like sling-shot, a skin's thickness from Young Grandfather's eyes. Young Grandfather used his granite club to break the enemy's knees, then his jaw, then open his head to the crows. Coyote ran with him afterwards, disguised as a grey dog.

'I have saved your skull, and this is my gift for you. But don't forget my name. You must remember that you owe me a name.'

The day came when Young Grandfather was growing old. Not so old that he couldn't disturb his wives in their sleeping skins, but old enough that the paint ran in many furrows on his face. He wished to fly with eagles, so he went out to Coyote Rock, to remember his birth.

When he had been born, White Eagle, his father, had stepped from the lodge and stared around the wide land. Three crows had been flying towards a high rock and woods where the carcass of a coyote lay, gored by a buffalo. He took the child up to the rock. But the coyote was not quite dead yet, and it watched the man and the child as the crows settled and began to feast.

Coyote said, 'I'm glad you've come with the new child, to give him my name, the name of the first thing you saw when your child was born.'

'I saw three crows, flying to eat,' White Eagle said. 'The boy will be named after them.'

Coyote was furious and the picking crows flew up to escape the slashing claws. 'He must take my name or my spirit cannot rest. I saw you come from the lodge. I saw you look up at me. You watched me haul myself to this place to die. The crows were still in the north wind. You saw me first. He must take my name.'

'Never!' said White Eagle, and Young Grandfather was then named for the crows.

The coyote died, his spirit entering the woods as his bones bleached. And from here, over the years when the people passed this way on the hunt, he crept out to watch over the child, and then the man, who had not been named for him by words, but who was tied to Coyote by first sight.

Now, years later, the spirit of Coyote came out to sit with Young Grandfather, in his new paint on the old face, at his new age, searching for eagles. Coyote said, 'I ran with you through the tall grass when you were a child who wished to be a man.'

'I remember you. You saved me from a trampling.'

'I remember you when you first went below the skin of your first wife. You were very clumsy.'

'I don't remember you. And I had no complaints.'

'From the look of you, the grass-hunting time is finished, and the inside-the-skin time; and the skull-cracking time is finished too.'

Young Grandfather shook his head as he thought of his wives. 'Not the inside-the-skin-time, but the others, yes. All finished. I wish to fly with eagles, and with crows, to see the tribe and their hunt-trails through other eyes. I wish to see the long-to-come through the eyes of other dreaming things. But something stops me.'

Coyote chuckled. 'You have the name of crows, and not coyote. You have the wrong name. Your father was at fault and I killed him.'

'My father ran up onto high rocks and fell.'

'I pushed him. He gave you the wrong name. It's not too late. Here I am.'

Young Grandfather had been expecting this. He knew from his father, from his grandfather too, that to take Coyote's name would be to be in Coyote's grasp, and Coyote was tricky. Sometimes his visions would be real. Sometimes they would be lies. It was the same with young women and old men. It was a dangerous thing to take Coyote's name, and no matter how sincere Coyote sounded, sitting there on the spirit rock, with the sun setting and the feathers in his grey hair waving in the wind, Coyote could not be trusted.

Young Grandfather scratched in the earth on the rock and found the skull of the dead coyote. 'You must come back into the eyes and the ears and the jaws of these bones,' he said to the spirit, 'so that I can honour you, and take your name.'

Coyote hesitated. Was he being tricked? No, the old man was too eager to fly with eagles. On the grass below, the lodges were spread widely, and smoke rose from every teepee. Children were making games, their laughter thin on the late evening air. Coyote sighed and went into the skull, and Young Grandfather carried the bones reverently to the village. There were many drums in the night, and a great fire, and a tall ash-pole with the spirits carved upon it and the dead coyote was placed on the ground. When the drums stopped, Young Grandfather drove a buffalo horn through the skull, then buried the bones in the earth where a stream split and made an island.

'May your ghost stay there forever,' Young Grandfather taunted. 'I will never take your name. Now at last I can fly with eagles.'

Coyote was furious. The buffalo bone, stuck through his skull, had made him insane. He danced on the island and screamed, but he was trapped.

But a time came when Young Grandfather's youngest daughter came to the island at night to give birth. She had lost her way in the darkness, and Coyote had sung sweetly, and rustled the leaves on the trees to make it sound like a good shelter for her labour, so she had crossed the water. As she crouched and felt the weight of the child, Coyote whispered that she should tug the buffalo horn from the ground and lean on it. She did so, and Coyote was freed from his buffalo coffin. Coyote helped with the birth, still singing softly, but as the child put its head into the world Coyote pinched its cheeks to open its eyes. He jumped into the open eyes and entered through the bone. When the child slipped out onto the soft skins of its cradle, it grinned. 'Now I have my name,' it whispered.

The mother was terrified to hear the new-born speak, but after a while she thought it must have been the pain in her loins and the cool of the wind making her dream, because soon after this the child began to cry, like any child.

But Coyote was now in the blood of the family, and already planning his revenge for Young Grandfather's trickery.

The rain had stopped and they shook out the tent, preparing to move on. As they worked, Helen said, 'We became the most wretched of families. We were known as the Mad Dog People, because nothing ever went right for us, and sometimes we killed each other in a fury of desperation.

'Coyote took the best of our hunters and made them crazy with potato whisky. He danced round the best of our warriors during battle and made them kill each other. Our children were sometimes born with the heads of dogs; the most beautiful of our women would mutilate themselves, or start to bay like hounds as soon as they were married. Coyote caused starvation, even when there was plentiful game and fish, interfering with nets, cutting lines, warning animals. He distracted fathers and warrior sons during war-party raids on other tribes, and left them with their skulls bashed open and the crows on their eyes. He brought disease and cancer. He struck children dumb, and our mothers blind. He dried up their milk. He caused fire in teepees, even in the rain. He appeared as a disembodied dog-skull, the jaws grinding, and when we saw that we knew that Coyote had come to claim another prize. For generations my family has been terrified of the dreamworld, where this malevolent shadow stalks us. We never know *when* he will strike.'

No one had known what to do. The old rituals were long-since forgotten, and the precise nature of the magic that Young Grandfather had used to torment Coyote in that time-before-horses had died with him.

Then Alexander Lytton had visited the university where Helen and Dan were teaching, and she learned of his obsession with a strange wood in England. He had been looking for an expert on Palaeolithic hunter-gatherer societies. He found a woman and her husband who were specialists in that subject and who were living a nightmare. He had welcomed them to the team.

'So that's all there is to it,' Helen murmured as she led Richard into open land, where a white-walled castle gleamed distantly. 'If I can get Trickster to come out into the wood, to be made solid, then I can kill him. Dan tried. I think he's failed. I'll grieve for him in good time. I can't think of anything, yet, except destroying the shadow.'

White Castle

From images of the ancient plains of North America, Richard suddenly stepped into the early Middle Ages, approaching the castle through patchy woodland, impressed by the height of the walls, suddenly aware that the purity of colour was not due to paint but to the white berries of a spreading thorn, grown so completely across the stone that it had covered the castle entirely.

The drawbridge had long since rotted. Across the scum-covered moat, a stagnant pool filled with decaying wood, a felled tree had been placed to make an awkward bridge. Inside, sheltering in the watchgate, Lytton and McCarthy huddled round a fire, McCarthy fussing with food on wooden skewers, Lytton smoking his black pipe and scrawling in his notebook. He glanced up as they arrived, grinning broadly. His rich Scots tones rang out to greet them. 'Glad to see you! Did y'have a good journey?'

'Wet!' said Helen irritably.

'Indeed! We saw the storm from a distance. Have you any food, Helen? As you can see, we're down to our last two dormice – tasty enough, but I'd kill for rare roast beef with all the trimmings.'

'Can't help you with beef, but I'm happy to go hunting.'

'God bless you,' Lytton said with a second yellow-toothed smile. 'I'd sing a song of luck for you, but I'm so damned hungry I haven't the energy. I saw wild pigs in the woods, across the way, there.'

As Helen prepared her bow, and spoke softly with McCarthy, Lytton glanced at Richard. 'You look as dishevelled outside as I feel inside. I wish I could say that your son was here, but he isn't. This place is deserted. He's discarded it. And nature, as you see from the walls, is regaining it, stone by stone, passage by passage, chamber by cham-ber. Explore it by all means, but this is a ghost place. First, sit down and tell me how close you *feel* to Alex. We *must* be close.

McCarthy here feels his shadow, but the boy is damned good at keeping hidden.'

Richard told Lytton of his experiences with the 'presence' of Alex, and the Scot mused and pondered, and smoked his vile pipe. 'There's something not right,' he said. 'Something I'm missing. I thought I had your son clearly in my sights, but something must have happened. If you can bear to indulge me, tell me again about his death, about the man Keeton. You saw him suddenly on a road, near his home, a year after he had vanished . . . and he was only days older . . . Tell me again . . .'

Richard recapped the events of that long-gone autumn night in as much detail as he could remember, from the songs in his son's adaptation of *Gawain*, to the state of James Keeton as he had stumbled from the Otherworld, half-naked and very frightened.

Keeton had gone somewhere 'out of time', Lytton mused. It had probably not been a form of fairyland – if that had been the case, his return still young would have meant time catching up with him. He would have aged a year suddenly. Keeton had been *suspended* from time, exactly like Alex, or at least, the Alex that could be sensed by McCarthy, probing the sylvan shadows, and Richard himself through his dreams.

'But damn!' Lytton said, leaning back against the wall of the watchgate. 'I'm missing *something*.'

'Time might *well* be playing tricks,' Richard offered, and for the first time told him of the Helen look-alike who had been at his house on the afternoon of Keeton's return, leaving a message that had been incomprehensible. Under Lytton's questioning he accepted that he could have been mistaken. 'But when I mentioned it to Helen, when she came to visit me the other day, the thought seemed to disturb her.'

'Did it?'

'I'm not sure it was her. I don't suppose I ever have been. But if it was Helen, then she visited me seven years before she'd even come to England . . .'

'Yes,' Lytton said. 'And she appeared on the night when Keeton came back from the Otherworld. Like Hallowe'en, maybe a night when the gates went down for an hour or so . . .' He scribbled in his pad. 'Time *always* goes forward in Ryhope Wood. Not necessarily at the same rate in different places, but always forward. Nevertheless, there's an odd coincidence here . . .'

McCarthy watched the inner walls of the castle dreamily, singing softly to himself. Richard realised Lytton was talking to him. The man repeated, 'The ur-Helen . . . what did she write in the note?'

Richard confessed that memory had failed him. 'Something that you had found. Something that needed my attention. Odd words. When I lost the note, I lost the sense of its contents completely. I'm sorry.'

Lytton wanted to think. McCarthy, shrinking in his clothes, pale and wan, yet always ready with a smile, nibbled at the thin flesh of their last catch and stared out through the watchgate at the wetland and far forest, where Helen could be seen, prowling the thickets at the edge-wood, listening for game.

Richard stalked the decaying corridors of the castle, feeling the cold silence, the dank stone, the sense of being in an abandoned place among dull shadows. He could not even imagine the sound of voices, of laughter, of the growling of the great hounds that must once have lazed in front of the huge wood fires, until required to bound through the forests in search of game. There was nothing here for him, and he started to return to the watchgate.

A moment later a shadow passed swiftly through the chamber, an odd touch of warmth, like a breath on his neck. He realised suddenly that he had lost his way. He passed from chamber to cold stone passage, down worn steps and into a sequence of wide rooms, where traces of the wooden partitions could still be seen. He called out for Lytton, but his voice was deadened by the stone walls. He was suddenly back in the main hall, a vast space, echoing to his quickening pace. It smelled of woodsmoke, and he saw the smouldering logs in the wrought-iron grate. On the wall above them he recognised the stone carving of a knight and a giant, clashing swords above the leering, foliate face of a Green Man, replete with branches for its mouth, and fruits and berries in a fringe around the face.

The atmosphere in the Great Hall suddenly became stifling. Richard reacted to sudden movement in the air, half-aware of hounds, of swirl-ing cloaks and skirts, and the steamy aroma of food in clay pots. He saw nothing of this activity but the smoke in the fire and the cracked, grey carving above.

And then, whispering startlingly from the shadows, a child's voice urged at him, 'Go back!'

'Alex? *Alex?*'

Somewhere a drummer struck the taut skins in a staccato, military beat. The stone carving shifted, rustled, and as Richard called his son for the third time, the foliate face stretched forward, peered down at him. 'Go back!' it hissed, and Richard stumbled towards the doorway. The face twisted on its long stone neck, eyes gleaming in the grey rock, stone leaves falling noisily as the giant head trembled.

'Go back where?' Richard shouted. 'Alex? Are you here? Go back where?'

The face withdrew and a sudden cold descended. The side-drum had faded, the fireplace was empty. Only Richard's skin was hot, burning with the shock of the encounter. He ran quickly through the passage-ways and abruptly found himself stumbling into the light, where the skies still drizzled rain.

Lytton was just outside the castle gate, staring towards the distant wood. 'Richard!' he called without turning. 'Quickly! Something's up.'

'Alex *was* here!' Richard called, as he scampered over the muddy coutyard and into the sheltering gate.

He stopped and drew breath as he saw Helen running to wards the castle, shouting, pointing to her right. As she came close, stepping awkwardly across the narrow bridge, she looked at Richard, breathless and excited: 'The cathedral – Alex's cathedral! It's over there . . . I've seen it!'

'That close?' Lytton gasped. 'So soon?'

McCarthy struggled to his feet, running out into the light rain and staring into the distance, his eyes half closed. He walked quickly to the thorn that draped the high walls, and crouched down, his hands running down the broad, ridged wood of the lower branches. He was tracing shadows, hunched and cold, feeling his way through the earth towards the defended site.

'I can't touch the shadow!' he called. 'He must have put up another barrier.'

'It's there!' Helen cried. 'I saw it when I climbed a tree to get woodcock eggs. It's *there!*'

'Then let's fetch him out,' Lytton said. 'And let's do it *quickly*. Are you ready, Richard? Are you ready to face your lost past?'

He grinned coldly as he slung his small pack across his shoulder and followed Helen to the open land. Richard said nothing, but caught McCarthy's quick glance, a look of uncertainty, of apprehension. There was something of a warning in the frail Irishman's expression. Richard whispered, 'Is Lytton still armed?'

McCarthy held up a hand with four fingers raised, indicating the number of rounds. 'It's only a pistol. But he's a bloody fine shot.'

'Go back!' the green face had said, and it occurred to Richard that he had been urged to leave the castle because Helen had now seen the way to the cathedral, and the castle itself was becoming dangerous as shadows crept back into the lifeless shell.

Lytton had not heard the drumming. It had been sound for Richard's ears only, a memory of the legends of ghostly drummer boys, and as such, a certain signal from Alex that he was close to his father again. But 'Go back!' . . .

The whispered words unnerved Richard as he entered the woodland, following Helen as she pushed through the lush, summer growth toward the light again. It was too still in the wood, too quiet. Was this simply anticipation affecting him, making him dread the moment of contact again with a boy from his past? His stomach churned violently, his legs shook, and he stopped for a moment, listening to the others ahead of him. He felt tears in his eyes and the pulse of blood in his temples and a moment later was sick. He wiped his mouth with wet leaves, then jumped as a gentle hand touched his shoulder.

'What is it?' Helen asked. She recoiled slightly from his breath, but touched, a finger to his cheeks, her eyes watching his. 'I guess that's an idiotic question. I can imagine how hard it's going to be to see him again. If you don't think you can face it just yet . . . if you need some more time . . . to watch from a distance for a while?'

'I don't know,' Richard confessed awkwardly, still shaking. 'He whispered to me. In the castle . . . he whispered "go back". I wonder if he meant go back from here? I remember in his school play, the words were used as a warning.'

'Against what?'

'The Green Knight, I think. Someone was trying to stop Gawain entering the Green Chapel and finding its secrets.'

'But Alex *wants* you to find him. You've felt this strongly. He wants you to help him out . . .'

Distantly, Lytton called loudly, summoning Richard. Helen kissed Richard quickly on the cheek, whispered, 'Courage!' and led him to the edge of the wood.

The cathedral rose high and ruined, grey through the heavy mist that drowned the steaming land. Richard crouched beside Lytton and followed his pointing finger to one of the arched windows, below the craggy line of the wall where the roof had been torn away. A boy's face watched them over the stone sill. A second later the head vanished, but reappeared lower down in a circular portal where once there had been stained glass.

'I can't get a touch,' McCarthy was saying. 'He's not allowing contact.'

'Call to him,' Lytton said, pushing Richard forward.

Richard called out his son's name twice, and a moment later came an answering cry, not a word, more of a sob, a high-pitched sound that was filled with longing, and relief, and fear.

'My God . . . he's in danger!' Richard gasped, and ran from the cover of the undergrowth, through the grass, to the gaping doorway of the side porch.

Lytton came after him, crouched low. The saturating mist swirled about them as they entered the bleak and deserted interior of the ruin, Lytton running to the centre of the space, Richard touching one of the broken columns that marked the side aisle. Helen came through the door, looking quickly round, then up to where the boy had just been glimpsed.

'This isn't right,' she said.

Outside, McCarthy yelled, 'Get out of there!'

'*Daddy! Go back!*'

The sound of his son's voice startled Richard. For a moment he couldn't locate the source of the words, and then the small figure stepped forward, a grey statue, up on the altar space. It had seemed to detach from the stone, to come away from the hard surface, and now raised its arms sideways. The boy's eyes sparkled, his mouth stretched wide, though not in a grin, nor a grimace – something oddly expressionless. But it was Alex, long-haired, naked, undeniably Alex, a small boy, frail in build, watching his father with an expression that suddenly shifted into Anguish.

'Alex! Come on, lad. Get out of here!'

The cathedral shuddered, the walls bending inwards, the floor dropping so that the rising columns seemed to buckle. Helen yelled and grabbed at Richard. The boy on the altar started to scream, and Richard pulled away from Helen, only to feel her foot kick his legs from under him so that he sprawled headlong.

Lytton was running towards the altar. Alex screamed again and crouched defensively as the man raced towards him.

'Don't touch my son!' Richard bellowed, and struggled to rise.

Lytton's first shot stunned him. The second made him cry his pain. The bullets penetrated Alex's head, blowing muddy tissue across the altar. The boy kept standing. The cathedral seemed to be falling down around them, and Helen was tugging at Richard, her words meaningless, even though he knew she was shouting at him to *get out, get out!*

Lytton emptied the final two shots into the brain-dead boy on the altar, then swung his staff so that it crushed the skull, then knocked the small figure sideways. The walls around him flowed down and bulged, grey stone melting into an organic flow that began to swell and surround the screaming man, tendrils of liquid rock reaching out and wrapping around him. The shape of the boy was absorbed into the floor. A new human figure erupted like new growth to tower over the struggling form of Alexander Lytton.

Dark, piercing eyes stared across the shrinking cathedral from below a shock of green hair, above a body that was clad in coloured rags.

'The Jack . . .' Richard hissed.

Stone tendrils probed for him and he used his staff to strike them away. The whole building was drawing into the Jack, a giant trap, shrinking, now with its human prey.

The door through the porch was closing down, but Richard felt a final tug on his shoulder and this time turned and followed Helen through into the rain, where McCarthy stood in shock at the woodland edge. He shouted, 'Alex is close. He's shouting for you! That's not Alex in there!'

A moment later the earth itself rose up around him. McCarthy screamed once, struggled, shouted 'Christ!' and was gone, sucked down below the yellow grass.

Richard ran for his life. He glanced back once to see that the cathedral now had the shape of a grinning stone head, watching him below flowing hair. From the huge open mouth two snaking branches erupted and raced towards him, sprouting side shoots as they came, full-leafed trees that formed a consuming tunnel as the tendrils bore down upon him. Somehow, somewhere above the roar of the earth and the rustling of this hunting growth, he could hear Lytton's death agony, shrill and desperate.

Where was Helen?

He saw her in the distance, leaping the moving earth like a cat, outrunning the snares the Jack was sending at her. There was a moment when she hesitated, caught sight of Richard in the distance and waved at him furiously: Get the hell away from here!

And a moment, later she was gone.

A towering man-shape loomed in the mist, stepping forward, arms outstretched and holding two tall poles. Richard sobbed with exhaustion and fear as the Long Man barred his way. But then the figure beckoned, shouted words that could have been 'Come on!' The Long Man turned his back and braced his legs apart, the poles held to each side.

Aware that everything behind him had suddenly stopped, that all was silent, that the Jack-chapel head had disappeared beneath a tangle of hawthorn and oak from which the hedges grew, he ran at the Long Man's back, and grabbed for the figure's shoulders. Long Man and frightened man stepped forward together, and the world closed around them.

A moment later they were stumbling against a red-brick wall, start-ling pigeons in the trees and a wild cat, that hissed, spat, then bolted into the dense undergrowth. The Long Man brushed himself down, peering up and around at the glade. But Richard recognised instantly where they were.

'Oak Lodge,' he breathed. 'You've brought me back to the starting place.'

The Long Man rubbed his eyes as he looked nervously at the ruined house and the rotting wooden statue that leaned against the wall. Perhaps he could feel Lacan's defences. In any event, he didn't like this place. His expression showed it. He picked up his staffs and stepped away from the wall of the lodge.

'Thank you,' Richard called. 'Thanks for bringing me home . . .'

Alex. Oh God, Alex. Was it you! Or the Jack? What happened? Helen. I've lost you. Helen! What happened? This can't have happened!

The Long Man shook his head sadly, long hair waving. By word and gesture he invited Richard to follow him back, but Richard shook his head, too disturbed by what had happened to contemplate returning to the nightmare.

The Long Man grinned, touched a finger to his right eye, then turned and stepped between his poles. The air popped, sending a gust of wind around the small clearing that had once been a garden, and the giant had gone.

Crying softly, suddenly very weary, Richard left the wood and stumbled along the bridleway to Shadoxhurst, to his house, to the silence of the grave.

The Green Chapel: 5

'He's gone!' Alex screamed, and erupted from the sharp embrace of the hollyjack. He climbed the creepers to the high window and stared out across the wood.

'Don't go!' he cried. 'Daddy! Don't go!'

There was no movement. Everything was still. His father had been close – Alex had shouted his warning about the giggler, setting his trap, and his father had escaped the snare.

But he had *gone* – just *vanished* from the Little Dream. He had been running. There was the tall traveller. And his father's shadow had disappeared from the wood, just yards from where Alex was sheltering behind his defensive wall.

He had been so close . . .

The hollyjack whistled from below. Alex went back to her and cried in her arms. She was very weak. She clattered and chirruped.

Winter is coming. There will be danger. We must draw deeper, to protect ourselves.

Alex closed his eyes. The wood in the chapel shivered, then seemed to freeze. Light caught the broken coloured glass above the doors, a last glimpse of the knight and the monster, before the shadows closed in on him. The window had grown – the glass had filled out, the colours deepened. He could see so much more of the scene of battle.

Something was not right. The knight – Gawain – not right.

The hollyjack trembled.

They slept for a long while.

PART THREE

Long Gone, Long to Come

Spirit Rock

(Two months later . . .)

There's a fire up by Hunter's Brook – they're dancing by the fire –
'Daddy – wake up – there's a fire—
   'They're dancing—'
   'Daddy!'

Richard woke with shock, yelling out into the pale dawn light. The room was cold and damp, dew-encrusted. The window was wide open and he could see rolling clouds, threatening rain. It was four in the morning. The crows were flapping and cawing in their roosts and Richard's head was pounding as the image of Alex, reaching out to shake him awake, began to fade.

He was fully clothed, having slept sprawled on two blankets on the floor. The bedroom was a mess. Downstairs, from sitting room to kitchen, the chaos was far worse. In the month since he had resigned from his job in London and returned permanently to Shadoxhurst he had become a slob through distraction. He walked the perimeter of Ryhope Wood every day, and filled his evenings in the local pub, writing an account of his experience at Old Stone Hollow and points beyond, and getting very drunk.

The more he wrote, and the longer he stayed out of the wood, the more dreamlike the events became. It began to seem as if he had been the audience at a film. The characters were vivid, but they were all actors. Arnauld Lacan, McCarthy, Alexander Lytton – a fine cast, certainly, but they were now playing other roles in other films. Ryhope Wood was a small, dangerous, marshy woodland, far bigger than it seemed, but surely just a wood, tricky, deceptive, but as tame, in its way, as everything in England. His son was not hiding there. His son was dead. His bones were in the earth. Even Helen had become an artificial memory of beginning love. She filled his waking dreams and occupied his thoughts obsessively: they had grown so close, in those few days in the wood, but now she too was dissembling into image, voice, laughter, becoming detached from him.

But the dream – it had been so real – it had been his first real dream since coming back here.

Standing stiffly, rubbing the small of his back where it ached from the hard floor, he staggered to the window and greeted the misty dawn. He saw, at once, the column of smoke that rose steeply from Hunter's Brook before being whipped by the cross-winds. Was that a figure standing on the grey skyline? He squinted, trying to make out the detail, and a moment later the shape had vanished.

'Christ! Oh Christ – Helen!'

He tugged on his shoes and windcheater, walked groggily down the stairs and splashed cold water over his face. He was unkempt and unshaven, but gave no more thought to this than to the ants that crawled over the sink where his dirty crockery was heaped, ready for cleaning. Outside, he relieved himself against the elm at the bottom of the garden, then walked briskly along the bridleway. Soon he saw the orange lick of flame below the shifting smoke, and as he came over the low rise towards the brook and the trees, he saw the crouched, black-caped and hooded figures, one in front of the small fire, two below the trees, mostly in shadow. The moustached face of the nearest man was very bronzed. Slightly oriental eyes watched Richard from below the hood. Somewhere in the trees there was movement in the mist and Richard was distracted. When he looked back at the crackling fire, the hooded man was standing and holding out a wooden object. Richard approached cautiously.

It was a cricket bat, six inches long. Richard was astonished. He accepted the gift, and was at once aware that the other man was pleased. His companions stood and drew back among the alders at the edge of the stream, pulling their capes about their slender frames. The hooded man beckoned to Richard, who followed him to the brook and along its dry bank.

A human shape, covered in leaves, lay on its side on a crude litter of poles and cross-woven twine. The body didn't move. One of the caped figures brushed leaves from the face to expose graying-black hair over deathly white skin. A further brushing aside of leaves revealed an arm in splints and the curve of hips, unmistakably female.

When Richard looked more closely he could make out the dead body of Elizabeth Haylock.

Across the brook two further dark figures appeared among the trees, then ran quickly towards Ryhope Wood. The moustached man clapped his hands and said sharp words. Both language and gesture were clearly designed to communicate 'She's all yours now.'

Then he followed his friends, away from the stream and onto the grassy rise, where more hooded shapes rose from cover and joined the easy trot back to the wood. There were nine in all. Before he vanished from sight the leader turned, a silhouetté against the brightening day. He raised both hands vertically, watching Richard and uttering a shrill, broken cry.

What had happened?

Richard pocketed the tiny cricket bat and leaned down over the woman's corpse, nervous about touching it. The leaves on the litter by her face shifted, as if blown. A moment later she groaned and her eyes opened slightly, focusing painfully on the brook. Richard cleared the hair from her face and she turned to look at him. When she saw him she allowed herself a thin and pallid smile.

'Richard – am I out?' she whispered.

'Of the wood? Yes.'

'Thank God. Oh thank God . . .' She grimaced with pain. 'I'm in a bad way. What happened to the Pathanan?'

Richard glanced at Ryhope Wood, thinking of the small figures. 'Gone. Can you walk if I helped you?'

'Sorry – sprains in both ankles. *Christ*, I'm cold. Please get me warm. Please . . .'

She drifted into unconsciousness again, and mercifully remained so as Richard dragged the litter along the bridleway – he hadn't wanted to leave her alone while he went for help – taking nearly an hour before he was able to unroll the damaged woman onto a blanket and haul her into the relative comfort of his sitting room. He called the doctor and made tea. Elizabeth revived again and allowed herself to be stripped and examined. Her ankles were bandaged and her arm placed in a better splint. She would go to the hospital for a proper cast the next day. Given painkillers, antibiotics and strong tea, she began to feel human again.

The doctor, although curious about her clothing and general condition, did not question Richard too closely. And as soon as he had gone, Elizabeth appeared to relax. Richard helped her to the bath, where she soaked for an hour, unbothered by his presence as he sat on the toilet seat, helped wash her back, and waited for her to talk.

She was very thin – Richard remembered her as being quite robust –

and her face was lined, her breasts badly bruised. She had shallow but extensive cuts on her legs, and Richard replaced the iodine that had now washed off. To compound her physical deterioration, she seemed mentally exhausted, distant and depressed, speaking in a slow, quite breathless whisper.

'What happened to you?' Richard asked after a while.

'The wrong sort of hero,' was all she would say. 'It doesn't matter. Don't push me on it. The Pathanan found me and helped me, thank the Lord. I was just trying to get out – just trying to get away. I've had enough.' She lay back in the water, one hand gently touching the deepest bruising on her chest, her eyes closed.

'They were camped in Oak Lodge, coming right to the edge.' Hesitantly, she added, 'I think they were looking for you. They were carrying a little cricket bat. It was a gift, either came from Helen or Alex—'

'They gave me the bat. Nothing else. Just the bat – and you. No message, no hint of anything else.'

Elizabeth sighed again. 'Someone wants you back in the wood. But there's nothing there now, nothing to go back to.'

Again Richard asked what had happened, and wearily the woman said, 'It all went wrong. We lost too many, too much. Maybe if you'd come when we asked it wouldn't have risen again. It overwhelmed us.' She opened her eyes slightly, frowning. 'That wasn't meant to sound like an accusation. Sorry. I *can* understand why you didn't want to go back. The way I feel now—' She rubbed her face with her hands. 'If this is how you felt, then it's not surprising you hid from us.'

Confused, Richard leaned forward, his gaze on Elizabeth's face as she breathed softly and soaked her aches away. Her words were coming out in a jumble – he didn't understand 'risen again', or being 'asked again'. Was she delirious?

'When was I asked back? I left the wood two months ago. I went back to London, couldn't face the job I was in and came back to live here. I've not heard from any of you, from the Station, for two months.'

Elizabeth Haylock frowned from behind half-closed eyes. 'Didn't you get Helen's note?'

'Helen's note? No.'

'Damn. She said she left the note for you here. You were out.'

Even as she spoke, a memory of 1959 screamed at him, memory of a previous encounter with Helen on a rainy day, the woman running from the house, leaving behind a scrawled note, now lost.

'When *was* this?' Richard asked.

'About a year ago. Station time, that is. This will probably come as a shock, but you've been gone from Old Stone Hollow for nearly three years . . .'

He felt more alarmed than shocked. Three years to his two months – so much had happened, then, while he had been suffocating in isolation.

The note – could it have been the same one? He asked if Elizabeth knew what message Helen had brought him, and his mind raced as she said, 'It was something Lytton had worked out – how to find the protogenomorph. Alex's, of course. It's most likely to react to you, so it would have been good to have you in the wood. Also – forgive me for gossiping – but Helen was missing you. You made quite a hit.' She became aware that Richard was very pale, very shocked, and sat up in the bath, using her good arm to draw a towel around her shoulders and over her breasts, perhaps self-conscious for the first time.

'Are you OK?' she asked.

'Yes. *No!* I don't know what to say. Is Lytton alive? I saw him killed by a jack.'

'I heard about that. It spat him out. He did some good work. Helen came to tell you about it . . .'

Confused, almost dizzy, Richard held his head in his hands and said, 'I think I *did* get the note. It sounds like the same one. Only I got it eight years ago! My time. 1959, to be precise. Helen had short hair, right?'

'In 1959? No idea.'

'I meant when she brought the note, a year ago . . .'

'That's right. She'd cropped it back after getting a tick infestation.'

Too much, too fast . . .

Lytton alive! An odd fury crept into Richard's heart. He had spent weeks trying to forget the moment, the wonderful moment when he had seen what he believed to be his son. And the same painful memory was linked to the sight of Lytton's murderous rage – the man had started to kill Alex *before* he'd realised the trick. He had wanted Alex out of the wood with such a passion that it had never been his intention to rescue the boy.

But when he said this to Elizabeth she simply shrugged. 'Helen told it differently. He was killing the Jack, not Alex.'

Helen had made her own slow way back to the Station, and

McCarthy and Lytton had turned up later. Although they had been tricked by the Jack, they *had* been close to where Alex was hiding, and it was when McCarthy had been submerged in the shadow world of the wood, unconscious and half-eaten by the wood, drifting in the flow of stored memory, quite bosky, that he had seen the inner shadow of Alex, the primal shadow that Lytton called the 'protogenomorph' – 'The first form of the dreaming mind of the boy, or something. A reference to first consciousness. McCarthy saw it playing near a Mask Tree, which Lytton thinks is a focus for it. He thinks it leaves Alex to explore, and returns to him. It's quite literally the boy's "free spirit", so if you can find it, and follow it, you'll find Alex.

'Help me up, please.'

Richard lent an arm and Elizabeth eased herself out of the bath. As he wrapped his towelling robe around her battered body, she said, 'Eight years! Christ! She *said* she felt something was wrong. She must have gone through one hell of a hollowing – but then how the hell . . . how did she transit back? It doesn't make sense.'

'Everything about that evening was strange, that much I remember. Strange all round. An odd note from a cropped-haired woman. An odd play at school. And it was the night James Keeton came back from the dead.'

'I've had enough,' Elizabeth Haylock said, her voice almost forlorn. 'I need to sleep. I need to repair. Then I need to go. There's nothing left in the wood for me, now. Everything I once loved I saw killed . . .' She glanced at Richard: 'It's not the same for you, though. Maybe you should go back.'

'I've made up a bed for you.'

Richard supported her as she walked painfully to the sitting room and sat heavily on the couch. He was burning with curiosity. 'Where's Helen now? What happened at the Station?'

'I don't know where Helen is. She vanished. Wakeman's dead, McCarthy too. Lytton was taken, probably dead. Nobody has seen Lacan since he left through the cave, the time you were with us. Heikonen drowned, we think, trying to retrieve a Finnish talisman from the lake, and Sinisalo went crazy and went deep. It all fell apart. Something came through out of Old Stone Hollow. It affected everyone, and it all just fell apart. I think I'm the only one who got out.'

She slept. Richard sat in an armchair and listened to her breathing, the words she murmured in her sleep, and her cries of pain, coming not from her broken body but from her broken memories.

At midnight he abandoned the vigil and went to bed. He lay awake for ages, staring at the moon, thinking of Helen and his son and the broad, good-humoured Frenchman.

Three years!

Lacan had expected to be gone on his own journey for six months, so he was far too long overdue. The thought of his loss brought tears to Richard's eyes. Should he have stayed with them? Should he have waited for Alex to come back? If he had stayed, would Alex have returned? Perhaps he should have *believed* in his son more. And yet, in a way he *had*. How could he have known about the trickster figure of the Jack, drawing his own needs from his mind, making them real . . . ? He should have *believed* in his son. The voice had been there, warning him. Not everything had been deception.

He drifted into sleep. His last thought was that he would invite Elizabeth Haylock to stay for a few days, after taking her to the hospital. He would piece things together with her.

He woke, in the dark, to the sound of horses and murmuring voices. Light flickered in the garden and he went to the window, looking down at the torch, held by a cloaked rider on a grey mount. The man saw him and called out a warning. There was a sudden flurry of movement in the house below and Richard ran downstairs to where Elizabeth Haylock had been sleeping. The couch was empty. At the back door he watched helplessly as the band of riders cantered back towards Hunter's Brook, the flame from the torch streaming behind the leader, Elizabeth held in the arms of one of the riders, slumped or curled against him, asleep perhaps, or unconscious – perhaps content? – he would never know.

She had been removed from him, and from her own world, and this time she would not return.

He ran frantically along the bridleway, shouting at the raiders, not thinking of the possible consequences of his action, but by the time he reached the edge of the wood the torch had long since vanished into darkness. He eavesdropped the silence. He brushed through the undergrowth, a night shadow between two worlds, listening for horses, or voices, hearing only the breeze.

At first light he went back to his house and cried, partly for the woman, whose terrible journey to freedom had so suddenly been frustrated, partly for himself, for the loss of a contact with both Alex and Helen that he realised, now, he had needed desperately.

From Richard's notebook:

—*many signs of activity in the ruins of Oak Lodge. A large pit, filled with charred wood and bones – axe and knife marks on trees, dried excrement (both human and animal) and discarded raggy clothing, all suggest that the place has been in regular use recently.*

No sign of Lacan's machinery, although there are traces of the wires he used to create the boundaries. Usual feeling of being watched, but feels like a girl . . . No sign of her.

—*round and round in circles again, but suddenly came to the Horse Shrine. The monolithic stone was overgrown with ground ivy, which I cleared to expose the carved image of the horse. Found a feathered arrow, point missing, and two rusting cans, the remains of Lacan's encampment. From here I can at least begin to follow the right path to Old Stone Hollow.*

—*back to the shrine again, but this time climbed a tree and saw a high cliff in the distance, and am hopeful that this is the Station. Have made a friend of a Roman legionary carrying a treasure and shared his food. He's a splendidly tanned man, black hair cut short, face weathered and full of good humour. His helmet is lost, but he carries a bronze-bladed spear carved with running animals, and a well-used and battered short sword, plus an equipment pack complete with tin and copper kitchen gear. His 'treasure' is the Eagle standard of the Twentieth Legion. He himself is Catalonian, of a local royal birth, banished by his father. He joined the Legion in a town called Burdigala, which I think is Bordeaux, and was separated from his troop after a terrible skirmish. He carries the standard as a rallying point for the scattered men of his army.*

—*he shared crusty bread, made very palatable by dripping olive oil onto it, strips of very tasty dried meat and spiced sausage, and used leaves from his pack and water from the brook to make a sharp drink that tasted remarkably like spiced wine. All the time we ate he talked and gestured, made maps in the air, quizzed me and laughed. I learned this little about him, but not his name. His name he will not reveal.*

—*the Roman accompanied me along the river and probably just as well. Bone-armoured man, heavily painted, wild grasses attached to arms, shoulders* and legs like bunches of quills, dropped on us from the heavy bough of an old willow. Murder clearly in mind, and the Catalonian dispatched him with great ferocity and determination, a massive strike from his spear, and then a series of punitive stabs, demolishing the stone axe of the opponent and splitting his bone corselet as easily as a butcher cuts through the breast cartilage of a chicken. One grass-bedecked head left hanging from the branch, turning in the wind. The Catalonian made a charm of one of the bits of our assailant's protective bone, I thought for himself, but he presented it to me, an animal's tarsal, now scratched with the sign of Mars.

—the cliff again, seen from a high bank through tall beeches, closer now. To my surprise, the Catalonian knows the place and is frightened of it. He calls it Spirit Rock, or Ghost Rock, and describes it as the scene of a terrible massacre, perhaps referring to the remains of mythagos at its perimeter. When I tried to question him more closely be became agitated, quite irritable, then whispered (using small signs too) that he believed in the Gods, but had never thought of magicians as anything but market-place charlatans. But many magicians had lived below the rock, and had been destroyed by their own evil charms. The ghosts of that magic remained, like a honey trap for a bear. He advised me against going there, but smiled and seemed philo-sophical when I shook my head. 'You are part magician yourself,' he said, and prodded me in the chest, 'Make a charm for me!'

—the Catalonian pointed me along a trail to Spirit Rock and I have finally broken the circular defences of this watching, thinking wood. I wrote my telephone number on a page from this notebook, folded it and inserted the paper roll into a section of rush. The legionary seemed pleased. It will be as useful to him as will his image of Mars be to me.

—going deeper. Claustrophobia is my constant companion, and faces in the undergrowth, so many of which seem familiar. I call for Alex and Helen, and am answered by shrieks, the beating of wings, or silence. Mosquitos and other insects are a permanent and excruciating nuisance. The Roman was good company. I wish he hadn't gone. Where is Lacan? I hope he's not too deep. Where the bugs have bitten me, the skin is raw. I try all leaves, and mosses, to soothe.

—three years and I have dreamed for days only . . .
    Where is Helen? I feel confused. The buzzing and the biting in this moist heat is infuriating. I am watched from inside my dreams.

Hungry – I have been six days. Very tired and faces everywhere. Someone is calling me from inside my eyes. My arms and hands are weak.

—to write down. The cold.

Lacan has the hare, skin round his ears, and fire, and elegant forepaws. Fire is dancing. The bats. Is elemental of course, and quite corrupt, like bone marrow, and Alexander as the knight.

Cold is coming. Slopes up and down. Is this it? The dying place, the dust, the cold, and the lake and down, swimming. To the castle where the pike rules the lake.

A fire was burning, up at Hunter's Brook. They were dancing round the flames . . .

With a cry, his body twisting to relieve the cramp in his thigh, Richard woke from a fever dream, drenched with sweat and frozen. He was in a crude shelter, naked from the waist down.

He knew at once that he had been here for three days, increasingly delirious. The notebook was open and damp, and he read his last ramblings with painful embarrassment. He had a clear memory of writing, and of feeling such *sense* in the entries. The fever, perhaps from the insect bites with which he was covered, had turned him quite crazy, however.

He was starving, and desperate for water.

Through the trees he could see tall stones and recognised them at once, as perhaps he had recognised them days ago, but through the obfuscating barrier of delirium. He was in the Sanctuary. Ahead, the river flowed; and on the far bank of that river, Old Stone Hollow waited for him.

He collected his equipment together and stood, still shaking from the days of fever, still weak. His mouth tasted foul, his face itched with stubble. He walked cautiously into the Sanctuary, looking for hollow-sticks but finding none, concentrating on remembering where the dangerous areas had been, the one-way hollowing.

The graveyard was a soft, mossy swathe of woodland corruption, all features gone save for the occasional jaw, or socketed face, that might easily have been the decaying bark of a fallen tree. To walk across the dead was no different to walking in the deep, soft mast of a beech forest.

He slipped down the incline to the river and tears surfaced. He waded through the deep water, hauling himself up to the broken palisade, desperate to hear the sound of voices. And with a sense not so much of foreboding, but of deep loss, he walked into what was left of Old Stone Hollow, moving first to the crumbled ruins of the longhouse, then to the shreds of the canteen tent, where glass shards among the claw-torn canvas told of the last of Lacan's wine. Eventually, he sat down in the mouth of the painted cave itself, below the streaming, running shapes of animals, and gave vent to his grief and frustration, letting all the tears flow, all the anguish frighten the birds with his shouts and sobs of fury.

Later that day, more composed, he wrote in his notebook:

Damage Report:

the outer wooden palisade has been smashed down, the poles left scattered and re-erectable. The wooden guardians have been burned. Traces of wires, and infra-red and laser generating equipment remain. The generator looks serviceable, but I have no idea how to service it, or the amplifiers that control the defences themselves. Plenty of oil.

The longhouse has been demolished from the inside with apparent ferocity and very little subtlety. The roof torn down and scattered, the walls pushed through in places with a large battering ram, perhaps a log. Fragments of maps, chairs and tables litter the place. This house is renovatable, at least in part. I can make a new roof from the old turves. The canvas tents have been shredded all save that over the generator, which can be patched up and made good. There are several tins of food, stacks of firewood and a good amount of kerosene; also, metal objects such as a shield, rusting swords and decorations. The compound is high with grass and thistle, which I shall leave, making a crazy path through it for extra defence. I shall search it for other items left after the attack and perhaps also will find a clue as to what happened here.

The good news is that the kitchen garden has flourished, with tomato and marrow plants, apple trees and scattered bushes of raspberries and blackcurrants. There is a small olive tree, a rosemary bush, wild garlic and onions and potatoes everywhere.

The lake: I can see the hollowing. Lytton's Viking boat hull is out in the water, close to the danger area, apparently untethered but motion-less. The sail is furled, but appears to be intact.

Proposal:

1. *I shall use pieces of the palisade to make a defensive wall along the river gully through the rocks that leads to the lake, and across the path that winds up to the top of the overhang.*
2. *Rebuild one end of the longhouse. Fetch boat to safety.*
3. *Learn about generators by trial and error.*
4. *Collect and reconstruct all that remains of the electronic defences around the hollow.*
5. *Build a new Guardian by the river, as grotesque if not more so than the previous incumbents.*
6. *Make hollowsticks in case of the need to travel.*
7. *Construct fishing equipment and hope for a good catch.*
8. *Wait for something to happen, someone to contact me, and try to contact Alex or Helen by power of dreams, belief and shouting loudly!*

Salvage:

Heinz Baked Beans × 2
Marinated Herring × 2 glass bottles
Old Oak Ham × 3 (one with spear-point damage)
Gentleman's relish × 1
Meacham's Potted Beef × 1 (looks disgusting)
Cans without labels × 7
Cote de Roussillon Rouge, 1962, × 2 (cheers, Arnauld!)
Olive oil 2 pt × 2
Colgate toothpaste × 2
Plastic hairbrush × 1
Silver cigarette lighter (working) × 1 (Lytton's?)
Leather shoe, left foot, size 7 plus bones × 1
Mirror glass fragment 6" × 5"
Effigy in willow of dancing man × 1.

When he had finished this 'log' he walked again to the lakeside and spent a long while letting his thoughts drift across the bright blue water. Herons stalked the reed banks near by and he watched them until suddenly they spread wide, black-fringed wings and ascended with much noise, out across the lake and back to their high nests.

At dusk he entered the overhang of the hollow itself and touched the cold stone walls, the fading colours of the running creatures. And it was then that he found the hollowstick. It had been placed at the deeper entrance to the cave, to mark its creator's passage inwards. Its legs had been snapped, its body slightly chewed, perhaps by a fox or wild cat, but the black and silver lock of hair was still tied to the roughly painted face at the tip of the curve of willow that formed the body.

Old Man, Old Lake

He had almost finished rebuilding the last part of the longhouse roof when the central pole buckled and snapped and the whole wood slat and turf structure collapsed below his weight. With a cry more of frustration than pain, Richard tumbled into the grassy, earthy chaos, spat out dirt, sat up and bellowed for the boy.

'Taaj!'

Above him, the sky was greying into winter. His ankle throbbed and he scrabbled for his stick, using it to haul himself up before hobbling out into the clearing. The sprain was almost healed, but each time he jarred the foot he spent a day suffering. It seemed to Richard that in the six months he had been back at the Hollow, not a day had passed without *something* biting him, fighting him or tripping him.

Where *was* that boy? Hadn't he heard the cry?

He rang the bells ferociously. The empty tin cans clattered together dully, and the stones inside them rattled. A system of rope pulleys connected with one set of cans at the cliff top, another at the lakeside. He tugged on the lake-bell several times, hoping that Taaj would hear, but he heard no answering shout.

It had been such a long morning. He had prepared the turfs with pegs for the holes he had so painstakingly gouged in the willow slats. He braced the walls and checked the attitude of each of the supporting poles. The roof should have gone on, over what had once been the Station's community room at one end of the longhouse, as easily as the piece of a known jigsaw. But the central pole had been weak – he could see the black stain of the fungal growth – and several hundredweight of turf and Richard himself had proved too much.

Again he rang the clattering bell and bellowed the boy's name. Then he remembered that Taaj had gone out on the lake, fishing. The boy had seen the movement of large fish during the morning and had returned to the Station excited and hungry. Something had been driving them into the lake – perhaps through the hollowing? – and they had thrashed on the surface, white bellies plump, fins flashing in the grey light. Their backs had been dark purple, like sloe berries. There had been blood-red streaks along the gills. The fish were half the length of an adult man, and one catch would last a fortnight, when smoked or salted.

'Catch the biggest,' he said as the boy ran to him, shouting excitedly. 'In the meantime . . .'

'You must help me, Rishar! Come and help me.'

Taaj was jumping up and down, his brown eyes glowing with pleasure. He was holding the crude ladder on which Richard was precariously balanced, and his leaping action made the whole structure wobble alarmingly.

Richard looked down. 'Easy. Easy! Why do you need *me* to come fishing?'

'I can catch the biggest, Rishar – but I don't want to catch the spirit that drives them! Can't you come onto the lake with me?'

'What spirit are you talking about?' Richard asked, and Taaj calmed down, looking apprehensively at the gully to the lake.

'Hold the ladder as I come down,' Richard said.

He sparred with the boy for a moment, touching the long hair, making flicking movements at Taaj's feather earrings. The boy ducked and weaved, laughing, then followed his friend into the longhouse. They kept the rods and hooks here, and Richard picked out the best. 'There. You'll catch a whale with this lot.'

He noticed the second look of apprehension on Taaj's face as the boy whispered, 'I don't want to be eaten by the spirit. I'm afraid, Rishar. I think I have less than the day's fight in me.'

'Nonsense,' Richard said, again tousling the lad's hair. 'What spirit can get the better of *you*?'

All he could think of was the longhouse. He needed the roof. In the six months he had been here he had made Old Stone Hollow into a magic place again, with a protective wooden wall, reconstructed from the old palisade, totems, talismans, a working generator, a latrine, a fire-pit and a longhouse to be proud of. He had rebuilt this lodge in stages, and today he would complete the turfing of the last room, a place for the hanging of furs, fish and game. He had no time to go fishing. Besides, the boy had been on the lake a hundred times before: he was a superb fisherman.

'Listen. *You* catch the fish – *I'll* gut the catch. I know how much you hate doing that job.'

Taaj went outside, slightly forlorn, Richard thought. He walked over to the river and undressed, and Richard followed, watching as the boy knelt down in the water.

He went back to the roof, for a while, but an hour later sought his mythago friend at the river, by the new gates.

Taaj was kneeling in the water, a girdle of flowers floating round his waist, a small piece of dark wood held in each hand, turned by his fingers as he sang a quiet, repetitive song. Richard crouched on his stick by the stream and watched the hunting ritual. It was so hard to date the lad to an historical time, but Richard believed he must have been from a mesolithic society, lake-dwelling hunter gatherers.

He was brooding on this point when Taaj 'drowned' the flowers, then strained to relieve himself in the water. He came ashore and dressed quietly, fixing his lines, hooks and baits. He smiled at Richard, then ran silently through the gully to the lake.

That had been this time yesterday!

It almost took Richard's breath away as he realised how long Taaj had been gone. All of yesterday afternoon, while Richard had prepared the turfs, then drunk potato mash to go with his dried meats, aware that the boy was away, but not concerned, because Taaj was always vanishing for a day or two at a time. Drunk, and full, and weary with work, he had slept a long night, and in the damp morning had set to the task of putting on the final roof. Only when he had suffered the mishap had he started to *need* Taaj. Only now did he become conscious that Taaj's words had seemed strange, that the boy had been in a strange mood, that for the first time in their short relationship the boy had *asked* for something and Richard had refused him.

With a terrible feeling of foreboding he hobbled to the river, shouting for his young companion. His ankle niggled him, but the stick was a nuisance and he used it almost like an oar as he waded into the water, ducked below the branches and squeezed through the gully between the 'clashing rocks', as he had named them.

Did you catch a fine fish? Are you sitting there, gutting it? To surprise me, to make me ruffle your head with pleasure? Oh God, don't let it happen again—

He staggered out through the broken wood and boulders onto the reed-fringed shore, scrambling down to the water's edge as he bit back his cry of distress. Then he stood for a while, shocked and sick, staring out towards the hollowing and the huge lake creature, the frozen moment, and the dying boy.

Slowly he edged to a water-slick boulder and leaned against it, squinting against the light on the lake, the glitter of the calm lake that must have recently been in a state of turbulent disorder as the battle had raged. He could imagine how the hunters must have thrashed, out there on the water, their struggle throwing waves across the rocks so that everything was wet, everything slick, with weed and broken rushes decorating the crusted oaks and the fallen willows, the gritty sandstone teeth of the shore.

'Taaj . . .' he called, but his voice was a mere whisper. Perhaps, even as he planned to help his friend, he knew that his betrayal would cost the life of the boy.

Again, 'Taaj! Hold on! I'm going to help. Hold on – we'll eat a fat slice of your friend for supper.'

If the boy heard, he gave no sign, not even a turn of his dark-haired head or a movement of his muscles, standing out so hard, so proud against his slim frame as he held the serpent through the jaw. It was like a blue-painted canvas, a scene from an ancient battle between a young David and the Goliath of the sea, a creature half fish, half reptile, its jaws stretched in a toothy rictus, its eyes slowly blinking, the frills and spines around its neck and gills waving, beating, slowly, like the oars of a galley. Reds and greens, and stripes of livid purple, pulsed on the coils of neck that tensed below the head, and in the small boat, Taaj knelt on one knee, the great harpoon upright, the stone point fixed in the throat of the serpent.

The tail of the beast was curled twice round the skiff, and once around the boy. Only the sting at the end of the tail moved, and it flexed in fury, suppressed and restless fury, and Richard, at the shore, intuited that somehow this battle had become a test of strength. Stalemate! The boy's weapon was close to something vulnerable in the creature. But the beast would not release its grip.

I'm afraid, Rishar. I think I have less than the day's fight in me—

Richard groaned, beat the rock with his bare hands, rugged at the cords of his plaited beard and hair, rent at the faded garments on his tanned chest.

It was as if Taaj had known of his fate. He had sensed it! That the fish would be driven from another world by a creature that was from the realm of monsters. He had *known* his destiny lay in a bitter fight to the death, perhaps one of many, and he had sensed that he was unequal to the task. He had asked his friend, the old man of Spirit Rock, Rishar, the screaming, dreaming, frantic, frightened *Rishar*, to come with him, just in case of danger.

Out on the water the monster foamed bloodily, the lake shifted, the skiff bobbed and Taaj pushed harder against the jaw, felt the muscular tail of the beast tighten, squeeze more life from him. The hollowing was a haze of white and grey – shapes moved there, out of vision, a disturbance against the dark treeline of the opposite shore.

I have less than the day's fight in me—

A day, then – *the* day – a full day to defeat the serpent, according to the story that had 'birthed' Taaj from the forgotten womb of a human mind, and already the brave boy had used up most of it. There were minutes left. Richard had only one hope of helping, and that meant using Lytton's boat, the old longship, and the harpoons he had kept there, and which were still strong in shaft and point. The vessel, with its death's-head prow, was moored close by, the sail furled. There was a good breeze. The boat could circle widely and come upon the serpent from the farther side.

Stripped to his trousers, all thoughts of pain long gone, Richard boarded the sleek longship and tugged the rigging that held the white sail, catching its ends as it fell and holding them at arms' stretch, body braced behind a rail of oak, leaning back to take the strain as the breeze filled the canvas, billowed the sail, nudged the dark hull across the water. A wave rippled out, covered the sparkling grey, tossed the skiff, and the serpent foamed bloodily again, thrashed its body as much as it could, but then stiffened. The wood of the skiff creaked as the muscles tightened, as the coil slid round Taaj's braced body, scales grating at his skin, but he held his own harpoon firmly, pushed against the creature, and brought mortality closer by the sliding of an inch of stone through bone, and an inch of flesh, to a heart in the skull, to the brain itself.

I can't lose this boy. Not this boy too. His fishing is too good. I should have learned his story. I should have been ready to listen, and then I would have been ready for this.

The longship glided through the icy waters, Richard braced, leaning back, muscles taut as he held the edges of the full sail, tugging to guide the low hull, watching the shoreline as it slid across the high prow, slipping across his vision with just the *lap* and *slap* of the lake and the rumbling protest of the nearing beast to remind him of movement and goal.

'Hold on, my lad – these Vikings built for speed, not subtlety.'

I can't lose him. I don't even know his culture. He's such a good fisher. He hunts so well. He sings raucously, and it reminds me of Lacan. I know he is comfortable with stone. He seems unfamiliar with metals, can launch a spear from a hollow pebble held in his palm, is frightened of the moon when it's full, talks of his sister with affection, seems to understand me. I can talk to him, although his words are meaningless. He can talk to me, though all I do is shout.

The carcass of a fish floated past, rolling in the lake, blind eyes seeing Richard, harpoon scar bleeding still. Streaks of bright purple ran along its side as far as the wide tail-fins – the dorsal fins were flecked with black. It was plump and no doubt the boy could claim the killing, but this creature of the sea had been driven here by a serpent from hell, and it would be some time yet before the catch hung out to dry . . .

He had rounded the hollowing, caught the strong breeze, shifted his stance and now built up speed again, coming in on a hard tack, prow cutting the water—

clop – swish, clop – swish, clop—

The voice of the lake urged him on, waters parting, breaking and the mast creaking with the strain, the canvas flapping when he let the tension drop, but strong again when the wind took it, tugging him forward, off balance, until he braced and the boat surged beneath his feet, listing on the water, then righting, and closing on the fisherman and his weakening attacker—

Another boy called to him, a voice from another time. 'I'm going fishing, Daddy. Will you come? Will you come with me?'

He had had so many other things to do in his lifelong pursuit of doing nothing. 'Have a good catch. A trout for each of us, please. I'll help gut the fish. Your mother would run screaming—'

'I'm fishing for perch. We can't really eat them. It's just to see them, really. It's fun . . .'

There was a cricket match to watch. He had waved the boys good-bye, Alex, Simon, a third lad with ginger hair. Their catch had been spectacular. Alex had hooked a pike. The greatest struggle had not been the bringing-in of the catch – who would ever want to eat pike? – but the release of the two-foot-long fish, which had given the boys a look with its piscine eyes that had haunted Alex for months.

'It was angry! It looked like you do, when you have nothing to say, because it's all been said before, and we ought to know better. Very cold.'

'I do *not* give you a cold look. Do I?'

'Sometimes . . .'

'Like a pike's? Really?'

'Not so . . . fishy . . . not quite, anyway.'

He had grabbed the boy, laughing, and they roughed and tumbled, but still he had only *heard* about the expedition and adventure, and that the pike was *this* long, and one of Simon's perches had had two heads – *honest!*

The water was thrashed, the longship rocked. Richard dropped one end of the sail which billowed and flapped uselessly, but momentum carried the vessel towards the struggling serpent, and Taaj allowed himself a quick, grim glance at the old man, bearing down on him.

'Don't come close!'

'I'll help. Hold on!'

'Let me go down. This was in the dream. Don't come close!'

In the dream? Had Taaj told him about the dream? If so, he'd forgotten . . .

Richard could smell the serpent now, a rank stench of weed. The huge body rippled below the scales, air puffed from its feathery gills. It was like a salamander, but its head alone was the size of a bullock. Eyes that were prominent swivelled and glared at the coming man, and the skiff rocked, the coil around the boy slid more loosely, and Taaj grunted loudly as he thrust the stone harpoon more deeply into flesh.

The longship slid by the rising neck and Richard flung the harpoon, finding the creature's watery eye, flinching as liquid spurted as the point struck. The cameo dissolved, the beast flexed, the tail shattered the skiff and Taaj was flung into the lake, still holding the spear which had been wrenched loose. The longship rocked to its side and Richard clung to the rail, wondering what he had done. The water around him foamed white and red, the air resounding to the serpent's screeching cry of pain and anger.

Its coils slid through the water, breaking the surface, then descending. Richard held the rail, stared out over the suddenly placid lake, shouting for the boy.

Taaj's face watched him from the crystal pool. He still held the spear. His arms were stretched out, his eyes wide as he slowly sank towards the deeper structure of the castle below.

'Oh no you don't. You don't escape me this easily!'

That he felt sick with fear did not register on Richard, as he stripped naked and leapt from the longship, aware of its dark shape moving past him, away towards the shore. The lake was icy. He dived down, wriggling like a fish, turning to try to find the boy and saw him as he descended, like a statue, arms out, hair streaming, face a mask of fear. Richard swam towards him and the dark eyes watched him with what might have been urgency—

Help me . . .

I'm coming. For Christ's sake why don't you swim? Alex! Reach up for me. Swim! It's too far . . . my strength . . .

The air burst from him.

Why doesn't he swim?

His ears jarred. He panicked suddenly and swivelled in the water, ascending to the reviving day.

Then down again, and swimming hard, directly down to the frozen face, the white face, the guileless features of the descending boy. He came close again, fighting the water like a thrashing catch on the line, urging himself deeper, refusing to let the lake float him up again, fighting down, reaching down, fingers in the drifting hair, trying to get a grip, to pull the boy up. Taaj smiled, his eyes wide with hope, although his arms were stiff and his right fist clenched the stone-tipped harpoon.

Fight, damn you. Alex! Swim! Don't give up now. Let the spear go. It's no use. Swim for your life. Why do you look at me like that? I'm doing my best. Help yourself too! I can only do so much.

He grasped the boy's hair. *Got you.* He reversed his swim, tugged at the youth, felt the small, tough body rise with him.

A shadow passed across the face of innocence. The immense length of the serpent flowed around Richard and descended distantly, towards the ruins. Richard's lungs began to burst. Air bubbled from him and he turned in fear and the fight for life, let go of the boy's hair and stretched for water and the light until he broke the surface and gasped for breath.

He went down for the third time to fetch his friend.

Now the boy was in the gloom above the ruins of the castle, far deeper than Richard had been able to go that time when he had swum with Helen. He glanced around, looked for the serpent, but saw only the movement of weed and eels, the occasional flash of deep light on the silver scales of fish. The boy's air was still inside him. There was still a chance. He swam vigorously, dropping vertically, pushing back the water and meeting Taaj's dying gaze. The boy's eyes watched him with great sadness. That look was so familiar! The faces were the same. He had always known it, always seen it, from the first moment the boy had appeared by the gate. There seemed to be such hopelessness there, now, and the sort of sad smile that might have been goodbye.

Lungs straining, Richard strove, kicked, flung himself through the chill and was triumphant when he felt the brush of hair on his fingers, and he spread his hand and grasped, tugged hard, tugged up, found a better grip and held the boy.

Taaj smiled and let the harpoon go. (Alex reached for him—)

We're going home. I've got you now.

Richard turned in the water and kicked, tugging at the boy's hair, feeling the body come with him.

Then the water swirled and twisted him. He looked down, saw the huge eye, the open mouth, felt the tug, the hair in his hand snatched, then torn away. Taaj's face had contorted into a mask of shock and pain. The serpent had come up from the dark of the castle and taken him round the waist. It dropped down again, fish-eye cold and expressionless. The half-boy reached from its jaws until it jerked and gulped and Taaj was gone, and only the closed maw, with its terrible grin, could be seen among the battlements, soon lost in the weeds, though light sparkled on a watching, silver orb.

The boy's air had left him. Richard swam with it, embraced it, twisted in the bubbles, scrabbling at them, consuming them, tasting the sour breath, the last of his friend. Man and boy reached the surface together, and the cry that sounded over the water was as much the pain of the drowned, released at last, as the despair of the living, who then struck for the shore and the empty camp at Old Stone Hollow.

To the Forgotten Shore

(i) Ship of Sorrows

All night Richard sat by the lake, hunched inside his clothes, staring out at the moonlit water and the haze of Wide-water Hollowing, thinking of the dead boy, and of Alex, indeed, of everything that was lost, like a life, like a story. He kept remembering Lacan's words of so many weeks ago: *harden your heart. These creatures are dying, but remember – they are alive, elsewhere in the wood.*

So somewhere else Taaj was still alive, perhaps the companion to an old man who this time might not reject the boy's plea for help on the fishing trip, and the serpent would be subdued and brought home in triumph. But that other Taaj did not belong to him. It would not have the same face, Alex's face. It would not watch him with sadness, would not need him in the same way, in Alex's way. He had watched a mythago drown, and he had been watching an aspect of his own son, consumed by a creature from the icy hell of a legendary deep, bitten in half, two gulps, a brief life savagely ended. He was not unaware of the irony of the situation. During the long night he thought hard about Alex, perhaps still alive in the wood and waiting. Had Alex sent Taaj as a test for his father? Or had Taaj formed from the Old Man's guilt, a conscience in need of a kick-start, creating an echo of that time of agony when Alex had been taken from him and he had done so little to resist?

He had not felt this alone for years. When Alice left him there had been a few months when he thought he was going mad with loneliness, missing his son, missing her, despite their relationship having been quite distant. The anxiety had passed, of course; he had adapted to his solitary life and moved to London. Now, however, he felt that same claustrophobia – he was in a vast world, but without voices. He might as well have been in a dungeon, hidden from sight and sound. Night birds chorused, water lapped restlessly, and somewhere, just out of earshot, Arnauld Lacan still roared, bearlike, Helen Silverlock sang her

187

charms to Trickster, and Alexander Lytton murmured his exhortations to the only hidden entity of the wood that mattered: George Huxley.

The memories of his lost friends were strong in Richard.

Something moved on the lake and his attention was snatched from dreams to the reality of Old Stone Hollow Station. He narrowed his eyes, concentrated on the hollowing, and saw again the grey shape moving in the haze. For a minute or more it was quite still and he thought of a sail, then it faded, although the lake became turbulent, the waves reaching the outcrop of stone where Richard huddled.

There was a presence beyond the hollowing, he felt sure, and it was approaching the lake.

At dawn, a drumbeat pulsed from the hollowing, a steady strike, two beats a second, a determined rhythm that might have come from a war-galley. As if carried on a shifting wind, the drumbeat faded for a while, then came back, and at times there was a deeper, slower rhythm superimposed, a second ship perhaps. The shape in the hollowing darkened to become an indented square, quite definitely a sail, and the lake reacted to whatever was on the other side, and the waves coming like billows, drenching the shore.

He went back to the longhouse for a while, but returned at the height of the day to find the lake literally *echoing* to the double thunder of wardrums. Shapes passed across the hollowing in a tantalising display of shadow movement, suggesting a sea battle. Indeed, at some time in the afternoon the smell of fire came from the lake, partly the fragrance of burning cedar, partly the acrid and choking stink of pitch. As if through a sound-shutter, opening and closing, the drumbeats surged and faded, and with them came frequent sounds of screeching, like tortured gulls.

For a while, then, there was silence, but at dusk and into the early evening the dark sail appeared again. Richard stood at the lake edge, chewing dried fish, waiting for the drums to start.

There was a sudden screech, like metal rending . . . and the screams of men dying—

A *thunder* of drums, and a white wave surged from the hollowing, spreading widely across the evening lake, bringing with it the sharp scent of the ocean—

Astonished, Richard stepped quickly back as the water broke over his feet. The black sail deepened in the frame, became sharper as the frantic rhythm of the drum grew louder. It was coming toward him, rising, filling the hollowing, but motionless for the moment, oddly frozen.

When the galley broke through the gate it so surprised Richard that he fell backwards. The ship came onto the lake at terrific speed, oars flashing in the dusk light as they rose and fell into the water, drum loud, sail straining in the last of an ocean wind, then dropping fast. High-prowed, deep-hulled, of classic early Greek design, the galley shot across the water, directly toward the frozen figure of the man on the shore. Richard heard voices scream, the sail was slackened, the oars dipped to skim the lake and slow the headlong approach, but too late, the great vessel struck the shore and with a smashing of wood and beams rode up over the rocks, into the trees, lifted from the ground, oars snapping, the mast breaking in a billow of canvas and rigging. The whole vessel came to a sudden halt, then subsided to the right. Half-armoured, grim-faced men jumped from the deck, yelling; out on the lake, one mariner was swimming awkwardly to the shore; below the deck, animals screeched. The wooden hull began to sing and whine, cracking and snapping as it settled and slipped until it was suddenly and eerily silent.

A shape scampered along the soaking shore and came up to the gully. Richard found himself staring at a creature from his wildest dreams: a man's scarred body on a black beast's rump, a striking animal form that urinated copiously with fear before looking round in panic, then leaping over the rocks and into the trees. Richard scrambled into cover just as a brawny man, dressed in gleaming breastplate, greaves and leather tunic, face half-hidden behind a white, slant-eyed mask, thundered past him, carrying a slim and deadly spear. The man screamed out in anger, patrolled the rocks where the beast had vanished, then turned back to the beach in fury, flinging the javelin, which struck and stuck in the ship's hull, quivering for long seconds.

Other men were spilling from the wreck, light gleaming on the scraps of Greek armour and coloured and grotesque face-masks they wore. They shed this metal to appear either naked or wearing filthy loin-cloths; all were old, Richard saw now. They were muscular, but heavily lined and paunchy, the flesh hanging on them; thick, dark hair spread over their chests and shoulders. A horse whinnied and was suddenly quiet. Then a woman cried out, a high sobbing sound that responded to a gruff order. A man sang sweetly for a moment, a brief lament, and somewhere below the deck there was a flurry of disturbance and distress that was soon quelled with barked orders and the sound of a lash.

A hand grabbed Richard's shoulder and he cried out, startled, rising from his crouch and turning, fists flying. The man-beast stood there, terrified. It was a centaur, of course, but like no such creature that Richard had ever seen depicted. The elements of man and horse flowed through the whole body. Richard felt he understood the being's fear – these new arrivals looked dangerous, and Richard was wary and frightened of them himself. He led the way from the lake into the narrow gully that led to the Station. The centaur followed, crying in a weird fashion. Spittle ran from its black lips and through the wiry hair of its beard. It shivered on the river bank by the Station gates, looking anxiously at the darkening trees, the defences and particularly at the tall, grotesque effigy that guarded the entrance through the palisade.

'You'll be safe,' Richard said, although he was aware that mythagos did not survive the electronic defences. 'At least, you'll be safe from me—'

The centaur suddenly cantered through the palisade and into the tall grass, following the path to the longhouse, stooping to peer inside. It dropped dung at the entrance and as if embarrassed stepped back and reached down to gather up the three hard pellets, tossing them into the wood and brushing its hands together. It prowled about the house, then curled up in its entrance. It feigned sleep, though as Richard stared down its eyes opened slightly, like a child's when sleep is necessary but curiosity remains.

Who were these new arrivals? He could hear shouting and banging, a drumbeat, and a moment later the area was pierced by the shrill tones of a horn, high-pitched, rising in note, repeated ten times while the drum was sounded. The centaur shivered, curled up on its side, its almost-human arms wrapped around its bearded head.

Richard crept back to the lake, night gathering around him. Torches burned everywhere and there was much activity. He could hear furtive movement around him and kept low in the gully, alert for any sudden attack. All he could make out in the gloom was that a skin tent had been erected, tied to the gunnels of the stranded vessel at one end and to the exposed roots of a willow at the other. A cauldron of water was hearing and women's voices came from that area of activity. Two men were swimming out across the black lake, calling to each other, others were hauling lengths of rigging into the tree branches. The great sail had been dismantled and folded. Three figures, heavily built, long-haired, were lifting down a huge wooden image from the stranded ship. Richard could see a woman's face and breasts, an expression of fury carved and luridly painted. This image was erected at the water's edge, facing towards the woodland, and two tall braziers, flaming brightly, placed on each side of it.

Further along the shore, flames that glowed brighter than a cooking fire suggested a primitive forge had been established. A large man fussed over this flame-pit in the high rocks and it was he who saw Richard, as if by far sight, and moved stealthily towards him. As the giant loomed up, Richard saw that he had only one eye. The beard that fringed his broad face was grey-streaked auburn. His arms were huge, each tattooed with a winding snake. Through the white hairs of his chest a brand had marked him, a wheel around a cross, with wings on each side. He stank of sweat and honey, and breathed hard as he stepped closer and closer to the crouching man, dragging one lame leg behind him.

He was just close enough when Richard said, sharply, 'Come any further and I'll kick your other leg away. Do you understand?'

The giant hesitated at the sound of the voice. From the beach he was called and shouted back. The words were guttural, strangely unfamiliar since they were no doubt a form of early Greek. Again he dragged his bad leg towards Richard, who fumbled in his clothes for Lytton's lighter, which he raised and struck, with the flame set to shoot high. To the other man it would have seemed as if the flame had come from Richard's clenched hand, and he was satisfyingly startled. Richard flicked the fire on and off twice more, then said menacingly, 'Get back to your forge!' indicating the flame in the rocks.

The smith glanced over his shoulder, then frowned and began to back away.

On the lake shore, an old man in a long, dark cloak, holding a long spear, watched what was happening and called again. The glint of firelight on this tall character's eyes reminded Richard of the light on the serpent's gaze as it had consumed Taaj, illuminating a soulless curiosity and aggressive determination. Richard shivered as he looked at the man by the water.

The smith spoke to this figure again, and this time Richard thought he heard a name: *Yar sun*.

The name was familiar. He played its sound in his mind. It was *distinctly* familiar, and when the smith repeated it the sound became clear, and Richard felt a thrill of excitement as he realised who was confronting him on the shore.

Jason!

*

The argonauts had worked all night and by dawn the *Argo* was secure and upright, still impaled on the rocks but ready, now, for the first planks to be repaired. At the water's edge the effigy of Hera was a grim depiction of the manipulative nature of the Goddess. Her face was pinched, her eyes wide and angry, and although there was beauty there, the effect was disempowering. One would not enter lightly into a relationship with a woman whose need for gratification was so determinedly portrayed. Ten feet high, wreathed in the coils of black smoke from the braziers, the statue gazed across the bowed, crouching shape of a man in a black, wool-trimmed cloak: Jason himself, but a man now long-years-since finished with the quest for which he had become renowned.

He was talking occasionally and nodding, as if in communion with the idol. When he stood it was a sudden movement and he turned quickly to look directly at Richard, hidden among the rocks. Richard started with shock as the dark face broke into a cruel grin and a brawny hand lifted, finger extended, pointing. The idol had drawn attention to him.

This was an *old* man. Below the dark fur hood, Jason's hair and beard were grey, and the naked torso that was now revealed was sagging, the belly full over a wide sword belt, like a girdle, the thighs still strong, but loose-skinned. He was in his seventies, by the look of him, and his companions not far off, their women friends too; they formed a gap-toothed, grey-haired, crouch-boned crew of adventurers, but strong in arm, and still strong in menace.

The smith was attacking rigging rings and bolts, sending sparks flying. The dull sound of hammered bronze pulsed along the lake shore.

Richard returned to Old Stone Hollow in time to see the centaur moving furtively away up the river. It glanced back as it heard movement and raised an arm in thanks before trotting jerkily into the shadows.

An hour later the first of the argonauts edged cautiously through the gully and approached the giant effigy which Richard had constructed at the gateway to the compound. The man had no beard, just a wide moustache. His grey hair was lank, but held back by a simple purple headband. He carried a bow, a quiver of arrows and a wide-bladed cutting sword that reflected greenly as he held it at the ready. Apart from sandals and a belt fringed with leather strips, he was naked below the heavy cloak of stitched skins that he wore, opened at the front.

They had come from hot Aegean weather into this brisk, chilly autumnal world.

The man stood across the river and peered into Old Stone Hollow, observing the cliff, the longhouse, the height of the palisade, the wooden Guardian. He was nervous, curious and perhaps only an advance guard. From hiding in the long grass Richard scanned the cliff top and the other paths, but he saw nothing. As the argonaut stepped into the river, to cross it and enter the compound, Richard darted quickly to the tent that protected the generator and increased its power to the wires, ground tracks and laser channels around the Station.

The effect was astonishing. The man stopped suddenly, very puzzled, then began to scream, stumbling back in the water, falling, dragging himself up onto the bank again. Around him, the land heaved, the trees shuddered. He jerked his hand away from the sudden tug of green tendrils that had emerged to wrap around him. Again he screamed, this time in terror, his voice taking on a strange quality, deepening, until it was not recognisably human. He was still standing, but he had become grey. Gradually his spine arched and he tumbled back. There was a scurrying of activity around him and ground-ivy flowed to cover him. Below this unlikely shroud he continued to struggle and breathe for some time, occasionally emitting a cry of intense pain, occasionally calling helplessly for Jason.

As he had fallen, so there had been a quick movement back towards the gully. Richard darted round the palisade and peered out, in time to see Jason and two others returning in haste, and certainly in confusion, to their lakeside camp by the *Argo*.

Later in the day, one of the women and another argonaut edged through the gully. They called out repeatedly, advertising their presence, and took a wide arc up the slope, above the river, before cautiously coming to the water's edge, grinning and nodding, there to place a gleaming jug and a roll of fleece on the ground. They were unarmed and crept away. Richard watched them go, then fetched the offerings into the compound, delighting in the fact that he was clearly regarded as some terrible creature that would need placating. He remembered the Gorgon, however, and was not unaware that to these ageing adventurers, placation might only be a first ruse in the eventual tricking and destroying of the mysterious, magical life-form that they had encountered.

How did Jason and his crew regard him, he wondered? They had adventured against cyclops and titans, gorgons and sirens, the guardians of magic groves and serpents. Here, now, they had beached by magic on a cold lake shore, after passing, perhaps, through an odd storm, or clashing rocks, on the sunny Aegean. They were in a mysterious land, and threatened by a wild man, a wizard, who summoned the very earth to consume one of their men by touching a bizarre, metallic monster that hummed a single note, and whined to call for more prey.

The jug was of beaten gold. It contained a sharp wine, flavoured with lavender, and he was immediately suspicious, risking no more than a taste on the end of his finger. The vessel was exquisite, decorated with figures of heroes, and the full and leafy features of the god of all things indulgent. The roll of fleece did not reveal gold, to his disappointment, but was beautifully soft, white with fine streaks of grey, and cut carefully to make a shoulder wrap, the ties at the front being the small, scaly horns of the creature that had perhaps once worn the hide more naturally. The horns were not pronouncedly like a goat's, nor sheep-like – more in the fashion of Pan, he thought.

The sounds of repair were loud. Richard heard trees being felled, the wood then chopped and shaped. The forge rang continuously and sometimes the breeze brought the smell of cooking and Richard sighed as he remembered good, tasty stews and succulent Sunday roasts of lamb and pork.

Perhaps his hunger carried on that same breeze. In the late afternoon, Jason and another burly fellow, both unarmed, both in sheepskins, brought a small copper cauldron to the river's edge and left it there. A tantalising aroma of fish and Mediterranean herbs came from the pot. Jason's companion withdrew nervously, but the leader of the argonauts remained. He produced a wooden spoon and consumed three mouthfuls of the soup and fish, then drew back so that Richard could cross the water and take the container. Jason made encouraging sounds, grinning, his mouth full of black teeth.

'Thank you,' Richard said, and added, 'Daksi.'

Jason shook his head thoughtfully, crouched on his haunches, eyes alert for every movement, every twitch of the forest. Richard carried the cauldron back into the compound then came to the river's edge again, dropping into the same tense crouch as his visitor. He was conscious of being explored carefully, examined in every detail, from his tennis shoes to his denim shorts, from the ragged affair of blankets that he wore around his shoulders for warmth to his braided hair and the bone slivers and egret feathers with which the boy had decorated him in recent, happier times.

Jason indicated the crumbling mound that was his dead companion and said a few words. Richard spread his hands and shook his head, before hunching forward again. 'I didn't know it would happen. There's a defensive field around Old Stone Hollow—' He waved his hand behind him and repeated slowly: 'Old. Stone. Hollow.' Jason nodded and said, 'Hollow.'

Richard went on, 'The field kills in different ways. It didn't kill the centaur at all, and you seem safe enough. You're mythagos. All of you. And you're all vulnerable in different ways. This is a dying place, for mythagos. It's dangerous for you to be here.'

'Hollow,' Jason said. 'Mythaaga . . .'

'Mythagos, that's right.'

Jason shook his head, looking beyond Richard, then scanning the high rise of shadowy cliff. He stood and stretched, rubbing circulation back into his tanned and muscular legs. His bones creaked and cracked as he straightened, like the *Argo* on the beach, and he grinned broadly, an acknowledgement of age. He pointed to the stew and said something encouraging, then raised a hand in temporary farewell.

As he left he glanced back twice, his face an open book of thoughtful planning.

What was Richard's significance to them? Were they afraid of him? Did he represent some goal in their adventure? Did they believe that he might be in possession of a magic that would aid their greater quest?

The *Argo* had been pulled down from the rocks, and was now suspended by ropes. Its stern was in the water, but its prow, and the damaged area of the hull, were more accessible to the carpenters and metalworkers, and Richard, watching from above the gully, could see how the planks had been cut back to expose the great tree that formed the keel.

An aspect of the Jason legend came back to him: the *Argo* was built around a sacred oak. He had always assumed that the keel had been shaped from the tree, however, not that the tree itself had been incorporated into the vessel. Yet there it was, its branches like veins, reaching up and through the narrow space below the deck, winding around like roots, a cage of branches containing strength and magic, a cage of branches within the man-formed sleek shape of the ship itself.

Two of the argonauts were at work repairing several broken branches, applying an unguent. Smoking censers had been placed inside the tree, and the vapour wafted out across the lake. Looking carefully, Richard could see movement inside the oak cage, acts of propitiation, perhaps or repair to the main trunk.

It was as he watched the bustle of activity that he heard the sound of a girl crying out in anguish. A harsh male voice barked an order. Much of the work on the ship stopped for a moment and there was a clattering, somewhere below decks, the sound of hooves, or stamping, and then a rattle of metal followed again by the girl's shrill cry.

One of the argonauts laughed. A length of rigging slipped, uncurling as it plunged, and was caught by a man below. The new mast was up, the sail being hauled to its cross-bar. The accident broke the moment's mood, and activity began again.

Five minutes later, one of the planks at the rear of the ship began to move. Curious, Richard moved closer through the rocks and trees. The panel had been loosened by the force of the beaching. It opened along three feet of its length, and a dark, frightened face peered out at the shore. Daylight glinted on wide eyes, then a second face, this one more animal than human, glanced out anxiously before withdrawing.

The plank snapped back into place with a crack, but the sound went unremarked by the busy men around.

In the evening Richard built a fire just inside the gates of the Station and racked up the generator. On the far bank, where the argonaut had died, an odd tree had grown. It shivered despite the lack of wind, and carried four small, yellow fruits, round and shiny. Richard declined to go across the river and investigate them.

Movement in the gully alerted him and he quickly strung his long bow, then nocked an arrow. Over the weeks since he had found this weapon he had become adept at its use, though the flights and heads were getting battered now and he had so far failed to make a successful arrow himself.

From the long grass he could see the gleam of light in the defensive field, and in places the glitter of the thin wires that carried the current. Water splashed, a man's voice barked, a girl's voice protested. Richard drew back into the grass, crouching, and soon Jason and three others appeared across the river. Jason had a small, dark-skinned girl with him, chained around her neck, her face open and frightened. She wore a thin wrap that scarcely covered her skeletal limbs.

Jason called to him and Richard came out of cover. 'What do you want?'

The girl immediately closed her eyes, concentrating hard. Jason just grinned and watched the other man. His companions shifted uneasily, tugging skins around their chests. One of them kept a weather-eye on the huge bow, which Richard had drawn, the arrow turned only slightly to the side. Richard felt his arm twitch with the effort of holding the weapon, but he sensed menace in the air and was taking no chances.

Again Jason spoke. He slapped his chest, his mouth, and indicated Richard. He wanted to come over the water and talk. He wanted to bring the girl. Was that permitted?

'Just you, then. Not your friends. They must go back to the *Argo*.'

'*Argo*?' Jason repeated. Richard stabbed a finger at the other three men and then towards the shore. Jason grasped the message. His friends withdrew. Jason tugged tie protesting girl and they waded through the deep water, shivering as they came ashore, crouching gladly by me fire in the gateway below the menacing glare of Richard's totem.

Closer to, when Richard met the gaze of Jason's prisoner and saw the etched lines of experience and humour, of pain and defiance all around the sparkling eyes, the corners of her mouth, he realised that it was only her slightness that had made him think of her as a girl, rather than the subdued but still defiant young woman that she was.

Jason produced a piece of cloth and unwrapped a rare-cooked and juicy shin of mutton. It gave off an aroma of rosemary and garlic and as Jason saw the hungry look in Richard's eyes, so Richard saw the look in the woman's. She was starving. Jason hacked off a portion of the meat and ate it, then carved a slice for Richard, who took it and consumed it with gusto. The woman accepted a small slice, behaving as if she were surprised to be offered such a treat. There was wine too, a clay amphora containing about two pints. Jason took a long draught, then Richard, and this time he appreciated the drink, with its honeyish aftertaste and warming effect on his stomach.

'Thank you,' he said, and the woman repeated, 'Thank you.'

'To what do I owe the pleasure of this visit?' Richard went on, then frowned as the woman said, in perfect imitation, 'To what do I owe the pleasure of this visit?'

Jason watched her, nudged her, but she shook her head and scowled, rattling the thin length of chain with which he held her. She looked hungrily at the lamb and the big man sliced more for her, then for Richard. She chewed gratefully, dark eyes sparkling. Her skin tone suggested the Middle East. Her hair was jet black, but cropped short. Her ear-lobes gaped grotesquely with holes where heavy rings had once hung, and indeed, there was a distension in the flesh of her nostrils too. A thin covering of dark hair spread from her ankles to her knees, and bushed from below her arms. She was boyish in shape, her face seeming older than her breastless body. The wrap that covered her was purple, and the designs were of broad-headed lions, winged dragons, and sharp-beaked eagles.

'Why are you repeating what I say?' Richard asked.

'Why are you repeating what I say?'

'Are you trying to understand me?'

'Are you trying to understand me?'

'My name is Richard. What's yours?'

'My name is Richard . . .' She trailed off, looked down.

Jason leaned forward expectantly, watching her. He said something and she nodded.

She murmured, 'I know him now.' She looked up, brows dark, head cocked. 'It's a strange tongue. I know you though, I know how you speak. Many tongues muddled. What do you call it? Your language . . .'

'English. You seem to have learned it very fast.'

'I already knew it – I just had to find it. It's a long-to-come language. They float in me like dreams. There are so many. The languages of the long-gone are easier. But I have him – you – I have you now. I have your tongue. You are Richard.'

'Yes. And you?'

'Sarinpushtam. My sad companions, below the deck of the *Argo*, call me Sarin. This is Jason.'

'Yes. I know.'

'Don't trust him.'

'I'll try not to.'

'I'm hungry. Please indicate that I should have more meat, or this man will deny me. He's very cruel.'

Aware that contact had been established, Jason tightened the chain around Sarin's neck, tugged her and growled at her. She spoke to him in his language and he glanced at Richard, nodding, then smiling grimly. He released the girl, who touched her neck tenderly and started to ask questions. He expected Sarin to translate, but the girl just watched Richard, eyes haunted. Richard pointed to the lamb and to the girl and Jason's features darkened, but he got the message, sliced a thick piece of meat and passed it to Sarin. He watched her impatiently as she ate it, seeming to chew longer than necessary, licking her lips exaggeratedly, closing her eyes in ecstasy when she wasn't watching Jason carefully and tauntingly. When she had finished she wiped her fingers on the ground, looked hard at Jason and wiggled her tongue between her lips in an odd gesture. She smiled 'sweetly' as Jason passed her the wine amphora, and drank so deeply from it that Richard was surprised to hear the slosh of remaining liquid when she passed it back.

'That's better,' she said. 'It will ease the pain later, when he punishes me.'

'Why will he punish you?'

'Mostly because I don't like him and he knows it, and I make life difficult for him. Partly because I'm a woman, or what's left of one, and ever since Medea killed his precious lover and his boys, he doesn't much like the female sex, although he doesn't prefer his lusty companions. He has very little choice. Boys, boy-shaped girls, and . . .' She sucked her fingers pointedly. 'Well, I hope you don't mind eating meat from a carcass that Jason has raped.'

She was grinning mischievously. Jason suddenly lashed out with his hand, a stinging blow to her cheek, drawing blood from the corner of her mouth. He spoke angrily, she translated quickly.

The business session had begun.

'What magic did you use to kill Peleus? And make Tisamenus disappear . . .'

Which one was Tisamenus, Richard wondered, but he said, 'A magic that surfaces out of dreams. The dream lives in the skulls of certain men, and also in the earth. The light of the sun, and the terror of lightning, can be controlled by this magic, and made to dance at my orders.'

It was sufficiently garbled for confusion, but Richard was proud of his invention. When Sarin conveyed this information, Jason began to look hungry in a different way. Predictably he asked, 'What will you trade for knowledge of this magic?'

'Nothing,' Richard said. 'The magic is known only to me. The very earth in this place is at my command—' Jason had seen something that would not give the lie to this lie— 'No one else can have the knowledge.'

It was some moments before Jason answered, his gaze burning into Richard. When he finally spoke it was in a whisper, and Sarin had to listen hard as she gave voice to the old man's thoughts. 'Will you come with me, then? Will you sail with me on the *Argo*, as my honoured companion, and work your magic for me? If you believe this, you're a fool.'

It took Richard a moment to dissect Serin's commentary from the translation. As he glanced at her she raised her eyebrows, quickly and pointedly. He said, 'No. Thank you, but the Goddess Hera directs your fortunes. You must ask her for all the magic you need.'

Jason turned his head and spat angrily. His face literally darkened as he met Richard's gaze again. 'Hera? She rations me. In some ways I'm no more than her shadow, and she dances at her own whim to make me move.' He scratched the grey stubble on his chin, smiling thinly. 'But I like the tone of your magic. I like its effect. There are places I wish to go, there are treasures to acquire, achievements that would be easier with a magician like you. I will offer you a *palace*. I carry a treasure in the hold of the *Argo* with which I could buy two such places. I will give it to you.' He grinned hugely. 'And gladly! Just come with me for one year. No more than that. One year. Come on – what do you say?'

Without taking his eyes from Jason, aware of the face that Sarin was pulling, Richard said, 'No. This is my home. My gods watch me from the woods. The forest and myself are as one. I seek something that only I can find. My own adventure will take me deep into the wood, not onto the high sea.'

Jason was very tense, the fingers of his right hand gouging at the earth. He said, 'Then I will help you find what you seek. Myself, my friends. We'll be at your service for . . . two years. If you will spend just one year with me.'

'No. I must find what I seek alone. There is a god called *conscience*, and he needs to be placated.'

The word was hard for Jason (for Sarin, too, Richard noted). The argonaut came from a time when the notion of conscience was still raw-formed, still a confusion, of the will of gods and predestined actions. Richard went on, 'More importantly, there is a life called Alex, a life that is in limbo. Like Orpheus—'

'Orpheus? I'll introduce you—'

'Like Orpheus, I have to enter hell to bring him out. I can only do it alone.'

Jason was angry, but he tried to hide the fury. He stood, kicked the lamb to Richard, then tugged Sarin to her feet, dragging her to the river. 'You should give me the chance to help you!'

'Leave the woman here for a while!' Richard called, and he heard

Sarin translate, but Jason snapped a negative and pushed the frail creature into the water ahead of him, splashing through the shallows towards the gully. As he disappeared from view, he shouted out, and Sarin's voice echoed the words: 'Perhaps your magic is not as powerful as you think!'

(ii) Dancing with Shadows

Somehow she slipped her chain, and came back to the compound after dark, huddling by the glowing embers and calling softly for Richard. He ran around the grass path, peering over the weeds until he saw who it was, then went to her, picking up one of the still-burning branches and leading her by the hand to the longhouse. She was shuddering, wincing with pain, and he wondered if it might be the defences, so he turned down the generator and indeed her agony diminished.

He had been huddled in the longhouse without a fire, but he set light to the pile of wood, now, and they sat and listened to the crackle of dry bark, watching the smoke stream up to the roof hole. There was food left, and unsurprisingly Sarin went at it like a hound. She sat cross-legged, her robe riding up her thin legs, and as the light grew with the fire Richard saw the bruising on her thighs. Distressed and disturbed for her, he reached over and tugged the cloth to conceal her wounds. Her neck was black and blue where the chain had been.

'He's sleeping. He put me back in the hold, without the chain, but there's a loose plank and I'm small enough to get through it. I mustn't let him know I'm gone. It would be too terrible for the others.'

She was not the only prisoner, then. But Richard hesitated to ask her who else was locked below the deck of the *Argo*. He wanted to know more about Sarin herself. How had she grasped his language so quickly? What was her myth?

By firelight, relaxed and warm, with a friend at last, she told him about her life. To her, of course, it was a natural life that had ended abruptly when she had been taken by Jason.

She had lived in a town called Eshmun, close to a city and sacred site where the priests had ordered the construction of a great tower to reach to the gates of heaven itself. A place called Babel. As a child, she had seen her grandfather broken by the work, sent home to die once his bones had cracked and his muscles become like rags. Her father had been taken. When he too was broken by a fall, his dying words had been that from the top of the tower he had seen a place where the sun shone from every horizon.

Sarin, her mother and sisters were now alone, and unsupported. Sarin had been six. One day they had been taken by other women, and moved up to the base of the tower itself, which was so wide, so huge, so high that it blocked the light from the west. They lived among the tents. Sarin for a while had helped prepare food for the builders, carpenters and stonemasons. But soon she was old enough to follow her sisters into the tower itself, and climb one of the twenty flights of spiral stairs. This led to the ornamental rooms where jade lions watched over shallow pools of water, and those men with the *Vision of the Tower* came to bathe and relax, and take their various pleasures. And Sarin, for a year or more, was one of these.

Because of the nature of her work, because she would need to talk to men from all across the world where customs and the secret languages were different, she was trained in the language of the Tall Grass. The Tall Grass language had been the first language, spoken in the long-gone by the first adventurers. Over many generations the Tall Grass tongue had become rich and complex and all men the known world over spoke it; a small part of it, however, had become divided and secret; each and every man and woman had a secret language, which they spoke alone, to the moon, or to hidden forces, or to God.

Once Sarin had learned the ancient Tall Grass tongue, she could see deeper into the wisdom of the men of Vision, further into their hearts, further into their humour, further into their fears. She became one of the Comforting Mouths, women whose conversation and under-standing was like magic. Her head was full of language, and those languages were like windows onto long-gone worlds. Sometimes, too, there were long-to-come worlds, showing themselves in dreams. This was the nature of the Tall Grass tongue: so simple that it was the key to everything human beings thought in their secret worlds. The women kept this secret closely guarded in their hearts.

One day, Sarin made the mistake – the only mistake she would ever make, until she failed to kill a man called Jason who came to abduct her – the mistake of mentioning her visions of the long-to-come.

One of the Tower Builders, aspiring to the priesthood, was jealous of her dreams. He asked her to reveal the names of God in the worlds of the long-to-come. Sarin refused. He beat her, then dragged her to the stone drop, a hole in the wall through which the blasphemous were sent to their death on the rocks and tents, an hour's fall below. The Builder held Sarin by the hair and dangled her from the stone drop. From here she could see the sun at every horizon, and she remembered her father's dying words, and that made her think of her grandfather, and her mother and sisters, now lost in this great structure in the service of the Builders.

She felt at peace despite the pain and hung there, talking to the memory of her father, while the Builder's arm tired. He demanded to know the names of God in the long-to-come. She asked him why he wished to know. He told her that in names there was great power, and when the tower reached to Heaven itself, those men in possession of the not-yet-known names of God would be as Kings in that great place.

That was when the tower cracked.

Sarin declined to let her secret knowledge be known.

The tower cracked again, and this time she felt the whole world shake, and reached to the Builder just as he released her hair. She clung to his arm, then found a grip upon the lintel of the stone hole. The tower trembled and the Builder was thrown out into the air, to fall for a long time, robes flapping, his scream outliving his body. As the tower began to collapse, Sarin scrambled into its ruined bulk, and scampered down the spiral stairs, dodging the rocks and stones, the cedarwood beams, the jade and golden idols. Eventually she was struck by masonry and lost consciousness, save for a dream in which, with thousands of others, she was falling through the ruins to her death below.

She woke among those ruins. Her mother was bathing her face. Everything was in chaos. The world was full of sound, and the sounds jarred and flowed and screamed, but as Sarin came to full alertness she found that she could understand those sounds. The secret languages of every man, woman and child were now the *only* languages – the greater part of the Tall Grass tongue had been torn away! – but each was different. She could understand her mother, but her mother could understand none of her daughters, save Sarin.

Sarin was the Tall Grass Lady, and she was depicted on many painted and carved surfaces, vases, and sacred stones. She knew all tongues. When she had denied the Builder his obscene request, she alone had been spared by the fateful and vengeful force that had destroyed the language of the world, the tower, and its blasphemous intent. Sarin dwelt in a temple, and was visited often, to interpret between new peoples, new clans, new tribes. Her visions continued. Her fame spread . . .

And then – to this Sarin at least – a strange thing happened . . .

Out of the long-to-come came a ship like no ship she had ever seen, men like no men she had ever seen, carrying swords and spears with terrifying blades, speaking a language that she recognised, but talking of her own life as if she was long-gone, long in the past. They were collectors, and they had come to collect her. They would sell her for a high price to a king whose desire for power could make use of this Witch of Tongues.

They took her, abused her, beat her and chained her in the cargo hold of the *Argo*.

Sarinpushtam. Tall Grass Speaker. A woman with the gift of language. One of Jason's readable treasures.

'There are two holds,' she said after finishing the last of the sour, lavender wine. It hadn't done Sarinpushtam any harm, so Richard too had indulged from the golden jug, and now felt light-headed and aggressive towards Jason. 'To get to the hold where the living are chained you have to go through the dead treasure hold. It's stuffed. You can hardly move for fleeces, skulls, statues and bits of armour.'

'Fleeces? Is there a golden fleece among them?'

'They're all golden,' Sarin said with a little laugh. 'He collects them compulsively. I don't know why – nobody seems to want them.'

'What about guards?'

'They're all drunkards. They'll be vigilant during daylight, but they eat and sleep like lions, and drink like Old Vineface . . . I don't know how you remember him in your long-to-come. They'll soon drift off, but Richard, they're not fools. If they sleep readily, because of their age, they sleep lightly, they wake fast, they're stronger than they look, and they've lost none of their skills. They're mean-tempered, ferocious old men.'

'I'll be careful. At least Hercules didn't come back.'

'Four of his illegitimate sons are among them, though, and one of the women is his daughter. The sons of the Dioscuri are among them too. And the shade of Aeneus, of whom you should be very wary.'

'The unsung heroes of Jason's later legend,' Richard mused aloud, and was about to speak again, to ask who the rest of the argonauts were, when he noticed that sweat was pouring from Sarin's face. She seemed to be in pain, and almost immediately she arched back and began to howl. Richard leapt to his feet and picked her up, astonished at the fact that he could hardly feel her weight. Her breath was bad, but her eyes, now wide, were terrified. 'Something's happening to me . . .'

The defences! Christ!

'Hang on to me. I have to get you out of the Station.'

She began to weep, biting back the sounds, gnawing at her lip to frustrate the anguish of pain that she was suddenly experiencing. Richard cut straight through the grass, wading through the tall grass, crossing his winding paths. He hardly glanced around him as he passed the gates, and entered the water. If Jason was here, now, then he was in trouble. Sarin's grip on his neck tightened, then relaxed and he was shocked, dropping her to the ground, slapping her cheeks, pulling her face round to see if life still existed. She was breathing shallowly. Her mouth was slack and wet. He picked her up again and stumbled up the bank, running fast towards the Sanctuary, to get her away from the humming defences, the totems, the talismans, the forces of the earth that could so unpredictably take the life of a mythago.

He fell to the ground, his legs too tired to work any more. He covered Sarin with his body, hugged her, his mouth against her neck not for pleasure, but so that he could feel with his lips for the pulse of life. She groaned, was sick, and he drew away, holding her hand, massaging her thin fingers, waiting for her to come back to full strength.

'What happened?' she whispered after a while. 'I felt like my life was being sucked into a great hole. There were running creatures, running men, all being sucked down into a great hollow in the ground . . .'

The reference was clear. She had experienced Old Stone Hollow itself. So did that mean that it was the camp's defences that had attacked her suddenly or had something reached to her from the cave? In any case, it would be dangerous for her to return to the Station.

'How do you feel?'

She wiped a hand across her mouth. 'Too much wine,' she said. 'I feel shaky. I don't want to be beaten again. I'm going back. From what I've heard Jason say to the others, the *Argo* will not be seaworthy for four days, perhaps five. So don't act hastily. If you really want to help, then we must wait for a good moment.'

She was staring at him. It was an odd look and he couldn't interpret it. Suddenly she flung her arms around his neck and cried on his shoulder. Helplessly he patted her back, alarmed by the prominent ribs. 'I *will* help,' he said. 'As best I can. But you mustn't come back to the compound. It's too dangerous for you.'

'He'll drag me back. He needs to control you. He wants your head. Jason believes that the source of all magic is in the jelly that fills our skulls.'

Clever man . . .

'Richard . . . ?'

'What is it?'

She drew back, peered at him through furrowed brow, licking her lips and grimacing at the taste. 'If you can't help us. If it seems Jason will win . . .' Her eyes gleamed with passion and desperation. 'Richard, I would rather not be alive than with Jason. Do you understand what I'm asking?'

'Yes. I do—'

'The knowledge has only just become important to me. I can't stand it any longer. I don't belong with him. I don't belong here. I dream of long-gone and long-to-come, but the dreams are wrong. It's as if I am not in the right world. Can you explain that?'

Richard could have spent an hour explaining it, of course, but he shook his head. Suddenly Sarin was on her feet. She slipped off her colourful wrap and merged with night shadows, a pathetically slim shape, slipping down the bank to the gully, moving like the softest breeze back to her prison in the *Argo*.

'*Riiich* – aaaard! Good morrr-ning. Brek-faaast, *Riiich* – ard. Braaaaak – fust!'

The sound of Jason's call, his shouted invitation to come to the river, woke Richard from a deep and dizzying sleep. He was in the longhouse, wet and cold with sweat. Jason's voice, the accent pronounced, the laughter a clear indicator that he was amused by the strange words (no doubt taught to him by Sarin), was nightmarish.

'Riiich – aaaard!'

He dressed and ran in his crouch through the wind-stirred grass, finally peering through the gate at the crouched, cloaked shape on the far bank. Sarin was there too, but not in chains. On a skewer, Jason held two crisply black fish, plump of body. Fish for breakfast. Why not? The pain in Richard's head was a sufficient warning not to accept any alcohol, however.

He thought of turning up the generator, but the memory of the previous night, and the possibility that Sarin would not survive the destructive field, decided him against such a move. Jason as ever was unarmed, but Richard nocked an arrow and skulked forward, finally standing in the open gates.

'Why the bow?' Jason asked through the woman.

'Because I relish the idea of living to be as old as you.'

Jason laughed and nodded. 'But that's too much caution, Richard. Men like you are too fearful of their backs. I'm old because I don't care. I just trust to Hera. She bargained with me years ago. A long life, said I. Then pleasure me, said she. How do I do that, I asked. I like to see you *find* things, she said. The world is full of hidden treasures. And like a man finding the secret places of a woman for the first time, so to the gods there is a satisfaction in seeing men discover the secret places of the earth. Hera is my love, my life and some might say my tormentor. But what torment? I have the fullest of lives, and I am unquenchable. I have the vigour of a youth, and the experience of age. I can drink like Old Vineface, and plan a strategy for the ache in the head the next day; and at the whisper of my voice I can summon a hero to sail with me, or a king to charge me with a task. I *like* being old. Memory – experience – these are the truest sources of *power*. Make your own pact, Richard, and that way you need never look behind your back again. But for the moment, it's breakfast and conversation that I want, and a bargain, not a fight, so do put down that bow.'

They ate fish, and Richard noticed that Sarin was given an equal share. Jason was treating her with much greater respect today. His old man's temper had got the better of him yesterday, but in the harsh light of retrospect he had clearly decided that a way to get Richard's confidence was to show consideration for the woman. Sarin's smile, as she ate and watched her friend, was cynical, a signal that she knew the situation.

'What's the order of business for today?' Richard asked eventually, and as if understanding him Jason laughed, slapped the woman on the back and indicated that she should talk.

'Firstly, I'm yours to do with as you want for the duration of the repair to the *Argo*.'

'I accept. I could do with some intelligent conversation.'

Sarin shook her head grimly. 'That's not what Jason means . . .'

'So what?' said Richard with a smile. 'What does it matter what Jason means? It's not what I mean. I'd like to have your company. I accept the deal. I'll find a way to get you deeper into the wood, away from him. I need company, chat, and a sense of humour, and you fit the bill. Yes please, I will have your company for the duration. If *you* agree, that is . . .'

'I agree! But don't think about smuggling me away. If I betray him, he'll kill his best friend, who happens to be mine too. I'm sorry, but this man knows his business, and there are other friends below the deck . . .'

Richard glanced at the smirking man. Did Jason follow the drift of the conversation in English? It was hard to tell.

Sarin said, 'The main business today is that you are invited to inspect the *Argo*, to see its goods and treasures, the creatures that he carries, the magic that he has stolen from the earth. He wants to convince you that to join him on the *Argo* would be in your favour. Of course, the whole point is to take you and subdue you. He has already gathered that your strength only shows in this magic place, this *hollow*. He's afraid of your magic, certainly, but he has guessed correctly that your skills are limited. He still wants to use them. So if you go to the *Argo*, don't expect to come back. That's my advice, anyway.'

'Thanks. I think I'll take it.' Richard looked at Jason and shook his head vigorously. 'Tell him that if he releases all that is living on the *Argo*, and waits a full day, then I'll talk to him again and consider his offer. Tell him I do not travel with prisoners.'

Jason raised his hands, on hearing this, then patted his groin as he crouched, a clear signal that Richard could take his request, perceived as the lie it was, and post it back to Shadoxhurst.

A look in Jason's eye alarmed and alerted Richard. There had been the faintest of glances upwards, the merest shake of the man's head. Richard twisted quickly, at the crouch, and was in time to see the faint shadow of a man pull back from the top of the cliff above Old Stone Hollow.

Damn! They had found a way up. Perhaps an arrow had been nocked and pointed at Richard's exposed back all the time that he had been talking. The compound was totally vulnerable to attack from above.

For a moment Jason picked at his lower teeth with thumb and index finger, examining the fragments of fish that he hooked from his blackening ivories before sucking them away. At length he said something to Sarin, who announced, 'He's sorry you won't see sense, but in fact your magic is probably of less use than he'd thought. He'll not bother you again. He has a centaur to hunt, an escapee. He's sorry, but he has decided not to give me to you. The *Argo* will be repaired in a day – I can't believe that's true – and then they'll be gone. If you can help me, please help me soon. Death or release, I don't care which. That bow looks like a giant's, but if you can shoot it, shoot it.'

'Be in no doubt of that,' Richard said, and as he spoke he realised, was almost shocked to realise, that he *would* kill her. 'I'm in no doubt that it's what you want.'

'Try to board the *Argo* tonight, to talk with our oracle. It might help you plan a strategy. I'll be waiting for you.'

Brutally, Jason tugged the Tall Grass Speaker to her feet. Again, as the night before, he tossed the remnants of the food to the dishevelled man in Old Stone Hollow, grinning, waving a hand goodbye.

Throughout the day the noise of repair continued, and the day passed. As night drew in, and torches were lit, Richard armed himself with sword and knife and spent nearly an hour approaching the shore with the utmost caution, his eyes so acutely tuned to the darkness that not even a fly could have moved without his seeing it.

Hera watched him from between her braziers; the lake water lapped calmly; a slight breeze shifted the *Argo*, which creaked in its 'dry dock', the rigging moving and slapping against the wood.

All things were quite peaceful, the argonauts sleeping below their skin tents, one man on watch, but his gaze fixed on the shimmering light of Wide Water Hollowing. Richard crept aboard the ship, past the heavily slumbering form of the smith, and swung through the deck hatch, where Sarin's tiny hands held his legs as he descended.

'Do you have the small fire?' she asked in a whisper, and Richard produced Lytton's lighter, striking flame to a compact torch, which illuminated the cramped hold and displayed the clutter of purloined goods.

The rolls of fleeces were stacked against one wall. Richard picked his way carefully through a crate of armour, mostly helmets patterned with designs that seemed to move with a life of their own. Clay discs, and papyrus scrolls were in another box, the lost languages of lost kings. There were bone horns, glass vases, gold amphorae, necklets and circlets of glittering gemstones, woven carpets with intricate and puzzling designs, such simple things as bunches of reed and rush, two sets of pipes as played by Pan, drums with patterned skins, horribly reminiscent of the shaman drum that the Sons of Kyrdu had once destroyed, and in the far corner, tossed aside as if of no interest, a set of bone pipes with a leather air sac that Richard recognised at once, and with a terrible shock.

They were Lacan's! He saw the black rings on the bass pipe, recognised the peculiarity of the design, felt sick with fear and apprehension. Lacan's favourite possession, here possessed by the butcher of the Aegean.

'What do you know about these?' he whispered urgently to a startled Sarin.

She peered at the bagpipes, then shrugged. 'They came on board with Tisamenus, just two days ago. They were taken from a dead man. Jason thinks they can summon the gods, but he doesn't know which gods, nor how to make the right sounds with them. He's keeping them in case someone recognises their function.'

Richard's heart had sunk at Sarin's words. His eyes filled with tears, his mouth went dry, as he thought of the big man, with his broad sense of humour, dead now. He said quietly, 'A dead man? Are you sure?'

'From a corpse. Yes. Peleus had watched the fight from a distance. I was in the hold when I heard him talking to Jason. Whoever it was, he put up a huge fight and broke Tisamenus' voice box, a rib or two, and two fingers. Tisamenus cut him almost completely in two. I'm sorry . . . I think he must have been a friend.'

'A dear one. The very best . . .'

As he placed Lacan's pipes down, a touch of breath passed through the bag and the deep pipe whined briefly, a last lament, shocking Sarin and reducing Richard to a posture of frozen terror. They listened for movement above, but after a few minutes all remained quiet. 'Be careful,' she said, and led the way to the rear compartment.

In the half-light, the sad figures shifted; a centaur tried to rise, but failed, watching Richard through eyes similar to the creature's that had escaped two days before. This one was female, though. A woman with small horns curled up in a corner; two men, wearing the sort of leathers and greens that suggested they were forest outlaws, were breathing softly as they sat against the hull, all life gone from their eyes. They were chained, but the most protection was afforded to a brawny, silver-haired, silver-armed man, who was held by arms and legs to the floor; the glint of metal on his right arm, the gleam of silver in his mouth, the anger in his eyes, the silence of him, all confirmed that this was Silver Arm, of Irish myth, and Jason was lucky indeed to have subdued him.

There were others, slender, broken shapes, some dressed, some naked, none of them recognisable as to their mythological or legendary natures, all story drained from them, stripped from them, leaving them not fairylike, as Lytton might have imagined, but dead, corrupt in that most human of ways in which, all hope is taken, and all life is made meaningless.

A voice sang sweetly and softly, and by the faint torchlight Richard looked at the far wall and saw five heads dangling by the hair, two of them clearly rotten, two others, red-bearded, alive but silent, watching him through furious eyes, the fifth a thin, youthful face framed with curls of golden hair, beardless, smiling, eyes sparkling as it sang.

But as Richard drew closer so what had seemed signs of youth fell away, and he realised that he was looking at a skull so drawn that it seemed smooth, and yet there *was* vigour in the eyes, the same vigour as in the tumble of thick, sweet-smelling hair. The mouth worked, the thin lips puckering, licked by a yellowed tongue. No breath could have supplied the voice, since the neck was ragged and blackened with blood. Still, though, the head sang, a soft voice, the words meaningless, until suddenly it sang, slowly and carefully, 'Two bloody nicks . . . to the back of his . . neck . . . all for the sake . . . of his lady's green . . . girdle . . .'

Alex's song, from the school play!

The head's eyes filled with sadness and followed Richard as he dropped to a crouch, staring at the monstrosity, asking 'Who are you?'

The sad gaze swivelled toward Sarin, who said, 'It's Orpheus. He's my closest friend. Once he was Jason's friend too, but no longer. Jason says he still loves him, but he searched for a year to find the rocks where this head was wedged, after being torn off by wild women at the gates of Hades, and he stole it, and will sell it. Orpheus can see the fates, so if you help him he will help you. He can see into men's hearts.'

'I know. It just happened . . .'

Behind him one of the green hunters stirred, reacting to the sound of voices. He spoke weakly, the words fluid but incomprehensible for a moment, 'Kenna thow helpa? Kenna thow helpa?' until the dialect resolved into the desperate plea for help that it was.

Sarin shushed him, then turned back to Orpheus, stroking the skull through the tight flesh. 'Sing for our friend. He can help us.'

Orpheus spoke in his own language, and Sarin looked grim as she replied to the wounded hero. Turning to Richard, she explained, 'I told him we'd take him too. We'll find a wizard to build a mechanical body for him. Does your magic extend that far?'

'I'm afraid not. Sorry. And my belief systems are stretched to credibility just seeing what I'm seeing.'

Orpheus sang again, a haunting tune, his eyes closed for a moment, then opening widely and staring at Richard. The voice changed, the words were English, and spoken, now: 'He is with the stone faces, in a place of stone. He is with the tree that runs and speaks. He watches and waits for his father by the oak shroud where the bird spits. He is imprisoned by his own ghosts.'

'Alex? Can you see my son?' Richard crouched eagerly before the head, all thoughts of the impossibility of this situation gone as he detected a reference to Alex again. 'Tell me more. Please! How do I get to him?'

But Orpheus was singing softly again, and in his own language, tears running from the hollow eyes.

A living head. No breath being pumped from lungs to activate the vocal cords, but a head, nevertheless, that sang and spoke, and gave oracles, and had seen Alex. Was this a dream? Had Jason spiked the wine with so subtle a drug that Richard was now existing in two states of consciousness, the real and the falsely lucid?

He scrambled back through the gully and into Old Stone Hollow.

A talking head! Orpheus himself, rent by the nails of the Thracian women after he had offended them in some way. Was it because he had looked back into Hades after abandoning Eurydice? Richard couldn't remember the legend. The head had been thrown into the river Hebrus, had become wedged between rocks and continued to sing for years. Jason, in his new profession as collector of oddities, had sought the oracle that was his old friend, and would trade it to the highest bidder. Richard, in his own way, needed to purloin the head, to have it, to hold it, to use it to find Alex.

But how could he alone invade the *Argo*, destroy the argonauts and liberate the oppressed creatures in its dungeon? The only way, surely, was to entice the crew of the *Argo* into the defensive field around the Station. But they would be wary, now, having seen the earth itself consume Peleus.

At dawn, the nesting herons in the woods behind the Station woke him with the clattering of their bills. A hard wind was blowing through the high grass, and from the cave below the cliff, from the hollow itself, came the sound of voices, distorted and haunting. He had spent a night dreaming of Alex and Helen, and in those dreams he had felt effective in their rescue. Now, in this breezy, mournful dawn, he felt the wood tug at him, sensed smells and detected the minutiae of movement in the forest that suggested he was becoming more attuned. His edge vision was restless again, and the breath was tight in his lungs. He felt happiest with his hands spread on the cold earth, as if this allowed strength into him. The taste in his mouth seemed to be satisfied by lapping quickly at the dew on the tall grass and he scampered on hands and feet, over a rough hummock that he didn't recognise, letting the moisture drench him, freshen him and invigorate him . . .

He stood suddenly, slapping at his cheeks.

What the hell am I doing? I can't afford to go bosky!

The bill-clattering faded. The breeze still disturbed him as he walked through the grass to the closed gates and eased them open. There was a cloth-wrapped object on the far bank, another gift perhaps from the nervous argonauts. Had they come during the night, or at dawn? He had slept so heavily . . .

His mind's eye began to clear, and the hummock in the Station resolved into the unnatural and new feature that it was. He had crawled right over it, moments ago, when he had been lapping up the sun-dew. He went back, now, back through the maze path, looking for the crushed grass that told of his bosky-transit, and there, suddenly, was the body of the man. It was overgrown. The suckers of ivy and grape-vine had penetrated the crumbling flesh. The man was sprawled on his side, one arm behind his back, still holding a bronze sword. His neck was bent back, his mouth agape and sprouting dog mercury. The grey hair was still visible on the decaying skull, a purple headband identifying the dead man as one of the argonauts.

So; you brought me a gift, then crossed the river to kill me . . .

He picked up the sword, removed the headband from the skull, which puffed into dust as he struck it with the back of his hand. With the band around the hilt of the bronze sword he crossed the stream and investigated the offering; an elaborately decorated long bone, the etchings ingrained with gold, the bulbous head, where it had once articulated in a hip joint, shaped into a grinning face. Richard covered the grotesque bone, unsure whether this was intended to frighten him, or had been offered as a gift in exchange for some of his own magic.

Distantly, a hunting horn sounded, not the shrill, metallic sound of the twentieth century, but a duller, more resonant call that ranged in tone and was clearly produced by the bellowing of a man through the grooved horn of an animal. The sound came from beyond the Sanctuary. Richard's hearing was acute, perhaps because of the isolation he had experienced for the last few months. He sensed that there were five men running. A creature on four legs fled from them. They crashed through undergrowth and cantered over clearer ground, and for a few minutes Richard stood by the slope, turning to follow the distant action.

Jason was determined to have his centaur back.

On the beach, the *Argo* was now half in the lake water. The mast was up, the cross-beam tied, the sail rigged and furled. The effigy of Hera had been replaced on board, and glared inland across a deck that was piled high with supplies, ready for stowing. The tent was still pegged to the shore, and several argonauts moved about domestic business, while a circle of four guards crouched, weapons in hand, very alert as they watched the wood. One of them was certainly aware of Richard, who observed the proceedings from his special place, but the man made no movement towards him. The smith was in the small skiff with another man, peering down through the lake waters, a hundred yards from the shore.

The hunting horn sounded again, a fluctuating note on the shifting, rising breeze. There was quite a wind, now. The lake water was choppy. The fires on the lake shore shed smoke in gusting streams. Richard eased his way back along the gully, and approached the Station, aware of the sighing and creaking of the forest around him. The wind was almost sinister. The tall grass in the compound rippled: the huge effigy outside the gate swayed on its stand, rags flapping. The gates of the Station banged on their hinges.

As Richard approached his home, the centaur suddenly appeared. It had been lurking inside the palisade. Its eyes were huge, its mouth slick with saliva, and it was dropping dung uncontrollably, as if terrified.

'They haven't got you yet, then? Are you looking for sanctuary?'

'Hide me . . .' the pathetic creature whispered, repeating the request three times.

Richard tugged its mane, trying to avoid its breath. 'Of course I will. Jason can't harm you inside Old Stone Hollow. There are defences here . . .'

The centaur seemed to relax, even though it couldn't have understood the words: its request to 'hide me' was almost certainly part of its education from Sarin. It shuffled nervously, its tail waving, its human chest expanded so that ribs and cords of muscle showed through the black hide. It backed away from Richard, back into the compound, eyes oddly imploring.

'The defences,' Richard said again, and the herons clattered their bills, distracting him, and a shrike called, and rooks, nesting in a high elm, cawed, while the wind brought the scents of sweat and groin, powerful smells that made Richard nervous. Yet when he looked around he could see nothing but the black man-beast, backing away from him.

The defences . . .

He realised with a terrible shock that the humming of the generator was no longer part of the sounds of the wood. Glancing quickly to the right, he ascertained that the glint of red light, the infra-red, was not there.

The generator was down!

He stepped quickly into the Station. The centaur made a sound, half fear, half laughter, then galloped behind him. Richard turned to watch the creature, which now pawed nervously at the ground by the gates, watching him, saliva streaming from its lower lip, eyes blinking furiously and nostrils twitching.

'A trap,' Richard said calmly. He turned back to the compound. There was an odd sound, a swish of air, followed by a second, then a third. He saw nothing in the rippling grass or among the waving trees that hid the path to Old Stone Hollow itself, but when he glanced back at the centaur he saw an arrow protruding from the creature's mouth. The man-face was wide-eyed with shock as it collapsed onto its forelegs. A second arrow jutted from its chest, a third dangling in the shallow skin of its shoulder.

And then Lacan's bagpipes wailed, the sound like a mocking sigh, breaking into the rhythm of a mocking laugh.

The fourth arrow, loosed now, sliced the air as Richard turned back to the cave. He saw it coming, but it was too fast. It struck the superficial flesh of his left arm and passed all the way through. The pain was strangely remote, and he lifted his forearm as if nothing had happened, then held his hand against the flow of blood as the bright woodland near the cave darkened with movement, and nine men, cloaked and hooded, all but one masked, stepped into the open and walked slowly through the wind-whipped grass towards their prey.

It was a moment of silence, oddly peaceful, nothing but the murmur of wind, the susurration of the grass, and the flap and slap of skins as the nine figures moved in a wide arc, closing on Richard. Jason was foremost, carrying a spear and the bone pipes, his glittering eyes filled with amusement as he watched from below his hood. 'Your magic is finished,' he said in stilted English, waving a hand at the generator tent.

'Don't be so sure,' Richard said, the wound in his arm beginning to hurt.

Jason shrugged. Sarin would have given him the words to speak, but he couldn't understand the reply. He simply repeated, 'Your magic is finished. Richard. Hollow. Magic finished.' And laughed, coming right up to Richard and striking him a stunning blow to the face. Richard fell and was sick. Jason squeezed the leather bag of the pipes, making a series of punctuated howls, like a tuneless jig, that caused laughter among the argonauts. As Richard half rose he saw one of them working the arrows from the cadaver of the centaur. When the weapons were recovered, he kicked the body into the river.

Poor betrayed beast. It had perhaps been promised its freedom if it helped entice Richard into the compound, where Jason was waiting. Its usefulness gone, its worth on the market limited, perhaps, Jason had decided to lighten the *Argo*'s cargo load. He had a new object to sell, now.

But if Richard entertained the idea that he was now one of Jason's objects of interest to the citadels of the Aegean, he was mistaken. Though led through the gully to the *Argo*, he was paid scant attention. His wound was treated and bound, and from Jason's murmured words Richard got the sense that the arrow hadn't been intended for him at all.

He was more concerned by the fact that the ship was now afloat. The below-water repairs were complete, and carpenters were working on the upper hull from the inside, braced among the branches of the sacred oak.

The wind brought rain, a dark thundercloud that poured across the lake, and made the morning seem like night. The tent was rapidly re-erected on the beach, and two small fires lit. Richard huddled in this miserable place, ignored by Jason for a while, free to run if he wanted, strangely reluctant to do so.

When Jason eventually came into this billowing shelter again, he was leading Sarin by a leather leash, tied tightly around her neck. Through the drum of rain, the woman said grimly, 'The gods must have helped him with the *Argo*. The ship was unseaworthy yesterday: now it's sufficiently repaired that he's proposing to sail back through the storm channel.'

'The storm channel?'

'The passage here, a raging storm between sea rocks, too narrow for large ships. It's how he escaped the war galleys of the Titan Polymnus, which were about to ram us and destroy us. The gateway is out on the lake, he knows that. But he's frightened. He thinks there must be a trick, and he believes you can help him understand the nature of what happened. If he sails into the lake, will he pass back to his own world? Will Polymnus be waiting for him? Or will he sail into another of the god's cages, like this place? Hera hasn't spoken to him for days. He thinks he's being tested, but he doesn't know for what.'

Jason watched Richard all the time, his face quite expressionless, waiting for the other man's response.

It occurred to Richard in an instant that there might be a way to separate Jason from his crew. He tried not to look too apprehensive. It would be difficult to contrive.

'There are many worlds beyond the lake,' he said, and Jason frowned as Sarin informed him of this. Richard described the dark lakes of Tuonela, the wild, icy seas of the Irish coast, the endless rivers through dense forest, marshes filled with brackish water that were home to heron-people, and offered no comfort at all. To pass back to his own, warm seas Jason would have to worship at a shrine. The shrine was on the hill, above Old Stone Hollow. It was a sanctuary of stones, and the far-sighted might be privileged to glimpse their destination.

Jason thought long and hard, staring at Richard with an almost corrosive gaze, grumbling in his throat, winding and unwinding the leather of Sarin's leash around his brawny fingers. Richard felt his knees begin to tremble as he crouched, damp and cold below the sagging, dripping hides of this crude shelter. Jason was not convinced.

'Tell him,' Richard said, 'that I have lived in this place for many years. I have seen heroes pass through, some wary of me, some befriending me. He has destroyed the source of my magic, but not my vision.' Sarin translated as Richard spoke. 'Tell him that Hercules camped for five days in the Sanctuary and told me in detail of the quest for the fleece and that he had seen Medea dismembered and hung in pieces, still alive, from a giant cedar tree, where silver-crested crows feed upon . . .'

Jason half rose, his eyes widening. 'Where? Where did Hercules see this?'

'He saw it through the shrine. There is a place of vision on the hill. Medea did not live long after the murder of your sons and second wife. A simulacrum took her place.'

This clearly conflicted with Jason's own knowledge, but he was intrigued. 'A simulacrum? Medea dead?' There was spittle at the edges of his mouth, and his skin, below the stubbly beard, was flushed. Tiny creases in his forehead gave the lie to his calm: he was furious, he was angry, he wanted this vision for himself.

'Medea dead!' he repeated, staring into the distance.

'Medea among the living dead, all magic gone, the object of ridicule from passing heroes.'

And Jason smiled! He stood, tugged Sarin roughly to her feet, then eased the pressure, rubbing a thick thumb over the bruising around her neck as he glared at Richard and said, 'Then take me to see this place.'

He bellowed orders. The sons of the Dioscuri cloaked-up heavily and picked short spears from the weapons pile, walking through the downpour to pin Jason. Aeneus came too, the rain running from the smooth, yellow-metalled helmet that covered his face to the gaping mouth, where broken teeth gleamed between thin greying lips.

These three guardians followed Jason through the gully, and Richard led them to the Sanctuary, to the ruined stones.

Where was the hollowing? It had only been a few months, but the wood had changed, grown denser . . .

He swept a stick through the ground elder, slapped at the carved pillars, ducked and weaved through this overgrown place of ruins. His eyes were alert for anything familiar, and he knew, too, that a hollowing led away from here, and that it was essential not to step through it.

A glimpse of red caught his eye, and he moved aside the ivy at the base of a standing stone to find a small hollow-stick, a much-rotted doll, but the red fabric of its body still tightly tied. Triumphantly he picked the effigy up and held it to Jason, who backed away, raising his spear.

Now Richard could orientate. The stone was part of the original arch, but the top had fallen. Was it still the gateway that he had taken with Helen, that time in the past? He began to move about the clearing, while the Dioscuri watched him suspiciously and Aeneus stared at him through the sinister eyeholes of his helmet. Sarin smiled, chewing on her finger, half aware that Richard was trying to trap her master.

Richard moved round the arch, then faced Jason, his arms wide, his head thrown back. 'It's here,' he said loudly, and Sarin whispered the words.

'I can't see anything,' Jason said.

'Come here, then, and look between the pillars,' Richard urged, backing away and beckoning to Jason. For a moment he thought Jason would bring the woman with him, but the argonaut let go of Sarin's leash. He glanced at the Dioscuri arid whispered something to them. Then, with his spear held ready and his black cloak wrapped tightly against the drizzling rain, he walked toward Richard . . .

For a moment Jason seemed to hesitate. Richard thought he had begun to move in slow motion. The light around him changed and the Dioscuri shouted in alarm, backing away. Sarin gasped and crouched, like an animal about to flee. Jason stared at Richard then spoke quickly and with meaning before his face slowly melted into a scowl, becoming a rage, the flesh blackening, the eyes deepening, radiating a terrible if futile menace, a menace touched by a sudden death's head smile.

He was still walking. He had been caught by the hollowing, and a second or so later he vanished completely from view. Richard had the sensation of being struck, but it may have been a leaf blown on the wet wind. The Dioscuri had fled. Aeneus stood, staring from behind his helmet mask, then he too turned and walked quickly down the hill.

'Where did he go?' Sarin asked in the sudden silence. 'I heard the statue of the goddess, screaming.'

'A long way away. Where Hera cannot control him. And for Jason there's no coming back, now. His newest adventure is one that no one will sing about.' He hesitated, watching the rain-drenched woman. 'What did he say? What were his last words?'

'He shouted, "I didn't see the trap. Well done! Though it won't hold me. So now you *should* start watching your back!"'

She shuddered, arms around her body, dark eyes enthralled by the silent stones that had consumed her tormentor.

'You banished him. I thought your magic was dead. Jason killed the humming rock, the source of your power. I thought you were finished.'

'He should have believed his own insight: true magic is in here, in the *jelly*.' Richard tapped his head. Scents and sounds swirled around him. He was dizzy with triumph and the wood. The rain had different odours, different textures. It ran down his skin, through his hair, through his clothes, and seemed to converse with him. Sarin's small hand tugged at his arm.

'Are you leaving me?'

He stared at her, frowning. 'Leaving you?'

'A spirit has you. You have the look of faraway. Are you leaving me?'

'I'm trying not to . . .'

She led him quickly back to the river, then through the gully. They had heard shouting on the shore, the sounds of frightened men. The *Argo* had been launched and was out on the lake, drifting slowly towards the hollowing, its sail furled, its oars out and steady, ready to strike. It was running away. On the shore, a motley collection of creatures huddled in the rain. Aeneus, or whoever had taken command, had decided to empty the hold of living creatures, perhaps unnerved by the thought of the magic they possessed. The two forest hunters were already moving surreptitiously around the lake, scanning the woods, looking for a pathway in. The female centaur was drinking at the lake's edge. The horned woman, wrapped now in a fleece, was cradling the open-mouthed head of Orpheus.

Even from the gully, Richard could tell that Orpheus was dead, that his singing days were finished.

The centaur bolted suddenly, disappearing among the rocks and calling out as it entered the forest. The *Argo* was rocked and the waters thrashed. Sarin cried out and hid her eyes as the serpentine tail of the lake creature wrapped suddenly and sinuously around the broken hull of the vessel, knocking men and women from the deck, snapping the oars like matchwood. The creature's head emerged and the argonauts shrieked. The *Argo* buckled, cracked, the sail spar shattered. As men and women dived for the unlikely safety of the lake the creature rolled, taking the *Argo* with it, vanishing suddenly amidst a storm and explosion of blue water.

Then one by one the swimmers heading for the shore screamed and were gone, the last being the shade of Aeneus himself who made it to the shore and was standing when the open-mawed beast flung itself suddenly through the shallows and dragged him back. Others had swum for the hollowing. Richard watched them reach the grey water and slowly vanish, emerging no doubt into the middle of a wild sea, to face a terrible drowning.

The hunters had gone, merging stealthily with the wood. The horned woman came up to the gully and gave the head of Orpheus to Sarin. Then she kissed the other woman, touched a rough-skinned hand to Richard's beard, before wading into the water and walking steadily into obscurity.

'Will I be safe?'

Sarin's words pulsed on the wind. Richard had a scent, though; it was coming on the rain. He crouched and brushed the water against his nose, smelling, lapping at it. The woman touched him, the ridges of her fingers sliding over his bristling skin. Her odour was strong, and the head of Orpheus was a faint sound as its final songs sang in the jelly of its skull, though no sound came from its mouth. The wind turned, the breeze stroked and curled, the rain shifted, the scents and touches of nature embraced Richard, and the stink-trail suddenly touched him in his heart.

He straightened and cried out. *It was her!* He sniffed hard, then breathed slowly and deeply, waving his hands through the drizzling rain, touching the play of aromas. She was signalling to him. She had touched his heart once before, now she called to him. The scent-trail rose from his groin to his throat and he cried her name. *Helen!*

Frightened, the dark-skinned woman scampered away from him, into the Hollow, through the rain-lashed grass and into the longhouse. Richard followed, a part of him wanting to see that she was safe. Then he closed the gates, howled his pleasure and moved with the scent into the overhang below the cliff, huddling there until the night came, the rain eased, the wind dropped and the stink-trail hardened, gusting from the hole in the ground, below the running creatures . . .

Bosky

The paintings flowed; they were not paintings at all. They were alive, they were vital, they were shadow herds, moving in a great, steaming mass across the rock, across the face of the world, thundering across the grasslands.

He rose to his feet, turning as the huge shapes drummed and billowed past him, and he ran with them, following the broken ground, his face wet with the rank foam that sprayed from their stretched mouths, their lolling tongues. He drew a new strength from the power of the great beasts and grasped at the thick and heavy hair that streamed from their dark hides. He followed the movement of the sun as it glinted on the curved horns and was carried by the power of the herd. Smaller creatures ran too, white-backed, grey-flanked, high-horned, slender-legged. He pranced with them on the rumbling earth, then loped with grey wolves that raced across the grassland, all moving towards the great cavern. The world was vibrant, the earth a deep and resonant drumbeat, the air thick with mud and spray, the sky darkened by huge backs. He ran with them, the scent-trail strong in his nostrils despite the dung and sweat and animal breath of the running herds.

When the earth of the hollow closed around him it was cold. The sounds of the herds became faint. He plunged through darkness into the coiling passages of the world underground, squirming and crawling through the narrow spaces, every finger alive to the smooth, damp rock, the slick stone, his body like that of a snake as he pulled himself deeper through the dark. The earth around him still thundered and shook as the herds of bison and gazelle found their own paths down into the odd world, not of dreams, or the real, but a place between the two. Water fell, hard and cold, from a high ledge in a great dark cavern, into a second system of passages, and he slipped down, following the flow, hands briefly brushing marbled human figures, his eyes glimpsing the stony faces, his nostrils flaring as he again responded to the scents of the wood that lay at the far end of the cave system, and the sweet and beckoning woman who waited for him there.

The cold water carried him. It entered him, bathed him, washed him, clothed him. He slipped and slid, ducked and crawled where the cavern narrowed, ran blindly when it widened, shedding everything that was false upon him, a trail of clothes like skins, letting the stone air and rock spray form a miasma around his taut and sensitised flesh.

He was aware that time passed, but in the absolute dark he measured its passing by the flow of dreams and voices that ebbed and surged, touching his eyes, his heart, his laughter.

At last he crawled out of the earth, emerging through the rock and the turf, clinging to the swollen root of a massive tree. He had been following the root for many dreams, through the lower darkness, embracing its softer texture where it emerged from the icy stone in which it was embedded. The trunk of the tree extended above him, filling his whole view as he rose to his feet, naked and filthy. The colours of the interlocking masks were bright despite the gloom cast by the huge spread of the canopy. He stumbled and jumped across the spread bf surface roots, then scampered into the brush at the edge of the Mask Tree's vast glade, looking back at the faces carved there, old faces, weathered and stained, overlain with newer, brighter shapes. The more he looked the more he was able to see among the horned heads, the wide eyes, the oddly gaping mouths, the grins – a thousand masks etched and gouged on the black trunk of the oak, each one watching him from its own forgotten time.

The tree affected him strongly. Somewhere in the maze of faces a sweeter face watched him, a boy, an earnest child – but he couldn't see the eyes, only sense them, and he curled down into the leaf litter, rubbed soil and crushed grass over his skin, smelled the ground and let the miasma strengthen.

After a while the vague sense of distress and loss that affected him in the glade passed away and he moved at ease through the wildwood, through the dappled light, gathering the scents of rose and wood anemone, bud and sap, gathering all of these to the miasma that flowed with him. The scent-trail which he still followed was strong, and he knew the woman was close. When the land dropped towards a moist hollow, filled with thorn and hazel thickets, he knew he had found her. The place was warm and hazy, the ground marshy, in shifting light as the taller trees that crowded and loomed over the dell moved to an unfelt breeze. A stream flowed at the bottom of the hollow, separating two banks, where briar and thistle grew densely, and as he looked from one bank to the other he saw her bower, a thickening in the copse of hawthorn and hazel, where grasses and dead branches had been woven into the thicket to create a protective wall, and a warm shelter.

He went to the stream and the miasma flowed around him, attracting more scents. The light from above made the fine mist in the hollow seem to glow. Through that bright, gently shifting veil, he watched the bower, and if he concentrated he could see her moving. She watched him too, but drew back into deep cover when their eyes met.

He couldn't decide if he should approach or not, and he crouched by the stream, splashing at the water, letting the heavy stillness of the dell envelop him, learning from the faint sounds where the nests were above, and the warrens and passages through the earth and hollow boles around.

At last he crossed the stream, drawing the miasma with him like a cloak, and ascended the bank, through the briar and bramble that she had laid in lines and patches where the ground was more open. The hawthorn bower shook to her sudden movement and a dart penetrated his flesh painfully, then another, thin slivers of white wood tipped with a blue stain. He turned and scampered back to safety.

He constructed a warm, dry place in a thicket, making a bed of ferns covered with grass, a crude roof of dead wood and the broad leaves of sycamore. From here, each dawn, he watched the hawthorn bower.

At first light the grass-covered woman slipped through her own defences to the brook, to crouch, sing, and drink, her body tense, her head always cocked, her eyes and ears alert for danger. Her hair was black and streaked with more silver than his dream-memory of her recognised. It fell loosely around her face, where bright, dark eyes flashed and a full and sensuous mouth opened to sing or drink. She was always moist, and light sparkled on her body. She was adept at brushing small fish onto the bank, stunning them and storing them in a leaf pouch. She always carried the thin pipe with its poisoned darts and if he stirred she raised it threateningly.

His arm and neck itched infuriatingly where the fungal toxins had penetrated his skin.

Each dawn when she had finished she would return through the haze, the thick miasma of heat and scent, and it was his turn. She would watch him from cover, sometimes singing in her reedy voice.

Animals came to drink, and he learned to snare hares, (he occasional, incautious fowl, a heron, and on one occasion a small pig. Without fire, the flesh was chewy, that of the hare strong and bloody, but exquisitely reviving.

The days in the dell were long, the moist warmth stifling at times. There was a silence and a stillness about the place, broken only by the brook and the restless murmur of birds. The nests of herons woke him each dawn with the clattering of their bills. Huge crows cawed and cackled from a colony nearby, and somewhere in a thicket deer were living. He could hear the male bark, the doe cough. But he never saw them, though their air flowed into the dell and mingled with the miasma of odours that formed each dawn above the brook.

Each dusk he returned to the Mask Tree and sat among the sprawling roots, staring up at the ancient faces. There were many things that tickled memories in his head, such familiarity, but no words or names came to him, only images of strange men, strange creatures, hints of stories, and the occasional thought of a bright boy running through tall grass, holding something wooden above his head that suddenly escaped him and soared into the sky, an unflapping bird.

He felt sad sometimes, but the sadness lifted as night shadow made the tree faces invisible, and only the monstrous black bole faced him. At this time he would stand against the trunk, his body almost enfolded by one of the deep channels in the thick bark. If he listened hard, if he blocked from his mind the chatter of nightjars, the rustle of voles and weasels, the furtive movement of cats and pigs, the flutter of nestlings, he could hear songs in the tree, but the words meant nothing. When he himself sang he sang with words that shaped the tune, and stirred feelings in his chest and stomach, yet meant nothing to the mind above – he had ears and eyes and thoughts only for the woman in the hawthorn bower.

One dawn, the scent miasma had changed. It stirred him deeply. It was sour-sweet, exciting, and he ran along the brook, splashing furiously, circling through the underbrush before crossing the brook and staring expectantly at the bower.

The leaves moved, eyes watched. The new scent flowed down the bank, encompassing him. His body reacted with pleasure and he closed his eyes for a long moment. But the bower remained shut. He whooped, called and sang, then returned to his shelter. When he was back, and out of harm's way, the bower opened and she came down to drink.

He watched her hungrily, silently. There was something different about her. She had tied her hair into a single frond at the back. Her breasts were naked and she washed them carefully. Her legs and waist were still thick with grass, but when she turned to run back up the bank, he saw that her buttocks were naked too, and without the usual caking of mud. When she stooped to enter the bower the breath caught in his throat before he could *whoop* his call. Sweat suddenly beaded his skin.

As he watched the strutting of birds by the brook, and later two hares on their hind legs, boxing and rolling in the grass, memories surfaced from the edge of dreams of men dancing by the light of high, roaring fires, which gave brilliance, by reflection, to the colours of cloaks and the gold of masks and helmets. As the dream dissolved he went to scavenge for leaves and feathers, to make himself the ritual garments of display, a primal urge impelling him to decorate himself.

All day he constructed his display. He used thin splinters of tough grass to sew leaves of birch down each of his arms, and of oak across his chest, and of shining beech, emerald green, down the fronts of his legs. He was careful to pierce only the surface skin and not draw blood, which would add the wrong scent to the miasma.

He selected long heron feathers for his chin, working them through the long, thick hairs of his dark beard so that they hung like a white fringe. Black crow tail feathers formed a fringe across the base of his belly. He used chalk and light clay on the exposed skin of his body, then dabbed the purple and red juices of sloe and belladonna to make eyes on the clay-white.

Instinct told him that this would make a good impression.

Finally he used a mixture of resin, sap and clay to stiffen his long hair, raising it into a crest that spanned his head from ear to ear. It took a long time, and it was almost dusk before he was ready. When he moved at last to the brook, the first of night had descended. A bright moon made the water gleam, the leaves on his body shine, his whitened skin glow. As he crawled to the brook, watching the hawthorn bower, he saw the leaves rustle and part, and he stood up slowly, arms stretched, legs apart. When the bower window remained open he grinned and wiggled his hips, then did a slow turn, and so began his first dance.

At the end of the dance he sang the first calling song. His voice was loud in the still night air and the herons clattered above him, irritating him as he summoned forgotten words and melodies from his other life.

But when the song was over, the bower window closed. He frowned, thought hard, then turned twice and started his second dance, drawing the miasma around him, feeling the condensing moisture with its stinks and perfumes of the wood. He danced a wide circle through the wood and returned to the bank of the brook. The bower window was open again. He cast quick glances at it as he turned and whistled, and when his back was to the bower he allowed a smile to touch his face. His heart was racing with anticipation.

At the end of the moon, however, she was still inside the hawthorn wall.

Disappointed and exhausted, he returned to the shelter, though as he stooped to enter the dry place she emerged and sang slowly and sweetly from the top of the bank, a brief call, thanking him.

Delightedly, he whistled back.

He couldn't sleep. The earth shook below him, sounded strange. The trees that surrounded the dell, its brook arid bowers, trembled and shifted, as if a storm was coming. At some point, in the depth of the dark, a horse rode through, breathless, burdened by a man's shape, which struck at the low branches. Later, four foxes came to drink, barked, fled when something stirred in the hazel scrub. He watched that dark shape apprehensively, the faint gleam on tusks. He had sensed it, but not how big it was, and for a while he wondered if it was watching and waiting for him as prey. He was relieved when, after a few hours, he heard it move away.

At dawn, he danced again, before drinking from the cold water of the brook. Then he returned to the Mask Tree and stood with his back to the carved and painted faces, feeling the enfolding bark, letting the air and aroma drift across him, watching the day's shadows pass with the sun, the light on leaves, the movement of trees and fern, the restless passage of clouds in the far distance, at the edge of the great canopy overhead.

And then at dusk he danced for the hawthorn bower with renewed energy. He crossed the brook and ventured up the bank to the lines of briar, turned and called, sang a song that had arisen in his soul like a dream, when he had been standing by the Mask Tree.

He retreated to the stream and waited for the night and dark. When the dell was bright with moonglow he danced again, in his own miasma, singing vigorously, and this time she emerged from the bower, approaching the brook slowly, entering the scent cloak around him, her body wrapped in grasses, her hair flowing, the streaks of silver bright.

She did a quick dance of her own, then laughed as he responded vigorously, encouraging him, before bounding off, disappearing into the night, following the curving bank of the brook, out of the dell and into the deep wood.

He leapt into the air and raced after her, drawing the miasma with him.

All night she led him on a wild and sensuous chase through the deepwood. He had known her in another dream. He remembered her pleasures, and they sang to each other from oak, ash, glade and earthen bank. Soon – it was that deathly time before dawn – they came to a high stone rise, a sheer wall of grey rock, carved with grim faces, and draped with ivy. She turned back from this rain, then led the way to a dry-earth place, among small trees without thorn or rose briar, and here she danced and sang for a while, before beckoning for him.

He stepped quickly through the trees, grasped her and they fell to the ground. She shredded the leaves from his arms and chest, tore the crow-feathers from his belly and held him. He bit through the grass knots and uncovered her, entwined his fingers with her hair, pressed his body against hers. Her mouth was soft and wet, her taste familiar and exquisite, the touch of her skin thrilling as they rolled together on the dry ground.

Midges plagued his back, biting hard; a mosquito droned faintly near his ear; an earthworm slid through the fingers of his hand as he grasped the raw earth for support; but he was in the earth with her, and the smells of earth and sweat, of blood and her mouth filled his senses, filled hers, and they moved frantically, then gently, then vigorously again, but always together, his mouth going down on hers when she began to scream, so that he drank the sound and the pleasure, sucking every cry, every tremor, every arching thrust of her body against his own, until after a long while she fell back breathless, holding his skin, his damp flesh, easing him to the edge of her body, then tugging him deep again, giggling and teasing.

When she had finished kissing him she lay below him, peaceful, breathing gently, looking up through the canopy, at the stark light, the shifting light, but listening to furtive movement inside the cold, false stone of the ruin close by.

The miasma flowed over them as the night changed, and the death-less dawn crept through the grass and the fine roots of the trees, and the pores of the leaves. Everything was suddenly very cold, very wet. A new vibrancy flowed suddenly about the lovers and the earth wrapped them with tendrils, feeding on the chemicals on their skin before drawing back.

And as dawnlight replaced the dark, Richard rolled away from the curled woman beside him and entered a lucid dream state in which he murmured her name and his own, and began to remember who he was, and the events at Old Stone Hollow.

He was cold, and curled into a ball, and he was tired, so he dozed, aware of movement and whispering all around.

Skin of Stone

At some time during the waking of their bodies and the reawakening of their minds, Helen had risen and left the clearing in the trees. Fully conscious again, Richard followed her and found her by the high stone wall, a greyish, naked shape in the morning haze, her long hair thrown back as she stared at the stone faces above her. Richard approached and she turned, stared darkly at him for a moment, then smiled and reached for him. They hugged for a long time, shivering slightly, rubbing each other's backs for warmth. 'I have a feeling you were glad to see me,' she said dryly.

'You remind me of someone I once knew. Helen Silverlock . . .'

A tighter hug, a longer shiver.

'I hoped you'd find me,' she said. 'It's been a hell of a long wait. I buried Dan a long time ago, back at the Station. I've missed you.'

Her words reminded him of the note she'd left, in another time, a misplaced time. Should he mention it? He decided not, saying simply, 'When Lacan described the process of going "bosky" to me, he made it sound dreamlike and silent, a great deal of communing with the rustling leaves and lapping lake waters. It wasn't like that at all. First I went on a mad stampede with herds of bison and gazelles and packs of wolves, then I followed your smell, acted out some sort of mating ritual, hunted you through the wood and became totally and absolutely rampant.'

'And so did I,' she said quickly, perhaps sensing the apology that was about to be expressed, and silencing it with a grin and a direct look. 'I wanted you very much.'

'Me too.'

'And wasn't it wonderful?'

'I certainly feel a lot better. Thank you.'

She pinched him very hard, sharing his smile. He went on, 'My mouth is full of mud and leaf mould. I'm scratched and bitten . . . and

I think I jabbed a crow's feather into your rump . . . at one of the more passionate moments . . . ?'

'You did. I forgive you. Try to control yourself next time.'

'I coated myself with clay and feathers. I pranced around by the brook like a prize prat, singing to you. God knows what I was singing . . .'

She suddenly laughed, dark eyes wide with delight, then kissed him on the mouth. 'But you were *wonderful*! I was half aware of the songs because they were familiar from *this* life, and half responding to them like a bird responding to a mating call. Sound pheromones! But you really aroused me – the primitive me – even though you were singing such funny things. That's what brought me out of the bower, dragged along by my own instincts.'

'For God's sake – *what* did I sing?'

She did a little bobbing dance, arms slightly out from her sides, knees bending, silver-dark hair falling over her breasts, eyes twinkling with mischief as she sang, 'Love, love me, *DO*.'

'*Beatles* songs?' Richard cried. 'I sang *Beatles* songs? You're joking!'

But memory came back; full, horrifying and embarrassing memory.

'Christ. I *did*. And Presley: *There's a place for us*.'

'Uhhuh.'

'And then suddenly *you* sang. *I can't get no satisfaction*.'

'Which at that time I couldn't. But you seemed to remember how much I liked the Rolling Stones. You chased me through the wood singing "Jumping Jack Flash"!'

'I did . . . I remember now. Oh my God . . .'

Laughing, she said, 'I thought that was great. You almost blew it the first evening, though, singing Beach Boys stuff. And something about, *I am the very model of a modern Major General*.'

He groaned. 'Gilbert and Sullivan? Dressed in leaves and feathers, in the middle of the night, in the middle of a wildwood, I tried to seduce you with *The Pirates of Penzance*? Oh God. This is going to be hard to explain to our children.'

'Talking of which . . .'

She pulled away from him, walked towards the stone wall. 'Do you recognise this place?'

'Yes. But it feels dead.'

It was a hard feeling to articulate. It was not just that it was ruined, but there was no *life* to it of any form. The trees that grew over it, the ivy that spread across its walls, the space between its stone buttresses and the nearby woodland, all these things were *silent*. There was an emptiness of spirit. It was an abandoned place.

'Dead, yes,' Helen said. 'But not dead enough. There's someone inside. He's been watching us. I think I know who it is . . .'

With a frisson of both excitement and apprehension, Richard whispered, 'Alex!'

But Helen said, 'No. Not Alex. A more recent arrival at the ruins.'

In her time in the bower, in her time in the otherworldly state of nature that the Station knew as 'bosky', Helen had become adept at creating warm and protective clothing from the living and dried fabrics of nature. Ivy, both thin and thick, could be used to create a clothing frame, then cross-stitched with grasses, or strong plant stems, and in-filled with soft litter, or broad leaves. She dressed them both in minutes, and though the vestments itched and scratched, the hard chill that had begun to become intrusive became limited to hands and feet.

As she worked, Richard enthralled her with details of his encounter with Jason and the *Argo*. Then he asked her about the last three years of her own life, after the Long Man had snatched him away and carried him back to Oak Lodge. 'It was as if he knew where I wanted to go.'

She nodded agreement. 'That's what I eventually realised. I'd passed him twice, trying to find my way back to the Station, but he didn't see me. I couldn't get out of that land no matter how hard I tried. I must have been there six, seven months. Eventually I confronted the Long Man, said yes when he asked me "Helpen?" and he took me back to the Station. That's his function in legend: to lead you home. I don't know his full story.

'McCarthy found his own way back, following shadows of course, but he died soon after. He was never very strong. And then one day, Lytton turned up. I thought he'd been killed by the Jack-chapel, but no. It spat him out . . .'

'That's what Elizabeth said.'

'You've seen Elizabeth?'

'Briefly.'

Richard told her of the encounter that had brought him back to Ryhope. When he described Elizabeth's abduction, Helen closed her eyes and shook her head. 'Poor woman. She had it so hard those last few months . . .'

When Helen had finally returned to Old Stone Hollow, there was news of Dan. 'That's why I didn't come and find you. I was missing you very much.' She smiled almost wistfully. 'I felt I'd known you for a long time. But I went off looking for Dan, and that was a year's journey, and I found him, what was left of him. And buried him. Lytton by then had scoured Huxley's papers again, and worked out how Alex's shadow might be loose in the wood. He sent me to get you . . . you weren't there . . . I don't understand what went wrong, yet. But anyway, I left the note, came back, and Trickster struck at us from the cave. It was no more than a shadow, all claws, tusks and destruction. It tried to eat Lytton. It killed Wakeman, and pursued me for days. I couldn't handle the confrontation. I wasn't even sure this was *my* Coyote. Then I went bosky, came here, close to the tree covered with faces, and made my home. God alone knows how long I've inhabited that dell. But something stirred in me, waking me up, when you came along. Singing your little songs . . .' She laughed again, shaking her head, then looked up at the grey stone wall.

'I think it's time to take a look inside . . . Find our old friend.'

They entered the remains of the cathedral through the vaulting arch where great oak doors had once opened to the sanctuary within. Richard stared into the vast, silent ruin and began to recognise it, though its name escaped him. He had been here before, however, and Alex too, a long time ago in another world, his son at that time a tiny child, awestruck and silent, staring up at the vaulted ceiling, at the light through coloured windows. Alex had called out in the heavy stillness, listening to the sound of his voice passing through the high spaces, an echo creature that had delighted him as much as the grimacing faces that had watched from the stone, and the serene figures that had moved in the glass.

'I know this place – I've been here before – but I can't remember it – but I do remember these from our last journey! The agony figures. Do you see?'

He walked between the first broad columns, each with the statue of a dying man, St Sebastian on one side, the stone of his face melting, the stubs of arrows still visible, the twisted Christ on the tree on the other, features faded as if dissolved in acid, but the musculature still defined, so that tortured limbs and a deeper pain communicated powerfully from the dead marble.

The roof of the cathedral had long since fallen in. Broken window arches made a jagged line along the walls, high above. Carved pillars, once richly coloured, now grey, rose to crumbling and broken bosses, massive structures reminiscent of the majestic ruins of Greece. Crows flew noisily across the open sky. Stone cracked and fell, clattering on the heaped floor, the whole building rotting before Richard's eyes.

He walked along the nave, between pillars, through the grey, petrified trunks of trees, thinking *a wood once grew here!* but though the gnarled boughs twisted up from the cracked floor, now they flowed into the stone of the cathedral itself, all life squeezed from them, pallid, fractile organic shapes in the architecture, roots spreading, branches flattening against the limestone, leaves like flakes of chalk, falling with every footstep.

There was no frost or ice, yet the place was deathly cold and his breath misted. From the altar he looked back into the body of the building, at the shreds of paint that showed where frescoes had once told stories, at the gargoyles in the high corners, some with faces intact, but broken bodies, others just stubs of proud stone. And at the statues: here, the robes of a woman, her face blank, her hands still precisely carved; and close by, eyes and mouth in a face, surmounting the body of a saint that seemed to melt through the white marble. And everywhere the shadows of dead branches, breaking the sky. And everywhere, stone that crumbled like rotten wood.

Helen was a dark shape, watching from the door at the far end of the church, motionless but for the icy mist that formed a halo round her head.

Suddenly she stepped forward, between the statues of the martyrs, and called sharply, 'Alexander?'

There was silence for a moment, and Richard called, 'I thought he was dead.'

Helen advanced through the cold place, walking cautiously between the stone pillars, the stone trees. 'He's here all right. I saw him from my bower, watching us. Lytton! Don't be shy, now.'

There was sudden movement in the fallen stone. Broken branches were dislodged from a heap of rubble, small shards of marble and rock rolled down, and a shapeless mass of rock and dust began to rise, to reveal itself as a grey man emerging from hiding, heavily dressed, holding a long staff. Through the lank hair that fell around his face, piercing eyes stared at Richard and a mouth twisted into a death-mask grin. Then the head dropped as the figure coughed violently, spots of blood falling on the dust-white chest before the man could block his mouth and stifle the sounds of pain.

When the fit was over, Lytton looked up and laughed, stepping more into the open.

'I've been here for four days,' he said hoarsely. 'I'm damned if I know what to do next. Your son has had the second laugh on us, Richard. But he'll come to the tree. He'll have to. He'll come to the tree. And when he does . . .'

Helen had been approaching quietly, and Lytton sensed her now. He turned quickly, his filthy cloaks swirling, his staff brought defensively down to the horizontal. As she hesitated, he backed away, turning again to Richard.

'You have the look of a man who's seen a ghost. And maybe you have. And that's a fine set of clothes . . .' Lytton laughed as he spoke, but again broke down into a violent, bloody coughing fit. Staring at Richard, he wiped the red spit from his beard and lips, then looked at it. 'I've been too long in the wild. It's slipping away. But Huxley will survive, mark my words. Huxley *will* survive. Damn it!' He looked up hard again, banged the staff on the broken floor. 'You've *got* to get him out. One of us. Somehow. He's running us like puppets on strings, Richard. Why didn't you come *back* when we called for you?'

Richard was confused and cold, and his heart was racing. The last time he had seen Lytton, the man had shot and smashed his son, not realising the trick, and been consumed by the shapechanger. Then Haylock had said he'd been killed at Old Stone Hollow. So indeed his words were right. For Richard, there was the distinct sense of looking at a ghost.

'Was he here? Was Alex here?'

Lytton struck at one of the marble columns, cracking the stone and watching as dust and fragments fell. The hollow sound reverberated in the space. 'In the same way that a snake sheds its skin, so Alex has shed this building. Can you *imagine* that, Richard? Like the Jack-chapel that tried to swallow us, this was a *part* of your boy, living stone, living armour. Certainly he was here. But he's long gone. This cathedral has been discarded, like a dying dream. Like the White Castle – do you remember? He's moved to another place, the same place, but a *living* form of it. And it's close. And it's hidden from sight. Why he abandoned this particular nest, that I cannot tell you. Perhaps because of me. Perhaps because of fear of me – or something else that was closing in. It's probably a part of his defences. He can create, discard, re-create. He can disguise himself in the world of the wood. So yes, Richard. Your son was here, a year ago, a thousand years ago, hard to tell. This place is as much a mythago as any of the Hooded Men, the Jacks, the Bone Carvers we might encounter. Once the life is taken from it, it will collapse back into itself, rot down like the dead thing it is. What *we* have to do, now, is look for a wrongness in the wood – a clue as to where he's hiding.'

Helen came through the drifting dust, circling Lytton widely, alert to the huge and heavy staff he carried so tensely, so threateningly. A stream of pink saliva ran from his lower lip as he watched her.

'You need a doctor,' she said.

'No time for that.'

'At least let me help you.'

'To a poisoned dart, on behalf of Mr Bradley, here? Thanks, but no. If I find Huxley, if I can bring him into this world, see him, talk to him, then what does it matter how ill I am? He can tell me the way to peace. He can show me the direction. I'm sure he knew it.'

Richard listened to the words, the obsession, only vaguely understanding what drove Lytton. The man's breath rattled in his lungs. He had known of Helen's poisoned darts – had he been watching events in the dell?

Helen, frowning at Lytton's defensiveness, said, 'I have no desire to hurt you. You should know that. Richard thinks you tried to kill Alex. Maybe you did. But if you help *us*, if you help us get to Alex, then you won't need to kill him. We should work together.'

Lytton mocked, turned away from her, always cautious. He ran his tongue around the inside of his lips, emphasising his hollow face, the emerging skull. But his eyes gleamed as he approached Richard and said, 'I knew it was the Jack. But I can't deny my first impulse was to settle it there, to get rid of the cancer. That was years ago and things have changed, but the boy will still come to the tree. I'm sure of it.'

'The Mask Tree?'

'You saw it. They're Alex's faces, the faces of his private heroes, his magic friends. Did you see Arthur there? And the Green Knight? And Guiwenneth of the Green? And Jason?'

'I've seen a little too much of Jason recently,' Richard murmured, and Lytton hesitated, thinking, before going on: 'Then you saw his pleasures. But there, also, is everything that is older, older, all the nightmares, all the elemental forms that haunted Alex as he lay kicking, terrified, in the womb. Did you see *them*? There are hundreds of them. And he'll come to them. He *has* to.'

'The protogenomorph?' Richard said, glancing at Helen.

Lytton straightened, looking impressed. 'Indeed. The protogenomorph.

The guardian in Alex, the part of him that has waited for you, the part that has been fighting the battle . . .'

'What battle?'

'Against everything that was released from him when his dreams and his imagination were sucked through the mask.' Lytton frowned through his filthy, matted hair. 'You've not been fully briefed, then.'

'He got my note,' Helen said, 'but under difficult circumstances. We've only just met again . . . in the dell, as I'm sure you saw.'

Lytton's look darkened, his lips pinched, though his gaze remained steadfastly upon Richard. 'Are you going to kill me, Richard? If I turn my back will you club my brains out for trying to kill your son, as you believe?'

'Of course not. Not unless you attack him again.'

'Then I'm relieved. I can't watch you both. I'm tired, I'm ill. And I need food, and rest. However . . .'

He dropped the staff, shrugged off his filthy cloak to reveal a second layer of stitched hides, with a grimy wool ruff. This he removed and tossed to Helen, who grimaced at its stink, but wrapped it gratefully around her shoulders. Below this second cloak, Lytton was wearing stained cotton shorts and a torn tennis shirt. He put his outer cloak on again and shrugged as if to say, Sorry, not enough rags to go round.

In his slow voice, breathing hard, he said, 'There's a tragic painting by Manet: *The Execution of the Emperor Maximilian* . . . Have you ever seen it?'

Frowning, Richard said, 'Yes. Of course.'

'Four attempts, Richard. Four attempts at depicting the moment of a man's death, two feet from a firing squad. A year and a half of the artist's life, of his mind, his sweat, his madness. All that time to get a single *moment*. A tragic moment. A violent moment.'

'It's a powerful painting . . .'

Lytton nodded thoughtfully. 'A year and a half of hell, for Manet. When he had completed the painting; he wondered, in a letter to a friend, if such a moment of violence, perhaps of evil, when subjected to such concentration, to such need to be expressed, might literally escape from time itself . . .'

Richard was perplexed by the earnestness and subject matter of Lytton's conversation: why were they standing in the discarded stone-skin of one of his son's mythagos, talking Art History?

Lytton chuckled hoarsely, wiping his mouth, his gaze on the etched and cracked face of a stone green man, whose piercing eyes watched through a mask of acanthus leaves. The sinister figure peered from below the marble legs of a horse, whose body and rider had long since broken away. He said, 'Because unless my understanding is wildly wrong, such a moment is waiting for *us*; in some way it's all around us; we've been inhabiting it for years. Alex has waited for you for several years of your time, but for just weeks of his. He exists *outside* of time. He's frightened. He's watching. You've felt it – McCarthy touched it on several occasions. He has constructed worlds around himself, through which you and I stumble, all of us, stumble. And at the heart of that world, there is a moment. *The* moment! He has guarded it jealously, or a part of him has. The moment of his death, or transition, as seen by the wood! When it occurs, we *must* be there. Because a primal part of Alex – which Huxley called the protogeno-morph – will be looking for *us*, to lead us to the hiding place. The protogenomorph will be a shadow, and the shadow behind it is the danger. Follow the small shadow, the guardian, and you will find Alex. I'll be following it too. It's the greater shadow that we must be wary of.'

'And the greater shadow is what, exactly? Or don't you know?'

'I'm certain it's Trickster,' Lytton said simply, with a half-glance at Helen. 'The trickster in Alex. The manipulative manifestation of our first consciousness, our first awareness of the potential for deceit. It exists in all of us, blocked by the small shadow to the best of the small shadow's ability.'

'Conscience?'

'Yes – but more *control*. The part of us that always recognises the danger in trusting to our own needs, in believing that our lies might never be found out. It's a primary quality, there are many legends and heroic figures associated with its existence. It's a gatekeeper between states of mind, states of behaviour, and is very deeply buried. Like dark and light, Trickster and Control cannot exist separately. Unfortunately, these aspects of your son are free in the wood and fighting each other. The primitive Trickster has been released and doesn't wish to return – but like all mythagos it is drawn to its maker, Alex. As Alex's protector, you threaten it and it has attacked you, most notably in the form of Jack-the-Chapel.'

He had talked so much he had weakened his already damaged lungs, and he collapsed suddenly to his knees, leaning forward to retch blood-ily and painfully into the stone dust. Helen crouched with him, arms round his broad back.

'You're a dying man, Alexander. We *have* to get you help.'

'I'm an ill man, not a dying one. I'm closing in on Huxley. He and I are fated to meet, I'm convinced of it. Something in his journals. Once I find him, my health will turn for the better.'

'I'm going to take you back to the Station. There's nothing here for us. Let's go back for a while, behind the lines, and catch up on what's been happening to us in this place. Get your strength back.'

Glamour

They retraced the steps of their lunatic dance to the dark glade formed below the branches of the towering Mask Tree. Richard stared at the jumble of forms, some so old that they were little more than shadows in his consciousness, others bright and new and recognisably Alex's. He told Lytton of his experience with the tree, when bosky, of the feeling of Alex singing.

'You saw deeper than us,' Lytton surmised. 'The masks are there, all of them. Alex is deeply in the tree, coming slowly to the surface. In time, all the masks will emerge. What then, I wonder?' He doubled up, coughing badly, and Helen tried to lead him away, but he shook her off, quite angrily. 'We mustn't leave this place,' he said forcefully, and for a while he stood in the overpowering rise of the bole, his hands against the dull colours that filled out the scratching and gouges in the bark. 'This is where it all began,' he whispered, and beat against the faces as if by sheer brute force he could strip away the brighter colours and reveal the primal ochres, the oldest of the masks, the deepest of the journeys of the spirit that was reflected, recorded in the tree.

'This is your son,' he said softly to Richard. 'Look at him! Images of the higher mind. This is the history that makes us all. This is Alex. Without it, he is just a hollow man. We cannot leave it. We may never find it again.'

Helen rugged Lytton from the tree and led him to the path. 'You have a flair for the melodramatic, Alexander. We must go back – we need clothes and I need an old Coyote. The tree won't go away. We'll come back in a few days.'

'The tree won't go away,' Lytton murmured, defeated. 'But we might miss the moment . . .'

Lytton's own route to the Mask Tree had not been through Old Stone Hollow. He had discovered the place a year or more ago, after searching widely, carefully, following his instincts and the map of the layers of the wood which he had compiled at the Station. He had found the cathedral, but no Alex, and for a year had obsessively scoured the land around the Tree, becoming ill, becoming weak in limb, attacked by the wild, frozen by winter.

He had returned just once to the Station, marking out a gruelling four-day trek through freezing birchwoods, raging rivers and deep valleys haunted by shadows and heavy with oak and elm, which closed above him until he had felt stifled in the heat, almost too frightened to continue. When he finally reached the camp, it was deserted, the haunt of scavengers, and he had retraced his steps.

Now he led Richard and Helen back along that same route, looting a mortuary enclosure on the way, for clothes, caps and tarnished knives of bronze.

And it was clad in this way, in the trappings of the dead, raw with itching from the coarse cloth, that Richard arrived at the edge of a lake on the fifth morning and recognised Wide-water Hollowing and the Viking vessel that he had used against the serpent. Half a mile away around the shore was the gully to Old Stone Hollow.

Now he thought again of Sarin, whom he had abandoned so abruptly, instants after his deception of Jason. Would she still be in the Station, waiting for him, warm and safe? He felt suddenly apprehensive. For the last few days he had been dogged by thoughts of the drowned argonauts and by a curious anxiety that some of them might have survived. And indeed, perhaps this had been a process of premonition at work, for as he entered the gully, aware that there was indeed someone inhabiting Old Stone Hollow, his heart was squeezed with fear as he heard the tuneless wail of bagpipes, sounding from somewhere inside the Station. An image of a grinning man, wrapped in black furs, squeezing the leather bag to make the sound of dying came to him . . .

'Jason,' he whispered. 'Oh Christ no . . .'

The pipes whined again, a long drawn out howl of pain, a mocking call to Richard before they were discarded, their challenge finished. Noticing Richard's sudden agitation, Helen led Lytton up the bank, to cover in the rocks, before returning to the wooden palisade. 'Trouble?'

'An old man with a big grudge – he must have found his way back.'

'You mean Jason . . .'

Richard thought of Sarin, and of the brutal man, and closed his eyes.

But perhaps it was Sarin herself who was trying to extract music from the ancient instrument. Richard dismissed the thought – she had been too apprehensive of the pipes before, believing them to be a call to the shadow world. And to confirm his anxiety, as he walked into the tall grass he saw a black cloak, hanging, from the branch of a tree, washed, wet and drying. A skull mask hung over the longhouse door. Two spears and a round leather shield had been placed on one side.

The breeze rustled grass, branches, and the wet cloak. Otherwise the Station was silent. A thin stream of smoke rose from the longhouse, more dead than alive. Richard motioned Helen down and then ran quickly, bent low, to the entrance to the lodge. He picked up the shorter spear and the shield, which had a cracked and heavy wooden back, and stepped inside, advancing stealthily into the first room. A fire had burned here recently. Its ash, the trickle of smoke, still swirled through the light from the small window. The discarded pipes lay nearby, plus two rolls of fleece and a tunic of patterned leather.

Certain that the thunder of his heart could be heard clearly, Richard stretched out the spear towards the rough curtain between entrance and inner room. When he tugged it open he saw only gloom, a deserted place, illuminated thinly from holes in the roof. He stepped forward and a hand gripped his shoulder, spinning him round.

'Have mercy! Have mercy!' Lacan roared through his belly laugh, as Richard made to strike. 'It's only me! Spare my life!'

'Arnauld!' Richard flung his arms around the big man.

'My favourite Englishman! You *stink*!'

'I thought you were dead. Oh God, I thought you were dead.'

'I should be. I struck a hard bargain! Sweet Virgin, what *is* that smell?'

'I was told you'd been killed on the *Argo*!'

'I wish I had been. I'm embracing you firmly, out of joy, yet asphyxiating with nausea. What have you been *eating*?'

'Mud and leaf litter, mostly.'

Lacan was beside himself with mirth, slapping Richard stunningly on his left shoulder. 'I should have expected no less from the English! Terrible cooks, terrible taste in food. Ah well, each to his own.'

'I could murder a hare stew, right now. Christ it's so good – so wonderful – to see you – I thought you were dead!'

Lacan detached himself from Richard's second hug. 'Enough of this excessive male bonding. There are limits, even for a Frenchman. Are you alone?'

From behind him, Helen murmured, 'Any hare's blood left?' and jabbed the second spear gently into the big man's rump.

'Helen!' Lacan roared, with his second peal of genuine delight, and the ritual hugging and asphyxia began again.

With Lytton fed, washed, warm and sleeping, they sat in the longhouse around the new fire, prodding at the burning wood, feeling the glow of comfort, pigeon stew, and nettle tea course through their bodies. For Richard, the whole thing seemed normal again, and it took an unwelcome effort of will to construct an idea of the world outside the wood, where time ran from one hour to the next, and the seasons obeyed the spinning of the globe.

'You said you struck a hard bargain – how do you mean?'

Lacan picked at his yellowing teeth. His hair rattled with shells, newly tied into his black locks. 'One of Jason's social workers – Tisamenus by name – pursued me for my pipes. He offered to strike off my head. I struck off his arm, then divided his skull – not without difficulty – into two uneven pieces. A *very* hard bargain.'

He looked at Helen who was very solemn, watching him and frowning. Lacan nodded. 'Before I left I had never killed a man. This man, this Tisamenus, was my third in the years I was lost. I have rarely been frightened, but in the hours after a killing fear becomes like an illness. Fear of what, exactly, I don't know. I am just afraid, and very sick. And very lonely . . .'

Helen reached out and squeezed Lacan's toes through his thick boots. There was some silent conversation between them, a reference to a time before Richard's acquaintance with them, perhaps, and he remained respectfully quiet. Helen asked, 'How did you get here?'

'On the *Argo*,' Lacan said. 'Disguised as Tisamenus. The ship came through Wide-water Hollowing, although I didn't realise this for a while.'

Lacan had been lost on the shores of a hot sea, having strayed through a hollowing two years after he had left the Station. He had adventured like Hercules, loved, lived, sinned, sunned and consumed the local wild life with a gusto that even he, now, found hard to believe. When the *Argo* had beached, and an expedition come ashore, the adventurer called Tisamenus had become envious of the pipes, which he had heard being played in the caves above the shore. The *Argo* was being pursued by two war galleys of sinister demeanour and intent. When they had appeared on the sea horizon Tisamenus called back to the ship, had masked himself and attacked the dark-bearded man, to claim the mysterious booty.

Lacan had then struck his deadly bargain.

Disguised as Tisamenus he had entered the *Argo* – 'I was lost. I had nothing better to do' – and had kept his identity behind the mask during the ensuing battle.

'I was aware that there were living beings below the deck. Richard, this man, this Jason, was the worst of men. A true monster. If not for the battle he would have unmasked me and slaughtered me – although I would have exacted a terrible price! As I'm sure you both realise.'

'Terrible,' Richard concurred.

'Awesomely so,' agreed Helen.

'Indeed! But the *Argo* plunged through a sea cave, which turned out to be a hollowing. On the other side it was cold. I jumped for the shore. Only days later did I discover that it was this shore, this place, my old home. Someone had been here recently, but had gone. Now I realise it was you two! I *knew* there had been a woman here . . .' He grinned at Helen.

'Not me,' she said. 'Been eating earthworms for a season or more.'

Lacan frowned. 'Who, then?' And his words reminded Richard that Sarin should be near.

'A small woman, very thin, very chirpy,' he said. 'She's called Sarinpushtam. She was on the *Argo* with you, but below the deck, and too often being abused by Jason.'

Lacan shook his head. 'I saw none of the prisoners, only the cooks. But I heard a young woman crying out sometimes, and not with pleasure. I'm glad I was only aboard for a few hours. I would have had to kill that man.'

Declining Lacan's offer of help in locating Sarin – assuming she was still in the vicinity and hiding – Richard left the longhouse to look for her.

She was hiding beyond the Sanctuary, sheltering below an arch formed of two fallen pillars. Terrified and cold, she had been about to give herself to the lake, but Richard's call reached her hearing and confused her determination. When Lacan, disguised as Tisamenus, had come to Old Stone Hollow a few hours before, she had fled, remembering the cruelty of that particular argonaut, not willing to experience it further. When Richard explained that Lacan was a good and trusted friend, she wept. When he told her that Lacan was a fine cook she stopped weeping.

'Since you left I've eaten nothing but mushrooms, dried fish and something from your house. It was in a fragile crystal vessel and I had to break it.' She closed her eyes at its memory and half smiled. 'It was like the food eaten by the gods. It drove me mad with pleasure. But there was very little of it.'

Meacham's Potted Beef! Good God. An English horror had appealed to a Bronze Age appetite.

'There's plenty more where that came from,' Richard said. 'Shops full. Unsold. Unwanted.' Sarin was delighted at the thought, and Richard led her back to the river.

It was close to dusk. Helen had made clothes from the cloaks of the drowned argonauts and Lacan had gone to the lake to peer into its depths. He was obsessed, now, with the idea of dredging the vessel from the castle ruins below and refloating it. Being a sensible man, he was wary of the lake serpent, but for most of the afternoon, Helen said, he had been sitting in the gathering gloom, thinking of the possibilities of voyaging aboard so famous a ship.

Sarin washed, ate heartily and kicked the bagpipes, as if to reassure herself that they were not, as she feared, the source of summoning of evil shadows (which she called night feeders).

Another shadow had to be summoned, and Helen sat with Richard and Alexander Lytton and recalled the day she had journeyed to the edge of the wood and delivered the note to Richard's home.

'I went out through the old Lodge. There was a strange feel to the place, like movement, like ghosts. I assumed everything was mythagos. I wasn't happy about it. Arnauld's snares and probes were everywhere, so maybe they were having an effect. He always said that Oak Lodge had more than its fair share of ghosts.

'I rested in the clearing for a while, and a young girl appeared. Again, I assumed this was a mythago, although my first thought was that she was a local. But she didn't speak. She was very willowy, very moon-faced, silvery, and beckoned me. I followed her through the wood, and came out into the field, above Shadoxhurst. No sign of the girl, but she was at the edgewood when I went back in, and again vanished as I followed her. As I say, a mythago of some sort.

'At Richard's house? I noticed that a woman was living there, which irritated me.' She cast a glance at Richard. 'I was tempted to leave a more loving note, but I didn't.' She leaned toward him. 'I did *miss* you, though.' And after a pause, 'That's about it. It was a flying visit to Richard through the ghost zone.'

Lytton had been scribbling furiously, and thinking hard. Without looking up he said, 'The moon-faced girl was silent. Do you mean she didn't speak?'

'Not a word.'

'And when she moved? Could you hear her?'

With a shudder Helen suddenly shook her head. 'No. No, I didn't hear her, come to think of it. It was quite eerie. I followed her by light. She didn't glow, I don't mean that. She sort of radiated. Ethereal, I guess. What do you think she was?'

'An elemental,' Lytton said quietly.

'You and your elementals!' Helen was amused, glancing at Richard.

Ignoring her, Lytton went on, 'What I don't understand is how she got there. Except that James Keeton re-emerged from the wood by way of Oak Lodge, hours older after an absence of months. Are you *sure* he said he'd come through the Lodge, Richard?'

'Quite sure. Like Helen, he said that he'd felt the presence of ghosts, many people. It had felt unearthly.'

Outside, from the direction of the wooden defences, a sound cut into the conversation. Richard stood and went to peer into the evening gloom. 'It's Arnauld. At last.'

Lacan had returned and was formally closing the gate, critically inspecting the crude hinges that Richard had contrived during his rebuilding. The Frenchman entered the longhouse and flung his cloak to one side.

'We must dredge up the *Argo*,' he said. 'It's an opportunity too good to be missed. What's cooking? *Who's* cooking?' he added with a nervous glance at Richard.

Then he saw Sarin. For a second he froze completely. Richard began to introduce the woman properly, aware that Sarin's face had registered an expression of startlement. He was startled himself when Lacan mumbled, 'Excuse me. Nature calls.'

The Frenchman reached for his cloak, almost angrily, and left the house abruptly, leaving Richard puzzled and Sarin disturbed. She stared after the big man for a long time, not responding to Richard's words. She was in a dreamy state, a daze, concerned and anxious, her face, usually so thin and pretty, now furrowed. Richard touched her shoulder and she jumped, then shook her head and crawled across the floor, to curl up on her furs and think.

When, after an hour or more, Lacan had not returned, Richard went out and called for him, but without success. After dark, with the fire dead, Helen curled up against him, below the fleeces from the *Argo*, and while Lytton groaned in his nightmare sleep and Sarin chattered like a bird, twitching and shifting below her covers, they made love side by side, very gently and with almost no sound.

'I'm beginning to like you, Mr Bradley.'

'Then why do you keep calling me Next-Buffalo-Dinner?'

At some time during the long night Richard was disturbed by the sigh of the bagpipes. Helen was sleeping against his chest, her hands holding him intimately. He detached himself without waking the woman and followed the dark shape of Lacan out into the tall grass. The night shadow of the big man was fleet as it passed through the moonlight to the open gates of the Station.

'Arnauld!' Richard called softly. 'Arnauld! Where are you going? What's the matter with you?'

'Leave me alone!' the Frenchman whispered furiously, his eyes gleaming in the moonlight. And with those brutal words he was gone again.

Richard couldn't sleep, and imagined that he had stayed awake all night, staring into the darkness of the longhouse, breathing the fading scents of woodsmoke from the fire. And yet at first light, when he stirred from the fleeces again, he saw that Sarin was not in her corner. He went out into the dewy morning. There was a slight breeze and the air was chill on his skin. The brightening sky was cloudless, still purple over the eastern forest. The gates to the compound were open, but it was to the overhang above the cave system that Richard went, aware that he had heard furtive movement high above him, where the rock curved out of sight.

He pulled himself up the steep path and came onto the cliff top, caught for a moment by the richness of colour, the spread of fire where the sun was rising over Ryhope. Then he saw the hunched figure of the girl, a few yards away, so dark against a tree that for a moment he had missed her. She was watching Lacan, who was hunkered down on his haunches, supporting himself with a heavy staff, his ringleted hair hanging lank around a bowed head.

As Richard moved up to Sarin he saw tears in her eyes and blood on her lower lip. He put a comforting arm on her shoulder and felt her tremble through the thin cloth of her dress.

'How long have you been here?'

'Since he called me. Before first light.'

'He called you?' Richard watched the motionless figure on the cliff top. Lacan might have been a statue, save for the fact that the wind rattled the shells at the ends of his ringlets, and occasionally his broad back, below the draping black cloak, heaved deeply.

'I heard his voice in my dream. I was so afraid of him when he came to the camp. He was still wearing the mask. But when I saw his face, I knew him. But I don't know from where. He just makes me feel wounded . . .'

Wounded? Richard watched the anxiety on Sarinpushtam's lean face, the furrows on her high forehead, the well and ebb of tears in her richly dark eyes. She was Lacan's mythago. That had to be the answer. But there was something more, and Lacan was in distress about it.

'Have you tried approaching him?'

'I've called to him. He just growls and crushes into himself.'

'Why don't you go back to the house? I'll try and talk, to our bear-like friend. Whatever it is, it can't last.'

Sarin hesitated then stood and ran, almost angrily, back down the track, swinging from trunk to trunk, slipping and skidding out of sight, occasionally slapping the trees and regretting with a cry that she'd been so angry.

The sounds of her departure disturbed Lacan, who turned his head slightly, caught Richard approaching and looked away.

'Arnauld? Call me a nuisance, throw me over the cliff, tell me to mind my own business. But tell me what's wrong, if you can. It hurts us all to see you in such pain.'

'Two hours more,' Lacan grunted, shaking his head. Beyond him, the sky was dazzling. He leaned on his staff and the wind blew his hair. The sun caught fire in his eyes.

'Two hours?'

To think. To be alone. Don't worry about me. Please, just bugger off. I'll be down in two hours. Don't let her get distressed.'

'Sarin?'

'Please. Look after her. I smelled blood on her, Richard. Don't let her do anything foolish.'

'She was only biting her lip. She's confused. She's yours, of course. Your mythago . . .'

'Of course. Go away, Richard. I need to be alone a while longer.'

A hind had come down to the lake, but bolted as Richard reacted to its presence with a cry. The hunt, with Helen, took several hours, and it was Helen's accuracy with the short bow that claimed the kill. She paunched the steaming beast with a confidence that left Richard amazed, and she rebuked the man for his teasing.

'Fresh meat, Richard!'

'It'll have to hang for a while.'

'Not its liver, my man. That we'll have tonight.'

'You're beginning to sound like Lacan . . .'

As they carried the carcass back to Old Stone Hollow, skirting the lakeside, they saw Lacan walking among the distant rocks, his hood drawn over his head against the drizzle. Richard called to him, but he kept walking, glancing occasionally across the wide water, his face grim.

They hung the deer, and prepared a stew pan of the liver with wild vegetables. Lytton was writing furiously in his notebook. 'It's so important to record everything. *Everything*. When I write, ideas come. That's how I worked out the function of the protogenomorph, after McCarthy's shadowy encounter with it. Explanation later, Richard. And I would like to hear an account of what has happened to you as well. Alex is everywhere. Can you feel him? He's watching still. He will pick the moment to come to us, and we must be ready, not just physically, but mentally as well. Where's Lacan?'

'Still brooding. Still upset.'

'Upset? About what?'

'I'm not sure.'

From the other room, where Helen was stitching hides together, she called, 'Matilde!'

Lytton nodded, said, 'I see. Where is she?'

'Somewhere about. Waiting for him.'

Without further response, leaving Richard infuriatingly confused, he returned to his notebook.

Richard went through the curtain and watched Helen at her task. 'Matilde? Sarin by another name?'

Helen cocked her head. She had a length of coarse thread between her teeth, and was using a bone needle very effectively. Her dark eyes engaged Richard for a moment, thoughtfully, perhaps making a decision. Then she nodded. 'I guess so.'

'His daughter?'

'His wife. He'll talk when he's ready.'

Lytton came through, his notebook closed. He rubbed his chin as he watched Helen work, then sat down, cross-legged on the floor, indicating that Richard should do the same.

'It's making a sort of sense, now, as much as anything in Huxley's first forest can ever make sense . . .

'The way Keeton described his sojourn in Ryhope reminds me of the land of faerie – unlike Ryhope, in the *fey* world you age *less* than the world outside, and that is what happened to Keeton, and what has happened to Alex. Alex has created his own time, and to do this he is using the elemental in him, the earliest myths, the earliest part of consciousness, when notions of time itself became defined, both in the terms we would understand it, and in the mystical time of gods and faerie that these days we would call fantastic.

'When Keeton lost his daughter in 1957 his anguish, his desperation, entered the wood as an entity *apart* from him, crystallising – *condensing*, as Elizabeth Haylock used to say – into the complex matrix of energy and time that underlies this place.

'Is it possible that Keeton was protected by a form of "glamour"? Held out of time by a protecting, sheltering cloak of faerie magic? When he left the wood, the glamour remained behind, an echo. It had formed into the shape of his own daughter, and lingered there for years – it's still there! When you encountered it, Helen, you followed it to the edge, you passed *through* it, because it was another form of hollowing, only this passage connected with a time eight years before. It was waiting for you on your return, after leaving the note, and again you tried to encounter the moon-faced girl, and so you passed back to the present.'

Helen was hunched over her work, her head shaking slightly, the silver locks on each side glinting in the candlelight. She said, quite simply, 'If that's right, then I'm frightened. Too much of my life has been interfered with by time. I've wasted too much time. Time has wasted me. Time has wasted my family. By fear, it has tricked us out of our lives. If Coyote is Time, then I'm going to be done, with him now.'

She looked up at Richard. There were tears in her eyes not of sadness but of anger. She reached out and touched his hand, and without even understanding what he was doing Richard folded his arms around her and kissed the moist, warm parting in her hair. 'Don't lose me,' she said. 'Every hour, every day – it's ours, not Trickster's. Don't lose me. Don't let it all go.'

While Lytton frowned restlessly, watching the kiss, unable to continue because of the sudden passion, the sudden need, Richard embraced Helen with all his heart. As their mouths parted and they smiled, their eyes lingering on each other, Richard had an image of Alex, smiling and clapping his hands in delight.

'My son's going to adore you,' he said.

Alex wouldn't know about Alice. He wouldn't know his mother had gone—

'Glad you've come to believe in him.'

She turned back to Alexander Lytton. 'So this "echo" Keeton created was like the "moment out of time" you talked about, like the Manet painting. So much anguish that it formed a focus—'

'Drawing to it everything that was related to that anguish – shaped like the daughter, but calling to anyone or anything that was associated with Tallis.'

Richard tried to absorb the images and ideas that were raised by Lytton's half-distracted account. The man was thinking aloud: he was unfocused, but he hardened that gaze as Richard said, 'How does Alex fit in?'

'Alex was the substitute for Tallis. When Alex stared through the Moondream mask – a hollowing mask, don't forget – he was torn through it, stripped of everything but flesh and bone and *dragged* through that mask.

'Keeton's anguish, Keeton's need, his need for his child – he reached from inside the wood through the mask, reaching to the moment of his real-time death and clutched at the memories of Tallis that he could feel there – all of them in your son.

'A reflection of Alex's mind, in the wood, is in the faces on the Mask Tree. That's where the boy will come – that's where we'll see the moment of his transition, a moment that we'll follow to the cathedral, where Alex himself is hiding.'

At dusk Lacan called from the river, and Richard went out through the tall grass to find him. He was aware that Sarin was among the elder bushes that concealed the deep cave. She was watching furtively. Lacan, swathed in a dark cloak, eyes glistening with cold, leaned against a heavy tree, staring distantly towards the gully. He acknowledged Richard, then walked away, up the steep bank, back to the Sanctuary, through the place where once the underfoot had been a graveyard of decaying creatures.

By the hollowing, by the marble pillars where Richard had tricked Jason, he turned and worked his staff into the ground.

'I am very lost,' he said quietly. 'You must help me.'

Richard started to reach a reassuring hand, but drew back as angry eyes caught his. He said only, 'I've offered friendship. Helen and Lytton are very discreet. I know that Sarin reminds you of your wife. I have a half idea that you've been seeking her . . . that she died, and you've been seeking her . . .'

Lacan seemed to collapse slightly, nodding, as if both relieved and comforted by Richard's simple intuition. 'I remember telling you – so many years ago, now – but I remember saying in answer to a question of yours that I was looking for the moment of my death; Richard . . . if you had known Matilde . . . if you could have once seen her, heard her speak, been touched by her glamour . . . she was ethereal. I know that, now. I always have. I loved her so much. When the wood killed her, it should have strangled me with its creepers too. But it left me to mourn her, and to die and be reborn, as it were, and then to hunt for her with a force of life that is all that protects me from the shadowland.'

Richard was about to make a comment, a naive interruption questioning why, if Lacan had now found his beloved Matilde, he found it so hard to speak to her. The Frenchman silenced him angrily, then apologised and walked stiffly back to a point, beyond this copse, where the ridge of the high cliff could just be seen.

Softly, he said, 'I didn't expect to find her like this. I've spent so long looking, I need her so much . . . and suddenly I am aware that she is dying. She has no life, only an appearance in our world for a few days, a few weeks. Like all these things we summon, she is no more than a shadow, strong in the sun, doomed to dusk beauty and then annihilation. I've always known it. Of course I have. But I've never accepted the truth of the matter, that when I found her she would be wood and earth, she would be transient. Oh God in Heaven, I can't bear to lose her again, I can't bear to lose her again . . .' He started to shake and Richard squeezed his shoulder, helpless and distressed as his friend's emotion began to surface.

'She's strong,' he whispered. 'I've got to know her. She's strong.'

'Not strong enough. Look at her. There's nothing on her, no flesh even for the crows. But it *is* her. After so long . . . she *has* surfaced from the wood. And I know, I just *know*, that she will never surface again . . .'

'Then go and be with her while you can. What more is there to do?'

'What more? Why, to save her from Matilde's fate, of course. I couldn't bear that. I feel lost. I think I must become lost again.'

There was a fleet movement ahead of them, and both men ducked slightly, scanning the trees, the ruins. Richard strung his bow, drew a flighted arrow. Lacan glowered at the shadows, hands caressing the blackthorn staff.

He looked at Richard abruptly. His sadness was overwhelming, but now there was almost anger painting his features.

'Were you born close to this wood?'

'Far away. I moved to Shadoxhurst when I married Alice.'

'There's the difference between us, then, since I *was* born near a wood like this. In Brittany. A vast forest through which you could only follow certain tracks, certain paths, much as we experience in Ryhope. It was a wonderful place. Huge stones circled it, hidden by the edge: it was a wood that had grown inside a stone circle and had reached out its skirts to hide the grey markers. It was a place of ponds and lakes, and deep, moist hollows. It was a place of magic.

'I lived in a cottage at the bottom of a hill. Some nights, winter nights especially, people came from the wood and passed along a lost track, close to my garden. They walked over the hill and to a vanishing place on the other side. Sometimes I followed them, but I could never see where they went. Perhaps I didn't have the faith, the belief in them, perhaps I simply didn't have the right way of looking.

'When I was a child I would explore the lakes, hiding in the bushes and watching the grey shapes, like mist creatures, that would come and stand by the water, staring into the depths. They were ghosts. Many of them cried silently before returning to the wood. All seemed to be searching for something. I have no idea what.

'When the war came, my father fought and came home wounded. I was too young, but eager to fight. In 1943 I left Brittany by fishing boat for England, to join a French Canadian command. I was sixteen. Before I left I went back to the lake. It was dusk. A woman came out of the shadows, a grey woman, and touched my eyes and my lips. She had appeared so fast, and she disappeared so fast, that I was too shocked to think. I remember only that I had been kissed on each eye, each cheek, each lip.

'When I arrived in England, I was there for only two weeks and suddenly the war ended. I came home, dizzy and confused, because I found that two years had passed.

'The cottage was shuttered, my parents were gone. Neighbours told me that they had followed a laughing woman into the wood one winter, and that was the last they had seen of them. I had been held safe in some sort of spell. Or had I? Two years had passed and I have memory of only two weeks.

'Then, in the edgewood, I met Matilde. I thought she was from a local village. Perhaps she was. She looked very like the woman who had touched me with her glamour, but Matilde was only sixteen. She was delicious in every way, sensuous in every way. Her laughter a joy.

'We lived together in the cottage. I stopped grieving for my parents. I was consumed with love for her, with her smell, her voice, her teasing. Then our son was born, but he was not born well. In a few months we realised that he was blind. And although he made an infant's sounds, he didn't speak as he reached the age when other children begin to chatter. He had no language. By the time he was four . . . it was terrible. I can't tell you how terrible, Richard. Matilde was – well, there is only one word: she was ruined. The boy gradually began to see – only colours at first, then shapes, then the whole world, except for shadows. He began to speak – little words at first, then wild descriptions, then haunting accounts of what his mind's eyes could see. At the same time, Matilde faded.

'In her dreams she screamed and fought with shadow creatures. She barricaded the cottage obsessively. She gradually lost her sight, until all she could see were shadows. She lost her speech. As the boy learned words, so they vanished from her, until she could only say two words aloud, my own first name being one of them, the other, something I never understood. It was such a terrible thing. She saw the world as shadows, and the shadows were alive in ways that were not right. She tried to communicate this to me. The shadows of trees chased her. The shadows of foxes prowled around her on moonless nights. It was as if she was being punished for having the badly-born child. I called him ghost-born, but as Matilde faded, so he grew stronger.

'When he slept, my passion for Matilde was always in earnest, and she responded with such need, such longing, such desperate physicality, clinging to me without break, that I began to realise that these moments of intimacy were her only way of expressing the love she felt, at a time when she was safe. And yet she never opened her eyes, never uttered sound, except for my name.

'I was heartbroken. I was dying was an endless battle with her to stop her sealing the house, with wood, with corrugated iron, with animal skins, with sheets of plastic, with anything she could find.

'Then one day she was gone, and my son had gone too. I searched for them desperately.

'I found them in the lake. When I dragged them to the shore, when I pushed the wet hair from their faces, when I kissed the white flesh on each face, the eyes, the cheeks, the lips, I could not tell them apart. I obliterated my son's name from my memory, because at that moment I believed he had never existed. It was the moment of my own death, and I entered the lake and fell into a sleep without pain.

'I woke in my own cottage, on the couch, covered by a blanket. I had been found by one of the villagers wandering aimlessly, not drowned at all. The man knew nothing of Matilde. He knew nothing of my son. He said I was a hermit, always barricading my cottage, and he was terrified of me. Indeed, I looked frightful.

'And the rest you know. She dwelt in my dreams continuously, but I began to snare and trap the ghosts of my wood, in the hope of finding her. I became famous for it, and word spread. One day, Alexander Lytton found *me*. I learned of mythagos. I clung to his invitation to come to Ryhope Wood because it was a last chance to resurrect Matilde. Maybe Lytton exaggerated the possibilities. He wanted what he wanted for his team and he saw possibilities in me. I came gladly, Richard. Life was then, and still is, as nothing without that lovely woman.'

'Then go to her.'

Lacan turned furiously. 'But don't you see? After all I've said? She never existed! I was touched by something, some charm . . . my life was a charm, and Matilde a part of that charm. She was only my dream, made real. I have tried to make her real again, but she is still just that, a dream, a shadow. There never was Matilde. There never was a son. And now there is a woman who is everything my heart longs for, but she exists only because I needed to fulfil my selfish needs in *one* life. Long gone! I have created the shadow of a shadow. This Sarin is less even than a mythago. She's the hopeless object of desire of an ageing Frenchman. If I touch her, she'll die, I know it. She'll die.'

Richard shouted his frustration with the big man. 'And maybe she won't! If you even have a few days with her, then have them, Arnauld. Sarin is very moved by you. She feels strongly for you. Tell her what you've told me. Maybe the two of you, maybe together you'll *find* the strength to survive. How can you tell until you try it?'

Lacan glanced at Richard, frowning, his eyes filled with sadness. 'There is more to it,' he whispered, looking away. 'But perhaps only things that should be forgotten. Ryhope Wood, the wood in France: they are the same wood, they share a common time, a common space, a dimension we cannot really see, the same shadows, the same dreams. We have no way of defining it, this imaginary time, this *sylvan* time. It's beyond our language.' He was in despair again, sighing deeply. 'What do I do? I couldn't bear to see her die through grief and fear, like Matilde . . .'

Remembering the encounter of a few days before, Richard said, 'Sarin nearly died when I switched on the defences, but she survived. She's strong, Arnauld. One of Jason's argonauts only lasted seconds. Don't underestimate her. Love the shadow while you can . . .'

And suddenly, perhaps because she'd been listening, Sarin was there, standing a short way away, her wiry body wrapped firmly in a thick wool cloak, her face dark with anguish and curiosity, and perhaps a touch of longing. Her gaze was fixed on Lacan. The Frenchman watched her, then smiled, extending his arm, hand outstretched to her. As Richard took his leave, the girl came over to the marble pillar and entered Lacan's deep embrace.

Curious, which is to say nosy, Richard watched them from the shadows. The two of them cried for a while, then laughed. Lacan began to speak and they walked away from the Sanctuary, deeper into the wood. Their movement disturbed birds, but soon there was silence. An hour later, crows erupted from the canopy a half-mile or so distant. As the sun began to set a nest of herons set up a clattering of bills, a vile objection to movement below.

At dawn, Richard was woken by the strident sound of bagpipes playing a jig, just outside the palisade, where two people were washing in the crisp water of the river.

He and Helen went out to join in the icy fun, and it was then that they saw the first signs of the world dying around them.

The Triumph of Time

Winter, like a branching white scar, had begun to streak the green-wood, patches and lines of frost in the verdure that slowly spread, ice killing the summer leaf and the hardwood trunks, stone turning into the same soft, crumbling decay that had infested the cast-off cathedral.

Sarin scampered naked from the river, grabbing for her cloak. Lacan, rotund and hairy, crawled out after her, using his hand self-consciously to protect his groin. Around them, leaves fell like ash. The air was winter crisp, and their breath steamed.

From outside the longhouse Lytton shouted excitedly, 'This is Alex's work! He's calling to us!'

Helen looked at the encroaching winter, frowned, then whispered to Richard, 'How the hell can he always be so sure?'

'I don't know. But I'm not about to argue. Are you?'

'To what end? Lytton knows what Lytton knows; Huxley's shade whispers to him . . .'

She turned and ran to the longhouse, to find warm clothes and food supplies. Richard thought of Old Stone Hollow and curiosity took him through the ice-glazed elderwood.

Below the cliff, the paintings on the overhang had faded, the rock flaking away and taking the colours and the shapes with it. The flow of water had dried. The cavern was a barren place. Lytton entered the overhang and stared around him, taking his weight on his staff, his grey locks iridescent with frost. 'I suspected as much: this place was from Alex's imagination, and like the rest, he's killed it now. What else I wonder? He'll be killing all his creations.'

Anxiously, Richard thought of Sarin, but the woman, bulky in her new furs, was following Lacan towards the Hollow. She looked, vibrantly alive.

'What's happening?' the Frenchman asked.

'We need to return to the Mask Tree,' Lytton murmured, his face to the sky as he sniffed and tasted the whiter air. 'Alex is close to us again. I can feel it. He's calling to us. He's *coming* to us.'

'He's coming here?' Richard asked.

Narrow eyes in a bone-white face glanced briefly, irritably at him. 'No. Not here. He's trapped in the cathedral. But I think he must be breaking from the moment of frozen time . . . He'll come to the Mask Tree. I'm sure of it!'

'We'll have to risk the hollowing,' Helen said. 'Through the cave.'

'Too dangerous. Besides, Richard only got through because he was bosky, and his son was able to guide him. Perhaps he did the same for you, when *you* went through the pipe. But we can't risk the cave, now. Too many outflows . . .'

'But it's a four-day trek along the land route,' Richard said, appalled at the thought of the return journey to the Tree.

Lytton smiled at him, a gesture of dry amusement. 'Then let's waste no time. If we miss him, Alex may have no choice but to stay hidden forever. And what he's shed to the wood will stay in the wood, and I simply can't have that.'

While the rest made their brief preparations, Richard scoured the area around the Station. The Sanctuary was intact, although the white and frozen corpses of a man and a woman were crouched nearby. In the summer wood beyond he found the icy mass of a boar, the broken spear with which it had run for most of its life still embedded in its flank. From the lakeside, where Jason had landed, he watched the Viking longship become engulfed in frost and slowly crack. Warm, summer air gusted, followed by the frozen blast of deep winter. The clouds, the water, all seemed to be divided between the seasons, and Richard marvelled at the way his son was drawing back his creations, sucking the magic forests, lands and creatures of childhood back toward the cathedral, and the giant elm, with its shallow faces, the place, Lytton now believed, that had been Alex's first entry into the world of Ryhope Wood.

The last thing he saw, before Helen came up behind him putting her arms around his chest and whispering, 'Stop brooding. It's time to go and find the boy,' was the frozen body of the serpent. It surfaced suddenly, a coiled iceberg, the head twisted up and away from the rest of its body, the haunting eye glazed-over and lifeless now. The creature floated there, melting slowly, disintegrating. As it decayed so it turned, seeming to watch the shore, then subsiding, taking the last memory of a terrible encounter, the last memory of Taaj, as it condensed back into the lake above the stone castle.

It was such an odd feeling: the realisation that Alex had created both the courageous boy, a powerful reflection of himself, and the monster that had consumed him.

Richard's thoughts turned briefly to the *Argo*, on the lake bed, but if that vessel too had been Alex's creation, now consumed by frost, it held its secret in the depths.

'Come *on*,' Helen urged. She had Richard's pack, his new cloak of crudely cured skins, a hood against the rain.

He followed her, followed the others, round the wide lake shore, to the valley between high, crumbling cliffs, which led back to the dell and the carved tree.

To avoid freezing, they followed, as far as possible, the pockets and zones of spring and summer. Inevitably there were times, lasting for hours, when they were forced to trek through winter woods, deep with snow and silent, or ice-locked and dangerous. A new life had begun to generate in these landscapes, to replace the vast creatures that now lay or stood like ice-carvings: mastodon, cave bears, elks, shaggy bison and snarling wolves. Darker, livelier forms of these beasts of the frozen world now emerged, including dire-wolves, which dogged their tracks with obvious intent and wilful abandon of strategy. Lytton confidently declared that these new creatures were 'condensing from our own minds, appropriate to the land around us'.

As ever, he seemed in his element, trudging through snowdrifts, cloak swirling, staff bearing his slight weight, white-haired head always turned to the far horizons as he absorbed the world around him, a magus leading his doubting followers.

In the summer wood they had to use force to avoid the dire-wolves, which attacked in groups of three, acting without caution, easily driven back. Helen shot game birds, but they avoided heavier meat since they were travelling fast and light. And they indulged in wary, careful exchange with the mythagos that emerged, usually at dawn or dusk, to share their food and fire, or chatter in strange tongues. There was usually time for Sarin to comprehend the languages of their guests; when she failed, she proved to be adept, as indeed was Richard, at interpreting meaning from sound and gesture.

Their most successful encounter was with a mailed knight, a young man on foot, a blue-eyed and blond warrior from the early Age of

Chivalry who entranced Helen with his smile and his descriptions of the river-barge he sought, where his lady's heart was hidden in the body of the black dog Cunhaval. The hound slept on the afterdeck. A ghost steered the barge. Its destination was a fabled castle.

The knight was named Culloch. He was Durham-born, but had squired at the court at Caer Navon, before taking his oath and shipping out to fight for the liberation of the Holy City in the Crusade.

'How big is this dog?' Helen asked.

The knight licked his fingers as he finished eating and pointed to the tree tops. 'As tall as the Cross, lady. It has eaten a king's ransom in gold from our new minster, and swallowed the purest heart that ever beat within the court and summer-tower of Caer Navon. I shall cut my way with iron into the body of the black dog and release that heart. The Cross will be my strength.'

'Sounds messy,' Helen murmured dryly. 'But good luck. God's speed.'

Culloch lowered his gaze. 'You give me courage with your smile and your faith in the Cross. God's speed yourselves.'

Helen watched him go, a glittering shape in his iron mail, swallowed by shadows within moments.

'In his situation, I think I'd prefer a large lump of poisoned meat.'

Sarin had begun to feel the cold; her exuberance faded, her energy sapped, and Richard and Lacan took it in turns to carry her through the worst of the frozen wastes. Her loss of defiance in the teeth of winter disturbed Lacan, depressed him. He showed a side of his character that Richard found hard to accommodate, a too-easy resignation, a fatalism that perhaps was protecting him against the anticipated grief of the girl's death.

When he could, Richard bullied the man into exercising a more cheerful and optimistic attitude, at least in front of Sarin herself, and Lacan said, 'Damn! You're right!' hugged Richard, but continued to behave in exactly the same gloomy way.

Helen whispered, 'The man's tired. Deep down, he's exhausted. To the core. He's been too many years in his own company, too many years hoping. Give him time.'

'Of course I will,' Richard said irritably. 'I understand Lacan well enough. It's Sarin I'm concerned for. If she needs *his* strength to extend her life, right now she's dying faster than she need.'

In the summer woods Sarin cheered up, found fresh heart, fresh strength. And at these times it was she who teased the big man, and over the days Richard saw the relationship between the two of them deepen and intensify.

Four days after they had begun their journey inward, they emerged in a downpour from the saturated forest into the heavy ground-haze of a clearing below wide canopy. The robust and serpentine roots that flowed across the ground marked the place as the Mask Tree, and the huge, dark trunk ahead of them was the place where Alex's imagination was embedded.

Already Richard had seen what Lytton had been shocked to notice: there were no marks now, no masks, no faces on the trunk, nothing but ridged bark, stained with white lichen, infested with black and orange fungal growth, rotting.

Lytton cried out in frustration. 'I knew we should have stayed!' But a moment later, as he moved towards the tree, he changed his tone. 'No! There is something here.'

He began to trace his finger round a shallow oval scratching, throwing his staff to one side, spreading himself against the trunk. 'Yes! There's something . . . Richard. Quickly! Come here . . .'

He had found a single design. It was Moondream. Richard recognised it at once, from the bark mask that James Keeton had been clutching on his return from the Otherworld, so many years ago, now: a half-crescent, sharply focused eyes, a half-smile, the same outline. It was Keeton's daughter's mask, his only memento of the lost girl.

Richard stared at the crudely carved face, touched its eyes, its mouth. *This has nothing to do with Alex.*

He wondered aloud what had happened to the rest of the faces and masks. Had they been re-absorbed, as all of Alex's creations in the wood had been sucked back? Then why had this particular image survived?

Lytton tapped at the bark, curious for a moment, then enlightened, and he confirmed Richard's intuitive thought. 'This design was not from your son.' He looked back at the face, spread his hands over the shallow tracing. 'But if not from Alex – then who? Who could have carved this face? You can see that it's old. But it's not ancient.'

The answer was not so much obvious as suggested by memory. If Richard recollected his son's account correctly, Moondream had been Tallis Keeton's favourite mask. And it was Moondream that she had dropped for her father to find at the entrance to Ryhope Wood, at the hollowing where Hunter's Brook entered the forest. Had Tallis herself, then, carved the face that was now etched across the growing and gigantic tree?

A few hours later, with the rain easing off, Sarin came running into the half-light below the spreading branches. Lacan was noisily cracking wood, constructing a temporary shelter along the lines of Helen's bower. He heard Sarin's loud call of, 'Someone coming!' and pulled into deeper cover. Richard and Lytton followed him, slipping on the wet underfoot and sliding onto their bellies in the cruel embrace of thorn and briar. Sarin pointed to where the undergrowth was moving, and a man stepped out to face the Mask Tree. He seemed dazed: his hair was dishevelled, his face streaked with dirt and blood.

He was wearing a red dressing gown, tied at the front. He was barefoot.

'My God,' Richard whispered, 'it's James Keeton. That's exactly how I found him, years ago. He ran in front of my car. James Keeton . . .'

The figure of the man walked unsteadily into the clear space below the high, wide canopy. He was clutching a piece of wood in his hands, holding the object close to his stomach. He stepped up to the trunk of the tree and stared at the face, silent for a long while, shivering with cold, his right hand occasionally reaching out to stroke the heavy bark.

And suddenly he called out Tallis's name. He repeated the cry, and the name extended into a howl of pain, a wail of despair. Again and again he called for his daughter, dropping the mask, leaning against the tree, hitting his forehead against the wood. His agony reduced Sarin to tears, and Lacan, who was crouched beside her, folded her into his cloak. Richard felt moved to tears himself. He wanted to go to the man, began to do so, and almost struck Lytton when the grey-faced Scot forced him back.

'Don't interfere. This is not his moment. It's *Alex's*. If you want your son, you'll have to let him come. I *know* he'll come . . .'

Lytton quickly scanned the surrounding forest, listening hard for a second approach. Helen held her head in her hands, half watching the screaming, sobbing man at the tree, wincing as the wailing grew louder, shaking her head helplessly. When Richard put a hand on her shoulder she leaned towards him, but still tried to block her ears against Keeton's appalling sadness.

The ground below them trembled. By the tree, James Keeton had stopped crying. He took a nervous step back, then reached quickly to pick up the Moondream mask, clutching it to his chest as he stepped away from the elm. At the same time the air turned chill and dry, and the noises of the world around them receded, as if the atmosphere had suddenly rarefied.

The tree shimmered with light.

The face of Moondream stood out against the black bark, a thin trace of silver light. No sooner had it been defined, clearly enough for Richard to see the details of the eyes and mouth, than it was lost below other lines and slashes that seemed to burn out of the wood, one face after another, then a proliferation of features, haunting, frightening attributions, male, female, animal, some from the dream world. The montage of masks spread rapidly to cover the whole tree. Silver light spilled like a fine spray up into the canopy, down to the distended root-mass where James Keeton still stood, half hunched, in shock and wonderment, his pale skin reflecting the rich colours of the emerging faces.

Suddenly Keeton again screamed out Tallis's name, a raw and primal cry of such need, such anguish, that the whole wood seemed shocked and silent for a moment.

And then the trunk of the tree exploded soundlessly, enveloping Keeton in elemental shapes!

Figures streamed through from the dark trunk, ethereal and huge, some running, some riding, some gleaming with armour, others in a swirl of cloaks or skins, colours bright. The ghostly forms flowed around the shattered form of James Keeton, but as each figure reached the edge of the clearing and entered the wood, so it became solid. Around Richard the forest was suddenly alive with movement.

Lytton hissed, 'Great God, I didn't think of this – he's coming from *inside*!'

A purple-painted man ran towards Richard, a round shield held in one hand, a short sword in the other, hair flying, lips drawn back to expose brilliant white teeth. The figure leapt across the crouching man, crashed into the underbrush, and with an ululation of triumph raced away into the gloom, leaving Richard with an image of faces and whorls and swirls decorating the body from head to feet.

'What are we witnessing?' he asked loudly.

'Witnessing?' Lytton repeated. 'Alex's death! The moment his history was sucked from him. You were in the room at the time. Remember? Look at it! This is an encyclopaedia of what we have *all* inherited. Everything is here! And I can never remember it all. There's just too much! We must watch for the boy! Watch for the shadow.'

He turned to Lacan and Helen, repeating the instruction. 'It will be small, no more than the *shadow* of a boy. When you see it, follow it. Don't lose it!'

The procession of forgotten heroes continued for a few seconds more and Richard recognised what Helen had called the 'Hood' form, and Jacks, and an axe-wielding Viking, and a woman with hair like flowing fire, dressed in chequered leather trousers and jerkin, leading two grey mastiffs on long leashes. This might have been Queen Boudicca, a particular favourite of Alex's. A wagon and horses came through, driven by hunched, shrouded figures. Warriors walked out of the tree, some of them Greek, some Roman, some painted, some with helmets of striking horror. Women flowed from the tree, green girls, cloaked matrons, women with the look of magic about them, or of the fight for freedom.

Alexander Lytton, his face shining with delight and colour, was uttering a catalogue of recognition as each hunter, warrior, crusader, wizard or wild man passed: 'Peredur . . . Tom Hickathrift. And that's Hereward the Wake! Fergus, from the Cattle Raid of Cooley. Where's Cu Chullain? Morgana! Jack the Hound Killer there! Guinevere. And Kei, from Arthur's court. That's the Henge Builder of Avebury! A crane hunter . . . Dick Turpin! The Woman of the Mist. That's Llewelyn!'

To Richard, they were an army of blindly running ghosts, streaming silently from the tree and vanishing noisily into the woods.

The explosion of life ceased as abruptly as it had begun.

At some point in the procession, James Keeton turned and walked away, Richard was half aware of his departure, but no one had followed the man. He had stepped away, into the oblivion of memory, into an encounter that was now years in Richard's past.

Still stunned by what he had seen, Richard watched as the Mask Tree darkened; the carved faces once again had vanished. He imagined they would not return. Whatever their function, that function was now fulfilled.

And yet – a movement in the darkness told of a struggle. A moment later a small shadow burst into the empty clearing and scampered to the left. It was so fleet, so undefined, that for a moment even Lytton hesitated, his gaze on the great creature that was stretching from the trunk, striving to free itself from the tree.

Then he was on his feet and running after the shadow. Richard delayed for an instant only, astonished at the writhing tree-man, its face and body a mass of leaves, glistening branches like tusks twisting from its gaping mouth. Behind it, other twigling limbs were reaching for the cold air of the clearing. A shrill clattering began to sound from them.

Richard raced after Lytton, following the man by sound alone. To his right he could hear Lacan and Sarin taking a different path through the forest. It was only after some seconds that he realised Helen had stayed at the Mask Tree, watching the final emergence from Alex's devastated mind. He called for her, but she didn't answer, and when Lytton shouted angrily, 'Richard! Come on!' he continued to follow the elusive protogenomorph through the wood.

They struggled through the tangled darkness, tripping over roots, forcing their way through thickets so dense that they almost suffocated. When they suddenly emerged into open ground, it was into an overgrown cemetery, where stained grey stones poked from thistle-covered mounds. The wall of the cathedral rose before them, white and frosted, already beginning to shed its surface layer of stone.

Richard's cry of triumph gave way to a howl of frustration and disappointment. 'It's just another shell! He's tricked us again.'

'I don't think so,' Lytton said calmly. 'Look!' He pointed to the ivy-covered porch. The depthless shadow of the boy moved there, then seemed to seep into the stone, vanishing. 'This *is* the place. But how do we get in?'

To their left, Lacan burst from the wood, his hair in tangles, ribbons of briar hanging from him like a bizarre May Day veil. Sarin crawled on all fours from the cover, her breath misting in the intense cold.

Where was Helen?

Lacan called out in alarm, 'The place is dead. We've been led off the track . . .'

'This is the place all right!' Lytton called back. He was scanning the high windows, the jagged line of the wall where the roof had fallen, the buttresses, the porch, the steep rise of what had once been a bell tower.

And as Richard followed that gaze with his own, he saw the falcon. It stretched from below a high arched window, a rain gutter, its mouth the opened beak of the bird, which stared down at the man with an almost teasing gaze. *The bird that spits . . .*

'The bird window . . .' he whispered. 'Into the chapel, disguised as a falcon . . . That's how Gawain did it in Alex's play . . .'

Lytton was exhilarated. 'If this is the Green Chapel, then we may find a way through to the Otherworld. *Our* world, that is.'

Lacan shouted, 'We're being followed! *Daurog*, I think, but they're changing. We have to find safety.'

'Is Helen with you?' Richard called back, but Lacan just shrugged.

Richard led the way, climbing to the roof of the porch, then ascending the slope of a buttress to gain access to a statue niche, the figure long since rotted. From here it was a dangerous climb, using fingerholds in the pitted stone, to the stretched neck of the falcon and the wide sill, carved with oak-leaves and acorns, below which it extended. Behind him, Lacan grunted and heaved his weight, reaching back for Lytton, whose arms were no longer strong enough to accomplish the climb. From high on the wall, Richard scanned the black forest below, and saw how winter crept, a growing silver crystal, towards them.

He could not see Helen, and the concern he now felt for her began to make him shake.

It started to snow, the dull sky deepening into a grim, grey cover, shedding flakes that began to swirl about the church.

From the sill, Richard saw the greenwood that had grown to fill the centre of the cathedral. A wave of warmth and moisture ascended from this summer place, although the first snow crystals were already wetting the higher foliage. He called for Alex and succeeded only in disturbing a roost of rooks, away towards the closed doors, where a tangle of vegetation suggested a huge, spherical nest.

As Lacan arrived on the stone sill, there was suddenly less room than before, and Richard almost lost his grip. Lacan steadied him, pointed to the ropes of creeper that covered the inside wall, and carefully Richard lowered himself to the chapel-wood below. Lacan dropped next, then Sarin, then Lytton, who immediately pushed his way through to the massive structure. Richard followed, aware of the terrible stench that exuded from the mound of dead wood and grass. Lytton had entered the nest. He emerged, brushing black feathers from his face, looking around. 'Empty,' he said. 'A *daurog* birthing place – she's shed, probably dead now.' He saw something, below the statue of the crucified Christ. 'There!'

The hollyjack had been laid on a crude bier. Her arms were outstretched, but had risen in the first moments of death so that her thorn-fingered hands seemed to be clutching at the open sky and the gently falling snow that was settling on her. Her mouth was hideously agape, the four branch tusks dry and mouldering. The leaf on her head had turned yellow-brown. Her body gaped, was arched as if in pain. A small, dead rook was entangled in the dry ribs.

Someone had placed a small straw effigy of a bird above her head.

From the chapel-wood Lacan hissed, 'Something below us!'

Richard felt rather than heard the movement below the marble flooring. The disturbance was brief and he wondered if it might be Alex, so he called for the boy again and from the far end of the ruin he heard a voice call questioningly, 'Daddy?'

With memory of the shapechanging Jack freshened by apprehension, Richard forced aside the foliage and approached the altar. Something gold was gleaming there, and after a few moments he recognised a crucifix, as tall as a man, rising above the consuming swathes of holly.

'Alex? Where are you?'

The boy moved suddenly from the green. He was unkempt and naked, a frail figure, his skin as white as the snow that drifted down around him, eyes fierce in a feral face, hair to his shoulders. He was trembling like an animal caged.

Richard began to cry. Alex was so young, so old. Despite the long hair, he was almost exactly as Richard had remembered him over the years, the Alex of those last terrible months in the long-gone when he had looked at the sky with blank eyes, when he had lain listless and content on the grass, responding with nothing more than reflex actions. But this boy, this Alex, had a light in the terrified eyes that spoke of intelligence, of awareness of the long-to-come; and best of all: of recognition.

'Daddy!' he yelled suddenly, and ran to the crying man, to Richard, who dropped to his knees to gather in his son. 'We're in danger!' Alex shouted. 'Gawain's coming!'

The Green Knight

Green light played on the white ceiling and walls of the hospital room. Alex lay and watched the swirling colour for a while, then rose from his small bed and walked to the window. He watched without wonder or fear as a knight emerged from the wood and rode across the dew-bright lawn. The knight was huge, on a massive white horse with flowing green trappings. His hair and beard were green, as was his scaly armour and the rippling cloak that unfurled behind him as he cantered; he left a spreading fan of glowing green that reached back to the tangle of the dawn wood.

He came close to the hospital, then reined in, reared up and turned twice on his charger, grinning at the watching boy above him. He beckoned. Five spears were strapped to his saddle, and a curved axe, its cutting edge smothered in leather, swung from his belt. Tusked faces formed his armour, which looked more bone than metal. Alex felt drawn without really comprehending the compulsion to follow. He saw the colour and the patterns of the knight, but felt no fear, no pleasure, no curiosity. Compelled, though, he left his room and went out into the early morning.

Once outside he could smell the rank sweat of the horse, and hear its heavy breathing. The ground vibrated as the beast turned, shook violently as it reared and fell back with a jangle of trappings. The huge knight reached down with a green-gloved hand. His breath smelted of earth. Alex accepted the grasp and was swung into the saddle behind the green man. No words were spoken. Alex held on to the thick cloak. His legs were stretched hard over the broad saddle. Faces of the dead, branches growing from their gaping mouths, watched him from the armoured back. When he touched one, its eyes narrowed and it snapped at him, giggling.

He gasped, then, as the horse charged back to the wood. It entered the trees without hesitation; the knight ducked, laughing as branches tore his flowing hair. Alex turned to glance briefly at the grey and silent building behind him. Then darkness closed about him and thorns began to tear his hands.

It was a wild ride. Silently, the knight rode through the woodland edges, sometimes using a knife as long as a scythe to cut a path. He crossed fields and roads, shouting encouragement to his steed, uttering a shrill cry when he saw a game bird, or hare, and running it down with almost magical speed, snatching and catching the creature more often than he missed. The horse pounded the country lanes, foaming at the mouth, complaining noisily when its direction was changed so that it had to plunge into marshy forest, or canter along shallow brooks.

A moment came when Alex passed his house in Shadoxhurst. He watched, aware yet unaware. There was movement in the garden, someone digging. He glanced back once, but without pain or longing, only recognition. The digging man had looked up, looked round, perhaps aware of the distant canter. But the knight was on the bridleway to Hunter's Brook, and his green aura was dispersing in the fog that filled this lower, marshy land.

They were soon at Ryhope Wood. The knight rode carefully into the edge by the old Lodge. Here, in a clearing by the ruin, he dismounted, to gather wood and grass, bits of rag and bundles of leaves. As Alex watched from the saddle, he shaped a boy on the ground, gave it Alex's features, then lifted it and made Alex spit into the wooden figure's mouth. The false-Alex stood and ran to the edge, then across the fields, uttering a meaningless gabble of sound. Alex watched it go without thought, without question.

He rested his head against the knight's broad back as they rode through the forest, his face cushioned from the bone scales and living armour by the thick cloak. This he wrapped around his body for warmth. His knuckles were white where he gripped the knight. His backside and legs were bruised and aching from the hours of cantering. He rode without a murmur though, embraced by his rescuer.

The forest opened into wide hills, then closed into stony valleys. They waded through deep snow, skidded on winter ice, were drenched with rains that soaked them for days.

One dusk, they came to a wide lake. A black barge was moored there, its sail furled. Three women stood on the shore among the tall rushes, watching. The knight kicked his horse forward, then stretched round to help Alex from the horse, down to the soft earth. The smallest of the women, a girl of about Alex's age, came forward and wrapped her red cloak around the boy. Alex stared into her eyes for a moment and she smiled. A second woman, who looked like his mother, robed in brown, turned to the barge and reached for the tethering rope. The third, clothed in black, was old. She climbed into the barge and unfurled the sail, then sat, facing the shore.

The Green Knight leaned down and tugged at Alex's hair. His breath misted as he spoke, his accent odd, 'I heard your call. I was the first to come back to you. I have to find the other knight, to bring him back.

'You need time now, to heal. These ladies will take you to the place where that healing can be managed. They will heal you with Courage,' he pointed to the girl, 'with Love,' the woman in brown, 'and Magic.' He scowled at the woman in black. 'But mostly you will be healed by Courage. I shall send a small spirit to be my eyes and ears as you recover. Don't do anything to hurt the wolves in winter! Each nick in their flesh is a nick in mine.'

And with that, he turned and rode away, axe swinging at his thigh, cloak billowing.

The girl held out her hand and Alex stepped with her aboard the barge. The woman in brown pushed the vessel from the reeds, knee deep in the mere, then clambered in. She picked up the oars and rowed the vessel across the silent lake until a breeze caught the sail and the eldest of the women leaned forward to hold the ropes.

After a while, as if in a dream, they drifted through fog, but emerged, oars stroking gently, to see tall trees and a craggy shore. The girl scrambled from the barge. She ran into the hidden land, through the mossy rocks of the shore, then came back and beckoned to Alex. As the older women stayed with the boat and watched, he held hands with the girl and let her lead him. They emerged from the wood to face the towering wall of a church. It was in a state of ruin.

'This is your place,' the girl whispered. She looked round anxiously. 'Go inside quickly. It's not safe on this side of the window.' She kissed him, first on his cheek, then his chin, then ran back into the undergrowth, toward the lake and her companions. 'Go inside!' she called again, and Alex turned to face the grey wall.

Inside the ruin he could hear the sound of birds . . . They had gathered on one particular window.

The doors were all blocked. He climbed the wall and went inside. It was warm but empty, yet as soon as he arrived, the wood began to grow from the crypt below, saplings at first, then a bristling, rustling forest.

Nothing had any meaning. He explored the ruin without interest, instinctively seeking warm places, and shelter. Faces watched him from the dark benches, from the stone figures on the walls. Light caught the tints of coloured glass from shattered windows. He scavenged for food, was drawn to water in a well, outside the wall.

At some time in the sequence of days and nights, he heard movement in the heavy wood, where the girl had left him. A sinister presence had arrived, that changed its shape, sometimes wolf-like and howling, sometimes tusked and giggling, sometimes a grinning knight who called to him with a mocking human cry. It meant him harm and attacked him when he came too near, and he became afraid to leave the sanctuary of the place of stone.

The hollyjack came, rustling in through the window where a stone face with feathers spat water when it rained. And it was soon after she had come that he began to dream again. The dreams came back to him, at first ugly and distorted. But one by one they passed the giggler in the wood, creeping into him through the doors and windows of the sanctuary. As he dreamed, so things found names again, and small figures danced out from the wooden benches, and the coloured window where the greenback lived began to grow, to reveal the knight and the green man, and the great mound of green turf through which a bright land gleamed. Everything was almost real again.

He dreamed about his father.

Alex huddled in his father's arms. Richard stroked the boy's hair, touched his cheek, tugged him more tightly into his embrace.

He could hardly believe that Alex was here. He kept cradling the boy, kept looking, remembering, reminding himself that this *was* how Alex had been, this unkempt, dreamy boy, this smiling, loving boy who grasped his father in the manner of a kitten, nervous and determined. What was Alex thinking? What did he feel?

His words, as he had told his story – his dream – had been stilted, as if he was struggling to find the language to convey the wonders and horrors of his existence. He was like a child waking from a deep sleep, half-coherent, strangely real, still unfamiliar.

He was not complete.

But he was Alex Bradley, no doubt about it, and his father held him with all the energy of a man who cannot bear to lose a dream, who cannot quite believe the dream, who wants to feel the dream forever, never to wake.

Richard whispered, 'You've been so missed. You've been so lost. It must have been terrifying for you to go through all of that.'

Alex touched his father's face and smiled. 'The hollyjack was sent by the Green Knight. She was my friend. She helped me dream. She was a small part of him, a small spirit. I thought the knight was Gawain at first. There's a window where the nest is. It grew back while I watched it. All the colours came back. All the reds and greens and golds. When the window healed, I remembered the knight. I thought it showed Gawain killing the green monster. But it's the Green Knight who's our friend. Gawain is cunning. He's the giggler. He trapped me here. He doesn't want to come back. He doesn't want you to take me away. He likes being outside.'

Richard looked up from his son, focused on the far window where sunlight illuminated the fitted shards of colour, predominantly green. The stained glass showed a classic duel between chivalrous knight and man-eating monster, a human form, a wild man, green-cloaked and massive, barring the way to a summer-wood, just glimpsed through the door in a mound that rose higher than the trees. Yet instead of the knight spearing the wild man, this window showed the wild man exacting the life of the knight. It could have been a portrayal of martyrdom. But Richard now saw that it depicted the triumph of nature over the despoiler.

Alexander Lytton had listened with fascination as Alex recounted this dreamlike memory of his 'rescue' by the knight. Now, he looked up, looked around, murmured, 'His dreams came back to him by all the doors and windows of the sanctuary . . .'

Alex, exhausted, had begun to drift into sleep in his father's arms. Richard cradled him, rocked him, but watched the gaunt features of the Scot.

'Where are we, Alexander? Where the hell are we? We're in a wood, I know that. We're in a reflection of a ruin that Alex once visited, a cathedral, a sanctuary, a holy place. A *haven*. I know that too. It's the Green Chapel, in its way, and Green Knights come and go, and dreams, enter and pass through—'

'Exactly,' Lytton murmured. 'This is the passing place. Exactly that. Old dreams pass out, new dreams enter. The Green Chapel in the old poem was a place of testing. To the medieval world, the tests were of honour, of chivalry, of courage. The Cross against the witches of the pagan world, the world of forgotten gods, forgotten lore. The Green Chapel itself was described as a burial mound, an access to the

Otherworld of "faerie". Your boy recognised a long time ago that the Christian story was a convenience to suit its times. I remember you telling
me how he subverted the story in his school play to make it not a test of honour by benevolent trickery, but a double-cross by Gawain himself, to get access to an older land and older treasures. And what treasures!

'The chapel is the frontier between instinct and conscience, the place which tests dreams, and by testing dreams, by testing the faith a mind *puts* in its dream-state, tests the mind itself. There is a magic in dreams that these days we can't value. They can express combinations of experience. They can create vision. If the vision is clear, is lucid, if it can be controlled, if its symbols can be comprehended, it gives power through something we take for granted. Intuition! But that ability has to be won against more basic instincts.'

Lytton glanced at Richard and smiled. 'Think of this place as your son's version of the "passage" between primal and higher minds, between unconscious and conscious. That's certainly what the Green Chapel itself represents. This is a natural place to come when you are stripped of dreams, and need to heal. How I would love to know the *dreamtime* story of the Green Chapel. What an understanding that might give us into *insight*. Your boy was given the briefest of glimpses. So have we been. But because of the appetite of Alex's imagination, which means he absorbs a lot of junk imagery, we only get to see Jack the Giant-Killers, and Gawains, and sturdy knights etcetera, Tennyson-esque queens in barges (an interesting aspect of the mind's notion of self-healing, incidentally). The hollyjack is primitive, though. *That* was close to something very old . . .'

From the window through which they had entered the cathedral, Lacan called down, 'There's something coming through the woods! Can't make it out, but whatever it is, there's a lot of it. Not creatures . . . not as such . . .'

Alarmed, Richard said, 'Christ! Helen! We've got to help Helen.'

Lytton grabbed his arm. 'Helen stayed behind in the glade for a reason. She's a capable woman. If she sensed Coyote, you should let her be . . .'

'She's in danger. I can't lose her! Not now.'

'She'll have to face Coyote on her own. You can't help her.'

'She's not facing Coyote. She's facing Gawain . . . If what Alex says—'

The greenjacks,' Alex whispered. 'Only it's winter. The Green Knight in winter can't be trusted. The hollyjack told me so. Until the spring comes, he'll try to kill us, just like Gawain . . .'

Increasing his grip on Richard's arm, Lytton said grimly, 'Gawain and the Green Knight are part of the same creature. But they're Alex's — Coyote is not. Helen wouldn't have stayed behind unless she was sure her own time of testing was coming.'

Winter developed into a storm. Snow blew hard against the cathedral, swirling icily into the wood inside the walls. Richard joined Lacan on the falcon sill, staring into the gloom, and saw the spread of movement across the black forest. Like the lights and shapes that had emerged from the Mask Tree, elemental forces were flowing towards the sanctuary, streaks and swirls of colour in the blizzard, faces and forms that existed at the periphery of vision.

Richard returned to the shelter in the Lady Chapel. When he told Lytton of the impending attack, the man swore loudly, raised wide eyes to the broken walls.

Moments later the elementals seeped into the cathedral, Lacan yelled suddenly from the window-ledge and almost plummeted to the snow-covered floor below, just keeping his grip on the thick, slippery creeper. Above him, faces stretched from the stone, statues shifted, and the cracked figures in the wooden pews emerged and ran through the shivering wood.

Through it all, light pierced the stained glass, making the figures of Gawain and the Green Knight appear to writhe within the crystal. Yet they remained in place, while the stone figures all around them, birds, gryphons and grinning monks, became animated, their voices emerging as a meaningless chatter, muffled by the stifling snow.

Alex laughed at the antics. His eyes glowed, despite the cold. 'It's like the first dream. They danced for me! They danced!'

Richard hugged his son, not understanding the enthusiasm, the excitement. The cathedral flowed with movement. Every thorn and hazel, all the gnarled oaks and slender birches that formed the chapel-wood seemed to move, to shift a little, to join the dancing figures.

'They're coming back to Alex,' Lytton said from his hunched position in a niche where a statue had once stood.

But even as he spoke, so the effect seemed to vanish. The figures froze, the sense of a massive elemental intrusion into the sanctuary withdrew. Lytton's eyes widened. He glanced at the boy, then murmured, 'Not Alex's at all! Someone watching us, someone outside.'

He stood and waded through snow to the ivy-covered wall, pulled himself up the thick strands to the icy ledge. Richard followed him. Lacan and Sarin huddled for warmth; Alex was swathed in the big man's cloak.

From the falcon window, as the snowstorm eased, a figure could be seen at the woodland edge. Richard was certain that it was not Helen, nor a knight in any shape or form. It was a man in a long, black overcoat, his white head bare, his face full-bearded. He carried a staff; a backpack was slung over his left shoulder. He was staring up at the cathedral.

The air cleared, a sudden lull. The man stepped forward, shaking snow from his hair to reveal darker locks, a younger face.

'My God,' Alexander Lytton breathed. 'It's Huxley. It's George Huxley!'

The man by the wood turned away. Lytton called his name. The man hesitated, frowning as he glanced back, but then turned again to pursue his path through the trees.

'Huxley!' Lytton cried desperately to the winter wood. 'George Huxley! Wait!' He scrambled down to the floor of the chapel, grabbed his rucksack and found his oak staff. He tied his cloak around his chest and tugged the hood over his head. 'I can't lose him now . . . I've spent too long looking.'

'You're mad!' Richard said. 'You'll never find him in this storm. And how can you be sure it *was* him, and not a mythago?'

Lytton laughed dryly, as if recognising the irony of the situation. 'How? Because I've seen more photographs of the man than he ever knew existed. I gained access to them. I've stared into his eyes, into his soul, using a lens, using my imagination . . . I've stared at that face for more hours than I've stared at my own, Richard. You could show me the shaved whiskers of his cheeks and I'd know they were his. Don't doubt me, lad. I'd know him anywhere. For Huxley, it's the 1930s. This is the middle of his deepest journey, his longest absence. I didn't expect to find him. He found *me* . . . our meeting is recorded in his journal – he doesn't name me, so I can't be sure, but everything fits with what he wrote when he returned to Oak Lodge in September 1937.

'I *will* find him, Richard; he can't get far in this snow. I hardly had the courage to believe it would happen. But it has. And it's time for me to leave you.'

He hugged Lacan powerfully, then bowed to Sarin. He ruffled Alex's hair and finally extended a hand to Richard. 'I'm glad we *both* got our wish. I learned a frightening lesson about myself, that day with the Jack . . .'

'Gone and forgotten,' Richard said quickly. 'As will Huxley be, if you don't get a move on.'

Lytton glanced down at Alex. 'Don't let your father do anything foolish. His friend, Helen, knows how to handle herself. She's a match for *any* trickster. To help her,' this for Richard again, 'might be to frustrate *her* wish.'

'There are wolves in the wood,' Alex said anxiously. Lytton frowned.

'*Scarag*. I know. The greenbacks in winter.'

'Try not to hurt them. When spring comes, they'll be our friends.'

Lytton smiled thinly to reassure the boy. 'Laddie, I have no intention whatsoever of challenging a scarag. I saw what they did to a friend of mine.'

He scaled the wall again, crossing the sill by the falcon gargoyle and skidding heavily to the ground outside. Richard followed him to the window, leaned out of the stone and watched him go, a fleeing figure, cloak swirling, entering the snowstorm again, soon lost in the wood, his final cry for Huxley sucked hollow by the winter world.

During the night the sounds and vibrations from the crypt were a constant, muffled reminder that the cathedral was not a complete sanctuary. The snow had ceased to fall. At dawn Lacan took his spear and climbed to the window to watch for danger. Sarin and Richard investigated the entrance to the crypt, but found only a sealed wall, riddled with roots and faint inscriptions. Alex wouldn't go down the stone stairs. 'They're coming back to me. My friend told me. But they frighten me—'

'Who?'

'The winter-wolves. They're finding a way to get to me . . .'

Richard strung his bow, fingered the tip of one of his arrows. 'We'll fight with everything we've got. Which isn't much, admittedly, but we'll use it!'

'They're our friends in the spring. Don't hurt them—'

'You seem to know a lot about them, Alex. But none of the rest of us do. You seem afraid of them, but afraid *for* them. What do I do if they attack?'

'Don't hurt them,' Alex whispered, but he shivered as he said it, looking nervously across the snow-laden trees, feeling the sudden vibration of a large creature below the altar.

'What is it?' Sarin whispered apprehensively. 'Something's happening.'

'I don't know.'

Richard took a step away from the altar. The whole wood was quivering, snow being shed from winter branches. 'Arnauld!' he began to shout, but he managed no more.

The floor in front of him buckled below the spreading roots and silver trunk of a birch, forcing the tree to lean sharply. It heaved again and the birch fell. A black marble slab thrust vertically from below it, scattering snow and exposing the darkness of the crypt.

The head that pushed up from the hole was bone-white, huge, with four tusks curling from its gaping mouth. Below folds of bone and gnarled ridges, black eyes glittered as the creature looked quickly around before heaving its lithe and sinewy frame from the pit. It had a wolf's features, despite the protuberances from its mouth. Its rib-cage was vast, gruesomely defined above a stomach that was hollow and taut, although it rippled as the muscles were tensed. The creature was twice the height of a man. Its arms hung heavily by its sides, fingers spread and ready as it watched Lacan on the high window, then howled at him.

Lacan hurled his spear. The scarag didn't flinch. At the last moment it snatched at the weapon, allowing the blade to make a shallow nick in its breast. It howled again and its tusks clattered. It tossed the spear across the cathedral, toward the altar where Richard watched in horror. As the haft clattered on the stone, Richard reached for it.

The scarag moved away from the vault. At once a second head appeared in the hole, this one broader, flatter, one tusk broken. The lame thing that hauled itself from the crypt was grey and bony also, taller than the first, but stooped. It watched Lacan curiously, then growled and turned to forage in the chapel-wood.

A third and fourth winter-wolf emerged from the hole in the floor, each looking around as it rose, hesitating, watching first Lacan, then Richard, before stalking through the trees. The fifth scarag, a smaller version but no less menacing, remained at a crouch by the gap in the marble floor, emitting a sound like a low growl. Without moving its head, its eyes shifted restlessly, sharing its scrutiny between the huge Frenchman and the crouching trio by the golden cross on the altar. It seemed to be guarding the hole to the underworld.

The first scarag soon found the body of the hollyjack. It gathered the dry, dead evergreen into its arms and lifted it to its chest. One of the others picked up the straw bird and placed it in the open body. The wood filled with the sounds of mourning and the winter beasts moved stealthily toward the cathedral's main doors and entered the decaying nest.

Last to go was the Guardian, the shaman of the group. It pointed three times with its carved staff to the passage through to the crypt, its feral eyes fixed on Richard. Then it rose and backed steadily through the snow to the maw of the nest. Here, with a series of cries that were almost human, it turned and crawled inside.

Three days later, at the height of the day, as Richard returned from a fruitless search for Helen, the nest by the tall doors began to exude bird-cries and chattering. At once, Alex ran to the ramshackle structure and stood in the wash of green light that began to flood from the circular mouth. There was a great deal of movement inside the nest and the same sun that had transformed the winter world into one of spring flashed blindingly through the crystal window above the doors.

Alex started to move towards that light but Sarin put restraining hands upon his shoulders and looked around for Arnauld, signalling to Richard as she saw the man drop over the access sill.

'Something's happening,' she called urgently.

Alex shrugged her off, then turned, eyes wide, lank hair flowing about his grinning face. 'They're back. They've come!'

Before Richard could do anything to stop his son, Alex had jumped at the hole in the mass of wood and grass and bundled himself inside. The eerie light flickered. There was movement and a sudden breeze, like a breath.

The entrance to the nest closed! It seemed to snap shut, and Richard flung himself across the cathedral to stand by Sarin. She backed away, horrified and appalled, her hands to her mouth.

'It's eaten him,' she whispered. Richard held her, shaking and afraid.

'No. No, I don't think so. I think this is the end of it.'

Dear God, please let it be so.

The nest shrank. The wood and bramble melted down, became hair, became eyes, became a nose and a grinning mouth that opened and emitted a low chuckle. The eyes watched stonily, the hair waved like rushes in a high wind. Richard panicked.

'Arnauld! Quickly!'

The Frenchman came running. Richard tried to thrust his spear into one of the Jack's eyes, but was blown back by the stench from its mouth, and the hollow laugh. *Don't hurt it . . .* his son seemed to say. A moment later the face seemed to calm down. It dissolved into a kinder head, a sad-featured visage that Richard remembered from the Argo.

Vast, grotesque in its way, Orpheus fleetingly watched the trembling man below him, and sang words in a whisper.

'*One bloody nick . . . side of his head, all for the lady . . . the love of the lady . . .*'

Then Orpheus too dissolved, the wood and bracken crumbling into dust, the whole nest collapsing down, dissolving, dispersing into the feeding green shoots of new growth that reached from the tall doors, and from between the cold stone flooring. Soon there was just a curled human shape covered with ivy and ground elder, which writhed over the boy's naked form, then drew back, taking the black rot, the orange fungal growth, the shards and fragments of decay, taking it all back down to the rootweb.

Curled on the floor, Alex opened his eyes. He unfurled like a leaf at dawn, his arms stretching, his legs flexing, his back arching. He greeted the high sun, the grey-green shadows, and smiled. He passed water and sat up, watching the steam from between his legs, slightly embarrassed. Then he looked at Richard, who was standing shocked and in tears. He stood up, brushing self-consciously at his wet thighs, trying to hide himself from his father's gaze. There was a strange fire in his eyes. Green light seemed to touch his skin.

'I need clothes.'

At once, as if kicked into action, Richard ran to the boy and placed his cloak around Alex's shoulders. He could hardly speak, managing a tear-choked, 'Dear God, you give me some frights!'

The nest had sucked all dead things away, including the ends of hair and strips of his nails. But there was something *whole* about the boy, now: trickster and conscience had come back. The two faces of the Green Knight had returned.

Alex stared at Richard with a searching curiosity. 'Your hair's gone grey. You've got lots of grey.'

Richard kissed the boy's forehead, then with his arm tightly around him led him back to the altar. 'I'm getting old. Too many adventures.'

'I've been dreaming, haven't I? It was such a funny dream. Can we go home?'

'Of course we can go home,' Richard whispered. He glanced down. 'You'll find things a bit changed, Alex. You've been in a long sleep. It's been a long dream.'

'I saw Mr Keeton. He was very sad. Is Tallis all right?'

Shaking his head, Richard said, 'Tallis went away. Mr Keeton was very sick, and he died.' He couldn't help his tears. He hugged his son to his chest. Alex struggled for breath, pushed at his father's embrace.

'It's all right,' he said. 'I'm grown-up enough to know that Mr Keeton was very ill.'

'Mummy's gone away too. But you'll be able to visit her. It will be very important for you both.'

Alex looked grim. 'You were always arguing. I could hear you from my room.'

'We were always arguing,' Richard agreed gently. 'We weren't happy.'

'Are you going to argue with the new one? The Red Indian?'

'*American* Indian! We don't say "red" any more. And no, I'm not going to argue with her. I know what songs to sing these days . . .'

'Is she a real Indian?'

Richard laughed. 'Of course! Helen Silverlock is an almost pure blood Lakota. Or did she say Dakota? Minnesota? Anyway, she's Sioux. I think. Maybe Cherokee.' *Damn! He couldn't remember.*

Alex was looking puzzled. 'What does "pure blood" mean?'

'She had a tough grandfather. She's got a lot of courage.'

'What's Lakota and Dakota?'

Richard sighed. 'I don't know. Signs and signals of my ignorance of any history that isn't our own. But what does it matter? I love the "new one" as you call her because she's making history with *me*. Silver hair on each side of her head, feathers up her nose, Rolling Stones and all.'

Alex looked blank, and Richard reflected ruefully that the boy had ridden away with the Green Knight before the Rolling Stones had given their 'Mummy' her 'little helpers', before the Beatles had 'please, pleased' themselves. If they could ever get out of this wood again, it would be 1967 . . . maybe 1968, eight years since Alex's healing had begun. And there was a climate of healing in the world beyond Ryhope now, a mood of peace, societies angry at the war in Indo-China; and the

Seventies were looming, and things were going to be so much more interesting! Alex would enter that new world, that brightly blossoming world, like a young leaf unfurling to make his mark on the tree, to suck in the sun, to add his voice and his dreams to the dreams and voices that were striving so hard to make their courage and their vision known.

Richard was startled by Alex touching his eyes. 'You're crying,' the boy said.

'Am I? So I am. I was just thinking how much you had to look forward to. I was just thinking of being home.'

'Me too. I think the Green Knight just showed us the way.' Alex wriggled away, and drew the cloak around his tall, thin body. He used a piece of creeper to tie the baggy garment at his waist, and hauled the extra length up and tucked it in the belt.

He went back through the trees to the broken floor and peered down into the crypt. Arnauld Lacan crouched beside him, spear held firmly between his knees. Alex said, 'When I was dreaming, I moved through strange corridors, through the roots under the world. I could dream of you. I saw you.' He glanced at Lacan. 'I could also dream of the hollyjacks. Sometimes I dreamed of the world outside, and I think this is the way home. It's down through the dead, but I think the dead only frightened me because they were coming back. They're all back now. There's nothing to be frightened of.' He looked up at Richard. 'I'd like to go home.'

'I know you would,' Richard whispered, looking desperately at the falcon window. Helen was still out there! He couldn't leave until she came back. But he couldn't leave Alex again, not now, not having found him. He was too precious a treasure ever to leave again.

He could hardly think straight. He wanted Alex home, and safe – he wanted Helen safe, and coming home.

Before he could speak a word, Alex looked up sharply, quite alarmed.

'What about your friend? She might be in trouble! Are you going to help her?'

'Yes,' Richard said quietly. 'I'm going to try and find her. I won't have to wait long. I can hunt for game. There's plenty of water in the well . . .'

'Is she hunting down a wolf?'

'Coyote.'

'Sounds like a wolf to me. I've heard him crying. He's there now, out in the woods. Can you hear?'

And indeed, as Richard fell silent and raised his head, as he listened hard through the trees and stone, he could hear an odd baying, a triumphant and frightening wolf-cry. A battle was being fought. He reached for his bow, but Sarin stepped forward and held him. Her dark eyes glistened.

'Let her be. Let her *be*. If you lose her, it will be because she's dead. But if you find her, it will be because she's won. Just let her come back in the way that will give her release from her nightmare. She knows the way out of the wood. And you've already proved enough. I will never forget how you defeated Jason! Now sit between the worlds and wait, and pray, wait for what happens. Now take care of Alex. Take him home . . .'

Lacan loomed behind the Tall Grass Speaker. 'I've just been down among the bones. There's certainly a hollowing below us. It has that feel. But if this giggler thing has gone, we might do better to go the land route.' He sensed the awkward silence. 'What's happening?'

Sarin said grimly, 'I think Richard is staying. To help Helen.'

Lacan smiled broadly. 'Of course he is! And we're staying too. Four are better than one! Besides, what's the alternative?'

Richard said, 'You could take Alex back to my house in Shadoxhurst – wait for us there . . .'

'Your house?' Lacan said, horrified. 'Where no doubt there is nothing to drink but tea and medicines?'

'You might find some red wine in the sitting room.'

'In the sitting room,' Lacan breathed with a despairing shake of his head. 'In the light, no doubt. By the fire. In the warm. To keep it happy. A very fine vinegar, I'm sure, but if I want to drink vinegar I'll go to a British fish-and-chip shop. There is no hope for you. Please immediately return to the *bosk*. I shall save your son from the humiliation of you being his father. Come on, Alex.' He squeezed the boy's ear gently, teasingly. 'Come on. We have a long journey. We have to hunt before we leave the wood. To *eat*, you understand! We have to prepare for your home – and for all the horrors it no doubt contains.'

Alex watched his father all the time. 'I'm staying,' he said, and Lacan laughed quietly.

'Of course you are.'

The boy came over and took Richard's hand. Richard smiled at his son, tightened the boy's cloak across his chest, noticed what brightness of spirit, what sudden awareness and maturity had etched the edges of the smooth face that stared at him.

'Perhaps you *should* go home. Arnauld is only joking when he says the things he says.'

'I know!' Alex said in frustration. 'I'm not stupid. But Sarin told me that she can't live outside the wood for very long, and Arno' wants to stay with her, so they wouldn't be with me for long. So we should stay.'

Outside the cathedral a wolf whined, a long, plaintive and sinister sound that made Richard's skin crawl.

'I'm frightened for you!' he said, standing.

'Don't be.'

Later, Richard went up to the window, to sit and watch and wait, listening to the whining call and the mocking laughter of the creature that Helen, perhaps, was hunting.

The night deepened. A fire was burning in the distance, a single beacon which Richard watched with an almost hypnotic fascination. It was hard to tell at this distance, but occasionally it seemed that a figure passed in front of the flames.

The wolf bayed in the wildwood, then chuckled and chattered. No wolf, then.

A flight of rooks swirled noisily through the cold night, stags coughed and barked, wide-winged water birds flapped noisily, moonlight grey as they circled their high roosts. The wood was a restless yet motionless expanse of dark and at its farther end the fire burned, the figure moved, the sky glowed, Coyote prowled. Above its nearer edge, at the threshold that separated two worlds, Richard Bradley lay on his side, curled up like a child asleep, thinking, of the son he'd found and the woman he loved.

He was startled by movement behind him and grabbed for his knife. Something had been climbing the ivy ladder to the falcon window. Half-dazed, he turned and reached down to defend himself against the intruder.

'It's me,' Alex said.

The boy scrambled the last few feet and huddled on the wide stone ledge, shivering slightly, watching the fire in the distance, close to where his Mask Tree grew in the forest. 'Arno' and Sarin have gone down into the crypt. I think they're sleeping. I'd like to stay up here while you're waiting for Helen. If that's OK . . . ?' He seemed apprehensive.

Out in the wood the sound of a wolf triumphant split the night. An instant later the sound was cut off. There was something chilling, something very final about that sudden silence.

'*Is* it OK?' the boy asked.

Richard smiled and reached to pinch Alex's pale cheek. He glanced back to the fire, which had now begun to fade.

'It's OK,' he said.

Appendix

Editor's note: *George Huxley recorded numerous folk tales, myths and legends, mostly obscure, which he heard or interpreted during his explorations of Ryhope Wood between 1928 and 1946. He dates* Jack His Father *to 600* BC, *an early Celtic version of a much older* Kurgan *tale.*

R.H.

Jack His Father

Jack was sowing the last of the summer wheat when the smell of smoke told him of the raid on his village. His sister, who had better hearing than a hound, yelled 'Horsemen!' and ran quickly to the cover of the woods. From the tree-line she called to Jack to hide. The boy followed her as far as the first tree, but stood with his back against it, strong against the coming storm. In the distance he could see the smoke rising from the enclosure where his father's house would now be burning.

'I still have a father, a mother, a sister and three brothers,' he said desperately to the birds that circled the field. The ravens departed noisily, mocking him. The geese descended to eat the summer seed, and Jack's heart sank.

The armed runners came first, searching for crops and cattle. They led three calves with them, and two horses, which trotted in silence since their jaws had been tied. These men were young. The horsemen and the warlord's chariot came after, riding suddenly from the trees, hooves drumming, chariot wheels creaking. Two of the horsemen saw Jack and galloped down upon him. Jack stood his ground, his right fist clenched around the last of the wheat. He saw the sacks that were tethered and slung across the withers of the horses, and thought at once of the pigs and fowl that he and his sister had so carefully raised.

'Don't tell them I'm here!' whispered his sister from hiding. 'Since you're so stupid that you won't hide, then your head it'll be, but don't give me away.'

'You'll give yourself away, if you don't shut up.'

The man in the chariot was Bran, resplendent in dark leathers and a red cloak. He wore a crested war helmet, and the silver curve of the moon was stitched into his corselet. He was black-haired, big-handed, clean of face. The blue and black symbols of his clan, the Boar and Eagle, spread richly across his cheeks and chin. Now he crouched in front of Jack, amused by the boy, and of a mind to bargain.

'I see you wear good shoes,' he says. 'Cowhide, is it? Well-stitched, I think.'

But Jack blows a hard breath at the man. 'Take them from me or leave them on me, it makes no difference. If you've done us harm I'll follow you faster than cloud shadow.'

The horsemen laugh, but the man with the crested helmet does not.

'That's a fine talisman, that bone carving, that boar, on the leather there, around your neck.'

But Jack blows a hard breath at the man. 'Take it from me or leave it on me, it makes no difference. If you've done us harm I'll come at you from a hawthorn thicket faster than the breeze.'

The horsemen shift nervously now, horse-chains rattling, sacks of booty swinging in the cooling day. The crested man draws a small bronze dagger and meets the defiant gaze.

'That's a brave tongue you wag at me, that lip-licker, there, that loud proclaimer.'

But again Jack blows a hard breath. 'Cut it from me or leave it in me, it makes no difference. If you've done us harm I'll sing in your ears as the crows feast on your eyes.'

The dagger points at Jack's right hand. 'I'll have what's there, then. I'll have what you hold, or cut it from you, that clenched hand.'

'Cut it from me, then. It's the only way you'll get it, and what I hold will vanish.'

'What does that fist conceal?'

'Seeds,' says the boy.

'What sort of seeds?'

'The seed of a tree that takes no more than a day to grow and can make a house where there's always a feast of pork roasting on the fire.'

'I'll certainly have that,' says Bran hungrily. 'And I'll have more. What else?'

'The seed of a tree that takes no more than a day to grow and can make a boat fit to cross any haunted lake.'

'I'll have that too, and more besides. What else?'

'The seed of a tree that grows faster than the hair on a man's face, and can give shelter and fruit to a host of men. From its top can be seen the Isle of Women.'

'I'll have that, and twice over!' says Bran, his eyes lively, his hand patting his balls. 'Or die in the trying.'

So Jack says, 'What will you give me for them?'

He can hear the sound of women crying. A cold wind brings the smell of smoke and slaughter over the fields, where the geese stalk the new seeds, and the ravens cast dark shadows.

And Bran says, 'I'll give you the best singing voice a man could wish to hear.'

Jack laughs. 'I'll certainly take that from you. *And* I'll have more.'

'Then I'll give you the prize of all pigs taken in this raid.'

'I'll certainly take that from you,' says Jack hungrily. 'And I'll *still* have more.'

'Then I'll give you back your father,' says the helmeted man, this Bran, with a scowl, slapping his knees to signify an end to the bargaining. 'And promise to make you a better man than him. There, now, it's done, this game. That's all.'

Jack agrees and holds out the seeds to the chieftain, who takes them and looks at them angrily. 'This is wheat!'

'Not everything is as it seems,' says Jack with a laugh.

'Indeed, but that's right, that's very true.'

The chieftain shakes his head and scowls, then goes to his chariot and fetches a sack, which he tosses to the boy. When Jack opens it, his father's head, half-lidded and bloody, grimaces at him from its cold grave.

Bran and the horsemen laugh and turn to ride along the river. The chief calls from his wicker chariot, 'Indeed, Jack, you were quite right there, correct in what you said. Not everything is as it seems. But I kept my part of the bargain, that bargain there just now, which you cheated on! Your father was the wild pig of your clan I prized the most, and he sang for his life more sweetly than your three brothers, who I'll be taking with me, in those sacks, there, which you thought were pigs. And since he's dead, your father, then it takes no magic to make you the better man!'

When they've gone from sight, though, Jack kisses his father's face and consoles his sister. Then he crosses to the field where the fat geese are almost finished with the wheat.

'You've taken my last seeds!' he shouts at the birds. 'Now you must pay for them. There can never be a better man than my father, so make me my father now, and return me to that chariot, that armoured man, who killed him, to follow him.'

And he catches a goose by its legs, holding the bird down, while the crows circle and chatter with amusement at Jack's cleverness. The goose is ashamed at its greed, the eating of the wheat while Jack had fought for his life. The air is suddenly full of feathers, and the sound of the Screech Owl that has been summoned, and by her magic Jack takes the shape of a raven which feeds upon the sad eyes of his father. Then the raven becomes the head. Only a goose is strong enough to carry the head in its sack, and this goose flies up above the furrows, and then to the west, following the chariot. Jack's sister takes their father home, to the burned village.

When the goose is above Bran's chariot, it lets the sack fall.

Then Bran opens the sack, and Jack-his-father opens his eyes. And he says, in his father's voice, 'Give me back my sons.'

'Never!' says the chief, but he ties the sack again and rests his foot upon it as he rides, frightened by what has happened.

The first night after the raid they camped on open land. Bran planted one of the seeds, more by way of humour than expectation, and pissed upon it. But Jack-his-father rolled unseen from the chariot and changed his shape again. He sang as he grew, a head becoming a tree, a strong oak, spreading out over the camp, reaching boughs to the ground and using leaves as a roof. When he had enclosed the raiders and there horses, he made the fire spring up and the wood spit and hiss with the rich fat of a spitted pig. He made sap run as honeyed ale and watched as the men below him fell into a pleasant stupor. The crows in Jack's branches flew down and stole back the severed head of his eldest brother. 'Carry it safely,' Jack said, and the sound of his voice woke Bran, but too late to stop the birds from flying off, out of this unknown region.

On the second night, Jack-his-father taunted Bran. 'One of my sons is safe again, taken home. Give me back the others.'

'Not even if the flesh rolls from my bones and I catch my death of a cold.'

They were by a lake. Jack waited until Bran planted a second seed and pissed upon it, crying, 'To see the Isle of Women, that would be a fine raid!' then, when the man had laughed scornfully and retired to sleep, he rolled from his sack and grew into a strong willow. He reached out over the deep water and shaped his prow, then his hull, and used branches as oars. He became a low, sleek galley, and the raiders found him in the morning and imagined it had drifted to the shore by night. They clambered aboard and rowed to the middle of the take, towards the forest trail beyond that led to their own land.

But half-way across the lake, Jack opened the branches that formed the hull and the galley foundered. Man and beast swam to the shore, but a great pike caught the hair on the head of Jack's second brother and carried the head up the river, out of this unknown region, back to the land of his birth. Jack-his-father was gathered in and slung across the neck of a horse, to be carried on. He felt like singing, but kept silent.

A third night, then, and Bran placed Jack-his-father in the ground, placing the last of the wheat seeds from the bargain into its mouth. 'If you make a tree that can shelter and feed my companions, and from which I can see the Isle of Women, then you shall have your third son back.'

Jack grew. He was the oldest of oaks, wide and strong, trunk dressed with creeper and a place big enough for a house in the angle of every branch. The host of men camped below the spreading lower branches. There were fallow deer here, plump geese, and sweet, young pigs. The hunting was good. Sharp-juiced apples grew from the middle boughs. Strong-breasted fowl nested higher, within bow-shot. Wild wheat bristled from the swathes of ivy, and made good bread. It was a great place to be, below this solitary oak, and they stayed here for the better part of the season, growing fat and thinking themselves on the Island of Ease.

Each day Bran climbed higher into the tree, but turned back before reaching the top out of fear, not liking the way the birds sang. But all the time he was thinking of what the Bold Boy had said to him: that he would be able to see the Isle of Women from the higher branches. It was a place Bran hungered for. To know its direction would give him great power over the land. He would not be caught by the spirit tracks that confused mortal men if he knew where, in the west, he was heading.

Jack-in-the-tree waited.

One evening, when the skies were clear and the air still and warm, Bran climbed the tree to the very top. From here he could see to the edge of the world. He saw the Isles of the Mighty, the Land of the Young, the

Isles of Women, and when he had learned how to get to them all he began to climb down. But as fast as he climbed down, so Jack-in-the-tree grew, until the oak became so heavy above the ground that it began to wave and bend in the wind. Soon it cracked across its roots, and fell heavily to the rocks on the shore of the Isle of Women, where the body of Bran was smashed and broken.

Jack became himself again, the Bold Boy, Loud Proclaimer, and picked up the head of his youngest brother. He could never run faster than the hound, so he became a hound in form, and ran from this unknown place, back to the lake, back to the open land, back to the ploughed field and over the rise of forested ground to the place of his father's lodge. His brothers were there, but his sister had disappeared the summer before, and he would not find her again for many years.

He spat out the last of the seeds and planted them, then rebuilt the house. A town flourishes there now, and it is still the best part of the island for growing wheat. A white figure, carved on the hill, marks the place of Jack's defiant stand against the raiders. From its head, looking towards the setting sun, his sister's strange tomb can sometimes be seen at dusk.

GATE OF IVORY, GATE OF HORN

For Annie,
our glimmering girl

Take, if you must, this little bag of dreams;
Unloose the cord, and they will wrap you round.
W.B. Yeats, from *Fergus and the Druid*

. . . there are two gates through which dreams reach us. Those that come through the Ivory Gate cheat us with empty promises that never see fulfilment. Those that issue from the Gate of Horn inform the dreamer of the Truth.
Homer, from *The Odyssey*, Book XIX

PART ONE

In the Valley of the Crow

Prologue

This morning, when I opened my eyes and saw the spring sky above me as I lay in the shallow boat, I realised that my long journey from the heart of the forest was over, and that I had come home again.

Oak Lodge was there, across the meadow, empty and silent. And yet I could not step through the trees and go to the house, as if the wood, so difficult to enter from the outside except along the brook, was now reluctant to let me go. So for a while I walked back into that consuming gloom, following an old track and coming after an hour or so to the clearing my father had called the 'Horse Shrine', after the crumbling, ivy-covered statue of the animal that stood in that place, a wooden shield propped between its forelegs.

Here, I decided that I must write down what had happened to me, to give an account of it, something that I might refer to later when the details will have faded, since I cannot believe that I will not be returning to the heartwoods again and again. Though I am tired and confused now, I shall keep going back. I have left someone behind and I intend to find her.

And I will start this account with a truly haunting memory, the memory of a boy watching his mother dance furiously on the lowest branch of an oak. A day that ended a week of wonders. A day that shaped the boy for the rest of his life, although he couldn't know it at the time.

And because that day is no longer mine, though it once belonged to me, I shall tell of it briefly, and in a different voice.

George Huxley was on his knees by Christian's bed, his hand resting lightly on the boy's shoulder. Chris woke quickly, aware of a pale, predawn light on the man's unshaven face. He could smell the water-proofing on his father's cape, the leather of the bulky backpack, the polish on the heavy blackthorn staff.

'I'm going into the wood again,' the man said. 'Just for a few days.'

'Hunting shadows?' the boy asked quietly.

His father smiled. 'Yes. Hunting shadows. Shadows of the past, strange and wonderful shadows of the past.'

'Shadows in the wood.'

'I'll be gone for a few days only. Take care of things. I trust you to take care of things. Of your mother . . .'

All night Chris had listened to his mother's shouting, her sobbing, the crash of crockery, the bass grumble of his father's voice.

'Mummy's upset,' he whispered, and Huxley frowned. The man's breath was cheesy, the black stubble along his lip flecked with crumbs. There was sadness in his pale eyes, the lids hooded, lines of discomfort on his brow, on his temples. A watery gaze, but a glance or two of affection, something that Chris's brother, Steven – away, staying with an aunt – never received.

'Don't go away again,' Chris whispered, but Huxley merely kissed the boy's cheek.

'I've left a note for you in the journal. The latest one. Read it, don't get it sticky, don't tear the pages. Do you understand? When you've read it, put it back on the shelf and lock the cabinet. Put the key in the drawer of the desk. Do you promise me?'

'Yes.'

'I'll be gone a few days. Just a few days. The torches you saw by the wood last night are important. Someone of great interest to me is very close to us. You'll find his name in the journal, too.'

'And the horse?' Chris said. 'I saw a grey horse. There was a girl on it, a girl with white hair. She was watching the house.'

'Be careful of her,' his father said. 'If my ideas are right – she's no girl. I shan't be gone long, Chris. You *must* promise me to comfort your mother. She's a bit . . . upset.'

Chris remembered the desperate voice: *Don't go, George! You've only just come back. How do you think it is for me? To see you covered in mud and dung. And blood! Stinking like a farmyard! I'm going out of my mind, George! Don't go to that bloody wood again . . . What do I tell the boys?*

'I'll make her some breakfast,' Chris said to reassure his father. 'I'll tell her everything's all right.'

'Good boy. I know I can depend on you.'

'Daddy . . . ?'

'I have to go, Chris.'

'How *far* do you go? Into the wood . . . ?'

George Huxley's hand swept gently across his son's unkempt hair. 'Very far indeed. There's a river at the very heart of Ryhope Wood, a river that flows from the beginning of the world. Strange ships sail there, and strange sailors watch me watching them. I'm learning so much, but I've only just begun. One day you'll know. One day your brother Steven will understand as well . . .'

He leaned forward and kissed his son, then rose and stepped away. At the door he murmured, 'Don't play with the white-haired girl, if she comes again. She isn't a girl. She's older by centuries than she seems. She's dangerous. Promise me?'

'I promise.'

By sunrise his father had gone. Chris put on his clothes and made a pot of tea. His mother, dressed for some reason in her Sunday suit, was huddled by the dead fire, staring at the ashes. She didn't respond when her son put the cup and saucer on the table and touched her shoulder. The boy walked quickly to the study and opened the bookcase, taking out a thick leather volume, his father's latest journal. Turning it to the last written page, sitting by the window that looked onto the brooding edge of Ryhope Wood, he tried to understand a little more about what he had seen over the last few days.

Huxley had written:

I am as sure of this as I am sure of anything – which is to say, not sure at all. But my guess, on the evidence, is that the group which has ventured beyond the Horse Shrine and is gathering at the edge of the wood is of the *Iron Age*. I suspect aspects of classic Celtic *questing*, the searching for cauldrons, grails, swords, great pigs, emblems of magic and mystical attribute.

I am tempted to think this may be a form of *Kylhuk* and his entourage of knights from King Arthur's court, obsessed with the many strange and wonderful tasks he must accomplish to win the fair Olwen, or die at her father's hands. To these questing men (and their ladies!) the edge of Ryhope is the edge of the world. What they seek lies either *beyond* that edge – in *this* world – or behind it, and they are lost, they have come too far.

I must leave poor Jennifer again to go in search of them, but Christian is a sensible boy. He will 'guard the fort'. I know he will exercise caution in all things, and make Oak Lodge safe for my return in a matter of days. He is not a curious boy; I trust him not to interfere in things he doesn't understand.

When Chris went back to the sitting room, his mother was no longer by the fire. He saw she had drunk the tea. He found her in the kitchen, bottling tomatoes. The front of her green tweed suit was splashed with juice. The red liquid squirted over the table as she pressed a lid into place and snapped down the iron lock of the preserving jar.

Chris wanted to ask if she was all right, but the words wouldn't come. His mother hummed to herself, increasingly drenched in the red juices. She should have been wearing an apron. She was bottling unscalded tomatoes; they would go rotten in a matter of days. She was doing nothing right and Chris felt like crying. His mother's mouth and eyes looked bloody where she had wiped her hands across her lips and brow.

'Go outside and play,' she said suddenly, looking at her son. 'You know how your father hates to have you under his feet when he's working.'

'Daddy's in the wood . . . He's gone into the wood.'

'Nonsense!' She turned away from him angrily. 'Daddy's *working*. And you should be playing. Go on, now. Go and do something constructive with your time. Make a model ship. You make good models. You'll be an engineer one of these days. Off you go.'

'Why are you in your Sunday clothes?'

'Why do you think? It's a special day. Now off you go.'

What special day? he wanted to ask, but the words dried in his mouth. He reached out to her, hoping for a quick kiss, a warm pat on the cheek, that little smile that always reassured him, but she went on squashing fruit, her head shaking as if thoughts were tumbling inside her head.

After a moment, Chris quickly left the house, drying his moist eyes on a sleeve, then kicking angrily at everything he could see before running to the stream which he and Steven called the sticklebrook.

Here, last year, the two of them had launched HMS *Voyager*, a two-foot, single-sailed model ship that had swept into the wood so fast they had hardly had the strength to follow it and see it vanish. Lost for six months, the vessel had turned up again, almost as good as new, caught in the mud on the Shadoxhurst side of Ryhope.

The return of the ship had thrilled his father and sent him into a fever of work and writing. Even now, Chris wasn't sure whether the hours of questioning that early spring had meant approval or anger from the man whose moods and obsessions dominated the atmosphere in his home.

By the millpond, later that day, Chris sat for an hour or more, hoping to see the furtive movement across the water that usually denoted the 'Twigling', an odd creature, disguised in the dull greens and browns of an outlaw, and with sticks and twigs tied about his head to make a crude and hideous wooden face. Today, all was still.

He wanted Steve. His brother was full of dreams and full of stories. His imagination had fuelled the brothers' games. Without Steve, Chris felt isolated. He longed for night, when the wood might again become alive with fire and voices, horses and garish human figures.

By the evening, he had walked as far as Shadoxhurst, playing on the village green for a while with friends from school, spending his meagre allowance on chocolate before heading back along the hedges towards the sprawling estate on which his parents had their lodge. The fields were waist high with barley, the seeds about to burse. It had been a fine summer and the harvest would begin two weeks earlier than usual.

When he came to the sticklebrook, he followed it to the thistle field and the dense border of scrub wood and nettle that made Ryhope Wood so hard to enter. He saw an owl swoop in flight, and a hawk of some sort hovered above the trees, turned towards him. A deer moved furtively, red-brown flank just visible for a second, then gone. He started to walk towards home again, surrounded by a bosky and eerie silence that thrilled him.

Suddenly, out of that silence, out of the wood, a white-haired girl rode towards him, cantering along the bank of the stream, leaning low in the saddle. As she passed the boy, she reached out to strike him on the head with a thin stick, strips of red rag and white feathers streaming from its shaft.

She laughed as she achieved this deed. Then the horse reared up, leapt the stream, and she trotted back on the other side, the coup-stick held loosely in her left hand while the right tugged at the crude bridle, slowing down the impatient grey.

Chris stared at her in astonishment. The ride had been so sudden, her appearance startling. Her face was so pale that she might have been a ghost, but there were thin dashes of colour at the edges of her cheek and he realised that she was painted. Her hair, too, was whitened with some paint or other; it was long and quite stiff, not flowing freely as she moved. Several braids had been wrung through these sculpted locks and tied with string or cord. One braid alone was decorated with leaves and feathers, and at this she tugged absently with the hand that held the crop as she gazed at her prey.

She was wearing a short tunic of red-and-green check and cloth shoes. Her legs were otherwise bare; there was a glistening sheen of sweat on her throat and arms.

This girl was *centuries older than she looked*, according to his father. But she seemed to Chris to be no older than some of the girls in the village, though there was something that he thought of as 'boyish' about her. He said to her, 'Why did you hit me?'

Instead of answering him, she shouted angrily at the wood behind him, and when Chris glanced round, he saw a tall man in a white cloak, standing with a black horse and gently stroking its muzzle. The man frowned, growled fierce, warning words at the girl, then pulled back into cover.

The next thing Christian knew, the sweating grey was splashing through the brook, snorting loudly, and the girl was reaching down to grab him by the shirt. She hauled him up with astonishing strength, verbally abusing him in a way that suggested he might help himself a little, and he grabbed at the rough saddle and the coarse mane, somehow righting himself astride the beast's back. Suddenly they were off at a heavy, painful canter through the fields of barley, ploughing a trail that wound and weaved towards the glowing sky where the sun was setting. The girl laughed and called out, kicking the young grey until it was galloping dangerously fast. Chris felt bruised by the saddle, but was more aware of the firm touch of the girl's fingers around his waist, and of her breath, sweet like fresh fruit, as she cried with delight and urged the horse along.

Her gaiety ended quite abruptly. She screamed, tugged so hard on the reins that the horse reared and the young riders fell heavily into the soft crop of corn. The girl was shaking, clearly in pain and very frightened. She tugged at her tunic to cover her legs, then twisted round to a kneeling position, breathing hard and shaking her head.

Chris tried to touch her, but she pulled away. He could feel a bruise on his knee and blood in his mouth, but the girl was in much greater distress, though the reason defied his eyes and his understanding.

Riders were coming across the cornfield, five of them, their faces painted a violent scarlet, white hair in spikey crests across their crowns, colourful cloaks streaming behind them. They rode in silence, spreading out to form a wide arc around the boy, long spears held loosely, points grazing the ears of the corn. The girl stood up and whistled for her pony. One of the oncoming men pulled up, shouted, the others swung round and dismounted quickly. The field of corn stooped to a sudden breeze that chilled Chris as he stood nervously, watching the events.

With a sharp word, then a laugh at him, the girl swung onto her grey's back and kicked towards the wood. One of the red-faced men slapped at the horse as it passed and his companions began to follow her. This one, though, beckoned to Chris, and the boy walked slowly towards him.

Close up, the apparition was frightening. The red paint was cracked across cheek, brow, and chin, and looked like dripping blood where it had been rubbed into the full, curling moustaches. The horse was edgy, held by its reins but wanting to return to the trees. Below the full-flowing cloak the man wore a chain-link coat of dull grey metal and patched rust-coloured cloth trousers tied below the knee. A broad, intricately patterned scabbard was strapped to his left thigh, and the jutting pommel of the sword it enclosed was shaped like a dead man's face, blind-eyed, long moustaches drooping around a gaping mouth.

This protecting warrior talked angrily at the boy, his free hand waving, punctuating his points, emphasizing the sibilant, fluid words that flowed through Christian's head like a smooth, welcoming dream. He recognised something about this man, but couldn't place it. The lesson was stern, but somehow forgiving. Whatever had angered the red face, it had more to do with the foolishness of youth.

Eventually the man slapped his heart and said, 'Manandoun.'

Christian said his own name. Manandoun nodded, puffed out his cheeks, and exhaled in exasperation, then pulled the horse round, mounted up, and rode quickly back to the wood, while Chris ran in pursuit, through the deep path left by the wild rider.

There was silence at the edge of Ryhope, where the sticklebrook flowed into the gloom.

But a moment later he heard the girl's whistle. Ducking below branches, she came quickly out of the trees on the grey pony, shrugging off the angry cries from behind her, and flung something towards the watching boy before vanishing again. He ran to fetch her gift, and held the feathered stick, her skull-cracker, her pony-whipper, and felt a sudden sense of wonder and joy.

He wanted to show the crop to his father. He wanted to stand in the light from the desk, watching as his father turned the piece of decorated wood in his hands and nodded with satisfaction.

This is much more than just a riding crop, Chris; it's a talisman capable of calling for power, a magic stick, something I've never seen before . . . Priceless, wonderful . . . I'll analyse it and display it in the cabinet . . . A real treasure . . .

But his father was in the wood, called by his own obsessions.

In the evening, while his mother stared silently at the fire she had laid, sweat beading on her skin as the unnecessary heat in this scorching summer made the room like a furnace, Chris prowled round his father's study, circling round the desk that occupied the middle of the room and staring at the glass-fronted cabinets, where the labelled, numbered exhibits were displayed in quantity. George Huxley was a man of application and orderliness, but his museum was cluttered.

Chris had always been fascinated by the weapons and crossed the room to his favourite display. Five longbows were arranged side by side; the first, with crude carvings of antelope and bison, was labelled *Cro-Magnon*, ca. 50,000 BC; next to it was a smaller, simpler piece of wood, with gut string, marked *Hittite*. The tallest of the bows, blackened with charcoal and decorated with simple bands of red paint on either side of the arrow-nock, was labelled intriguingly: *An Agincourt Bowman called Alan Leanback (note pun in name): cannot find story attached to him.*

In another cabinet, figurines in clay and bone, bronze and wood were arranged by subject, rather than period: Snake Goddesses, Lords of Animals, Power Figures (made of wood, their bodies wounded with shards of bone or metal to release their anger), Keepers of the Hearth, grotesquely obese icons For Fertility and Fecundity, Battlefield Guardians with hawk or owl attributes, Animal Totems, Spirit Houses, and others. Chris stared at the range of homed faces, fat-bellied women, crouching ghouls, terracotta statues with their arms raised and snakes, or ropes, draped around them, and distorted animal faces that peered malignly at him from dulled ivory, or greened bronze, or the battered, ragged grey of flint, and something reached out to tug his heart, drawing him closer to the cabinet until he found his nose against the cold glass and his breath misting to obscure these grim and gruesome tokens of so many lost and forgotten peoples.

It took a moment for him to realise what it was that had attracted his attention. Then his mind focused where his eyes were staring: at the dead face, blind eyes, gaping mouth, identical to that which had adorned the grip of Manandoun's sword. The effigy was clearly part of a similar weapon, Chris now realised; it was not the same face; it was *akin* to the Manandoun face; brothers in death, perhaps.

For reasons he couldn't understand, he felt unwell, disturbed. He started to leave the study, but became weary and sat down behind the heavy oak door, staring across the room, across the wide mahogany desk at the garden windows, at the gathering dusk.

He fell asleep and woke when the desk lamp was switched on. His mother was sitting there, hair awry, head shaking, her hands moving over one of his father's journals like scurrying, frightened animals. She was flicking through the pages, whispering words, hissing sounds, scanning the tight and tidy writing. She hadn't seen her son, although she was facing him. He remained curled up, half hidden by the open door, listening to the stream of words.

After a while he drifted into sleep again, huddling into his body, feeling chilled, aware of a flickering but persistent light beyond the glass door opening onto the garden.

He awoke again, this time to the sound of breaking glass. The study was alive with shadows, cast by torches held by figures which emerged slowly into the room from the garden. He could see his mother, but only in silhouette. She was standing by the desk, facing the intruders, her arms limp, her body quite still. A tall man walked about the room; a sharp, unpleasant odour followed him. He leaned down to Christian, bringing an acrid flame close to the boy's face. Chris saw grey eyes, black beard, scars across a high brow, glittering rings in the man's ears, the sharply stylised face of a horse on the bulbous pommel of a sword that was slung across his belly.

'*Slathan!*' the man breathed, and then repeated the word, as if questioning, '*Slathan?*'

A woman's voice answered from behind him, the words like a low growl.

'*Slathan . . .*' the man said again, menacingly, then reached out and used a tiny knife, a green metal blade, to nick the edge of Christian's brow, at the same time touching the healed scar by his own right eye. The boy sucked in a breath and touched a finger to the gash, but he remained quiet, watching as the shadowy figures smashed the cabinets, rifled the exhibits, laughed and shouted at the things they were finding, and all the while his mother stood in frozen silence, staring through the open garden doors at the flame lit wood.

A cry of triumph, and the scarred man turned away from where the boy crouched. There was a moment's laughter and the invaders left the study, all save a strangely long man, a figure so tall that he had to stoop below the high ceiling of the room. He smashed the cabinet containing the bows and drew out the one which had been labelled *An Agincourt Bowman called Alan Leanback*. He flexed the yew and listened to it, then nodded with satisfaction and followed the others to the wood, cracking his skull on the lintel and complaining loudly to the amusement of his comrades.

A cowled woman came back into Huxley's den and faced Jennifer's motionless figure. Chris thought it might have been his friend from the horse ride, but he briefly glimpsed a face below the cowl that was gaunt and moon-silvered; and old. While outside, horses were led away from the house, men shouted, and torchlight flickered and streamed into the night sky, this matron whispered something in Jennifer's ear, then moved quickly around the room, marking each wall with ash symbols, shapes that Chris couldn't fathom. Finally, she used a knife to spend several minutes hacking a criss-cross of lines along the vertical edge of the door frame, before backing away from the study. Outside, she stuck a carved pole into the lawn a yard from the house, then turned and ran after her fellows.

By the desk, his mother had started to wail, and when Chris went to her, touching her gently on the arm, she turned, shrieked, and ran. She fled to her bedroom, locking the door behind her and refusing to respond to her son's urgent and frightened questions from the landing outside.

What had the old woman whispered? What could she have said that could have so terrified his mother?

It was the longest night he had ever spent, though in years to come he would know greater fear and a greater need to see the light of a new day, to banish shadows. He kicked through the glass of the smashed cabinets, picked up the artifacts that had been scattered, trying to place them back where they had once been displayed, and studied the smeared symbols and the cuts on the door. He shuddered as his finger felt the vertical line of tiny scars, a premonition of the meaning that would come some days later, when his father interpreted them:

Kylhuk turned away from the Ivory Gate and broke this place. He took what he had been seeking. He marked the boy as slathan. *The burden of quest is now lighter for the ever-searching, fearless man, Kylhuk.*

The journals, six volumes of his father's obsession, were still on their shelf and he reached to take one down, but got no further than this before the sound of running upstairs made him push the volume back again and call to his mother. In fact, she came into the study, furious and frightening, chasing him out.

'Look at this mess!' she cried, kicking at the broken glass. Her son watched her apprehensively. She had washed her face, combed her hair, changed the juice-stained blouse for a new one. She looked *smart*. But something was dreadfully wrong.

'Are you all right?' he asked her. She hesitated for a moment and he thought he saw tears in her eyes. Then she spoke sharply:

'Go upstairs, Chris. I'm going to lock the room. Heaven knows what your father will say when he comes home. Go upstairs, now. Go to bed!'

She was speaking as if the lines were learned and familiar, mouthing the words without any real feeling; she was acting, Chris thought; her mind elsewhere as she paced around the study, murmuring her annoyance. And yet she was aware of him, avoiding his gaze.

'Mummy? What's the matter?'

She turned on him, her face like stone, stunning him with the hatred in her look. 'Go to bed, I said!'

He fled from the room.

His mother closed and locked the broken windows to the garden, then locked the study door, pocketing the key as she moved away into the darkness of the house. Chris had watched her from the landing; now he crept into his room, crawled beneath the covers on his bed, and cried with loneliness.

He woke sharply at first light, alert and clear headed, as if someone had shouted at him. He was still dressed in his holiday clothes. He rubbed at his eyes, then went to the window, aware that it rattled, that a stiff late summer wind was blowing from the east. There were rain clouds looming over Ryhope Wood. The gate to the garden was swinging and several chickens were pecking in the hedgerow, their feathers bristling. Somewhere in the house, a door banged.

Then he saw the figure in the distance, and recognised his mother, moving like a shade through the rippling field of barley, her direction towards Shadoxhurst. The awkward way she walked, leaving a dark, snaking line behind her in the field, whispered to Chris that something was terribly wrong.

He followed her, running into the barley, picking up her path across the rise and fall of the land. Was she running too? The faster he went, the more she seemed to be ahead of him. And he noticed, too, as he brushed at the windswept corn, that she was bleeding; she had cut herself, perhaps; there were regular spots of blood on the flattened stalks.

Then the trail divided and he stopped in astonishment, aware that someone had walked at right angles to his mother's route, heading directly for the wood. Indeed, as he stretched on his toes to see who had made this second trail, he thought he glimpsed a dark shape entering the underbrush. A familiar head, a determined way of walking, his mother certainly. And yet he could see her ahead of him, emerging from the barley onto the low rise of ground that led towards Shadoxhurst, the path running close to the tall, broad oak known locally as 'Strong Against the Storm'.

The blood trail led towards the tree and, confused though he was, he moved past this second path, noticing that the ghostly figure had vanished now, and soon he was walking over the field towards the sombre spread of the summer oak, where his mother stood facing him, dark against the brightening dawn sky.

She watched him approach. She was still in the stained Sunday suit, and had combed out her long hair, pinning it back only above her ears to reveal pearl earrings, bright like drops of dew. Her mouth was a slash of garish red. A rope was round her neck, slung over the lowest branch and waiting to be tied.

'What are you doing? Mummy!'

'Go away!' she shouted, but Chris began to run towards her. As he moved, so she jumped, reaching up to grab the branch, tugging at the rope to shorten its drop, dangling one-armed as she threaded a securing knot, a wild, mad dance on the lowest bough, then taking her weight with both hands, hanging there, watching him, her fingers digging into the grooves and knots of the umber bark.

He stood a foot away from her, staring up as she stared down, aware of the tears in her eyes and the blood on her shoes.

'What are you doing? What are you doing?' he wailed.

'Ending the pain. Starting a new life . . .' As she spoke her gaze flickered briefly to Ryhope Wood. The wind gusted strongly and the tree swayed, his mother's body swinging left to right. Christian went up to her to put his arms round her legs, but she kicked out savagely, her right foot connecting with his face and sending him sprawling.

'What are you *doing*?' he screamed again, adding, 'What have I done?'

She laughed as she dangled.

'Nothing. Yet. But it will turn out very badly for you.'

Her strength was giving out, her face strained, her fingers slipping on the branch.

'What did that old woman say to you?' the boy wailed.

'Nothing I hadn't dreamed of already. Nothing that wasn't already pain.'

'Tell me what I've done,' Chris said again, fighting tears and struggling to his feet. 'Please don't die . . .'

He couldn't bear the thought of it. His mother gone; no smile, no laughter, no knowing hug and gentle words after his father had raged and ranted about some madness or other. She couldn't die. She couldn't leave him.

His mother shook her head, blood suffusing her cheeks, her eyes watering with effort. 'My son is gone,' she whispered. 'I have seen what you will do! My poor boy. My poor little boy . . .'

'No! I'm here! I love you!'

'He's gone; they're both gone. Now it's my turn . . .'

She dropped and the rope stopped her fall, making her gasp, making her instinctively scrabble at the hemp around her neck, her face bloating almost at once. Chris sprang to her again, screaming in his panic, throwing himself at the dangling legs to take their weight, his voice an animal howl as he held her, aware that she was limp, now, limp and warmly liquid, her eyes unfocused, everything about her at peace as she swung in his arms.

He let go. Climbed the tree. Crawled up the branches to the heart of the oak, where he and Steven had often made a camp. Here he curled into a warm and huddled ball, listening to the wind and the creak of branch and rope below him.

After a while he heard voices. Several men were coming from Shadoxhurst. They didn't see Chris in the tree as they lifted down the corpse and carried it on a stretcher back to the village. Two of the men, one a policeman, set off round the cornfield towards Ryhope and Oak Lodge. Chris watched them go, watched them cross the two trails in the barley, the one that had brought the woman to the tree, the other that had taken the image of his mother into the wood.

He wondered if she was watching from the underbrush; or had she followed her husband inwards, to the cauldron of strangeness that Huxley claimed to have found at the heart of the forest?

And he was aware, though distantly as he huddled in the tree, that the seed of a great and terrifying knowledge had been sown – but like a butterfly that flits beyond the net, the precise form of that thought eluded him as he tried to grasp it through his grief.

One

I stayed in 'Strong Against the Storm' for a day or more. The manor
cooperated in the search for me, and had called out the hounds and the
local hunt, scattering widely to search the fields and woods around the
heart that was Ryhope. None, of course, entered Ryhope Wood itself,
where the paths were known in local lore to turn back on themselves
and confuse the senses.

It was my own father who found me, and then only because I think
he intuited I would be there. He had come from the wood and discovered the tragedy. He had walked across the barleyfield at dusk, to
stand below the tree and stare at the branch where the body had
recently kicked.

Whether or not he saw me, I shall never know. But after an hour,
with the light now gloomy, he suddenly called out to me, 'All right,
Chris. Down you come. Your brother Steve's home. We have to go
home, now. We have to face this together.'

He started to walk away and after a minute or so I swung down from
my hiding place and followed him back to Oak Lodge.

A silence more oppressive than that in the gloomy study pervaded the
house for more than a year. Steven mourned for our mother. I anguished at the loss of a woman who had been a friend. My mother had
always stood between me and my father, protecting me from his occasional anger and frustration with me (though he always seemed to have
more time for me than for Steven). Her words, her caresses, had
reassured me that all was not as bleak and terrible as it seemed. And in
this way, and after picnics in the fields, and games and laughter with a
woman who seemed to have so much time for me, so the sounds of fury,
the gasping cries of pain and indignity as Huxley used her (Yes, Huxley!
That is how I often think of my father, now), blindly, callously, and
without love, all became as no more than bad dreams.

A hand gently stroking my hair, an ice-cream cone, a walk, hand-in-hand through the meadows as the sun dipped below the trees and the distant spire of the church in Shadoxhurst, these from my mother were enough to banish the shadow of my father's darker moods. Her violent and angry words to me, as she died, had been shocking and incomprehensible.

When at last Steve began to accept that she had gone, so Jennifer Huxley crept back into my own dreams, crouching by me at night, whispering to me, almost urging me to remember her, to find her. Suddenly, these were frightening encounters with my mother, though I longed for her to come home again and would have welcomed a ghost in *any* form.

Over the years, I often woke to find myself standing at the very edge of Ryhope Wood, damp with sweat, convinced that the shade of my mother had beckoned to me urging me to enter, to follow, to find her, to bring her home! And she seemed to call out: *A girl, centuries older than you think, took you on a wild ride. Chris! She, too, was ghost-born. Open your eyes! If you listen to me, it may not be too late!*

Her warning, I now realise, came in my dreams, insubstantial, yet affecting.

And yet, how quickly I dismissed these sensations as no more than guilt and grief at the loss of a woman who had mattered to me so much.

There was something else which struck me as strange, in those last years of the 1930s, before the war in Europe would change our lives for ever whenever the field by 'Strong Against the Storm' was ripe, with corn or beets, or grass if fallow, two trails would appear on the anniversary of my mother's death, one leading towards the tree, the other leading to the wood.

To stand where the track divided was to hear an unearthly song, the sound of wind from a cavern; it was to smell the deep earth, to hear lost voices. Perhaps I was catching a glimpse, by odour and touch, of the twin gates that would one day confront me: those of Horn and Ivory, of Truth and the Lie.

I have often wondered if my father at this time entered into an odd form of dialogue with me, he writing in the pages of his journal, me responding with naive, awkward questions which he dismissed to my face, but seemed to answer later in his ungainly scrawl.

Frequently, I prowled the closely written pages of his journal and fought the wildness of his mind, finding, in my reading, a certain satisfaction, since my awareness of the wood and of events was slowly broadened. In this way I discovered the meaning of the *ogham* inscription that Kylhuk's 'marker' had left that time before . . .

He has masked the slathan . . . *the burden is lighter for the ever-searching, fearless man, Kylhuk.*

And I read that Kylhuk, according to legend, as a young man had arrogantly enlisted the help of Arthur of the Britons and his knights – Kei and Bedevere and the rest – to help in his marriage to Olwen, a 'giant's' daughter. Olwen's father had set Kylhuk a series of wild and wonderful tasks, from the ploughing up of whole forests in just a day, and the finding of magic cauldrons, to the rescue of an entombed god and a confrontation with animals older than time.

But there was nothing in Huxley's journal to suggest a meaning for the word *slathan*, which settled upon my youthful shoulders like some silent, watching bird of prey.

Only the reference to 'the Ivory Gate' openly puzzled my father. All he wrote was:

According to Homer and the Roman writer, Virgil, false dreams, dreams that delude the sleeper, enter the world through the Gate of Ivory; and true dreams, truth, if you will, through the Gate of Horn.

This legend does not link with the other, that of Kylhuk, and the reference is perplexing.

I noted this entry with interest, but was too young at the time to understand the significance of these mythological 'dreamgates.'

All of the entries in Huxley's journals, convoluted and confused as they were at times, related to manifestations of mythological creatures and heroes that my father called myth imagoes or 'mythagos' (I shall keep the man's eccentric spelling of the coined word).

The 'forms' of these mythagos, he believed, arose in Ryhope Wood as a result of being *seeded* by the human minds close by. They would first appear at the edge of vision, in the peripheral area of awareness where imagination and reality co-exist in shadowy tension. But the very fact that they could be glimpsed here, haunting ghosts, vague, startling movements seen from the corner of the eye, meant that in the deeper forest they were being given *form*, and *life*, and certainly a *past* . . . a history and a role in myth, born with the solid flesh, and a life that functioned as it had functioned in prehistoric times, perhaps. They could arise time and time again, conforming to memory and legend in many ways, but utterly unpredictable. And dangerous.

Indeed, there was a short entry referring to my mother that saddened me deeply, though again I couldn't grasp its full significance:

Jennifer sees her. Jennifer! Poor J. She has declined. She is close to death. What can I do? She is haunted. The girl from the greenwood haunts her. Jennifer more often hysterical, though when the boys are around she remains coldly silent, functioning as a mother but no longer as a wife. She is fading. Giving up all hope.

Nothing in me hurts at the thought of this.

The girl from the greenwood? Not the 'whispering woman', I imagined. And surely not the impish girl on the grey horse! So to whom had he been referring? And what role had this 'greenwood woman' played in my mother's suicide?

There were no answers to be found at the time, and life at Oak Lodge settled into an uneasy and grim routine.

Two

Years passed. A devastating war swept across Europe, and when Steven and I came of age we were both called up and saw action on the Front. When the war ended, I returned as soon as possible to Oak Lodge, and the brooding and obsessed presence of my father. I'd hoped Steven would be there, but he sent an enigmatic, oddly sad letter: he was staying on in France, with the family of a nurse he had met in the field hospital.

He was well, recovering from a shrapnel wound, basking in the warmth of the South of France and quite at peace with himself.

This announcement made me feel very melancholy, very alone, but I couldn't help remembering Steve's frustration, those few years before, when he'd received his summons to duty. I was home on leave at the time and had come down, sleepily, to find my brother angrily turning the pages of Huxley's journal.

I stood in the doorway, smoking, watching Steven, his grey suit smartly pressed, his hair short and shiny, his eyes almost feral as he glanced at me.

'What *is* all this shit?' he said. 'Jesus! What *is* all this rubbish?'

There were tears in his eyes. 'Chris, he didn't even bother to say goodbye. He's gone off somewhere again, one of his "explorations". He just looked at me, then waved me away. Waved me away!'

'He's in a world of his own,' I consoled. 'I thought you knew that by now.'

'I suppose so,' he sighed. 'Yes, I suppose I do . . .'

'I'm going to make some tea. A last cup before you go?'

'A last cup before I go,' he echoed morosely, and I turned away to the kitchen.

I heard the tear of paper. I glanced back into the study to see Steven folding a page from the journal and tucking it into his pocket. He might not have understood his father's obsessions, but he was going to take a fragment of that obsession with him into France, into the war, damned if he wasn't! I smiled, admiring the spark of anger. I could imagine what Steven was thinking about Huxley: *I may be a long way away, but I'll have a little bit of you with me, even if it means nothing to me. I won't let you go from me like you've let me go from you . . .*

And I was still wallowing in a similar feeling of loneliness and pointlessness on the day, in December, some years later, when my father finally turned on me like a wild creature.

A heavy snow had fallen during the night. I'd stayed in the village, sleeping on a couch at the crowded local hotel, but woke at six, made tea, then gratefully accepted a lift on a passing truck as far as Ryhope Manor. The main pathways on the estate had already been swept clear of snow, right down to the farm, and from there I followed the tracks of the tractors that had been out at dawn with hay for the animals.

By following the hedges and the stream, where the snow was thinner, I came quite soon to the garden of Oak Lodge. As I jumped the gate, I noticed what I can only describe as a *panic* of footprints in the snow of the garden, as if there had been a chase, or a wild dance, circles of impressions leading from the kitchen door, through the spiral formations and then to the gate. The single trail then crossed the field to the wood. The impressions were small. Deeper marks in the snow showed where the person had fallen or stumbled.

These were not my father's footprints, I was certain of that. Whose, then? A woman's, I felt.

The house was in chaos; someone had ransacked the kitchen, opening and emptying cupboards, battering at cans of food, smashing jars of preserved fruits and vegetables. There was blood on the surfaces, and in the sink, and a towel was blood-stained where it had been used to mop at a gash. Nervously, I walked through the rest of the house. My bedroom too had been ransacked, though nothing seemed to be missing. In his own room, Huxley lay naked and in a deep slumber, face down on the bed, his skin scratched and grazed, his eyes half opened. His right hand was clenched as if holding something, or frustrated by the loss of something which he had been gripping firmly.

'What *have* you been up to?' I whispered at him. 'And what have you been eating?' I added, because I had suddenly become aware of the odour in the room; not a human odour, not animal at all; no smell I could associate with winter. Indeed, there was the scent of summer grass and autumn berry in the atmosphere of this disrupted room.

'Where have you *been*?'

I left him where he was, went downstairs and laid a fire. The house was freezing. And it was as I struggled to light the kindling in the grate that my father suddenly lurched into the room, still naked, his flesh pitted with the cold.

'Where is she? What have you done with her?'

His appearance was startling. The growth of greying beard on his face and the strands of dishevelled hair made him look wild. The watery gaze was hypnotic; the wet slackness of his mouth after he screamed the words at me stunned me into silence. He looked quickly round the room, then lurched for one of the two shotguns stacked in the corner. He grabbed the weapon and swung it round.

'Don't be mad!' I shouted at him, throwing up my hands as he pulled the triggers. The two dull clicks brought me back to furious reality. In the past, those guns had been kept loaded, the breeches broken.

He advanced on me with the empty weapon, his thigh bruising against the edge of the table, his eyes still shining.

'Where is she? The girl! What have you *done* with her?'

'There's no one here. Dad, put the gun down. Get some clothes on. There's no one here – just you and me.'

His answer was to swing the stock round to crack against my head, but I was too quick for him, avoiding the desperate blow and grabbing the barrel. We struggled for a few seconds and I was astonished at his strength, but I had learned a trick or two in the last few years and disabled him with the briefest of kicks. He howled, hunched over his battered flesh, clutching himself in agony. Then, like some berserk creature of old, he was on me again, hands at my throat, musty breath in my face.

'Where is she? Where is she? I've waited too long for this encounter . . . I won't let you interfere with it!'

'There's no one here. You. Me. An unlit fire. That's it. Dad, stop fighting me.'

He seemed shocked, staring hard into my eyes, his own eyes wide with alarm. '*Fighting* you? I'm not fighting you, Chris.'

'What, then?' I whispered.

And he answered quietly, 'I'm frightened of you.'

His words astonished me. I was too stunned to speak for a moment as I stared at the grey, apprehensive figure of my father in all his filthy glory. Then I simply asked, 'Why? You have nothing to be frightened of . . .'

'Because you saw me . . .' he said, though he said it as if the statement should have been obvious. 'Because you know . . .'

'I don't understand.'

'You know what I *did*. You saw me!' He was suddenly exasperated. 'Don't pretend!'

'You're making no sense.'

'Aren't I?'

He was shaking, now, tears spilling from his eyes. I held him close to me. His body slackened, his gaze dropped, fatigue catching at his strength. I didn't understand his words, but they had distressed me. There was an emptiness in this cold house again, a hollow sense, that I had last known when my mother had danced for me on that terrible day and I had felt that – because of a whisper – I was the cause of her anger, her hatred, and her suicide.

I tried to speak, but the words caught in my throat. I wanted to be anywhere but here. For some reason the fire, which had refused to light at my urging, suddenly caught, and the dry kindling crackled in the flame. I helped my father down onto the sofa, now more than conscious of his nakedness and of the bruising on his groin. His hand stroked and soothed the wounded limb and he slumped to one side, tears rolling on his cheeks, glowing with the sudden fire. I pulled the cloth from the table and covered him, and like an old man he clutched at the edges, drew the warming blanket up to his throat.

'She was here,' he said quietly, and for a moment I thought he meant Jennifer Huxley, but he had never referred to my mother with such tenderness in his voice.

'Who was here?'

'She was here,' he said. 'I went with her. She was everything I had expected. She was *everything*. Everything I'd imagined. Everything . . .'

'The girl from the woods?'

'The girl . . .' he whispered, touching a shaking hand to his eyes to wipe the tears.

'Guiwenneth, you called her . . .'

'Guiwenneth,' he repeated, clutching at the blanket. 'Exactly as her story had said. But she is mine. Created from my own mind. I had known that. But I hadn't known what it would mean . . . Poor Jennifer. Poor Jennifer. *I couldn't help it*. Forgive me . . .'

'What does that mean? The girl was yours, you said. What does that mean?'

'They reflect our needs,' he answered, then turned his head to look at me, and suddenly all weakness had gone, only the canny look of the thinking man that I had known for all my life. It was as if his face tightened from the flaccid mask of despair to a stone-hard look that concealed all emotion. 'They *take* from us. I should have known that. They reflect us, and they *take* from us. We are them. They are us. Mythagos! Two shadows from the same mind. I was curious; therefore, so was she. I was angry. Therefore, so was she . . . I longed for her in certain ways. Why should I have expected anything different from her?'

Suddenly, he threw the tablecloth aside and leaned towards me, hands at first seeming to go for my throat so that I pulled back defensively, but I think he had merely wanted to embrace me. He said, simply, 'Did you see her? Any sign of her.

'She danced in the snow.'

'Snow? Is it snowing?'

'Last night. It's quite deep out there. She went back to the wood, but she'd danced first.'

'Back to the wood . . . If that's so, then I can follow. There'll be a way in for a moment. Into the wood. The way is open more clearly for a moment . . . Chris, make me some tea. Please! And a sandwich or two.'

'Yes. Of course.'

And the man, so recently mad, so recently feral, walked from the room, a tablecloth for modesty, reappearing minutes later dressed for a winter's walk, indifferent to me once again.

Three

I watched him go. He inspected the disturbed snow in the back garden, then quickly followed the strange trail into the scrub that led up to the wall of oak and elm that marked the near-impenetrable wood. He didn't look back; he was swallowed by the winter darkness of the trees in an instant.

My curiosity got the better of me and I resolved to follow him. But first I entered the study, found his journals, and read the entries for the last few years.

They were very matter-of-fact, and I was struck by how repetitive many of his observations were. There were also several macabre references to my mother, written as if she were still alive.

I put these out of my mind. It was the recent visitor to the house who now fascinated me, and I had a name to go on. I leafed back through the volumes and found entry after entry referring to Guiwenneth. The two that excited me the most were these:

The girl again! From the woodland, close to the brook, she ran the short distance to the chicken huts and crouched there for a full ten minutes. I watched her from the kitchen, then moved through to the study as she prowled the grounds . . . The girl affects me totally. Jennifer has seen this, but what can I do? It is the nature of the mythago itself . . . She is truly the idealised vision of the Celtic Princess, lustrous red hair, pale skin, a body at once childlike yet strong. She is a warrior, but she carries her weapons awkwardly, as if unfamiliar with them. She is Guiwenneth of the Green!

Jennifer is unaware of these details, only the girl and my helpless attraction. The boys have not seen her, though they have certainly seen strange activity at the edge of the wood . . .

And from a later entry I learned this:

She is a warrior-princess from the time of the Roman invasion of northern Europe, but her characteristics, the essence of her story, are older of course. She is beguiling, intelligent, fast and vulnerable. Is she a benign and seductive form of the enchantress we know as Viviane? Or Morgan le Fey? This is an interesting heroine indeed, and she is as curious about me as am I of her. It is not surprising that my heart leaps to see her.

This time I cannot fail. She will be my guide to a greater understanding of all that rises from the past and is sustained inside Ryhope Wood itself.

I was intrigued. I dressed warmly and went into the woodland, following precisely along the line of the girl's tracks, ducking below the branches and following the winding route between the trunks, aware that the snow was thinner here and that the light from above was rapidly fading – not because the day was advancing into dusk, but because the whole nature of Ryhope was changing with every pace.

Suddenly, the winter had vanished.

Bemused, I stood and smelled spring. A brighter sunlight beckoned me forward and I entered a wide glade, a leaf-strewn clearing, criss-crossed with bramble, a fallen tree, now very rotten, cutting across its heart. All was stillness. All was silence. But this was not winter and my body was pricked with apprehension, my head whirling with the sudden sense of being watched. It was stranger and more chilling than the night patrols I had made in France, at the end of the war.

By closing my eyes, the fear subsided. But to stare steadily ahead was to experience movement, an intriguing movement, at the very edge of vision, figures and shapes, human and non-human, some of them leaning close as if to peer at me. And sounds, too: voices and horses, rattling and drumming, ebbing and flowing as if caught on a gusting wind.

To search for that movement with a more direct gaze was to see nothing but shadow and woodland. To hold steady was to experience a whole world of life and attention, so far into the corner of my eye that it might have been heat or light playing tricks on the budding leaves that had no business on the branches in this deep, December day. But I was being watched. I was in the presence of a life-force that defied rationality – time and space were wrong, here, and I remembered something else that Huxley had once written: that the wood somehow *turned you around*, confusing the senses and sending you back to the edge.

Small though Ryhope Wood was, it guarded itself against intruders, and I was now an intruder.

And as I thought of this, so a sudden panic gripped me. I turned and ran, bruising and grazing myself against the trees, trying desperately to escape the haunting voices and surreal glimpses of the watching figures, who dogged my steps like the bad dreams they were. Finally, I burst from the edge of the wood, falling in the welcome and familiar snow, scrabbling and swimming in the cold, refreshing mush.

'Dear God . . .'

Sitting up, after a while, I stared back along the way I had come.

For the first time in my life I had experienced the sensation that I was sure had first intrigued my father. Encounters with strange figures had featured large in my childhood years; but never this sense of being drawn in, turned inside out, scanned, approached, scrutinised and finally kicked *back* to the reality of snow. Huxley had never truly shared his understanding of the wild realm beyond the edge. He had kept us all quite blind to the truth, and that passing thought made me angry for a moment.

But the simple *wonder* of what I had experienced made me suddenly almost drunk with excitement.

'Wonderful!' I shouted to the 'shade' of my father in the wood. 'You're on to something wonderful! I've always known it. It's always been there! I've lost never felt it so strongly, until now.'

What strangenesses we can take for granted in chilfhood!

I flopped back in the snow, laughing loudly, giving in totally to this moment of release and exhilaration.

'What *have* you found?' I asked the memory of my father. 'What *is* going on?'

And I sat up abruptly, remembering Kylhuk, *slathan*, cuts to my face . . . and my mother's urine soaking from her shoes onto my shirt as I held her and tried to keep her back from that terrible valley where the carrion birds gathered.

'And what have you done to *us*? What have you done to *me* . . . ?'

Later, seated miserably in the cold enamel tub, washing in murky, lukewarm water, I heard the tentative movement of someone in the house. The bathroom looked out over the garden and I shivered and peered from the window, noticing a new set of tracks from the wood. Wrapped in a towel, I crept out onto the landing, peered over the banister, and was at once struck on the back of the head by a stone. As I slumped in confusion, I glimpsed and smelled the woman who darted from my father's room. She crouched briefly on the turn of the stairs, staring at me as she breathed in that shallow way that denotes fear and flight, then was gone, leaving me to a slow recuperation of my senses.

Dried and dressed again, I searched for her, found only traces of her presence. I added wood to the fading fire and crouched in its welcome warmth. Then I sat in the chair where years ago my mother had stared into her future through similar flames.

The girl was still in the house. When I walked through the rooms I knew she was watching me, but she stayed out of sight, darting and supping through the shadows, adding to my sensory confusion.

I could smell her.

I called to her. I tried everything. I tried to make myself non-threatening. I even sang a jaunty song and cooked a pot of broth, hoping that the smell of food would entice her from her shifting lair.

She was biding her time, no doubt watching me, trying to work me out.

She confronted me in the late afternoon, as the light was going and I had switched on the lamps in the sitting room. Movement in the kitchen caught my attention and I went to investigate. The kitchen was empty, the pot of barley and chicken broth gone, the back door open into the snow-shadowed dusk. My breath frosted as I called for her again, then closed the door. But when I returned to the blazing fire, there she was, sitting in my own chair, the pot held to her lips as she drank the cold soup. Her eyes watched me over the iron rim. A vicious-looking weapon, a leather sling tied around a stone, lay in her lap. She was clad in loose woollen trousers, vaguely patterned, and with a heavy cloak still tied around her shoulders. Her feet were bare, small, pale toes warming at the fire. When I smiled, she nodded, then lowered the pot; a yellow froth of soup lined her upper lip and she briefly frowned into the vessel before placing it to one side and letting the fingers of her left hand twine with the leather of the skull-cracker. She made no effort to move, simply stretched out her feet a little more, wriggling with clearly implied satisfaction.

In all this time her gaze never left me, green-eyed, slightly frightened, very wary, her face a pale oval between long locks of fire-reflecting auburn hair.

'I can make you a better supper,' I said. 'The soup was very thin.'

'Huxley,' she said, and I fancy there was a question in the word.

'Yes. Huxley. Christian.' I patted my chest. 'Christian Huxley. My father is George. George Huxley . . .'

'George,' she echoed, her eyes narrowing, her grip tightening on the stone skull-cracker.

I raised my hands in a gesture of pacification, but she had risen to her feet, every muscle tense, her gaze on mine, but her awareness wider, now: listening, sniffing, alert for betrayal.

'He's not here,' I said to her. 'I promise you. He followed you into Ryhope Wood . . .' I was making dancing and walking motions with my fingers, simple gestures to emphasise and direct my words. 'You're quite safe with me.'

What arrogance! What assumption!

She smiled at me, bowed slightly, and started to walk past me, the soup pot in her hand, for all the world as if she were going to wash up her dirty pan. As I stepped to one side I saw the blur of her fist, heard the exhalation of her breath, felt my head cracked and my world go black.

This time when I roused myself, I found the fire burned low, the carpet charred where embers had spilled from the blaze and not been extinguished, my head sore from the blow, and Oak Lodge filled with the sound of breaking glass. Weak and shaking, I hauled myself to my feet, and cautiously walked through the house to the sound of mayhem. Guiwenneth had found framed photographs of my mother and was systematically smashing them, screaming abuse at them as she did so, flinging the buckled, splintered remains across the study floor.

'What are you doing?'

At my feet was the crushed portrait of Jennifer Huxley that for all my life had adorned the mantelpiece of my parents' bedroom. She was young here, smiling brightly, half turned to the camera, her cheeks highlighted from the studio lights. This was a woman perhaps no older than myself, her life ahead of her, her dreams filled with beauty, her hopes so legion that she had no hopes at all, simply expectations, anticipation, the exhilaration of looking forward.

Now smashed, now ruined by this creature from my father's furious, feral mind!

'Stop this!' I shouted. 'These are precious!'

The stone sling blurred towards me and I snatched it from the air, flung it to the floor where the handsome, youthful woman watched me from the creases in the photographic paper, through the jagged edges of the glass, the twisted metal frame.

'Enough!' I hissed.

She crouched. She launched herself at me, her feet striking me, her nails raking me, her teeth gnawing me, her voice piercing. And then she was gone, out into the evening snow, floundering in the deep drifts, cold and lost and frightened, calling for something or someone, desperate in her loneliness, desperate in her fear, oblivious of my calls to her to *come back, come back*, that I really wouldn't hurt her.

She was a frail shadow against the crisp and moonlit field of snow, falling below it and flailing within it, like a fish leaping and splashing in an icy river. She stumbled and vanished and at once was quiet. It was too cold to follow, and I was too disturbed by the thought of the reception I might receive if I made to pursue her.

I found enough kindling to make a crude torch, tied it together, lit it, placed it in the open kitchen door to the house. As the evening passed, I kept feeding the simple beacon, but soon the meagre supplies from the woodshed were exhausted; and I was exhausted too; and the night was black and bleak, and the snow came heavier.

My father came home at dawn, and he was not a happy man.

By the beard on his face, he had been away a week, I thought; he quickly checked the calendar, then – as if not quite believing me when I assured him of the day – he turned on the wireless and sat hunched beside it, listening to the voices, waiting for the first chimes of the new hour and reference to the day itself.

'I was here only this morning.'

'Yes. And she's been and gone . . .'

'Guiwenneth?' he shouted, startled and angry.

I picked up the loaded shotgun and faced him across the room. 'Guiwenneth,' I said. 'She's kicked the hell out of me, and fled.'

The animal in his eyes was back and I snapped shut the breech of the shotgun, keeping it pointed away from him, but my fingers close to the trigger.

'She was here looking for *you*, not me. She's gone. She's angry. Whatever is happening to you, please either sit down and talk about it, or go away and leave me alone. Do you see the bruise on my face?'

His watery, wild gaze flickered to accommodate the yellowing and painful mark that was still aching and distracting me.

'She did that?'

'She's a bit of a fresh one, Dad. More than a touch lively. You taught me not to walk behind a lathering mare after the hunt, in case she kicked; you forgot to mention trying to pacify one of your . . .'

I hesitated, then used the word: 'Mythagos . . .'

'Myth*aa*goes,' he corrected. 'From "myth imagoes".'

'I've read what you've written,' I said patiently. 'I know the source. I don't understand what they are, these *mythagos*, but I know the coinage. And I know that you think they come from the wildwood, beyond the house, and from our own unconscious minds.'

'Primal woodland, Chris. Unchanged for twelve thousand years. The hiding place of *living history* . . .'

'I don't know much about that. But I *can* tell a woman who's jealous of another . . . she's smashed my mother's photographs.'

'Smashed them.'

'Went berserk, in your study.'

He seemed startled. 'She's smashed them all? All the photographs?'

'Not beyond repair.'

'Not beyond repair,' he echoed, a curious smile on the unkempt face, in the sad, tired eyes. 'No. Of course not. Not beyond repair. Pictures and statues, the earth itself . . . all can be damaged. But not beyond repair. Not like us . . .' He sat down behind the desk, slumped forward, head in hands. 'I'm weary, Chris. And hungry. And cold. Is there anything to eat?'

'Not much. I'll fix you something. A hot drink.'

'Wine,' he said. 'Bring me anything red. Don't bother about letting it breathe. Just pour it.'

'Barbarian,' I said as I left the room to follow his instructions.

The wine was a mistake. He got drunk and aggressive and at two in the morning was raging at me in the darkness of my room, where I lay in bed. 'What did she say to you? Tell me everything she said! What are the two of you doing behind my back? I told you, Chris . . . leave us alone! I've waited too long for her. She doesn't belong to you.'

Frightened that he might have the shotgun with him, I stayed quite calm, watching him carefully. He was holding a blackthorn walking stick, a deadly enough weapon if used deliberately, and I gently prompted him to put it down. He did so but came towards me, leaning down and hissing like a cat through near-clenched teeth, his lips drawn back. 'Don't touch her. I won't let you touch her. I know your game! I've always seen it in your eyes. You know what I did. You saw me—'

'I don't know what you mean, Dad. All I know is, you're drunk . . .'

His breath reeked of wine. I suspected he'd opened a second bottle.

'You saw me,' he repeated nervously, his words of yesterday. 'That frightens me.'

'I don't know what you mean. Go back to bed—'

But before I could say another word, he had leapt at me again. His hands closed on my throat briefly and I threw him back, flinging off the counterpane to defend myself more effectively. But again, like a cat, he had slipped from the room, an angry shadow, taking the stairs two at a time, banging below me through the house and finally trudging out into the snow. From my bedroom window I watched him go, a sad, lonely man, a hunched shape, head bowed, using the staff he always carried to help him through the deep snow of the field, back to the wood, back to his dream.

The snow kept falling and I decamped to Shadoxhurst again, to the room above the Red Lion Inn. Whether or not Huxley returned to Oak Lodge in that time I do not know, and at the time couldn't have cared. When I went back myself, on the last day of the month, the snow was on the melt. I laid a new fire. The photographs of my mother were still where they had been smashed. The wine cellar had not been further raided and I removed several bottles and locked it up again.

In the evening I heard the sound of carrion birds and went out into the garden. A small flock of crows was circling a part of the field, where a dark shape was half exposed as the snow melted around it. Shocked and apprehensive, I ran across to it, waving my arms to scatter the noisy birds. I had expected to see my father's grim, dishevelled features staring from the ice, but it was the girl who lay there, her pale face white as the snow around her, the skin drawn in to expose the skull, the eyes dull below half-opened lids. The crows had not yet started to feed, and though they mobbed me, screeching, I kept them off and covered the corpse while I returned to the house for a blanket.

I hauled the fragile body into the woollen shroud and was surprised that it was as light as a doll. Indeed, she might have been made of hollow wood, her skin as brittle as an autumn leaf. It was as if I handled a broken mannequin. I stored the sad remains in the empty coop, wondering what to do about reporting it. If my father was right, this woman did not exist in our own world. If he came back and found her dead, he would assume the deed to have been of my own doing. Better to bury her, perhaps, leave her in peace, and forget that she had ever existed.

And though my conscience plagued me for some days after, this is what I did, interring her where the chickens once had run, where the earth was deep, well away from the house itself, forgotten bones in a forgotten corner of the garden.

Four

It should have been easy to forget her. Who had she been, after all, other than some strange woman from a strange place, hostile, uncommunicative, beautiful, yes, but an entity nonetheless that had in no way impinged upon my senses?

So why, then, did she haunt my waking hours, and whisper to me in my dreams? Sometimes I woke crying; my mother seemed to drift away, a shadow in the room, her words fading into obscurity, but my muscles and stomach still clenched with the pain of the loss. Other times, it was Guiwenneth who called to me, and there was something in the look, something in the smile I should have recognised but for the moment could not.

These edge-of-the-mind intrusions became increasingly distracting. I realised, some time in the spring, that I had become as obsessed with Guiwenneth as my father had been, and this prompted me to read his journals through again, to commit to memory great tracts of what he had written, to think more deeply about the things he'd seen, the lands he'd visited, beyond the gate and the brook, in this tiny patch of English woodland.

I tried to find the entrance to the wood, but nothing opened in the way that Huxley had described. Nevertheless, if my father had been right, there ought to be some gap, some opening in the wood's defences. Huxley himself had used various strange, hand-held devices which he had called 'residual aura detectors' or 'vortex focusing sensors' or other such nonsense. I found two of these in his desk drawer and tried to use them, but though they responded, I had no idea what they were signalling to me.

I decided to sleep on it, and explore the edge of the wood first thing in the morning, with or without the 'strange detectors'.

I'm glad I waited.

*

A sound like the bellowing of a metal bull woke me from a spirit-haunted sleep, disorientated and cold. When the sound came again – a short, rising call – I went to the window to peer out through the crisp dawn at the dew-covered trees of Ryhope Wood. And at that moment I had my first glimpse of visitors from the deep for more than two months.

Pale light reflected off gleaming metal, a strange and hideous animal's head, open-mouthed, swaying in the tree line at the end of a long, curved neck. This metal grotesque pulled back into the underbrush almost instantly. A man's face, pallid and beardless, replaced it for a moment, peering at me hard, then that too was gone.

I had never seen an instrument like this vertical horn before, though I had heard them several times in my childhood. I imagined they had been used in war to frighten the enemy; they certainly made the pulse race.

The two blasts had been a summons to someone in the house, but not for me. I sensed rather than heard the doors to the garden open and a few seconds later a woman ran lightly from my father's study towards the gate. Her long, red hair had been tied into a single braid; she wore a leather tunic of the Roman kind, and sandals. When she glanced back at the house I could see she was in her war paint, purple spirals on her cheeks, a band of black across her eyes. Even so, she was both beautiful and recognizable.

I had buried the bones of a form of this woman last winter. Here she was again, the same and different, and altogether less feral.

The girl again, from the wood . . .

And this time she was *mine*.

As she caught my eye, she hesitated at the gate; the smile that touched her lips was both enigmatic and impish. She seemed to have taken something from the study, but what she raised to me in acknowledgement was a riding crop, feathered and brightly painted, similar to that which she had used to 'count coup' on me as a boy.

For the first time I realised that the white-haired girl rider of my childhood and 'Guiwenneth of the Green' were the same, separated only by the span of years of adolescence.

I felt both stunned and elated. There had been something in the look of this Guiwenneth that was more than familiar – it had been *knowing*. The girl rider had come back. And she was signalling to me to follow.

She had gone then, running fast over the field and into the wood, and though I waited a few seconds, hoping for a further glimpse, I knew there was not a moment to lose. If my father was right, mythagos left trails through the dense and convoluted defences of Ryhope Wood, openings into the deep that would grant me an access so often denied. Even now, this new doorway, like a wound in flesh, would be slowly closing up.

Grass and decaying leaves were strewn across the floor of my bedroom. The heady scent in the room was alarming and arousing – more than just flowers, then. Dust danced and swirled through a thin shaft of light from between the curtains.

The woman had been in here, I realised, and had charmed me in some way, sending me deeply to sleep. Waking me *just* at the moment of her departure. Had she *wanted* me to see her as she made her escape from the dawn raid upon Oak Lodge? Of course she had. Why else wave at me? She had spent time exploring while I slept. Now I was being called inwards.

An hour later, strange detectors in my pack, I reached the glade where previously I had been turned about. This time there was no such attack upon my perception and I pressed on, deeper into what was now a forest of great and ancient growth. If I was following a track, I was not conscious of it, but my path seemed clear, and my journey, if claustrophobic, seemed directed.

And in due course – by now time had ceased to register – I came to the greater, darker clearing among the massive oaks, the shrine, well known to my father, that was the place of the Horse Goddess. I had heard the rattle of the skulls tied to the lower boughs and that morbid sound drew me from the darkness into the circle of light that illuminated the massive statue at the centre of the sanctuary. Made of bones and branches, the Horse faced me, eerily watching me from the eyes that had been shaped in the bridled head. There was a strong breeze and the leather trappings that adorned the hundred skulls around the edge of the clearing whipped like tendrils, clattering where their metal decorations clashed.

I hated this place; I believe Huxley had hated it. But it was the entrance to the inner forest, and all things passed this way, and therefore Guiwenneth – *my* Guiwenneth, the wild girl grown older – had passed this way, too.

A sudden shaft of daylight, released as the canopy rolled and shifted in the wind, illuminated the brilliant shield that stood between the statue's legs. And I remembered something that my father had written about just such a shield, which changed according to who or what passed by:

If there is significance in the restless decor and patterning of the shield, I have yet to find it. But that it *does* change is of great interest. The designs seem to reflect the latest visitor from the heart of the wood: Wessex warrior-priests of the Bronze Age fading into the figures of Aegean dancers, and then to Viking dragonships or lost Roman legions – each mark, each picture, each symbol telling a tale, or suggesting a route if the puzzle can be pieced together.

The shield was oval and as tall as a man. Rimmed and with a central boss of iron, patterned in bronze on the outer leather, it was made of oak so thick that I could not lift it. It was certainly not meant to be used in war or combat, at least not by men of my own physical stature.

I examined the detail of the latest design to cover its face. Five ravens circled the top of the shield; a white horse, curiously elongated and catlike, graced its centre; and a white-faced mask, framed in luxuriant auburn hair, stared at me from the lower quarter. This mask appeared to be the object of desire of two crudely drawn wrestling warriors, whose interlocked arms and grimacing faces formed a circle above it.

I stared at that image for a long time. I couldn't help feeling it signalled that Guiwenneth had passed by this way, but also that my father was still in the deep, still searching for the woman who obsessed him.

To the naked eye there was no way of telling which direction among the great oaks the party had taken some hours previously. But Huxley's inventiveness, his residual-aura-detector, should at least have been able to indicate the general direction of the departure. This small gadget, like a flashlight but with neither bulb nor glass at its end, only a series of copper needles fanning out like a pin cushion, functioned (he had claimed) by responding to the residual life energy of those who had passed by. Huxley had been infatuated by the notion of ley lines and patterns of energy and memory both in earth and in the confined spaces of glades and clearings, even in the root network of the heartwood itself. A small dial indicated the highest source of this residual aura by the simple device of a needle flicking to maximum and then dropping again, as a magnet might respond to a lodestone.

To my surprise – and to my admiring delight – the needle duly flicked and I began my journey to the heart of the wood, passing to the right of the statue of the Horse, following the route suggested by this unlikely piece of electronics. There was a heavy scent of mould in the air, and a claustrophobic darkness for a while, but in a minute or so the oppressive sense of enclosure dissipated, as I had known it would, and I was on a wide track, a summer sun overhead, the land opening before me and dropping away, perhaps to a river. In the distance the land rose again into the great swathe of primal forest that would soon be my home for as long as I remained in Ryhope Wood.

The ridge ahead of me was like the hunched back of an animal, topped with a spine of conifers that reminded me of quills. This was the Hogback Ridge, a place which Huxley had often visited and referred to in his journal. Indeed, as I tentatively explored the rocks and wind-curled thorns that fringed the rise of land, I found the rusting remnants of more of his strange detectors, fragments of metal, broken dials attached to trunk and branch, their function long since dead with time.

How often had my father paced to the summit of this ridge, I wondered? And what had his machines told him about the ebb and flow of myth and legend in this place? It was a strange sensation to know that the man had made his camp here, surveying the inner wood perhaps from this very spot.

But Huxley was now deeper, engaged on his own journey. He was beyond this ridge, and beyond the river that I knew curved around the bottom of the hill, taking the traveller through deep gorges and towards the setting sun. To dwell on the flux of time and space in this realm was to go mad with confusion. At any moment, the man might come striding through the spine of trees, aged by tens of years, perhaps by days only.

These thoughts occupied me for a while. I was reluctant to leave this place of open hill and rusting intellect; it was my father's shrine, in every sense and in every way as significant as the gruesome Horse that marked the multitude of crossroads into the past.

But after an hour I had made a sort of peace with this place and ascended to the spine of the ridge. Rarefied, clean air, a crisp breeze, a wonderful silence, these were the sensations as I stood between two tall conifers, my arms outstretched like a man on a cross, or a man embracing the far horizon. I was heady with triumph and with anticipation. I had already seen a coil of smoke curling from the forest below me. Light shimmered on movement for as far as the eye could see across this ocean of wildwood. Something was out there waiting for me, and the thought of this was both frightening and exhilarating. And I assumed, also, that Guiwenneth herself would be there, at the edge of the inner forest. And it was with confidence, if caution, that I began the walk down to the hidden river, and that enigmatic curl of smoke.

I had begun the journey, and I had made my first mistake.

PART TWO

The Forlorn Hope

There is no limit to my foreignness, every word means something to someone somewhere. I will find one you know.

Alanna Bondar, from *Agawa host*

Five

I had expected to find a camp at the riverside below me, smouldering embers signalling its position. In feet I found a funeral pyre, crudely and hurriedly erected, only half consumed by flame, sufficient to char but not cremate the long body that lay upon it, its hands on its chest. The pyre was still glowing and in time the journey of this particular dead soul would be achieved, but for the moment it stood in a clearing among smoke-blackened crack-willows, both a tribute to the loyalty of friends and a consequence of the need of those friends to travel quickly.

Everything about the arching corpse, its grim mouth gaping, suggested that it was a man. Four crudely shaped wooden poles had been erected at the points of the pyre, and ogham symbols had been hacked upon them, but without a knowledge of that code the meaning was elusive. I noticed, though, a fragment of bronze, a segment of tube that had been placed upon the dead man's chest, perhaps, before rolling off as the cadaver had writhed in the first, fierce heat. And at once I was reminded of the vertical bronze trumpet I had glimpsed from Oak Lodge. This might have been the mouthpiece.

How this man had died I couldn't tell. I approached, but a gust of wind enflamed the smouldering embers and the fire licked high for a few seconds before dying down. I stepped back to a respectful distance.

In a second clearing, however, some way from the river, I gained a fair idea as to how the trumpet-blower had met his end. There had been a hard fight here, and the sour-sweet smell of it was strong on the humid air. A severed hand lay in the protecting curl of an elm's root; long locks of black hair, scalp attached, were caught in cracks in the bark of the same tree; slices of blood-stained leather and linen clothing lay everywhere. The trees showed the marks of slashing blades, powerfully deployed. And huddled together, as if asleep, two dead men had been placed in the overhang of a thorn bush, side by side, heads tucked down, knees drawn up, arms folded. They might have been Buddhist monks in deep contemplation. They were naked, no doubt since clothing and weapons were always of value to someone, somewhere, and I guessed that these had been the enemy of those who had built the pyre.

There had been an encounter, then, but with whom it was hard to tell. That the two dead men were tattooed was not surprising. Huxley had written several times that: *it seems all life in prehistoric ages boasts body decoration of this type; like a coded script, the designs contain more information than is at first apparent.*

But I could not read them.

Their hair was long, formed into braided locks interwoven with strips of leather and colourful beads, all bloody now. They were fly-ridden and beginning to stink and I didn't linger long. But I was sure that Guiwenneth had been taken by surprise by these men, and she and her group had fought hard for their lives, losing the trumpet-blower before continuing their inward journey, the direction of which I soon discovered as I prowled the edge of the river.

An exposed bank of sand stretched out from below the low-hanging foliage and I saw where people had passed, walking towards the setting sun. A hundred yards from the spit of sand, the bank was furrowed where canoes had been stored and launched.

One small boat remained, without paddle or seat, like a floating coffin, perhaps, but a hulk of oiled wood and patched hide that at least was river-worthy. Had it been left for me? Who could tell? But surely, had there been a fear of being followed, my party would have taken the boat to frustrate my pursuit.

I was to drift with the current, it seemed to me, and await further contact.

What Fates, what forces were guiding the flow of my own journey? It hardly seemed to matter. To enter Ryhope was to enter a confusion at the *edge* of things, a sensory jumble of sound and vision — glimpses and echoes that could not be grasped — that was both frightening and seductive. I had experienced these feelings on a previous occasion, and had become determined to fight through the fear, to fight the dizzying defences of this semi-sentient wildwood, to find that certain moment when a definable and welcome peace replaced the screams of the anxious intellect and the tricks that the forest was playing. It was a moment when a hand seemed to reach out and soothe everything, from mind to brow. There was a certainty attached to it, a feeling that the direction was right, that the events which were being witnessed, and the loss of control, were all being carefully monitored. I was like a child, secure in the assertion and confidence of a parent, unaware, of course, that the parent was trained to respond to my fears in just this way.

Previously, I had turned about when this catharsis had occurred. Now, with the rediscovery of Guiwenneth as my goal, I fought against the feeling to return and let events take their course.

I thought of Longfellow as I launched the short canoe; I lay back, my pack at my head, my arms over the side of the simple, smooth-hewn craft; I let the river take me and watched the sky through the over-reaching branches of the trees. I let the motion of hull and water become the movement of time itself, taking me backwards, ever backwards, into a distance of which I had only dreamed.

This was the edge of the Wilderness. It was the true entrance to the past and to the Otherworld and I became afraid to watch it, aware of its beauty and its confusion. To try to see it, to document it, would perhaps have been to find that it ceased to exist; and it would spit me out, hurl me back into the bright air near the cornfield by Oak Lodge, drifting again on a stream in England rather than on a river that flowed into the realm of ghosts.

I thought of Longfellow, and his Hiawatha.

I thought of Arthur on his way to Avalon, stretched out in his barge, three queens attending to his mortal wounds. And I rued the lack of women, black cowled or otherwise. How nice, how pleasant it would have been, to have had their strange company on this sluggish journey to the past.

And so this simple boat of fate brought me, by the hour, towards my first encounter with the bloodied, angry group that had been to the edge of their world to find me, and had suffered a terrible loss as they returned to the garrison that protected them.

I drifted for a long time, though precisely how long is hard to know. For a while I stared at the watch on my wrist, noting the second hand mark the passage of minutes, but this objective observation soon ceased to relate to the subjective experience, and within a few hours the mechanism had wound down and I left it so.

Like a leaf on a stream, the canoe turned slowly in the deeper water. Later, it grounded in the shallows and I lazily reached over the side to push the craft back into the flow. Night descended then departed, and at dawn I was dew-covered and shivering, but still at peace. That same dawn, as I stared through the broken canopy over the water at the brightening sky, a massive, human shape stepped across the river and across my boat, startling me. He was untrousered and massive – I saw no more than the legs and the bulbous droop of the swinging genitals as the stride was taken, and heard a sound like rolling thunder that might have been his voice. Sitting up, shaking languor from my eyes and mind, I began to take more interest in the direction of my travel.

A while later a second figure appeared in mid-river, walking towards me, waist deep in the water. The current carried me rapidly towards this bearded human male; he was large, a giant, though not like the river-striding man I had seen before, and he grinned as I came towards him. He carried ropes over one shoulder, each attached to a boat, ten in all, some small and sleek, some simple, one ornate and masted, like a royal barque. From what I could see of him I reckoned him to be ten feet tall at least. His hand, as it reached ahead of him to stop my own canoe, was the size of a dinner plate. Strong fingers gripped the prow and he struggled to keep my craft from turning and twisting away from him. He had kindly eyes, lank black hair, a water-saturated beard and gleaming teeth. He wore a green and patterned shirt that gaped open to his huge meat-fattened belly.

'Elidyr,' he said, his voice deep and loud, and repeated the word. I slapped my chest and responded with, 'Christian.'

'Elidyr,' he repeated, then pressed the boat's prow against his belly, releasing his hand for a moment to make an odd little walking move-ment in the air, then touching the tips of his fingers to his chest and cocking his head. 'Elidyr,' he said softly.

'Christian,' I said in the same soft tone. He looked puzzled.

I could learn little of the man at this stage of our encounter, of course, but because he would stay with me for a while, I would learn that Elidyr meant 'guide', though the nature of his guidance was far more complex than I realised. He certainly seemed confused, however, standing there with the river flowing and soaking him, and the ten small boats shifting restlessly in his wake. Bodies lay in them, I could see, and smoke rose from two.

Elidyr kept looking back downriver, to the east. (The sun had risen in that direction, so I considered it to be the east.) Then he would look ahead to where I had come from, and frown and sigh. It was decision time, that much was clear, and he was having a terrible time with it. His sighs made the leaves tremble. The anxious beating of his free hand against the water made waves break against the rocks. Had he been looking for me? Did he recognise me? Had I arrived unexpectedly?

Whatever was inspiring this indecision, it was clear that Elidyr was confronting a situation he had not anticipated.

After a while he let go of five ropes and let the boats slip away from him. The river turned them, the low branches snagged them, but they were swept away downstream and had soon vanished. When they had gone, Elidyr waded to the bank and tied the other boats to the bough of a fallen tree. He unfurled a coil of rope from his waist and secured my own canoe, then walked up into an outcrop of rocks, stripping off shirt and trousers and slapping them against the stone, beating out the water. He was certainly about ten feet tall and I was in awe of the man.

As he attended to his rough ablutions, I inspected his charges, and was shocked by what I saw.

In a round coracle decorated with the eyes of animals on its oil-skinned sides, a grey-haired brute, clad in tooth-decorated buckskin, lay as if softly sleeping, a fistful of thin-shafted, flint-tipped fishing spears by his side. A mangy-looking hound, more wolf than dog, was draped across his belly, eyelids fluttering to expose the dark eyes that struggled to see from its hunt-dream. It was the breathing of this hound that gave the illusion of life to its owner.

By contrast, in an ornate riverboat painted in sumptuous blues and reds, with an eagle-prow and roaring-lion stern, a man lay on rain-saturated and now mouldy cushions, a scimitar across his bloody body, one hand on the gash that had opened his belly and stained the green and purple silk of his shirt and billowing pantaloons. His beard was neat, in ringlets, his hair tied into a tail and draped over his shoulder. Gold and rich blue lapis-lazuli adorned his wrists, ankles and ears. I thought immediately of Saracens.

A third boat, shrouded in white satin and filled with red flowers, was occupied by a sleeping beauty, pale skinned, her closed eyes shimmering with purple dye, her lips glistening with rouge, her hair jet black and shoulder length, her clothes similar to the Saracen's, loose and light. A strange,' symbol-covered staff was all she had with her in the way of a weapon; and a small, red-beaked carrion bird was tethered to her wrist. Very much alive, its eyes flicked and flashed as it watched first my movements, then those of Elidyr, away in the trees. Small though it was, I felt it was protecting her, even though her life was lost.

The other two canoes were similar to my own. In one of them, his face still twisted with the pain of the mortal wound to his breast, lay a man in an iron-studded leather jacket and a pair of cloth trousers that were striped in the dull green of moss and the fading purple of dying heather. A thin, bronze torque was wound around his neck, the heads of wolves on the overlapping ends. His moustache – saffron-coloured, like his hair – was elaborately fashioned, curling down over the grim set of his mouth. His hair was odd, drawn up on each side of the crown of his head, the parting in the middle shaved in an inch-wide line, the bare scalp pricked out with purple chevrons. He lay, in death, noble and magnificent, and with all the despair of his lost life etched into the frown and gape of his face.

And in the last, small boat, his companion perhaps during the journey to the edge of the wood when I had seen her, Guiwenneth lay asleep, her left hand still holding a bronze dagger, a small oval shield on her breast, its pale wood painted with the image of a leaping stag. Her face was intricately decorated with circles, spirals and other symbols. As I looked at her, I began to cry. I couldn't help it. There was a truth I had to face and I couldn't face it.

I had met her as a child and glimpsed her as a grown woman for only a moment from my bedroom window. But the look she had given me, and the way I now felt for her – whether by guile or magic, or simple love at first sight, I could not imagine, I did not care – I knew only that I was in pain, and that I longed for that gentle face to *open* again, to look at me with a wink and a knowing smile, a look of longing that would echo my own.

It was not possible that she was dead, rather than asleep. There could be no point in her being dead!

Tearfully, I leaned over her. I could see no wound on her, but neither could I detect any breath from her mouth, and for a few moments I was confused, and perhaps this helped to keep despair at bay.

I was still staring at her when a hand like a giant claw wrenched me by the shoulder, pulling me back from the tethered boats. The naked Elidyr scowled at me, pushed me aside, then bent over each body in turn, patting the cheeks, tugging the ears, touching the gashes on the 'dead'. As he probed the belly wound in the Saracen, the man stirred and growled. Ironjacket's mouth opened as his ribs were parted by the probing fingers of the guide, an expression of pain half felt through rising consciousness.

I laughed out loud with relief and delight, since Guiwenneth too was stirring. They were still alive, then. All of them. They had burned their dead, the trumpeter, back below the Hogback Ridge. These were the wounded survivors of the skirmish.

But who was Elidyr, and why was he dragging them back along the river?

I had no answer to this at the time, and to my disappointment, the five sleeping figures continued to do just that: sleep soundly, though the hound, like the red-feathered bird, was now alert and very noisy. I crouched by Guiwenneth's boat and stared at her. And for the first time a shadow passed across my vision. I remembered the woman whom my father had summoned, as beautiful as this sleeping figure, but warped and made sinister by the man who had brought her into life.

It was not possible . . . was it? . . . that Huxley had left others like her in the wood? It was a cold thought in the mind of a drowsy man.

I was being called by name and came out of my reverie.

Elidyr was watching me closely, leaning down towards me, his big hands making gestures that I thought were pacifying.

'Chris! Chan! Chris! Chan!'

He was waving me towards my boat, indicating that I should enter it and – by his elaborate gestures – that I should fall asleep. I declined vigorously, pointing to Guiwenneth and referring to *her* by name. This surprised the river-walker and sent him again into an agony of indecision. He stalked back among the trees, scratching at the fungal rings that wreathed his waist and buttocks, slapped at the branches, swore at the air, then grabbed his damp clothes and dragged them over his limbs, returning to the water's edge.

'Guiwenneth!' he agreed loudly, nodding. Then he moved his pointing finger to Ironjacket, the proud Celt, and raised his hands in that universal gesture that says, 'I just don't know.'

I think he meant that he didn't know his name.

The dark-haired woman was 'Issabeau', and he added a word that sounded sinister, waving a hand towards the sky, then simulating the cutting of his throat three times, his eyes popping with meaning.

'Thanks. I'll be careful of her.'

The Saracen was 'Abandagora'. The buck-skinned primitive was apparently called 'Jarag'.

'Thank you for the introductions. But why are they all asleep?'

Elidyr stared at me. 'Huh?'

I tried to ask my question with gesture. The big man grumbled and said with emphasis, 'Gureer! Gureer! Gwithon. Angat. Ankaratha! *Gureer!*'

I repeated, 'Gureer?'

Elidyr waved a hand in front of his mouth and repeated, 'Gureer,' then tapped a finger from his lips to my ears.

An interpreter! He was ruing the absence of an interpreter, a *gureer*, or a human of that name.

I made walking motions with my fingers and said, 'Let's go and find this *gureer*. You lead the way.'

He seemed delighted at my decisiveness and busied himself at the tethers on the fallen tree, waving me to my canoe as he did so. I stepped in gingerly and sat quite still as he untied his sleeping charges and slung the mooring ropes across his shoulder. I had expected him to continue up the river, but with a loud sigh and a grumble that seemed to go on for ever, he let the six boats float out ahead of him and drift downstream, tugging them back against the drag of the current, leaning back and taking their weight before slowly returning the way he had come, waist deep in the water.

For a while, facing Elidyr, I was fascinated to watch the big man at his work, reminded of stories of the Irish hero Bran, who had dragged great ships across the Irish Sea to effect an invasion of Wales; reminded of the boatman of the Styx, and all the boatmen of all the rivers of the Underworld; and I wondered what role in legend this worried giant filled, and why, indeed, every action he took seemed to fill him with an anguish of indecision.

As he walked through the deep river, tugging at the ropes, struggling to prevent one small vessel from drifting to the bank, or snagging on a broken branch, so he watched me, the furrows in his brow as restless as a sea of snakes as his mood and thoughts changed.

After a while he reached a hand towards me: 'Go to sleep,' he seemed to say.

I remembered *Treasure Island*. 'Neither oxen nor wainropes could make me sleep in this terrible place,' I asserted, and tightened my grip around my knees.

'Huh?'

'Never mind.'

He sighed wearily, hauled at the Saracen's barge, brushed aside the heavy bough of an over leaning willow, then grunted with effort as the river suddenly deepened and became more turbulent, running through glistening granite rocks formed from gigantic, broken statues.

But I could not stay awake. One moment the sweating, bearded face was staring down at me from above the burden of coils of rope . . .

. . . the next, the sun was dappling my vision through a breeze-blown lacework of high foliage. I was on the ground, my pack below my head, the sound of voices and laughter touching my awareness as I surfaced from swirling dreams of my mother's death and my father's anger.

The chatter stopped; a man's voice spoke in tones of alarm; a woman's sounded calming. A moment later, Guiwenneth crouched over me, her hand a gentle touch on my chest, her hair a tickling presence on my face. She smelled fresh. Her cheeks were pale, the painted spirals washed away, and from the way she looked at me, and smiled at me, she certainly knew me.

'Guiwenneth,' I whispered and she cocked her head, raised her eyebrows, repeated her name in an accent that I knew I would never reproduce. And then she said, 'Christian,' and I agreed quickly, adding, 'I'm glad to find you.'

And now I was certain: this was not the angry woman I had met before, my father's diabolical creation. At least, she was not the same manifestation. Something, certainly, connected the one with the other, but the look in her eye, the sense of familiarity and belonging, was comforting and warming. She helped me to my feet, brushing at my clothes, talking in her fluid language to the Unnamed man, the Iron-jacket, who leaned on his sword and regarded me coolly, answering his companion in monosyllables.

The others paid me brief acquaintance, the Saracen touching his hand to his head and heart, the sorceress Issabeau repeating her name to me without much interest, the elk-skinned hunter slapping his hands together as if crushing shells, which it turned out he was doing. He tossed me the river-food that he had been processing, a gritty, slimy mollusc that he indicated I should eat.

I ate.

It was an unpleasant snack, but it seemed the courteous thing to do.

These introductions over, the band went about their business, allowing me to observe what I soon realised was a coming-to-terms with a new situation. In truth, they were amazed to be here. Their laughter came from astonishment. Watching their body language, it was clear that Abandagora and Ironjacket did not expect to be alive, and were discussing the reason for this sudden return to the mortal world. Jarag had formed a ring of stones and sat inside it, whittling heavily on a piece of bone with a flint blade. Beside him, apparently ignoring him, Issabeau crouched and whittled at her staff, and as she whittled, so her appearance changed. The staff, I could see, was damaged, mostly by burning. She was reshaping the symbols using a thin, iron blade, cutting down to the wood again, refreshing the magic.

But what magic!

As she touched here, then there, so her face became a shadow of a beast, now a wolf, now a lion, now a snake, hints only, glimpses only of the power of the animal world that was condensed into this patterned shaft. Jarag watched her suspiciously, and when her face briefly transformed into a dark-furred dog, she growled, when a cat she spat, when a deer she blinked, when the features of a monkey shimmered on her eyes and lips, she chattered; and as Issabeau herself, she smiled darkly, keeping to her task, bringing back a craft and a talent that had perhaps died with her on the occasion that had brought her to the river, in her funeral boat, drawn by her otherworldly guide.

Six

In the late afternoon, the lassitude in the group as they recovered from their river journey changed to fierce activity, hunting for food, the building of a basic camp, mostly a foraging for dry wood to construct a fire at the river's edge. By dusk, Ironjacket and the Saracen had constructed a clumsy pyre as high as the tall men themselves. Jarag stripped off his skins and swam twice across the river, dragging his clothing and four lengths of newly hewn birch behind him. Dry and clothed again, he erected these posts in a row on the far bank, then chipped at them, making symbols, before crouching down in front of them, staring up the stream.

As dusk became twilight, Issabeau lit the fire, and when it was blazing she too went to the river's edge and sat down, singing softly as she cast small stones into the water.

It was a cool, breezy evening. I sat on the ground, close to the warming flames, and drifted into the sounds of fire and river. After a while, Guiwenneth sat down beside me, flicking mischievously at my legs with her feathered riding crop, firelight shining in her eyes and on her lips as she watched me.

'Christian, Christian,' she whispered, and I responded, 'Guiwenneth, Guiwenneth.'

Then, to my surprise, she leaned her head on my shoulder and took my hand in hers. My world closed down to encompass her body and her fragrance and nothing else. Her touch was gentle and curious, her fingers squeezing each of mine in turn, then running lightly over my wrists and arms. And she talked to me in that soft and sibilant tongue that I supposed to be the language of pre-Roman Britain. It was a mellow and comforting sound. Sometimes she seemed to be emphasizing a point; once she slapped my hand as if in reprimand. Twice she said something and turned her face to mine, and when our eyes met, and when she looked down at my mouth, I wanted to kiss her. I think she saw my longing.

'I've been with you but not with you,' I said quietly. 'How do I explain it? I was with the *wrong* you. But truthfully, you *are* that wild rider; you *are* the white-faced, chalk-haired girl who galloped me through the barley, all those years ago. God knows, it's good to find you again, even in these strange circumstances. And you have cast a spell on me, and I certainly won't complain about it . . .'

'Agus acrath scathan,' she said by way of agreement, then pointed to the river. 'Gwyr. Ambath criath. *Gwyr*. Hoossh!'

'How can I be *hoossh* when I want to kiss you?'

She relaxed into my arms again. Ironjacket walked past in the firelight, glancing darkly at me, then at Guiwenneth. He muttered something and she told him off. He laughed and made a quick movement with his right hand and Guiwenneth growled at him again.

'He's big, looks very strong,' I said with a smile. 'But useless with a sword, I expect . . .'

'Hoosshh . . .' was the reply to my nervous observation.

I had already made connections between the Saracen and Issabeau, a pair, I thought, despite their different origins; perhaps part of the same story? But their intimacy, what little had been demonstrated, might equally have been that between brother and sister – or people in the same business? – as between lovers in dire circumstances.

Ironjacket was intrigued by Issabeau, I noticed. And she seemed perturbed by his presence, and they kept apart. But the proud man kept a protective eye on Guiwenneth, especially where I was concerned, and again I was unsure of his relationship with her. They spoke the same language, I had easily noticed that. And though they spoke different words from the Mesolithic hunter, the Saracen and the mediaeval Sorceress, all five understood each other, and very little in the way of signs and gesture needed to be used.

As Guiwenneth relaxed in my tentative embrace, awaiting the results of river-fire and totem poles, I watched the tall, saffron-bearded Celt. He was very fussy about his appearance, continually stroking his moustache and those weird and wonderful wings of hair above his head. I had noticed earlier that rings of tightly interwoven snakes were tattooed or painted on his arms. Though his clothes stank, and were ragged and battle-torn, something in his demeanour suggested that he was less a tramp, more a warrior.

It may seem strange to observe this, but all of this motley group suggested more than they displayed. I might have been in the presence of royalty (as much as a Mesolithic hunter might be described as royal), or in the presence of knights of their age.

I had to remind myself constantly that I was in the presence of *legend*; and if Huxley was right, then these people, each in his or her way, had been a hero of their time, even if forgotten by later generations. But a hero once, and now alive again.

That thought indulged me in a moment of inappropriate paternal protectiveness; for they might all have been of my own creation. These wildwood warriors might have come from my own unseen dreams.

Certainly Guiwenneth had. I was in no doubt about it. The woman had touched my heart from the moment I had seen her at Oak Lodge, and then again, wounded, perhaps dying in her boat of fate.

And if she was my creation now, then she had been mine then, those years ago, when she had disobeyed her guardian – Manandoun, was it? – and galloped headlong from the forest. And if she had been part of the raiding party that night, then they too were from my deep unconscious, my most secret dream, and I had called them to mark me.

Slathan! Whatever it was, whatever it meant.

I had not thought of *slathan* for years. The two nicks in my brow were all but invisible, though now, as I remembered how they had been inflicted, they began to itch again.

'Slathan,' I breathed softly and Guiwenneth looked up sharply, frowning; then touched a finger to my lips and nestled down again. I remained hypnotised by the flame, aware of Issabeau's crouching figure and the murkier shape of Jarag on the other bank.

I fell into a light sleep, but was roused by a sudden cry. Guiwenneth stood up quickly, then tugged at my hand. I followed her to the water's edge and stood with the others, watching the approach of a boat whose hull was illuminated by flaring torches.

It sailed towards us slowly, turning in the flow. A tall, familiar shape stood in the stern, tugging and twisting at the rudder; a leaner, harder-looking man, trim-bearded, occupied the prow, regarding us coolly. I noticed that Issabeau had put her hands to her mouth and was staring in shock. The Saracen and Ironjacket were dismayed as well. Guiwenneth was shaking her head, smiling at some secret realization. She raised a hand and acknowledged the man in the prow, and he raised a hand to her, a grim smile touching his lean features. She glanced at me and whispered, 'Gwyr.'

I got the distinct impression that whatever this group had been calling to, with their fires, they had summoned more than they had bargained for.

Jarag and Ironjacket waded into the shallows and Elidyr cast a rope to the Celt, who caught it and pulled it taut, helping to slow the drifting vessel. Jarag swam back to the fire and all of us helped to draw the boat onto the bank. Elidyr unloaded several small, clay amphorae and four sacks of foodstuff. The newcomer tugged at the reins of two grey ponies which had been lying on sacking in the deeper part of the vessel's hull. They were small animals, shaggy-maned and ungroomed. They struggled and stumbled to dry land, protesting loudly, but became calm when Guiwenneth embraced them like old friends, whispered to them, and gave them a thorough once-over by the light of the fire.

The Saracen had opened one of the sacks and laid out food of varying types on his shield, inspecting the morsels critically and without much enthusiasm. Ironjacket cut the beeswax seal on one of the flagons and took a long draught of its contents. I smelled sweet wine on his breath and he spoke to me in a much warmer tone of voice than before. Guiwenneth was crouched by the shield, picking at fruit and chunks of grey meat. Jarag and Issabeau joined her, but Issabeau selected only an apple and walked back to the river to join the sulking Saracen.

Elidyr watched all this from the gloom of the woodland behind us. His arms were crossed, his body hunched, as he stood, his face drawn into a worried frown. The man seemed plagued by uncertainties and concerns. When Ironjacket carried the wine to him he nodded his thanks without a smile and took a drink. He bent his knees to tower over the Celt by a mere two feet. They talked for a minute or so and from the giant's quick glances towards me I knew that I was the subject of that conversation.

Agreement on something was reached between them, and Ironjacket went to Guiwenneth and quietly talked to her as well.

I was too tired to be further wearied by all this mystery. I assumed that if something was happening that involved me, I would be told about it in due course.

Ironjacket called to me. He was crouched by the shield, beckoning to me, grinning broadly, though I had to guess at that fact since his drooping moustaches were so enormous. I sat by him and he pointed to the various meats and fruits, naming them and indicating that I should eat. Everything smelled of decay! From the rancid stink of fatty meat to the heady, suspicious odour of failing fruit, this feast was stomach-churning. But I picked at it, and welcomed the wine, which was savoury, pine-scented, and slightly sharp; perhaps one of the resinous wines from the Aegean that I had read about but never tasted.

And it must have been strong in alcohol too; soon, all of my companions were curled up next to each other, close to the fire, beneath the cover of a hastily erected tarpaulin.

The embers flared and glowed, and the river beyond glittered with reflected fire. Drowsy, aware that Elidyr still watched from his place among the trees, I lay down behind Guiwenneth and tentatively let my head rest on the spill of hair that covered the roll of clothing she was using as a pillow.

A voice called to me and I woke in the silent night to see Elidyr standing over me, his eyes bright with the moon. There was a strange atmosphere in the clearing, an ethereal presence in the trees, which reflected a pale, ghostly light. The others still slept, their bodies covered with dew, a sleep so still and quiet that for a moment I felt a touch of panic, and reached to Guiwenneth. But Elidyr stopped me, taking my hand in his and helping me to my feet.

He beckoned me to follow him. When I walked it was an odd sensation, as if the ground were cushioned. Something was not right about this midnight rising. The big man walked ahead of me, passing into the gloom beyond the trees, and as I followed him, and glanced back, my heart skipped as I saw that the fire and my companions had disappeared.

Elidyr said nothing. I experienced the sensation of being touched and stroked by tiny hands; it might have been insect wings. It alarmed me at first, then I grew used to it. From the corners of my eyes I seemed to see faces, eyes, movement, watching creatures, never there when I turned to look at them.

The pre-mythago forms first appear at the edge of vision . . . Words remembered from Huxley's journal. Was I being taken to see the place where mythagos were born?

Suddenly the woodland brightened. Elidyr glanced back at me, his face friendly. The brightness grew stronger, and with it the verdancy of leaf and fern. We had passed into a summer wood, which burgeoned and ripened around me as I stepped deeper through its spaces.

And then, remarkably, flowers started to erupt in increasing swathes of colour and bloom. They grew up from the ground, and out from the massive trunks of oak and elm. Reds and yellows, trailing greens, and vibrant whites, the forest bloomed until it was so rich with colour I was dazzled.

A step further and a pricking on the skin of my face and hands made me realise that from these surfaces, too, flowers were sprouting. Elidyr was swathed in briar-rose, with lines of white petals down his back. Luxuriant, spongy tree fungus grew out from his legs; white-capped mushrooms from his shoulders – and from mine too! A step further and he was so swathed in red rose and green fern that I had to struggle to see his eyes when he turned to me. Archimboldo had never painted so strange a sight! I brushed at my hair and leaves shed their dew across my face.

Elidyr spoke to me and the words flowed around me meaninglessly.

Holding up hands covered with red orchids, I said, 'I know people who would kill for a gardener like you!'

And Elidyr sighed. He hesitated, looked in the direction of travel, then back the way we had come. He shook his briar-cloaked head and came to a decision, indicating that we should return. He had wanted to show me something but had changed his mind.

'Where are we, Elidyr? What place *is* this?'

He raised the mossy stumps of hands and shrugged. I turned again to follow him, shedding nature, returning to moonlight, to the fire, and to a sleep that took me faster than I could realise, Elidyr fading from my eyes even as I lay down by Guiwenneth, entering at once into the same dream of my mother that I had recently deserted . . .

I was awakened in rude and painful fashion, Gwyr kicking me in the buttocks and grinning as he barked incomprehensible instructions. My face was wet with dew. The experience with Elidyr had taken on the strangeness and the insubstantiality of a dream, and I truly wondered whether that indeed was what the whole adventure had been.

I had ho time for reflection, though. Gwyr was holding the two ponies by their rope bridles and was certainly urging me to my feet.

Already Issabeau was bathing in the river, and the Saracen was crouched at the water's edge, his head stretched back as he looked at the sky. Guiwenneth and Ironjacket slept in each other's arms, the tall warrior snoring loudly through open mouth, the long hair of his moustache fluttering like a leaf in the wind. I felt a long moment's shock and irritation at this display of intimacy and Gwyr saw my look; he slapped me on the shoulder, still smiling, and shook his head.

Was he saying: Just the way they ended up in sleep?

More important to this man was that I got into the saddle and rode with him, and this I did, uncomfortable on the broad but drooping back of the smaller pony, my feet practically touching the ground. Gwyr showed me how to grip the rope rein with one hand and the creature's mane with the other; a kick at the flanks made the ponies canter, but the blanket tied over the coarse hair was not thick enough to stop my bones from jarring, and my flesh from bruising.

After a while he slowed the canter to a gentle walk, through sun-dappled glades, following a narrow track away from the river. At this point we began to exchange names for things, with Gwyr indicating or slapping those parts of nature or his own body that he wished me to describe. His own words, similar in sound and intonation to Guiwenneth's, were forgotten by me as soon as I heard them, but Gwyr echoed what I said, sometimes frowning, sometimes laughing as if he had just realised a fact that should have been obvious to him.

For an hour or more our conversation was a listing: 'Arm, hand, chest, breast, or bosom . . . leaf, ivy, bark, twig . . . oh Lord, *gallop*, trot, snort – whinny? Sneeze! – sigh, weep, laugh . . . sap, sweat, blood!'

He explored more difficult concepts by inviting the expression with gesture and play-acting.

'That looks like love-making, making love; that's cuddling or hugging . . . throat-cutting, beheading, disembowelling – you certainly change the subject fast! – um, duelling, sword-play, stabbing or cutting, admonishment, anger . . . affection, heart-throb, longing or needing . . .'

The thesaurus came in a shifting, startling way, each phenomenon of nature that we passed causing a change in the direction of his questioning.

'Sunlight, sheen or shimmer, rustling leaves, gloom . . . That might be a shady grove – that's *sudden* movement, edge of vision . . . stink or stench, a fart, flatulence . . . I think you mean *long ago*, the past, history, time . . . the future . . . wildwood! Legendary figure? Understanding . . . language . . . communication, chatter . . . interpretation or interpreter? Interpreter of Languages?'

And suddenly, my companion astonished me by talking to me:

'Interpreter of *Tongues*!' Gwyr said in English. 'That is what I am. That is what I was born for. To take the knots out of gabble and see it for what it is. And I am here at last, and you and I are together at last I *have you*, as the saying goes. I have you now. I have touched the magic in your tongue.'

At which point of triumph he fell from his pony, thudding into the fresh fern. I jumped down to help him up; the man was shaking, his body drenched with sweat, his pulse racing. He was exhausted and I dragged him into the shade, propping him between the massive roots of a tree. I carefully pursued the ponies, which had run astray, and persuaded them back, leading them and tethering them close to where Interpreter of Tongues lay recovering from the effort of the past few hours.

When at last he woke, he stretched and scratched, urinated with a great sigh of satisfaction, then drank from his leather gourd before turning to me, his face still showing the effort of his work.

'Well, that was difficult, and I will not pretend otherwise,' he said, dark eyes glittering as he watched me, dark heard still wet with sweat. 'I am tired to my bones. But I was born with the ability to disentangle the tongues of strangers, and I have disentangled yours, and know you, now, for your thoughts and your words. I will instruct the others in your language and then they will be able to tell you their own stories, which have nothing to do with me, though of course I am aware of them.'

'How do you do . . .' I said, extending my hand, which he ignored.

'For the moment,' he went on, 'you should know this: that you have been accepted by us, and are now a part of our group. We are known as the Forlorn Hope, because of what we do. We are at the head of Kylhuk's Legion. We have had two terrible encounters, on each occasion with the Sons of Kyrdu, who are a malign and evil presence in this time. It is only by your arrival that we have survived, and for that we thank you.'

'How do you do,' I said again, dizzy with the spill of words, my hand waving towards him in a vain attempt to be courteous. He glanced at my fingers curiously, then again ignored me.

'I, in particular, wish to thank you, Elidyr fetched me back from the pyre, where I was already charred bone and ash according to his own words, and this was a great deed and a great concession . . .'

'Your arrival was a bit of a shock, I think.'

'Indeed. They had been signalling to Legion. Because of you, though, Elidyr has looked kindly upon me. I have a reprieve from the pyre!'

'You were the trumpet blower, I think. I saw you at the edge of the woods, near to Oak Lodge. A terrible sound. Like the dying of bulls.'

'Somebody has to do it,' Gwyr said, pain etching his face as he stared at me. 'Blowing the war horn, that is. The "trumpet" as you call it. And I have the strongest lungs. It is said that I can make the call of the bull's mouth speak to everyone who hears it.'

'You certainly can.'

He looked away from me. 'I had thought the effect more musical than you seem to have heard.'

I realised he had been stung by my comment. 'I'm sorry. I have no true appreciation of music.'

'Clearly. It's of no consequence, however,' he said with a smile. 'My only objection is that the *horn* is so heavy! I'm glad it's gone, lost in the river.'

'You called Guiwenneth back from her raid on my house.'

'The sanctuary?'

'Call it what you like. I followed you into the wood, through a place that is a shrine to horses.'

Gwyr shuddered noticeably, shaking his head. 'That is a strange and evil place. At the edge of the world – I had heard of it and came to it without realizing it!'

I didn't know how to pursue that observation, so I completed my question. 'You were together, then, the two of you. And all the others.'

'Indeed, we were together then, the two of us. And all the others. And now I am here because of your arrival, and for as long as I am here I am in your debt. Truthfully! Despite your insults, your coarse appreciation, your lack of tact, your lack of—'

'I'm *sorry*. I'm sorry for my lack of tact.'

'Well said. Your words are accepted. And make no mistake,' he went on airily, 'you have friends with you even if they scowl and grumble and put you to the test.'

'I hope I shall prove worthy of any and all tests to which I am put.'

'I share that hope,' he said with a serious look at me, and for a few moments I felt warmed by his companionship, but he quickly treated me to the comfort of Job, saying, 'And be assured, a terrible time awaits you, and a terrible discovery if you fail to keep your wits about you. A strong arm would help.' He glanced without much enthusiasm at my physique. 'And we have time to improve on that, but you must be prepared to be strong in all aspects of heart and mind. That is the purpose of the Forlorn Hope, and it is why we scout ahead of the Legion.'

'Am I part of the Forlorn Hope, then?'

'I have told you that already.' He peered round at my right ear. 'The hole in your head appears to be open, but perhaps there's a sparrow's nest inside! Pull your horse round, now, and get on its back. It's time to return to the others.'

I stood my ground for a moment. 'If you can talk to me in strange tongues, tell me what *slathan* means. The word is meaningless, but it gnaws at my neck like a bird of prey.'

Gwyr scratched at the back of his own neck, perhaps in response to my metaphor, and thought hard before saying, 'It's a word that Kylhuk uses, but not a word from his own language. It's older.' Irritably, he added, 'He's always doing things like that. He thinks it gives him stature with enchanters.'

'And does it?'

Gwyr tugged at his thin beard. 'Now you mention it . . . yes. I suppose it does.'

'And *slathan*?'

'Slathan. Yes, I'll try and find out, if it's important to you.'

Truthfully, it is important.'

'Put it from your mind, Christian. It is a question that will be a long time being answered. And now we have a long journey ahead of us and it will be bad for us if Kylhuk abandons all hope and changes his direction as a consequence. Without his Legion, we are all lost.'

Seven

Gwyr's anxiety that we would be abandoned by Kylhuk and his Legion was unfounded, as I would shortly discover, for even as we rode back to the camp, the great beast that Kylhuk had formed around him, the entity of flesh, stone and legend that would soon become my home, was moving in its ponderous way towards us, tacking away from its steady progress through time and the forest, drawn, I am quite sure, by a scent from Elidyr, some otherworldly call from the Guide that attracted Legion (as I would come to know it) as powerfully as flame attracts a moth.

It took us several hours to find Guiwenneth and the others, the paths Gwyr and I had ridden having subtly changed, causing us to lose our way on three occasions; but the river was there, and each time we reached it Interpreter of Tongues seemed to find his bearings. I was exhausted with the ride and the humidity of the moist wildwood, and fell gladly into Guiwenneth's embracing arms.

There was a buzz of excitement among the Forlorn Hope. Issabeau was almost in a trance, darting here and there around the boundaries of the glade, peering into the forest, snapping her fingers in quick, sharp rhythms, cooing and calling to her red bird, even as she shouted crisp observations and instructions to the Saracen, who responded in kind. Whatever difference in their magic, they were combining their talents expertly! Though the results, if any, eluded me.

An air of anticipation, then, and indeed there was a crackling atmosphere around the small fire, as if the whole glade flowed with unseen energy.

Guiwenneth left me and went to talk to Gwyr. Their conversation was animated for a while. Guiwenneth was listening hard, repeating words that I gradually understood were my own. Ironjacket was listening too, frowning at me as he concentrated. Jarag and his mangy hound were not around, and when Gwyr came over to me, dropping to his haunches and picking at the undercooked wildfowl that had been grilled on the wood, I asked him of the Mesolithic hunter's fate.

'No fate,' Gwyr said. 'Just hunting. Without him our diet would be poor indeed.'

I looked at the string and sinew on the charred bone of the moorhen and thought of times past when Steven and I had been instructed on how to distinguish between the birds of the riverways, the coots and moorhens, the ducks and the waders. I also thought of what I knew about the prehistoric past, and guessed that Jarag's idea of a hunting trophy would be a pile of bivalves and a clutch of gull's eggs.

Ironjacket joined us and sat down, cross-legged, his arms folded across his belly. He stared at me solemnly, his voluminous orange moustache moving side to side as he chewed thoughtfully on the remains of his meal. Gwyr said, 'Christian, I must make this man known to you, he has requested it. He is Someone son of Somebody, unnamed at birth because of a tragedy that you will soon hear about, though his true name runs before him, waiting only for the speed of the man to catch it and claim it.'

'Pleased to meet you . . . Someone . . .' I said, and extended my hand which the man looked at, then shook. He nodded with satisfaction, still staring at me, and scratched at his shaven chin before muttering a question which Gwyr translated.

'He wants to know where you come from. Guiwenneth has said that you come from the same islands in the west as she does. Is that right?'

'Yes.'

Someone son of Somebody would not recognise the name England, I guessed, so I said, 'Albion. South of Hibernia? No, that's Ireland. East of Hibernia! South of Caledonia? Britain. *Prytain*? Logres . . . ? West of Gaul . . . ?'

Someone, listening to these words, suddenly indicated that he had understood. He spoke to me through Gwyr and I learned that:

'Someone comes from the east of you, where two great rivers join near high mountains. The strongholds of his land are many, and the kings are rich beyond measure. Great war-chariots often raid across the rivers into Gaul, but his people take ships along the coast to your own country, where they celebrate at the great circles among the forests. His forefathers sailed further west, to the Island of the Great Boast, where five Queens ruled and may still rule and every head taken in battle can sing for five seasons after being severed.'

This sounded like Ireland, where everything in those days, and even now, was larger than life, from its generosity to the battle antics of its warriors. This Someone himself, I gathered, was an unnamed and banished Lordly. One from early Celtic lands east of the Rhône, in modern-day Germany, his homeland perhaps below one of the great cities that had so recently been devastated by war.

There was indeed something regal about the man's appearance. Even the hacked and scruffy leather of his jerkin, I now saw, was studded not simply but with the bright iron heads of mythical animals. The short knife he carried was wide-bladed and leaf-shaped, more ceremonial than offensive. (His sword was very offensive indeed; I had watched him clean and hone it.) And the way he wore his beard and hair, those elaborate coils above his scalp, shaped and made secure with grease, certainly suggested an attention to appearance that went beyond the traditional Celtic warrior's vanity.

I had not suspected it, but there was a slight ulterior motive to Someone's first, friendly contact, the warmth he gave me. Gwyr said, 'He wonders if you know him; if anything about him is familiar? It may help him.'

'I'll try,' I said, but nothing about the man's look inspired me with any sense of recognition.

Someone spoke briefly about his birth, using Gwyr as translator.

'As far as I am aware, my father was summoned to combat before he could name me. The combat was by chariot, and along the eastern edge of the river that divided our land. The dispute was about the stealing of a bull and five cows that were being taken to honour Taranis. It was the beginning of the winter and when the snow came in that place, one in every three of us would die of cold and hunger. This was an important sacrifice, and my father had intercepted it – the white and black bull was a very famous creature, well regarded and envied among our clans – and made the offering himself. He had no time for the other king, who was his brother-in-law, but that didn't matter. A challenge was issued and had to be acknowledged.

'So – as I was told later – the two kings arrived at the river to fight first with spear and then with sword. They rode up and down the sides of the bank, shouting insults at each other until the horses were tired. Then they threw off their cloaks and prepared to hurl spears at each other across the water as a preliminary to the main combat.

'Unfortunately, my father was killed outright by Grumloch's first throw.

'All that saved my life, when Grumloch came to take possession of the fort, was the fact that I hadn't been named, otherwise I would have been killed along with the selected five knights who were used in place of the animal offering. We were taken to a lake in the forest and out onto the water in small boats. The five knights were stripped, tied, bled from the throat, skull-cracked then tipped into the lake. I was left in a coracle with a wet nurse, forbidden ever to return to the fort.

'When I was weaned, the woman left me in one of the glades dedicated to Sucellus. She never told me my father's name, only that he had known which name to give me, though the secret had died with him. She placed me in a hollow between the feet of the great wooden idol, where it was warm and protected from rain and wind. At night, the great gods roared at each other across the forest, and Sucellus strode around the glade, beating at branches. But he, like all of them, was tied to this place.

'Every so often, masked people came and sacrificed or left offerings at the feet of the idol, I ate whatever was left and Sucellus never complained. Only later did it occur to me that because I had no name the god could not see me.'

He stopped speaking and looked at me expectantly, almost hopefully. I think I grimaced and shrugged. Grumloch? Not a name to ring the bells of romance and chivalry.

'No, I'm sorry,' I had to say. Truthfully, if I could help with a name I would, but I know only of Perceval, Kay, Bedevere and Bors, Gawain and Galahad, the knights of Arthur and Guinevere, of Camelot, of Merlin, Morgan and Vivien, all of them introduced to me in stories by my mother when I was a child.'

As I recounted my limited listing of Malory's heroes I watched Someone for any sign of recognition, but he simply shrugged, sighed, bade me goodbye and went back to where Issabeau was still engaging with the woodland in her strange way.

Whatever was then said, within a few minutes Issabeau had cried out in what may have been despair, but which was certainly a voice of fear, and run into the gloaming. Someone took off his leather jacket and flung it to the ground angrily, then stomped away in the opposite direction to the distraught woman, swearing volubly, and slapping his left hand against his left buttock. Gwyr seemed to be as bemused as I was by what we were watching. Then he called for Guiwenneth, but without success. The Saracen was agitating to move on, and had been held back only by the antics of Issabeau, but now Gwyr came over to me and said, 'We shall have to start walking towards Legion. It's quite close now, but it's well protected and we must be ready for encounters with its defenders.'

'We can't go without Guiwenneth or Jarag . . .' I said. And indeed, where was Elidyr, the mournful guide?

The jarag,' Gwyr said, using that form of the name for the first time, 'is beyond my knowing. His magic is too strange, his life seems inviolable, and he has become the rock on which this unit of Forlorn Hope has stood; so I doubt if he is lost; he sprouts from the earth like a new shrub, full and green just when you think the earth is barren. Guiwenneth is more vulnerable. We should look for her at the river.'

We started to retrace our path to the water, but Gwyr turned back. 'You should stay here, I think. I can always follow later if she returns and you then feel the need to move on.'

And *so he* had gone.

I stood in this firelit place, utterly confused by the random and seemingly pointless movement of this small band of travellers. My heart longed to see Guiwenneth again, but my head was full of apprehension now, with Gwyr's departure, since he was my voice in this wilderness of incomprehensible sign and song.

A light touch on my shoulder from behind startled me. I turned quickly where I sat and saw Issabeau's doleful face, staring down at me from its frame of luxuriant night-black hair. She was holding a small branch of white-thorn, stripped and trimmed so that only a single thorn remained, like an elongated nail at the end of a withered arm. She kept this pointed at me as she walked round and sat down demurely, arranging her skirts around her, pulling her cloak across her breast. With the wooden arm of thorn between us on the ground, her liquid eyes almost unblinking as she gazed at mine, she began to murmur words. I heard 'Merlayne' and 'Vivyane' and asked her to repeat what she had said. There was something indefinably familiar about her words; I was on the edge of understanding, it seemed, and these noticeable names had helped me focus on the tongue, and I heard that it was a dialect of French; and Issabeau was a name that came from the time of Chivalry, eleventh-century French, perhaps, or some variant local to the peninsula of Brittany, a land where so many legends were held in common with the legends of my own country.

In a voice that was as deeply husky as it was sad, she whispered slowly, 'Merlayne eztay mon mayder. Vivyane eztay mon *covrz mord!*'

This last was said angrily, with her right hand extended towards me, gripped into a fist.

'Merlin and Vivian,' I said. 'Are you part of their story?'

She shook her head, not understanding, then went on, 'Merlayne ez *mord*. Enabre, enterre, envie ettonmord pondon tomp ayterne! Moie, onfond treez d'onzhontrayz, de courz noy, de fay ett onzhondmond moivayze!

'Zharm ett *onzhondmond*!' she muttered furiously, staring at the branch she held. 'Layze yeuze voie surlmon lay monzonge.'

These sounds were run together, sharp and fluid, teasing my awareness, communicating nothing but her passing despair, a sadness that had suddenly surfaced in her. I would ask Gwyr about her as soon as I could.

When Someone reappeared he was wet from the river, stripped to the waist, wringing water from his moustaches. He crouched by the fire, looked around, glanced quizzically at Issabeau, then grunted, 'Is Guiwenneth . . . here?'

'Gwyr is looking for her. Gwyr . . . looking! Guiwenneth!'

He understood.

'Kylhuk.' He stabbed a finger at the forest. 'Men! Chariot! Warrior!'

'I understand! Men and chariots and other warriors . . .'

'Legion! This way is.'

'I know. They're coming to find us. I'm glad to be able to talk to you, Someone son of Somebody.'

'Uh?'

'What language is Issabeau speaking? It's later than your own, I think. Is it early French?'

'*Uh*?'

'Never mind.'

We weren't quite as far along the path of understanding as I had hoped.

But a while later, Gwyr returned, Guiwenneth and the jarag with him, the two absentees carrying fish and birds across their shoulders. Jarag grinned through his unkempt beard, twirling his snares around his finger, rattling his small, bone-tipped spears in the loose grip of his other hand. His horrible hound was panting with exhaustion, its head shaking from side to side as it recovered from what I intuited had been a triumphant hunt.

I told Gwyr that Issabeau had been trying to speak to me, that she was mournful. He nodded wisely, spoke briefly with the woman, then told me, 'Merlayne was her master; he taught her many ways of charm and enchantment; but Merlayne has been tricked by the black-hearted Vivyane, and is entombed in a tree in the earth. Issabeau has many talents in the way of magic, but there are times when her eyes see only lies, and this is because Vivyane's dark magic is still attached to her. She was upset for a while when you mentioned Merlayne. She thought you were Vivyane's spy. But now she knows better.'

'What does she know?'

'That you, like the rest of us, have heard of the two enchanters. They are widely talked about. The terrible things they did when they were together were more devastating to the countries they passed through than war and pillage.'

I thought of Merlin, the white-bearded wizard, and his haunting presence in the corridors of white-walled Camelot, a benign figure, voice of advice to King Arthur. We were clearly not talking about the same old man from the stories *I* had heard.

And I had no sooner processed this thought than the whole glade seemed to shift.

The fire guttered, then flared high again. The trees had bent in a strange way, as if pressed upon by an unseen hand. The sensation in the earth was that of a mild tremor and I felt shifted sideways, though I had not moved in space, at least as far as I could see; but now, as stillness returned, there was a new electricity in the canopy and on the ground, a tension, as if creatures ran among us, hands touching, fingers pinching, tiny teeth nipping, not unlike the sensation with Elidyr, the night before. If a flock of curious carrion birds had invaded this glade, I could have understood the feeling; but there was no sign of the disturbance, simply the *touch* of it.

It was enough for Gwyr.

'Elementals,' he said quickly. 'They are damned and a nuisance, though in truth, they always precede Legion and are useful. We've been spotted.'

'Is that good?' I asked.

'Of course. Eventually. But for the moment, we are unknown because it is assumed we are dead. So we must make ourselves known again, or be attacked.' And he shouted to all around us: 'Get your things! Issabeau, take a brand from the fire, then flatten the embers. Guiwenneth, start calling to Kylhuk. Saracen, sing to your sword. Jarag, go ahead of us and enter the shadow of the wood, tell us when that shadow changes . . .'

Everyone in the glade except for Guiwenneth was staring at Gwyr blankly. He realised with some embarrassment that he had been barking orders in English, perhaps, because his head was still full of his latest Interpretation. He repeated the instructions – he was in charge then? I hadn't known this – this time in the tongue they spoke in common, which was his own.

Even as he issued orders, I could sense some small meaning in the words. Gwyr, then, had not just learned from me, but had implanted the seed of new language in my own under-educated language centres.

As activity commenced, Guiwenneth came quickly over to me, brushing at my cheeks with quick fingers and smiling. 'There were things I had to do,' she said in careful English. 'I have been with Gwyr. To know how to talk to you. To know you better. I'm glad to have you now – *Christian*,' she said, then repeated my name as if savouring it. 'Do you remember me?'

'Oh yes . . .'

'It was – a long time ago. I was a girl. Very small. Manandoun was still my . . . *guardian*. I was so frightened. Remember? The horse reared and we fell into the corn. I felt . . . so strange . . . as if a cliff had struck me where there was no cliff, and hooks dragged at my limbs where there were no hooks . . . dragging me back to the wood . . .'

'I remember you well,' I said, and though I remembered also that Huxley had written how mythagos could never journey far beyond the edge of Ryhope, they simply died and decayed, I chose to keep this knowledge to myself. 'I think I must have been waiting for you from that moment on. I was entranced by you, despite your chalked hair and white face. Remember?'

She laughed as she agreed.

'But I hadn't realised how much I was thinking of you until you came back and called to me from the wood, with Gwyr blowing that strange bronze trumpet, the bull horn or whatever it was. There had been a war. I had been fighting in a foreign land. I'm glad you came when you came. And I'm glad to have followed you here, even if it's cold and wet. And the food is grim.'

She sighed, partly content with what I'd said, but partly through anguish, I thought. Indeed, there was a quick, strange look in her eyes that I couldn't fathom. But she said, 'This is not the best time to meet again. Though truthfully – I'm glad you followed me. If I had remained in the sanctuary . . . where you were sleeping that night . . .' she sighed wistfully, then shook her head. 'But I was afraid the Creature was there, and the Creature frightens me. I am glad I saw you. I am truly glad you followed me.'

The sanctuary? She must have meant Oak Lodge, my home. Gwyr had used the same word. The Creature? Did she mean Huxley? My father? He hadn't been there that night, but perhaps some scent, some shadow had remained.

I said nothing. Indeed, I could have found no moment to say a word, for Guiwenneth had gone on brightly in her growing confidence with the English she had learned from Gwyr, 'Once we are in Legion again, everything will be as it was. Kylhuk is intimidating.' She shrugged. 'But if you leave him alone, he will leave you alone. There will be a job for you . . . and we can be together. When this great task is finished, Legion will rest. Kylhuk has assured me . . .'

'What task?'

'No one knows. Kylhuk keeps it secret – except from Manandoun! He has sworn secrecy on his life. But Legion is first searching for the Long Person, and when we find *her* we will know. The great task will begin . . . Kylhuk has gathered Legion for this very purpose.' She looked at me quickly. 'And it is a very great task indeed, the hardest of all that Kylhuk has been set.' She put a delicate finger to my lips. 'Enough of that. Time to talk about it later. First, follow me, do exactly as I do. And don't at any cost leave the Forlorn Hope. If you do, it will be worse for you than you can imagine.'

'So I was told by Gwyr. I hear you. And I understand!'

'Good. I'm glad you hear me. And *understand*. Follow me . . . Christian.'

I was amused and delighted at the thrill my name seemed to give her; and by the mischievous look in her green eyes and on her mouth as she teased me.

Another day passed, and another glade found and flattened, protected with a few sharpened branches, a fire started and grim food eaten. The hunt had been poor, and Jarag's hound old and failing.

We ate the dog.

Elidyr settled at the edge of the camp, knees drawn up to his massive jaw, fingers fiddling with the coils of rope he still carried round his shoulders.

I was uncomfortably aware that he was watching me.

As if touched by magic, the Forlorn Hope suddenly lay down on their blankets and drifted into sleep. The fire guttered and I stoked it, putting on a log to make it burn a little brighter, fighting against the drowsy influence of drink, silence and peace.

The next thing I knew I was being called from a dream. I sat up, blinking through my tears, and again found Elidyr reaching for me, the same otherworldly glow all around us.

'This way,' he said. 'Something for you to see. To understand.'

Perhaps that was why he had turned back previously. He had felt too alienated from me without Gwyr's mediating interpretation.

And so we walked again, through a ghostwood that suddenly began to bloom. Since we had travelled several miles from the river during the day, and since this wood was identical to that of the previous night, I knew we had stepped out of the space and time of the Forlorn Hope.

I couldn't help laughing as again we underwent our floral trans-formation. The air was scented and sublime; the light was gorgeous, and we walked between its pools and shafts like manifestations out of Eden.

Elidyr was not indecisive now. He led the way with a sureness of foot and a firmness of purpose. Once we had become flowered and fun-gused, the transformation was complete. When Elidyr stopped and crouched he became like a rotting trunk, vibrant with parasitic growth in full colour. I nearly tripped over him.

'Sssh!' he said, and pulled me down by the fern on my arms.

I listened carefully, and heard the sound of a woman singing, and running water.

Knee deep in iridescent bluebells, we stepped closer to the pool. On one side of it rose a cliff, and a thin waterfall tumbled through the trees that crowded its edge. The woman was dressed in black and was rinsing pots and pans at the water's edge. Her red hair was combed but undecorated. Her feet were bare.

Elidyr pointed to the right. A stone tomb, made from roughly hewn rocks, rose among the trees, whose roots were entangled with the stones, as if drawing it closer to their gloom. A small red pennant hung above the low entrance, and simple dolls had been fixed to the lintel, though from here it was difficult to see what sort of dolls they were.

This was a magic place, a luxurious garden in the vibrant forest, and everything but that crumbling mausoleum was alive with brightness.

Elidyr sighed and the breeze he caused flowed through the fern and passed away. The woman looked up, looked towards us, then returned to her pots, beginning her song again.

'Can she see us?' I asked.

'No. Not looking for us,' Elidyr muttered. 'I must show you.'

He walked into the clearing by the pool and I followed. We crossed the rocks to the tomb and Elidyr ducked down and crawled inside. I glanced at the woman again, but she was quite unaware of me.

Inside the tomb, a man lay on a marble plinth. He was garbed with chain mail over heavy shirt and trousers, and clutched a bunch of flowers to his chest. His sword, which was broken in half, was by his side. A doll lay below his feet, which were crossed at the ankles.

I touched the white face. It was as cold as the stone on which he lay. His hair had been combed. He smelled of flowers, not decay.

After a while, the woman came into the tomb. She walked straight past us, carrying fresh flowers for his hands and a pot of water, with which she washed the dead man's face. When this was done she kissed his lips, knelt down and prayed to an icon of a woman in white, then left the mausoleum.

Elidyr, in his green disguise, rustled over to the corpse and blew on its mouth.

The knight stirred and opened his eyes. The flowers dropped from his hands and he started to breathe, a ghastly sound as he returned from the dead. One hand reached for the handle of his sword, found it and gripped it as a child grips a finger. But he lay there, on his back, his unfocused gaze upon the corbelled ceiling of his resting place.

A sudden stench made me look down at my body. Everything was rotting where it grew. Elidyr's luxuriant growth of fern and briar had browned and shrivelled; insects burst from the fungal swellings. The flowers the knight had dropped wilted then putrefied.

I ran outside, ducking to avoid the lintel, brushing the small cloth dolls, which I swear made sounds like children waking. Elidyr followed me. The woman was on her feet, looking up at the waterfall, where the trees had begun to die, the leaves shedding in a rain of russet, autumn fall. Winter curled through the forest and this pool with a malevolence and a speed that shocked me. Ice grew on the pond and spread along the branches of the wood. The cold was so intense I thought the woman had frozen where she stood, but she slowly looked down, then at the tomb, a crease of confusion forming on her brow.

At once, Elidyr was furious with himself. He went back into the chamber. The winter faded, life returned to the pool, flowers bloomed and the dolls swung in the breeze that came from the big man's breathing. The woman ran to the tomb – I followed – and knelt by her dead lover, but he had gone again, as cold as the marble on which he lay. She cried silently, her hands clasped in prayer across his chest.

Elidyr walked quickly from the place and into the woods, and when he was a long way back towards the region where the forest changed, he howled with anger and with sadness. I had chased after him, shedding my summer's growth, and found him huddled against a mossy rock, tears streaming from his eyes, his great brow furrowed, his fists clenched in his lap.

'Had to show you. Bad to do.' He muttered fiercely to himself. 'Poor woman. Sad enough.'

'You brought life back to him.'

'Yes. Not again. Poor woman. Sad enough!' He looked up at me, grey eyes misting, his mouth grim below the straggling hair of his moustache. 'You must think about it. *Christian*. I live with it. Waking to sleeping. You must think about it.'

'Who are you, Elidyr? Who *are* you?'

'Elidyr,' he said unnecessarily, frowning and touching his lips. 'I take boats down rivers. Remember?'

'Yes, I know. The wounded and the dead. You carry the wounded and the dead. You guide them to where they must go in the next phases of their life. I understand. And you brought Gwyr back. Back from his pyre. You gave him life.'

Elidyr stared at me for a moment, then said softly, 'You will *need* the gureer. He will need you. Care for him.'

'I will. I surely will . . .'

He had said, *I had to show you*. Why? Why had he been under such an obligation?

And what significance had there been in that strange fluctuation from summer to winter? The answer eluded me, and perhaps this was because another thought was on my mind, and this I mentioned to the anguished man, trying to be as tactful as I could.

'Elidyr . . . did you once take a boat with a woman who had hanged herself . . . killed herself after Kylhuk had assaulted her? A woman called Jennifer . . . ?'

'Guinevere?'

'*Jennifer!*'

He stared at me, the tears drying in his eyes, the furrow in his brow deepening. He put a big hand on my face and I flinched, wondering if he was going to do me harm, but his fingers brushed my eyes, his thumb my mouth—

And suddenly I was walking in the river, waist deep and hauling back on long ropes attached to the boats that floated ahead of me! I had become Elidyr.

The vision was startling. The bright sun glinted through the canopy. The narrow river was icy. My feet were slipping as I walked with the flow. The ropes cut into my shoulders, rubbing and bruising me. I ached with the effort of this walk, tugging back against a current that was trying to drag me faster. I was hungry. I longed for rest. But there was so far to go, such a huge river to find, so many small boats to tether carefully, in hidden places, ready for that final pull, that massive guiding of all these floating coffins towards their final destination, beyond the twin gates . . . And I could rest . . .

But I leaned forward, now, and through Elidyr's eyes looked at the sleepers in their boats.

Fair faces and old faces, and strange faces and masked faces . . .

And suddenly I saw my mother! Her hands were crossed on her chest! Her suit was still stained with the juice of tomatoes. Her hair was still combed and pinned for the Sunday service. She was resting on cushions, and though her face was white, and her chest didn't rise or fall, I could see no sign of the strangling rope with which she had taken her own life. I was twelve years old again. At any moment my mother would sit up, yawn, rub her eyes and see me; and she would smile and tease me. And she and I and Steven would walk around the edge of Ryhope Wood as far as Shadoxhurst or Grimley, and sit on the village green . . .

'Elidyr,' I begged, breaking the trance. 'That's my mother! Bring her back. Take her back to Oak Lodge! Don't let the twin gates take her! She still had so much life to live.'

'I can't,' said Elidyr.

'Why not?' I cried.

'She has already passed the two gates. Besides . . . her death was not as you think.'

'Not as I think? What do you mean by that?'

I had seen her death. I had been there! And I had experienced Elidyr's memory of taking her along the river.

And I had seen Gwyr brought back from the pyre, and a dead knight briefly raised, though what message I was supposed to take from that I couldn't quite imagine.

'If you know so much,' I yelled at him, 'answer my question! What do you mean: her death was not as I think?'

'I cannot bring her back,' the big man said, staring at me stonily. 'Only you can. After all, that is partly why you're here!'

I could bring her back?

He rose and stalked away, leaving me crying and staring after him, shouting, 'And what does *that* mean? *Partly* why I'm here! *How do* I bring her back?'

'Ask your father . . .'

Huxley?

'Where is my father in all of this?' I screamed at him.

'Waiting for you.'

'Waiting where?'

'Go to sleep,' Elidyr called back gruffly. 'I'm bored with you. Until Kylhuk finds the Long Person – nothing you can do!'

I followed him for a while, but I became lost and confused, blinded by the silver-bright reflection from the trees, a lost soul in a winter's nightmare. I seemed to see my mother's face in every patch of shadow, every shimmering, moonlit fern. She called to me and I cried for her, cried for the life with her that had been taken from me by Strong Against the Storm. How much I longed for her quiet counsel, her gentle reassurance. I had been too young when she died, too young to know what Steve and I were losing. Now, having glimpsed her through the boatman's eyes, a sense both of acute loss and hope snatched at my breath. For some reason the awful words of a hymn came to mind: *she is not dead, but sleeping* . . .

And I laughed, because the words were associated with a memory of my father singing them, during the funeral of his sister, his mind elsewhere, his eyes focused elsewhere . . .

And then I panicked, not seeing Elidyr ahead of me any more. I ran after him in this moon-gleaming wood, shouting for him, but I could no longer even hear his long, steady stride.

I finally accepted the truth – that Elidyr had gone – and curled into the hollow of a rock to sleep, only to discover that the rock was Guiwenneth's back, and I had returned to the dead fire, the crude camp, and the slumbering forms of the Forlorn Hope.

Elidyr had gone.

Eight

Kylhuk, thinking my companions dead, had formed a new 'point' to his legion, a new Forlorn Hope which had been probing steadily towards us, attracted by the signals that Issabeau and the jarag in particular had been emitting, the calls and summonings of the enchanted parts of their lives.

We were running in single file along a thistle-strewn stone road that had been laid between the edges of the wood. It ran in a winding fashion. Overgrown monuments, probably tombs, lined it on both sides. Gwyr ran behind the rest of us, leading the two horses. He had muffled their hooves and muzzled their jaws, but they still made a loud noise as they trotted, though the rest of us padded through the wood in silence.

Abruptly, Issabeau raised her arm, waved us back. I could see nothing ahead of us save the bend in the road and the dense wall of greenery, but I didn't doubt for a moment the truth of Issabeau's urgent shout that: 'Eelzond ici! Ontond! Payrill ezbroje . . .'

They are here. Listen. Danger is close.

Almost at once, a part of the forest shimmered and changed, becoming silver and white, resolving into the form of a mounted knight, a grim-raced man in gleaming mail. He was riding with thundering speed towards us, lance-arm raised. A javelin sped towards Someone son of Somebody, who stepped aside and almost disdainfully plucked the weapon from the air. The white charger reared, the knight turned, fair hair flowing as he reached for a second spear then rode at us again, this time stabbing low, going for Issabeau, who turned her back and bowed her head. Her red bird flew at the knight, who raised his weapon and stabbed at the screeching creature, sending it to the ground in a storm of feathers. Then he wheeled around and flung the spear at the Saracen, who stooped to avoid the blow.

After that the knight returned to the edge of the wood and sat there motionless, side-on, stretching up in the stirrups to peer at us more curiously.

'Peril!' Issabeau urged again, her dead protector held to her chest, her eyes glazed with tears. But this time she was looking behind us.

Out of nowhere, it seemed, two sleek male figures came running towards us, hawk-faced, green skin gleaming. Someone intercepted them, fighting furiously. His sword struck a face and I realised that the men were wearing tarnished masks of bronze. Even as one reeled back, so the other ducked and the air about him shimmered. Someone became wreathed in fire, his face grimacing as he held his hands outside the consuming flame. I ran towards him, but Issabeau growled, 'Stay back!'

A second later, the fire gathered around the warrior's shoulders, formed into something like an animal and jumped into the trees, where it flowed amorphously, hovering in the lower branches. Quite suddenly, it resolved into a white-robed woman, silk clad and with white, silken hair.

There was much shouting. The hawks drew back. The knight kicked cautiously towards us, then sheathed his sword.

Our friend Someone was standing with his arms raised, a gesture of welcome and peaceful intention; indeed, of surrender. Issabeau adopted the same posture. Jarag growled but grinned, mocking us for a weakness that only he could understand.

Gwyr said to me, 'It could have been worse than that. It was an easier encounter than many. They recognised us for what we are despite you, and now Kylhuk will hear of it and soon you will meet him.'

'Again,' I added.

'Again?'

'I met him when I was a child. He marked me. As *slathan*. I told you before.'

'Indeed,' said the Interpreter. 'The strange word. Slathan. Indeed, you have met Kylhuk before, so he will be expecting you. I'll stay close to you when you meet him for the first time, if you wish. If he marked you, he may be intending to kill you. He often does this.'

'He *often* does this?'

'He's an unpredictable man. But I am in your debt, so you have only to ask if you wish me to stay close to you.'

'Stay close,' I said, my whole impression of Kylhuk shifting into a new and darker form. 'Your absence made me uneasy, that time before, when you went back to the river to look for Guiwenneth. Now, even the thought of it, the absence of your understanding tongue and wise counsel, makes my head spin.'

He seemed pleased with my comments, patting his breast above the heart, and tugging at the horses with greater enthusiasm.

We followed the knight and the woman along the road. The woman walked in an ethereal way, as if floating, her robes drifting in the light breeze. The knight slouched in his high-backed saddle, his attention on the woodland around him, his hand resting on the pommel of his sword. The horse dropped dung at regular intervals and the small file that followed this imperious chevalier wove one way or the other to avoid it, though during the early part of the march, both Issabeau and Jarag stooped to inspect the remains, Jarag flicking pieces of the spoor into the bushes that crowded the boundaries of this ancient road. They showed no sign of alarm or concern at whatever they might have detected.

Someone watched the performance with appalled dismay, however, but when he stared at Issabeau she simply taunted him by shape-changing into a grimacing animal. The two walked next to each other after a while, but in disdainful silence. When the proud Celt offered to take the dead bird from Issabeau and carry it in a small, cloth bag, she reluctantly agreed. It was an odd moment.

Though the two of them were still not talking, they kept glancing at each other curiously.

The two hawks ran beside us, out of sight in the woodland, but not out of hearing. They called to each other, a regular series of screeches and shrill whistles, imitating the birds of prey whose features they had adopted in paint and mask. Listening to them, still remembering their lithe figures running and somersaulting towards us, metal hammers raised for the attack, I wondered from which culture they had arisen as heroes. They seemed unlikely for any role in legend that I could imagine.

But then, by the sound of it, Kylhuk himself – who as *Culhwch*, in love with the fair Olwen, was recorded with great affection in the mediaeval Welsh romances – was not quite the youthful and proud arrival at King Arthur's court, the determined suitor needing only Arthur's assistance to achieve his conquest, with which my own generation was familiar.

And as I walked in the file, alert to every sound and every sight, I began to appreciate one of the earliest comments in Huxley's journal (it wasn't dated, but must have been written some time in the mid-1920s; he could scarcely have been older than I am now. I certainly hadn't been born at the time):

Curiouser and curiouser. I must repress my expectations and beliefs. I mast forget everything I knew and thought I knew. I am in an unknown region, walking unknown paths.

In the words of the poet, all is a blank before me. There are no maps, no paths to follow. This is the wilderness.

And yet no society of primitives inhabits this wonderful WILDNESS of unshorn hill and rough-banked river I penetrate day by day, adventure by adventure. But rather, a mixture of forms and figures, and strangely familiar images from my studies, that seems to suggest ALL of myth, something timeless yet ever-changing, fragmented, and at any time, in whatever place I occupy, somehow ever-present. I am so curious . . . I must not too quickly interpret what I see . . .

'Then why did they attack me?' I wanted to ask my father from this distance in time, and yet – perhaps – from no distance in space that might be counted as significant on any map. After all, Ryhope Wood was not the broadest or deepest stand of ancient wildwood in the country.

But these thoughts were rattling drums, no more than that, a reflection of confusion, fear and curiosity – how often I thought of that jibe in Huxley's journal! (*Neither boy seems curious.*) How often I wonder whether he was tempting me, Satan to my Eve, taunting my intellect with an encouragement to question what I could see around me. And I wonder: why did he not take me into his confidence? Why taunt me when I would have been such a willing student?

'Why did they attack me? If these people are the memory of heroism, why are they so brutal?'

All is a blank before me. There are no maps, no paths to follow . . .

'Yes, yes. The easy answer . . .'

'Who are you talking to?' Gwyr asked, startling me from my reverie.

'A ghost,' I answered, adding in Gwyr's way of speaking, 'truthfully! If I was talking out loud it is because a man walks beside me whom I never understood, and who wishes me harm when I wish only that he would talk to me without secrets. And I don't mean you!'

'Your father?'

'My father.'

Gwyr rolled his eyes and sighed. 'I know. I know. They get old before they're ready. Women get wiser because of this, men no less so, but fussier. But I don't think I can help you on this occasion. I'm getting too old myself!'

Before I could comment – he didn't look *that* old, though he was certainly older than me – the horses tugged at him, or he made them seem to, and he turned away from me, calming the restless animals as he led them in a soothing circle.

At the first opportunity, I talked to Guiwenneth about Elidyr. She took my hand as I recounted the strange trip into the forest, the far stranger transmogrification of Elidyr and myself, and the lush, luxurious garden around the stone tomb of the knight.

'I remember a story like that,' Guiwenneth said. 'It was told to us when we were children. It's an old story:

'A man lies dead in a fairy hill, his body guarded by his wife who will not let him go into the valley beyond. The hill is in the bend of a river, surrounded by a deep forest filled with rich fruit, strange herbs and wonderful flowers. The wife will not let her husband go until she has had a child by him, but the man is dead. There is nowhere for her love to go except into the land, and the land has flourished on this love for years, and is abundant and beautiful, mysterious and welcoming.

'Then, one day, the wife finds a herb growing over the body of a fledgling bird that has fallen from its nest. The bird comes back to life and starts to sing. She takes the herb and plants it in earth in the mouth of her dead husband. He comes back to life and they fall in love all over again. She declares love for nothing and no one but this man and their children.

'But without her love, now given back to her husband, the land becomes wasted and blighted. An eternal winter covers everything. And that is the lesson . . .

'Each of us has only so much love to give, so we must share it carefully between everything that matters to us, no matter how small. That's what my mother told me when she told me the story.'

She squeezed my hand, but didn't look at me when I glanced at her. She went on, Elidyr has shown you this terrible scene for a reason. And by the look of you . . .' she looked at me, now, 'there is certainly something distressing you.'

'He showed me a vision of my mother. He said – he said I might be able to bring her home.' *Back to life* . . . 'And then he left. But *how*? How do I bring her home?'

Guiwenneth said nothing for a while, and we walked in awkward silence. She was thinking hard, still occasionally squeezing my hand, gestures of affection that I reciprocated.

At last, she sighed.

'Elidyr the Guide has shown you his dilemma. He is always torn between guiding the dead or giving them further life. He is showing you that there is a consequence to everything. The woman's happiness would blight the forest. Her sadness sustains nature. Elidyr always agonises over the choice he must make.'

I thought of his crisis of indecision in the hours before he had brought Gwyr back from the pyre. And I watched Gwyr, walking with the horses, and wondered if he knew.

'Gwyr was dead,' I said. 'Elidyr brought him back. So is he now living on borrowed time?'

'It depends on the consequences,' Guiwenneth said. 'He might live to be old. Elidyr might take him back tomorrow. It all depends.' She looked up at me with a smile. 'I like your words, Christian.'

'What words?'

'Living on borrowed time! It's a good way to talk about the gift Elidyr has given to Gwyr . . .'

'Thank you.'

'You use so many wonderful images in your talk . . .'

'I do?'

'They make my head spin. So soothing and charming, so . . . unusual.'

Clichés, I thought, but said, 'I'm glad.'

'I loved the way you talked about our first night together, by the river, by the fire.'

'Remind me.'

'You said that it was like . . . like a *midsummer night's dream* . . .'

'Ah . . .'

'And that's just how it seemed!'

'It did,' I said. 'I can't deny it.'

'You have such a way of using words to make visions. Sometimes when you speak, it's like listening to a poet.'

'It is,' I agreed. 'I certainly can't deny that either.'

Between one step and the next we had entered the twilight of the day, and the wood seemed to crowd suddenly upon us. Flocks of birds circled above the canopy, angrily noisy, perhaps because they were being disturbed by activity somewhere ahead of us. Guiwenneth rested a hand on my arm to draw my attention, then whispered, 'It's here. Just ahead of us. It's watching us, making sure it recognises the armoured man.'

We waited for a long time, standing in a line across the road, on the chevalier's instruction, silent but for Gwyr's muttered words of calm to the animals. Then, astonishingly, the wall of forest *split apart*, the edges stretching towards us like a sucking mouth, widening as if to eat us, fires and human figures revealed within its maw; and two men on black horses cantered towards us. These riders came through the mouth, turned back suddenly and beckoned us to follow, and the chevalier led his own steed forward, the rest of us close behind.

The smells of cooking and animal ordure, and the noise of a military camp, greeted us as the hidden gate closed behind us. We were in night and in the forest, and dazzled by the brightness of twenty fires.

Almost at once, a group of runners, two women, seven men, ran towards the forest wall and appeared to merge with it, or pass through it, vanish from view in any event, a new Forlorn Hope sent to their uncertain fate.

There was so much movement of men and animals, so much barking, shouting, laughing and clashing of metal on metal, that it was hard to detect who or what was paying attention to us; but the knight was in earnest conversation with a group of men and the ethereal woman was standing, palm to palm with a second woman, who scowled as she listened to what was being said, one eye watching me, the other closed, and I guessed I was being discussed. Gwyr and Guiwenneth were in deep conversation too, peering deeper into the camp that was spread through the wood. I sensed they were expecting an arrival. Jarag sat alone on one side of a fire, his skin clothes stripped from his muscular body, whittling happily at a piece of bone with an elegant flint blade. On the other side of the flames, three grim warriors were leaning forward, idly talking as they ran whetstones lazily along their iron knives, taking scant interest in the prehistoric man who was using their firelight. All members of the same team, I thought, even though there would be no playful banter in this particular stadium.

Of Someone and Issabeau there was no sign, and I hadn't even seen them slip away. I was puzzled by what was happening between the two of them, this odd flux of hostility and affection, with a common tongue continuing to elude them both, although the Saracen seemed able to talk to each of them in turn without difficulty.

I liked Someone. I liked his swagger, and the sudden doubt that seemed to plague him.

Guiwenneth had told me a little more about the proud Celt, who had been recruited to Legion at much the same time as she, though she had been a child at the time and placed in the care of Kylhuk's friend Manandoun, and Someone had been a youth, wandering and making his living as a mercenary as he searched for his identity . . .

At the moment of his birth, with horns sounding and silver hawks circling above the house where his mother laboured, his father was being struck by the spear that had been flung across the river by his challenger. The name his father had been about to announce flew from his lips and was caught on the wind. A woman hovered there, disguised as a great bird of prey, and she caught the name.

'I know someone who will pay well for this,' she screeched from the clouds.

Men ran and dogs ran, following the bird, and after a day the hawk faltered and fell to the rivet. But before they could fend the name it had stolen, the name had been swallowed by a salmon. The salmon was pursued but was caught and eaten by an owl; the owl then fell prey to a dog-wolf. The wolf was hunted but gored by an old boar. The boar was hunted but eaten by a creature that no man or woman had ever before encountered.

And in this way, the name was lost. And because his father had died before naming the child, the father's name was forgotten too.

It all seemed very unfair on the mother, but that was that, that was the way it worked.

The men gave up the hunt, returned, only to find themselves servants of his father's killer. The boy was exiled. But when Someone came of age, he set out to find the single word that would make him whole.

The way Guiwenneth told it left me in no doubt as to why the man was ill at ease. A great deal indeed was placed on a name.

And as I stood listening to the sounds of the night camp, I realised that I was surrounded by people who seemed ill at ease, continually unsure, always looking around them, always questioning. I wondered whether this was to do with the fact that they were part of what appeared to be an unnatural union in this land of fairy, fey and fiction. Times fused together, stories welded one upon another, an uneasy alliance of destiny and determination that could only exist because . . .

Because what? Because one man had deemed it so? This Kylhuk?

Legion was not itself a memory of myth and history, like the people and creatures that occupied it. As Huxley scoured the wood for mythagos, to gain brief glimpses of the forgotten past, one such mythago – Kylhuk – had found a way to raise these entities *unnaturally*, to gather them like flowers, subverting their *own* stories to his own, transmuting their legend to his own quest, whatever that quest might have been.

How was he doing it? What 'source' of magic or myth was he using to so shape this already supernatural wildwood?

I became dizzy with noise and movement and strange smells, and the sensation of being alone in a huge place, with a crowd which was somehow walking *through* me, as if it were I who was the ghost, and not these ghostly recapitulations of the hopes and wishes and stories of long-gone generations.

I seemed to draw the wood around me, to become the narrowing focus of some creature, invisible to the eye, bending the trees and the forest with its presence as it closed down upon me, sniffing, licking, quizzically eyeing its captive, then pulling back, letting through as if from nowhere a tall man in bright clothes, a man with hair as white as snow, and with a face as hard as ice. He strode towards me, rooting me to the spot with his fierce gaze.

And I knew him. It was Manandoun, Guiwenneth's guardian, and the last time I had seen him I had been twelve years old.

Without a flicker of emotion, Manandoun reached up to grip my face in his rough hands, his thumbs running along the two small scars by my eyes. Then the hard expression on his face broke and he grinned broadly. He jabbered excited words at me, then fell silent as he realised I was failing to understand him. But when he spoke more slowly I began to get meaning from his words, though my frown finally encouraged him to shout for Gwyr, who came running over to us, wiping the back of his hand across his mouth. His beard was greasy and he was chewing and swallowing hard, ready to act as interpreter again.

Manandoun said, 'I didn't think you would come. You were so far at the edge of the world that we didn't expect to see you again. But I'm glad you're here, and Kylhuk is delighted too. It has been a good day for Kylhuk. The return of friends we thought were dead,' he glanced at Gwyr with a slight frown as he said this and Gwyr stumbled in his translation for a moment, 'and the discovery of a boy who is now a man and come to help him in the most difficult part of his quest.'

'For the Long Person,' I said and Manandoun slapped me on each shoulder, delighted.

'That's just the beginning of it. But if you know that, then you know it's dangerous. That's good. You know what you're up against.'

'Truthfully, I don't,' I said, still trying to imitate the way of speaking of Manandoun and Gwyr (which at that time was an effort for me, though it is an effort no longer). 'I know very little, though I am eager to learn.'

'Then don't worry for the moment. Kylhuk will tell you everything, everything about himself, from his childhood to wise warrior, of his deeds and his disappointments. Kylhuk has lived for a long time and not one breath of wind has passed that hasn't seen a great deed or a great fight or a great song from that man. Nothing is wasted, not time nor wit nor the strength of his arm. He is a living legend, every moment of his life packed with interest.'

'When will I meet this man Kylhuk?'

'Tomorrow,' said Manandoun, glancing away from me, almost as if embarrassed. 'When he has finished shaping the great delights of today into a story.'

And in English, Gwyr added, 'He's drunk.'

Manandoun, clearly understanding what had been said, scowled at the interpreter and reprimanded him. 'He is in the Delightful Realm!'

'I'm sure he is.'

'The Delightful Realm!' Manandoun repeated. 'From where he can see events from all sides at once!'

'Especially from on his back, looking upwards,' Gwyr retorted.

Manandoun stared at the other man. 'Truthfully, I should take you to task for that insult. But Kylhuk would want me to be forgiving, now that his friends have returned from the far frontier.'

'No fight, then,' Gwyr said, disappointed.

'No fight,' said Manandoun.

Then a thought struck him. He reached out again to embrace me with his fists, feeling my arms and shoulders. '*Can* you fight? Can you throw a spear? Can you drink and run at the same time? Can you use a sling? Does the pain of a wound slow you down?' He peered more intently at me, whispering, 'Can you summon the frenzy? Are you willing to shoot an arrow at the Scald Crow? It would be good for us all if you could!'

Before I could attempt any answer to this tumble of questions, Gwyr said, 'I can give him some basic training. The man is fast, I've seen him run, but he's younger than he looks, and drinking will be his greatest training.'

Both men looked at me and laughed, though I couldn't see the joke. I said, 'I have a few tricks of my own, which I'd be glad to demonstrate.'

I was thinking of the training in unarmed combat I'd been given in '42. I was certain that I could throw even the burly Manandoun, but had decided to wait for the right moment to demonstrate my skills. I might make a fool of myself using their own crude weapons. It would be useful to have a come-back which might earn me more respect.

'Show those tricks to Kylhuk,' Manandoun said. 'He is very fond of tricks.'

And again both men laughed.

Then with the words, 'Legion is an animal that moves on ten thousand legs. But two extra are more than welcome . . . Christian . . . Huxley,' Manandoun bid me goodbye and went in search of Guiwenneth.

He had given me a strange look when he'd used my name, but I thought no more of it.

Gwyr watched him go, then turned to me, tugging at his thin, trimmed beard. 'Until recently, he was Guiwenneth's guardian, but now there are others who will begin to care for her. Despite Kylhuk's rage, pomposity and inclination to visit the Delightful Realm, he truly does see the future, and with Ear son of Hearer and Hergest Longsight, he can often tell who or what is to come into our lives.'

'Did he know that I would come into his life? And into Guiwenneth's?'

'I don't believe so. And this is why Kylhuk must be watched, and his mood determined with great skill. He will be afraid of you, and fascinated lay you. He marked you, after all; he needs you for something, that is clear. I very much doubt if it's for your head as a trophy, but I hardly see how it can be for your throwing arm. There is something that disturbs me about all of this, so I shall stay close. Guiwenneth, though, will be parting from Manandoun, so there may be a mood of sadness. Manandoun was in despair when he thought she was lost. Now he must face a different loss. According to Kylhuk, a band of hunters – the Jaguth – are rising from the earth, twelve in all, and Guiwenneth will spend time with them before the next adventure in her life.'

'The Jaguth,' I repeated.

Gwyr shrugged, saying, 'I have heard of them. But Legion has never encountered them, or captured them, so they are not within its gates. They may not even arrive until this adventure is over.' I think he was trying to reassure me. He went on: 'But *you* are here, and Manandoun has told me to show you the garrison. Tomorrow, you will meet Kylhuk himself, but tonight – are you tired?'

'Not at all.'

We had only been travelling half a day before Legion had swallowed us and shifted us away from daylight to night. It was remarkable that Gwyr and the others seemed so accepting of this phenomenon.

'Then we can begin now,' said the interpreter. 'Legion is a garrison that moves during the day and settles into the forest by night. You must come to know it intimately. You will have to work for your stay here, and you must know of your position inside the beast at any time, otherwise you will be snatched away by the forests of the Long Gone. Stop looking so forlornly at Guiwenneth. She is leaving Manandoun, not you! She has plans for *you*!'

There was a twinkle in his eye and an impertinent edge to the grin on his face as he added, 'All things in their time.'

'Yes. All things in their time. Unlike this place, Gwyr. Unlike Legion. This is not a *thing in its time*.'

But he pretended not to understand my point, though I'm certain he did, and simply led me to the horses.

PART THREE

Legion of the Lost

Nine

I had once read a description of a Roman legion on the march, mile upon mile of cavalry, armoured infantry, surly auxiliaries, archers, trumpeters, pack animals and their handlers, siege machines, smiths and cooks and carpenters, baggage wagons and camp followers, an orderly, organised, relentlessly advancing and thoroughly dusty column of battle-weary men that would take a day to pass, and would continue to shake the earth for hours after it had disappeared into the distance.

Kylhuk's Legion was not like this, though it was ordered in its own way and was huge, seeming to stretch forever through the forest, a sprawling beast (now mostly sleeping) laid out according to Kylhuk's needs.

In a Roman legion there were traditionally six thousand men of war. Manandoun had referred to this one as 'an animal marching on ten thousand legs', but Gwyr thought that four thousand was more like it, two thousand men, women and children, although if Manandoun was including the dogs and horses, each of which had four legs, he may have been closer to the truth. Kylhuk's Legion had whole packs of dogs scattered through, its line, hounds of all types and mastiffs the size of bulls; also, four herds of wild ponies, which would be broken in and used as the need developed.

Indeed, as we rode down the line later, there was an outburst of angry shouting from some of the fires as a spike-haired boy astride a black, narrow-muzzled wolf-hound came bounding past us, leading five angry, kicking horses by rope tethers. He was whooping and laughing, holding the dog by its mane, kicking the beast's sweating flanks with bare feet.

We watched them go and Gwyr said, 'One of Kylhuk's first tasks was the capture of the hound Cunhaval from its master, Greidos son of Eiros. That hound has mated with every bitch in Legion and the place now swarms with its bastards. Like the one you've just seen. The children in Legion organise hunting parties – for its fleas!'

And then, as if the moment had not happened, he continued his thought on the number of legs in Legion, saying that as well as horses and dogs there were also weasels, foxes, sacred hares and bulls, not to mention owls, eagles and hawks, none of them tethered but flying free, attached to the column by magic and by instinct.

'And there is a woman who keeps cats,' he added as an afterthought, but said no more, looking distinctly uncomfortable even at mentioning the fact.

That first night, as Gwyr and I rode slowly down the line, I became overwhelmed by the size of the column, the dazzling fires with their chattering, laughing or sleeping groups of fighters and their mates, the confusion of armour and weaponry, the chaos of tents, some of them ornate with pennants flying, some made from bent willow and animal hides, some nothing more than a few skins wrapped around the yellowing long-bones of mammals.

We rode through a forest that was alive with light, that droned with voices, and which also flexed and flashed with distorted perception: on many occasions, during that first tour of the defences of the Legion, I saw people emerge from nowhere, trunks giving up the shapes, or the earth opening to disgorge a human form, afire sucked down then flaring up again as a man or woman stepped through the flames as if nothing had occurred at all.

If I asked Gwyr a question along the lines of, 'Who is that?' or 'How on earth?' or 'In this forest can someone step out of the fire?' he would most often shrug and say, 'Truthfully, if I knew the answer to that I'd be a wiser man than I am,' which became such an incantation that I began to laugh when he said it, or even voice the words along with him. On an occasion or two he explained that these apparitions were part of the perimeter force that used the secret ways, or the charmed ways, or the ghost-born ways, legendary and mostly forgotten forms of magic, to hold the flank of Legion against those malevolent forces that surrounded the garrison like so many predatory animals.

The flanks were also defended by groups of armed men. These, as in any legion, were formed from groups of warriors of the same culture, and so Viking patrolled with Viking, and mail-clad Norman stood arrogantly debating his fate with shorn-haired compatriot. I saw soldiers with muskets who might have been from the seventeenth century, Saracens and crest-helmeted men from the near east, Greeks and Goths,

Scots and Sumerians, all of them recognizable because history and the carvings on rock-tomb, pottery and chalice have preserved the form and shape of their beard, hair and armour. And I saw dozens of other groups whose dress and attitude confounded me, all of them spread down the line, band upon band of them, becoming hundreds, all of them resting now that Legion had dropped to its haunches for the night.

When Legion advanced, the Forlorn Hope spread out before it, and the Silent Towers, as they were called, behind it, for reasons that I would learn later. Behind those scouts at front and rear was a formid-able defence, divided between armed warriors and specialists in the ways of magic. Gwyr listed them for me, and I became dizzy with these specialist functions, but I remember that he talked of earth-walkers, spirit-travellers, shadow-fighters, shamans who could become hounds, eagles, salmon or stags, running or swimming through the forest with an animal's sense. There were 'Oolerers', who opened and closed hidden gates, called Hollowings, so that the Legion could slip briefly into another time before slowly flowing back again, avoiding danger. And the woman who kept cats, he added, shuddering.

There were Arthurian knights, their heavy armour gleaming as they rode, their horses huge compared to the smaller ponies that Kylhuk owned in multitude; and these knights were either ghost-born or holy (Gwyr used the expression 'hallowed', which I took to mean the same thing).

Ghost-born were not to be interfered with. They were reluctant additions to Legion, parasites on the back of the noble column, seeking a totem that was as dark in its meaning as it was in its appearance. A Dark Grail? I asked.

'Truthfully, if I knew the answer to that—'

'You'd be a wiser man.'

He looked at me irritably and I smiled, then laughed as he walked his horse below a low-slung bough and cracked his head.

'Perhaps we have seen enough for the night,' he said, composing himself after he had rubbed the area of the blow. 'The heart of Legion is around Kylhuk himself,' he pointed into the forest. We had ridden ten miles or so in one direction, and returned half-way along the other flank. Circling the heart had taken several hours and my impression was that Kylhuk and his train lay a mile or so from this rim, behind more circles of defences.

And I was certainly tired now, my backside sore, my thighs aching from the stretch across the horse.

Legion slept. Gwyr and I rode slowly between the fires, returning to where Guiwenneth lay below a woolen blanket, her back to Someone son of Somebody, who lay with his hand on Issabeau's outstretched arm (a pale limb in the night, everything about her so delicate). Guiwenneth stirred as I lay down beside her, Gwyr again having taken the horses to their own station.

She looked at me sleepily, then touched fingers to my cheeks and smiled. 'I wanted to come with you,' she said. 'But you went before I knew it.'

'Gwyr has shown me the defences of the legion,' I said. 'I've learned a lot.'

'I've missed you,' she murmured, then stretched to kiss me, putting a hand round my head and holding my face to hers, her lips on my cheek, then, after a moment's hesitation, her lips on mine. 'Come under my blanket. Keep me warm.'

I went under her blanket. She was a slender shape in my arms, wriggling and snuggling closer to me, reaching a cold hand inside my shirt for my warm flesh. But if I'd hoped for passion I was disappointed. She mumbled and murmured, drifted into sleep again, her hair covering my face. I had to move it away with my chin and nose, since my arms were entwined with hers.

And I slept. And I slept well.

And at dawn, when I woke, I woke to the sight of Guiwenneth beside me, her eyes open, her breath in rhythm with my own, our faces still very close.

'Good morning,' I murmured.

'You sleep very peacefully,' she said. 'I've been watching you.'

And then she kissed me again. But before I could kiss her in return she had thrown off the blanket, risen lithely to her feet and scampered into the cover of the bushes.

A horn sounded. A long, low note, then the frantic beating of a drum. Distantly, I heard the whinnying of horses, the angry barking of dogs and the shouts of men.

Legion came alive. Its fires were extinguished, its tents dismantled, its human occupants put to their stations after snatching breakfast from wherever they could. Manandoun, white-cloaked, white-haired, his face painted scarlet, rode up with an entourage of two, one a striking woman, yellow-haired, solemn and with a plethora of weaponry slung across her shoulders, from her waist, even strapped to the high, leather boots with which she gripped the heaving flanks of her sleek and feisty mare. I was not introduced, but in any case, she had eyes only for the distance, as if dreaming of the fighting for which she was clearly well equipped. The other was a man in a silver helmet with stylised face-plate and leather armour – 'the Fenlander', Gwyr informed me later.

'Good morning to you from Kylhuk, and indeed from me,' announced the scarlet-faced Manandoun, as he tried to control his restless steed. 'He hopes you slept well on your first night here, and indeed, I have that same hope.'

'I slept very well. Thank you.'

'Kylhuk feels that you must learn to walk with Legion, which will take some time and may surprise you. I share this view and would add only this: that when you cease to believe your eyes, your legs will find their true rooting on the earth.'

'Thank you for the advice. I don't understand it, not a word of it. But I'm sure I will.'

'I am certain that you will. We have all, in our turn, had to find the truth in our eyes and the steadiness of our legs. When you feel confident with the motion of this great Legion, ride back with Guiwenneth to Kylhuk's tent and Kylhuk will embrace you and answer all your questions. There is trouble following us and later you will test your arm, or at any rate, learn the smell of Kylhuk's vengeance!'

'What sort of trouble?' Guiwenneth asked from behind me.

'Kyrdu's sons. What else?'

Nothing more was said. Nothing more needed to be said. Guiwenneth was biting her lip. Gwyr, standing also, had heaved a deep breath.

'Legion will move at the next sound of Kylhuk's horn. Be ready!'

And Manandoun and his companions swung round from us and galloped away, merging with the forest, swallowed by the trees ahead of them.

'She came to get a look at you,' Guiwenneth said with a sly smile. 'I thought she would.'

'Who was she?'

'Kylhuk calls her Raven. They're not lovers, though Kylhuk would like them to be.'

'What raven has yellow feathers?' I asked, thinking of that tumble of golden hair.

Guiwenneth shook her head. 'He named her for her black heart and the darkness of her humour.'

'Magnificent, though.'

'Yes.'

'And she came to get a look at me . . .' I said, standing a little taller.

'Yes. And it seems she was not impressed.'

I had not understood Manandoun's advice to me, about the truth of eyes and the sureness of legs, and Guiwenneth shrugged my question off when I asked her to elaborate.

A few minutes later Kylhuk's horn sounded, distantly but sonorously, and everyone around me turned to face the front of the column, horses held tightly, dogs restrained, wagons ready, armed men in groups of twenty-seven, a number which seemed important but which Gwyr could not explain. A silence such as that at dusk fell briefly on this gathering; it lasted a second or two only, a caught breath in time, and then the second blast of the horn sounded through the camp and everyone stepped forward—

And the whole world lurched with them, like a ship casting off into a turbulent sea.

How can I describe the sensation? The earth began to shudder as Legion, spread for miles through the wildwood, began to advance with a steady step. But the forest *itself* seemed to be dragged forward, each tree and bush, each rock, each gully, shedding a ghost of itself, which progressed with us, then faded. I stumbled to avoid hazards that were only images. I struck wood and rock that had seemed ho more than illusion.

Two worlds, then, occupied the space of Kylhuk's legion, one drawn from an underworld that flowed up to surround and accompany us, the other the dissolving reality of a world I knew well, but which was made insubstantial by the power of the advancing beast.

A cliff face suddenly materialised ahead of us and the whole column shifted away from it, not just those who walked and those who rode, not just the wagons and carts and animals, but the ground itself, the *whole of the space around us*. In doing so, we walked through broad-trunked oaks as if through images projected on the air; and a shimmering after-image of the cliff would come with us for a while, detached from the reality, then fading into nothing.

It must have been like this to walk along the deck of a galleon, swinging in the wind and with the waves. And it was a kind of 'sea-legs' that I strove to find for balance, and a 'focused-sight' to tell which of the forests we passed through was real and which was not.

Though even that is wrong, because it was not the case that *any* of these wildwoods was illusion (I learned this later from Kylhuk), simply that Legion moved forward outside what you or I might think of as ordinary space and ordinary time. These were woodlands and rivers and massive stones that in various forms had occupied the space through thousands of years, new and vibrant, eroded and rotted, and the cleverness of Legion, supernatural entity that it was, was that as it marched it used these times to *hide* itself from all who pursued it.

Only when it rested was it vulnerable.

And what strange effect, I wondered, might it have had on any passing prehistoric group, hunting or travelling up the rivers in the past, when Legion flowed for a few seconds through their space and time, pursued by those forces of Nemesis herself that Kylhuk could not shake off?

By such encounters – and Huxley would have agreed with me, I'm sure – were stones begun and myths evolved!

(How quickly I was coming to accept 'magic' in my life. But then, like dream, in Ryhope anything could happen, though unlike in dreams, in Ryhope Wood the presence of the peculiar was defined and *ruled* by its existence in fiction!)

I walked in my group of twenty-seven, aware of the joking, the arguments, the groans as bodily functions needed to be addressed 'on the hoof', as it were, the mocking jollity, the lies and exaggerations of the claims and stories told to conquer fear and boredom as Legion advanced into the unknown region, nosing for the first trace of the Long Person, who would guide us to Kylhuk's final task.

The wildwood flowed about us and our ship rocked through time and half-glimpsed worlds, swaying as it moved, settling steadily into its forward rhythm.

How long it took to find my legs and eyes of truth I cannot say. I was suddenly hungry, breaking from my column to seek the crude wagon where the cold carcasses of roasted birds and mammals were stacked, ready for distribution. The bread was as hard as rock, baked on hot stones during the nights when Legion rested. But it melted eventually when held in the mouth long enough with wine or water, and we were not short of these commodities, and I was glad to get half drunk like everyone around me.

Riders came through our ranks, and running men, stooped low, heading for the forward tip of Legion, to where the Forlorn Hope was spread out in the unknown world, scenting for danger and for the right path. Behind them came Manandoun, without an entourage. He spoke to Guiwenneth, glancing at me. A horse was brought for each of us and Guiwenneth asked me, 'Do you want Gwyr with us?'

'Yes!'

She signalled to the Interpreter, then said, 'He'll follow us when he can. Come on now. Come and meet your *marker.*'

Ten

Some colourful, some grim-faced, some wild, some silent, the raiding bands, the solitary adventurers, all the warriors of Legion marched steadily past us as we rode furiously down the line. Baggage wagons trundled and swayed through the shifting, ghostly forest, burdened beneath screeching children who clung to each spar and beam. Naked, painted men in wicker chariots charged at us, taunted us, tried to race us as we passed. Spectral figures flickered in and out of vision. Sombre, armoured knights, some helmeted, some wild-haired and youthfully bold save for the dark look in their gaze, kept their great horses on a tight rein, matching the steady pace of Legion's lumbering walk.

Soon we saw tall pennants rising from narrow, ornately-tented wagons, the flags mostly black, but one above all displaying the symbol of a boar's tusk crossed by a rose. There was a confusion of activity now, horse riders, dog riders, masked runners, all taking messages and orders between all parts of the garrison.

And there were frightening moments of disorientation: the feeling of plunging into a ravine where no ravine existed, or of being suddenly caught in a burst of fire; birds clawing at our heads, arrows being fired at us . . .

Guiwenneth had forewarned me of this, the unseen defences that Kylhuk's enchanters and enchantresses had erected around the heart of Legion, like glowing embers ready to be 'ignited' if the pursuing forces broke through the outer walls and came close to the Keep.

So many defences! So much magic, which Kylhuk had painstakingly recruited at every opportunity during the years in which he had strengthened his army.

'He has spell-casters,' Guiwenneth had told me. 'Controllers of Time and of Fire, Controllers of Seasons, so we can shift within a year; there are summoners of spirits, speakers to animals, fire-starters, swimmers with fish, runners with hounds, fliers with birds, and cave-walkers –

they tread carefully, and only ever walk at the edges of the worlds of the dead, since most of the dead seem to be on our tail!'

Manandoun reined in suddenly, interrupting my efforts to identify this magic, a worried frown on his face. 'Kylhuk is not with his train,' he whispered nervously. 'Something has happened.'

He raised a short hunting horn and blew three blasts. After a while, two riders galloped out of the wall of the forest, emerging like black-cloaked phantoms from the greenwood. Both had their faces painted scarlet, and one was suffering from a wound to his right arm, which he had tied across his chest.

'He is at the Silent Towers. Eletherion and his brothers have breached them.'

'How many killed?'

'Less at that time, when we left, than now as we sit talking.' A glance was cast at me. 'He will be in the way.'

'He should see this,' said Manandoun harshly. 'He should *see* Eletherion, since the bronze man has sworn to kill the *slathan*.'

Guiwenneth hissed with anger, distracting me from the shock of that revelation, that I was the target of a death squad. I imagine I was ashen as I looked at her, and she looked hurt and sorry, her hand on her left breast.

'Modron's Heart, Christian, I was keen to tell you that Eletherion also has you marked, but there was a right time to do it, to give you a chance to decide for yourself . . .'

'Decide what for myself?' I asked.

'To return or to stay. To confront Kyrdu's sons. I'm sorry.'

'There is nothing to be sorry for. Later, you can tell me about him in greater detail. Now, I think I should accompany you to the Silent Towers.'

The riders were unhappy about this, but clearly there was no time to sit on restless, tiring horses and argue the point.

Some time later we began to smell death. I have no words to describe how awful that aroma is. There is something about it that is familiar, and yet which instantly tells you the dead await. After that, the sky darkened, another shift in space and time, and we were suddenly in a brightly lit night, the moon low and gibbous behind an earthen mound where a single tree grew, its branches winter-dressed, bare and stark. Steel clashed and men were screaming. There was an odd hollowness to the sound. The skirmish was ferocious, but involved few warriors. Torches streamed, illuminating frantic shapes engaged in combat.

Ahead of us, framing the hill, was a wall that rose sheer to a turreted summit. It was shaking with the movement of Legion, of which it was a part, and crumbling before our eyes.

Manandoun at once flung himself into the fray, disappearing into darkness. Gwyr uttered a bloodcurdling cry and also vanished into the gloom, towards the silver gleam of a river, where people were fighting in the water. Suddenly deserted, I turned anxiously to Guiwenneth, but a wildcat leapt at me, silver-flanked, black-maned, came right into the saddle, crouched there before me, a carved staff in its mouth. At once it transformed into Issabeau, who slapped my face hard and hissed: 'Attonzion!'

Then she dropped to the ground, crouching low, sniffing the air and shaking her black mane like the cat whose features she was adopting. She was looking for something and abruptly cried out, following in Gwyr's tracks towards the gleam of the river, where metal rang and eerie light played.

I looked again at Guiwenneth, in time to see her reel from the saddle, the sound of a stone from a slingshot cracking against the bone of her skull echoing loudly in my heightened consciousness. Stunned in my own way, I was easy prey for the silent figure that rode at me, face hidden behind the mask of an owl, chest bared, legs protected by strips of hide wound round to create a crude armour. I saw the spear stabbing at me and recoiled quickly. The blade glanced off my face but didn't cut. Nevertheless, I tumbled from the uncomfortable saddle and hit the thistles on the ground hard and my frightened horse cantered away and vanished.

The rider had turned and was coming back through the darkness, silhouetted by the moon, screaming a challenge, or an insult, something in any case that chilled my blood. I rose unsteadily to my feet to face him, watching the gleam at the spear's tip, anticipating how I would snatch it, but before he reached me another rider thundered past, flinging a javelin that pierced the attacker through the shoulder, turning him and sending him screaming from the field. My saviour swung round and reached down for me, gripping me painfully by the arm and suggesting by every motion of his large, smelly body that I should jump up behind him. I did this, cracking my undercarriage against the wooden bar that marked the rear of the saddle, gripping onto the rolls of fat that warmed the waistline of this half-naked rider.

He slapped at my hands with a yelp of pain. 'Hold my hair if you must!' he roared, and I did just that, gripping the long locks, silver and black in the moonlight, jerking his head back as I got a better grip, then leaning against the tickling jungle of hair on his sweat-saturated shoulders as he cantered again towards the hill. He had a torque around his neck, and he rattled with earrings and bits of metal tied to his hair.

'Manandoun!' he shouted. 'Manandoun!'

He rode this way and that, snarling angrily, then drew out a leaf-shaped sword and struck and hacked at an oak branch in pure frustration. He seemed to be talking to me sometimes, but I couldn't understand him, and when I leaned forward and asked, 'Say that again?' he just pushed me back with the muscular ridges of his shoulders. When he suddenly kicked the charger into a gallop and I reached again for safety to the ample flesh of his flanks, he again slapped my hand away with an irritable shout. I rode behind this man, using his hair as reins, noticing that as *he* rode, he used the mane of the horse. The earrings jangled. The gold torque round his neck struck me time and again in the teeth and I was lucky not to lose enamel. I hardly had time to think of poor Guiwenneth, struck down by the slingshot, but my anxiety would have been grief had I not noticed her slowly standing even as my fat friend was rescuing me.

Hopefully, then, she had escaped back to the inner lines.

'Manandoun, you dog! Manandoun! Great Hound! Come to my side! Old friend . . . call to me!'

My guardian's voice deafened me.

We had reached that turbulent river, the water thrashed by running men, dogs and horses, the far bank stalked by shadow creatures, wolves and stags, upright, monstrous and shifting in and out of vision.

One such apparition was locked in a strange embrace with Issabeau. She was ankle deep in water, her face and breast fused with a man whose face and form writhed through the shapes of animals, as did Issabeau herself. Only her right arm was human. She held tightly onto the left hand of Someone son of Somebody, who was backed up against her, stark naked save for the golden torque around his neck.

The two of them were protecting each other.

He was fighting against three men in the curious, skull-like helmets of the ancient Greeks, all of them naked too, but pushing from the river at the proud Celt with shields and long, bronze blades which he was parrying with difficulty, though he screamed abuse at them. When his iron sword was struck from his grasp I thought it must be over for the shouting man, my companion from the Forlorn Hope, but my guardian flung his own sword into the fray, a spinning weapon that Someone grabbed from the air and, without hesitating in the movement, used to cut down his nearest opponent. The sword was flung back to my paunchy companion, who caught it with equal dexterity. Someone grabbed the dead Greek's sword and shield and rampaged against the others on their own terms. As he forced them back into the river, Issabeau followed him, breaking the spell from her own opponent and sending him flying like a dark bird, screeching into the night, where shapes reached for him and seemed to shred him like a cloud ripped on the wind.

I saw this over my shoulder. We had cantered uncomfortably along the river, the horse unhappy with our double weight. I saw the Fenlander, and Raven, fighting furiously from horseback, their shouts and challenges bloodcurdling and ferocious.

And again came the anguished cry from my host: 'Manandoun! Fall back! Come back! I can't ride to you!'

Then a terrible scream pierced the confusion of night. My blood went cold. I know now how that feels. The scream was short-lived, but my guardian had broken from hot sweat to cold fear, and his mare became agitated almost beyond control, eventually becoming still under the gentle persuasion of her master. I realised the horse was now limping.

It was as if the whole skirmish had come to a sudden pause, an awful silence. Somewhere in the distance I heard a rider approaching, but my gaze was fixed upon the hill with the moon full behind it. A man was climbing to the summit, coming into view, dragging the body of another behind him. When he stood there, to one side of the winter tree, he was taller than the lower branches, a giant of a man, then. I struggled to see in this silver light. It seemed to me that the man on the hill wore a helmet with a high, vertical crest and a face-plate fashioned with the grimacing features of a church gargoyle. White skin gleamed from the clean-shaven face that showed through the frame of the mask. Hair flowed on one side only from below the helmet. He seemed to be kilted to the knee, but bare-chested like my guardian, though moonlight picked out the shine of bronze in a lacework across that body.

He had raised his sword to the heavens.

'No!' said my guardian softly. 'Not now . . . Old friend . . . Don't leave me . . .'

The sword moved down savagely, then cut again, and then again. The body in the bronze man's grip slumped away from the head, which the bronze man swung round and round by its grey hair, then released, so that the spouting ball came towards us and struck the tree a few feet away.

'*That* is Eletherion,' whispered Gwyr grimly from behind me, and I turned to look at the interpreter, glad not to be looking at that black hill. Gwyr had ridden up to us with a second horse, the great chestnut charger that Manandoun had loved, and my heart sank as I realised who had been slaughtered by this Son of Kyrdu.

'I saw Guiwenneth struck,' I muttered, 'but she was still alive—'

'She is alive. She is safe,' Gwyr said. His eyes were narrowed with pain.

'Where is Kylhuk in all of this?' I asked, suddenly angry, and the man whose lame horse I straddled reached round and grabbed me by the shoulder.

He half swung me from the saddle, but held me, his face inches from my own so that I could see clearly how his lower lip had been ritually cut to make it broader and angrier. Circles of blue dye covered one side of his face, the other was white with chalk. The teeth of small animals and glittering links of bronze were tied to the fringe of his hair. His eyes were dark in this light, but his cheeks glistened with a stream of tears, which dripped from the trimmed beard around his jaw and fell upon my hands . . . hands which still gripped him around the belt-tine for balance.

'Kylhuk is *here* in all of this,' he said in a whisper. 'I am Kylhuk. And truthfully, I have looked forward to our meeting, and indeed called you to it earlier today. But this is not the right time, now. I have just lost the closest friend a man could wish. His head is in that tree, caught among the branches. His life is in that man on the hill there, that bronze man, and I must find a way to get it back. Now . . . *Let go of my skin!*'

I obeyed and he dropped me like a stone, then turned away, dismounted and disappeared into the night, leading his unsteady horse.

Gwyr handed me down the reins of Manandoun's steed. 'Kylhuk will want you to have her. But she will be grieving for Manandoun, as indeed will we all. So ride her gently, and if she springs for the canter, let her have her head and wait until she finishes the Grieving Ride. I know little about you, but I have seen you gallop, and I have seen your concern for those around you. I know in my heart that you are a man who can understand this creature, and her needs, and her instincts. Her name is Cryfcad, which means "Strong in battle". She is brighter than any of Uther's sons, which is not saying much, but she will respond to affection, and to a resolute instruction. Is that clear?'

'Who are Uther's sons?'

'The Three Arthurs,' Gwyr said, and shook his head despairingly. 'All born together when Uther had prepared only one name. I would have thought you would have known of them.'

'Truthfully, I know of only one Arthur, a great king.'

Gwyr looked at me for a moment as if I were mad, then said, 'Never mind that now. Go and fetch Manandoun's head.'

'*What?*'

'Pick up the head,' Gwyr repeated sharply. 'Kiss its lips and eyes and tie it to the mane of his horse. Bring it back to the heart of Legion.'

'Why?'

'*Why?* So that you can learn how to honour a great friend. Or even a great enemy, though Manandoun was no enemy of anyone save a coward. Kylhuk will expect this of his *slathan*.'

'What *is* this *slathan*?' I asked again irritably.

'*You* are this *slathan*,' Gwyr said coldly. 'Clearly, you are this thing that you keep questioning me about. But I have no knowledge of it beyond what I have told you. Pick up the head. Do what I have told you. Then follow me.'

I had found my legs and found the truth in my eyes, and though Legion made its ponderous way forward towards the Long Person through overlapping worlds of time and the forest, I was now accustomed to the dual movement, and approached the heart of Legion with Gwyr and without difficulty.

As it moved, the heart was no more than a train of wagons, each pennanted with the identity of its owner or the task it fulfilled. The forest was opened before each cart or wagon by either a roadmaker, or a pathfinder, some of these functionaries forming into gangs of labourers, laying logs and stones at the front of the column, then picking them up behind, others using the wiles, tricks and magic of their own ages, from prehistoric to mediaeval, to make passages through the tightest thickets and the densest groves of ancient oak and elm.

In this part of Legion, the true specialists that Kylhuk had gathered around himself lived, worked and journeyed as the garrison forged forward in its final quest, not just the cooks and brewers, weavers, leather-workers, saddlers and all the rest, but stone-shapers and metal-smiths, who used every bit as much sorcery in their craft as those sorcerers Kylhuk had cunningly stationed behind the Forlorn Hope and at the Silent Towers, at the rear of the column.

But here as well were Kylhuk's accountants, who traded spoils for assistance and exchanged quests with passing knights, or passed on the acquisitions of successful tasks to those who had asked for them. For Kylhuk was now a mercenary and took on challenges on behalf of the fainthearted, or the overburdened, or the just plain frightened.

Since there was often a 'hand in marriage' at the end of a task, he had a team of Shapechangers who could appear as the triumphant knight, claim the marriage bed, and then be found 'dead' in a few weeks' time. These were called the Marrying Men, and their position was keenly sought by all heroes who were blessed with the ability to alter their looks. There were Marrying Women too, but since they were often required to sleep with Giants, there was less demand for this particular station.

Perhaps most important of all were the Cleverthreads, Kylhuk's name for them, a group of women who could hold and weave the complex strands of fate that these many quests and tasks unravelled. Since any one action seemed to involve a host of other actions – as I was soon to find out from Kylhuk himself – these clever, silent women filtered and fashioned the consequences of each deed by each hero or heroine in the column. Without them, there would have been Chaos, and a grim ending to Legion.

Far more powerful than sheer walls of stone, water-filled moats or armoured men, the Cleverthreads were the true fortifications that kept at bay the great enemies of Time, Confusion and Nemesis. And among them I thought I recognised the woman who had whispered to my mother.

'Who *is* she?' I asked, and Gwyr answered, with an ill-concealed shudder:

'The dolorous voice. If she has a name, I don't wish to know it. She whispers bad news or good news. Usually a simple word that gives a vision either of hope or despair. It is a double-edged gift since its whole purpose is manipulation. We can all act to change the vision – or not! Why do you ask?'

'My mother died because of a word that woman said to her.'

Gwyr thought hard for a moment. 'Then take back the word.'

'Can that be done?' I asked, my heart pounding.

Gwyr glanced at me. 'Tell me how she died.'

'Hanged by her own rope. From a tree.'

'Who *saw* this act?'

'I did. I tried to stop her. I saw it happen.'

Gwyr laughed. 'I doubt that you did. Not if the dolorous voice had been there first. But take back the word! That's what you have to do. If you can do that, you might find things aren't as you believe.'

Elidyr had said that to me!

'How do I take back the word?'

'I don't know. Others have done it,' Gwyr said simply. 'But don't expect help from the Cleverthreads!'

I was anxious to see Guiwenneth and she had asked to see me. Gwyr led me to the wagon where she was being cared for. Someone son of Somebody rode behind the cart, facing backwards on his horse, his sword drawn and held across his lap. He was glad to see me and let me pass. I noticed that he had trimmed his beard, combed out his hair and changed his clothes. On the dimples of his shaven cheeks he had painted two small images of long-necked birds, one in red and one in white, their beaks towards his eyes. Gwyr whispered to me, 'That's interesting. He has done something without knowing what he is doing. That is the prerogative only of certain men.'

'The birds?'

'It is a powerful charm to protect Guiwenneth. Interestingly, he has learned it from Issabeau, the sorceress. And the backwards riding! And the hair hanging to his shoulders! Very significant. But our handsome friend is using magic without the knowledge of its power. As long as I live, I'll pay more attention to his quest for his true name. He is certainly noble and what you're seeing is a *geisa* . . .'

'A geisa?

'Yes! A courtesy he is bound to show, or a taboo he is bound to honour. He will have several of them, perhaps as many as ten, so if he ever behaves peculiarly, that is probably the reason. A man's geisas are born with him, like a birth mark, but usually he hears of them from his family as he grows older. Someone, of course, was abandoned at his birth, so the geisas return to him like bad dreams.'

'Which geisa are we seeing now?'

Gwyr shrugged, leaning forward in his shallow saddle, legs dangling by the heaving flanks of his pony. 'My guess would be that he is bound to ride backwards and ward off enemies – using any means he can – for seven days after the death of an honourable man. Manandoun was certainly honourable. It will be something like that. I may be wrong. But enough of this. Go and kiss the woman in your heart.'

Guiwenneth was awake, her head resting on a fat, feather pillow, a wet pouch of herbs pressed against the bruise from the slingshot; her breath, was sickly with some medication that she had willingly consumed. Issabeau sat beside her, dark eyes watching me, one slender hand on the pale forehead below the tumble of luxuriant red hair of the wounded woman. She smiled at me as I closed the flaps of the covered wagon behind me. I wondered if it was for *her* that Someone now rode backwards behind the wagon.

'Ellez trizda,' she said in that deep, slow voice. 'Ellez trayze trizda, mayze ellez *sauve*; le sonje *ez forta*.'

Issabeau left the wagon. I came closer to Guiwenneth who reached out for my face with both hands, smiled and mouthed a kiss to me. There were tears on her cheeks and after a moment she looked at the sack I carried and asked to hold the head of Manandoun for a while, and though she kept it inside its leather bag, she talked to him as if he were there in front of her and answering back.

'Trim his beard,' she said suddenly and gave me back the bag.

'Every whisker,' I avowed, and kissed her on the lips. 'Guiwenneth . . .'

'Trim his beard!' she said again, gently dismissing my moment of longing, and I left her, following Gwyr to the oilcart.

Here, under a cover made from the skins of wildcats, a solitary man supervised all such ritual as the oiling of heads and the preparing of corpses. That he was a so-called 'druid' did not impress me, since he was neither exaggeratedly dressed for some festival of poetry and singing, nor a wild man, hair dishevelled, eyes glowing with the effects of hallucinogenic mushrooms. He was scruffy, his hair long and uncombed, his face covered with a grey stubble and heavily wrinkled, but his hands were very smooth, like the hands of a youth. His whole body was running with sweat (though this was deliberate, I suspected, since every so often he scraped the sweat from his skin with a curved, iron knife and let it run into a small, pottery receptacle). His manner was very matter-of-fact.

Gwyr explained that it was Kylhuk's wish that I prepare the head for Manandoun's funeral. Although it was customary for a man like Manandoun to be interred with his horse and chariot, it was in Manandoun's fate that he would be burned after death so that he could ride to the Islands of Fire, where a quest was awaiting him, so a pyre had been erected. The druid spread a wolfskin blanket on the floor of the wagon, fur side down, then told me to place the head upon it. Manandoun looked ghastly and bloody, his face still in its final grimace, hair plastered to the skin with gore. Next to it, the druid placed a crudely hewn block of elm wood, approximating to the size and shape of Manandoun's head.

The first task, then, was to wash the head and comb through the hair and beard. I did all of these things, the druid patiently showing me how.

Whatever I did to the true head, I mimicked on the block of elm.

When the cleaning was complete, a long iron knife was used to trim the end of the neck; then the neck was covered with a woollen cloth, dyed blue, and tied tightly with a leather thong, to stop any further seepage.

A sharp flint blade was used to shave the stubble from the cheeks, and with a pair of iron shears I trimmed the beard, moustache and hair into a neat and precise style. On the wood, I scoured simple lines.

With the eyelids closed, and a small stone carved with Manandoun's totem wedged below the tongue, the head was ready for oiling. The druid guided my hands as I massaged the cheeks and the scalp. The cedar oil was pungent and enlivening. An iron awl was used to pierce the septum of the right nostril, Egyptian fashion, and oil was poured into the brain cavity before the entrance was sealed with beeswax.

The wood was then oiled, its crude nose pierced with a knife. Finally, a chalk and water mixture was combed through the washed hair with fingers, making a fan, a peacock's display of stiff, white hair, a crest around the head. The same mixture was caked on the block.

When this had dried and the hair was rigid – it didn't take long – Manandoun was ready. I picked up the head and presented it carefully to Gwyr, who took it away and returned it to the dead man's wife.

'Well done,' he said as he departed. 'Since the way you have made him look is the way he will live for the rest of his life, he will be more than pleased with you. Don't forget the trimmings of his hair. His wife will need them. And the block, that tree-head, is to be buried with the widow when she goes, so treat it kindly.'

The druid had already gathered up the trimmings and put them into a cloth pouch. Like a Victorian pharmacist, he was now busy stoppering pottery jars of unguents and potions and sorting out the wagon, where no doubt soon he would receive another corpse to dress.

*

And that was that for the better part of two more days, during which Legion lumbered forward towards the Long Person and the secret she held, and Issabeau and Someone son of Somebody became increasingly intrigued by each other. Of that, more later. But then Kylhuk sent for us all, all of the Forlorn Hope who had become my friends, to be his guests at the funeral of Manandoun. Jarag had vanished into another season, helping to guide the garrison, but the rest of us went back to where Manandoun was laid out on his pyre, his proud, chalk-whitened head on a stone beside it, ready to be replaced with the wood when the fires were lit.

I rode there with Gwyr.

Eleven

As we approached the tent with its four pennants, each of a boar's tusk crossed by a rose, Gwyr said to me, 'I forgot to mention something. Kylhuk is very angry with you.'

I slowed the pace of my approach and looked at the man, who was behaving in a slightly shifty way. 'Angry about what.'

'About your comments that he is a fat man, and would be a better warrior and a keener fighter if he were not so heavy around the waist, the flesh hanging on him like great folds of tree fungus, and all because he eats too much and drinks too much and prefers to ride horses, or travel in chariots, rather than running like the younger men you have cruelly compared him to.'

I stopped the horse completely and turned it round.

'Is there some problem?' Gwyr asked.'

'Yes. I made no such comments, and I have suddenly lost my appetite. Again.'

'You made no such comments?

'Would I dare make such comments?

'Comments must have been made, why else is the great man Kylhuk so furious with you?

'I made no comments! Tell the great man that I'm ill. I'm returning to the Forlorn Hope. I feel safer there!'

'You cannot do that. You must face Kylhuk and explain your insulting behaviour, and your cruel slaps and pinches to the fat that you have complained about.'

Ah! That was it, then. When he had buried Manandoun in his heart, though the funeral had not yet happened, but when the tears had become private and not public, he had begun to remember my inadvertent attempts to hold on safely as he rode around the Silent Towers, looking for his friend. He had been made painfully aware of his burden of flesh by my painful grip, and in his fury, being the man he was and from the type of warrior caste that he was, he had invented stories and insults to displace and reflect away his own embarrassment with himself. As a Celtic warrior, from whatever period of time or from wherever in Europe, he would have been ostracised for his lazy weight. Because he was a leader, and greatly feared, he was tolerated and respected, but the degree of sarcasm that I had already detected in conversations about Kylhuk, the great man, clearly suggested that this respect was being tested, and indeed, that his own self-respect was being challenged.

The Celts simply did not tolerate a paunch on a man, especially not a young man, and certainly not a king. (Kylhuk was not young, but he *was* a king in his own domain.) And on such dissatisfactions as being overweight, regarded as a discourtesy, were changes in kingship made.

I wasn't sure that I was the young blood to take on such a challenge, but from what Gwyr had said, Kylhuk had fashioned a grand account of my insults with which to test me.

'I didn't say a word,' I said to Gwyr, adding, 'I grabbed his belly for balance. He slapped me down.'

'I know,' Gwyr said. 'Everyone knows. And it would certainly have been better for us all if you had found something more *heroic* to hold on to. But there it is, it is done, you have failed us. He is now so aware that he must stop eating and drinking if he is to run with the hound like CuCullain, the fleet-footed CuCullain, the iron-bodied CuCullain, and not run behind the hound like Dubno, the thorn-snagging Dubno, the breath-gasping Dubno, he is so aware of this that he is sarcastic at all eating and drinking, no matter who the eater or the drinker might be, man, woman, child or dog, sarcastic at all feasting unless it is with plums and water.'

Plums and water?

Events became even clearer to me! The great man had gone on a diet.

And for 'sarcasm' read 'criticism'.

And the great man's companions were not happy about this. Any of this.

It wasn't Kylhuk, I suspected, who would be angry with me, but the warrior guests at his nightly, knightly feast.

'And you, Gwyr,' I ventured, turning back to finish the ride to Kylhuk's hold at the centre of Legion. 'Are you angry with me too?'

'Let's see what he offers in the way of hospitality,' the interpreter said with ill-disguised disgruntlement.

I believe I laughed, thinking at the time that the man was referring only to meat and mead. To Gwyr, though, and to all who were of a high caste in the society which had made them heroes, hospitality was as complex a concept as any I could ever wish to know, and single, mortal combat could and would be initiated on so sublimely senseless a notion that a man wearing a red flower, who had not shaved for three days, had been denied the first cup of mead at the moment the king sat down to drink after the death of his champion in combat in a river.

Gwyr hinted this to me as we rode through the thorn and wicker fence and the lines of flaring torches that defined the oval funeral and feasting area. The strange notion he had described to me was another *geisa*, that taboo or demand on a noble which might need to be addressed once or many times in life, not one of Kylhuk's in this instance, Gwyr had simply been giving me an example.

For the moment, though, Gwyr led me through the wicker fences, through the shielding torches, through the grim-faced guards, to the cluster of crude tables, piled with bread, fruit and clay flagons of sharp-smelling liquor, where we found ourselves to be not just guests but *honoured* guests at the funeral feast for Manandoun, seated with Kylhuk himself, and so at last I met the man face to face and not cheek to spine, or fingers to fat!

'Most of this celebration is for my friend, the Wise Counsel, Man-andoun, I miss him, I will miss him all my life in this world—'

He looked into the night sky and roared: 'Taranis hear me, strike me with thunder if I lie! Modron, bring us together to hunt the great-tusked, ever-bleeding black boar, wounded after I put my spear in its side, and Manandoun put his spear in likewise, though less effectively, that deadly boar, the hunter of our world, the silent peril of our woods!'

He looked back at me, softer, sadder. 'Yes! That is how much I miss him, and this feast is for him, and on that pyre there, if you look closely, you will see my friend about to burn, to go into a place that I will soon know well, as will you, as will we all. But Christian . . . *Huxley* . . .'

He scratched his chest and stared at me, looking me up and down as he sat there. 'Huxley*oros*? Huxley*aunii*?'

Clan names!

'Where do you come from? Huxley*antrix*? Huxley*uranos*? What are you, I wonder? What clan? Why did I mark you? Why did I go so far into the netherworld to find you? Was I mad? I can't remember for the moment. Can you help?'

Before I could respond, he went on, 'Anyway, though Manandoun will soon open the gate to a fairer land than this – and a fond goodbye to him, I weep to see him go – this feast is partly for you, Christian, to welcome you, even though you seem to have nothing to say, since you have not said a word since I started speaking, but you are welcome nonetheless, and here is the food, you must eat what you want, you must not hesitate to demand what you want, whatever Legion can offer is yours, have you tried these?'

He held a plum towards me, watching me keenly.

'It looks like a plum.'

'Very well noticed,' he said, holding it closer. 'It is better for you than that foul stuff over there, that roasting pig-meat and the racks of hot-peppered chops for those men in iron . . .' He scowled at the Courteous Men, the chivalrous knights in their colourful tunics and chain-mail protection.

I took the plum, ate it, spat the stone into my hand and tossed it over my shoulder. Kylhuk watched me through furrowed brows. The aroma of roasting pig was making my stomach sing. There was a honeyish, alcoholic smell from flagons being surreptitiously passed around, but between Kylhuk and myself there was only a wide dish of crystal water, with rose-petals floating. He pushed the dish towards me.

'Drink your fill. I am told this tastes very good.'

I drank from the dish. Kylhuk studied me carefully, leaning forward. 'Well?'

'It's water.'

'I know it's water. Are you content?'

'No.'

The whole feasting place was suddenly silent, all faces turned towards us.

Kylhuk's voice was a controlled whisper as he stared at me. 'Why are you not content?'

'Because water satisfies a thirst. But as drink goes, it does not satisfy the need to show a great man like Manandoun the respect he deserves. It is not the right drink to hold up to the flames that will soon accompany a great friend into the Otherworld.'

'I agree!' Kylhuk exclaimed emphatically. He rose to his feet, staring down at me darkly. 'You speak with the same Wise Counsel as Manandoun himself! Yes . . . the same wise counsel . . . And I agree!'

He flung the rose-water onto the ground and stamped on the clay dish, breaking it, kicking the shards all around the feasting area. He seemed very satisfied with the act.

In the middle of the tables, over an open fire, the pig was a poor sight now, being no more than bone from skull and spine to upper haunch, and at the lower part of each leg. Like two obscene growths, the rumps, the prime cuts, were intact, untouched, since it was these portions that were Kylhuk's to enjoy first. With a single stroke of his wide-bladed sword he cut the gruesome carcase across the backside, sending shards of bone and flaming charcoal among the cheering host.

I had expected Kylhuk to cut from the haunch and eat, but instead he flung his sword onto the unlit pyre, calling out:

'That another man has come to take your place does not mean that your place can ever be taken. Not here, old friend. You and I will always hunt for the heart of the beast, and if Trwch's tusks take us, if the beast is too strong, then we'll ride on its snout and tell stories for a year and a day! Manandoun! Wise, gracious Manandoun! Truthfully, I would not have seen you go, and certainly not on the end of Elether-ion's sword!' Then he turned to the pyre-makers, snapping, 'But he's gone and that's that. So burn him, and burn him well,' before beckoning me through the gate in the wicker fence.

As I went to follow, Gwyr flicked his fingers, drawing my attention, and pointed towards the hacked but still unused hind-quarters of the fat pig, crisping slowly in the charcoal where they had fallen.

I went over and cut two thick slices of the tender meat, laying them out on a wooden platter. I carried this offering out to the silent man who stood, staring up at the waning moon.

'Have a little piece of one of Trwch's bastard offspring,' I said, holding up the slices. He looked at the wooden platter for a moment, scooped up the meat in his hand, squeezed the flesh until the juices ran, then slapped it down again, wiping his palm on his clothes.

'No. You eat it. I have no taste for it now.'

'Kylhuk! If you offer me this meat, this best cut, then I will eat it to the memory of Manandoun. I met him when I was a boy, when he was Guiwenneth's guardian. And again recently, when he impressed me as a man of wisdom.'

'Yes,' Kylhuk said, turning to face me, his big hands on my shoulders, his dark eyes gleaming but not, now, with tears, 'Yes. He was a man of wisdom! And the best friend a man could wish for. And you are not yet a man of wisdom, though from what you say, I believe you will soon become one. You are a man of impulse and recklessness, of shallow delights and shallow appetite, but you give me hope and heart, because once I was the same. And though you have insulted me I forgive you. You were right to say about me what you said, though I am certainly not as bloated as the corpse of a dead bullock swelling up on a hot summer's day, as you so coarsely described me . . .'

On Madron's Heart, I did not! I wanted to cry, but mere was a great warmth for me in this man at this moment, or so I thought. And the crackle of the pyre, the passing away of Manandoun, was casting a gentle and doleful sound across us, and I said nothing.

And Kylhuk concluded, slapping his portly places, 'You were right. This great man needs to run with CuCullain's hounds, and I will do it, though Manandoun would have thought otherwise! We have time to run as we move towards the open legs of the Long Person. Time to talk, to get to know each other. Time to run with the hounds. Time to *fast*, you and I, to fast as no two men have ever tasted before, and ignore the greedy brutes who have gathered around me, those who feed only on succulent pig-meat, tender roasted venison, roasted fowl birds, all of it!'

Still on a diet then, I thought grimly. But I said, 'Is it this Trwch Trwyth, then, this giant boar that is your great quest?'

'No. Though I long to hunt it down and take its head. And *will* do so before I ride to the Islands. But no. It's something else.'

He grinned at me, then embraced me, a full bear hug. Then he slapped the platter of meat I still held into the air and announced, 'I have so much to tell you! And while my dear friend is still alive with the movement of flames, he can listen to me and clip my ear if I tell one word of a lie.' He stared at me hard, for a moment, then said softly, 'Gwyr tells me that you are confused by what *slathan* means.'

'Yes.'

'Shall I tell you or shall I not?'

'Tell me.'

'But shall I?'

'Please do.'

'Once I tell you, you are bound to it, so if I tell you, you must stop me quickly if your courage fails you and you become frightened, because I expect my greatest friends to be true to me until the moment of the pyre.'

I ignored the taunt, the insult. 'I'll be sure to do that. Truthfully. On Modron's Heart!'

'On Modron's Heart,' Kylhuk repeated softly, amused and thoughtful, his gaze meeting mine for a long, too-long moment.

And then, without a further word, we went back into the stronghold, where everyone at the funeral party, for reasons no doubt to do with Kylhuk's cutting of the prime of the pig and the consequent opening of more flagons of a drink stronger than rose-water, was in a rowdy and vibrant mood.

Twelve

The pyre blazed. Manandoun was lost inside its fire. I watched the wind-whipped smoke rise to the stars. I scented the cedar oil as it burned that trimmed beard and hair. I tried to imagine what Manandoun was seeing as he passed through the hinterland, that place of shadows and tricking gates, and approached his chosen realm.

Manandoun's wife Ellys sat on a stool with her back to the flames, a safe distance away, her arms crossed over her breasts, her husband's battle-torque over her wrist, his small knife on her lap, a pouch containing the trimmings of his hair around her neck. The wooden head was mounted on a stone beside her. Her two sons, both youths, knelt beside her, scowling at the ground, no doubt thinking of Eletherion and his brothers.

Each woman in the host went over to the widow and stood before her for a while. Then each man in the host went over and gave her a token, kneeling as they did so. Kylhuk watched all this, talking to me so softly and angrily at times that I couldn't understand him above the roar of fire and the spitting of burning wood. There were moments when I felt the poor woman who had lost her husband would be incinerated herself, but the sons brushed all cinders and flaring shards away, and I could see by the pyre's light that each was crying.

At last Kylhuk went to the widow and knelt on one knee on the flattened ground before her, his head bowed. Ellys put a circlet of white flowers on his head and he passed her a ring, which she accepted. The two youths, surly in their expression, hugged the big man when he stood and he spoke to them for a few moments, one boy listening, the younger looking angry, and this boy rode away soon after, and I saw that his mother was distressed and being comforted by her elder son.

Kylhuk led me back to the table where Gwyr sat among Kylhuk's closest retinue, all but one of whom was drunk, all of them wearing short, colourful cloaks, bright torques around their necks and arms, and the white streaks of grieving on their cheeks and breasts. Two of the ten were women, including the hard-faced Raven, who sat apart from the others, adrift in her own thoughts, seemingly unbothered by the chatter and wild laughter that was again rising around her now that the courtesy to Manandoun's family had been completed.

'Where's Guiwenneth?' I asked Gwyr. 'I'm worried about her.'

'Issabeau is with her,' the interpreter replied. 'Not far from here, by a shallow stream. Someone son of Somebody is close to them, keeping watch. The strange oyster-eater too.' He meant the jarag.

'Does she know that Manandoun's pyre is burning?'

'Of course. While you were elsewhere, she carried the body here herself. She spent time with him, and brought the head to Ellys for the last kiss. Her own father, a man of high rank, was killed a long time ago and Manandoun adopted her. But because of a *geisa* that Manandoun won when he was a younger man, she cannot be here while he passes to his Island. That is why Issabeau is with her.'

'I should be with her too,' I said, and I meant it. Nothing that had happened so far had moved me to tears, but the thought of Guiwenneth being banned from the funeral of a man she had loved made me angry because I could imagine her sadness and I wanted to be by her side, even with Someone and Issabeau, and help her through her grief.

'She will want you later,' Kylhuk said through a mouthful of fruit. I hadn't realised he'd been listening. 'She'll be glad of you on her cloak of grass. Have you been there already?'

For a moment I didn't understand the words. Then the meaning came to me.

'I am more than fond of Guiwenneth,' I said to him, standing from the bench. I was incensed at his comment, and my head had started to whirl with drink and rage. 'And it is none of your business how she feels for me. None of your business at all! All I know is, she is distressed and I feel for her. Your cheap jokes, your callous tongue, your . . . your *fat* tongue and your *fat* wits, you should be ashamed! Gwyr, take me to Guiwenneth. I want to be with her!'

Every warrior in Kylhuk's retinue was standing, staring at me, none making a move to draw their weapons, every one of them waiting like a hound at the start of the course.

Kylhuk spat out the plum he had been eating, stood and faced me. How hard he now looked, how narrow his gaze, how grim his scarred lips. His breath was slow and even. He towered over me, his gold and bronze funeral decoration rattling on the hair and the ears that held it.

He looked very powerful, and he was very angry, and I flinched as he drew his dagger and held it by the blade, handle towards me. But his words were very soft when he spoke them.

'What was said was wrong. I will have none of what was said. A tongue spoke, but the heart did not mean the words. If you sit back at my table, I will be the richer man for your kindness. As this good man Gwyr will tell you, Guiwenneth asked to be alone with Issabeau, but she will be glad of your company later. And I will be proud to ride behind the two of you when you share one saddle.'

I noticed that his retinue were relieved by this gentle declaration. When I sat, they sat, and when they had sat, Kylhuk sat, and when he was seated, he poured me a cup of sweet-sour honeyed liquor. Gwyr waggled his eyebrows at me, then pretended to be engaged in eating.

I found out soon after that one of Kylhuk's *geisas* was that he should always apologise for the first angry words, whether his own or someone else's, spoken after the death of a friend.

And when Guiwenneth told me this, I wondered what might have happened if that particular *geisa* had already been 'called in'?

The offer to ride behind the two of us when we shared one saddle was his self-invitation to be (in whatever terms the society of six hundred years BC thought of it) my 'best man'. On this subject, I had my reservations.

And when he had said, 'A tongue spoke, but the heart did not mean the words', whose tongue was he talking about? Mine or his? Had that been necessary apology or infuriating forgiveness? I decided on 'courtesy' and kept the thought to myself.

Legion was at rest, and the wildwood it occupied was alive with fires and the conversations and laughter of many different times, protected by the subtle, concealing magic of twenty thousand years. As Manandoun left us, and Ellys and her companions danced within a ring of thorns to the thunderous beat of bone on skin drums and the wailing and howling of bronze trumpets, so Kylhuk broke his short-lived fast, and with the first intake of meat and the first swallow of beer he too passed on from this funeral, remembering that he had a special guest to whom he had made promises; and in the way of a storyteller, he told me a little of his life, and I'm sure you will not mind if I present it in the formal way that Kylhuk expressed it.

But it was only later that I realised how he had used the story to answer my question: 'What is a *slathan*? Why have you marked me?'

Thirteen

(as told by Kylhuk himself)

When the child of a great man is born, and Kylhuk's father was a king in his land, there is usually a portent: a star falls from the sky, perhaps; or a great storm washes away a fortress on a high cliff, a cow gives birth to a lamb; a poem cannot be made to rhyme.

There were no portents when Kylhuk fought his way to life, though a storm that had been building in the west suddenly vanished, and if this seems remarkable, bear in mind that Kylhuk, even when in the womb, could affect the world around him.

Kylhuk was born with the portents *inside* him; he had swallowed them by using his mother's mouth, and they would be useful later.

As the unnamed child lay in its applewood crib, one of the sons of the giant boar Trwch Trwyth burst through the palisade wall and attacked the dogs in the stronghold, killing six on its tusks. Badly wounded by a spear thrust from the child's father himself, the boar rampaged into the round-house and shook the child from its crib, screeching angrily as it did so, trying to impale the infant but succeeding only in wedging the tiny boy between its tusks.

The boy clung to the tusks as the boar ran from the stronghold and into the forest, pursued by hunters and hounds. The chase lasted for an hour, and though the boar tried to shake the child from its tusks to see where it was going, the boy held on. Eventually the boar ran blindly into an oak and stuck there fast, to be quickly caught and slaughtered.

Seven days later it was roasted, and Eisyllt Cleverthreads, the king's favourite daughter, cut the hide so skilfully that she made four cloaks and two masks from the skin of the pig.

The valiant child was named Kylhuk, which means 'running with the pig', a very great name, greater than CuCullain, which means 'running with the hound'; though these two heroes would meet one day and become great friends.

When Kylhuk's beard had begun to itch but not to sprout, his father married another woman, his first wife having died.

At the games to celebrate the marriage, Kei Longthrow challenged Kylhuk to a spear-throwing contest. Kei cast the first spear and after several hours it was seen to strike the side of a distant mountain, seven days ride to the east. Then Kylhuk threw and after several hours his spear was seen to glance off the summit of that same mountain. But Kei cast again and the spear sailed over the summit. It killed an ox that was peacefully grazing on the other side, though this wasn't known until the complaint arrived, some time later.

'You will not do better than that,' said Kei in triumph.

'I will,' said Kylhuk, 'though you think otherwise.'

And Kylhuk circled four times where he stood, summoned the storm he had swallowed as a child, and cast his spear. The spear disappeared into the distance, flying over the summit of the hill.

'It is a tie,' said Kei Longthrow, 'since we have no way of seeing which spear has gone the furthest over those hills.'

'Be patient,' Kylhuk said. 'The throw is not finished.'

The sun set, and the host slept, and in the morning Kylhuk and Kei were still in their places.

'You are a bad loser if you do not accept the draw,' said Kei.

'Be patient. The throw is not finished.'

At dusk, Kylhuk turned his back to the hills. In front of him a flight of geese was suddenly disturbed as a javelin came flying out of the setting sun. He snatched it from the air and tossed it to his challenger.

'There. I win. Keep the spear, Kei. It is my gift to you. It will come in useful.'

'I am impressed by that throw!'

But the contest had consequences.

Kylhuk's stepmother was also impressed by the throw. She was still a young woman herself and fell quickly in love with her stepson. Kylhuk, being the man he was, rejected her interest, but out of kindness to his father kept the betrayal to himself. Angrily, that night his stepmother cursed him.

'By my head, you will wed no one until you have first won Olwen, the daughter of Uspathadyn, and you will not win her because Uspathadyn is a champion in his country, and a giant besides, and twenty-three severed heads, all brothers, all of them still singing of Olwen's charms, make up his table decoration! When Olwen is won, he must kill her lover, or be killed, as part of a *geisa* that he carries, but he is keen to live and has no intention of letting his daughter go. So there. That's that.'

'I will win her,' said Kylhuk coldly, 'though you think otherwise.'

Kylhuk had accepted his first challenge, but to Kei he confided, 'I could have wished for a better start to my life of adventure. Olwen's father is a giant of a man, and will be hard to kill, though I can do it, I'm in no doubt about that. But Olwen herself is half again as tall as me, and though she is certainly shapely, I have heard that her thighs are like Greek columns and can easily crush an ox; when her teeth chatter it might be rocks falling from a mountain. And she makes oak logs into kindling by *twisting them into knots*! Kei – as a man, and with a man's passions, I fear those hands more than I fear her father.'

'By my head, Kylhuk, I'm glad it's you and not me that must sleep with this woman.'

'What shall I do?'

'If it were me, I would chain her hands to the bed-posts!'

'I mean, what shall I do *now*?'

Kei scratched his chin. 'Go to Pwyll. His fort is only ten days' ride away. Ask for help there. That is my advice.'

'I shall take that advice, though I'm sure I am wrong to do so.'

So Kylhuk went to Pwyll's fort, but hesitated at the gates, again reflecting that to ask for help in his first task was a cowardly thing, and might have consequences. But he was too young to think it through clearly, and too eager to win and then dispense with Olwen, so that he could continue his life of adventure.

He begged his way through the gates, then rode to Pwyll's hall. He was so nervous that he forgot his manners and rode straight into the hall where the meal was being taken.

When he had stepped down and been seated and fed, and had told Pwyll of his quest, the king stood.

'Kylhuk, you are the son of Kylid, who once took a blow that was intended for me, but that is neither here nor there. There are a hundred men in this fort, and a hundred women, and every one of them is a great man or a great woman.'

And he proceeded to name them all, which took some time.

Then he said, 'Kylhuk, you are welcome to take one or all of them to help you in your task, since I am bound to grant the wish of any beardless man who rides his horse into this hall without his weapon drawn, which you have done. But if you take more than two I shall know that you are younger in heart than you are in body, and that will not be good for you.'

'I will take two men only,' Kylhuk said, but in his heart he knew this was also a grave mistake. He should have taken no men at all, accepting only the good advice he would have been offered and Pwyll's hospitality.

He picked one of the older men, and one of the younger, Manandoun and Bedivyr, and some days later Manandoun used his wiles to gain them entrance to the fort on the white hill where Olwen was the favoured daughter of Uspathadyn.

Uspathadyn gave them hospitality and a chance to abandon the quest and keep their heads. When he spoke, the whole of the hall shook from floor to rafter. Olwen looked longingly at Kylhuk, and Kylhuk looked nervously at her hands. But he smiled at her and she smiled back, blushing and lowering her gaze.

Manandoun and Bedivyr teased Kylhuk until he silenced them. On the table, twenty-three oiled heads, their beards trimmed, sang mournfully of their love for Olwen.

Olwen's father stared at Kylhuk for a long time along the length of the table. Then he said, 'Of all the men who have come here to ask for my favourite daughter, you have the fairest face and the best manners. Why, you have not even drawn your sword, which is quite unusual for visitors to this household.'

'Give your consent to my marriage to Olwen and my sword will never reflect the flames of your fire, that great fire over there, where the ox is roasting.'

'Well said indeed,' said Olwen's father, slapping a hand on the table so that all the heads jumped and lost the rhythm of their song. 'The more you say to me the more I like you. It is a shame, then, that I must ask you for three wedding gifts. And since you will fail to get them, it is a greater disappointment that I must kill you and put your head here, on this table. But I will place you at the top of the table, where I can talk to you like a father to his battle-slaughtered son. Yes! That is how much I have come to admire you.'

'I will get your wedding gifts, whatever they are, and at the wedding it will be your own head that is at the top of the table and singing, and *I* will talk to *you* – as a son to his battle-slaughtered father.'

Uspathadyn roared with laughter. 'By Olwen's Hands! The more you speak the greater is my admiration for you, Kylhuk son of Kylid. I have never had so nice a man here. Your manners are impeccable. Your spirit is everything a proud father could wish for. And so it grieves me even more that you will never get the wedding presents that I insist upon, but there we are, that is that, your head will still be a comfort and joy to me and to Olwen.'

'I will get the gifts, though you think otherwise, just as soon as you tell me what they are.'

Olwen's father sighed. He was enjoying this company, but now business had to be done, and necks made ready. 'The first gift is that you will plough and sow the great field that lies to the west of this stronghold. It is bordered by four tall stones, and there are other stones inside it. And a few mounds of earth, as well as trees in groves, and pits with swords and shields and pots . . . a few bones, some trinkets, other bits and pieces . . . nothing to concern you. The wheat that you will then grow there will make the bread for Olwen's wedding, since as her father I must supply the bread for the feast.'

'Ploughing a field is a task for lesser men than me,' Kylhuk said. 'I will find it no hardship at all.'

Olwen's father stared at his nails, each the size of a dagger. 'To be done by morning. I forgot to tell you that it must be ploughed and sown by morning.'

'It will be easy to do that,' said Kylhuk.

'I don't think you will find it easy,' said the other man.

'What else do you want me to fetch? Quickly, I must get on with the ploughing.'

Olwen's father thought hard for a moment, then said, 'If this marriage is to take place, there will be so many guests that I could not possibly afford to feed them all without Cerithon's hamper.'

'Cerithon's hamper?'

'Yes. A small thing, made of briar and willow. Four men can carry it easily and, once opened, it can feed everyone with their particular delights.'

'I have never heard of it. But I will get it for you easily.'

'I don't think so.'

'Oh, but *I* do . . .'

'And the horn and silver cup of Votadinos, which will supply strong, sweet drink endlessly, and therefore save me a great deal of money. Yes, you must get that too. Neither man will part with his treasure, though.'

'They will be easy to get.'

'Don't be so sure. Others have tried it.'

'It will be easy to get them,' Kylhuk declared. 'But you must tell me where they are.'

'That's a good question. They are hard to find. You must ask the houndsman, Mabonos son of Modron, who was stolen from his mother when a boy.'

'And where is he?'

'I'm not sure. You should ask his cousin, Yssvyl, who lives with the oldest animals.'

'And where are they?'

'I'm not sure, but if you can find the boar called White Tusk, you will find the hunter Othgar in close pursuit, and he will help.'

'And where shall I find him?'

'I'm not sure, but the houndsman Gordub, son of Eyra, will certainly know.'

'And where is he?'

'Again, I'm not sure, but if you can find the Long Person, she may answer your question.'

'Enough!' said Kylhuk. 'We could stand here all night only to grow older by ten years. I must get to the field and plough and sow it'.

'I forgot to tell you. You'll need the spotted oxen of Amathaon, son of Don for that.'

'I'll get them easily. Where are they to be found?'

'I'm not sure, though Caratacos the Wanderer will know.'

'And where is *he*?

'I'm not sure, but if you find . . .'

'Enough!' shouted Kylhuk.

'Remember your manners,' Olwen's father said angrily, and Kylhuk apologised. He glanced at Olwen who rose to her feet, her cheeks blushing, her eyes filled with love. Kylhuk stared up at her and felt the muscles in his neck straining. He tried to think of an endearment, something romantic to say to the Tall Woman, a love token.

'I'll be back,' he said in his strongest voice.

'Hurry,' said Olwen. 'And be careful of tricks.'

'Tricks? What tricks?'

'I'm not sure,' she replied. 'But the brother of Dillus the Bearded will know . . .'

'Good*bye!*' said Kylhuk in exasperation, and with Manandoun and Bedivyr he hastened from the hall and set about his task.

He had ploughed one strip of the field when Manandoun rode up to him from the west, his face whitened with chalk, a white pennant tied to the blade of his spear. 'Kylhuk! This is not a field, this is a burial ground.'

'I know,' said Kylhuk as he hauled on Amathaon's spotted oxen, keeping the second furrow straight.

'Those are not piles of earth, they are mounds covering the tombs of kings.'

'I know,' said Kylhuk. 'And they are harder to flatten than I'd thought.'

Now Bedivyr charged at him from the east, wheeling round nervously, white pennants of protection on shoulders, elbows, knees, ankles and around his neck and waist.

'Kylhuk, these are not pots and bones and bits and pieces. You are disturbing the dead!'

'I know. I can hear them shouting as the iron shares cut through them and turn them over.'

'Those are not rocks at the edges of the field, they are carved stones, older than time.'

'I know, Bedivyr. I have seen them. I will haul them down later.' He turned the oxen to begin the third furrow.

'You must leave this place alone. As you plough the field, the dead are being called back from their islands!'

'I know! Do you think I can't hear them riding towards me?'

'You are bringing terrible consequences upon yourself!' shouted Manandoun as his horse reared with sudden fright.

'I will confront those consequences later. First, I must plough this field.'

'Olwen's father has tricked you!' pleaded Bedivyr.

'I *know*! And when I have finished ploughing the field I will think what to do about it!'

They left him alone and he got on with the job. When he returned to the gates of the fort on the white hill, Kylhuk found them closed. Manandoun and Bedivyr were there. Inside, there was music, a great feast, and the sound of Olwen's grief and her father's triumphant laughter.

'You were tricked,' said Manandoun.

'I know. But knowing *that* I was tricked is less of a burden than knowing *how* I was tricked.'

'You should not have ploughed over the tombs in the field.'

'There's more to this trick than just that,' said Kylhuk, trying to think through everything that had been said in the hall earlier.

'Nevertheless, you should have stopped the ploughing.'

'When I start something I have to finish it.'

Bedivyr slapped him on the shoulder. 'Well spoken! Such a quality in a man is both a good thing and a bad thing!'

'Thank you,' said Kylhuk.

'And on this occasion it was a bad thing,' Manandoun muttered pointedly as they rode away, the angry dead in slow pursuit.

Unable to find hospitality that night, they camped in the forest.

'I have learned one thing at least from this difficult encounter,' Kylhuk said as he drank from his cup.

'That you are a fool and easily deceived?' Manandoun suggested.

Kylhuk finished the cup, then wiped his lips.

'I have learned two things at least from this difficult encounter,' he amended. 'Manandoun has referred to one of them, and I have learned that lesson and no one will deceive me again.'

'Ho ho,' said Manandoun.

'Indeed. Ho ho. But we'll see about that. The other thing is that something has been passed on to me, some burden, and Uspathadyn is celebrating because he is a free man. He has tricked me into calling down the anger of the dead. But he has also set me the task of finding this hamper and the silver horn.'

Bedivyr muttered darkly, 'There is more to those gifts than meets the eye.'

'There is more to the *pursuit* of those gifts than meets the eye,' Kylhuk said, and Manandoun added:

'By the head on my shoulders, you are right to say that. The danger is in the pursuit of the beast, not in the beast itself! I am game for this, Kylhuk. I was born for this hunt. And may my arm fail me if I ever call you a fool again.'

The two of them embraced, while Bedivyr shuffled uneasily by the fire, saying, 'I have come this far and God Knows, it is not a long way back to the place where I started . . .'

'Which particular god are you referring to?' asked Manandoun.

'Whichever one follows me noting my deeds in combat.'

'I'd noticed a certain absence of gods,' Manandoun said dryly, looking round at the night as he stoked the fire.

'I will ignore that discourtesy. My point is, I will not return to Pwyll until this man Kylhuk is free of the burden.'

'Thank you!' Kylhuk said. 'Manandoun . . . Bedivyr . . . My good friends! This is just the *beginning* of something!'

'Indeed!' said Manandoun.

'I have no idea what that something is,' Kylhuk went on, 'except that it involves a hamper of food and a silver horn filled with drink. When it is ended, we will all three of us look back and celebrate its ending. We will *rejoice* in its ending. Whatever it might be that has ended. I cannot say fairer than that. Shall we stay together?'

'I will not leave your company by my own will,' said Manandoun.

'Neither oxen nor the wain-ropes they pull will drag me away from this small band,' agreed Bedivyr, 'terrible though this situation is.'

'Well spoken,' Kylhuk said. 'And my head on this: I will not abandon either of you until Olwen's father's own head is on the end of my spear.'

'That's that, then,' said Manandoun. 'We are all agreed. And you will certainly need a big spear for the head you propose to sever. But now we must think about what to do next. I would suggest that the three of us are not enough to take on everything that is behind us, and everything that is ahead of us.'

Manandoun's counsel was wise. And besides, on the hill behind them a line of men had risen and stood watching their fire, but try how he might, Kylhuk could see no features on them, only shadow, and he knew that they were ghost-born.

He, Manandoun and Bedivyr fell to thinking.

Fourteen

A fight had started at one of the tables, a disgraceful insult to the memory of Manandoun, and Kylhuk had been increasingly aware that he should intervene on behalf of his friend.

When he reached the point in his story which signalled an end to the beginning and an anticipation of the ending, where the three of them were 'falling to thinking', he stopped the narrative.

'Gwyr may feel inclined to explain what happened next,' he said to me, and rose and crossed the forest glade, where the two men, naked but for kilts and metal torques on their arms, were hacking at each other with great determination, shouting insults and laughing in each other's faces. Blood had not been drawn, and would not be drawn, since among the clans that these people represented such an act would bring instant execution. But the duel was rowdy, and the watching crowd was becoming excited. Outside the taunting ring of Celts, puzzled legionaries, dour Saracens, ice-eyed Vikings and dismayed Courteous Men kept a watchful gaze on the proceedings, but did not interfere.

Kylhuk entered the fray and the fighting stopped.

I had thought that would be that, his authority stamped on the squabble, but he was not in a good mood and he snatched the sword from one man and beat him unconscious with it (without drawing blood).

The other man backed away, then walked stiffly through the gates in the temporary palisade. I never saw him again, and suspect that an act of contrition had occurred that had left him for the forest to reclaim.

Gwyr said, 'You have heard the first part of the story and now have the general idea. Sometimes, when Kylhuk recounts his tale, I wonder about Olwen, that poor Tall Woman who was so attracted to the feisty youth. Is she still waiting? Does she know how fat her Beloved has become?' He grinned, then went on, 'Truthfully, Kylhuk was so afraid of her he would never have completed the tasks, those simple tasks as he thought of them, he would have found some way to delay the ending of the adventure. But as you have heard, Kylhuk's quest is a harder task than anyone would have thought. We seek the hamper, we seek the horn, but that was just Uspathadyn's way of tricking Kylhuk into adopting something very dangerous, which Uspathadyn had sworn to do and was unable to do, despite the consequence of his failure.'

'What consequence?' I asked, disliking the word.

'A rather final one,' said Gwyr pointedly, 'and with no prospect of an Island at the end of it.' He meant death without the Otherworld. Then more brightly, 'But Kylhuk will achieve the task, now that he has you.'

'So I'm to be tricked too.'

'In one way, you have been tricked already, but Kylhuk is a different man to Uspathadyn, and if you choose to abandon him he will let you go. But without you, the great task he is sworn to accomplish will never be accomplished.'

'Because I am marked as *slathan*,' I said, remembering that Kylhuk had still not told me its meaning.

'Yes. Whatever it is, that term he uses and will not explain.'

'Gwyr, I fear that word more than I fear Kylhuk himself, or this quest that he has drawn me into.'

'Well said; bravely admitted,' Gwyr said with great affection. 'And as long as there is a head on my shoulders and a foot on the end of each of my legs, I will stay close to you and make sure there is no further trickery. But my feeling is, it is some magic, or a certain knowledge or memory that you possess that Kylhuk needs.'

'What is the task, Gwyr? Has he told you, now that Manandoun is dead?'

'Yes. But only a handful of us must know. We will accompany Kylhuk himself. We have been chosen for our various skills.'

'And what exactly are we to do?'

'We are to undertake a rescue. We are to attempt to rescue Mabon, who is imprisoned at the very gates of the Underworld, in a place that is savagely defended. Mabon! Son of Modron! I heard about him as a child and just to say his name makes my hair stand on end and my skin crawl. This is a *terrible* task. But that said, you must believe me, Christian, this rescue – which many have attempted, but none with success – will have a wonderful consequence for each man and woman who takes part in it. Kylhuk is undertaking a great task, perhaps the greatest of them all. No one is born who doesn't soon hear about and grieve for the cruel way Mabon was entombed alive.'

'Entombed alive?' I repeated emptily. Why did that sound so familiar? Echoes of Merlin from my childhood's reading!

'What happened after Kylhuk and his two companions had ploughed the field and unleashed the dead?' I asked.

'A good question, Christian, well asked—'

'Get on with it, Gwyr,' I snapped.

He was taken aback. 'Your first discourtesy. I'm surprised by that. However, to continue:

'Manandoun advised that before they did anything at all they should try to understand precisely what had happened, and the first task was to work out precisely what tasks had been set them by Uspathadyn. Although the field had been ploughed, the whole journey to fetch Cerithon's hamper and the drinkhorn of Votadinos involved a total of thirty-six individual deeds, and buried among them was the Great Deed, the rescue of Mabon from his terrible prison.

'Most of the tasks were simple. *Tall Men* had to be killed for their *whiskers* for use as *leashes* for great *hounds* to run with great *horses* to be ridden in great *hunts* on enchanted *saddles* that only *dead men* could fashion . . .'

He paused for breath and I took a chance and said, 'The whiskers of Giants? It sounds ludicrous.'

'I agree,' he said, shaking his head. 'You are not the first to comment on it. But nothing will work without them.' He went on, 'Kylhuk and the others worked steadily through the list, finding some of the tasks hard and others easy. But everything, no matter how simple, had a *consequence.*'

'Consequences,' I said bitterly. 'Yes. This is certainly turning into a game of consequences.'

Gwyr stared at me, thinking about my words, perhaps, and their modern allusion. Then he nodded abruptly. 'Indeed. When Kylhuk caught the hound he released the Hounds of *Hell*, which now follow behind us! And wherever the hounds run, they summon the ghost-born of their kind so that it is not one pack of hounds that pursues us, but hundreds, a legion of them, and all slavering, all with great eyes—'

'Yes, yes,' I said. 'I get the picture. Get on with it, Gwyr.'

He raised his eyebrows. 'Your *second* discourtesy. You are not quite the man I thought you were. However, to continue:

'When the hamper of Cerithon is finally taken and opened – Yes, I see you are surprised by the thought of this quest. But the hamper is said to be of endless capacity, so it seems quite reasonable for Kylhuk and the rest of us to eat our fill before transporting it to Uspathadyn – when the hamper is finally opened, the ghost of every man and every woman and every child and every dog that has fed from that hamper will rise from the earth and come in pursuit. This has already happened with the silver horn of Votadinos, which Kylhuk found last summer. It was a worse experience than could be imagined, because the ghosts were drunk, and a drunken ghost is less reasonable even than a drunken man . . . they are argumentative and confused . . . and I feel that you are experiencing this feeling even now, even as I talk to you, answering the question that you put to me—'

'Get on with it, Gwyr!'

'Three! Three discourtesies!' He looked me steadily in the eye. 'I feel a fight is coming on.'

'I will not fight with you.'

'Will you not? We'll see. But to continue,' he said warily:

'One of the tasks within the task was to hunt the great boar that had sired the boar that gave Kylhuk his name . . .'

'Trwch Trwyth,' I said.

'Indeed. And to hunt Trwch Trwyth, a huntsman was needed, and this was Kuwyn, son of Nodons. Kuwyn was a young man in whom were imprisoned the thousand ghosts who had first ventured into the Underworld. These ghosts had ruled the shadows and the islands of the Underworld from the beginning of time. But one day their time was up and they were routed and cast out, to be passed from one man to another among the living, any man who had the strength to contain them – there are many stories to do with this, I can assure you—'

'I have no doubt about it. Even a maggot in this Legion has its story it seems.'

'Four! Four discourtesies!' Gwyr looked delighted. 'My sword hand is twitching! Your white throat looks so exposed! But to continue:

'When Kylhuk found Kuwyn, the demons were released from him. Kylhuk was not a fit man to accept them, however, so there they are, behind us, with the dogs, the risen dead, the Sons of Kyrdu and all the rest, a great army of shadows and evil that presses close to us and is kept at bay only by the forces that Kylhuk, Manandoun and Bedivyr sensibly began to muster around them as they rode through the wilderness of woodland, river and rocky crag, shortly after that moment when they had fallen to thinking, that moment Kylhuk told you about.'

'And how did they muster those forces?'

'A very good question, very well asked . . .'

Gwvr waited for my response, but I kept a prudent silence.

He frowned and went on: 'He could not go back to Lord Pwyll, though Pwyll, being the man he was, would not have hesitated to help. But the consequence to Kylhuk would have been too great in terms of the repayment of the favour. This has all to do with courtesy and honour, as I believe you are beginning to understand in your simple way . . .'

Gwvr waited for my response, but I kept a prudent silence.

He frowned and went on: 'There was only one other stronghold with sufficient brawn to supply Kylhuk's needs – an army of swordsmen and spearmen, charioteers and horsemen, runners and jumpers, madmen and brutes, strategists and the far-sighted, those who are sound in hearing and vision, smellers, sniffers and frighteners of the shadows that occupy this great wilderness, these old trees, these timeless woodlands, and that stronghold was held by . . .'

I leaned towards him questioningly, as courteous as I could possibly be.

He leaned towards me and concluded: 'Uther.'

'Uther?'

'Uther!'

'Arthur's father?'

'The father of all the Arthurs, Uther Pendragon himself.'

'Arthur's father Uther. No other?'

'No other. Only Uther.'

'Uther and his little Arthurs.'

'Yes. Are you mocking me?'

'I'm joking with you. It's not the same thing.'

But unfortunately, to Gwyr it was.

As he stood, he struck. When I had regained consciousness it was to the awareness that my lower incisors were loose and my mouth was full of blood. Gwyr stood over me, looking anxious. Kylhuk was by me, holding out a hand, which I accepted. I was hauled to my feet.

Looking around, I saw that the whole of the host, that feasting host, those who had come to say goodbye to Manandoun, were gathered around in a ring. I took silent comfort from Gwyr's earlier information that at the funeral of a friend blood should never be drawn in any personal combat. I resolved not to let Kylhuk see that blood was flowing from my battered gums. It might be the worse for Gwyr.

'Are you ready for the fight?' asked Kylhuk, and I mumbled: 'What fight is that?'

'Gwyr has counted it against himself that he struck you in anger, and therefore you may have the first blow.'

I mumbled through my swelling jaw something further to the effect that I was sorry, very *very* sorry for any insult that might have been perpetrated on a man whom I heeded in my life like air itself, and that I was simply under the influence of strong drink and not in control of the lively horse called 'impatience' that was currently bucking below me.

Kylhuk laughed.

'Well said, Christian! Well said indeed . . . Whatever it was you said,' he added as an afterthought. 'But I have decided that Manandoun would want to see this fight, and would want to see a head taken, since the two men who have decided to fight during his long ride to the Island he has chosen are such fascinating men, and each with different skills and different *tricks* . . .'

He looked at me as he said this. A very pointed comment!

'. . . tricks which can be tested one against the other.'

'Please don't ask me to fight,' I said, bitterly regretting my earlier conversation with Gwyr, or had it been Manandoun, about my combat skills.

Kylhuk ignored me. 'I am relaxing all rules of courtesy and hospitality in order for you to have this fight which I know is important to you both, though I have changed my mind and will not allow a head to be taken, nor more blood to be drawn.'

'Thank you.'

'But I expect this matter to be resolved, and at the end of it I will expect to have two friends who are still friends with each other, even though their bones may be broken and parts of their body twisted into strange shapes.'

'By Olwen's hands, I hope that does not happen,' I said, and Kylhuk went white, giving me a look that combined alarm with unwelcome memory. He stepped up close to me.

'That is a good thing you say,' he said softly. 'I had forgotten about Olwen's hands in the excitement of seeing the two of you about to fight.'

'So the fight is off?' I asked hopefully.

Gwyr was waiting impatiently, stripped naked, all weaponry out of reach. 'Hurry,' he said to Kylhuk. 'I want to get at him.'

'That is a discourtesy you do to me, asking me to hurry!'

431

Gwyr fell silent.

Kylhuk scratched at his beard as he stared at me, then said, even as he was thinking, 'Why are you still wearing your weapons? Take them off.'

I unbuckled the belt which held my sword. But the further look he gave me made me realise that I was expected to strip naked, and I performed this task with as much indifference as I could muster, which was not very much at all, since Guiwenneth and Issabeau were watching from the outer circle.

Guiwenneth smiled at me. Issabeau whispered in her ear. Guiwenneth giggled. I felt humiliated and let my stomach relax. Guiwenneth watched me with affection.

'There,' said Kylhuk. 'We are ready for the fight. But I still have to decide on the rules.'

I spoke quickly. 'Knowing Manandoun for the short time that I did, I would nevertheless say that he would want us to fight only with our feet.'

Kylhuk stared at me in bemusement. Gwyr frowned.

Kylhuk asked, 'Why would he want to see that?'

I thought very fast. Very fast indeed. 'Because of Cryfcad his mare, his great horse, that great beast that is now in my charge and which has taken to me gladly though with sadness, but will allow me to ride her. She is a feisty creature, and her kick can disable four men, one behind the other. I'm sure Manandoun would want us to use only our feet. It would amuse him.'

'I am impressed with this explanation,' Kylhuk said, and it was Gwyr's turn to look shocked.

'Go to it,' said the Overlord, and slapped his hands together.

Gwyr approached me. I summoned all my strength, remembered the training in unarmed combat I had been given in '42, and kicked out to disable him when he was least expecting it. He went down, stunned, conscious, and in pain.

'I have never seen that done before,' Kylhuk said thoughtfully as he stared down at Gwyr's groaning figure.

'It is not often that I have done it,' I said in triumph.

I should more truthfully have said, 'I've never seen it done before either. And I've certainly never done it, except to a straw-filled dummy.'

So that was that, and Gwyr and I became friends again, and everything went on as if nothing had happened, except that afterwards he nicknamed me 'Quick Foot'.

I would never come to a full understanding of the way nicknames were used in Legion, those at least among Kylhuk's Celtic gathering. For example:

'Carried a King', 'Fought in the River' and 'Survived Gae Bolga' had all done these things.

'Leapt over Trees', 'Savaged the Boar' and 'Makes Women Sing' were named because the opposite of these events had happened.

'Face of Stone' was a woman who never looked at the man who had let her down. 'Face of Shadow' was the man who had slighted her. 'Face of Moon' was a woman who aspired to greater things. 'Face of Horn' was a woman who had passed her prime but would not accept the fact. 'Spear of Horn' was a man with the same reluctance to accept his age, the reference to Horn being to 'the truth that is there for all to see'.

(Horn for truth, Ivory for the lie. If I noted these things at the time, I let them pass.)

Everyone had many nicknames and by those nicknames you could summarise an individual. If you were a man you were named by your children, by your wife, by your parents and your wife's parents. Also, by your closest friends, by the chief, by the chief's first wife and by the druid and any tale-teller who might be passing.

Respect for an individual was often reflected in the balance of courteous nicknames ('Reliable Spear') to discourteous ones ('Stabs his own Foot'). If the balance was unfavourable, a combat could be arranged to win back an unfavourable nickname and convert it to a favourable one. No nickname ever stuck for long and new ones were adopted constantly. Everyone seemed to be attuned to these changes. Indeed, to refer to someone with a nickname that was out of date was an insult.

After death, one nickname would linger and would come to reflect the person, and around this particular name the 'bright story' would be told, which is to say, the story of that person's life. 'Wise Counsel' for Manandoun, for example. ('Thinner than the Willow' for Kylhuk? I wondered idly.)

But in short, it was best to think of people as they had been named at birth, although this might cause problems, since if a nickname was used in a conversation about a third party, and you failed to recognise that party, the man or woman who was doing the talking could accuse you of discourtesy.

In short, the less said about anything the better . . .

A few minutes after our brief combat, however, Gwyr had relaxed again, taken a drink, and concluded his summary of the formation of Kylhuk's Legion.

During the years following that first encounter with Uspathadyn, Kylhuk completed all but a few of the tasks set him by Olwen's father, but had turned Legion into an industry, accumulating and accomplishing the quests set to others, and exacting a very heavy fee, though always inheriting the consequences. Bedivyr had died because of one such screeching Nemesis. Legion itself had become dedicated to one thing: finding the Long Person; opening the gate to the rescue.

Early on, he had negotiated with Uther, and Uther had supplied horsemen, charioteers and runners, all well-trained and eager for adventure, and they had been a great help in the beginning. But none of Uther's knights could resist undertaking their own quests whenever the opportunity arose, and more often than not the tragic or sinister consequences of their actions came to burden Kylhuk.

Uther's sons – the Three Arthurs, all of them identical – were particularly difficult to handle. They had been born fighting, Gwyr told me, little fists in faces, tiny feet in mouths, and it had taken nearly a week for the midwife to separate them and stop the squabble.

Because Uther had prepared only one name for his son, only one child ever spoke at any one time. They passed a small sword between them to indicate whose turn it was to voice his opinions on this or that, usually a criticism of their father, or an expression of love for their father's sorceress, whom he had housed in a cave below the hill.

As they grew up, the Three Arthurs rode together to the far north and south of the land and gained a reputation for great actions, great battles and great conquests. They joined Kylhuk's legion for a few years, then one day had a fierce argument with each other and rode off in different directions. But because they were identical, their exploits far and wide became known as the exploits of one man only, and Arthur's name became associated with magical appearances and the ability to ride the length and breadth of Albion in a single night.

Kylhuk had been glad to see the back of them. I was fascinated, but Gwyr was unforthcoming on any further details of this unlikely legend.

By this time, Legion was already like a great whale, nosing through the ocean of the forest, sensing for danger ahead, trailing behind it a great wake of angry ghosts, the armoured dead and vengeful sanctuary spirits. Riding among these, using the powers and insights of this spectral army, came Eletherion and his brothers, Kyrdu's sons, seeking the entrance to the Underworld, to begin a course of plunder and outrage in the caverns of the earth that, according to legend, would change the earth itself.

Kylhuk tried to shake them off, but the Sons of Kyrdu were jackals that had found the scent of prey. They stalked around the marching garrison, attacking at the front, sometimes at the flanks, sometimes from the rear, killing and taunting, holding on to Kylhuk with teeth of bronze, because they had seen that Kylhuk's quest contained the answer to their own!

The *Underworld*.

Gwyr used the word deliberately where usually he expressed the idea as 'Otherworld'. He seemed unhappy at the thought of a place so dark and dismal. Being Celtic, his own afterlife would be an Island of his choice, endless hunting, endless pleasure, occasional returns to the world of his birth to check on the behaviour of his family. The gloomy, ghastly caverns of Hades were not at all to his liking, and he was confident that only Greeks, Romans and the Sons of Mil would go there.

I intuited that Gwyr had little time for Greeks, Romans and the Sons of Mil.

But his mention of the Underworld brought back thoughts of my mother, and the strange thing Elidyr had said to me. *Her death, was not as you think*. I imagined her there, in the dark caverns, walking with the other shades.

And if the rescue of Mabon could unlock the gate to that Underworld . . . what chance, I wondered, of bringing her out of the Valley of the Crow, back into the light?

Was that what Gwyr had meant by 'the rescue of Mabon will have wonderful consequences for each man and woman who participates'?

Despite everything I had come to know, I chose to believe so.

Fifteen

I had paid my visit to Kylhuk, and my respects to Manandoun. I had fought with a man whom I regarded as a friend, and agreed to a fast that I had no intention of keeping. I had become almost anxious at the realisation that my father was abroad in this wilderness, and melancholy at memories of my mother, dizzy with the thought that she might be rescued. I might then understand what she had said that day, when she had dangled from the tree.

At the moment, however, I wanted to be with Guiwenneth. I needed her. I imagined she needed me as well.

I found her by the narrow river, half a mile from the centre of the camp where the bank was clear. Her feet were in the water and she was leaning back on her elbows, staring at the night sky. Issabeau sat beside her, idly flicking at the stream with her carved staff.

As I approached, Someone rose from where he had been keeping watch and greeted me softly, clearly glad to see me.

'How is she?'

'Doleful,' he replied. 'But the tears have dried. And she will be pleased to see you.'

'And how are you?'

'Hungry. But not for Kylhuk's plums and water.'

'There's meat as well.'

'I'm glad to hear it. But I'm not interested in eating, now.'

He stood before me, an imposing figure, gently stroking the luxuriant moustaches that framed his mouth. He was a man scarcely a year older than myself, and yet he carried weight and authority, from the steady gaze to the careful thinking, to the immaculate state of his garb, a simple kilt of green cloth, an open deerskin shirt, skin boots tied around his calves with twisted gut . . . and his sword, slung from a shoulder belt, its ivory pommel carved to suggest a bull.

He said, 'You have paid a great respect to a man you didn't know.'

'Manandoun? I did as I was told to do.'

'Nevertheless, you showed a great respect.'

'I feel as if I know him without ever having known him. I have a picture of him. It would have been nice to have known him better.'

Someone touched his right hand to his breast, a gesture of affirmation. But he said, 'Manandoun's death is terrible for us all. He was close to Kylhuk. He kept Kylhuk in hand. Without Manandoun, Legion is in a greater peril than even Issabeau suspects.'

He had pronounced 'peril' in the way of the Frenchwoman. And it was clear that Manandoun had been a controlling influence on Kylhuk, and that Someone – perhaps *everyone* – now feared Kylhuk's behaviour.

'Shall we send for Elidyr? The guide?'

'Elidyr has gone,' the Celt said bluntly.

'Do I have a role in this?'

'We all have a role in this.'

Someone looked away, frowning. 'If I could just find my name – if I could just understand the taunting words of the hawk. It sits on my chest while I sleep, pecking at me, and its demands are strange and frightening. Until I understand them . . .'

Again, that bright, hard stare at me. 'Until then, Christian – you must stay close to Gwyr, and think hard after everything you say or do with Kylhuk.'

'He is a fat man . . .' I began to say, but the Celt cut across me.

'He is no such thing. Neither fat, nor a man, in my opinion. He has played a fine game with you. Don't always believe what your eyes tell you. And if I could explain more then I would, but like you, I am a stranger in this Legion. But enough of that for the moment. Come and be with Guiwenneth. She's been waiting for you.'

We walked to the river. Issabeau looked up at me, then at the Celt. She reached out a hand and Someone took it, helping her stand. Issabeau looked at him and smiled, then said to me, 'Bonzoire,' before she and Someone walked away.

I sat down on the damp grass by Guiwenneth and put my arm around her. She nestled into me and sighed.

'So that is that,' she said, presumably meaning the departure of Manandoun.

'So that is that,' I agreed.

'I know he will be happy. But I shall miss him so much.'

'I know you will. But as you once held on to him, please now hold on to me. I am not wise, and I am not old, and my beard itches rather than grows, and his horse tolerates me, but only just. But I love you, I know it. It's a true feeling, Guiwenneth. Whatever happens to you, I want to be a part of it.'

She turned to me, put a hand on my cheek and urged me closer. Her lips on mine were sweet and soft. The kiss deepened. She sighed suddenly and lay back, her grip becoming firmer on my hair.

I sighed too. For all my inexperience, my hands found her, and my mouth found her, and nothing happened that needed to be thought about; everything that happened by that river happened as if we had known it all our lives.

A splash, a laugh, and the sound of 'Hoosh!' made us sit up suddenly, drawing Guiwenneth's cloak around our naked bodies to block the chill of the night air.

'What was that? I asked.

She looked at me delightedly. There was mischief in that glance.

'Quickly,' she said, and pulled on her clothes, shaking the grass from her long, auburn hair. Silencing my chatter with a finger to my lips, she led the way along the river, to where the stream widened and formed a pool.

From the cover of the underbrush we watched Issabeau and Someone son of Somebody swim lazily together, he on his back, she across his belly and between his legs, arms outstretched to propel them forward. They circled the pool slowly, whispering together, their pale bodies almost translucent above and below the water.

Guiwenneth tossed a small stone into the middle of the pool. Issabeau and Someone glanced towards us, then returned to their leisurely swim, eyes only for each other, laughing together.

'Come away,' I said, suddenly embarrassed. 'This is none of our business.'

'I knew it would happen,' Guiwenneth said as we walked hand in hand through the wood, back towards the Keep. 'There is something that connects them. I could tell that from the moment they were recruited to the Forlorn Hope. Anyone could tell it who had half an eye for love.'

'I thought she was with the Saracen,' I said. 'They were together when I first met them.'

'No. They shared a similar magic. They were powerful together. But Abandagora had no heart for love.'

Her voice was strange and I looked at Guiwenneth as we walked.

'*Had* no heart for love?'

'Has no heart at all, now,' she said quickly. 'Eletherion took it in that same skirmish when he took the life of Manandoun.'

Sixteen

And so I began my long march with Legion, a journey of many weeks, many months – I find it hard to be more precise than that. The column, as it progressed, shifted so often through time, and into so many different seasons, that even day and night became meaningless. And Kylhuk worked me hard at the various stations throughout the marching garrison, sending me on many night watches and occasionally on wild rides outside the forest wall.

He kept me close to Guiwenneth, however, and I was grateful for that. Her company was a comfort and a delight, and the mischievous sense of humour a great relief among this army of mostly dour and silent adventurers.

Only on two occasions did I come close to disaster. The first was one summer's day, when we finally discovered Cerithon's hamper.

Kylhuk had abandoned that particular task the moment he realised it was just part of Uspathadyn's trick to make him search for Mabon. But there had always been a grumble of opinion that the hamper should still be sought since it promised such a feast, and very often the food in Legion was worse than 'dog's paw and baked fur', as Issabeau so delicately put it. (She liked fine food, it was clear, and it was always very difficult sitting near her at mealtimes since she spent the time sighing with despair and sulking heavily as she contemplated whatever was on offer.)

So when the Forlorn Hope brought back the fattest child I have ever seen, a boy so rotund that he could have been rolled into camp like a beer barrel, his skin covered with rashes, stings and spots, a child who stank of honey and whose mouth and fingers were so sticky with the same that no matter how hard we tried we could not remove the dead leaves and grass from his hands, there was a sudden air of excitement among Legion's uncouth hordes. The word had gone round that this boy had been 'feeding at the hamper'.

'There is a slight problem,' said the Carthaginian woman, Dido, who had been given charge of the boy.

'And what problem is that?' Kylhuk asked irritably.

'The hamper is protected by a force of nature.'

'Then it will find itself assaulted by a force of *Kylhuk*!' said the grizzled man with a grin at me.

'The force consists of flying stingers.'

'So does mine!'

Without further discussion, our small band rode through the forest wall for a first look, the sound of appetites being whetted ringing in our ears. But as we left Legion a new sound struck us: the hum of bees, a buzz that rose in volume along with the black cloud that we could see flowing towards us as we entered the true wood.

The swarm was on us in a moment, wasps, bees and giant hornets, smashing into our faces, crawling through our hair, pouring through the gaps in our clothing to sting and die, or sting and sting again.

'Get the bee-boy!' Kylhuk shrieked in pain, using his cloak to sweep the air around him. 'Find him! Bring him! The *bee-boy*!'

Guiwenneth returned quickly to safety, her flowing hair seething with these flying stingers. The rest of us flung ourselves to the ground, covered our heads and bodies and rolled as best we could to squash the invading insects. How long this agony lasted I can't remember: it seemed for ever.

Then, suddenly, the swarm detached from us and the horses became calmer. The air was still electric with the buzzing of a billion wings.

The bee-boy had come, I realised, a tiny lad from prehistoric Crete, a country which had been famous for its honey from a time long before even the jarag had stalked his Mesolithic shores. In his kilt and loose shirt, the bee-boy was running in a zigzagging, circling dance, imitating the bees that he sought to control. Soon, the black swarm rose into a funnel, a whirlpool of wind and motion, widening around the dancing boy. We flung ourselves close to him, finding merciful shelter in the stillness at the eye of this storm, and the boy led us to a distant mound of seething black and yellow.

As we approached this restless hill we stepped among seated groups of children, all of them as bloated as the boy who had been brought to the camp, all of them encased in glistening honey, all of them red raw with stings. As the bee-boy danced up to the mound, the crawling mass of insects rose in a single movement to join the swirling vortex around us. Beneath the thick and sluggish flow of honey the vague shape of a wicker hamper could be seen. As the honey rose and spread like lava, so it carried flat, round loaves of bread, which lay encrusted all around, a landscape of crystalline, stone wheels.

'Well, well,' said Kylhuk irritably. 'And not a haunch of meat in sight.'

Gwyr talked to one of the children and came back to us, chuckling and shaking his head.

'Uspathadyn tried to play a second fine trick on you.'

'Did he, indeed?'

'Indeed he did. It seems that Cerithon was not a king at all, but a royal child.'

'I can hardly bear to listen further.'

'One day this child distracted two bears from their attack on an old man, who turned out to be Merlin.'

'I might have known it.'

'Merlin granted Cerithon a wish and the boy, being a greedy lad, asked for an ever-filling picnic hamper. And Merlin asked what he would like in the hamper. And Cerithon said, "Nothing more than bread and honey!" Which is what he got.'

'Children!' Kylhuk muttered, severely disgruntled. I expect he was thinking of his reception when he returned to Legion.

'Cerithon himself lies in the centre of the hamper,' Gwyr went on. 'Long dead, and preserved in the honey he so coveted.'

'Good,' said Kylhuk. 'It's where he deserves to be.'

'These children are visiting from their dreams, from many lands, since the story of the hamper is one of their great delights.'

Kylhuk looked around him thoughtfully. Then he reflected out loud that because these dream-visitors looked so much like pigs themselves, and were already fattened, perhaps we might pacify the hungry mouths of Legion by—?

He stopped in this reflection when he realised we were all looking at him in horror.

A few weeks after I had joined the column, Kylhuk attached me to a knight called Escrivaune, armoured as his squire, carrying his shield (a black gryphon), battle spears and axe. Sir Escrivaune had assumed the appearance of a questing knight called Mordalac and was returning to a castle called Brezonfleche where Mordalac's fair lady waited for him. Escrivaune, on Mordalac's behalf, had killed the son of a giant who was terrorizing the castle, and now carried the giant's gold-embroidered sword belt, an item of clothing so heavy it needed two pack-horses to transport it.

The belt itself was of no use to Kylhuk, but the terms agreed with the cowardly knight included a fourth of Mordalac's dowry, and a hundred head of cattle, which Mordalac had promised from his own estates.

Unfortunately for Sir Mordalac, he had become drunk after Escri-vaune's triumph in his place and indiscreetly revealed that he had no estates of his own and was simply a 'chancer', living by the lie, the worst sort of trickster since their guile was usually so successful.

Furious at the deceit, Kylhuk had challenged the knight and the challenge had been haughtily accepted. I counselled against such a combat – full metal jacket against a torque around the neck? – and Kylhuk squeezed my nose between thumb and forefinger, shaking his head.

'What do *you* know about it? Stay out of my business!'

He then stripped naked but for his blue battle kirtle and the bronze necklet, selected a narrow, leaf-shaped bronze sword only twenty-four inches long, and stood in the middle of a clearing, arms crossed, sword resting lightly on his left shoulder.

Mordalac, mailed and helmeted, had ridden down on Kylhuk with a pennanted lance, but at the last moment Kylhuk glanced at the horse which shied with fright and threw its rider.

Kylhuk helped Mordalac to his feet and gave him time to draw his sword, a four-foot long, half-foot wide, double-edged steel weapon of tremendous weight.

Nevertheless, Mordalac swung it with such speed that Kylhuk yelped with shock and had to dance quickly to one side. He had to leap four feet vertically as the sword sliced horizontally in a continuation of the first movement, then duck almost double as the blade flashed back in a blur.

'You're better than I thought,' Kylhuk said as again the broadsword swept through the air like a Samurai's blade, skinning him, shaving his beard, pricking the end of his nose.

'By the hands of that woman! You've been trained well!'

The silent knight came grimly forward, cutting swiftly. Kylhuk somersaulted over the blade and howled like a hound when a return blow bit deeply into his right buttock. Hand up his kilt to hold the wound closed, he danced backwards, the bronze sword held limply before him.

'Even your horse is well trained!' he shouted in astonishment. 'Here he comes!'

The knight drew back, glanced round (his horse was standing silently at the edge of the clearing) then looked back, staggering slightly before leaning heavily on his sword.

Kylhuk stood quietly before him, arms folded, the bloodstained leaf-blade resting on his shoulder again.

'In case you're not aware of it,' he said, 'I've just cut your throat.'

Sir Mordalac swayed twice then fell forward with a rattling of chain mail and a throaty gurgling of blood.

Kylhuk knelt on one knee beside him. 'Though I called you coward, you were a finer fighter than I'd realised, and the next few painful days in the saddle will keep me constantly reminded of the fact. Perhaps there were unspoken reasons why you asked Escrivaune to double for you. It's my loss, I know, to have killed you, Mordalac. The truth is, I could never have trusted you.'

Then, clutching his bloody backside, he left the arena, returning the sword to its owner who made an immediate gift of it to Kylhuk.

Kylhuk accepted gratefully.

But a certain deal had been struck with Mordalac to do with the Lady of Castle Brezonfleche, and Kylhuk being the man he was felt obliged to honour that Cherished Lady's request. Mordalac had been a chancer, but she would survive a broken heart better if she felt her suitor had died nobly, for a noble cause, rather than ignomtniously because he was a cheat.

It was a weakness in Kylhuk that he cared for this sort of chivalry, the sort that existed to diminish the hurt in people, rather than to celebrate the honour expressed to them. Which is why he had formed the Marrying Men, a band of stalwarts combined into knight and shape-changer, brute force and magic, to which I had just been assigned.

I had wanted Issabeau as our shapechanger, but Kylhuk had sent her to another part of Legion, to learn more about Mabon. The jarag would have done just as well for that, but Kylhuk had other plans for him too. So Sir Escrivaune and I rode through time and the forest to the Castle Brezonfleche in the protective company of that same ethereal woman who had greeted me on my first encounter with Legion, a silent figure, timeless, exquisite, somehow more elemental than human. She went ahead of us with instructions to leave a strip of rag, tied to a tree, on the path that led to the gorge where the castle had been built.

White cloth for safe progress; green for danger.

The castle seemed almost to be growing out of the depths of the gorge, tall, thin towers reaching from the dense forest below, rising high against the craggy, tree-strewn cliffs, their grey-weathered walls pierced by tiny windows. Hocks of crows circled the grey-slate, conical turrets. Mist hung halfway down, clouds too tired to rise higher. From far below came the sound of wind and the creaking of wooden gates and stretched ropes. Occasionally, as we listened hard, we could hear the sounds of dogs and horses.

'It looks safe enough to me,' said Escrivaune unconvincingly. 'It's a steep path down, though.'

We dismounted and led the horses. Half-way down, winding around the chasm towards the distant bridge across the river, we encountered a green rag tied to a tree, its edge cut by a knife in a significant pattern.

Escrivaune sniffed hard. 'Have you noticed?'

'Have I noticed what?'

'No wood smoke. No fires. No welcome.'

I looked at the green rag, at the discreet cuts that had been made in it. I struggled to remember my lessons in cypher from Kylhuk's sorcerers, and realised that I had become bewildered rather than enlightened during those long, concentrated sessions. But I was fairly confident as I articulated aloud each of the shapes of the jagged divides in the simple cloth, and summarised finally that the cuts implied: 'All not as seems.'

'All is not as it seems,' Escrivaune repeated, then looked at me quizzically. 'Meaning what, exactly?'

'Things are different to the way we look at them,' I hazarded, adding, '—don't trust your eyes. I'll not trust mine. Trickery is afoot. Beware!'

He scratched his jaw, tugged on the bridle of his charger, stared into the space between us and the magnificent and imposing stone turrets. 'Trickery?'

'Trickery!'

'Eyes untrustworthy . . .'

'Don't trust your eyes.'

'Beware, you say.'

'Be *very* aware. Trickery. Danger. It's all here.' I waved the green cloth.

'Seems safe enough to me,' said Escrivaune.

'They'd want you to think that.'

He glanced at me blankly. 'Who would want me to think that?'

'The people doing the tricking. The inhabitants of the castle.' I waved the cut, green cloth again, but Escrivaune simply frowned as he surveyed the castle.

'But I can see nothing wrong. Only the absence of wood smoke from the fires you might expect to be burning in this season. They must be a hardy lot . . . I hope they have a fire for *us* . . .'

'Where's our guide?' I asked nervously, and as if in answer to a prayer she appeared, suddenly, startlingly, misty and wan of race, stepping between trees.

Sir Escrivaune took the green rag from my hand and waved it. 'How dangerous is it?'

She said, 'I can't tell. But I can tell you this. That half the castle is overgrown with red and yellow briar-rose. The other half is rotting below black ivy. It is a desperate place. Its corridors are alive with snakes. Dogs are howling from the ivy towers. I can see dead women's faces in the towers of rose. There is the stink of corpses, the stench of moon's blood, the sweat of fear, the bristling tension of treachery.'

'It might be wise to be on our guard, then,' Escrivaune said thoughtfully.

I looked at the castle and saw only the stone, the wood, the windows, the drifting mist and circling carrion birds . . . and felt such a sense of ruination and desertion that I was inclined to think this was an abandoned place, all human life long since departed, only wisthounds, scald-crows and rats left to scour and haunt its passages and chambers.

'Which part is in the rose?' Sir Escrivaune asked.

'The main hall. And by the entrance gate, by the bridge over the river.'

He looked at me. 'We'll make the transaction there. Don't be tempted into the inner court.'

'I'll be sure not to,' I said, but since I could see nothing of the flower and ivy that was enveloping the castle, it was hard to know where safety ended and danger began.

Escrivaune was in control, a proud knight, proudly displaying. He was an older man, quite grizzled, but still lean and lithe and full of passion, with all the charm and power that goes with age and experience, though sadly lacking in common sense. His beard was cut like Mordalac's and dyed black and he had been treated with simple cosmetics to give him the look of the knight for whom he would substitute. Magic – the 'altering of looks' – was all very well, but it was an extravagant use of resources when dyes and dress and imitation could accomplish the same end! And anyway, Sir Escrivaune would not be expected to sleep with the Cherished Lady for more than a week, and in his own words, 'She'll not have time to take breath in that week! As long as my back holds out! So I don't expect to be tested on my nature or my honour!'

'You don't think she'll want to wait for a wedding, then . . .'

His quick glance in my direction suggested that he was not happy with my observation. But he said nothing.

'And her father?' I persevered.

'What about her father?' he grumbled as we slipped and slid down the steep, wet track, descending the valley walls.

'I imagine he'll want to entertain you. To talk to you. To learn your intentions. Is he going to be happy with your immediate and no-doubt vigorous – *congress* – with his daughter?'

'Congress?'

'Intercourse!'

'Conversation?'

'*Lovemaking!*'

'Sweet words? I only have a week!'

'You know what I mean, Sir Escrivaune! You know very well what I mean! Carnal lust!'

'Mind your manners! Is my shield polished?'

His comment confused me. He repeated it. 'Is my *shield* polished?'

'It is.'

'Then polish it again.'

'I will. But the question won't go away.'

'I don't feel inclined to answer your question. Polish my shield!'

'I'm leading the horses. I can't lead and polish at the same time.'

'Then just lead the horses. Stop talking about her father.'

'I will. But the question won't go away. And think as well of *mother*! What about her mother?'

He turned on me furiously.

'My task is a simple one, Christian! Do you understand me? Simple! I enter the castle. I become that *slit-necked* chancer whose quest I accomplished, that Beloved Knight, that *Mordalac* for seven days and seven nights. My armour shines! I drink, I eat, I laugh, I *service*!'

'Not in your armour.'

'Of course not in my armour! And at the end of the seven days and seven nights my squire brings me news of a challenge! Don't forget *that* part of the plan! *Squire!* I leave full of bravado, and I do not return! I have been defeated in fair combat. The *slit-neck's* helmet and sword are returned to the grieving Gracious Lady. In due time, when the grieving is over, she finds comfort and consolation on her back with someone else! In his armour or out of it! In that same time, I am getting on with my own life! *Don't condemn me, slathan of Kylhuk!*'

'Sorry. I'll shut up, now.'

'Polish my shield.'

'I'm leading the horses.'

'Then lead them better!'

'What about the rose and ivy? The castle is in disguise.'

'So am I. Two masks will surely be a block to the truth for as long as I need it!'

'Will they?' I asked nervously. 'Are you sure about that? Is that a Truth or a Guess?'

'It's a Hope,' said Escrivaune. 'And in case you're not aware of it, Christian, Hope is a two-edged sword every bit as dangerous as that sword of Mordalac's, that steel blade which Kylhuk danced around and still got stung by. Hope is both challenge and despair. We weave our lives around Hope, and succeed or die according to the pattern of that weave. Enough now, slathan. What little wit I have I'll need if I'm to secure the dowry. If you smell rotting ivy, retreat. More importantly: keep the horses on half-rations so that they'll run fast when we leave. But water them well; keep them gently bridled but not saddled, lightly tethered and facing the gate.'

'And your shield polished to perfection?'

'The shield is more than just a shield. Your *forlorn friend* is in the gryphon. The better polished, the safer our escape.'

'I'm glad you told me,' I said, wondering what friend he could have meant, and assuming he meant Issabeau, who among my 'forlorn friends' was the only one I was confident could assume the shape of an animal.

But a *gryphon?*

Our ethereal guide had seen a castle in two halves, covered with rambling rose and ivy; we had seen a castle that exuded an air of desertion. But as we came through the woods to the drawbridge we might have been stepping towards Camelot. The walls were painted white, the towers streaming with coloured pennants. The courtyard into which we were led was alive with the activity of animals, wagons and the inhabitants of the stronghold. Yes, the place stank of the farmyard, but the smell of fires was also a warm and welcoming odour; and the aroma of cooking, and of the honeyed ale that I had come to associate with this mediaeval period, soon overwhelmed our senses.

We were greeted by the baron, the Lord of Brezonfleche, and Escrivaune, in his guise as Mordalac, was received with grace and charm by the astonishingly beautiful Lady Brezconzel.

'God's Truth,' he murmured to me through the laughter as we stood in the mud by the main steps, 'I think I'll stay for ever.'

'I suspect that's exactly what they have in mind for you,' I retorted and Escrivaune glanced at me sharply.

'Meaning what?'

'Meaning this castle changes its look as you approach it. Please summon that little wit you referred to earlier.'

'S'Truth! You're right.'

I slipped away, leading the horses, and found the animals grain and stabling as close to the gate as possible. I did as Escrivaune had instructed, but noticed that I was watched by eyes expressing puzzlement, the castle's ostlers confused as to why I left the steeds half ready.

'It's the way we do things in my country,' I said, but without Gwyr to interpret, my words might well have been in the language of the Devil.

That night we feasted in style, seated at a long table, facing a roaring fire at the side of the hall. Eight immense hounds, fur the colour of bracken, lean-bodied, muzzles like the dead-eyed features of a python, prowled the hall, eating bones and fighting among themselves. Thin, insubstantial music was played from a gallery and Escrivaune and his Lady danced a sedate routine alone before circling the hall and drawing all the other knights and their ladies, the squires and the daughters into the spiral dance.

I was on my guard all the time, but when I finally succumbed to sleep that night – on a bench a few yards from the glowing logs, among others of my status – I dreamed well, and woke at dawn to find everything in its place, and all quite normal.

And except for the feasting, it was like this for five days.

I began to feel relaxed. Castle life was cold, busy, noisy and dull, but since my tasks consisted only of looking after our horses, supervising Escrivaune's bodily needs – water to wash in, if a quick splash of face and chest could be called washing, and a sharp blade for his cheeks

since his Lady's own skin was looking noticeably raw from his intimacy
– I managed to find time to myself.

But on the sixth night, as Escrivaune made his bed-time preparations,
he whispered to me, 'Polish the shield.'

The gryphon shield was hanging on the wall among the shields of
other guests and knights under the baron's protection. I took it down
and cleaned the soot and grime from its face, then lay it on the floor
below my bench as I slept.

In the dark hours, with the fire now a dull glow in the deep hearth, I
woke to find the gryphon standing over me, eyes bright, breath foul,
jaws open to reveal gleaming teeth. Its tail flexed angrily, its claws
flashed as they extended from the pads.

'Follow!' it whispered.

'Issabeau? I thought Kylhuk had sent you elsewhere.'

'Follow!'

Was this Issabeau in animal disguise?

The voice had not been hers. I crept after the shadow. It rushed
through corridors, down spiral stairs, then out into the yard, a shape
almost invisible against the night, so swift, so silent that sleeping dogs
stayed still and tethered horses hardly shifted from their stations.

The gryphon led me deeper into the castle.

Suddenly I could smell decay. Suddenly the air was full of desolation.
We entered a tower and ran lightly up its winding staircase . . . entered
a room where dark, still shapes hung from the rafters, turning slightly
with the breeze of our arrival. Discarded armour lay everywhere,
catching faint rays of light.

Above us, the wooden ceiling creaked and whined in erotic rhythm,
and I could hear a man's voice howling in pain, a woman's laughing.

'Get the skin!' hissed the gryphon.

I looked into the darkness, but the shadow had fled, though it
stopped in the entrance to the tower and repeated, 'Get the skin!'

Suddenly the ceiling opened and light spilled down. A shape tumbled
towards me, screaming, attached to a rope around its neck which
sprang taut and stopped the fall. In that moment of spilled light,
before the ceiling closed, I had seen the skinned men hanging around
me, the snakes around them, intimately entwined, bulging eyes turned
to me in anger at the interruption of their congress. Escrivaune's part-
flayed and bloody carcase swayed among them, now, his scaled Lady
wrapped around him like a python, her jaws holding a glistening, sickly
sack.

His skin!

I could hardly think what to do. The tower was alive with hissing. The hanging men were crying feebly, all save Escrivaune who was screaming with all his lungs.

The fall had not killed him, then.

I had only my sword and my strength. I ran to the Lady and tugged at her tail, pulled her from the knight and cut the hissing head from her body. The sack of skin seemed to wrap itself around me, hugging my arm like a terrified and grateful pet. I jumped and jumped again, slashing at the rope that held my friend, and eventually he fell down, screeching with pain as his raw flesh contacted my touch and the floor.

We ran through the night. The gryphon danced ahead of us, sending the bloodhounds scattering, and by effort of illusion, shape-shifting and pure determination, we found the horses. I had still kept them half bridled, and they reacted violently to the smell of my friend's half-skinned torso, but this only served to make them livelier. As the gryphon ran like a cat up to the ropes that held the bridge, loosening the blocks that held the pulleys and letting the wooden road fall across the river, so Escrivaune clung on grimly to his charger, galloped through the gate, his squire in frantic pursuit, dogs in pursuit of the squire, but dogs only, as if no human life existed that could be roused and riled to follow.

And that was that. A half-flayed man, who should have died of his wounds, was made well again when his skin was retrieved from the sack. His shield gleamed in starlight; the gryphon was gone; Issabeau, escaping her duties with Kylhuk to hide in the shield, Issabeau was gone.

Our guide appeared, a dreamy, flowing shape, narrow faced and beautiful, beckoning to us, encouraging us back along the path to Legion.

By morning, Escrivaune's skin had reassembled. Naked and humiliated, but alive and experienced, the man rode slightly higher on the bare-backed stallion as we finally encountered the forest wall, and the protective attentions of the Forlorn Hope. His awkward posture in the saddle had nothing to do with his pride.

'You did very well,' Guiwenneth whispered to me as she lay across me later that night, still warm and wet from our lovemaking. She had tugged the cloak over our heads and we lay, cheek to cheek, in moist and pungent darkness. 'But I was worried about you.'

'Is that why you asked Issabeau to hide in the shield?'

'I asked her to follow you. I didn't know how she'd do it, but she agreed.'

'She was wonderful. A gryphon!'

'A what?'

'A mythical beast. A shadow. Without her, Escrivaune and I would both be alive and in pain for ever, and for ever the source of food and satisfaction for those succubi.'

'Succubi?'

'Reptiles. Demons. *Lamia*. I don't know how to describe them.'

'Don't try,' the woman said and brushed her lips over mine. 'Don't try and remember. Just be a source of satisfaction to me.'

'A prospect that fills me with joy, since I love you so much.'

'I'm glad you think that way. And we still have so much time.'

'We have all the time we want in this strange, strange world.'

'We have the time we have,' she said quickly. 'Let's not waste it.'

But before I could think about her words, her teeth had closed briefly on my breast, nipping me to attention, and she had wriggled down, reaching below her belly to find me, gently easing me into a second conversation.

For a while, as my time with Legion continued, I was too busy and too confused to think clearly. I saw very little of Kylhuk himself after the funeral respects for Manandoun had been paid, and had no chance to push him on my strange role as 'slathan'. Most contact with Kylhuk was fleeting, usually on horseback as he brought me new instructions, or a new guide to my circuit of the garrison. He always brought me a gift, anything from honey or meat to a small knife, or a cloak pin that he had thought would appeal to me. And once: a bow of strong ash, half the length of my body, and a leather quiver of arrow shafts ready to be tipped.

'You should give him a gift in return,' Guiwenneth hinted one day, and in the absence of anything better I begged a slice of thin, polished birchwood from a carpenter, red and black pigments from my 'forlorn' friend Jarag, a strip of leather from the young Cleverthreads I knew as Annie, and to the best of my ability painted a snarling boar on the face of the wood, staring straight out of the amulet. In charcoal around this image, as if inscribing a coin, I wrote: From dream you came; to dream you will go.

'For me?' Kylhuk demanded when I gave it to him. The look in his eye was of surprise and suppressed delight. His companion, the silent Fenlander, was uneasy behind his bronze-featured face-plate.

'What do these runes say?'

Kylhuk meant the inscription. I was ready for his question.

'That you will one day return to the place from which you came.'

'One day I will return to the place from which I came?'

'I couldn't have put it better.'

'Nothing too profound, then.'

'Hardly. I'm too young for profundity.'

He gave me a quick, sharp look, almost quizzical. 'But not a curse . . . ?'

'Certainly not!'

He seemed relieved. 'I like this old tusker!' he said (he was referring to the boar) and kissed the red and black image on the black wood slice. He tied it round his neck and grinned at me. 'I'll hunt him one day. This big, bad pig. I'll bring you his crest! All those sharp spines in one crest!'

'I do believe you will.'

'I know I will.'

Then with the same ceremony he gave me the cut and battered leather glove from his right hand, which left his sword hand exposed, and I could see that Guiwenneth was astonished . . . and perhaps alarmed?

'I *like* gifts,' Kylhuk said loudly. 'I like gifts of food and I like gifts of love. But the best gift is that gift which can only be given once. So guard that glove!'

'I will. And thank you. I'll wear it with pride as I undertake my tasks for Legion.'

'You will! I'm sure of it. But you won't like this next task, slathan.'

'This doesn't surprise me.'

'You must do it anyway.'

'To the best of my ability.'

That was when he assigned me to Escrivaune, the adventure I have just recounted.

Two evenings after my return from Castle Brezonfleche I asked Guiwenneth about Mabon son of Modron, whose rescue lay at the end of Kylhuk's quest. I had tried to raise the subject before, not just with Guiwenneth, but encountered only shrugs, impatience, confusion or avoidance. Tonight, however, with some ten of us sitting round a good fire, succulent and spicy food and warmed sweet ale for company,

Guiwenneth stood up, brushed down her tunic, shook out her long, auburn hair and raised her hands as if to say, 'Silence.'

She was drunk.

'Mabon's story,' she said, 'is tragic. There are few people who have even heard of him, and few facts are known about him, though for some of us his fate is entwined in our lives like a braid of dried grass in our hair. When I was a child, my mother told me the story of his miraculous conversation just after birth. It went like this . . .'

And she began to act with her body and with different voices, to the amusement and applause of several of our dinner companions.

'So!' she said, looking at me with a grin, 'So! The babe is in his purple swaddling, still shocked from what his Mother, the Queen, has just proposed! And what has she proposed? His answer will make it clear.'

'It is not right that a young dog should lie with an old bitch; even if she is his mother!'

(Howls of horror from around the fire.)

'It is perfectly right,' shouts Mother. 'No *whelp* will result from the union. What will result is only that special knowledge that the Young Dog who is Divinely Born, as you are my son Mabon, needs to have about his *Mother*. How else will you inherit the knowledge of the land? More than *whelping* is achieved when Divine Son lies with Divine Mother.'

So! Struggling in his swaddling, Mabon's face distorts into a furious mask, the hairs sprouting on chin and cheek as the man he will become rages from the skin, fire dancing in his eyes for a moment before he is the peaceful babe again. 'This whelp is too small and too young,' he shouts. 'It would suckle gladly, since it is hungry, and its eyes are on those swollen paps! Milk! Milk! It is all I have on my mind, Mother. Is there nothing to be learned from suckling?'

Mother pulls her cloak across her rat breasts to deny milk to the infant. 'Suckling is for the ordinary dog,' she snaps.

'Then I am ordinary. Put me to your breast, or there will never be hair on my chin!'

'You are not ordinary and I will make you aware of it!'

'You may try, Mother, but you won't succeed.'

Furiously, she reaches for the babe to chastise him, but Mabon is too quick for her.

Confined in his purple swaddling, only his head exposed, he wriggles away from her and squirms like a maggot around the hall. Mother faces in close pursuit. Round and round they go, the worm wriggling faster, little rump rising and falling, until he slithers up a roof pole and sits on a rafter, out of reach, staring down at the dishevelled woman and her weeping breasts.

And Mother cries out, 'The ordinary dog has always howled when it loses the scent. But a Royal Hound should listen to that howling and should always know the scent that is trailed through time and the forest. You are a *Royal* Hound!'

'I am content to howl with the other dogs. I will be an ordinary man!'

'You are not ordinary,' roars the harridan. 'And I will make you aware of it.'

'You are welcome to try,' shouts the infant, 'but you will not succeed.'

'I *will* succeed,' says Mother, soft and grim. Then in a raised voice: 'In the forest, the strongest tree grows alone in the clearing where a great tree has fallen. Our family is that sunlit glade, Mabon! Hallowed, a place of worship. You are the sapling that will grow during the Mother Moon and outstrip the rest of the wildwood. Ordinary men will hang their trophies from your branches.'

'First hounds, now forests,' sneers the child with a coarse laugh. Oak leaves sprout from his ears and a hound's muzzle from his mouth. 'This world into which I have come through your gate confuses me.'

'Hounds or forests, there is always One who can run further and faster than the rest, or reach higher and wider.'

His face that of a babe again, Mabon says, 'Mother, listen to me. I am content to run in circles with the pack and grow in tangles with the thicket.'

'You are *not* content with that and I will make you aware of it.'

'You are welcome to try, Mother, but you will not succeed.'

'I *will* succeed, because I have already dreamed of what will happen to you!'

The babe laughs. 'That dream is for tomorrow and the days after, Mother. *I have time to turn your dream to dust!*'

'You are welcome to try, Mabon. But by the power of the gate that passed you into this world, you will not succeed.'

Guiwenneth was stroking my face, looking at me earnestly. 'What is it, Chris? You've gone as pale as the dead.'

'Something you said – nothing more than that . . .'

'Something I said? In the story?'

'Brought back a bad memory.'

She seemed to understand, fussing at me, but I assured her that I was well, just a little shaken.

I have already dreamed of what will happen to you!

When Guiwenneth had used those words as she had sketched out the story of Mabon, I had shivered with the awful recollection of my own mother, holding herself alive against the branch, watching me with eyes that expressed nothing but contempt.

What did that old woman say to you? I had wailed, thinking of the unkempt old woman I now thought of as the 'dolorous voice'.

Nothing I hadn't dreamed of already. Nothing that wasn't already pain.

My mother's words; the admission that had left me desperate.

What have I done?

Nothing . . . yet, she had said.

Please don't die, I had implored her.

And she had whispered, *My son is gone . . .*

And dropped.

And snapped.

And left me alone.

Mabon's tale was strange and frustratingly incomplete, like everything, all stories in this realm, from Someone with his unfinished name and Kylhuk with his unfinished tasks, to Issabeau with her unfinished passion, and Gwyr in his own form of Limbo, a man in a waiting place, both dead and alive.

'When did this happen to Mabon?' I asked Guiwenneth and she replied, 'When he was an infant.'

I'd realised that.

'I meant, how long ago?'

'That I can't answer. Not recently, I think. My grandmother knew the story, so it must be very old.'

It seemed that shortly after his bitter row with his mother, Mabon had disappeared.

Talking among the travellers with Legion, I heard various accounts of what might have happened:

That he had been sent for fostering for seven years to a neighbouring clan (a common practice among the early Celtic aristocracy); that his father had hired hunters to take him away from the stifling and sinister attentions of his mother; that he had crawled to the animal huts and suckled on a cow, but the bull that guarded its herd had hooked the child by its woollen wrap and carried it into the forest, passing it to one of the Oldest Animals for protection.

Mabon now became a hunter. He flew like a bird of prey, pounced as a cat, stalked as a wolf, lurked in the deepest of lakes as a pike, swam fiercely like a salmon and watched the world cannily and dangerously as an owl. The spirit and features of all these creatures he wore as a mask for his face and a cloak for his body.

There was a ludicrous element to the fragment Guiwenneth had enacted, which suggested that by her own time in history the story was *already* old and being recounted with typical Celtic exaggeration. Others in the circle that evening – even though they had laughed at Guiwenneth's eccentric performance – were adamant that the furious exchange with his Mother had occurred when Mabon was many years older. Two accounts made it clear that it was not just his mother, but his sister as well that Mabon was expected (because of his rank) to 'lie with'. In one version, Mabon had two sisters, both older than him, and he was expected to sleep with each of them once a year for seven years before going with them into the forest maze, at whose heart lay the Divine Gate.

The reference seemed clear: the sisters were both lovers to him and his chosen executioners, and Mabon was having none of it! He had fled the scene – he felt himself to be an ordinary man! – denying his royal status.

A cheerful, charismatic red-haired warrior called Conal had a tale from the cycle that was a little more ambitious. Perhaps it contained a grain of truth? I think it unlikely:

'It's a true fact that when Mabon was fourteen years of age, no more than that, he heard that his Mother's hunters were only two valleys away from where he was hiding, their dogs like mountains, their horses each with eight legs – I've *seen* such beasts, so I have! – carrying spears that could fly round corners! These are the facts, now, so pay attention!

'Mabon was hiding in the woodland when this news reached him. He began to eat stones and rocks, the trunks of trees, and to swallow clay from the river. And that's a big appetite in a man, in case you're not aware of it. As fast as Mabon ate these stones and trees, so he grew. The rocks built up around his belly, the trees formed into sturdy gates, the clay shapes into massive ramparts. He kept eating. Stone towers rose on the walls and an inner stronghold grew up. Do you now see what's happened? He had formed his body into a stone fortress!

'When the hunters came near, what did he do? He spat splinters of wood the size of javelins at them! The riders failed to recognise him, but the spears were cutting them to pieces, so they passed on by. Now Christian, listen to me! That's a wonderful achievement by any account, and a story that's as true as the feet that I'm sitting here telling it, though I may have got some of the details wrong, I can't be sure of that, it's a long time since my own dear mother nursed me. But it certainly saved Mabon's life on that particular day. That's the story I heard as a child, so I did, and it's a true tale.'

There was a period of silence, all eyes on Conal, then a sort of collective sigh.

Guiwenneth glanced at me. 'The Irish,' she whispered in exasperation.

I soon realised that knowledge of Mabon was very fragmentary and confusingly contradictory. The fate and ill-fortune of a young 'dream-hunter', as he was often referred to, was known from Ireland in the west to the mountainous land of the Kurgan in the east, and by the dishevelled heroes and heroines of many ages, in particular the Bronze Age Minoans, though the jarag from ten thousand years in my past did not recognise Mabon in any shape or form.

Mabon's story, at its heart, seemed to be that of a Princeling born into a matriarchal society, perhaps on one of the Mediterranean islands such as Corsica or Crete, who had refused to conform to the rituals of that society: marriage to his mother, immolation at the hands of his sister. He had escaped sacrifice as a youth, fled, survived by his wits and muscle in the wild, but had finally been tricked out of hiding and either buried alive or imprisoned – but certainly confined alive in a grim place.

He was 'divine' – half human, half god.

And by *all* accounts he had been born out of 'an animal's dream' on a mountainside, in the heart of a land surrounded by ocean.

In prehistoric times!

'How is it that Uspathadyn was searching for him?' I asked Guiwenneth, in bemusement. 'The man lived in the Welsh mountains, thousands of years later.'

'He'd inherited the task, of course. The task has been passed on since that terrible time in lost memory.'

'And Kylhuk inherited the task from him.'

'Tricked into doing so.'

'And now Kylhuk is waiting to trick me in turn.'

'You've asked this of Gwyr already,' Guiwenneth said slyly. 'And Gwyr still doesn't think so. You are not man enough for the task. You are too much an outsider. But your presence has persuaded Kylhuk that the rescue can be achieved. The result will be amazing.'

'Yes. And it still amazes me that until recently, I had never even *heard* of Mabon!'

PART FOUR

The End of Wandering

Though I am old with wandering
Through hollow lands and hilly lands,
I will find out where she has gone,
And kiss her lips and take her hands;
And walk among long dappled grass,
And pluck till time and times are done
The silver apples of the moon,
The golden apples of the sun.

W.B. Yeats, from
The Song of Wandering Aengus

Seventeen

A tall, black-maned cat came running at me from the bushes on its hindlegs, startling me as it flung itself onto my body, the feline features melting to reveal Issabeau in her wildcat furs. I fell to the ground, caught in her embrace. She straddled me, her dark hair flowing over my face, her breath sweet. 'If you value your life,' she whispered, 'don't fight against this kiss.'

And she pressed her wet mouth against my own, pushing my head to the ground. Her fingers squeezed my shoulders, keeping me still.

Eyes open as the kiss continued, I could see that she was listening. When I tried to move she urged me down again, her own gaze flickering left to right, her mouth eating at mine. It should have been intimate, but Issabeau was elsewhere and very frightened.

And an image flashed into my eyes: a raging sea, a rainswept shore, a girl running from horses!

A few seconds later, in the real world as I knew it, the woodland stirred. Something gigantic walked past in this lazy, summer's afternoon. I heard its growl. A second creature followed it, and to the other side of us a third, stalking through the forest. Turning my head slightly, I glimpsed a figure like an upright wolf, but its massive head was like the skull of a dog, covered with thin, grey skin. The skulled face turned to look down at me, came closer, a foul sight. It sniffed, snarled, licked at its bony chops, then turned away. It grumbled several words. Growls were answered. This awful troop moved on and Issabeau, after a circumspect few moments, disengaged from me, wiping a hand across her lips.

'They didn't see us. Kissing can be useful.'

'Thank you for the kiss.'

'Thank you for not moving. If they had sensed you, they would have sensed me, and we would both be dead. I could only protect us with that kiss.'

'What were they?'

'Good news and bad news,' she said, helping me to my feet. She was amused by something now, looking me up and down.

'What were they?' I repeated.

'Scaraz,' she said. 'Winter creatures. Like wolves, but like the *bones* of wolves. They eat flesh. In summer, they are green and often friendly. Then they are known as *dauroz*. I think it means "green man".'

'But this *is* summer,' I said, and she smiled.

'That's the good news. It means we are close to the Long Person. The Scaraz have come along her, that much is obvious. That's why they are displaced and not in their time or in their season or on their guard. Didn't you smell them?'

'No.'

'They smelled of *time*. The Long Person! We are almost there.'

'If that's true, we should tell Kylhuk . . .'

But Issabeau said, 'Wait a moment.'

She stepped up to me and put her nose against my neck. 'You smell of the ocean . . . the salt sea! What did you see when I protected you with the kiss?'

'A girl running. A wild sea by a rocky coast. Just a glimpse. Was it you?'

Issabeau had gone quite pale, a look of alarm on her face. 'Well well,' she said after a moment. 'I let you in. I let you see. I didn't mean to do that.'

'*Was* it you?'

'Yes,' she said. She was close to me, staring at my eyes. 'You are a strange man, and I don't understand who you are. But I trust you, which is saying a lot. Christian . . . we are almost there, almost to the Long Person, and when we have reached her, nothing will be the same again. There is something that puzzles me, something that haunts me. I don't know why, but I think you may have an answer for me. Will you try?'

'Yes. Gladly.'

'Will you take another kiss to see the kiss that saved my life?'

'What can I possibly say? I had no idea that magic was so stimulating.'

Issabeau smiled wryly. 'I thought you loved Guiwenneth.'

'I do!'

'Then put a little *winter* where it counts . . .' she said, wriggling on my hips pointedly as she lay down and embraced me again.

*

The sea again, surging against the girl's legs as she lay in the surf, aware of rain falling and a sky lowering and darkening. Her mother had crawled from the water, dragging her infant son. The crates with the animals in them were spread along the beach, among the spars and flotsam from the wreck. Too tired to lift her head, too dazed by concussion from the rocks, the girl could only stare across the billowing waves at the ship's stem, still high above the heaving ocean.

'My animals . . .' she whispered, but there was no sound from the broken cages, though she was half aware of the drowned shapes curled within them.

After a while, the cages were dragged away. She could hear them being moved across the shingle. The rain grew more drenching before it receded. Slowly the girl's senses returned. Distantly, she could hear the dull canter of horses, coming towards her.

She forced herself to her feet and stared along the shore. Seven or eight riders, still far away, one of them a woman with billowing black hair, one an old man. They moved almost eerily through the misting air, but they were riding hard.

She ran up the beach, into the shadow of the cliff, then scampered from sea cave to sea cave, looking for a hiding place.

In one, its passage reaching deeply into the hill, she saw her crates, her creatures, and she flung herself among them.

'Owl! Cat! Oh no! Roebuck! Eagle! Oh no, no!'

Each corpse she stroked or held, but there was no way of bringing life back to them. 'Who dragged you here?' she cried. 'Who tried to save you?'

A woman's voice shouted angrily. She crept to the mouth of the cave and saw her mother, terrified, dishevelled, running from the hunters. The corpse of her infant son lay naked in the tidal zone, limbs shifted by the waves. The hunters rode after the poor woman, passing the sea cave without a glance.

'I have to hide. I have to hide . . .'

Her thoughts selfish, now; all about survival.

She drew her skinning knife and slipped the feathered pelts from the owl and eagle, the hides from the deer and the cat, sticking the skins to her face and her arms and across her clothes. The skins moved into her, swallowed her. Her eyes sharpened with the owl, the eagle put murder in her mind, her senses heightened like a cat's, her limbs grew sinewy and strong.

Dressed as this strange, many-coated beast, she crouched in the sea cave and watched as her mother was ridden into the ocean, pushed back into the swell by a mailed knight and by the sorceress with the wild, black hair, who screeched abuse at her until the poor woman stumbled and slipped into the turning tide, dragged suddenly away, and down into the deep, and out of the world.

'I will kill you for that murder, Vivyane,' the girl-beast whispered, but it was a foolish thing to have done, since the old man with his tight growth of grey beard who had sat back from the troop of armoured men, suddenly glanced her way, as if her words had reached him. The girl felt her heart squeeze as the dark eyes spotted her and the mouth formed into a silent, triumphant word.

His glance was noticed fay Vivyane, who screamed angrily at her steed and galloped the animal up the shore.

The sea-cave girl in her skins cowered back. The cat snarled and the owl watched. The deer made ready to bolt. The eagle chattered, anxious to kill.

Vivyane appeared in the cave entrance, breathless from the ride, damp with rain. She looked into the darkness, eyes bright like a wilder cat than her prey.

'Where are you hiding?'

She looked to where the girl was concealed behind her creatures; she frowned, then took a step forward . . .

A youth moved suddenly out of the shadows of the sea cave. He was tall, wiry, dressed in brown leather and linen, stained black with the ocean and hanging with weed. What little facial hair he possessed was white with salt.

'Leave my pet alone!' he shouted defiantly.

Vivyane stood uneasily in the cave mouth, staring at the sea-crusted man who had risen from the darkness.

'I have never seen a creature such as this,' Vivyane said, pointing to the girl in her skins.

'You've seen it many times,' defied the youth. 'You should open your eyes. This creature is my pet and I will not see it harmed.'

'What's your name?' Vivyane asked. She was holding a short, pointed staff, wickedly sharp, its haft carved with the signs of her strengths.

'What's your *name*?' she asked again as the youth stood defiantly silent.

'If you can see it,' he said, 'then by the Good Christ, you can have it, and my pet as well. And me too for that matter. Because as God Knows, if you can see my name, nothing will matter *but* the name. That is my challenge to you.'

His words provoked Vivyane to a fit of fury. Her figure filled the mouth of the cave. But she didn't step inside, kept at bay by the challenge and by confusion. Instead, she screeched abuse at the cowering, pelt-covered girl and flung her staff at the crouching creature. The hard wood turned in the air like a knife and its point pierced the buck's skin covering the girl. A moment later, Vivyane was gone, riding furiously back towards the fort, the sharp-stubbled old man and his knights galloping behind her.

The youth ran out of the cave and threw stones after them, mocking them as he did so, then went back to kneel by the girl, pulling away the ragged clothing of skins and feathers, shocked by the wound he saw. Outside, the sea was still raging, the wind howling, but inside this place there was only calm, and the dying girl.

'Has she gone?' the girl asked.

'Yes,' said the unnamed youth. 'And I don't think the Good Christ is in her heart, but only the dark lady of the crossroads.'

'Hecate. Didn't you recognise her? That was Vivyane. And Hecate flavours her bile.'

He could hardly take his gaze from the blood on her breast. 'I would think so. There was an old man with her, but when I looked at him I had a strange thought: that he is either a young man pretending to be old, or an old man who would be young, because as God is my witness, he seemed ageless and frightening.'

'*Merlin*,' the girl whispered. 'He is training a new protégé. Vivyane. But he doesn't trust her and would prefer to be instructing me, having met me at my father's court, before it was destroyed. The protégé will not hear of it. She wants me dead. Merlin watches. Vivyane and I are pitted against each other in this cold-hearced young-old man's scheme. And do not mention God in the same breath as his name, because it is Hecate's Master that guides him, and all the Hounds of Hell.'

She looked at the youth gently, her eyes still alive with light, though she was slipping into darkness.

'My name is Issabeau,' she said.

'Well, well. Are you half boy, then?'

'I am *not*!' she chastised him as loudly as she could. 'I was christened *Yzabel*. But I was called Issabeau by my parents, and now that they are both dead, I wish to remain as they thought of me, in that fond way, that softer name. And there is *nothing* of the boy in it!'

'Issabeau it is.'

'I'm dying of that young hag's magic.'

The youth glanced furiously at the sea beyond the cave. 'She is dying of her own magic, though she doesn't know it.'

'You're very confident, to condemn a sorceress so easily.'

'Trust me.'

'I don't,' said Issabeau, gently amused, 'since it's only bravado that makes you say what you say. But thank you for trying. And I hope you're right. She didn't manage to guess your name.'

The youth sat back on his haunches, gazing through the mouth of the cave to the violent sea. 'By the Virgin's Prayers, she tried. She certainly tried. I felt her magic in my head. I felt stripped and beaten. I felt exposed and naked, with crows pecking at my eyes and ears and heart. The Cruel Saracen could not have inflicted more pain on me than did that hag as she sought my name.'

Issabeau was impressed. 'Then how did you hide it?'

The youth stared at the girl for a long time, a twinkle in his eye. 'There was nothing to hide, Issabeau. I was never named.'

'*Everyone* is named.'

'*Someone* was not! That someone was me. My father died before the name could be given.'

'How did he die?'

'The truth of that is lost with my name.'

'If he knew your name, then the name is still there, but in the heart of a dead man.'

'The Good Christ Knows, Issabeau, I have clung to that hope. But there is a good reason to never find it. Five reasons, in fact.'

'And they are?'

'*Because* I was not named, I was given five gifts.'

'That's generous giving.'

'I agree. One gift for each limb: one each for my arms, one each for my legs . . .' he stared at the girl, a mischievous look on his face. 'And one for the smaller limb that is speaking to me even as I look at you.'

Issabeau smiled knowingly and tossed a pebble at her companion. 'Put winter in that limb! I'm still too young.'

He grinned. 'I'll do my best. My very best. But as to the other gifts, the four that I can show you are as follows: that I can give back a life to one who has died. But this will cost me the strength of my right arm, which will be my sword arm, so it will be a gift given carefully.'

'A wise comment.'

'Secondly, I can give a kiss that will bring freedom. That's my left arm gone, though I can live with that. Thirdly: I can hold the Holy Grail of Christ as long as I fast from all things physical while I carry it. My left leg is the price for this privilege, when it's done.'

'When it's found!'

'Indeed. But the Grail has to be somewhere in the heart of the land.'

'But which land?'

'Indeed. A wasteland, apparently.'

'Among the many that we hear of.'

'Some knight will find it. Some day.'

'Much good may it do him.'

'I agree. The knights I meet often wonder what will be done with the Grail once its hiding place has been revealed.'

'Tales will tell, no doubt,' said Issabeau. 'And the fourth gift?'

'I can confuse sorcerers as long as my True Name is lost.'

'Amply demonstrated,' said the girl. 'Vivyane's head will ache tonight!'

'Indeed. But if I find my name, I lose a leg. So I think I'll continue to *confuse*. And as regards courtesy, you can call me whatever comes to mind.'

Issabeau sighed. 'Since I'm dying, none of your gifts are of use to me except the first, the bringing back of life, and you should save that gift for a greater friend than me.'

The youth smiled at her. 'I *will* save that gift, though I have no greater friend than you at this moment. But the kiss will suffice, I think, and I'll give it gladly.'

He leaned down to Issabeau, pulled aside the tunic over her small breast to expose the bleeding wound from Vivyane's staff. The blood was still flowing. He lapped at it, licked the wound, then put his lips against the torn edges, kissing fiercely.

Issabeau watched him, then reached a finger to touch his glistening lips. 'I feel stronger for that kiss.'

'And I feel a chill in my left shoulder.'

The left side of his body froze, became gleaming stone. They both marvelled at the transformation. Fingers flexed, wrist flexed, arm bent at the elbow, but this was a stone arm, now, white marble shot through with streaks of green and red; and yet he could feel with it, and was strong with it.

'God's Truth, by kissing you I've made myself invulnerable to attack from the left.'

'That's because the kiss was given gladly.'

'It was a True Kiss.'

'And stopped the wound to a True Heart.'

The youth leaned towards Issabeau, his brow creasing with love and desire, his crimson, rose-bud mouth soft with need. 'Issabeau, I feel so much older than I am . . .'

'And soon you will be,' she whispered, brushing her lips on his. 'And that will be good for us both.'

Then she pushed him back firmly, shaking her head, half smiling. 'But for now, I think I'll stay intact.'

'Must you?'

'Yes! I must! I wish I knew your name, though.'

'It will find me soon enough, no matter how fast I run.'

'Yes. I suppose it will.' She sounded forlorn. 'And then you'll be prey to Sorcerers.'

'But the Good Christ is in my Heart, Issabeau. His Enduring Cross will be my strength! And no one can kill me from the left.'

'Bravely said, stone-knight,' murmured Issabeau. 'And I think you must be of noble birth, with gifts such as yours; and also by your clothes and your confident look.'

Suddenly she was fighting back tears. The boy put his arms around her and hugged her. 'What is it?'

'Hell has just drowned my mother and is on our tails. I will miss her dreadfully. She had such wisdom. This will be a desperate time.'

'A desperate time indeed,' said the youth. 'But if Hell has taken her, Hell can give her back. I will do what I can for you to make her live again, and protect you from Hell in the process!'

The seascape faded and I emerged from the dream, dizzy with the images and heady with the scent of salt air. There was a weight on my belly and I became aware that Issabeau was straddling me, her hands resting on my chest. My mouth ached from the prolonged contact that had induced the memory.

She sat there, dark against the bright sky, staring do what me.

'Did you see?'

'Yes. What happened next? Between you and the youth?'

She sighed. 'We had different paths to follow. But we agreed to meet at the sea cave in a year's time.'

'And did you?'

'I was there. He was not. And I never found him again.'

But in a way she had, I thought to myself.

'*Haven't* you found him?'

She shook her head. 'I'm confused because . . .'

'Because of Someone son of Somebody? That proud Celt with his drooping moustache and golden hair?'

'The barbarian,' she said wistfully, repeating, 'barbarian!'

'But you think you recognise him. He's a good few years older . . .'

'He is not the same boy grown into a man!' she insisted. 'He is nothing like him. When I met him in Legion for the first time, I was frightened of him. Something about him was familiar. All I could think of was that it was Merlin, disguised to trap me. Or Vivyane, tricking me into complacency.'

Her sudden look at me was innocent and lost.

'But I am in love with him, and I feel I am betraying the Sea-Cave Boy I promised to find. Do you have an answer for me, Christian? Tell me what is happening to me!'

'I have an answer,' I whispered. 'I'm sure of it.'

Issabeau's body was tight against my loins and I was aroused and embarrassed. She wriggled on me, her fingers clawing at my breast, her eyes wide with anticipation.

'But I think I should talk to Someone first,' I went on. 'I need time to think. And if Guiwenneth finds us like this . . .'

'It will be bad for us both. I know. This isn't love, Christian. It's comfort. And very comfortable too. You make a good chair,' she added with a mischievous laugh before rolling off me, standing and brushing at her clothing.

I needed time to think.

I hadn't lied to her. How could I explain to her what was obvious to me: that she and Someone were part of the same story, but a story in two versions, hers from mediaeval France, his from a Celtic land hundreds of years before the Romans had conquered northern Europe, from before *Christ*, as she would have understood it. A story had been told generation after generation, and it had been adapted by the telling over fifteen hundred years.

What would happen next? I had no way of knowing. But perhaps it could help the love between these two people if I could find out Someone's version of events.

Were these to be star-crossed lovers? Or would they live happily ever after? I was amused and alarmed by the thought. If the story they represented ended sadly, it would be too bad for them. But if one version of the story was agreeable, they would need to push themselves in that direction, as long as they stayed inside this forest.

Distantly, a horn was sounding, but it came from the direction of the Long Person and not Legion. Issabeau shuddered noticeably.

'We *are* close,' she said. 'You find Guiwenneth and the jarag. I'll find Kylhuk.'

Eighteen

I found out quickly enough that the Long Person was a river, her 'parted legs' the place where twin streams joined, each flowing from the heart of the wildwood but bringing very different boats and travellers.

In the months that I had journeyed with Kylhuk's Legion, we had crossed many rivers. The Long Person was something different, however, and Issabeau, like all the enchanters, could 'smell' that difference since the river flowed not out of the hills of the world, but from the forgotten past of the world. And though Issabeau could not describe to me the smell of time, it was clearly something pungent and exotic to her, and that smell clung to the Scaraz, as it would soon cling to Legion.

Issabeau, small staff in her mouth, transformed into a fast runner and went back to the garrison, urging me to be cautious as I probed onwards towards the river itself. She whistled for Someone, who answered from a distance. Guiwenneth was scouting elsewhere with the jarag and I tried to call for them.

In the six months I had been marching with Kylhuk I had taken a turn at the Silent Towers, behind the column, watching that terrible darkness follow us, seeing men die by sword and spear and by unseen hands, or claws that snatched them into the black sky, shredding them like paper. There were always fires burning in that darkness, and to pass beyond the Silent Towers was to enter a realm of eerie sound, calls and cries, screams and howls, sounds that are beyond description, but which suggested primitive, angry language. And above all, the steady gallop of horses, an endless ride towards Legion, neither encroaching, nor receding, but someone keeping pace, the steady drumming of hooves, riders biding their time.

I had spent time as well in the centre of the train, dispatched on several small quests.

But in the end, something drew me back to the Forlorn Hope, and my companions from that first encounter. Kylhuk was certainly aware of the bond between us, and though Gwyr was often called away to help with interpreting the language of captives, or acquisitions to the garrison, the six of us worked well together, Issabeau and Jarag using magic as a defence against danger, Someone and myself using brute force. I had taught Someone simple martial arts; he had taught me to use the leaf-blade sword, the shield, the chariot and the javelin. He didn't believe in bow and arrow, a dishonourable weapon. Gwyr, of course, used his wits, his newly acquired trumpet, its mouth like a grinning bronze boar (which, though it sounded a piercing and terrifying bellow when used as warning, could also be played with delicacy, a sort of vertical horn with a range of seven or eight notes), and his speed – in retreat!

No fool, Gwyr, but a shadowed man, often to be found alone, silent and melancholy, his cheeks glistening until a sleeve wiped the sheen away and a quick smile broke through his beard at the approach of a friend.

It was Gwyr, now, who rode up behind me as I trotted along a rough track that had appeared within the greenwood, still calling for my companions. A river flowed ahead of me, out of sight, but not out of smell, though its odour was a familiar one to me from my boating trips along the Avon and the Thames.

I heard his horse thunder towards me and turned defensively, relaxing as the Interpreter jumped from the bare back of his mount, hauling on the reins to stop it grazing as he led the animal across to me, his gaze over my shoulder.

'Kylhuk is following,' he announced. 'Issabeau says this is the place . . .'

'I can smell a river ahead of us. Issabeau told me she can smell *time itself*.'

Gwyr was elated. 'We've found her,' he said in a delighted whisper. 'The Long Person. Now it begins, Chris. Now it begins.' And, with a quick glance at me, he added, 'And for some, it ends.'

We ran on, Gwyr's horse trotting behind us, glad to be unburdened. The woodland opened out; the way ahead became dazzling with reflected light. Soon we came to the tree-fringed, gravel bank of the Long Person and gazed at the broad ribbon of water and the crowded forest on the far side.

Gwyr looked to the left, towards the setting sun, to the source of the river where the forest was in gleaming, ruddy twilight. 'That's the direction we are headed. It will be hard rowing!'

At that moment, the forest shifted, the land heaved, Gwyr's steed reared in alarm. Legion's outer wall had arrived and as we turned, the wildwood opened and Kylhuk himself galloped through. He jumped from his horse's back, letting the beast walk free, reins dangling. He strode past me, prodding me painfully in the stomach.

'You should have kept me company!' he barked.

Kylhuk had not broken his fast, except to eat an occasional fish, game-bird and loaf of bread, since his diet of plums had soon given him diarrhoea. But he was lean and hard, now, wearing nothing but a dull green war-kilt and a short cloak, pinned over his heart. His sword was slung from its belt across the other shoulder, and his sandals were Roman, taken from a corpse.

He dropped to a knee on the gravel by the river's edge, put his hand out and tentatively touched the flow, trailing his fingers for a while and looking thoughtfully upstream.

Then he called to me.

'Touch the water,' he said as I crouched beside him. I obeyed and felt a strange flow of life from the fluid to my skin and up my arm, not a tingle, not a charge, but a breath of presence.

Kylhuk extended his hand and I took it, and the river mingled in that grip, and there was a look in his dark eyes that I couldn't fathom. 'You have come a long way,' he said to me.

'Yes.'

'I have come a long way too. Of all the tasks I was set, finding the Long Person was going to be the most difficult. Sailing her will be the most strenuous. What we achieve at her source will be the hardest. I had only the omens of my seers and Cleverthreads to get here: Issabeau could smell her; Ear son of Hearer could bury himself in the ground and *hear* her – he can hear an ant walk on a leaf when he is quiet like that – and Falcon died at the claws of the Scald Crow, ascending to let his Far Look gaze across this wilderness. All of them were right. And here we are.'

'Here we are,' I agreed. 'What happens now?'

He stood, slapped me painfully on the shoulder and barked, 'We build a boat, of course. By Olwen's Hands, you're getting fat, slathan! You're no good to me carrying such weight on your shoulders.'

'If I knew the full meaning of the word, perhaps I'd agree with you.'

He didn't respond. He had told me only that a slathan was the 'sharer of his burden'. He returned to his horse reached into a pouch and tossed me an apple, grinning before he rode furiously back into Legion.

I had seen no boats in the garrison. I had assumed that a period of tree-felling, carpentry, nailing and rigging would now occur, but I was wrong. I had forgotten the carts and wagons. And indeed, as these vehicles were dismembered like wooden puzzles, and rearranged to form a wide-hulled, low-masted ship, even the wicker chariots were pressed into use, to form row-locks, hatches and store-houses.

For several days the camp along the river's edge was a hive of activity as this bizarre transformation took place, and on the gravel shore, above the waterline, the lean, low-prowed longship was constructed, its shallow keel sharp so that it could cut the water as it was rowed upstream, sail slung low to catch any favourable wind, deck wide so that men could easily stand and handle the oars that would drive us up against the current.

There was no fussy design on the ship yet, no figurehead, no icono-graphy to challenge the world of myth and superstition into which we soon would sail. Just wood and metal, wheels, rope and cloth.

The vessel would carry a crew of twenty-seven (that number again!), I was certainly to sail on it, with my friends from the Forlorn Hope and with Kylhuk and his personal entourage. Meanwhile, a long and difficult process of selection was occurring behind the forest wall for the men and women who would make up the number. This involved games, tests, combat, trials of wit and the casting of lots. Guiwenneth watched it all with deep fascination and brought me lurid accounts of the activities and the often fatal consequences of the contests, some of which turned my stomach. I will not recount them here. At the end of it, the ship was crewed and a feast was held to celebrate the finishing of the task.

But as for the rest of Legion, when the celebrations were over it would have to follow along the edge of the river itself, a slow and dangerous journey and without a leader.

As I waited for Kylhuk, I glimpsed for the first time the extraordinary flow of life that was erupting at the river's source; and of the death that it was drawing back, against the stream, as if the impulse to life was the easiest, that to death the hardest, all notion of entropy ignored.

A broken tree floated down the centre of the river, turning in the flow, its roots high above the water, a man and a woman, exhausted and afraid, clinging to its trunk. They saw me and called, but the Long Person swept them on.

Later, dogs swam past, six or seven of the creatures, leashes trailing, baying in desperation, their owner drowned perhaps. And a glittering barge, light shimmering from metal on its hull, white sails catching the breeze and tipping it slightly as the helmsman struggled and four cowled figures stared into the distance, unmoving and unmoved by the voyeur on the bank.

Then upstream, rowing hard against the current as soon we would be too, came a ship that looked so grim I drew back, half into the cover of the forest. A low, mournful horn sounded at regular intervals as it stroked its way against the river. Its blackened hull might have been tarred or charred. Faces peered at the shore from jagged holes hewn in the sides. The rails around the deck were lined with men who watched the forest. I could hear the complaints of animals and the stamping of hooves from below decks. A single mast trailed a shredded sail, so holed and rotten that the opposing breeze hardly ruffled it as it hung, half furled.

The horn moaned as it passed me, and suddenly a man's voice shouted. There was immediate activity on the deck and a hail of arrows flew towards me, one grazing my cheek, another striking the tree next to me and spinning round to crack against my skull. A spear thudded into the ground, trailing red ribbons and black feathers. A second hail of arrows whispered past me, and stones struck and clattered among the rocks.

This terrible ship of the dead pulled away and I cautiously stepped out of cover to watch it go. A last arrow wobbled towards me in the air, a curved, crude shaft that was suddenly snatched from its flight as Someone stepped in front of me. He looked at the weapon then scratched his jaw with the chipped stone point as he stared into the distance.

'We go that way too,' he said after a moment. 'But I'll be glad to let that ship get ahead of us.'

'How many more ships like that on the Long Person?' I asked and Someone nodded soberly as he glanced at me.

'Very many, I imagine. The challenge of the twin gates is too seductive.'

Although I had talked to Someone about his life of adventure, I had never thought to ask him about his childhood after the events of his father's death by combat. The opportunity arose that night, as we camped by the open water, a few miles downriver from the main camp. Kylhuk had taken a hand of forty men and ten specialists to guard the bank, since omens had suggested that Eletherion was there.

A torch-lit barque drifted past us, lighting up the river. A woman's voice sang sweetly, though the woman was not revealed. A black hound watched us, paws crossed on the rails.

'What is your earliest memory of love?' I asked the Celt, and he glanced at me with a frown, tugging at his moustache.

'Why?'

'I'm interested to know. You've told me of adventure, and the search for your name; you've told me of the haunting presence of the tasks you feel obliged to perform. But you've never mentioned passion. Has it been a lonely life until you met Issabeau?'

He prodded the fire with his knife. 'Truthfully, it has, though not by my choice. When I was very young I met a girl in the dark forests that filled the valleys to the north of my father's fortress. I have never mentioned this before, and I don't know why I should tell you now, but I will. Perhaps you can answer a question that has been bothering me for some time . . . !'

'I'll do my best,' I said, and he drew breath, stared into the distance and began.

You will remember, from what I told you when we first met, that my father was summoned to a combat a few hours before my birth and before he could name me, challenged in a dispute about the stealing of a famous white bull and five cows that were being taken to honour Taranis. They were to be sacrificed, a sacrifice of great importance, and my father in his envy of the bull intercepted it with his warrior band and made the offering himself.

My father, you will remember, was killed outright by Grumloch's first throw across the river, a truly lucky strike.

Because I hadn't been named, Grumloch spared me. I was taken out onto a forest lake in a small boat. My father's finest knights were murdered there, and dropped into the pool. I was left in a coracle with a wet-nurse, forbidden ever to return to the fort, though of course being only a babe in arms I knew nothing of what was occurring.

When I was weaned, the woman left me in one of the deep forest glades, one dedicated to Sucellus. She placed me in a hollow between

478

the feet of the great wooden idol, where it was warm and protected from rain and wind. At night, the great gods roared at each other across the forest, and Sucellus strode around the glade, beating at branches. But he, like all of them, was tied to this place.

Every so often, masked people came and sacrificed or left offerings at the feet of the idol. I ate whatever was left and Sucellus never complained. Only later did it occur to me that because I had no name the god could not see me.

Then one day – I had lived in the shadow of this monstrous, shouting tree for ten years or more – animals began to visit the place, I remember a small, black bird that watched me for ages before flying off. And an owl settled on the wooden head, high above me, every night for a week. Then a grey-furred cat came slinking around the glade. And a small deer that I tried to snare, but it butted me and escaped each time.

These creatures all came through the forest from one direction, at the edge of the glade, close to where I had dug out my stink-pit. I found a hidden track there and one morning, after the statue had returned to rest, I began to follow the trail. And after a while I found a glade where two great wooden idols, one of a man the other a woman, stood locked in an angry embrace. They were wrestling, their legs stretched out for balance, their arms around each other's heads, their mouths gaping in pain, the wood of their muscles swollen with tension. During the night, they were clearly fighting. During the day, the trees had grown together. They cast a vast and sinister shadow in the sun. I soon recognised them as Cernunnos, Lord of Animals, and Nemetona, Goddess of Glades.

There was a stink-pit here too, and the trees were hung with knots of grass, the stems of flowers, with strips of hide, and dolls made out of feathers. Another prisoner, then. But who was she – I felt sure it was a girl – and where was she hiding?

I stayed at the edge of the clearing until nightfall. As the moon rose and the last of twilight was swallowed to the west, the statues began to detach from each other. The forest began to echo with the screaming of the wooden gods in their sanctuaries, and these two began to wrestle and scream until I was deafened. They staggered about the glade, tearing at the bark on their faces, clubbing at each other so that splinters and strips of wood flew like spears around me. At midnight they released each other and prowled the glade, pulling back the trees, prodding at the bushes, calling in their strange tongue. I cowered back as Cernunnos leaned towards me, gape-mouthed and slack-eyed, but the monstrous horned head moved away. It hadn't seen me.

They were looking for something, and I imagined it was the human occupant of this place. Cernunnos stalked off through the forest. Nemetona hunkered down, growling, then turned her head to stare at the bright moon.

And at that moment a voice whispered, *Don't give me away. This one will tear me apart if she finds me.*

I tried to speak to the girl, but she pressed a sap-scented finger against my mouth. *Wait until morning. It's not safe until then.*

And then she pulled me to her body, holding me against the cool of the glade. I felt a soft fuzz of hair on her face. Her breath was sweet with wild herbs. She was as thin as a carcase, bones prominent below the flesh. She stayed awake all night, I think, because when I came out of my own forest dream, in the dead, dark hours, the first thing I saw was her starlit gaze on me.

At dawn, the wooden idol rose and bowed its head, hardening into the tree from which it had been so crudely hacked.

'We're safe, now,' said my new-found friend. She ran to the stink-pit and squatted over it, then kicked leaves from a pile into the hole. I followed her example, fascinated by the way she had painted her body. She sat down against the heels of the idol, legs stretched out in front of her and face upturned, quite relaxed now that the night had passed.

What a sight she was! Not an inch of her skin was not painted with the tiniest of animals. What seemed like lines or circles on her face and arms were in fact a hundred creatures drawn so close together that each ran into its neighbour. I saw every creature I knew and a hundred that I didn't. They ran across her features like deer on a bare knoll, like a flock of birds, wheeling at dusk.

'What's your name?' I asked her.

'Mauvaine,' she replied. 'What's yours?'

'Only my father knows, and he's dead, killed by a spear on the day of my birth.'

'I shall call you Jack of the Glades. Who killed him? Your father.'

'Grumloch, his brother-in-law.'

'Why was he killed?'

'Over the matter of a bull and five cows, which had come his way.'

'You mean he stole them in a raid.'

Yes.'

'The Oldest Bull was called Tormabonos,' Mauvaine said. 'I have him painted here,' she indicated a spot on her left side, close to where her small breast scarcely stretched her clothing. 'All of the Oldest Animals are painted on me.'

'Who painted them on you?'

She sat quite still, hands on the ground, feet splayed as she stared at me. 'Taranis. When I was an infant. I think he knew what he was doing.'

'They're magic animals, then.'

'Yes. They're the Oldest Animals! Unfortunately, I can't raise all of them, only a few. I was trapped here when I was too young. Nemetona keeps me here, and she will kill me, given half a chance. Cernunnos tries to take me away for his own ends, but their struggle is an endless one. She is not as powerful as he, but she has a secret which drains him of full strength.'

'What secret is that?'

She looked at me with amused disbelief. 'If I knew the answer, it wouldn't be a *secret*,' she said.

'Indeed.'

'She steals his knowledge and his power when they fight at night. But the animals that rise in the wood from my painted skin stalk her and bring some of that power back to him.'

Because of their struggle, Mauvaine was caught in this wilderness, a piece in a game that was beyond her control. When I suggested this to her she snarled at me.

'Yes. But only if I fail to escape. And I intend to escape!'

'I feel the same. But whenever I try to leave the glade, I end up back where I started. Something drives me in circles. At least you can disguise yourself as an Old Animal and run.'

'Easy to say. Not easy to do.'

And she explained that Cernunnos had more control over her when she was in animal form than he could exercise when she was in her human guise. The animals ran, and her animal senses were heightened, but they were obedient to the call: a whistle for the hound, a song for the cat, a breath for the owl, a clacking of tongue for the ouzel, a bark for the buck. They could run and fly widely through the blackwood, but always came home at dusk.

'We must burn the idols during the day. Set fire to them!'

'I've tried it. As Nemetona burns, so I burn.' And Mauvaine showed me her right leg, where the skin inside the ankle was red and scarred by scalding.

'I am trapped here,' she added sadly.

'I had had the same thought. Then a cat enticed me away from my own prison.'

'That was me.'

'I know it was. Mauvaine, all we need is the way to break the charm that holds you here.'

'I am charm itself,' the girl said with a wry smile, lying back and stroking her body through her clothing. 'My skin crawls with magic, but not my dreams.'

'My own skin crawls with lice. So I'll look to my own dreams for a way to save you.'

I remember the way she laughed at that, but that night I crept into her arms, sheltering her from the raging giants, shielding her from the splinters of wood that flew from the angry gods.

And when the moon was high, and the idols were off somewhere, stalking the night forest, I dreamed such a strange dream: perhaps a memory of my time as an infant, after my father's death.

A face was hovering above me, old and wise, half-toothed, deeply scarred; a man who said: 'I am your grandfather. I cannot tell you your name, since my son is dead, but he would have told you that you must always welcome any scarred-faced man to your hall if he pays you courtesy during the rising of the moon, and pay heed to his words. If his hair is black, you must pay him tribute. If he has lost a hand, you must allow him to depart in his own time.'

Then a woman came, full of gall and spirit, grey hair like the glow of the moon around her shrunken face.

'I cannot tell you your name, but your father would have told you this: that at the beginning of each season you must offer advice to every child you meet in your fortress, even if they don't ask for it. Nothing you say to them will ever be forgotten, even if it makes no sense.'

A druid crowded in on me in my dream, black-bearded, hungry-eyed, foul-breathed, a gold lanula round his neck dangling and glittering above me. 'I cannot tell you your name, but you must give back a life before your death, or your death will be an ending and not a beginning. Give back a life! Don't forget that. And because of your rose-bud mouth . . .' he touched my lips with his stinking finger . . . 'a kiss from this mouth will put new life in a dying heart, but only once. Once only.'

I woke from the dream to find Mauvaine deeply curled into my chest, her face and mouth close to my own as she slept, her breath so sweet in the night that I could think only that with a kiss I could take her away from the torment of this glade: I could put life into a heart that was dying.

And so I kissed her. And as I kissed her, her mouth opened and the kiss deepened. And her hands ran over me as she slept, and her fingers were in my hair, and she had rolled back to pull my body on top of hers, lifting her simple dress to expose her belly and pulling me onto her, trying to pull me into her . . .

In her sleep.

But I woke suddenly to find myself in a coracle on a cold lake, surrounded by freezing mist through which the forest could be seen as a black, brooding fringe of winter limbs.

The kiss had not released Mauvaine, it had released me!

I spent years exploring that forest, searching for the glade where the painted child was imprisoned, but I found nothing but pain, loneliness, solitary adventurers . . . and finally Legion.

I have never forgotten that girl, though, and though the pain has gone, the betrayal remains.

I said, 'You dreamed of the taboos that would be placed upon you by your clan. These were your *geisas*. They have haunted you since your infancy. You cannot be blamed for using one of them inappropriately when you were still so young.'

I managed no more of the thought. The Celt rose angrily, glaring at me, and stalked away into the forest. I ran through my own words again, and realised that nothing could have been more inappropriate than my empty-headed advice to the man, and no doubt I would have to make amends.

But I had him!

I knew him, now. Though not his name!

The ship was finished. All of us who would sail in her stood in a circle around the sleek vessel on the shore, holding torches. Kylhuk stood before the prow, swathed in a cloak of feathers. The frightening woman, the dolorous voice, whispered to the wooden barque, moving slowly around the hull, her hands spread on the planking. The Fenlander and the grim-faced Raven cut notches on the wood with their blades and Kylhuk made his own mark between their signs. Each of us then carved a symbol on the right side of the hull and nailed a crudely fashioned shield above the mark. The shields were made from bark, or cloth, or shards of wood tied together, and were gaudily and variously decorated. Everyone seemed to know what to carve and what to paint on the shields, but when the blade was passed to me, Kylhuk gripped my hand in his, directed the point to his own crudely scratched symbol – a tusked boar inside an oak leaf – and made me carve a C.

'You don't need a shield,' he said with a smile, 'because you are protected by my own. I hope you can row,' he added quietly, as I gave him back the knife.

'I expect I'll learn soon enough. Are you going to name the ship?'

'What do you think we've just been doing?'

'That's a complicated name we've given her. Twenty-seven in all . . .'

'It will help to confuse the enemy.'

As supplies were put aboard the vessel, and a slipway to the river constructed out of logs, Guiwenneth found me and tugged me away from the river. She led me at a run through the tangled forest, saying only, 'What have you done to Someone?'

'What do you mean?'

'I'll show you.'

The Celt had hacked down small trees to make a glade. He had piled the trimmed trunks into a wigwam shape, with a gap so that he could enter. He sat inside, carving a statuette by the light of a single torch rammed into the soft earth.

'Do you have an answer for me, Chris?' he asked without looking up.

'I have an answer for you. But it will be hard for you to understand.' I glanced at Guiwenneth. 'Find Issabeau . . .'

But Someone said, 'Issabeau is here. She is in the forest. When I have finished the cat—' he turned his carving slightly and I saw that its features were feline, 'she will come back to me.'

And he was quite right. A while later the undergrowth was stirred by stealthy movement and the torchlight picked out two quick, green eyes. A moment later Issabeau stepped into the clearing, her stick-of-shapes held firmly in her right hand.

'Do you have an answer for me?' she asked. Someone stepped out of his dream lodge.

I made them hold hands, then reached out to take that loving grip in my own. Guiwenneth stood behind me, her arm around my waist.

'I am an Outsider in this forest. Everything is new to me. But of one thing I am certain: and that is that you are the same children who met in the sea-cave – Issabeau – and in the idol glades – Someone. You do not recognise each other because Someone is far older in time, because time has passed, and in a way which will confuse things if I start to explain it. But as Guiwenneth is my witness, and by the power of hindsight that I carry with me, I now pronounce you *versions of the same myth*. You have already had the honeymoon. Now you must start to find a common path. What the future holds for you I can't say. You have told me the early part of your story, but the end of your story is not yet resolved. Only Kylhuk can glimpse such events.'

They were looking at me blankly, then turned to gaze at each other, as if seeing each other for the first time, despite the fact that their relationship had been intimate for months. But somehow the difference in detail of that Celtic and mediaeval story had fallen away. They were not Issabeau and the Sea-Cave Boy, nor Mauvaine and Jack of the Glades, but Issabeau and Someone son of Somebody.

Guiwenneth and I left them to their embrace.

Besides, away by the river Gwyr was sounding his horn and there was something urgent about that doleful howl. We returned at once to find out what was happening.

Kylhuk had had a trance-dream, it seemed; omens had supported his vision; he had even drowned a dog with its rider and watched the way the fleas had jumped. He was in no doubt that the time was right.

The ship would be launched immediately, despite the darkness, to begin its journey towards the heart of the forest, where Mabon was imprisoned.

Nineteen

The simple ship had already been pushed out into the river, only the keel below its prow biting the mud of the bank; its aft was tethered to trees, which bent and creaked with the strain of holding the vessel still against the flow. A shaky ramp had been extended from the prow to the shore, and supplies were being carried aboard by torchlight. The oarsmen were at their stands below the deck, practising their stroke to the steady rhythm of a drum.

Kylhuk was standing impatiently at the water's edge, the Fenlander beside him. Gwyr was already aboard; he stood in the stern, occasionally raising the camyx and sounding the note that would summon all of the far-flung and the forlorn hopes who were attached to Legion.

'Where have you been, slathan? I told you to be at hand at all times!'

Kylhuk's fingers pinched my arm with irritation as he spoke, but he forced a smile as he waited for my answer.

'I've been learning about two of your best and most trusted scouts,' I replied evenly. 'And I've been helping the course of love.'

This took him by surprise. 'Love is a hard sort of thing,' he said bitterly, the frown on his face deepening as he thought, no doubt, of Olwen. 'You should not be wasting your time with it.'

Someone and Issabeau had gathered their belongings and with quick and furtive glances towards me were making their careful way up the ramp.

As if he had seen the edge of my vision, Kylhuk glanced their way, then looked back at me with a wry smile.

'The course of love?'

'The course of love!'

'Well, well. I hadn't realised. Are they in the Delightful Realm?'

'Indeed. They might have been made for each other.'

'Then for the moment,' Kylhuk said agreeably, pinching my arm again as he stared at the romantic pair, 'I'm all for love. Let's hope it lasts. I am very fond of that husky-voiced trickster. Now – Christian! – fetch your weapons, your blankets, find Guiwenneth, get aboard. I want to get moving on the river while it's still dark.'

'Because Eletherion is on our tail?'

Kylhuk exchanged a brief, amused glance with the Fenlander before saying, 'No, *slathan*. Because Eletherion has gone ahead of us. He has a quicker mind than I'd thought, and my Forlorn Hope – too busy journeying in their own Delightful Realm from what you tell me – have brought Legion to the river too far away from our final destination.'

To the sound of horns, high-pitched ululation and the sombre chanting of the knights left behind, the boat of shields heaved against the river, the water flashing as the oars struck and lifted, soon finding their rhythm: a silent, steady stroke that was at first unsettling and then became smooth, so that we seemed to drift through the overcrowding forest.

Kylhuk took us to the middle of the stream. Two men with torches leaned out on each side of the prow, watching ahead for trees or other boats. On the raised stern, two people marshalled the spirits of the night to guard our rear. One was an elderly man wrapped in a voluminous cloak of bearskin, the skull rising above his long grey hair. Around him the night boiled with movement, elementals summoned by him and kept under his control, sent darting to the forest to scent and sense for danger. The other was Issabeau, her face in its cat form, her eyes reflecting green in the torchlight as she sniffed and listened to the animal world. Someone sat close by, keeping a watchful and protective eye on her.

For the rest of us there was nothing to do but sit, or sleep, or love, and I found a place behind several crates where there was a degree of seclusion and wrapped myself inside Guiwenneth's cloak, huddling snugly against the weary woman.

I woke at dawn. There was no sound except the gentle splash of water as the oars dipped. The slight forward surge of motion with every stroke was hardly noticeable. The mist-shrouded forest seemed to glide past us. A flight of cranes swooped over us as we lay, staring at the brightening sky, shivering with the damp.

We were on a river journey to the heart of the world, and already I felt as if we were in the deepest wilderness imaginable. At night, the forest echoed with cries and growls, sudden movement and the violent shaking of great trees. By day, only silence, each bend in the river bringing us further towards the source, but showing us nothing but the wall of wildwood. There were no rapids, no broken water, no sand banks . . . only fallen trunks and statues, sprawled and broken where they had toppled from their sanctuaries on the shore. And an occasional boat, drifting downstream, its occupants invariably wearing the blank expression of the newly born, their gaze fixed ahead, their awareness not yet wide enough to encompass the boat of shields that stroked so lazily past them.

We drifted through space and we drifted through time. Winter came and passed away in a matter of hours; thunderclouds blackened the horizon, a drenching rain shattered the river, drummed off the deck; then a hazy sun warmed us. The forest shed its leaves, then went into green budding life, then was rich with the colours of late summer. Days had passed, perhaps weeks. Guiwenneth's cycle suggested more than two months, but again, how could I be sure? She was as much a part of this wilderness as the geese and cranes that flew above us, as the giant, ridge-backed salmon that occasionally broke the surface, swimming ahead of us, out of reach of the lines and hooks that Someone and the Fenlander cast in desperation for such a catch.

Every so often we passed a sanctuary, the forest cleared to make space for an idol, or a temple, sometimes rude constructions out of wood, sometimes shining marble, sometimes no more than a giant boulder, deeply carved with a symbol or rune that the sorcerers on the boat of shields anxiously tried to identify, their arguments becoming heated.

We put into the bank only once, at a shrine to Freyja, one of the northern goddesses whose weeping, falcon-faced statue in rough stone dominated the shore. A spring of clear, fresh water bubbled from the cliff behind the ring of stones and the weathered statues of wolves and wild pigs and we drank greedily. Someone had heard that this goddess wept tears of gold, but we found only mossy rock and rotting wood. Issabeau took on the shape of a monkey and scaled the cliff, then stood guard against the wilderness beyond as all of the twenty-seven came ashore in groups, to drink and wash, to touch the earth.

But after a while the spring turned suddenly sour and the sky darkened. The ground around the stones started to shake rhythmically, as if at a gigantic approach. Issabeau found her eagle's wings, came down to the shrine, alarmed and unashamedly in retreat. 'A falcon flies this way!' she said. We flung ourselves back along the ramp of our boat of shields and cast off.

Though we stared at the shrine for several minutes, we could not tell what or who had arrived there, and had soon left the place behind.

I took my turn at the oars and my back strengthened, my arms thickened, my mind deadened. Increasingly, we sailed through deep, cloying banks of mist, emerging to new locations, a river subtly changed. Reeds and rushes crowded the banks, then crumbling cliffs, their fractured ledges home to desperate thorns. But always we came back to the forest, meandering through the silent walls of summer green.

One dusk, Gwyr's cry of alarm roused me from lassitude and I joined the others at the starboard rail, staring at the indistinct shape of a giant, walking parallel to our course, away in the woods. We could make out its head and shoulders above us, a cape of patterned furs. It carried a staff. A deep, resonant booming was its voice, the words indistinct as it called to a second walker, on the other side of the river. This one was female, long hair flowing like golden water around a pale, pudgy face as she loomed hugely towards our boat, peering down at us, before turning deeper into the forest, her grumbling words like thunder. This stalking pair dogged our passage for a few hours, through the night, then, shortly before dawn, the male stepped across the river ahead of us, the wind from his swirling cloak of skins rocking us in the water, and the two of them disappeared into the wilderness.

We all became slightly mad.

Gwyr played his bronze horn in a rhythmic but melancholy way. Issabeau and Guiwenneth sang in a shrill, harmonizing duet, in a private, nonsense language that they had invented, laughing hysterically at some of the ululating trills they accomplished as Someone and I sat bemused and idle during our resting period. A grizzle-bearded hero from Finland, Vainomoi by name, constructed a six-note reed pipe and became quite accomplished on it. A crinkle-faced, weather-tanned, wolf-skinned shaman whittled a kazoo out of a long bone which he had tugged from a gigantic skeleton half submerged in the river.

And under the direction of Kylhuk, the rest of us made drums.

This combined voice, wind and percussion then commenced, under my guidance, to create a version of Beethoven's Fifth Symphony that would have had the composer jittering in his grave. We became crazy. The sounds filled the space of the river, sent whole flocks of crows circling into the night sky. The stroke of the oars changed to reflect the dancing around the many blazing torches that illuminated the upper deck.

At dawn we were still playing, entranced, tranced out, lost in time, lost in space, the beat of the drum filling our heads, our legs moving effortlessly as we circled and twirled, arms outstretched, moving slowly through the fires, chanting and stepping out to the monotonous, all-consuming four-note rhythm.

A shadow had appeared ahead of us, but none of us had seen it at that time.

The shadow grew, and if we began to see it, we could not accommodate it in the dream vision.

The boat of shields pulled onwards, up the river. The shadow reared, grew tall, grew more distinct.

We were dancing in a circle, like the Greeks, my arms around the delightful Guiwenneth and the pungently animal jarag, who had taken to this ritual formation with exuberant delight, grinning, singing and breathing on me at every possible moment.

'Good dance! Good dance! We dance this way on river shore before collect fish and shell. Good dance!'

I had never known the prehistoric hunter so vociferous.

Opposite me, the impeccably trimmed and dressed Gwyr was squashed between Kylhuk, who was half naked and very drunk, and Issabeau who was in a dreamy state, her face a fluid film of animal features, all vying for control over the darkly beautiful human.

When the circle juddered to an awkward stop, I looked up. Gwyr had ceased dancing and was staring beyond me, his face a depiction of pure astonishment. Slowly the music faded away. The oars struck relentlessly as the boat surged forward, but on the upper deck there was only silence as we turned to stare at the massive tree that had at last loomed large in our awareness.

'Olwen's Hands!' Kylhuk breathed in amazement. 'So that's where he is. I had no idea . . . no idea how vast!'

'It's drawing us towards it,' the jarag said, leaning over the bow and staring at the water. The river flowed past us *away* from the tree, but we were caught in a deeper current drawing us forward and the oars were struck, the effort of rowing being wasted.

Still the tree rose ahead of us, its dark trunk a writhing mass of faces, shapes and glowing fires, its girth blocking the horizon, its height and wide, spreading branches smothering the dawn sky.

'Divine Son of the Mother! The bitch didn't mean her bastard to escape from this!'

The words were again the astonished words of Kylhuk, a strong man again, eyes wide, sobering fast.

Then Issabeau shouted out, 'By the Good God! What is that?'

But we had all seen the swirl of water, the great whirling maelstrom that was sucking us towards its deadly mouth.

Kylhuk shouted, 'Back oar! Can you hear me below? Back oar now! Or the pool will suck us in! Get the rhythm! *Back oar!*'

With a clatter of wood and the uncertain beat of the stroke-drum, the oarsmen tried to find a reverse stroke. Several oars splintered, the boat lurched, the water thrashed as blades struck in confusion, the ship of shields beginning to twist and turn as it was sucked towards the pool.

'Drag it back!' Kylhuk screamed angrily, dropping from upper to lower deck. The drum had stopped. The oars trailed deeply in the water. We clung to the rails, the mast, even the flimsy hutches for support as our progress towards the swirling water below the bulging roots of this towering growth was slowed.

Again the boat of shields lurched, throwing several men over the side. The shields clattered against the hull, some detaching and falling away, taking their protection with them. The defences were weakened. Then the prow dipped, the hull reeled drunkenly, slewing to the starboard. The ever-determined jarag and two others leapt into the white water holding ropes, and tried to swim to the bone-strewn bank to find stones or trees around which to tie the tethers. They were sucked out of sight, whipped down into the deep like leaves in a storm drain . . .

The end came so suddenly I have little clear recollection: the ship broke in two, splintering across the hull and pitching everyone else on the upper deck into the swirling river. I remember seeing Kylhuk flying backwards, his face contorted with pain; I remember Guiwenneth grabbing for me, her saturated hair wound around her face, her eyes full of despair in the instant before she was flung from me and lost into the river. Someone grunted loudly, somersaulted as a spar struck him, and vanished in a plume of blood. I went under the water. The current had taken my feet and I was dragged down so fast that within seconds I was in the silent realm of the dead, my lungs bursting as I held my breath, my arms flailing as I sought feebly for anything on which to gain a hold.

Then my vision darkened. A corpse swirled past me, gape-mouthed, fish-white, dull-eyed. Issabeau's black hair floated in my vision, the woman turning almost peacefully, her arms across her chest, her eyes closed. She had resigned herself to death.

I reached for her but she was caught in the spiralling flow and spun away from me, and at that moment I too began to resign myself to the cold and to breathing out for a final time, my mind suddenly clear and calm—

When a force like a vice pressed into my head. A finger the size of a baby's arm blocked the vision from one eye. Something huge had risen up below me and grasped me in its hand!

I felt myself pulled up, then freed from the water, letting go of the stale breath and sucking in air gratefully and with a sobbing cry of relief. A second powerful hand was on my arm. A mass of dripping weeds *blinked* at me, eyes in the river wrack, a grinning mouth . . .

Elidyr!

Then he grunted with effort, heaved and *flung* me onto the bank, literally that: lifted me and threw me. A branch broke my flight and bruised my arm. I fell to the turf, next to the groaning bodies of Guiwenneth and Issabeau. A moment later the ground shook as Someone thumped down, his face twisted with pain, his soaking hair red with his own blood. Guiwenneth crawled towards me and slumped over me, her mouth on my cheek, her fingers digging into my flesh. She was still only half conscious. As I sat up, cradling the woman carefully, I saw Kylhuk some yards away. He was on all fours, retching up water and shaking his head. The jarag was beside him, slowly getting to his feet and staring at the weed-draped giant who had just hurled him to the shoreline.

Elidyr, the green-haired monster, stood in the maelstrom and stared back at us, the weed writhing like snakes. I shouted out, 'Where is Gwyr? We need him, Elidyr! We need our Interpreter!'

After a terrible moment of silence, the boatman grumbled words that were incoherent against the noise of the swirling pool.

Then he shouted, 'Gwyr!' and raised his arms. The lank shape of the Interpreter of Tongues was drawn from the water, draped across Elidyr's palm like a rag doll. A moment later Elidyr stepped through the wild water – he could not have been touching the bottom of the whirlpool! – and emerged onto the bank, the weeds drawing back into his body just as once the flowers and fruits of the forest had drawn back into his supernatural skin.

Elidyr turned the Interpreter upside down, holding him by his legs. Soon, Gwyr vomited water and twitched with consciousness. And soon he, like the rest of us, was sitting huddled round a growing fire, Elidyr back in the shadows of the wood watching us. His favourite place, it seemed.

When I was warm and dry I went over to the boatman, who frowned uncomfortably as I approached. He was crouching but still looking down at me through the deep ridges of his eyebrows, his jaw working beneath the heavy beard.

'I thought I was a dead man at that moment. Thank you for my life.'

He nodded quickly, then looked away.

'Have you been with us all the time, Elidyr? Are you following us? Why not stay with us?'

'Go away,' he grunted, then reached out and prodded me away from him as easily and indifferently as I might shift a cat that was snuggling too closely against me on a sofa.

Thank God for Gwyr! As the rest of us had succumbed to whatever spell had been cast about us, the Interpreter of Tongues had managed to stay in touch with the hidden sounds and sights of the world around him. Even from his own dreamtime, his function – to see the hidden meaning in words and sounds – had enabled him to surface suddenly and see the danger. Without that moment of vision the maelstrom would have taken us suddenly and devastatingly. I suspected that not even Elidyr could have saved us.

Kylhuk agreed with me. But for Gwyr, he said darkly, we would have been swept below the arching, giant roots of the tree, and would have been lost. Others before us had managed to break the spell, there was evidence around us to testify to that fact, but it was clear that even those had often fallen foul of the defences of this massive prison.

Stunned, disorientated, shivering in the shadow of the towering oak, we looked around at the desperate place on which Elidyr had 'beached' us. Ten or so others of the Legion had survived the drowning and dragged themselves to where they could smell the fire.

We were camped, now, among the sad and rotting hulls of ships, some extending above the water, some broken on the banks or among the trees of the forest's edge. There were bones of men as well, and of animals, some of them grotesque, many of gigantic size. This whole place was a graveyard and the roots of the tree had reached to encompass the remnants.

And it was not just ships and creatures that had fallen foul of Mabon's prison. A city had once stood here. As the light grew brighter,

Kylhuk pointed to its gates, its turrets, its once-proud walls, all of them now absorbed into the gnarled, black bark of the tree, sucked upwards as the tree had grown, broken into its components, but still recognizable.

We had come ashore in the corrupted remains of its harbour. The bridge to the land was still visible, impressed within the high-arching roots that spanned the double flow of the river.

At the tree, the Long Person divided; or rather, her two branches, flowing below the roots, joined, forming the whirlpool, to continue through the land to a long-forgotten ocean.

'Are those the Gates?' I asked Kylhuk in a whisper, glancing back as he stood behind me. His hand was a gentle pressure on my shoulder, his breath sharp and stale after the dream dance.

'The Gates? Ivory and Horn? No. That isn't how the Cleverthreads wove them for me. But the two branches of the river have flowed through them.'

'Bringing the truth and the lie,' I repeated, remembering our earlier conversation. I could see no difference between the two branches of the river, and no sign on the huge arches of wood and stone that might distinguish their origins, 'Which comes from which?'

Kylhuk's hand gripped my flesh painfully and when I looked round at him again he was grinning at me, his eyes twinkling.

'Why, *Christian*! That's for *you* to find out!'

'Because I'm *slathan* . . . I should have known it.'

'By the rough love in Olwen's Hands, I'm sure you will succeed! I have that much confidence in you. Besides, you ate hardly alone. I selected your companions carefully. And I notice that we are all here, all but Abandagora, and you can replace him adequately.'

'The Forlorn Hope?'

'Tried and tested in the fire, like Annanawn, my father's sword. I despaired only once, when I truly thought they – and you – had been destroyed by Kyrdu's bastards. But my *slathan* surfaced in the wilderness, as my dream had told me he would, and brought them back. And here you all are. Not Forlorn. Not dead. But alive! Determined!'

I looked quickly around me, at the activity, the shelters being built, the boats of past adventurers being looted for fuel, crude shields being hacked and shaped, idols and propitiatory structures being erected. I could see Guiwenneth among them, and Someone scraping the whiskers from his cheeks with a small bronze dagger as he stared up at the tree and its glowing, running figures.

Kylhuk broke through my distraction. 'What's on your mind, Christian?'

'Only that I have no idea what you expect of me, or what I'm to do.'

'Your task is to find your mother. Isn't it? Isn't that why you came here?

I couldn't read him. His voice was gentle, his icy gaze almost soft. The smile through his beard was neither triumphant, nor sarcastic It might almost have been encouraging.

But I didn't trust him!

'I saw her dead and dancing by the neck,' I murmured, and Kylhuk reached out to squeeze my arm.

'You saw what you were told to see, Christian. You were just a boy at the time. Now you're a man. What you saw is in the past. This is the present. And tomorrow is the future.'

I would have laughed at the simplicity, but his eyes were alive with energy and triumph. 'In the future,' he went on, 'dreams remain undreamed! Don't you see, Christian? If a dream is *waiting* to be dreamed, we can choose to *shape* it. There were men and women on the boat of shields, and in my Legion, who do such things all the time, only they don't know how to use their skills to the best effect – which is why,' he added quietly, 'they're all so scrawny, scruffy and obsessed with wild, familiar spirits!'

I saw what I was told to see?

'What did you mean by that?' I asked Kylhuk, whose attention was beginning to wander as the need for raising defences became more urgent. 'What did you mean that I saw what I was told to see? *Who* told me? *What* did I see? Are you saying my mother didn't die?'

'Mabon will show you.' Then he laughed out loud, and added, 'Just as soon as we can tease him out of the tree! Relax, *slathan*. Something wonderful is about to happen to you.'

And he walked away, as cryptic as ever – he had never explained the full meaning of 'slathan' to me – as dismissive as ever, a man drawn to the task, this final task, the rescue of Mabon from his tree.

Odd, though, the way he had said, 'tease him out'.

As if, despite our best efforts, Mabon himself might be reluctant to come.

Twenty

Where was Eletherion in all of this; and his brothers, the other Sons of Kyrdu? The question was asked repeatedly of Kylhuk, who simply answered, 'I imagine they are close by.'

It was oddly circumspect behaviour for a man who had recently seemed so confident, so aware of things in the future. And I guessed, before Guiwenneth suggested the same thing to me, that his true talent for far-sight and that uncanny sense of all-knowing had come from the Dolorous Voice and the Cleverthreads, none of whom were with us now.

Perhaps Kylhuk was on his own for the first time in a long time, although he had his Forlorn Hope at his side, the small band he had nurtured and guarded with his warriors' lives. He had sent all other survivors from the boat back down the river to set up camp and wait for his call.

But Eletherion was on our minds, and despite Kylhuk's almost violent objection, now that we were down to seven, Someone and myself scouted into the forest for a mile or so, while Guiwenneth went back along the river with Issabeau and Jarag who, his body daubed with moss and lichen from the damp rocks, crept as far towards the first rise of the towering tree as he dared, sniffing the air and tasting great handfuls of river mud, river water and the earth from the higher bank.

Strange things were happening, I discovered later, but for the moment I only noted the oddities in behaviour. I had passed through several forest glades, taking the *sinister* side (as Issabeau called it) while Someone took the other, and was waiting for my companion in a shaft of welcome sunlight when a towering, upright boar ran at me from the edge of the glade, and through the edge of my vision.

I swung round to protect myself against the jutting tusks and gaping muzzle of the charging beast, and found the Proud Celt standing there, breathless and hot as he quickly dropped to his haunches, recovering from his run.

He looked up at me and smiled, then frowned as he saw my shocked expression.

'Is something wrong?'

'I don't know. You took me by surprise . . . Is something hunting you?'

'This forest is alive with ghosts. They are from the prison, I'm sure of it. Kylhuk warned me that we might encounter them.' He looked round nervously. 'I reel strange,' he went on. 'My skin itches. I want to scratch against the bark of a good old tree. I can smell things below the ground, and they're making me hungry! I suspect that Mabon has sent his own defences into the wilderness. Can you feel them around you too?'

I couldn't, but didn't say so. Instead I closed my eyes, breathed deeply, turned where I stood, trying to experience the presences that had alarmed my friend, wondering again whether Mabon was trapped or hiding, or both. When I opened my eyes I was startled by the brightness of the sun through the summer foliage. And as I turned away from the glaring light, the boar was rising beside me, leaning towards me!

Again I stepped back, looked directly at the beast and saw only Someone, son of the Defeated King, reaching towards me anxiously.

'You seem disturbed,' he whispered.

'I keep seeing the image of a wild boar. On its hindlegs. Very big, very menacing. But when I look at it, the boar vanishes . . .'

I decided to say no more than that, to leave Someone temporarily in the dark about the apparitions associated with his own welcome features.

The Celt tugged at his beard, pale eyes glowing with agreement. 'Yes! I sense it too. Mabon is certainly aware of us – legend has it that he hunts boar in the form of that same creature! – he is probably watching us. Come on, we must turn back. If Eletherion is here, he's biding his time!'

The sky was darkening towards night and the massive trunk burned with the faces and shapes of the lost. Guiwenneth and Issabeau stood with their arms around each other, staring up at the *mélange* of movement, occasionally crying out as they recognised some beast or a figure from their own legend, sometimes startled as a face formed and leered at them, a boyish physiognomy, with flaring fire as its hair and a mouth that grinned then went hard; this apparition was fleeting and very rare.

Standing naked between two torches, close to the first swell of root, his hair caked in mud and his body still plastered with moss, Jarag stared silently at the same blaze of masks. He had been like this for several hours, now, and Kylhuk sat close by, watching him, wrapped in a heavy cloak, sword across his lap, as motionless as the prehistoric man.

This was the second strangeness. Someone by now was very disturbed and very remote from me, standing by the edge of the river, staring back at the tree-line, a deep furrow between his eyes.

I picked a little food from the spit over the dying fire and huddled down between the spread roots of a thicket, only to move quickly away as the roots kicked at me. It was Elidyr, disguised and silent, and he glowered at me from the foliage.

'Go away.'

'Sorry. Didn't see you there.'

I crawled to a less intrusive haven. But even here I was suddenly prodded in the back, which startled me so that I choked on my first mouthful of supper. Turning, I saw that Gwyr was sitting behind me, swathed in a horse blanket he had rescued from the river. He grinned at me through his trimmed beard.

'What are you doing here?' I asked him.

'Keeping out of the way. Elidyr is lurking in the woods and I don't like the way he looks at me.'

'Elidyr is ten feet away,' I whispered, cocking my head to the left. Gwyr glanced nervously into the gloom, then scowled and turned back to contemplate Someone, by the river.

'What's he doing?' asked. 'Do you have any idea?'

Someone was standing with his back to the river, ankle deep in the wiry grass that grew from the muddy edge. He was in trousers, bronze cuirass strapped to his breast, a gleaming torque around his neck, arms folded. His eyes were open. Issabeau, in her catskin cloak, her hair tied in a flowing ponytail, stood near to him, watching him carefully, but not moving.

'We have always looked after each other,' Gwyr said. 'Now more than ever we must be aware of what is happening in our group. Issabeau is guarding Someone. Kylhuk guards Jarag. You must pay attention to Guiwenneth.'

'Who guards *you*?'

He laughed forlornly. 'My task is almost done, if not done completely.'

'Interpreting.'

'Certainly. And keeping my eyes open. Once the Oldest Animals have
been summoned, if the jarag can speak to them, then all I'll be good for
is to fight against the Sons of Kyrdu, if they've survived the maelstrom,
if they're still around.'

The way Gwyr spoke confirmed that everything was happening
according to a plan of Kylhuk's devising. His own role was almost
finished. Someone and Jarag seemed to be coming into their own.
Issabeau and Guiwenneth were still behaving in an ordinary way, as
was I.

'But what does Kylhuk intend for me?' I breathed the words, watching the huddled man as he gazed steadily at the naked shaman.

I hadn't expected. Gwyr to hear me, but he whispered, 'Be on your
guard. From everything I see and hear, you are the key to Mabon,
though I don't know how.'

The same words, more or less, that he had spoken to me many
months ago, when we had first ridden through the wildwood together.

'Look. He's here!'

Gwyr's words directed me to Someone. A dark shadow flickered
around the tall Celt. The man's face dissolved into an evil muzzle,
torchlight on jutting tusks and a raised spine of quill-like grey hairs
on his head. The face of the boar was fleeting. The man wailed and
writhed where he stood, eyes bulging. Again the boar inhabited him, its
pizzle curling from the poor man's groin, lashing like a coiled whip.
Then gone again.

Issabeau was clapping her hands delightedly. Kylhuk was standing,
tensed and ready for something. The jarag was racing back and forth
along the river's edge, stooping, grabbing, touching and reaching his
face to the heavens to howl or bark.

'What the *hell* is going on?'

Gwyr said, 'Kylhuk said this would happen. Mabon has been nosing
for us, sniffing us out, testing us. But for some reason he can't fathom
Someone. The Celt has upset him. Kylhuk knew this in advance, but I
have no idea why it should be.'

I did, though.

And I told Gwyr, 'It's part of his *geisa* . . . or one of his *geisas*. I'd
never heard of *geisas* until I met your forlorn band.'

'A geisa?'

'Yes. He can confuse sorcerers until his true name is known.'

That particular talent, though, was not from Someone's own story but from the mediaeval romance of Issabeau and the Sea-Cave Boy.

'Having been unnamed before his royal father was killed,' I hazarded, 'when he is close to a sorcerer he must make himself available for their inspection, though he will confuse them in the process.'

Gwyr nodded as if everything was now clear. 'That sounds right. It's very much the sort of imposition that would be placed around the neck of a king under the circumstances you mention, being unnamed at the time of his father's death. It had never occurred to me before now that Someone, with his wild hair, is invisible to sorcerers. How useful . . . How very useful.'

So Kylhuk had used the Celt to draw Mabon, son of the Mother, to the edge of his prison stronghold, where he had reached out to probe and peruse the Forlorn Hope and found a man he couldn't recognise or fathom, inhabiting the Celt in his boar-shape as he tried to break the man's identity, failing in the task but revealing himself.

Mabon was both prisoner and ruler of his domain.

From everything that was happening by the river, both Gwyr and I agreed that Mabon's stronghold was weakened and vulnerable, and that we would soon be passing from the wildwood into the shouldering Tree of Faces, closer to the enigmatic hunter who was the object of our quest.

I *needed* to know what would be expected of me!

But before I could articulate this sudden, angry thought to Gwyr, Kylhuk had shouted, '*Slathan*! Show yourself. Now! They are rising all around us!'

'The Oldest Animals!' Gwyr gasped beside me, his face a mask of astonishment and admiration. 'By the Cauldron's Depths, the man has done it!'

'*Slathan*! Gwyr! Show now!'

Kylhuk was storming towards the forest's edge, great cloak flowing. He stopped when he saw us emerge from cover, waved us to him angrily. Someone and Issabeau were arm in arm, mutually enveloped in the faint phosphorescence that outlined the uneasy giant boar, Mabon's ghostly presence at the events now unfolding.

The jarag was walking backwards in a circle, eyes wide, mouth gaping, his beard and breast wet with the saliva that seemed to pour

from his mouth. Suddenly he wiped his chin, stopped the ↑
movement and grabbed for a torch, holding it above his h↑
peering at the river.

Beyond him, the vast, over leaning tree glowed more brightly, an↑
movement and action of creatures seemed to be drawn towards us, as if
we were the focus of that great stampede.

Kylhuk smacked me around the back of the head, impelled me before
him, dragging Gwyr by the arm until we were within scenting-distance
of the overripe shaman.

'They are rising around us,' Kylhuk said. 'The Oldest Animals. Jarag
has performed his task better than I could have hoped. When they turn
and run – the creatures – we must follow them. They will take us into
the land beyond these roots, and Mabon won't have time to flee.'

His grip on my shoulder tightened suddenly. 'There!' he whispered,
pointing to where the surface of the whirlpool was bulging as a silvery
shape rose through the water, a man-fish, a leering salmon!

'Clinclaw!' Gwyr muttered, then urged, 'And there!'

The turf close to the forest had swollen into the shape of a giant man-
like figure, resting on his back.

In the greenwood itself, the trees were arching and twisting, as if
being pushed apart by an unseen force. Feathers began to swirl and rise
on the breeze. An owl's face watched us from the darkness.

'Cawloyd . . .' Gwyr whispered. 'That's how the owl is known in my
country, but it will have an older name which Jarag has used.'

The swelling turf opened and the man stood, as tall as Elidyr, if not
taller. His face was a hound's muzzle below the broken, jagged stubs of
antlers. His body was clothed in the limp forms of pine-martens, rats,
weasels and stoats, all the vermin of the forest, attached to his body by
their teeth, clothing him in corpses.

This one was called Rhedinfayre, oldest stag, according to Gwyr.

From the river, the fish-headed man stepped to the shore, pike and
perch and carp and eels thrashing from his skin, where they hung by
their tiny, bony teeth.

And the owl too was clothed in the fluttering bodies of birds: ravens,
robins, iridescent kingfishers and the single, massive shape of an eagle,
its beak hooked through the ligaments of the man's neck, hanging
across his belly, wings stretched, like a living golden breastplate.

I was so enthralled by these monstrous visions that I failed to see
what was happening to the Mesolithic hunter-shaman, the naked jarag
whose forgotten talents had summoned these ancient echoes. He was

crouched on the ground between his three remaining torches, incontinent, terrified, shuddering with a fever of fear.

Kylhuk leaned over him quickly and ran a powerful hand down his back, then touched his neck and lank hair. Jarag looked up. I was shocked to see the skull leering from his face. Corpse-like, emptied, he lay quietly down on his side and Kylhuk spread his cloak across him, covering the ghoulish features.

'That is that, then,' said Gwyr.

'*Slathan*! Stay close!' Kylhuk bellowed. Good God, was that a sob in his voice? For all that the jarag had kept his own, strange counsel, was this inheritor of quests distressed at the dying of the primitive man?

'*Slathan*, he stay close,' I muttered archly. The Tree of Faces flared, the flow of movement represented by the glowing shapes in the bark quickening slightly, and the sudden light made the Oldest Animals seem starker as they stood in wood, on earth, by water.

Then the boar stalked past me, glaring at me, and when I met its gaze I saw my friend Someone. He stared at me inquisitively, head cocked, mouth working strangely. I turned away from him and the black pig was there around him, Mabon surveying the events from his attachment to the unfathomable Celt.

Someone stared at me, but his eyes were not his own. And those eyes were curious about me.

He asked, 'What do you seek.'

Gwyr nudged me meaningfully and I answered, 'My mother. I seek my mother.'

'How did she die?' Mabon asked through the lips of my companion.

'She took her own life. On a tree.'

'What is served by finding her?'

What was served by finding her? What did *that* mean? I stood and stared blankly.

Gwyr nudged me again and I pushed him away angrily. I didn't answer. I didn't know *how* to answer.

Someone stalked away.

But then a vague memory of a story came back to me, of Arthur and his knights and their Grail quest. I remembered my mother leaning down towards me as I snuggled below the blankets, my mind alive with those castles and gleaming knights.

'The *truth*,' I called to him. 'The *truth* is served by finding her.'

That was when the cat leapt from the river!

Sleek, lean, a blur of movement, the grey-furred feline snatched at one of the fish hanging from the body of Clinclaw, then crossed the bank to tear and snarl at the dangling form of an otter on Rhedinfayre's chest. But it was the eagle that was her target. As the owl-faced Cawloyd raised its arms defensively, the cat was on the eagle, chewing at the great bird's feathered neck.

The eagle released the owl and bird and beast rolled in a blur of feathers and angry movement, their harsh, hoarse cries and wails deafening as they struggled for supremacy.

Then the eagle took flight, a slow beat of massive wings, a slow rise, the cat held in its claws, still screeching and twisting. The eagle seemed to have doubled in size, the cat to have shrunk. It flew across the root of the tree, across the river and to the far shore. The salmon-faced man had returned to the river and his silver form could be seen swimming the edge of the whirlpool. The owl, and the dog-stag were running away from us, following the eagle.

'Come on!' Kylhuk cried. In his kilt and breastplate, with little else to cover him, he was in close pursuit of these oddities from the past.

Gwyr was running, Someone too – free of Mabon now, I imagined – and I could see Guiwenneth, spears in hand, head low, red hair streaming behind her as she faced towards the tree, having established with a quick glance that I was behind her.

Where was Issabeau?

I passed the covered body of the jarag in his half-circle of torches. I looked back along the river. And then I realised that she was the cat who had attacked the eagle.

We were running along the root of a tree that loomed immense and alive with fire above us, its branches reaching out to cover the sky. The trunk leaned away into the heavens, but the roots were formed from the broken stones of a city, and soon, as the river dropped further below us, I saw we were passing through a place of broken, petrified wood, and crumbling wood-cracked stone. Twisted iron gates, crushed wooden doors, echoing shafts and tunnels besieged the senses as Kylhuk led us in the heated pursuit of the eagle and the flowing, ghostly animal forms of the fish, the dog, the stag and the owl. Like spectres, their shapes shifting between the myriad forms of the creatures they comprised, they flowed ahead of us, returning to the security of the stronghold.

Kylhuk was a barking, baying hound at their heels, his laughter and his anger sounding in equal measure, and time and again I heard him demand that his slathan keep close to him.

In all of this, I would never have known which passage into the tree to take. The entrance was disguised not by subtlety but by quantity. We had crossed the river. Our world was the world of grey stone, fractured pillar and twisted wood, a labyrinth of alleys, paths and shafts that boomed with sound as we traversed them.

The eagle dropped the cat!

The cat snarled, arched up into human form, Issabeau naked and slick with sweat, padding quickly in pursuit of the giant bird of prey, then standing and pointing to the arch of marble, ivory and horn through which the bird had flown and into which the writhing shapes of the Owl of Cawloyd and the Stag of Rhedinfayre were passing.

The salmon, Clinclaw, was in the river, finding its own way home, no doubt through the maelstrom.

'Quickly! Quickly!' Guiwenneth called to me as she followed Kylhuk and the wary Someone through the entrance. I exchanged a nervous glance with Gwyr.

'You don't have to come,' I suggested.

'He hasn't told me to go back. And with Jarag dead . . . if these Oldest Animals need to be understood . . . who else is there but me?'

'You are too noble, Gwyr.'

'No, Christian,' he retorted with a grin. 'I am long lost!'

'Look after yourself.'

His sudden look at me was full of pain. 'I tried. But you should have found me sooner.'

'SLATHAN!'

Kylhuk was framed in the arch, bronze-bladed sword in hand and thrusting towards me, then used to wave to me, to *summon* me to him and, as if ropes were attached to the point of that sword and to my legs, I ran to where he waited. I entered the gate, Gwyr on my heels, Guiwenneth a sudden presence in my arms, her face radiant with the glow of this inner realm, a light that emanated from the ten towering statues that stood in a semi-circle about us, watching us with strange, stone faces.

'I have heard of these ten,' Kylhuk whispered in my ear. His blade was bright as he wove a pattern between the watching figures. 'You can see the fish, the hound, the bird of prey . . . their names come back to me: Silvering! Cunhaval! Falkenna! That is the Child in the Land, *Sinisalo*. That one is the shadow of forgotten forests. *Skogen*. Beware of it! And that's the shape of memory, the storyteller: *Gaberlungi*. And that one's old mother, and young mother . . . I can't remember what

they're called. And the face of death, *Morndun*. And of grief . . . look
at them . . . Look at them, Christian!'

I looked without understanding at these crude stone carvings, blank-
faced masks hacked out of the hard grey stone.

I listened without understanding as Gwyr whispered the strange
names himself, the names of these stone guardians:

'Skogen, Gaberlungi, Sinisalo, Morndun . . .'

'What are they, Gwyr?'

'The Oldest Animals. The oldest memories . . . I've heard of them all
my life. They mark the way to the realm of *Lavondyss*, the unknown
land, the beginning of the Labyrinth. It's a place of mystery. The
unknowable, forgotten past. These are one way inwards. They have
often been sought. Never found!'

He was almost breathless with awe.

But we were here, we had followed them to where Mabon was
imprisoned, and we *had* found them. Some reckless impulse in me
made me smile and think aloud that they could not hurt us now.

'We'll find out soon enough,' was Gwyr's wise and whispered
counsel.

Kylhuk turned to me. 'Look more closely. What do you see?'

Between the stone pillars he had called Cunhaval, the hound, and
Morndun, death, and between Gaberlungi and Sinisalo, memory and
the child in the land, I could see a cornfield, summer trees on the ridge,
blue sky. I suddenly realised I was looking at the field behind Oak
Lodge, the place of my mother's death!

'It's my home,' I whispered.

'One of them only,' Kylhuk said thoughtfully. 'One is the true dream
of that place, one a false dream. Look carefully, *slathan*. Everything
now depends on your making the right choice. These are those gates,
those Ivory and Horn gates, that test and torment us all. Which one
seems to speak most honestly to you?'

I was looking at the place of my mother's passing. Morndun, then?
Death? But I was looking too at a *memory* of that passing. So should I
choose the gate by Gaberlungi? For a moment I couldn't decide. I felt
like a child, confused and dismayed in the shadow of these towering
effigies.

And as I experienced that instant of fear, so Sinisalo – the child in
the land – drew my gaze, and the crude though gentle features calmed
me.

And at once – I'm not certain whether by intuition or instruction – I opted for the passage to the Underworld which passed between this child and the etched stone face of 'memory'.

Kylhuk grunted when I told him of my decision, then turned to Gwyr and prodded him in the chest.

'Go back if you wish. You've done enough.'

'I'll stay, if it's all the same to you,' replied the interpreter nervously.

'Don't move from this place, then. I'll make you my marker. You'll mark the way out when this business is done!'

'Take my cloak,' said Gwyr. 'You look cold.'

He removed his short woollen cloak and passed it to Kylhuk, whose flesh was pale with the chill in the air. Kylhuk accepted gladly and covered his shoulders and arms with the garment.

'When you pass this ring of totems, through the gate which we hope is Truth,' he said to Guiwenneth, 'you must remember that childhood ride you made, out of the wood, when you reached the end of the world, with the *slathan*, here. When he was a boy. Mabon will remember too. That's how we draw him out.'

'I remember the ride,' Guiwenneth said. 'Manandoun was my guardian at the time.'

'Indeed. He was an angry man that day. You rode too far. You did more than you were told.'

Guiwenneth glanced at me awkwardly. Without taking her eyes from me, she said, 'But I *did* the deed I was told to do. I obeyed your instructions. And I fell in love with the boy.'

'I'd noticed,' Kylhuk said. 'A little love will help. Everything now depends on Mabon himself. Remember that childhood ride. He will *catch on to it*. That's how we will draw him out, though that's all I can tell you. It was the last third of the tapestry . . .' he opened his hand to reveal a crushed piece of embroidered cloth. It fell away to dust as he held it. 'My life has been informed by a few threads of silk,' he said with a wry smile. 'But nothing lasts. Not even a promise. Go and find Mabon! Go!'

Twenty-One

It was that same summer's day, the fields of barley flowing in the warm breeze, the edge of the wood a dark, brooding wall. I had run here, on my way back from Shadoxhurst. I had used a stick to strike at thistles. I had jumped the brook, then heard something in the wood. For a while I had stood and stared at the trees and just as I turned for home, the girl had come, cantering suddenly towards me.

I was here again, a man in a boy's body, and I turned where I stood and stared at the sky with its drifting, summer cloud. My hands felt small, my face smooth, my ribs prominent. I laughed and explored this memory of my early youth. The scents of summer were strong.

Distantly, the clock on the church tower was chiming three.

Where was she? Where was the girl? From the wood again . . .

A flurry of wings drew my attention back to Ryhope. An owl was looping in the bright air, then a hawk, then a blackbird. A tall, red-brown flank moved through the underbrush, a stag edging too close to the open space. I heard a growl and a grunt, then the soft complaint of a horse being kicked forward, and a moment later she rode out of the wood, just as I remembered her.

She cantered towards me, white hair flowing, white mask solemn. The crop she held was trailing by her left leg. Her short tunic seemed simply draped on her, this girl child, coming towards me.

There was that same hint of boyishness, that same tension in limb and posture.

Suddenly she kicked the horse into a gallop, charged down on me, struck me gently with the feathered crop, laughed – a deeper laugh than I remembered – turned and came back, haughty in the saddle, peering down through the uncracked layer of white paint.

'Is this how it was?' a boy's voice asked. 'Do you remember her like this?'

'Who are you?'

'Who do you think I am?'

'Mabon?'

'Of course Mabon! Some people take on the shapes of animals. I take on the shapes of people! Through their memories,' he added. 'Climb up behind me, I want to remember the girl rider.'

He reached down, grabbed my arm and hauled me onto the broad back of the grey. He yelled out loud, kicked the animal, and we rode into the barleyfield, but it was no thin, soft girl that I held onto, now, but a hard-muscled man-boy. His breath was not sweet like Guiwenneth's, but sour and stale. Aged! His back, below the silly tunic, was covered with greying hair. He was so much older than his white mask made him seem. He laughed boyishly, though, as the grey stumbled and struggled through the tall corn.

'Was it here?' he shouted suddenly.

I didn't know what he meant, but he suddenly reined in, threw the horse to the side, sent me tumbling, went sprawling himself.

He stood and turned in the barley, striking the ripening heads with his hands. 'Yes, it was here that she fell. I can feel it. Where is the tree? Come on! I want to see the tree.'

Again he mounted the tired horse. Again he hauled me up behind him. He galloped to Strong Against the Storm, staring up at the dark branches, the rich green leaves.

'What a tree!' he whispered. 'Yes! A good place to die. A very good place to die.'

Then with a shout, 'But she isn't dead yet! Her death is still days away! Where is she?'

'My mother?'

'Of course your mother! Where is she? I want to see her.'

'In the house, I expect.'

'Show me!'

I pointed to Oak Lodge and he thrashed the flank of the grey and we galloped round the wood and over the fence, to ride right up to the windows of my father's study.

I had thought Mabon would stop there and dismount, but he kicked the animal viciously and the horse smashed through the windows. Mabon rode us twice around the empty room, hitting the cabinets with his crop.

'What's this?'

'His specimens. My father's specimens.'

'Is this where he worked?'

'Yes.'

He rode into the hall, through the parlour and into the kitchen, striking the metal pans hanging on the wall, sweeping the storage jars from their shelves.

'What's this?'

'The kitchen.'

'Did she work here?'

'My mother? Yes. She did the cooking for the family.'

'Why isn't she here?'

'I don't know. Perhaps she's gone to one of the villages.'

'She should be here.' He beat his crop against the pans, drumming on them and delighting in the various tinny sounds.

Then back through the parlour and stumbling up the stairs. The horse bucked and whinnied, but Mabon thrashed it. On the landing he paused, leaned forward over the grey's nape, looked at the doors, then made the animal kick into Steven's bedroom.

My brother lay fast asleep and Mabon rode round the bed, peering down at him, flicking the feathered crop at the face in repose.

'Who's this?'

'My brother. Steven.'

Mabon peered at him closely. 'His sleep is charmed.'

Yes, I thought. It is! But this was Steven several years after the time when young Guiwenneth had come from the wood, years after our mother's death. This was an image from later in our lives. I was confused, hanging on with one hand to the restless man-boy, nervous in anticipation of the next wild move or gallop. It would not have surprised me if Mabon had leapt the grey out of the window, a long drop to the garden below.

Had I chosen the gate correctly? Had I sent Guiwenneth – had I followed Guiwenneth – through the *Ivory Gate*, into the land of lies? Confusion tormented me, and yet . . . And yet this seemed *right*. From the moment I had smelled the field of barley, and the summer air, I had felt that this *was* the same place that I had once inhabited.

Mabon said, 'Stop talking.'

'I'm not talking.'

'You are! You are talking incessantly. *Is it true, is it real, is it a lie?*' His voice mocked me. 'My head is hurting with your doubts. All that matters is that we see the truth of her death.'

'My mother's death?'

'If you know of another death, I'd like to see that too. But yes. Of course! Your mother's death. Where is she?'

I tried to remember what had happened that day of Guiwenneth's wild ride. Had my mother stayed away overnight? Where had Huxley been? Steven had been away at school. This strangely isolated image from my past had so much that was true and so much that was false.

At last I remembered that my mother had spent the evening staring at the fire, the unnecessary fire that she had laid and maintained during the warm summer's night. But though the wood in the fireplace was newly set, there was no sign of her at all.

We had come through the wrong gate.

'Not at all,' Mabon whispered as he rode the horse back through the kitchen and out into the late afternoon, blinking against the light, staring at the silent wood.

There was no food in the house. In the evening, Mabon walked outside, whistled into the dusk sky, and a while later his eagle flew in with a chicken clutched in its claws. Mabon took the dead creature, stripped some feathers, sniffed the flesh disapprovingly – 'Smells young. No blood!' – then went into the kitchen, clattering among the pots and pans, running cold water from the tap, laughing and complaining, delighting in the long, sulphur-tipped matches, which he called 'fire sticks', finally boiling the stripped and gutted fowl, which we ate with our fingers after dark.

My mother did not return.

While the chicken was still boiling, however, the man-boy walked with me to the woodland's edge.

'I'm glad you brought me here,' he said. 'I like your house. I like the warmth in the rooms. I like the fire sticks, I like the iron pans, I like the way it is clean and orderly. I like this dry garden, that gentle field of yellow grass. I like the strong trees, the way they stand alone in the fields, like watching giants. This is a strange yet lovely place in which you live.'

'I never thought so myself. It always seemed very empty.'

'But what made it seem empty? Did you ever ask yourself that?'

'No.'

'Was it the land? Or was it the father? It certainly wasn't the mother.'

'No. It wasn't my mother. It felt very lonely in the house at times.'

'Because a father was missing!'

'Yes. Because a father was missing.'

'In the forest.'

'You know a lot about me, Mabon . . .'

He grinned through his white mask, which was beginning to crack, revealing the older face below. Every hour, the youthful and female look of his disguise was degrading into a harsher, ageing masculinity. 'I know nothing about you at all, Christian. That's why I'm here. Feeding from your dreams! I want to see for myself. I don't need to know you to know that your father was as distant as that cloud up there. I don't need to know you to know that you loved your mother to the point of fury with your father. I don't need to know you to know that you love Guiwenneth, whose shape I took, though I've shed it now, I prefer my own body to a woman's and especially to a girl's. I know you for the man you are, though you look like a boy. But I know that you did something in your boyhood that you cannot face. I did something in my boyhood that I cannot face.'

'What was that? What did you do?'

He laughed. 'If I knew that, there would be no point in all of this!'

I couldn't help smiling at this admonition, since it reflected Issabeau's words, from her own account of her story with the Sea-Cave Boy, the lad who had asked her the secret that kept her in the glade: *if I knew that, it wouldn't be a secret . . .*

This place was neither real nor false; it had echoes of many memories, and from what I had seen, the memories were accurate. I felt as if I had come home, but this was not my home at all, and Mabon was a visitor, creating the familiar landscape around us in order to explore my own childhood.

And yet, knowing that the place was both real and unreal did not discomfit me. Perhaps if I had passed through the Ivory Gate, there would have been terrors and nightmares gnawing at my consciousness as I surveyed this Dreaming Land. Here, though, there was familiarity, peace, and an impending sense of discovery.

Full of fowl, thirst quenched with strong tea, which Mabon also enjoyed, I lit the fire and waited for my mother, staring at the flames as they consumed the wood, feeling the sweat run from my skin in the stifling room. Mabon watched me from the corner, curious, quiet.

'Your father is here,' he whispered suddenly, and when I looked up he was holding out a hand to me. He smiled, then put a finger to his lips. He looked so odd, in his short tunic, his hair lank and white with lime, his face like a cracked, Japanese mask.

I followed him to the study. Huxley was hunched over the desk, writing furiously in his journal. He looked up as we entered, frowned, changed his spectacles from the horn-rimmed reading pair to the slightly larger, horn-rimmed lenses that he used to see into the distance, stared at me and stared right *through* me, then rose and walked to the shattered windows, his hands behind his back. He peered at Ryhope Wood for a long minute, then came back to his desk; changed glasses again; picked up his pen and continued to write.

I couldn't get over how *young* my father looked. His hair was full and dark, shaved smartly above his ears, parted precisely on the left side of his crown, hair-cream reflecting the light from his desk lamp. There were no lines, no shadows on his skin. His mouth was pink and youthful. He was enveloped in a cocoon of inspiration and enthusiasm. This was my father as he must have been when he first realised that he had discovered something wonderful, literally in his own back garden.

I saw him now through Mabon's eyes. Mabon and I were two ghosts, haunting the scientist as he recorded his latest insights, his most recent observations.

What date, I wondered, what day, what year was this? I peered more closely at the tight, neat writing.

. . . from the wood again.

I must keep calm. I must maintain control over the physical and mental environment. I have seen these creatures in the flesh, the forms of the Green Jack, of the Hoods and Arthur, Hereward, Finn, Tam Lyn, Tom Rhymer – all the brutal, stinking forms that have come down to us as heroes. I can smell the woman. She is around me always. She is watching me. Why? I cannot answer the question, but I know this: these myth images are watching me, and are curious about me, with the same intensity that I watch them and am curious for my own part. Here we are, at the edge of two worlds. My careful curiosity drives me to question their past. Their own curiosity drives them to question their present. And I must fight against the arrogant assumption that I am superior . . .

They haunt me every second of the day. They are here, watching me. I can glimpse them from the edge of vision, and because my mind is frail in its way, I think I see my son Christian; and the girl, of course. The girl from the wood.

Like laughing clowns, they crowd down on me and peer at my scrawl.
GET AWAY!

But why should I write that? I *welcome* these hauntings. My life depends upon them! I have not yet found the way into Ryhope Wood, the way deep. Perhaps these ghastly reflections at the edge of vision will harden into the true ghosts they are, and take me by the hand, and guide me gently into a place I wish to know so well, and which I do not know at all – I am an Outsider in my own life. I long to be inside the world of *Mythago Wood*!

I whispered to him, 'My son Christian is a sensible boy. He will "guard the fort" . . .'

My father wrote the line.

Mabon whispered, 'There is a beast that is at the heart of the world.'

There is a beast . . . at heart of the world . . . Huxley wrote, and I caught my breath.

'Shall we call it Urscumug? Call it Urscumug!' mocked the white-faced Mabon.

I call it Urscumug. Man-like, but with the tusked features of a boar. Ancient and forgotten, now. It is the first hero . . .

'Oh this is good, this is good,' said Mabon with a laugh, clapping his hands together across the hunched form of the young man, my father, that young-old man.

'What are you doing?' I asked. 'This isn't real. My father's discoveries were his own. We weren't here then, all those years ago, haunting him.'

'We are here now, haunting him,' Mabon whispered through Guiwenneth's crack-faced features.

'But we are not in the past. This is just a play on the past!'

'Really? Are you sure? Breathe on his neck. Go on. Breathe on his neck. He will feel that breath!'

'I know he will. Look at his writing!'

Huxley had written:

. . . they are near me. I feel their breath on my neck. They are watching. This is wonderful! I have no rational way of explaining it. It is as if inspiration is falling from a bright, yet unseen sky. I document not my own experience, but the whispered fears and fantasies of men and women long dead, heroes, heroines, the forgotten folk of time who have been waiting to express their hearts and their stories to someone, anyone who would listen. This wood, this wonderful, ancient forest, has waited in time for a moment when someone . . . someone like me – some man, some woman, some entity would sit quietly at its edge and hear its whispered tales of terror, of beauty and of great deeds performed in great times when there was no man, no woman, to remember that moment.

George Huxley is here, though. I am here! Whisper all you want, I will deny you nothing. Just tell me the names. Tell me the names of those ancient heroes . . . Urscumug? What in God's name is that? But I will write it down. I will remember it.

'Just a piece of invention,' mocked Mabon over the frantic, possessed figure of my father. 'Do you hear me? Just a piece of fancy. A piece of unreality. A little tale from the Ivory Gate.'

The ghostly whisper was confusing my father.

I raged at Mabon: 'You said we had come through the Horn Gate. The "true" gate.'

'We have. I'm teasing this fool! I know those gates well, in all their forms, and I have learned how to draw a little sustenance from each of them!'

'Was my father's work a lie, then? Were you here, years ago? Have you made his obsession into something that is false?'

'If only I had that power!' Mabon said. 'Alas! Only in our lives can we turn something true into something that is a lie. It's a human failing; and it is also a human strength. If Huxley did that to himself . . . if he created his own lies, his own visions in this place . . . then there was a reason for it. And that reason has nothing to do with my own interference, now *or* in the past.'

'Unless you are lying about it,' I whispered, and Mabon grinned boyishly from his ancient mask.

'We create stories to illuminate truth. We create lies to hide pain. Don't we?'

'Stories to illuminate truth? I would think so. Yes, Fables. Yes.'

'And don't we create lies to hide pain? The truth in *masquerade*?'

'Yes. I'm sure we do. But I can't think about this for the moment. Go away for a while, Mabon. I want to be alone with this dream.'

Like Puck making his exit from the glade, Mabon's light winked out.

I stared down at my young father and after a while he looked up at me, his focus not quite on my eyes.

'I've found her,' I said. 'And I've found love. I don't *care* from whose mind she came. We love each other. I'll never let her go! I know you loved her too. And I know you are looking for her still. But if you can hear me . . . if you can hear these words . . . stop looking for

Guiwenneth. You can never find her, not as *I* have found her. She will never love you, because you can't create the love you need!'

Huxley smiled at me, or seemed to; and a moment later bent to his journal, writing in an impassioned scrawl.

I half dozed, half dreamed in front of the roaring log fire, the sweat running from my body, hot on my chest, cooling on my back. The flames seemed to lick out of the wood, curling like mocking tongues about me. I shivered in that heat. There was movement around me, the murmuring drone of voices, the dull clatter of crockery. Touches on my shoulder . . .

Whispers in my ear.

But I half dozed, half dreamed, and I dreamed of my mother. Is this how she had felt, those last nights of agony before she had walked to the solitary oak and calmly, calculatedly hanged herself?

There was a crashing of glass, and a sonorous, moaning sound that might have been music on a gramophone slowing to a stop. I looked up at the clock, but the glass face was steamed up, time invisible behind the condensation. I rose and walked unsteadily to the study, stood in the doorway for a moment staring out at the night, and at the shapes that moved around the room.

I was beckoned to the desk and stood with my legs against the mahogany edge. The smells of the night mingled with the smell of the leather covering on the desk, where Huxley had written away his life and mind. I dreamed I was my mother for a moment . . .

An old woman in garish clothes, layer upon layer of skirts, a shawl above a shawl, the glitter of metal on her ears and nose, grey hair hanging in ringlets, walked up to me and whispered something in my ear.

The words were incomprehensible, but my blood turned cold, my heart began to face, my head filled with terror!

And a voice whispered, 'Is this how it was? Is this how it happened? Or should I say – is this how it *will* happen?'

Daylight flooded the room. I stepped into the garden, walked around the house to the yard, with its chicken huts and sheds. The wood was ablaze. Steven stood there, with Guiwenneth! And another man, staring at the fire, the forest fire, frozen in their movements as if statues, though their hair moved and the woman's dress flowed slowly with the heat.

I stood behind them, dreaming, a dream that made no sense, seeing events that were meaningless to me, though the way my body reacted, surged with fear, brought them horribly alive.

Golden shapes tumbled from the fire, hawk-faces on running bodies. Horses came through, and tall, dark men.

An arrow struck the stranger who was my brother's companion, sent him tumbling towards me, clutching at the shaft that had entered his chest. His face was marked, as if burned; he was in agony as he died.

Rough men struck Guiwenneth, bundled her over the back of a horse, led her away. An ageing, scarred man flung a rope around my brother's neck, pushed him against the shed, kissed his lips, then walked away. And a man I recognised – the Fenlander! – pulled the rope tight over the roof of the shed so that Steven hung there, limp and strangled. The fire consumed the figures again, but the ageing man looked back for an instant, blew a kiss, and through the beard that covered his face I recognised someone I knew.

I had seen myself!

I had seen myself through my mother's eyes.

I had seen her eldest son kill her youngest son. Myself killing my brother Steven!

And Mabon whispered again, 'Is this how it will be? Is this what must happen?'

She was running through the tall barley. I followed as fast as I could, calling for my mother, but she ran so fast, in her best suit, with the blood from her eyes splattering on the ripening ears and broken stalks. I called to her but she seemed not to hear. She ran to the solitary oak and wept for a few seconds, then saw me coming, tried to fling the rope across the bough but her throw wasn't strong enough, even though the branch was within jumping distance of her outstretched hands.

By the time I had reached her, though, she had secured the noose loosely around her neck and stood there watching me, tearful and blood-stained, sobbing as she swayed on her feet.

'What are you doing?' I screamed at her, but she shouted back at me.

'Go away, Chris. You can't help me – only yourself!'

She looked up and again flung the rope across the branch, and this time it curled over the bark and draped back down. I stood in terror, staring at the half-hunched shape of my mother as she racked with tears, blood on her shoes, her breast red with blood, her pearl earrings catching the light as she held the free end of the rope, as if still reluctant to complete the act she had planned.

'I don't understand what you're doing!' I wailed at her.

'Nor do I,' she said through her tears, her head shaking, her arms around her body as if she was cold. 'But I am in such pain, now. I must end the pain. I must start a new life, somewhere away from all of you, *all* of you!'

She was still not on the tree.

'I love you!' I shouted at her, and she cried and wailed more loudly, staring at me through a face that was crushed with grief and fear and tears.

'I love you too, Chris,' she managed to say, her voice small with despair. 'My little boy . . . oh my lovely little boy . . . how could you become such a thing – such a terrible thing . . . how could you kill him?'

I ran to her, put my arms around her, but she pushed me back as if frightened of me.

'What are you doing?' I shouted, terrified at the rejection. 'What have I done?'

'Nothing . . . You've done nothing . . . Not yet, not yet! You're too young. But it will turn out so badly for you. I have seen it. I have seen what you'll become. I can't bear it – I can't bear the pain—'

It hasn't happened, I wanted to scream at her! That fat, scarred man killing Steven wasn't me! I'm just a boy. The old woman lied to you. And if it wasn't a lie, it was nothing more than a prediction! She was giving you a prediction only. You can act to stop the dream from coming true!

What I said was, 'Don't believe what that old woman said to you. What did she say to you? Don't believe it!'

'You are your father's son. I had dreamed what she said already. It was already pain in my life.'

'I've done nothing! Nothing you think I've done ever needs to be done! Don't die. Mummy!'

'My sons are gone. My poor boys. My poor little boys.'

'I'm here! I love you!'

'Both of them . . . gone. I've seen their going. I've raised a *devil* and a *hanged man*.'

It hadn't happened like this. These were 'almost' words. They were 'not quite right' words. I didn't remember it like this at all. This day was no longer mine!

And behind me Mabon whispered, 'It was like this. And this day *is* yours, though you remember it with a different voice. You've come this far, now see it through. We always remember *part* of the truth. We always *forget* a part in equal measure. This is how it was, Chris. See what happens next! Face the truth. And *then*—' he laughed in my ear. 'And then I might let you have her back from the dead.'

'My mother? You can do that?'

'No. *You* can do it But to bring her back, first she has to die!'

I turned to look at Mabon and cried out with shock.

It was my father who stood there, but he was so dishevelled, so ragged, so filthy, his face painted black and white with the features of a tusked pig, that for a second I didn't recognise him.

Naked, his belly sagging, his beard scrawny, the muddy mask falling away from his features, all I could see was how he stared at Jennifer, his mouth twisted into a grimace of hate.

'Why don't you do it?' he roared at her. I closed my ears with my hands, ducking away from this terrifying, stinking apparition that had moved upon me so silently through the field of barley, coming from the wood.

His voice, and my mother's voice shrieking back, were just the drones of bees and engines, and I pressed my fingers hard into my head to stop the words of hate forming.

Listen, Mabon whispered. *Listen.*

My mother was screaming, 'Go back to her. Go back to that girl from the wood . . .'

'Don't you think I would? I can't find her. If I could find her do you think I'd stay in this love-forsaken place?'

'Look at you! Look at what you've become! Nothing but a beast. Leaves, mud, filth, the marks of the savage on your face and body . . . you are filth, George! You are savage! Go back to the wood. Go back to your filth. Go back to that girl!'

'Let me go!' my father roared. 'I beg you, woman. Let me go! Each time I get close to her, you call me back. Each time I find the scent of her in my nostrils, your stink, the stink of my house, the stink of my sons calls me back. Let me go for once and for all!'

'I will be glad to do that. And may God have mercy on your sons while they are boys; because as men they are doomed to a terrible death!'

'Then I will be free of them too. Dance for me, Jennifer! Dance and let me go! Come on! I'll help you!'

Like the wild animal he had become, this boar, this man, this *Huxley* leapt to the bough, pulled hard on the rope and wound it round the branch, knotting it. My mother screeched, then gasped, reached up to hold the tree, hauling with all her strength to take her weight. Her eyes, half closed with strangulation, half opened now to stare at me, and I rose from my crouch, stepped towards her, aware that she was imploring me silently to help her.

My father, legs splayed, urinated on the woman below him, leaping like a wild man on the bough, making it bend and buckle, making the woman dance below him.

I couldn't speak. My mother's lips moved and perhaps she would have reached for me, but she was gripping the branch until her knuckles were white while her husband rocked her, rocked her, the pale yellow piss streaming from the fat, slack stub of his ash-grey member and drenching her hair, running from her shoes.

All I could see was her face, bloated and bilious, puffing and pathetic, the eyes bulging, the nostrils beginning to seep blood.

And she dropped, and the rope stopped her fall, making her gasp horribly, making her instinctively scrabble at the hemp around her neck.

Still the beast danced upon the tree. My father inhabiting the primal form of the Urscumug.

They take from us. They reflect us, and they take from us.

And this is what my father thought I had seen as a child! This is why he had been so frightened of me.

I had to save my mother! I had to throw my father from his perch. I ran towards her, leapt to reach for him, tried to grab the branch, tried to get a grip on his feet, to throw him down, to stop this killing.

But my jump fell short I had jumped with the expectations of a man, and achieved only the success of a child. As I failed to touch the bark, my arms clutched for comfort around my mother's waist and my weight dragged her down suddenly before I could release her, and in that quick, sharp movement I heard the wet and sickening snap of the twig that was her life.

I fell down, wailing, my head drenched in warm and stinking water. The bough above me did not break but creaked, and the shadow of the woman swung across the tough grass below the old oak, a limp thing, drifting left to right, left to right.

'That's that, then,' said the naked man in the tree in a low voice, as if talking to himself. 'The boy has done the deed quicker than I could have done it myself. She's dead. No bringing her back. But he saw what I *did*. He knows what 'I've *done*. He was here, a witness . . .

what to do? What to do? He knows what I've done. Though by the look of him . . .'

Blows were struck at me as I lay in agony and I curled into my body. A boar's savage teeth gnawed at my neck, while fingers squeezed my throat.

'What to do? What *shall* I do?'

And the voice of this primitive creature, this Urscumug as my father had called it, this half man, half animal, whispered:

'I do believe you've been charmed. Charmed into blindness. Charmed to forget. Well that's good. Thank God for that. Better get dressed. Better wash and change my clothes. Can't be seen like this. Paperwork. There'll be paperwork to do.'

And I heard my father run through the corn like a young dog released from its leash, keen to use its new-found freedom.

'Dear God . . . *was* it like that?' I whispered in horror to Mabon. I was suddenly sick, retching and wretched with the vision of my mother's death that had been revealed to me. '*Was* it like that? Like *that*? No wonder the day is no longer mine! Did the two of us conspire in my mother's death? I don't want to believe it, Mabon. But I *do* believe it! Mabon! Mabon . . . ?'

But my answer was only the wind rustling the tall corn. As I turned over on my back, staring at the sky through the spreading branches of the oak, I saw that no woman's body hung there now. And no girlish man, face cracked with white paint, stood grinning at me.

I sat up and called for the wild rider, the strange man who had been the presence of my conscience in this imaginary place . . . my guardian to the truthful vision. But Mabon was nowhere to be seen. And when I stood and looked around I realised that I was not in the cornfield at all, but in a field of wild grass and thistles. Strong Against the Storm was only one among many great oaks that surrounded me, an open clearing, a bright glade with many bright paths leading away from it. The air was hot and heavy, fragrant and still, not the air of England but of the dry and aromatic islands of the Aegean.

I began to walk towards Oak Lodge, to where it should have been, and after a few minutes I saw stone ruins in this wildwood. I had crossed a stream to get there, but the 'sticklebrook', as Steve and I had called it, was wider and deeper and flowing in two channels, hard into the forest.

I approached the ruins through the undergrowth and began to smell honey and spices. Where Oak Lodge had once stood, now I could see a white-stone house, fronted by marble pillars painted in exotic blues and reds. The roof was made from rounded, terracotta tiles, gently sloping. Small windows, their shutters opened, seemed to watch me darkly. This was how I imagined ancient Greece might have been, the air so hot and dry, perfumed with rosemary and thyme and lavender, so still and silent that time itself might have been suspended for the moment of my passing through.

I stepped to where the door to the kitchen had once been, ducking below a stone lintel into a square, white-walled room, where a fire burned in the corner hearth, and a stocky, muscular man in a black tunic and leather sandals, his dark hair shining and tied back with coils of copper wire, his beard a thin line around the angle of his jaw, stirred the contents of a wide, copper pan slung above the flames.

He looked up as I entered, then beckoned me over, scooping some of the stew into his spoon and holding it out to me.

'Careful! It's hot. I think I've used too much honey. I could die for honey. But too much can spoil good meat. Taste it, Chris. Tell me what you think.'

This was Mabon, I knew from his voice, but without the mask, without the chalk-streaked hair and the clothing that he had copied from Guiwenneth. His legs were dappled with tiny red and yellow animal symbols, I noticed, like freckles, and I thought of Issabeau's tattoos of the Oldest Animals. Thinking of Issabeau, I noticed Someone son of Somebody's rough cloak in the corner. The proud Celt had been here too, then.

'It's fish,' Mabon said, still holding the spoon towards me. 'Pike, to be precise. A great lake-water hunter. I caught it from a pond while you were sleeping after seeing the truth of your mother's death. Go on, Chris. Taste it.'

His statement confused me. Had I *slept* after the vision of Jennifer's murder? It hardly seemed likely! And I certainty couldn't remember doing so. But I couldn't find the words to raise the question as Mabon stared at me, his offering held out towards me. I accepted the spoon and ate the morsel of pike. It was good, very succulent, a little sweet and aromatic for my taste, though again I didn't see the need to comment. I could see the fish's head on a platter, gawping at me grotesquely, all jaws, teeth and evil, still eerily alive despite its being severed from the body.

'It *is* sweet, but it's good,' I said after a moment.

'This is a dish we cook when an old friend comes home,' Mabon said, again stirring the pot. 'Or when a new friend arrives: a birth, perhaps; a union of families; or the return from war of a man who knew a dead son and has brought his armour and his sword-hand back to his village. The head of the fish, with its teeth and savage jaws, is cut away. That means no more pain, you see? Only the sweetness and succulence of the flesh remains, which symbolises the comfort of friends. The honey is important. The dead stay fresh for a long time if placed in honey. We preserve a lot of things in honey, from mothers and sisters to ideas and hopes. So friendship and life can stay fresh too, if preserved in the *idea*, of honey.'

What in God's name was he talking about?

'I don't understand what is happening,' I said sorrowfully. Then the tears I had been fighting back suddenly surfaced. 'I killed my mother! I thought I was trying to hold her up, hold her own weight against the pull of the earth around her neck. But I hung on to her like a child at her breast, and I heard her neck go. I heard the snap! I killed her . . . and my father, dressed in skins, danced on the tree, danced and sang on the tree.'

I think I cried out loud. I screamed at this black-clothed man for thinking about nothing but fish and honey and the preserving of the dead. He seemed a callous presence in a dream that was filled with pain and fear, and terrible grief.

I could still feel the boy's weight of my body, slung on my mother's waist, I had done to her – without intending it – what the families of hanged men in centuries past had been allowed to do to quicken the death, by execution, of a loved one.

After a while I felt gentle hands on my face. Fingers smeared the tears across my cheeks. Honeyed breath scented the air as Mabon crouched beside me and whispered: 'You must understand – before you could have her back, you had to know the way she died. There are no quick paths through the forest, Chris. No short cuts. You were "charmed" that day into forgetting the truth. That is why you called to me. That is why I am here to help you. Mabon. My name means Remembering Shadows. I am *Memory* brought back through the broken dream. You were charmed into forgetting truth. Someone cast a spell on you.'

'Someone? The Celt?'

'Not the Celt.'

'Of course not. Who, then? Who made me forget the truth? Who charmed me? My father, of course,' I added with anger. 'I don't know why I bother to ask . . . If he could hide himself on the branch of the tree, if he had been there, he certainly could have blinded me.'

But Mabon said quietly, 'It was not your father.'

'Well it was certainly not my brother. Not Steven!'

But as I said the words, I felt a moment's shock, remembering the raid on Oak Lodge, the girl on the grey horse.

'Guiwenneth! Oh God – Guiwenneth herself . . .'

My heart suddenly ached, and my chest tightened. She had certainly charmed me in my sleep. She had been present in my life as a brutal, feral savage; and then again as the woman I loved. A trickster! A charmer! Had she charmed me when I was a boy?

'Not Guiwenneth!' Mabon said with a frown. 'Not directly.'

'You, then. You seem to know all about me. Of course! You. But how? You weren't there . . .'

'*Not* me, though you have done me a service. I knew nothing about you until you came here. Once you arrived, you were as transparent as the waters of the streams outside . . .'

'Then as I have always suspected . . . *Kylhuk*. It was *Kylhuk* all along. Tricky, canny *Kylhuk*, a man consumed by the trickery of others, tricking me . . .'

'Not Kylhuk,' Mabon said, again adding, 'not directly . . .'

'Then who? For God's sake *who? My mother? Mabon! I'm running out of possibilities.*'

'Yes,' Mabon said coldly, his fingers on my cheeks, turning my tearful face to look at his own hard, bronzed features. 'Yes. It *was* your mother who charmed you. Just as my own mother charmed me.'

My last guess had been a flippant one. I was astonished by his calm answer.

'My mother didn't know the time of *day* most of the time,' I raged back at him. 'She was in a dream! She was in despair! She bottled tomatoes in her Sunday clothes, Mabon, her *best clothes*. She lit fires on hot summer days. She was lost in a world that my bloody father had created, and she could no more have tricked me, or charmed me, than she could have taken wing and flown south for the winter!'

'She took wing in her own way, though – and summoned help. Help *from* that world your father had created, used to get her *out* of it, I suspect.'

I stared back at the man as he sniffed at the copper vessel, stirring the thick lumps of fish and fussing with the height of the pan above the glowing wood. He seemed so confident in his comments to me. He knew so much about me, or appeared to. *My name . . . Memory brought back through the broken dream . . .*

A mythago! *My* mythago. Brought alive by my own need, from my own unconscious.

I watched him, and again heard his words: *she took wing – summoned help . . .*

I said angrily, 'Then tell me this: *whose* help did my mother summon?'

Mabon poured himself wine from a clay flagon and sipped it, watching me, half amused.

'*Your* help. Why else are you here?'

'*My* help? I'm helpless!'

'Hardly helpless,' Mabon said with a laugh. 'But as to mothers – mothers, you may have noticed, have a way of making things happen. My own mother, when she couldn't get her way with me, when she couldn't catch me in the chase after I had fled her stronghold, when she saw that I would not submit to the demands of her Sanctuary and spend my life a captive to her goddess, and my death as bleached bones built into her altar – my own mother contrived by pure genius to imprison me at the entrance to the Underworld itself! Which is where you are now, by the way, in case you weren't aware of it, Christian!'

No, I had not been aware of it. And as I looked around the kitchen of this ancient house, Mabon laughed and shook his head, rose to his full height and kicked some cold embers onto the fire to damp down the heat, then walked to the door, standing there for a moment before he said, 'It's this way.'

'The Gate of Horn?'

'The open mouth that will lead you to your Grail. You passed the Gate of Horn earlier. You saw that truth lay between Memory and the Child in the Land – two things which people often think are false, but which hold the seeds of our lives!'

I followed him back towards the twin streams, then through the woods, through sanctuary clearings, ruins, and between tall, mossy rocks.

Suddenly a face appeared ahead of us, carved from stone, a broad, narrow-eyed monstrosity of leaf and flower, a green-man's face looming hugely, its nostrils flaring, its mouth gaping darkly. A hollow wind blew from the cavern. The twin streams were running like tears from its eyes, the beginning of the river along which I had recently rowed.

Mabon placed a hand on my shoulder.

'When my mother trapped me here she made it so that I could never enter the Underworld, only *guard* it in whatever way I wished. I am old and tired, Christian, and I have longed to make the journey into that silent and peaceful realm. I could only do it when a man came and shared the truth of his mother's death. That was the spell she put on me for denying her my love. Love as *she* saw it. You have broken that spell for me and I am grateful. I will gladly lead you into this Beautiful Realm. Once you find your mother among the Shades, lead her out, but when you do so, don't speak to her, no matter what she says to you, nor look back at her . . .'

'I know the rules,' I said. 'I've read the story! Have you encountered Orpheus?'

Mabon seemed surprised and delighted. 'Yes! A long, long time ago. But he was impetuous and lost the woman he loved. He looked back . . .'

'I *know* he looked back. I'll be sure to take more care . . .'

'Come on then.'

But I stood my ground, nervous and edgy. 'Not yet, I must go back to the others first. I need to see Guiwenneth before I enter . . . will I be able to go in – to Hell – on my own?'

Mabon smiled. 'Of course. One trip inwards. One life returned. My gift to you. And my thanks for releasing me, Christian,' he added as he turned to walk towards the mouth of the green and monstrous, sighing head.

The air hissed sharply and an arrow struck him in the shoulder, throwing him forward, screaming. Behind me, horses thundered through the tall rocks. Two more arrows streaked past me, one clattering against the rock face, the other catching Mabon son of Modron in the arm as he staggered to his feet.

A man yelled triumphantly; riding down on me, a lance held low, its shaft tied with coloured streamers. I flung myself to one side as Eletherion stabbed at me and I felt the crack of the wood as he missed with the point and struck with the shaft.

I was defenceless, and Mabon was badly wounded. The five horsemen rode over him and dismounted at the mouth of the Underworld, peering into the windy gloom. Eletherion took off his hawk-faced helmet and flung it into the void, then laughed with triumph, made a fist and banged it against the stone lip above his head.

Raggedly dressed, save for their gleaming helmets, the Sons of Kyrdu turned to look at me. Eletherion's eyes were bright with blood lust, his teeth gleaming white through the heavy, russet beard.

Then he hefted his javelin above his shoulder, drew back his arm, aimed . . .

Reeled back as a slingstone caught him above the eye!

He turned where he stood and sent the javelin into the rocks, but it came back at him and struck one of his brothers. Kylhuk and Someone stepped quickly into the space before the gorge, armoured and smiling, Kylhuk in battle kilt and torques, daggers strapped to each thigh and each forearm, Someone in a purple cloak, his hair meticulously shaped above his crown, his whole bearing prouder and more magnificent than I had ever seen him.

'I will take your head and heart for the life of my friend Manandoun,' Kylhuk roared, and leapt at Eletherion.

The man's brothers barred his way and he struck furiously with his long, iron sword. Someone entered the fray, using sword and axe, sending a spray of blood each time he struck at one of Kyrdu's sons. But these warriors were harder than they looked, and they spun and danced, weaving between the two Celts, drawing blood on the enemy themselves, screeching in their ancient language from behind the bronze masks of their conical helmets.

'*Slathan*!' Kylhuk shouted at me, and a dagger was flung to the ground at my feet. Eletherion was standing in the very entrance of the cave. Mabon was still breathing, I noticed, but his body was crushed by hooves and split by arrows.

I picked up the dagger and hefted it. Eletherion glimpsed the movement and as the blade streaked towards him – a good shot, I was quite surprised – he raised an armoured forearm and caught the weapon, picking it up and grinning.

Kylhuk could make no headway through the four brothers and his roar became frustration.

'Fight! Fight me for the honour of the man you slaughtered!'

But Eletherion could not understand the words, though he certainly understood the anger.

Suddenly he barked an order. His brothers began to fall back, stepping nimbly, their bright blades deflecting the heavier, stronger iron of their opponents. With a quick laugh, Eletherion turned and entered the Underworld, the others following so fast that Kylhuk, unbalanced, could not reach far enough to strike at their backs. He faced to the mouth of the cave, screeched furiously into the darkness, but could not pass, of course. There might as well have been a stone wall there.

Someone son of Somebody was licking the wounds on his arms, looking curiously at the void that marked the way to Hell. Kylhuk threw his sword to the ground, then leaned back against the stone, holding out his arms as if crucified, his eyes closed with frustration; the water from the left eye of the face washed the blood from his left arm.

Then I noticed Someone grinning at me. He looked back at Kylhuk and said, 'Are you refreshed?'

'Why?' asked the man.

'Because if you are refreshed I shall call Eletherion back to you.'

Kylhuk stood up straight, then carefully reached down for his sword. He stared at the unnamed Celt quizzically.

'How can you do that?'

Someone scratched his newly trimmed beard. 'I'm not certain I can . . . but I can certainly try. This poor, dying man here, this Mabon, has released my name to me. I know my name, now! I know who my father was, who my mother was, and I know who I am, and I am astonished to discover the truth of my name, since my identity could hardly be more noble, more legendary, more famous in the world in which I have sought it. I am my own hero! I have sat with men and talked about the lost hero, and the lost hero was me! But of this triumph, more later. For the moment, all that is important is that I know who I am and what I can do. I have seven geisas on my life, *seven*! Only one man was ever issued with seven, and all my life seven has been a special number to me. I have always known myself without knowing the truth of myself. What a fool! How blind a man can be when he is lost in the wilderness. But seven geisas are mine to use, and I have only used one of them. A second is that I can summon to account for himself any man who sets his brother to fight against me in his place! When you are ready, Kylhuk, I shall call Eletherion back to account for himself, since he raised no weapon against me in this skirmish, but only set his brothers to do the task.'

'Do it!' yelled Kylhuk, standing ready, strong and tensed in front of the cave mouth. 'Do it, and my life is yours for the taking!'

'Thank you for the offer. If your life remains for the taking at the end of the fight, I'll make a gift of it to you.'

'I accept,' said Kylhuk impatiently. 'Now bring that bastard out of Hell!'

*

The proud Celt stepped to the cave. In a voice that boomed like thunder he shouted words in his own language, and over and over again the name Eletherion was embedded in that abusive, angry, *furious* exhortation, that exercising of his geisa against the eldest Son of Kyrdu.

After a minute of this shouting, Someone fell silent, stepped back from the entrance to the Underworld and crossed his arms. Kylhuk stood there, a hound straining at the leash, the muscles of the arm that held his sword standing out so strongly that I thought they might explode.

How long he waited I can't say; it seemed for ever, and then suddenly a figure rose in the darkness, the helmeted and masked shape of Eletherion, walking hesitantly into the day. Even though his face was covered it was clear that the warrior was confused by what was happening to him. He had stolen the secret of entering Hell – part of his legend – and now he was being dragged back to the world he had left.

Frustrated in his ambition to loot the Underworld, he now found himself confronting the looting of his life by a man whose friend he had callously and tauntingly murdered.

'This for Manandoun . . .' Kylhuk breathed and struck the helmet from Eletherion's head, revealing startled, bloody features.

'And this!'

He struck again, cutting deeply into the man's shoulder.

Now Eletherion came alive, spinning round on the spot, his bronze blade flashing in the bright air, catching Kylhuk off guard and sending him sprawling. Someone stood impassively, motioning me back as I involuntarily stepped towards Kylhuk as Eletherion charged down at him.

But Kylhuk turned, used his feet to trip his opponent, stood quickly and backed away. As Eletherion, too, found his feet they rushed at each other; there was a quick, sharp ring of metal on metal, then Eletherion's face went loose, his body went down on its knees, his arms dropped, and a moment later Kylhuk was sawing furiously at the sinews of the head he was claiming in triumph.

When it was off, he spat in its face, then tucked it into the belt of his kilt by the long, russet hair.

'Don't worry, Christian,' he said to me. 'I shan't ask you to prepare *this* one for the pyre!'

Then he faltered in his step, and Someone and I went to his aid. I realised suddenly that Mabon was nowhere to be seen. In the fury of the last few moments he had vanished completely, though a thick trail of blood led to the mouth of the stone head. I felt aggrieved and ashamed that in his dying moments, Mabon had had to haul himself to the place he had so longed for, and which for so long had been denied him by the sorcery of his mother.

I cleaned and bound the wounds on Kylhuk's body. He watched me all the while, a half smile on his face, then reached out to squeeze my shoulder.

'I had plans for you,' he said. 'But things have turned out better than I'd expected.'

'What does that mean?' I asked.

He closed his eyes. 'Goodbye, Christian. And the best of fortune. It won't be long until we meet again.'

And then he drifted into a recuperating sleep.

I went in search of Someone son of Somebody, and found him staring into the distance, away from the Underworld. He was restless, that much was obvious, and I guessed that he was as keen to get back to Issabeau as was I to Guiwenneth.

'How is Kylhuk?'

'He'll live. He has more blood in him than most of us, and I saw a lot of it in his face today, as he avenged Manandoun.'

'He fought like a boar cornered by hounds. He fought well. This is a good ending for him.'

'And he called me Christian,' I added with a smile. 'Christian. Not *slathan*. Though I don't suppose the courtesy will last.'

To my surprise, Someone laughed out loud. 'He's released you. He had told me he would. You are no longer the *slathan*. He will keep Legion for himself. For the moment, at least.'

What did the man mean? Kylhuk would keep Legion for himself? Had he intended to make a present of it to me?

'Yes,' the Celt said simply. 'Exactly that. Well . . . not so much a present. He was going to pass it *on* to you. To trick you into taking it. To rid himself of the burden . . . Legion, and the quest for Mabon, and all the consequences of his questing, have been a burden on the man for years, exactly as they were for Uspathadyn before him. Uspathadyn tricked Kylhuk into taking on the quest for Mabon; Kylhuk was *slathan* to the giant, you see? In his quest for his own *slathan*, however, he found a boy – Christian Huxley – who could become the key to the rescue of Mabon himself, a boy whose mother could shape the boy's life by a lie she was led to believe in, and who could have the truth revealed to him only after he had come of age. Kylhuk planted the lie in your mother, then harvested you later, to help end the quest.

'I'm quite sure,' Someone went on, 'that he would have left you the responsibility of Legion, and therefore the anguish of fighting and fleeing from everything that is crowding and looming on its tail. But he can't do it. His honour prevents him. As his *slathan* you were both his guide and his heir; the word means simply *disguise*. He had disguised your true nature from you. That was part of the trick. Now, though, you are free to go, free of him, free to enjoy the lusty Guiwenneth . . .' he clapped his hands together spiritedly, 'as I will enjoy that husky enchantress, that Issabeau, that divine, raven-haired creature to whom you have married me, Christian Huxley, and my thanks, my arm and my life for your life on that!'

'Don't forget,' I said to him quickly, 'that now you know your real name you can no longer confuse enchantresses!'

'So she has told me. But that particular change in my talent isn't in *my* geisas, not as I now know them. I will *always* confuse and confound enchantresses. One, at least!'

'And your name? This great name? I can't keep calling you Someone . . .'

He turned to me proudly, then made a small bow of respect. The sun shone sharply on his waxed hair. 'My name is that great name, the name I have always known, a name that will be as familiar to you as the sound of the lark on a hot summer's day.'

I waited almost breathlessly, my mind running through all the great heroes, all the giants of myth and legend that I had read or heard about in my scant years on the earth.

'My name is Anambioros, son of Oisingeteros!'

He paused for a moment, to let this information sink in. 'Yes, Christian. I am that man. And despite what I must now do to fulfil the immense ambition attached to that name, I am always . . . *always* at your service.'

'Say the name again?' I asked nervously.

'Anambioros, son of Oisingeteros,' he said quickly, with a frown.

'Anambioros! By Olwen's hands, I thought you'd be older!' I said with a laugh.

He seemed relieved. 'I'm still young. There is a great deal of adventure ahead in my life to put the years on me. I'm delighted you recognise me. I had thought – being the strange man you are – that you would not have heard of me.'

I didn't disabuse him. 'Pleased to meet you at last. Anambioros! And what *geisas* do you have left?'

He drew himself up to his full height 'Just these: that I must give a word of advice to every stranger I meet, even if they don't request it. I must address the first child I meet after the night of Beltane as if they are royalty. I must shave and trim the hair from the head of a proud enemy taken in battle, and have the head to my right at the first feast, and address it in conversation without mockery. I can give back one life before my own death. I must not enter the house or stronghold of a stranger unless a red-haired woman enters first.'

I didn't have a response that seemed appropriate. All I could think of was how strangely mundane they seemed, these *geisas*, compared to the elaborate and supernatural versions that had been devised fifteen hundred years later.

'We should let Kylhuk rest, now,' Anambioros said. 'He's quite safe. And it's a long walk back to the stones, and to the others.'

He paced off, walking with a new swagger in his step, cloak flowing behind him.

'Anambioros, son of Oisingeteros,' I murmured as I followed. 'I'll do my best to write your name into the storybooks when I get home. But if you had been called 'Arthur' or 'Mordred', it would have been a lot easier.'

Twenty-Two

From the confident way he strode off, away from the house where Kylhuk lay asleep, I thought Anambioros knew exactly where he was going, and jogged along behind him through the forest. He was fitter than me, despite his wounds, and his pace was furious, a combination of swift walking and steady running that soon had me falling out of sight of him, though he kept calling to me.

I caught up with him by a river. He was standing, confused and uncertain, looking to left and right.

'You've got us lost,' I said. 'And no *geisa* to help us find the right track.'

'Not lost. . .' he said. Around us the wildwood stirred with wind. There was the scent of flowers on the air, and above us birds circled silently, as if preparing to roost for the night.

'Do you know where we are?'

'I thought I heard Elidyr call. I was following the sound of Elidyr's voice. He told me to listen for him . . . as soon as I'd found you. But! can't see him. Why would he hide from us?'

We spent a minute or so calling for the boatman, but to no avail. Anambioros then suggested we went separately along the river for a few minutes, meeting back at this starting point. Knowing the realm as well as I did, with its shifts and uncertainties in time, I thought this was a very bad idea; but the Celt was insistent and we parted company.

After a while I came to a part of the river where flowers in full bloom and swollen fungi grew from bank and tree trunk, hanging in great loops, plates and fronds from the branches, even rising in full, red and yellow petalled splendour above the flowing water. Insects buzzed and fed on nectar, dragonflies swooped and hovered, birds chattered and took wing, and Elidyr came towards me through the water, huge and menacing, his gaze hard as he watched me. He was dragging three small boats behind him. My heart began to race as I realised, shocked and horrified, who lay in them.

'I have to take them now,' Elidyr growled at me as he passed. 'They have had long enough.'

'NO!' I cried, and stumbled into the water. I could see Gwyr's ashen face in the nearest boat, and the tumble of Guiwenneth's auburn hair in the middle one. I waded towards Elidyr, blinded by the tears in my eyes. 'Oh God, please no! Don't take her!'

'Time to go,' the boatman snarled again. 'One kiss. Quick!'

One kiss?

He had stopped in the stream. The boats swayed in the current. I wiped a hand across my eyes and peered quickly down at the Interpreter, his face peaceful now, no sign of the charring that had destroyed him, his hands resting over his waist.

'Gwyr . . .' I whispered quickly. 'Thank you for friendship . . .'

'Hurry,' Elidyr growled again.

I spent a moment staring at Issabeau. Her eyes were half open and seemed to shine, but she was quite dead, the blossom of blood on her breast from the wound that had killed her covering her heart.

I held the sides of Guiwenneth's boat and leaned down to kiss her cold lips. I reached out to touch her icy hands, folded on her breast. I didn't understand. How had they died? I didn't understand . . .

'All died before,' Elidyr said. 'Now I must take them.'

Before? In the skirmish? 'I thought only Gwyr had died,' I protested. 'The others seemed so alive in the boats.'

'All died,' Elidyr murmured. 'Gwyr first. Then Kyrdu's sons killed all while they burned him. I gave them back for you. For pity. But only for a while. I told you!'

Yes. Yes, Elidyr. You told me. You showed me the flower garden and the dead knight with his mourning lady. But I had thought you were warning me about Gwyr. Only Gwyr. I hadn't known the skirmish had eliminated the whole Forlorn Hope.

Guiwenneth! Dear God, I couldn't lose her now. I hugged her cold body and wept for her, but Elidyr reached over and pushed me firmly away, back into the water.

'All over,' he said harshly. 'Now go away.'

Anambioros appeared on the bank, a sudden, screaming figure, leaping into the water, his face filled with despair and fury.

'Issabeau!' he howled.

Elidyr transformed. His giant's body thickened even more, his face became that of a snarling hound, his pelt became wolf-grey. He lashed out at the Celt, who drew his sword and struck back, only to have the weapon snatched from his hand, snapped quickly and tossed away. Then Elidyr swiped a hand across the proud man's face, knocking him backwards, below the river.

Baying and howling, angry and frustrated, crying out, 'I *have* to do this!' Elidyr tugged at the ropes that held his burden and continued his journey towards the Underworld, to enter the place through the route of the dead, along the river that flowed below the gaping mouth of the green-man cliff.

I swam to Anambioros and dragged his unconscious body to the shore. After a few minutes his eyes opened to stare at the sky, then his face twisted into grief and rage, his hands clenched into fists as he lay there.

When he was more composed he went back to the water's edge and crouched down, crying softly, mourning the death of his beloved Issabeau. I stood behind him, numb and confused, my head reeling with memories of Guiwenneth, and with the events of the last few hours. I felt suddenly alone and totally helpless, aware that I was far from home and without the woman who had become such a part of my life that I had not noticed how much my fear of this wilderness had been soothed by her reassuring presence.

I didn't know what to do, now. I didn't know what to do next.

'I took it for myself,' Anambioros was saying softly, angrily. 'I took it for myself. I could have given it to her. I *should* have given it to her . . . the boatman didn't give me the choice . . .'

What was he talking about? I crouched down beside him, my arm round his shoulder. 'What are you saying, Anambioros?'

'I had the right to give back a life. It was one of my privileges. I died with the others, that awful day in the forest, when Eletherion attacked us. Elidyr has let me live because of my own *geisa*. But I would have willingly given it to Issabeau.'

And then she would have been alive and alone instead, I thought, but I didn't voice the words. Anambioros was almost inconsolable, and by helping him through his grief I was able to delay the onset of my own deep sadness.

Or perhaps my strength at this moment was not because of the weeping long beside me, but because I was increasingly aware that Guiwenneth, now, was in the same Underworld realm as my mother, a terrible place opened to me by Mabon for a single journey only, for a single rescue only, his thanks for releasing him from the prison that he had guarded and which had guarded him in turn.

I felt almost faint as I stood and stared back towards the stone house, the narrow passage through the rocks and the grotesque face carved around the entrance to the deep.

My mother was there. Guiwenneth was there.

And I could go into that Dark and see them. I could sit and talk to them.

But eventually I would have to choose between them.

Twenty-Three

I was not greeted by Cerberus as I entered Hell; no five-headed hound snarled and snapped at me. But Mabon was there, old and grey, robed in black and smiling through his beard.

'You took your time,' he said.

'It was about time I did something for myself,' I replied. 'I wanted to think. I wanted to be with Guiwenneth. From the moment I entered this wilderness of time, trees and gateways I have been led, pushed, shuffled, tricked, deceived, manipulated . . .'

'Loved?'

'Oh yes. Certainly that.'

'But love itself is also something that *happens* to you,' Mabon agreed. 'Not something you can make happen. Yes. I think I understand how you feel.'

'Love is wonderful. And I'm glad it happened. But now . . .'

He stood quietly as I struggled with my fears and feelings, staring beyond him to the bright land, a world of woods and fields, not at all the gloomy, grim incarceration that was the construct of Hell of his own, original time.

This was the Otherworld of the Mabon of my own legend, the Celtic Lordly One; I looked beyond him at the wonderful ideal of death held by the wild and optimistic clans of Iron Age Europe, and not at all the grey and dismal shroud of ancient Aegean philosophy.

'Well, well. At least I can agonise in summer.'

'Which, is more than can Eletherion,' my Shade-guide said, and I followed his gaze to the skeletal figure that was strapped by chains to a jagged rock in the gloom. Eletherion's wounds bled copiously, his eyes blazed furiously, but his mouth, though it worked angrily, emitted no sound, no sound at all.

'His brothers are finding their own deaths, deeper in the ground,'

Mabon added. 'But that is another story for another time. Look for it in your books, Christian, when you get home.'

'I will.'

'Home is where the heart is. How many times have you thought that, recently, I wonder?'

'Very many. Very many indeed.'

'Keep walking, keep following this path. Home and all your heart-beats are there, and if you remember the one simple truth: that you must not question your decision! If you remember that, then you can bring her out alive.'

'And how do we then get home? To my true home!'

'Elidyr will take you. He's the boatman, remember? He doesn't just transport the dead. You can trust Elidyr to take you home. Off you go, now. Time is passing faster than you think.'

I had run across the field from the wood and now stood breathless at the gate to the garden of Oak Lodge. Smoke curled from the chimney. Hens clucked and pecked, watching me nervously. Somewhere in the house music was playing, and I thought I recognised one of my mother's favourite symphonies, by Vaughan Williams. It was peaceful and beautiful, but I had never taken much interest in classical music and I could do no more than register the gentle, pastoral theme.

My spirits lifted. This was a wholly different return to my childhood than the encounter with Mabon. I might almost have been home, properly home, on a hot, still summer's day . . .

But there was smoke from the chimney . . .

I opened the gate and walked up to the house, then changed my mind about entering and continued to walk around the garden, peering in through the French windows at the study. Everything was intact, nothing broken, the desk polished and gleaming, my father's journal on one side, two books on the other. No Huxley sat there, however. The place was just a shrine, a memory of intellect.

And so I entered my home and found my mother by the fire, sweat on her face, her gaze focused on the flames, her shirt stained red with the juice of the fruits she had been preserving.

I sat down beside her, clasped my hands together and stared at the flames. We spent a long time in silence. I couldn't find the words to express my feelings. I looked around: at the clock on the mantelpiece, the pictures on the walls, the table with its thick green cloth, the shelves, dark-stained and ornate, with their wretched rows of plates and mugs. The room was stifling, and not just because of the fire blazing on this hot, still day.

After a while, my mother said, 'She's in the study. She's waiting for you.'

'Who is?

'Guiwenneth. Go and see her.'

'I've come here to see you,' I said, tears flooding my eyes as I stared at my mother's sad, bowed head. She was more forlorn than I could remember. She licked her lips, wiped her hand across her nose, clasped her hands in her lap, each tense, restless motion reflecting a thought or a memory that was haunting her and hurting her, and yet which she would not speak.

'Go and see her,' she repeated softly.

'I've come to take you home, Mum. I've come to find you. To take you home.'

She was suddenly crying, but her voice stayed strong. 'No. That's not true. It was true once, but it's not true now. And I wouldn't want it differently. Go to her, Chris. You only have one chance. I'll be all right. It's only while you're here that I feel the pain. Once you're gone, once you are finally gone, my life will go on . . . Go to her. She needs you . . . And you need her. If you take her home with you, then the terrible things I've seen might not come true at all.'

'I know what you've seen. It's not going to happen. I will not become like that man you saw!'

'I saw Grief make a monster of you.'

'I am not a monster.'

'I know. That's why you must trust me. You must take Guiwenneth. I love you too much, and I'm too frightened of what you might become, to let you take me in her place.'

'Everything you saw, all that horror, that vision of me as an old man killing my brother – just a dream! Just a lie! I will not kill Steven. I promise you, Mum! I will not kill Steven . . .'

'Not if you take the girl from the wood. Take her home, Chris. Do what you have said and make the dream a lie! Perhaps when the time comes, and the dream breaks and dissolves into dust, perhaps I'll know it. Besides,' she turned to me, put her hands on my cheeks and after a moment, a restless, moist-eyed and searching moment, kissed my mouth.

'Besides . . . you long for her more than you long for me. You have found love, then lost it cruelly. Now you can retrieve it. I long for your life to be long and loving. Go to her, Chris.'

*

There was someone in the study. I could hear the murmured words, the rustle of the pages of the journal being turned. I opened the door slowly and saw the spill of tight from the garden through the opened windows. Issabeau sat weeping at the desk, her tears staining the scrawled writing of the journal as she read. She looked up at me, sorrowful and forlorn, her face as pale as snow, a small, sad oval in the tumble of greying hair.

'She's been waiting for you,' the enchantress whispered. 'She will be so glad you came.'

'Where is she?'

'In the garden. She's been waiting a long time for you . . .'

I walked past the desk. Issabeau drew breath, fighting back her own sadness. 'How is he?' she asked in a small voice. 'Will he remember me?'

'Oh yes. He will remember you. Grief will not make a monster of him, he's too proud for that. But he will not be the same man again.'

'I loved him so much,' she said. 'I hope he knew that.'

'He knew it, Issabeau. And God willing, I will make sure he never forgets it.'

'Look after him.'

'As much as I'm able, I swear I will. Issabeau . . .'

She looked up at me, a lovely face crushed by pain. 'Go to her . . .'

Her fingers shook as she ran her nails down the lines of my father's writing, raking through his thoughts and observations, and I left her there, lost in her own considerations, her own world, her own magic.

I finally found Guiwenneth by the sticklebrook, sitting on the dried mud of the bank, her bare feet in the shallow water. This was the very place where, as a child on a grey horse, she had trotted round me and struck me with her feathered coup-stick. She seemed to be remembering that moment pleasantly, her head tilted up, hair still luxurious and full, face almost serene with delight, eyes closed.

'Hello,' I said, and she opened her eyes and looked up at me.

'Do you remember this place?'

'Of course. You whacked me with a riding crop. Then we rode together, into that field, there, and fell from the horse.'

'And Manandoun came to rescue me and was furious with me. I thought he was going to kill you, but I think he just wanted to make sure I understood how dangerous it was to come to the edge of the world and to go galloping off after gullible and gorgeous boys.'

'Is that how you thought of me? Gullible and gorgeous?'

'But you are, aren't you? Sit down beside me.'

I sat down, she reached a hand to stroke my face, then tugged my hair and pulled me back, so that we lay on the earth, our faces to the heavens.

'Once upon a time,' Guiwenneth said quietly, her fingers entwining with mine, 'there was a young man, fair-faced and full of life, who loved a girl. But the girl died. The young man rode the length and the breadth of his land, seeking in every forest and every valley and on every mountain for the way into the land of the dead. He sacrificed everything he could lay his hands on. He kissed every stone and undertook every quest that was asked of him. He slaughtered the beasts that inhabited the edge of the wood and the edge of the lake, even if he wasn't asked to do so. He fasted, then feasted, then fasted again, then turned himself inside out and upside down, walking backwards for a whole season, and speaking his words in reverse. And at last he had done enough to enter the world of the dead, and there he found the girl he had loved.

' "I've come to fetch you," he said, and she looked at him in horror.

' "Who are you?" she asked.

' "I am the young man you loved," he replied.

' "Well, if you are," she said, "you left him behind a long time ago. Things have changed. And you have certainly changed."

' "You are as beautiful as the day you left me," said the sad old man.

' "Alas, I cannot say the same to you. Go away. What we once had was wonderful. What has happened since cannot justify your waste of life. Go away."

' "I have spent my life trying to find you."

' "I was dead and in a wonderful place. You were alive and behaving like a dead man. You have wasted your life. There were better things for you to do. You have one life only, and there are always other lovers." '

She turned to me, smiling mischievously. 'Did you like my story?'

'Not very much. What are you trying to tell me?'

'You have one mother and you can take her back; you can start again; you can use her dream, her terrifying vision, to make sure that the dream remains unreal. As for me . . .' her face changed from happiness to sorrow, though she tried to hide it. 'As for me,' she repeated, 'you can find me again. I am always in the wood. There are more of me than you can imagine; all I ask, my dearest love . . . all I ask . . . just dream me well. Dream me beautiful. And dream me happy, and with a heart that can fulfil all your own needs and love.'

These last words had been spoken through tears and she crushed me to her, sobbing quietly, her fingers digging into my back and neck. 'Just dream me well, Chris . . .'

'I don't need to dream you at all. I have you here, in my arms. I can take you out of here, I can take you home. I have won that right, and I will claim that right . . .'

'You came for your mother. Don't imagine I don't know that. She is alone, Chris. She needs you, she needs this life more than I do. Chris . . . you can find me again so easily! Just dream me well,' she repeated firmly. 'We can *always* find each other again. You must take your mother out of here!'

'I can't leave you, Guiwenneth.'

'You can't leave her!'

'She wants me to take you . . . you want me to take her . . . what am I to do? I want you both. I want you both so much!'

'Good memory is a great comfort,' she whispered. 'Eventually, that is all we can ever hope for. I have loved my time with you. If you are sensible, we can find that time again. The same cannot be said for Jennifer. So go home, Chris. Go back to the beginning. *Take your mother home!*'

I had come to Oak Lodge across the field from Strong Against the Storm. As I walked back to the entrance to the Otherworld, I realised that I was following the same path through the tall corn that my mother had carved, years ago, when I had followed her to her death. This was not quite the same field; nor the same sky, nor indeed the same tree; though to my right, the edge of Ryhope Wood watched me with its hidden eyes as it had watched my family for years.

Somewhere here, I remembered, the trail through the corn divided, a part of my mother's spirit taking off to flee into the safety of the wilderness beyond the forest.

Or perhaps . . . the mark of a spirit joining her? My father's spirit, come to kill her? Invisible to me, though he didn't know it.

Eventually, walking stiffly and carefully, repeating to myself that I must not look round, I must not speak, I must not even hear the murmuring and breathing of the woman behind me, I came to the rise of land from which ordinarily I would have seen the spire of the church at Shadoxhurst, away in the distance.

This ridge of land, this focus of my memory, close to the hanging tree, was where the bright realm ended and the grim, gloomy passage to the surface of the world commenced. I stepped foward into this Stygian night, and behind me footsteps shuffled on the bare rock.

Ahead of me, the new day was a glowing circle, the inside of the mouth of the green-man's painted, stony face.

The walk took hours, or so it seemed.

No Mabon greeted me to say goodbye; no Eletherion screamed silently from his rock. The presence of the shrouded dead was visible literally as shadow, the movement of shape and memory on the walls on either side of me, and I dared not look too hard in case, inadvertently, I glimpsed my passenger with the edge of vision, and dispatched her back to eternity.

Silently and steadily I led her from the world of the dead.

Anambioros was waiting for me as he had promised he would, spear at the ready, his sword exposed and resting on its sheath in case any of Eletherion's brothers should make a bid for their own freedom, like bats flying from their roost.

He stood up as I emerged, grinning broadly. And then his face dropped in astonishment as he saw who was following me out of Hell.

'What's happening?' he asked blearily. 'What's going on?'

'Is she free of the cave's mouth? Has she emerged from the shadows?'

'Yes,' said Anambioros, and I took the chance and turned to look at Issabeau, who stood there, blinking against the light, as young, as husky, as raven-haired as when I had first met her.

'Go and kiss him,' I whispered. 'I think he needs it.'

'By the Good Christ, I thought I was dreaming,' she said, and I laughed, though my heart was breaking. I had wanted to amend her thanks to: By the Good Christian!

It was enough to see the two of them in each other's arms, re-united in love and purpose.

Later, Anambioros found me in the stone house. Kylhuk had long gone, returning to his Legion, pursuing his own fortunes. I had made a fire, polished the tarnished cooking equipment that Mabon had left who knew how long ago, and made a broth of vegetables and wild pig, speared at great effort with the Celt's own weapons, while he and Issabeau were lost in their Delightful Realm.

'My father was a king among men,' he said, 'and so am I. But I am a man with a true king for a friend, and I will never ask you why you saved the life of Issabeau and not one of the two people who mattered to you most. Christian, I will not die until I have saved your own life once! This is my promise to you. It is a *geisa* that I am willing upon myself, and the price is all the others, which I hereby abandon, send back, deny and part with. If I am ever asked to explain my actions, I will claim the friendship of a man of courage – and offer my own life as forfeit.'

'Thank you,' I said quietly. 'How many lives do you have, Anambioros? You seem to conjure them put of the air.'

'I do, don't I?' he replied. 'I seem to have the lives of a cat. And I have a cat in my life! Thank you again for that. My heart goes out to you in your loss; may good memory be a great comfort to you.'

'Gentle words, my Guiwenneth's words too, and I will cling to them gladly.'

He leaned down and kissed my cheek and chin.

'By the way. Elidyr has come for you. He says he can wait until you're ready, but not to leave it too long. He's by the river. I shall miss you, Christian. But I will make your name famous!'

And with that he left me, returning to his own world, leaving me to mine.

CODA

I have been in the Path of Stone and the Wood of Thorns,
For somebody hid hatred and hope and desire and fear
Under my feet that they follow you night and day.

from W.B. Yeats,
He Mourns for the Change . . .

Coda

We must all eventually awake from the dream, unless we have been stolen from our passage through the wood of thorns, from the path of scones. While I dreamed in my boat, Kyihuk passed by, together with his Legion, many on horseback, most on foot, some in chariots, some in wagons. They overtook my slow boat on the winding river, moving by on each side, each face peering down at me, smiling, bidding me farewell, blowing me kisses.

The last to pass were the woman, Raven, and the Fenlander.

Raven said wryly, 'You might have made more of me, but your mind was elsewhere.'

I didn't understand her words. She had already cantered on ahead.

The Fenlander said, 'Our time has not yet begun, Christian. I look forward to it!'

I remembered the vision through my mother's eyes, of myself as a fat, scarred warrior-chief, cruelly killing my brother Steven. The Fenlander had been there, my right-arm man, my friend . . .

'I don't,' I whispered. 'I don't look forward to it. Not at all . . .'

He grinned, held his masked helmet high, then rode on.

And so they had gone, and slowly the earth ceased to shake with the passage of that army. The boat drifted on.

Did my father pass me as I dreamed? I heard the growling of a boar and a dark shape leaned low, one dusk, an animal's face painted white below lank, black hair.

'It is not finished yet . . .' this apparition breathed. 'When you come back, I shall be waiting for you.'

'I looked for you,' I whispered.

'Not very hard.'

'I followed in your footsteps. I came into Ryhope Wood along the Hogback Ridge, but I couldn't find you.'

'I hid from you,' my father said.

'Hid from me? Why?'

'You had other things than your father on your mind.'

'It's true. I had Guiwenneth on my mind. And now I've let her go.'

The man leaned down towards me, but behind the savage, snarling mask of chalk, the eyes were sad and gentle. Almost like Elidyr's, I thought . . .

'Yes. You did. And now, like me, you will pursue a dream. We pursue the same dream, Chris. That dream will become your life. You don't know it yet. And that is why I will be waiting for you. *When* you return.'

He drew away, growling and grumbling, towering over my supine form, following the boat for a while almost protectively, until quite suddenly he turned away from me and was gone from my vision.

The boat rocked. If Elidyr pulled it, he was invisible. I saw only the moving of branches against the clouds and the changing colours of the heavens.

The journey seemed endless, a journey without hunger or sleep, without pain or pleasure, a journey through winter and summer, a gentle passage along a narrow stream, through an age of forests.

Eventually I succumbed to sleep, made drowsy by some hidden charm but delighting in the anticipation of oblivion.

And this morning, when I opened my eyes and saw the spring sky above me as I lay in that shallow boat, I realised that my long journey from the heart of the forest was over.

I had come home again.

If only for a while.

Acknowledgements

This latest visit to Mythago Wood was made all the more enjoyable for an encounter at the 1996 International Association for Fantasy in the Arts (and a near death experience in a convertible) with Chip Sullivan (rafters ring!), Roger Schlobin (wassail!), Brian Aldiss, Donald Morse, Bill Senior, Gary Wolfe and DD, Usch Kiausch, Alanna Bondar (thanks for the permission to quote!), Ellen Datlow, Beth Gwinn, two Clutes, one Shippey . . . I'll be back! My special thanks to Jenni Smith, Jim Rickards and Jane Johnson who helped very much during later, difficult times. And Kirsti Bambridge for Grail talks, Graham Joyce for a little 'Greek Correction', and the Library of Avalon in Glastonbury for just being there! And as ever, to the Badminton group, and Sarah, Chris and Fi, Garry and Annette: a fine band of players.

Embedded in this novel is the strange and surreal tale of *Kylhuk and Olwen*, from *The Mabinogion*, which certainly contains references to pre-Celtic myths, long lost. For those who might be interested, I have used the Everyman edition of *The Mabinogion*, translated by Gwyn Jones and Thomas Jones, and the Penguin Classics edition, translated by Jeffrey Gantz, which I slightly prefer. Also, the Oxford paperback of *The Cattle Raid of Cooley* (Cuailgne) (a.k.a. *The Tain*) translated by Thomas Kinsella. C. W. Sullivan's *Welsh Celtic Myth in Modern Fantasy* (Greenwood Press) was an inspiration! Barry Cunliffe's *The Celtic World* (Constable), and Anne Ross's *Pagan Celtic Britain* (Cardinal, but long since out of print) have always been source books of enormous importance, and no less so this time. And as ever, when in doubt: Asterix to the rescue!

Afterword: Imaging the world of myth

ROBERT HOLDSTOCK

I have been 'dreaming' Ryhope 'Mythago' Wood for more than twenty years, now. I live at its edge, half asleep in reality. I write other things, journey elsewhere. But then I hear the sounding of a horn, or the howling of a hound. Someone or some *thing* steps out from the edge of the wood, and beckons to me. And once again, it's time to live the dream. Time to journey.

Those journeys are difficult, intriguing and always revealing. The writer never quite knows what he's going to find. All of 'legend' is in Ryhope Wood, though the legends often exist as fragments, briefly glimpsed in a glade, by a river, across a valley; most often from the corner of the eye, something half seen, which vanishes when it is gazed upon fully. All of legend: that which we remember, and perhaps most importantly, the vast amount that has been forgotten over time. The tales fade from the oral tradition, and the events, which had once burned so fiercely in the story-teller's memory, have crumbled to ash.

But they are not forgotten. The wood itself remembers, and these ancient images of myth, these 'myth-imagoes', rise whenever a human mind becomes engaged with this oldest of woodlands.

The artist John Howe, in his illustrated *Beowulf*, describes the way that he sees the world of myth in his imagination as like looking through 'an arrow slit in a high tower wall, affording a few details but above all the knowledge that the view will forever be tantalisingly inadequate'. He has painted Beowulf, whose 'world may be remote, but is brought close by the very distance that separates us from him'. Time takes away the clutter of every day detail, but leaves a profoundly moving core of story, which can be embellished and represented in new ways.

When I'm imagining the ancient past, I always feel as if I'm sitting around a fire, outside a ring of men and women, listening to, but not understanding the words being spoken, but aware of the laughter, the cheers, and the gestures that are made as someone brags of a hunt or a battle, someone is teased, someone remembers a lost friend, someone asks for advice on love. I sit in the shadow of the time, and make my own tale from it.

As the two books in this omnibus illustrate, Mythago Wood is a place of memory, glimpses, and encounters. Nothing is as it seems, and no legendary figure, emerging from the edge of the wood, is ever the same twice: they are created from different minds with different sensibilities.

The Hollowing takes the exploration of Ryhope Wood forward in time to 1967, twenty years after the solitary scientist George Huxley has disappeared 'inwards'. I was intrigued by the thought of a team of scientists, mythologists and anthropologists entering the wood in an attempt to understand the supernatural forces at work there. (As an aside: having been questioned closely, a few years before, about what exactly my characters ate when in the wood – nothing but squirrels, nuts and wild boar? – I included a chef in the team! He's French, he's larger than life, and is an excellent cook!)

The main notion that appealed to me, when thinking about *The Hollowing*, was the idea of seeding the wood, creating mythago forms, from a damaged, now disturbed, adolescent mind. From there it was an easy step to introducing the 'trickster' element of the novel, disguising it in many mythago forms.

The book is in two parts: a narrative followed by a series of encounters for the characters. Each of the encounters is designed to illuminate an aspect of the young mind behind the 'seeding'. The sequence in which Jason and his rough-neck argonauts appear led to later work: *Celtika, The Iron Grail* and *The Broken Kings*. Those heroes of old haven't remained in memory just by chance; they are powerfully iconic, and always available and interesting to explore further.

Gate Of Ivory, Gate Of Horn brings the Cycle full circle. In *Mythago Wood*, Christian, one of the two sons of the scientist and explorer George Huxley, becomes lost in the wood in more ways than one, and ends up a brutal and almost unrecognisable version of his more youthful self, with extreme consequences for his brother Steven.

I had always wondered what event or events might have caused that terrible transformation, and in part at least, *Gate Of Ivory* attempts to answer the question. The book is set at the same time as *Mythago Wood*. In one section, it takes a tongue-in-cheek look at the nature of the 'hero' ethic. In the main, it deals with truth and lies: truth from the Gate of Horn, lies from the Gate of Ivory, and Christian's attempt to distinguish between them.

In the end, I didn't take the story as far as originally intended. A deeper and more exotic tale of love and frustration took over, that of Christian, Issabeau and Someone Son of Somebody. (The latter, by the way, is a real character from one of the Welsh myths.)

Christian's fierce and tragic tale remains to be written.

Rob Holdstock
London, May 2007